PUBLICATION/EMBARGO DATE:
- 6 MAR 2000
PENGUIN BOOKS AUSTRALIA LTD.

THE PENGUIN CENTURY
OF AUSTRALIAN STORIES

The
PENGUIN
CENTURY
of
AUSTRALIAN
STORIES

EDITED BY CARMEL BIRD

WITH AN INTRODUCTION BY
KERRYN GOLDSWORTHY

VIKING

If you would like to write to Carmel Bird, visit her web site at www.carmelbird.com

Viking
Penguin Books Australia Ltd
487 Maroondah Highway, PO Box 257
Ringwood, Victoria 3134, Australia
Penguin Books Ltd
Harmondsworth, Middlesex, England
Penguin Putnam Inc.
375 Hudson Street, New York, New York 10014, USA
Penguin Books Canada Limited
10 Alcorn Avenue, Toronto, Ontario, Canada M4V 3B2
Penguin Books (NZ) Ltd
Cnr Rosedale and Airborne Roads, Albany, Auckland, New Zealand
Penguin Books (South Africa) Pty Ltd
5 Watkins Street, Denver Ext 4, 2094, South Africa
Penguin Books India (P) Ltd
11, Community Centre, Panchsheel Park, New Delhi 110 017, India

First published by Penguin Books Australia Ltd 2000

10 9 8 7 6 5 4 3 2 1

Jacket design by Sandy Cull, Penguin Design Studio
Text design by Marina Messiha, Penguin Design Studio
Typeset by Midland Typesetters, Maryborough, Victoria
Made and printed in Australia by Australian Print Group, Maryborough, Victoria

National Library of Australia
Cataloguing-in-Publication data:

The Penguin century of Australian stories.

ISBN 0 670 89233 5.

1. Short stories, Australian – 20th century. 2. Australia – Social life
and customs – Fiction. I. Bird, Carmel, 1940– .

A823.010803

This project has been assisted by the Commonwealth Government through
the Australia Council, its arts funding and advisory body.

www.penguin.com.au

CONTENTS

This book is a collection of a hundred pieces of short fiction written by a hundred Australians. The stories are brought together here for the first time, and all have been published before in hundreds of different places throughout the twentieth century. To read them is to visit the sensibilities, memories and imaginations of writers in this country in the years between Federation and the new millennium. I used to hear the word 'century' when I was lying on the grass at the edge of the local oval while my father played cricket, and the word 'century' still resonates for me with the excitement of a hundred runs on sunny afternoons in rural Tasmania. They didn't often make a century, but when somebody did there was an enormous and most satisfying fuss. This book is in some ways the literary equivalent of such a celebration.

When I first dreamt up the idea of the anthology, I wondered if it would be possible to contain so much in one volume, for I wished the stories to sit together, to be browsed and read side by side without the need to juggle a couple of books. I imagined international flights where the passengers dipped into the century of stories between movies and drinks, the words and images taking them into realms that no aircraft could ever reach. Taking them, I hoped, into a place you might call the Australian psyche – a creature of many, many faces. For fiction is one powerful source of a country's truths, a deep pool of images and preoccupations, of moralities and attitudes which mirror and enact the history of the people and the place. Consequently, to explore the movement of fiction across a hundred years is to visit time and meaning, to listen to voices now silent, to survey perspectives no longer visible, to take pleasure in the narratives of Australians from Tom Collins who died in 1912 to Raimondo Cortese who was born in 1968.

In order to help readers find their way around *The Penguin Century of Australian Stories*, I have included a biographical timeline which shows the chronology of the writers. I have also provided information on the dates the stories were first published. The stories are set out alphabetically by author name. My selection was initially limited to works of fewer than 3000 words. Then I read stories by writers I believed to be significant in the history of Australian fiction and I chose those that appealed to me and that I thought would serve the purpose of reflecting the development of the short story in this country. I didn't set out to balance the genders or any other elements; I simply went in trusting the stories to sort themselves into a satisfying whole. And I believe this strategy has been successful. As it turns out there are forty-five women writers here, and fifty-five men. There is comedy and tragedy, city and country, beauty and ugliness, hope and despair. There is, above all, clearly a vigour and a sense of pleasure in the writing.

The world depicted in the stories of Henry Lawson and Barbara Baynton no longer exists, but it can be regenerated as we read and will connect – through the fiction as through a photograph – with the Australia of today. Although most of us live in the cities by the coast, images of the bush are still vivid and powerful not only in the international perception of the country, but in our perception of ourselves. A picture of a forest of gum trees still speaks, to the world and to us, of Australia, suggesting ancient forests which will burn up in summer and burst forth in bright young growth in spring. An image of constant regeneration and reinvention. There is much in the stories in this collection that is tender and green, much that is raw and brutal, and it is fair to generalise and say there is a sharp inventiveness and a wry humour, both of which are recognisable as Australian traits.

Two of the deepest sources of pleasure I know are the reading of fiction and the writing of fiction. The physical act of writing, for the early writers represented here, was a matter of pen and paper. Some writers of today still work in this way, but they do at least have the opportunity to use computers, to choose between the kinds of technology they might employ. Typesetting is different, publishing is different. We worry about sacrificing trees to make the paper to make books. It would be possible to put this book on the World Wide Web, but for the present it exists as ink on paper, bound between covers, an object to be touched, with pages of a certain texture to be turned and turned again. It is my hope that *The Penguin Century of Australian Stories* will be a volume that readers of the twenty-first century will read as a treasury of Australian fiction of the past, and also a source of pleasure and inspiration.

This collection looks forward to the next century, including as it does the work of young and daring writers who are fabulously free with their inventions. When their writing is seen in the context of the work that has gone before, readers can catch a resonance, hear a distant melody worked into a brand new song. The old laconic notes still move through the short stories of the nineties, with a range of voices so wide, so diverse. Enjoy reading these stories, following the common threads and the sharp differences that characterise them. I hope you will see how they demonstrate the vigour and diversity of the short story in this country, and that through the lens of this lovely genre you will perceive a shifting portrait of Australians and their country.

My thanks to the people who have played a part in the realisation of my dream for this book. They are: Camilla Bird, Fran Bryson, Matt Condon, Clare Forster, Lyndal Harrington, John O'Meara, Brenda Walker and Kate Wigney. They also include all the writers or their agents who agreed to have the stories included in the book. I also thank Kerryn Goldsworthy for her scholarly introduction to the work.

Carmel Bird
December 1999

INTRODUCTION

The Australian short story already had a lively existence in the nineteenth century. Many stories now lost and forgotten were published in newspapers, magazines and journals in both Britain and Australia, stories that documented the conditions of colonial life.

These stories worked out, through the course of their narratives, various ideas and problems that preoccupied Australian settlers and colonists. Much of the Australian short fiction of the nineteenth century was produced mainly for a British readership at 'home', and represented Australia as a foreign and exotic place full of strange animals, unpredictable 'savages' and haunting, sometimes threatening, landscapes. Some stories, like Ada Cambridge's 'Arriving in Melbourne', were of the 'sketch' variety: a kind of autobiographical literary journalism also frequently and brilliantly practised by Marcus Clarke and later by Henry Lawson.

Other stories were essentially a kind of travel writing that emphasised local colour. Stories of colonial adventure abounded, featuring convicts, bushrangers and gold; stories by women tended more usually to fall into the romance genre, often examining questions and issues of nationality and allegiance by setting up and then resolving some romantic problem or quandary for an Australian girl and her British suitor or, less often, vice versa.

Many nineteenth-century Australian stories fall into two categories beloved of late-Victorian readers: the detective story and the ghost story, genres that are in any case closely linked by their common basis in the mystery of death. With its eerie bush landscapes, its isolation and vast distances, and the sometimes terrible deaths it had in store for the unwary colonist or visitor, Australia offered a rich source of material for writers who wished to tackle the supernatural, mystery and crime.

During this period, all of the Australian short stories published in Australia, and many of those published in Britain, appeared not in books but in newspapers and journals. *The Australian Journal*, produced in Melbourne, was one of the longest-lived of these; it ran from 1865 to 1958 and it specialised in the publication of short fiction. *The Australasian*, a weekly Melbourne journal published from 1864 to 1946, also specialised in literature and literary matters and published stories by a number of leading Australian nineteenth-century writers.

Representative stories by some of the best of these nineteenth-century writers – John Lang, Marcus Clarke, Francis Adams, Ada Cambridge, Rosa Praed, 'Tasma' – were collected in several anthologies published in the 1980s, when the Australian publishing industry was flourishing and interest in the short story as a genre was high. Cecil Hadgraft's anthology *The Australian Short Story Before Lawson* (1986) and Fiona Giles' *From the Verandah* (1987) between them give an excellent overview of the kind of short fiction that was being written in Australia in the nineteenth century.

The title of Hadgraft's anthology suggests, and rightly, that the work of Henry Lawson represents a kind of turning point in the history of the Australian short story. The 1890s saw the heyday of the *Bulletin*, the astonishingly influential and widely read nationalist journal established in 1880 by J. F. Archibald. A. G. Stephens, hired as a sub-editor in 1894, began immediately to develop the journal's literary content and by 1896 – with the establishment of its major literary section, the famous Red Page – the *Bulletin* had become the focus of Australian literary endeavour.

What this meant for writers was that Archibald and especially Stephens became powerful figures in the development and directions of Australian writing. And Henry Lawson's work embodied the values they most prized: a nationalist world view offering a distinctive 'Australian' voice and concentrating on local themes and subjects not as exotic matter for British readers but as Australian stories for Australian readers. Lawson's work – with the exception of some of the stories he wrote in London in the first years of the twentieth century – is written for a readership already familiar with the characters and landscapes of his stories.

'The Loaded Dog' is rivalled only by 'The Drover's Wife' as Lawson's most popular and best-known story. 'The Loaded Dog' shows Lawson's mastery of a distinctively Australian form of storytelling: the yarn, an outrageously exaggerated 'tall tale' told in a relaxed, laconic, ironic voice, its underpinnings usually comic and sometimes slapstick. The judicious use of the 'yarn', and of the kind of character who tells it, is something that links Lawson's work to that of two of his contemporaries represented in this book, two writers who are otherwise very different from Lawson and from each other: Steele Rudd and Tom Collins.

'The Loaded Dog', despite its violence, shows Lawson at his most innocently funny; his humour is usually less physical and much blacker, residing more in an ironic tone and turn of phrase than in character or event. A story like 'The Union Buries its Dead', another well-known and much-anthologised Lawson piece, turns on a bleak view of bush life and an even bleaker view of human nature, its black humour residing in its oddly modernist satire of nineteenth-century Australian romanticism: 'I have left out the wattle', says the narrator in concluding his description of the funeral of an unknown man, 'because it wasn't there'.

'The Drover's Wife' is not funny at all, and in its concentration on the trials of a woman in the bush is one of the Lawson stories that comes closest to the work of his contemporary Barbara Baynton. Baynton was another writer approved of and encouraged by Archibald and Stephens at the *Bulletin*; though only one of her stories appeared there and was heavily edited first, she was one of the very few women writers to be published in its pages at all. Like Lawson, she wrote of Australian characters and conditions for Australian readers. Her story 'Squeaker's Mate' was published in her collection *Bush Studies* in 1902 and is a typical Baynton story in its grim view of human nature and gender relations, its representation of bush conditions as harsh and hostile, and its philosophical and aesthetic roots in nineteenth-century European naturalism.

The *Bulletin*'s fostering of literary nationalism around the turn of the century provided fertile ground for fiction writers, but between the early 1900s and the early 1930s, little happened in the way of Australian short-story writing; the emphasis in the early decades of this century was mainly on poetry. Between the late 1920s and the outbreak of the Second World War, however, a group of writers emerged who were mainly interested in fiction and whose highly developed political ideas and ideals added to the force of their work. Most, if not all, had left-wing ideals and as the 1930s progressed became more actively involved in the international resistance to the rise of fascism in Europe. The 1930s also saw a revival of the kind of literary nationalism that had been fostered by the *Bulletin*, with organisations like the Fellowship of Australian Writers becoming influential in the growth of Australian culture.

Katharine Susannah Prichard, one of the most prominent names from this period, was like Vance Palmer a novelist and short-story writer. Prichard was a founding member of the Communist Party of Australia in 1921, and her work during the 1930s and early 1940s demonstrates an intriguing combination of her socialist world view with the recognisable influence of the work of D. H. Lawrence. Much of her writing addresses itself to the evils of capitalism, and concerns itself with social justice and the need for social change; but within that framework, her writing is often sexually charged and informed by the techniques of psychological realism. 'The Grey Horse', one of Prichard's best-known stories, combines all of these aspects to some degree and somehow manages to be funny as well.

Henrietta Drake-Brockman, like Prichard, was a writer of that era whose fiction was ahead of its time in its understanding of some of the problems that beset race relations in Australia; her story 'Fear' shows how an atmosphere of distrust can be self-perpetuating and, like some of Prichard's other stories – 'The Cooboo' and 'Flight' are the two best known of this kind – shows how white Australians' treatment of Aboriginal people has a history of tragic consequences. Xavier Herbert's 'Kaijek the Songman', published eight years later than 'Fear', considers Aboriginal Australians from a different angle; here the story is about Aboriginal subjectivity with the Aboriginal characters at the centre of the story. Their values – highlighting the importance of community and culture – are contrasted with, and implicitly shown as superior to, the gold-greed of the unbalanced white man Andy.

Of the writers included in this book, others who were particularly influential in the 1930s included Vance Palmer, Frank Dalby Davison and Marjorie Barnard. Like Prichard, these three were primarily novelists and best known as such, though Palmer in particular was also a prolific short-story writer over several decades. Palmer's 'The Stump', Davison's

'The Woman at the Mill' and Barnard's 'The Persimmon Tree' are all stories that concern themselves with 'ordinary' people at some kind of crisis or turning point. The latter two stories in particular are also, like much of Prichard's work, exercises in psychological realism; the characters' interiority, their thought processes and emotional states, are at the heart of both of these stories.

In an era of burgeoning literary nationalism when rural Australia was widely regarded as the 'real' Australia, Marjorie Barnard's classic story 'The Persimmon Tree' is rather unusual for its period, and anticipates later developments, in being a wholly urban story, set in inner-city Sydney. Barnard's contemporaries, writers like Prichard, Davison and Palmer, wrote fiction with largely rural settings; but Barnard, who lived in Sydney all her life, was more concerned with the lives of urban characters, often of characters leading 'lives of quiet desperation' like the narrator of 'The Persimmon Tree', or in other stories from the same collection, like 'The Lottery' and 'The Party'. What Barnard shares with her contemporaries is an interest in the effect of environment on character, whether that environment be urban or rural.

The Australian fiction writers of the 1930s and 1940s mostly knew each other and were friends, reading and encouraging each other at a time when there was little in the way of supportive infrastructure for writers in Australia – not many publishing outlets, not many good critics and reviewers, no support from the universities and not much by way of government funding. Two Australian writers from this period who were working under very different conditions from this, however, were Henry Handel Richardson and Christina Stead, both of whom had left Australia as young women and were, in the 1930s, living in Europe. Although there is more than thirty years between them in age, their two stories included in this book – Richardson's 'And Women Must Weep' and Stead's 'Guest of the Redshields' – were published in the same year, 1934. Richardson's story seems to belong to an earlier time, perhaps to the era of her novel *The Getting of Wisdom* (1910), set in a girls' school in the late nineteenth century. 'And Women Must Weep', while seemingly late Victorian or Edwardian in its setting and subject matter, feels oddly modern in its treatment; Richardson's familiarity with the work of Freud is visible in this story. The main character Dolly's resentment of the passive, 'feminine' role she is expected to play, though she hardly understands it herself, anticipates the more overt feminism of stories published half a century later by a much younger generation of women.

The Stead story is written in quite a different mode from the realism that dominates Australian fiction of the period. 'Guest of the Redshields' comes from the first book Stead ever wrote, *The Salzburg Tales*. This extraordinary book is a collection of fairytales, fables, yarns, ghost stories and other varied genres held together, after the manner of *The Decameron* or *The Canterbury Tales*, by an embedding narrative in which a heterogenous assortment of people find themselves in the same place and take turns telling stories in order to amuse themselves and pass the time.

Gavin Casey's 'Dust' and John Morrison's 'Nightshift' are examples of the more overtly political stories of this era. They are stories in simple, unadorned language (Morrison's elliptical documentary style adding to its realist effect) that focus on workers and workplace disasters, on the physical dangers lying in wait for working men and women. Alan Marshall's 'Tell Us About the Turkey, Jo . . .' and Dal Stivens' 'The Man Who Bowled Victor Trumper' draw on the 'yarn' tradition going back to, and beyond, Lawson and Rudd; Marshall and Stivens, however, are writing not in the genre of the yarn but rather about it, in stories in which yarns and the telling thereof function as a method of characterisation. Frank Hardy, another writer of a later generation, also celebrates the 'yarn' in his short stories, again as a quintessentially Australian mode, differentiated from the 'tall story' that Americans also tell by its laconic, ironic, often mocking or self-mocking narrative quality.

All five of these writers – Casey, Morrison, Marshall, Stivens and Hardy – are among the most important names in the history of the Australian short story, all with something unique to contribute to the genre and to Australian literary culture. Although traditional and simple in their form, Morrison's stories are particularly original in their representations of the relationship between public and private life: his socialist beliefs are clearly apparent in his choice and treatment of subject matter, while his concern for individual freedoms and inner life is equally apparent in the dynamics of his plots. In a story like 'The Nightshift' he can sketch the contrast between different social classes without any hectoring or bitterness, but rather with the same documentary neutrality that characterises the descriptions of his waterfront settings.

The Australian short story was given a considerable boost in 1941 when Angus and Robertson published the first of a series of annual anthologies, collectively entitled *Coast to Coast*. It was published annually from 1941 to 1948, biennially from 1949 to 1970, again in 1973 and once more, finally, in 1986. Like the newspaper supplement *Tabloid Story* over thirty years later, *Coast to Coast* was a determined and largely successful attempt to provide a focus, a publishing outlet and a readership for the Australian short story. Each individual volume had a different editor – often people who were themselves short-story writers, many of whom are represented in this book.

Eleanor Dark and Kylie Tennant were two of the best-known fiction writers of the 1940s and 1950s; both were prolific and primarily known as novelists, but Dark was the more sophisticated writer with, like Prichard and Richardson, a strong interest in psychological realism. Tennant's story 'Lady Weare and the Bodhisattva' reflects the growing interest in fiction about cities that had begun with writers like Marjorie Barnard, and is typical of her work in being humorous with a strong undercurrent of serious feeling. Dark's 'Serpents' is from her last and rather uncharacteristic book *Lantana Lane* (1959), which, like the work of Steele Rudd half a century before, focuses on the comic aspects of rural life. It has been argued that in the politically repressive and conservative atmosphere of the 1950s it was no longer possible for Dark to write the substantial, broadly based fictions of social and political engagement and critique that typify her earlier work.

Ethel Anderson's 'Miss Aminta Wirraway and the Sin of Lust' is one of a series of linked stories entitled *At Parramatta* (1956) and is quite different from any of the other fiction written during this period. Best described as a non-realist combination of social comedy and historical fiction, this highly-mannered and very funny book about female culture in a highly patriarchal world is set in the 1850s in Parramatta and surrounding villages. This setting gives Anderson the full scope of both urban and rural settings for her pre-feminist reworking of the colonial period.

The most noticeable development in short fiction of the 1950s is the appearance of stories about the wave of postwar European immigration. This is reflected in two very different stories in this collection, E. O. Schlunke's 'The Enthusiastic Prisoner' and Judah Waten's 'Mother'. The first, like Xavier Herbert's 'Kaijek the Songman', uses comedy to frame an implicit critique of the Anglo-Celtic Australian character – and there are a number of such stories from the 1950s and 1960s, notably Thelma Forshaw's 'On Our Safari', a very funny story about a family of hardworking Viennese immigrant chicken farmers. By this decade, and in the wake of the Second World War, the literary nationalism of the 1930s – which had its roots in that of the 1890s, which in its turn had a number of negative elements including open racism – had begun to give way to a more self-reflective and self-critical view of the so-called national character.

By the 1960s it was becoming clearer that the three dominant characteristics of Australian short fiction for the last three decades – realism, social critique, and a preoccupation with 'Australianness' – were becoming less and less marked. The short fiction of this decade was much more diverse, and paved the way for the exponential increase in literary production and especially the boom in the short-fiction market that Australia was, for various reasons, to see in the 1970s.

Although the middle decades of the century were notable for the large number of gifted women writers, the 1960s and most of the 1970s were overwhelmingly dominated, especially in the field of the short story, by men. John Morrison's *Twenty-three Stories* (1962), Hal Porter's *A Bachelor's Children* (1962) and *The Cats of Venice* (1965), Patrick White's *The Burnt Ones* (1964) and Dal Stivens' *Selected Stories: 1936–1968* (1969) were the most significant and best-received collections of stories published in the 1960s.

Of these four writers, only Morrison was working in the social realist mode of the mid-century. Patrick White had begun to revolutionise Australian fiction with his international world view, metaphysical pre-occupations and modernist techniques. Some recent critics have pointed out that White's social criticism and concern with the development of Australian society and culture remain as acute as those of any writer from the previous era, and his political position no more conservative, broadly speaking, than theirs in spite of his own privileged background. His story 'Being Kind to Titina', like many of Hal Porter's, reflects his readiness to write stories with international characters and settings; his style is quite different from what he had rejected as the 'dun-coloured journalistic realism' of his Australian contemporaries.

Porter's story 'Francis Silver' is typical of his work in several ways: in its use of autobiographical elements, in its preoccupation with memory and the passage of time, and in the way that it uses objects, small details, and the density and quiddity of the physical world in general to evoke a specific time and place. Although he is comparatively uninterested in questions of nationalism and of nationality as such, the evocation in his writing of particular Australian places is sometimes breathtaking. His style, like White's, is a great deal more elaborate and colourful than Australian readers of the early 1960s were used to, or (sometimes) comfortable with.

The publication of Dal Stivens' *Selected Stories* in 1969 coincided with the publication of a first collection of short stories entitled *Futility and Other Animals* by a young writer called Frank Moorhouse. A 31-year-old journalist, Moorhouse had published his first short story in the literary journal *Southerly* in 1957, but had found it difficult to publish his stories during the 1960s because of their sexual explicitness. After the publication of his second collection *The Americans, Baby* in 1972, his name was to dominate Australian short fiction for the next decade.

Dal Stivens, meanwhile, is regarded by recent critics, with hindsight, as the forerunner of the kind of writing that was to dominate in the 1970s and beyond. Like that of Porter and White, his work had departed from the social-realist norm; many of his stories are self-conscious fictions in which the act of storytelling itself is central to the story, taking the form of fables and yarns.

The explosion of new writing, especially prose fiction, in the 1970s in Australia was a phenomenon with complex causes, but two of the main ones were the lifting of censorship restrictions and the establishment of the Australia Council, including the Literature Board, in 1973. The previous year, Moorhouse, with Michael Wilding, Brian Keirnan and Carmel Kelly, had established a short-story magazine called *Tabloid Story*, which provided a new publishing outlet for, especially, experimental fiction by younger writers. With new publishing outlets, new freedoms of subject matter and, most of all, new government support for literature, the amount of literary fiction published in Australia in the 1970s increased dramatically and exponentially. In the wake of the Vietnam War and the rise of second-wave feminism, there were suddenly a lot of new things to write about. Australian fiction became abruptly more internationalist in viewpoint, content and influence; more sexually and politically explicit; and more varied in its subjects and styles, as is suggested by the title of a book on contemporary Australian fiction by Ken Gelder and Paul Salzman called *The New Diversity: Australian Fiction 1970–1988*.

Short fiction was the dominant literary form in Australia in the 1970s, and those of its writers most recognised at the time were Moorhouse and Wilding, Peter Carey and Murray Bail. These four, with Morris Lurie, were enshrined as the writers of the decade in an anthology edited by Brian Kiernan called *The Most Beautiful Lies* (1977), in which Kiernan collected the fiction he saw as the most representative, and best, of the 'new' fiction. It was heavily influenced by European and American postmodern writing: experimental, sexually explicit, incorporating elements of fantasy, surrealism, fabulism, literary self-consciousness and the process of storytelling itself. Bail's story 'ABCD-EFGHIJKLMNOPQRSTUVWXYZ' and Carey's 'The Last Days of a Famous Mime' concern themselves with the riddles and paradoxes of representation itself, as do later stories in this collection like Beverley Farmer's 'A Man in the Laundrette' and David Brooks' 'John Gilbert's Dog'.

There were signs towards the end of the 1970s that the advent of second-wave feminism was beginning to show results in the kind of fiction, poetry and drama that was being written, published and performed in Australia. Towards the end of the decade, the publication of Helen Garner's *Monkey Grip* in 1977 followed by that of Jessica Anderson's *Tirra Lirra by the River* in 1978 – both novels won national awards and were, by high-culture standards, bestsellers – showed that something radical had begun to happen in the writing of Australian fiction. Both these novels had first-person narrator heroines called Nora, a name irresistibly suggestive of Ibsen's Nora and her quest for autonomy and agency; and both focused on the paradoxes of women's lives, on the competing claims of romance, domesticity, and the quest to live a useful and meaningful existence. The kinds of social change that followed in the wake of second-wave feminism had begun to produce a receptive audience for such novels – enthusiastic publishers and a growing number of readers – and their success was indicative of what would happen to Australian women's writing in the 1980s.

In the meantime, however, there was, as there had been all along, Thea Astley. Astley had been publishing novels and winning prizes for them all through the male-dominated decades of the 1960s and 70s; her only collection of short stories, *Hunting the Wild Pineapple* (1979), was one of the few by Australian women published in the 1970s. It was published, and well received, in the wake of Garner's and Anderson's novels, as were Jean Bedford's *Country Girl Again* and Glenda Adams' *The Hottest Night of the Century*, all in the same year. Their stories in this collection – Astley's 'Petals From Blown Roses', Bedford's 'Country Girl Again' and Adams' 'A Snake Down Under' – come respectively from these three collections.

From the early 1980s, the Australian readership for fiction by women – short stories and novels alike – began to seem inexhaustible. Elizabeth Jolley, who had been trying and failing to get stories published for many years, was suddenly recognised as a uniquely gifted writer and many of the stories she published in the 1980s had in fact been written years before. Younger Australian women who in the 1970s might never have found someone to publish their work (or who might never have written it at all) emerged as major forces in Australian writing.

Other women writers of an earlier generation found new voices in the new freedoms that feminism had given them to say particular things in particular ways. Olga Masters, after a long life as a working mother in the field of journalism, had a short but brilliant career as a fiction writer in her sixties, cut short by her death in 1986. Her story in this collection, 'The Lang Women', is representative of her work in the way that it harks back to the writing of the era in which it's set – the 1930s – in its realist detail and its compassionate but unsentimental treatment of poverty. Unlike the writing of the 1930s, it focuses firmly on female subjectivity and on women's lives.

A younger generation of women writers – some of whom had already been quietly writing, like Jolley, for years – also emerged in the 1980s, in short fiction as elsewhere; among the best known of these are Marion Halligan, Carmel Bird, Helen Garner, Beverley Farmer and Kate Grenville. Of these writers it is Halligan, Bird and Farmer who have given the most time and attention to the short-story form, though Helen Garner's 'The Life of Art' became what one critic called an instant classic and is one of the most frequently anthologised Australian short stories. 'The Life of Art' is a good example of the dangers of generalising about this generation of women writers; Garner's work has often been described as 'domestic realism', but this, her best-known story, is an explicit departure from both realism and domesticity.

Examination of the statistics will show that the popularity of women's writing in the 1980s did not make it more difficult for male writers to get their work published and read and favourably reviewed, though there were some who claimed that it did, even though the converse situation had clearly applied in the previous decade. The 1980s were a golden decade for Australian writers of both sexes. Support from the Australia Council had made it possible to expand Australian writing and publishing very quickly; the effects of increasing globalisation had not yet begun to be felt, and there was still a comparatively large number of independent Australian publishers.

So there was plenty of room for the publication of stories by male writers like Gerard Windsor, Barry Hill, Peter Goldsworthy, David Brooks and Tim Winton. But the changes wrought by feminism did affect male writers in one way; fiction by men in the 1980s (and even more so in the 1990s) not only concentrates more on gender relations but is concerned in increasingly sophisticated ways with gender differ- ence and the nature of masculinity. Hill's 'Headlocks' and Winton's 'My Father's Axe' offer two particularly good examples of the way that contemporary male writers have tackled the tangled connections among the subjects of masculinity, fatherhood and violence.

One of the most pronounced trends in Australian fiction of the late 1980s and the 1990s, perhaps precipitated or at least amplified by the 1988 Bicentenary, has been a preoccupation among the country's novelists with history: with the nation's troubled, ambivalent beginnings, with colonialism and its consequences, and most of all with Australia's race-relations history. Apart from several stories about Aboriginal char- acters and a few recent ones by Aboriginal writers, this preoccupation is not very apparent in this collection of stories. The reason is probably something to do with genre: the working-out of complex ideas about history, and the writing of historical fiction, requires far more space than the short-story form can provide.

It's too soon – and with the effects of global publishing and technological change, the shifts in publishing conditions are still too rapid – for it be possible to generalise about the new writers whose work began to appear only in the late 1980s and the 1990s. Some of those represented here – notably Gail Jones, Brenda Walker, Gillian Mears and, most recently, James Bradley – have published several books and have established their names firmly in the field of Australian fiction.

Each in his or her own way is a sophisticated writer with a distinctive style, but they are otherwise all quite different from each other in subject matter and approach. Mears' most powerful stories are about intimate relationships and their infinite complexities of nuance, detail and change; Bradley, Walker and Jones are more self-consciously intellectual in their approach but all from, as it were, different angles. Walker and Jones are both extraordinarily gifted writers of complex fictions who should be better known than they are.

Two of the youngest writers included in this book, Delia Falconer and Elliot Perlman, made spectacular beginnings to their literary careers in 1994; both won prestigious national short-story competitions, run by *HQ Magazine* and the *Age* respectively, with the stories included in this book. But in their setting, style and mode, Falconer's 'The Water Poets' and Perlman's 'The Reasons I Won't Be Coming' could not be more different; all they have in common is an air of having been produced by an internationalist sensibility in an increasingly global culture.

This is not to argue for a minute that this generation's writing has lost its specificity of location. Matthew Condon's 'The Sandfly Man', for example, is an intensely place-specific story in an unmistakably Australian landscape, a story turning on the difference between Home and Elsewhere. But the writing of this generation is not nearly as concerned with nationality and nationalism as Australian writing once was, for the excellent reason that it no longer needs to be. What is becoming clearer in Australian writing – as in so many other things – as the century ends is a shift in focus: a shift away from the idea of the national, and towards the dynamic between the local and the global.

Kerryn Goldsworthy
December 1999

BIOGRAPHICAL TIMELINE

The following timeline records the birth and death dates for each of the authors whose work features in this collection.

1843–1912	Tom Collins	*1904–1998*	John Morrison
1844–1926	Ada Cambridge	*1906–1960*	E. O. Schlunke
1857–1929	Barbara Baynton	*1907–1964*	Gavin Casey
1867–1922	Henry Lawson	*1911–1984*	Hal Porter
1868–1935	Steele Rudd	*1911–1985*	Judah Waten
1870–1946	Henry Handel	*1911–1997*	Dal Stivens
	Richardson	*1912–1988*	Kylie Tennant
1883–1958	Ethel Anderson	*1912–1990*	Patrick White
1884–1969	Katharine Susannah	*1914–*	Peter Cowan
	Prichard	*1916–*	Jessica Anderson
1885–1959	Vance Palmer	*1917–1994*	Frank Hardy
1893–1970	Frank Dalby	*1918–*	Amy Witting
	Davison	*1919–1986*	Olga Masters
1897–1987	Marjorie Barnard	*1919–*	Ida West
1901–1968	H. Drake-Brockman	*1920–1996*	Gwen Harwood
1901–1984	Xavier Herbert	*1922–*	Ruth Park
1901–1985	Eleanor Dark	*1923–*	Dorothy Hewett
1902–1983	Christina Stead		Elizabeth Jolley
1902–1984	Alan Marshall	*1925–*	Thea Astley

1928–	Elizabeth Harrower		Bruce Pascoe
1931–	Shirley Hazzard	1948–	Keith Butler
	Peter Mathers		Joan London
	Barry Oakley		Rosie Scott
1933–	Fay Zwicky	1949–	Barry Dickins
1934–	David Malouf		Garry Disher
1934–1998	James McQueen	1950–	Brian Castro
1935–	John Bryson		Kate Grenville
	Thomas Shapcott	1951–	Peter Goldsworthy
1936–	Brian Matthews	1952–	Janine Burke
	Herb Wharton		Jan Hutchinson
1938–	Sara Dowse	1953–	David Brooks
	Frank Moorhouse		John Clark
1939–1991	Barbara Hanrahan		Kerryn Goldsworthy
1939–	Terry Lane	1955–	Candida Baker
1940–	Glenda Adams		Gail Jones
	Carmel Bird	1956–	Susan Johnson
	Marion Halligan	1957–	Liam Davison
1941–	Murray Bail		Brenda Walker
	Beverley Farmer		Archie Weller
1942–	Peter Corris	1959–	Deborah Robertson
	Helen Garner	1960–	Tim Richards
	Janette Turner		Tim Winton
	Hospital	1962–	Matthew Condon
	Michael Wilding		Luke Davies
1943–	Peter Carey	1963–	Bernard Cohen
	Robert Drewe		Nick Earls
	Barry Hill		John Kinsella
1944–	Robert Dessaix	1964–	Gillian Mears
	Gerard Windsor		Elliot Perlman
1946–	Jean Bedford	1966–	Delia Falconer
	Penelope Rowe	1967–	James Bradley
1947–	Marele Day	1968–	Raimondo Cortese

PUBLICATION TIMELINE

The following timeline records the year of first publication for each story featured in this collection.

Glenda Adams

A SNAKE DOWN UNDER
1979

We sat in our navy-blue serge tunics with white blouses. We sat without moving, our hands on our heads, our feet squarely on the floor under our desks.

The teacher read us a story: A girl got lost in the bush. She wandered all day looking for the way back home. When night fell she took refuge in a cave and fell asleep on the rocky floor. When she awoke she saw to her dismay that a snake had come while she slept and had coiled itself on her warm lap, where it now rested peacefully. The girl did not scream or move lest the snake be aroused and bite her. She stayed still without budging the whole day and the following night, until at last the snake slid away of its own accord. The girl was shocked but unharmed.

We sat on the floor of the gym in our uniforms: brown shirts and old-fashioned flared shorts no higher than six inches above the knee, beige ankle socks and brown sneakers. Our mothers had embroidered our initials in gold on the shirt pocket. We sat cross-legged in rows, our backs straight, our hands resting on our knees.

The gym mistress, in ballet slippers, stood before us, her hands clasped before her, her back straight, her stomach muscles firm. She said: If ever a snake should bite you, do not panic. Take a belt or a piece of string and tie a tourniquet around the affected limb between the bite and the heart. Take a sharp knife or razor blade. Make a series of cuts, crisscross, over the bite. Then, suck at the cuts to remove the poison. Do not swallow. Spit out the blood and the poison. If you have a cut on your gum or lip, get a friend to suck out the poison instead. Then go to the nearest doctor. Try to kill the snake and take it with you. Otherwise, note carefully its distinguishing features.

My friend at school was caught with a copy of *East of Eden*. The headmistress called a special assembly. We stood in rows, at attention, eyes front, half an arm's distance from each other.

The headmistress said: One girl, and I shan't name names, has been reading a book that is highly unsuitable for high school pupils. I shan't name the book, but you know which book I mean. If I find that book inside the school gates again, I will take serious measures. It is hard for some of you to know what is right and what is wrong. Just remember this. If you are thinking of doing something, ask yourself: could I tell my mother about this? If the answer is no, then you can be sure you are doing something wrong.

I know of a girl who went bushwalking and sat on a snake curled up on a rock in the sun. The snake bit her. But since she was with a group that included boys, she was too embarrassed to say anything. So she kept on walking, until the poison overcame her. She fell ill and only then did she admit that a snake had bitten her on a very private part. But it was too late to help her. She died.

When I was sixteen my mother encouraged me to telephone a boy and ask him to be my partner for the school dance. She said: You are old enough to decide who you want to go out with and who you don't want to go out with. I trust you completely.

After that I went out with a Roman Catholic, then an immigrant Dutchman, then an Indonesian.

My mother asked me what I thought I was doing. She said: You can go out with anyone you like as long as it's someone nice.

In the museum were two photographs. In the first, a snake had bitten and killed a young goat. In the second, the snake's jaws were stretched open and the goat was half inside the snake. The outline of the goat's body was visible within the body of the snake. The caption read: Snake trying to eat goat. Once snake begins to eat, it cannot stop. Jaws work like a conveyor belt.

A girl on our street suddenly left and went to Queensland for six months. My mother said it was because she had gone too far. She said to me: You know, don't you, that if anything ever happens to you, you can come to me for help. But of course I know you won't ever have to, because you wouldn't ever do anything like that.

Forty minutes of scripture a week was compulsory in all state schools. The Church of England girls sat with hands flat on the desk to preclude fidgeting and note passing. A lay-preacher stood before us, his arms upstretched to heaven, his hands and voice shaking. He said: Fornication is a sin, and evil. I kissed only one woman, once, before I married. And that was the woman who became my wife. The day I asked her to marry me and she said yes, we sealed our vow with a kiss. I have looked upon no other woman.

I encountered my first snake when I went for an early morning walk beside a wheat field in France. I walked gazing at the sky. When I felt a movement on my leg I looked down. Across my instep rested the tail of a tweedy-skinned snake. The rest of its body was inside the leg of my jeans, resting against my bare leg. The head was at my knee.

I broke the rules. I screamed and kicked and stamped. The snake fell out of my jeans in a heap and fled into the wheat. I ran back to the house crying.

My friend said, 'Did it offer you an apple?'

Ethel Anderson

MISS AMINTA WIRRAWAY AND THE SIN OF LUST

1956

The weather, in the summer following the Bishop's visit, was hardly less beneficent than the autumn had been. The days were cloudless. A picnic was to celebrate Miss Aminta Wirraway's seventeenth birthday, chiefly because it was the one form of entertainment likely to be eschewed by the 'agéd'.

'Though I do not call people really old till they take their baths with the door open,' Victoria McMurthie had observed, 'people begin to be elderly when they look thoughtful after eating apple-dumplings –'

'Or when they refuse toffee –'

'Speak when you are spoken to, Alberteena McMurthie!' Victoria silenced her younger sister, and continued: 'But though we are not old, we will leave our bathing dresses behind. Why should we suddenly become stand-offish with each other when we have shared a hot tub every Saturday night until just lately?'

'And when Donalblain (who is four) thinks nothing of coming into the Nursery to borrow the soap?'

'Alberteena! How often must I tell you that speech is silver, silence is gold?' Victoria again quenched her younger sister. 'So why be squeamish?' she added, and before climbing into her place in the buckboard, she hid nine voluminous sets of garments, made of many yards of serge, and decorated with white vandyked braid, behind the hedge.

The Vicarage buckboard, an unwired aviary of chirping girls, and drawn with cloppy animation by 'old' Ruby, who was rising two, then set off, to creak, to hesitate, to side-slip in the ruts of the sandy track that led from Mallow's Marsh to Lanterloo Bay.

The road was often repaired with bridgings of wattle saplings laced together with rope or vines, yet over the creeks there were no bridges; these had to be forded with a great splashing of water and many shrieks of excitement.

However, Juliet McCree was a dashing whip – she brought her gay passengers safely to the harbour's rim.

And in Lanterloo Bay the sand's golden half moon, the calm yet mettlesome hiss of the placid sea, the entirely conventional sky.

Lying after her dip to dry her pliant body in the warm, down-soft sand, each girl paid her tribute to its beauty.

'Such a blue sky, such a radiant sea, not a cloud, not a wave, not a wrinkle on the water!' Alberteena, for once, was allowed her say.

'The sea is darker than the sky!'

'Where we lie, above high tide mark, the sand is as fine as icing-sugar, and it is never covered with seaweed or seashells.'

'What I like best is the smell of the umbrella fern coming from that creek.'

'The sea smells of lobster.' Juliet McCree, as usual, was seeking after truth. She sniffed, with a scientific expression of her glowing face, the hardly stirring waves that lapped her sunlit body, which, from top to toe, rivalled a ripe apricot in colour.

'Juliet!' Aminta felt it necessary to assert her age. Shielding her flawless complexion with a minute, hinged parasol (its ivory stick was chaperoned by a tell-tale silver bell) she lay, more beautiful than any Venus known to art, among the castles of sand Alberteena, Gussie and Octavia had built round her. 'Juliet! Come out! You have been in the water long enough!'

'Oh, no! I can't come out yet! The water is so delicious! I want to find out exactly what it really smells of! Sometimes it has a queer reek, almost like a noise, and at other times it has a whiff like Grandmama McCree's white Camellia –'

'Whose pink lawn handkerchief is this?'

'Mine, dear.'

'Tie it round your wrist.'

'Across the harbour Sydney begins to look like a real city, doesn't it? There's St James' spire – such an elegant candlesnuffer.'

'So many lovely sailing ships, too! I like them best like that, with all their sails set, drying in the sun, and all reflected in the water, as they just swing with the tide.'

'Dr Phantom does not really care for women.'

Gussie Wirraway had a younger sister's uncomfortable habit of introducing an unwanted subject.

'What a pity!' Victoria McMurthie became worldly. 'He's the only eligible bachelor between Mallow's Marsh and Hornsby Junction.'

'His three brothers all made such good matches.' Gussie was not to be outdone. Sitting on a sandcastle she searched, like 'The Spinario', for a thorn in a pink toe.

'Simeon married ten thousand pounds in bonds,' Victoria remarked, still in her role of woman of the world.

'And the handsomest set of buck teeth this side of the equator.'

'Ninian, the second boy, married twenty thousand acres –'

'What! More teeth, dear?'

'No. Goosie-Gussie! A-C-R-E-S! Of land! Covered in sheep, in Victoria.'

'And three sets of twins.'

'Septimus, the third brother – (what a cheat Mrs Phantom was, to call her third son Septimus) – well – he married a line of South Sea Whalers!'

'And a whale of a wife!'

'No dear, she was a minnow – a gold fish, merely. I was a bridesmaid at the wedding.' Aminta sadly roused herself from a reverie.

'My dears!' Victoria evaded contact with a flowering wattle which Alberteena was using to brush off sand. 'They all married Prosperity.'

'Yes! And look at them! Ninian at thirty with a barouche, a gig, five saddle horses, a Crown Derby dinner service with covers for forty, a tolerably handsome residence at Point Piper – right in the bush, really –'

'And the intolerable bathos of three sets of twins!'

'And Simeon, dear man! I'm very fond of Simeon! He's *so* rich, *such* a handsome property. Two thousand Merinos, a thousand head of cattle, all within a day's ride –'

'Of the nearest glass of rum.'

'And with a shambling progeny of fourteen daughters, and a face pockmarked with hen-pecks –'

'Dr Phantom cares for nothing but sport.'

'Yes! The minute he's free, off he goes on that sawney sorrel brute of his, and surrounded by all those curs, pariahs, dingoes, collies, kelpies! Yap, yap, yap! Bow-wow-wow! Oh, the din! Oh, the clatter! They woke me up at four o'clock this morning.'

'Where does he go?'

'Most often to that old Inn, "The Devil's Tail", at Doggett's Patch, about fourteen miles past Windsor, out by the Hawkesbury River.'

'He goes to shoot wallabies or dingoes.'

'No one really believes he goes simply to shoot.'

'Oh, keep away, Juliet! Keep away! If you shake yourself so near us you'll make us all wet again, and we are just drying nicely.'

Such was the chorus that greeted Juliet, who ran out of the water at last, to pirouette, to stamp, to squeeze the moisture out of her auburn hair, now black and sticky.

'All right, all right! I'll sit here on this hillock of sand with the mimosa tree to keep the sun off! Poor Dr Phantom says he has not the slightest wish to marry, much less to become a father –'

'Who told you that, pray?'

'He did. In Church. Of course we were sitting right at the back. No human being could sit silent through Grandpapa's sermon on the Hittites, the Jebusites and the Ammonites! It's too learned!'

'What! Dr Phantom a bachelor? He'll fall in love and marry just like any other man.'

'No. He says not. The trouble is, he says, that one is allowed no choice! And, really, it does seem to be so. My dear Papa used to say, "Sweet or dry?" or "Say when, old chap", and Mama says, "Milk and sugar?" Grandpapa asks anyone who goes into the Snuggery, "Do you prefer the window open or shut?" And that old waiter out at The Devil's Tail breathes over your shoulder and says, "Thick or Thin?" And we always think we are being asked to make our choice between things that do not matter in the least, which makes us think we are actually somebody with a will of our own, but God does not ask "Boy or Girl?" when we are waiting to be born – which is important, really. He knows we would all say "Boy", and then where would posterity be?'

'There should have been a third sex,' Victoria agreed, 'with the vices of neither men nor women and the virtues of both.'

'And without the bore of having to live like men and women.'

Juliet was emphatic.

'Of course there are the saints. They refuse to be men and women, but do they enjoy it? Look at St Lawrence with his gridiron, and St Catherine with her wheel, and St Sebastian with his arrows and St Stephen with his stones! They are always painted with calm, holy expressions on their faces, but I doubt if they enjoyed themselves. As things are, Dr Phantom says, nothing would induce him to marry.'

'Why, dearest Aminta! Tears! Oh, that scrap of pink lawn is useless! Take my handkerchief.' Even Victoria was concerned to see such grief.

'Yes,' went on Juliet, who was turned the other way, 'all Dr Phantom wants is to be free to go to Burragorang or to cross the Wollondilly, or explore the Nepean, or the Diamantina, or to go to the hills to shoot pigeons, or shovellers on the lakes, or to the Limestone Plains, he says, to shoot plovers and wild turkeys – there are flocks of them there, he says, and he wants to go to the Snowy River, to fish for trout – rainbow trout – that's the life for him, he says, and he's making a collection –'

'Of women?'

'No, silly! Of goannas! He has four beauties already.'

'Why – *whatever is the matter with Aminta*?'

'Oh, poor darling! Doesn't she look unhappy!'

'She's getting so thin, too! I can count all her ribs.'

'Why,' Juliet exclaimed, looking round, 'her backbone looks just like an oxtail, with all those knobs.'

'Oh, my dear! Tell us all your sorrows. A sorrow told is a sorrow halved, they say.'

'Oh, I'm in love!' Aminta's tone was desperate. 'Oh, love is a terrible thing, so sweet when it begins, and then, ah – the ache, the yearning, the longing! I get no rest. I toss and turn. I can't get *him* out of my thoughts, and oh! he doesn't care a rap for me!'

'Take up woolwork; it's so fascinating.'

'Knit him a smoking-cap, in double Berlin wool, and line it with plush. With *that* on his head he could not help thinking of you!'

'Embroider him a set of the new braces – like the curate's.'

'Don't tease her, girls. Can't you see this is serious?'

'I'm so restless. I can't concentrate. The world seems quite unreal! I wanted above all things to come to this lovely picnic, but now I'm here I keep thinking – "suppose *he* passed our gate and I was not there to see". Oh, and I lie awake all night making up conversations with him!'

'Do please tell us what you talk about. I've never been in love.'

'Nor I.'

'Neither have I.'

'Of course we haven't, yet.'

'I should never dream of falling in love, myself.'

'Let me rest my head on your shoulder, Juliet dear, then I'll tell you. I'm so weary, I suffer, oh, how I suffer! I have no strength left. Look at my arm. It's so weak that I could not even support the weight of my bracelet –'

'You mean that silver filigree bangle?'

'Yes. I left it at home.'

Aminta's was, apparently, a classic case! Her every symptom of hopeless love matched poor Phaedra's, who, through weakness, discarded her cumbrous ornaments, and let her auburn tresses fall over her shoulders – as Aminta's then were doing, for she had freed her chignon of its net – it seemed to ease her.

'I found its weight insupportable. I did not eat a bit of breakfast.'

'Do tell us, dear Aminta, about those conversations.'

'I imagine we are riding together on two most beautiful horses (a roan and a dapple-grey) and we talk about the flowering trees and the swiftly moving clouds –'

'Trees and clouds, dear? You are going quite the wrong way about it. *He* cares to discuss nothing but the price of hay.'

'Or I pretend we are sailing in a little yacht (such a pet of a boat with tan sails) and we glide across the water, and the sun shines and the breeze is as soft as silk on one's cheek –'

'Just like this! What could be lovelier than it is today?'

'But he is not here. *He* is not with me! Oh, I shall die! I know I shall! I cannot endure this nag, nag, nag at the very marrow of my heart one moment longer. I can't, I can't.'

'Oh, isn't it sad?'

'Oh, poor, poor girl!'

'Oh, it's agony, agony!'

'Have you tried getting Granny Smith to read your fortune in the dregs of your cup?'

'I did. She said she could not see a ray of hope.'

'I always think Granny Smith has such an amused expression on her face, don't you, Gussie?'

'Hush! I want to hear what Aminta is saying.'

'I bowed three times to the new moon and wished. I slept with a stocking full of apples under my pillow. Oh, such a dreadful thing I did! I stuck a flail up the chimney! Nothing was the least use!'

'Stuck a flail up the chimney! Aminta! What a dreadful thing to do! But that's Black Magic. Oh, you naughty girl!'

'The terrible thing is, I have grown quite shameless. I shock myself. Sometimes I have to get out of bed and say my prayers, however cold it is, and however bad my chilblains are! And that's not the worst! I saw *him* go into the chemist's! I did not want to buy anything but in I went! Just to see him smile – I felt my reputation was of no consequence! And he gave me such a cool nod. Such a respectful salute – just with two fingers.'

'Better get her dressed.'

'Better harness Ruby and take her home.'

'Juliet, you slip your clothes on and run and harness Ruby.'

'Yes, yes, I will, immediately! Someone come and hold the shafts. Ruby is so immense, it's a squeeze to get her between them. She's a pure-bred brewer's dray horse from Marseilles, and she's much bigger than any Flanders mare.'

'Get dressed, Aminta darling, and come home. And when we're all nine of us in the buckboard, and the hot sun is shining, and old Ruby is going at a brisk trot, with all her brasses clinking, and her hairy hooves clapping the stones, and all of us are chattering like jays, oh, darling, it might cheer you up, indeed it might.'

'Nothing could! Oh, dear! Oh, dear! Abigail has put too much starch in my chemise, and the frills are as sharp as knives round my armpits, and they cut my flesh to ribbons –'

'There, there, darling girl, dry your eyes, my pet, and come home.'

'A liberal dose of hartshorn, that will pull her round.'

Victoria, laden with the luncheon basket, paused. 'What about this doll, dear, that you made of milk and bread while we were all eating our sandwiches?'

'Shall we bring it?'

'It's not a doll. It's Venus. A votive offering. After all, you never know, do you? I'd like to leave it by the sea's edge – just in case!'

'Paganism, too!'

Even Juliet McCree was shocked, and she was almost a free-thinker.

'Miss Loveday Boisragon,' Gussie Wirraway volunteered, to change the subject, 'sometimes goes to stay at The Devil's Tail. The landlord's daughter was one of her Sunday school pupils. Yes, she drives over and stays a few nights sometimes.'

'My dear!' Victoria whispered to Octavia, who was next to Aminta in age, 'do look at Aminta. Directly she heard *that* she dried her eyes! If a kitten could look calculating – well! Just look at her! She has suddenly got quite a scheming air, hasn't she? I think she is far less innocent than she appears to be.'

'Nonsense! She is the dearest thing! I suppose you mean to infer that she will try to get Miss Loveday to take her with her next time she goes to The Devil's Tail?'

'What!' Overhearing, Alberteena, who was precocious for ten, ex-claimed, 'Aminta go with Miss Loveday to The Devil's Tail at Doggett's Patch! What would she do in Doggett's Patch?'

'Why, Dr Phantom goes there sometimes, Goose!'

In the haste of departure the bevy of girls trooped through the flowering wattles and stiff, aromatic umbrella ferns in the creek bed, and nothing was left of the picnic but a great many footprints and dimples in the sand, a branch or two of mimosa, lying golden in the sun, and the small image of Venus, made of milk and bread, which (the beach once deserted) soon attracted the seagulls and poddy-moddies, who, knowing no better, ate her up to the last crumb.

Jessica Anderson

UNDER THE HOUSE

1980

'If you don't wait under the house,' said Rhoda to me, 'she won't come at all.'

Sybil, at Rhoda's side, jumped up and down and said, 'She won't come at all if you don't.'

'And for all we know,' said Rhoda, 'another visitor might come with her. So go on, Bea, wait under the house.'

'Go on, Bea.'

At the foot of the wooden steps, which jutted like a ladder from the veranda of the house, the three of us stood in the solid heat. We all wore dresses of brown and white checked cotton made by our mother. Rhoda, who now took me by the shoulder, was ten, Sybil was six, I was four. I deduce these ages from my knowledge that when I was five we left that house, which, with its land, was known as Mooloolabin, having been called after Mooloolabin Creek, the secreted stream on its northern border, to which our brother Neal, the eldest of us all, was allowed access, and we girls were not.

Rhoda's long greenish eyes, as I pleadingly sought them with my own, did not regard me with her usual love, her almost maternal concern, but were made remote and pale by the projection of herself into her intention, by the heat of her imagination. I had had much delight from my sister Rhoda's imagination, but that day I was resistant. I felt she and Sybil were deserting me. 'I want to wait here,' I said.

'Not in the sun,' said Sybil. When Sybil asserted herself, she sought the backing of our mother. 'Mum would be angry if we left you in the sun.'

'And you would go to the gate and peep. I know you,' said Rhoda, turning me by the shoulder. 'You can't peep from under the house.'

Rhoda could be coaxing and implacable at the same time. She kept hold of my shoulder as she and Sybil walked me alongside the cool breath of ferns under the steps, and then beneath the floor of the veranda. In the vertical slats encompassing that area which is still called, in Queensland houses, the under-the-house, there were two gaps, back and front, and through the front gap I was now ushered, or pushed.

'And no coming out and looking down the front paddock,' warned Rhoda, as she and Sybil hurried away.

I could never go alone into the under-the-house at Mooloolabin without an uneasiness, a dogged little depression. Unless it was raining, no lines of washing hung there, and nor did my father use that space for his workbench, as he would do in the suburban house to which we were soon to move, for at Mooloolabin all such needs were filled by the Old Barn, the first shelter my father's parents had put up on their arrival with their family from Ireland.

So, in the under-the-house at Mooloolabin, there was no extension of the busy house above except the meat safe hanging from a rafter, the boxes of wood cut for the stove, and the tins of kerosene used for the lamps. These objects, dull and grey in themselves, left dominant to my eyes the sterile dust at my feet, the rows of tall sombre posts with blackened bases, and the dark vertical slats splintering the sunlight outside. Broken cobwebby flowerpots were piled in one corner. From a nail in a post hung the studded collar of the dog Sancho, who had had to be shot, and from another hung the leg irons dug up by my grandfather, relic of 'some poor fellow' from the days when Brisbane was a penal colony.

Feeling imprisoned, put away, discarded, I stood where Rhoda and Sybil had left me, waiting for them to get too far away to detect me when I ran out and peeped through the garden gate. Above my head, in the big front bedroom where the three of us slept, I heard Thelma crossing the floor, slow as ever in her clumsy boots. Thelma came in from one of the nearby farms to help my mother. By the brief muffling of her footsteps, I knew when she passed over the red rug beside my bed. My discontent with the dust and husks of the under-the-house made the bedroom upstairs seem packed with colour and interest, increasing the attractions of the embroidered bedcovers, the lace valances over the mosquito nets, and that particular red rug, so memorable because of that dawn when Rhoda had plucked it from the floor and flung it over my shoulders.

We had both been wakened by the silence, the cessation, after so many days, of the hammers of rain on the iron roof. Warning me to hold the edges of the rug together, Rhoda took me by the other hand. We crept down the front steps, stealthily opened and shut the gate dividing garden from paddock, and ran splashing down the broad rutted track towards the road. It was a quarter of a mile (my brother Neal has since told me), but memory, woven tight though I know it to be with imagination, insists that it was longer, showing me, beyond correction, a flat extended prospect crossed by those two running figures, one backed with red wool, the other with her long tangled brown hair.

I had no goal in mind. My elation in the expanding daylight was enough. But when we reached the road, a goal was provided. Heard before seen, the gutter was running with water, a miniature torrent, over stones a cascade. Instructed by Rhoda, I squatted beside it. Still holding the edges of the rug together, I put the other hand, cupped, in the torrent. I shouted to find myself holding a ball of live water. I was amazed, enraptured by such resilience, freshness, softness, strength. I had never seen a swiftly running stream, had never seen the sea. Rhoda took no part, but stood at my side, satisfied with my delight, with the rewards of the entertainer, until she judged it time for the scene to change.

'Come on. Come back. Quick. Or they'll catch us.'

Who would? I didn't ask, but gleefully connived, adding my own hints of danger. The sun was prickling the tops of the uncropped grass as we ran back.

Now I heard my mother enter the bedroom above my head, her footsteps also muffled for a moment by the red rug. I could not distinguish the words she said to Thelma, yet could hear the swishes and soft bumps as they gathered up the mosquito nets and tossed them on top of the valance frames, out of the way before mattresses were turned and beds made.

My mother's presence in the bedroom stopped me from running out and peeping through the gate. The bedroom window overlooked the front garden and the paddock beyond, and if she happened to look out and see me peeping, she would call to me in her pleasant commanding voice and ask why I had been left alone. Rhoda, when delegated to mind me, was gravely warned never to leave me alone, because of the creek.

So I fidgeted and waited while her footsteps crossed and recrossed the floor above my head, brisk and staccato above the indecisive steps of Thelma. She wore neat black or brown shoes (polished by Neal) laced over the instep. Her parents had emigrated from England when she was three. Both she and Thelma wore aprons, Thelma's of opened-out sugar bags, hers of checked cotton.

They went at last, together, but left me in indecision by standing talking in the corridor near Neal's room. I would feel safe once they were in there, working. Neal's room, like the creek, was forbidden to me, though in this case the risk was to him. I had drawn a margin of red crayon round a page in one of his exercise books, in emulation of his own neat margins ruled in red ink. The consequent hullaballoo he raised is my strongest memory of Neal at Mooloolabin. Visually, all that reaches me is the misty outline of a thin figure, not much less than man-sized, standing in profile, with the hump of a school satchel on his back.

Neal and Rhoda went to the local school, where the teaching was deplorable and they were likely to get nits in their hair. 'Are we to bring up our children among ignorant cow cockies?' my mother sorrowfully asked my father, by lamplight. They owned half an acre of suburban land, near a 'good' school. They could sell here and build there. But my father, though agreeing about the teaching and the nits, was reluctant to leave his father's meagre acres. From an office in Brisbane he instructed others how to farm, how to treat disease in stock and crops, but still hankered to return to farming himself, so that sometimes he would respond to my mother; 'Better a cow cocky than an office johnny.'

As soon as I heard my mother and Thelma go into Neal's room and begin work, I ran out from under the house and stood at the gate, looking through the palings. But no visitors were approaching, neither by the track across the paddock nor through the long grass from the clump of she-oaks to one side.

But suddenly, under the she-oaks, I caught a movement, a flash of shining blue. I jumped to the bottom bar to get an unimpeded glimpse between the pointed tops of two pickets, eager to see again the exotic high gloss of that blue.

Instead, I saw a boy emerge, in grey and white. For a moment he stood uncertainly in the sun, then ran back into the she-oaks. As he was about the size of Curly Moxon, from the adjacent farm, who was moreover the only child within range, I thought that Rhoda and Sybil had been diverted, the game of visitors abandoned, myself forgotten.

The sun beat on my back and penetrated my green-lined sunhat. I went back under the house and wandered drearily about. In Neal's room work was still going on. I passed beneath our parents' bedroom (which I remember only as white, starchy, insipid, and often locked) and wandered about beneath the other side of the house, longing for solace and company, tempted by the red and blue medallions on the kitchen linoleum, the blue and white crockery on the dresser. In the windowless living room, dimness would make magnetic the forbidden objects – the dark books on the higher shelves, the shining violin in its red velvet nest, the revolving top of the music stand. But the books on the lower shelves were permitted, and beyond the glass doors, on the veranda, stood canvas chairs with sagging mildewed seats wide enough to contain entirely my curled body.

Thelma and my mother crossed the corridor into the kitchen. I saw myself standing at the table (spoken to, tended, receiving something on a plate) and considered wandering out to the foot of the back steps and having a fit of coughing. Yet when I heard Thelma come out of the back door and embark on the stairs, I instantly took off my hat and slipped behind the nearest post, my heart beating in that manner so interesting when Rhoda was with me.

Thelma took a plate of meat from the hanging safe. I was much thinner than the post I stood behind, and I held my hat crushed against my chest, but I must have moved; she must have glimpsed me as I had glimpsed that flash of blue under the she-oaks.

'Hey, who's that?' she called out. 'Beatie? Syb?'

Behind my post, I did not move.

'One of you, anyway,' concluded Thelma.

She turned and started up the steps. With one eye, I watched her feet rising between the treads. Then I ran over and seized the tennis ball lying among the boxes of wood and, by the time my mother's feet appeared between the treads, I seemed engrossed in bouncing the ball against a rafter, and catching it and bouncing it again.

'Beatie?'

My mother stood in the gap in the dark slats, behind her an expanse of sun-yellowed green and the weathered silvery timber of the Old

Barn. The horse Pickwick was moving into the gap with his usual slow intent, cropping grass.

'Beatie, where are Rhoda and Syb?'

I resumed my game, saying they had just gone off for a while.

She came and took the ball from my hand. 'Gone off where?'

'You'll spoil it.'

'Spoil what?'

'It's a game.'

'What kind of game?'

Did she know about our visitors? She had sometimes stunned Rhoda and me (though not Sybil) with her knowledge of our secrets. 'I have to wait here,' I said with crafty vagueness, 'till they come.'

She looked dubious, but gave me back the ball. 'You *will* wait here?'

'I promise.'

'And not go wandering off to the creek?'

'I promise. God's honour.'

'Your promise is quite enough,' she said with a tartness I noted but did not yet understand. She twitched straight the hat I had put on in such a hurry. 'And that sandal is loose. Here.'

As she had crouched, I extended a foot and submitted to this service I could have done for myself. Her hair was already grey, making her olive skin look fresh and polished, and kindling her eyes beneath their dark brows. At that time she must have been in her early forties, about the age at which Rhoda died. She rose to her feet to go. 'Mum?' I said.

'Yes, dear?'

'Ro won't get into trouble for leaving me?'

'Rhoda has been told again and again.' My mother turned and started back up the stairs, adding, 'We will have to see.'

'We will have to see' meant that it was important enough to consult my father. I crushed the tennis ball between my palms, hoping that Rhoda would get off with a reprimand, chastisement being the alternative. As soon as my mother's feet disappeared, I dropped the ball and ran towards the front of the house. Warnings must be carried. But when I reached the ferns under the steps I heard the high affected voice of a visitor, and I stepped back under the house and waited.

Rhoda and Sybil came in from the sunlight. Rhoda wore a floppy-brimmed hat of shining blue crinoline and carried a little petit-point bag. Her cheeks and lips were pink with cochineal and her face white with what could only have been talcum, for our house was as unprovided with face powder as it was with lipstick and rouge. She held the bag at a dainty distance and swung her hipless body from side to side, while Sybil, dressed as a boy in grey pants, white shirt, and a tweed cap, tried to trudge.

'You are Beatrice, I believe?' said Rhoda, in a high, bored drawl.

But I could not rise to my part. I was distracted not only because I had betrayed Rhoda's dereliction to our mother, but also by the evidence which Rhoda and Sybil presented of other punishable acts. It did not matter that the clothes Sybil wore were Neal's, made to fit by many pins and tucks, nor that the tweed cap was my father's. Forgivable also were Rhoda's apricot silk dress, court shoes stuffed with paper, and little handbag; all were play property, donated by my mother's youngest sister, who was modern. And Rhoda's hair was not really cut, but looped and pinned to the top of her head, so that beneath the crown of the blue hat it approximated the look of the bobbed hair she longed for, but which was denied to her though granted to Sybil and me.

No, it was the hat itself that alarmed me, the hat, the hat. Not even the modern aunt would have worn it. It was the type called by Rhoda a 'see-through' or 'actress' hat. It was in fact by these descriptions of hers that I recognised it as utterly foreign, and certain to fall into the category of the forbidden. It looked brand new, too, and attached to its band was a bright pink rose of stiffened cloth. And then, to divert my attention (if anything could) from the scandal and mystery of the hat, were the military medals and regimental colours pinned to Sybil's shirt.

Rhoda's body was moving from side to side in a stationary sashay. 'The little girl must be shy,' she remarked to Sybil.

'Why don't you answer, little girl?' gruffly demanded Sybil.

I cried out at Rhoda, 'Where did you get that hat? It's brand new. And those are Neal's medals.'

'Oh, no, no, no,' said Rhoda with a laugh. 'Those are Johnny's father's medals. But goodness, I quite forgot to introduce us. I am your sister Rhoda's rich friend Maisie Lemon. And this is Johnny Pumper.'

Overhead, Thelma clanked a bucket down on the bathroom floor. By my mother's footsteps I could locate her in the kitchen. Under compulsion not to shout, I wailed instead. 'It's not Johnny Pumper. It can't be. And where did the hat come from? It's *new*. And those are *Neal's medals*.'

On my forbidden forays into Neal's room I had seen how he kept those Anzac decorations in little separate boxes, each laid out on a piece of card, with a border ruled in red ink. I was aghast at Rhoda's sheer nerve in having gone in there and simply grabbed them.

But Rhoda was looking at me with mild adult surprise. 'Who is Neal, little girl?' she asked. Sybil frowned and folded her arms.

'You'll get into awful trouble,' I said.

'What a silly little girl,' remarked Rhoda to Sybil. Sybil shook her head in wonder at my silliness. Rhoda turned again to me.

'Johnny's father was a war hero, killed at Gallipoli.'

For a moment I was arrested. At the nitty school there were many fatherless children. But the attraction of the word 'hero' could not conquer my distress, my confusion at having been presented with too many problems at once, so that I did not know which to tackle first. I said, trying to be calm, 'That is not Johnny Pumper. And how will you know the right boxes to put the medals back into?'

Sybil gave a gasp and turned shocked eyes on Rhoda. For a moment Rhoda's eyes responded in kind, but in the next moment she had converted her shock into the energy with which she patted her hair and thrust forward her painted face.

'Little girl,' she said with clarity, 'you are not very polite. I introduce Johnny and myself, and instead of saying how-do-you-do, you go on with all that bunkum. I will give you one last chance.' She indicated Sybil, who again folded her arms and set her feet apart. 'This is Johnny Pumper, and I am your sister's great friend, Maisie Lemon.'

Also with my feet apart, I flailed my arms around like a windmill. This reduced my impotence and anxiety, and enabled me to say, 'Those are stupid *stupid* names.'

Rhoda did not move nor speak. The hand with which she had indicated herself remained suspended in graceful limpness near her chest, a hostage to the game behind which she could withdraw into brief consultation with herself. For of course I was right. The names were stupid. Rhoda had reached that point in her creation where her characters had slipped away from her first flippant choice of names and now needed rechristening.

'It is true,' she said at last, 'that I am not Maisie Lemon.'

I pointed vehemently. 'And that is not Johnny Pumper.'

For very near the heart of my offendedness was Sybil's impersonation, which deprived me of the original Johnny Pumper, a foolish pigeon-toed redhead who resided in the sky and was often in serious trouble with his father. Whenever it thundered Rhoda said that Mr Pumper was roaring at Johnny, and demonstrated the terrified tumbling gait at which Johnny tried to escape his father.

'No,' admitted Rhoda, 'it's not Johnny. That's true, too.'

'Then why did you say it was?'

Rhoda's eyes were narrowing, her tone becoming threatening. 'I had an important private reason. It is something to do with the government. And now, dear –'

'And the hat!'

'And now, dear,' said Rhoda, in steady and overt threat, 'I have a little present for you.'

I was silent at once. After giving me a glare of warning, she opened the petit-point bag and took out a small parcel. Unwrapped, it disclosed three big lollies, tenderly pink, perfectly globular. We were seldom allowed sweets, and these looked as desirable as the kind bought in shops. I put my hands behind my back and stared at them. Sybil shuffled closer, licking her lips. I said, through my watering mouth, 'Where did you get the hat?'

'You may take one, little girl.'

Suddenly Sybil and I both plucked with greedy little hands at Rhoda's palm. Rhoda took the remaining sweet, raised her eyebrows as she examined it, then slowly and fastidiously put it into her mouth. With my own sweet still melting in my mouth, I flung both arms round Rhoda and clutched her tight.

'Ro! Tell me about the hat.'

'I shall never tell you about the hat,' said Rhoda blithely.

'Ro!'

'I shall carry the secret of the hat to my grave.'

One of Rhoda's eyes had a cast. It was extremely elusive. Like that flash of blue under the she-oaks, or the movement Thelma glimpsed of the child behind the post, you saw it, then doubted that you had. Even at her photographs I must look closely to detect it.

She can't have been physically punished – chastised – for leaving me unguarded, or I would have remembered it. At that time illness was taking hold of my father, stiffening and hollowing out his big frame, and sometimes, after he had made the long journey home from Brisbane, his coughing and exhaustion left my mother room for no other concern. In any case, it was certainly not one of those occasions when Rhoda, her face wet with tears, would hug me and whisper that she was going to run away, and would give me as a memento her cinnamon brown handkerchief with the clown embroidered in one corner. How we bawled and clung! The next day she would take the handkerchief back.

As for the medals, I recall only my mother saying, with absent-minded benignity, that no great harm had been done, and Neal could put the medals back himself, though Rhoda must promise not to take them again.

Maisie Lemon evaporated, as characters will when untimely exposed, and so did both Johnny Pumpers, the fake drawing the original with him. Rhoda's attempt to reinstate the original during the next thunderstorm met with my absolute stubborn and insulted resistance. Later, an attempt was made to bring on a Christabel Someone and a Cyril Somebody-else, but before they could take hold, we moved to the suburban house.

As soon as we moved from Mooloolabin it became Old Mooloolabin, by the same process as, when our paternal grandparents moved from their first stout unornamented shelter, it became the Old Barn. At the new house we had less need of outright fables. Relations and our parents' friends could easily visit, other children lived nearby and could be asked home, and we could see, passing in the street or standing behind counters in shops, persons of sufficient familiarity, yet sufficiently strange, for Rhoda and I to graft upon their lives our frequently outrageous speculations.

And in a bush gully at the straggling end of the street ran a creek frequented by children my mother would have called rough or even undesirable. We did not have that child-tracking device, the telephone; I would say I was going to Betty's or Clare's and would go instead to hang around at the creek, keeping a slight distance, shy yet fascinated. I kept the creek secret even from Rhoda, feeling that it would lose value if it were not all my own. Rhoda, now that she had friends of her own age, also had her secrets, but in spite of our different preoccupations a special fidelity to each other remained, and for me, the hat remained a marvellous apparition, ever blue, shining, and brand new. At first I continued to beg Rhoda to tell me where she got it, losing my temper and pummelling her when she wouldn't; but she would only give her former answer, or would smile as if at private knowledge as she fended off my fists. And after a few months, though I continued to ask, my question – Where did you get the hat? – became cabalistic, something to sing into a silence, to murmur for the mystification of cousins, or to whisper for reassurance if we found ourselves isolated in uncongenial company.

Only once did the ground of our tacit deceit shift a little. Now that we lived near shops we managed to get more manufactured sweets than before, but I continued to remember as so excellent those three pink lollies that one Saturday afternoon, when my mother was out visiting, attended by Sybil, and Neal was helping my father in the garden, I persuaded Rhoda to show me how to make them. I watched closely as she mixed icing sugar, milk, coconut and cochineal, and as she rounded the mixture between sugared palms. She covered it briefly – a magician's gesture – before presenting it. And I saw that it was imperfectly round and slightly grey with handling. Yet there was Rhoda's face, as confident and triumphant as at Old Mooloolabin.

I took the lolly, put it in my mouth, and twirled away through the house until I reached the front veranda. Here I rotated quickly and silently, the better to meditate on what I had just learned. Rhoda came out and twirled nearby. The wide verandas and smooth boards of the new house had set us dancing, and a Christmas play had given us our models.

Coming to a stop beside Rhoda, my speculation complete, my decision made, I advanced my right foot, curved my right arm above my head, and gazed upward at my hand. Rhoda, the backs of her hands forward, bowed low to the audience. Beneath our feet, in the under-the-house, the leg irons hanging from one nail, and Sancho's collar from another, were seldom noticed among all the stuff from the Old Barn. Outside in the garden Neal, now clearly defined as a tall youth with dark curls and a meritorious frown, walked in a strenuous slope behind a lawnmower. Gazing upward at my primped hand, I said to Rhoda, 'That hat wasn't new.'

'It's true,' she said, 'it wasn't *new*.'

Undefeated, she contrived to imply, by that slight inflection, that its lack of newness was a distinction, adding mystery, extending possibilities.

Filled with delight, I flung myself twirling away down the length of the veranda. Once again, as when we ran back from the marvellous torrent, I fully connived, this time by silence, so that together, twirling at different parts of the veranda, we put my new-found cleverness in its place.

Thea Astley

PETALS FROM BLOWN ROSES
1979

Down by the bar at the end of the pool Ella Fitzgerald was telling them to take love easy easy easy and the women with skin like bark kept taking the conversation easy with two gate-crashers from a lugger. No-one quite knew how they got there and by this stage no-one cared. By eleven the group had re-disposed itself under the chuk-chuk of the hi-fi whose avant-garde globular speakers dangled amid the fern baskets and allamanda vines like magenta carbuncles.

This is another house along the coast. And other people. And the same house and the same people. One party is all parties. Why bother? Why exist? There is only one *gaucho*, as Borges says.

The drink and the heartiness and the heat are taking them in and out of the water like yo-yos; and after a while, after a very little while, the younger women are flinging tops aside in a kind of brazen flat-chestedness and offering themselves to the gloze of half-light and aquamarine.

I watch Mrs Waterman sitting serenely in a corner perhaps expecting a parallel gesture or diagonal revelation from the men. It does not come. But in a flash I'm there at the Nature Club, in memory only, I assure you, where in pseudo-metaphysical release members ping-pong, hurdle, ball-net, divested of all civilisation's rags. In the club's wet tropic air, lotioned against March flies and mosquitoes, behind languid banks of jungle that shelter their philosophic inquiries, they had seemed vigorously mad, especially at tea-breaks when the sudden clutching of glasses of carrot juice stressed their nakedness. Oh, the strategy of plates!

'What can I get you?' Bosie Hackendorf asked, coming naked from the poolside. She was a stubby blonde with almost no breasts and her nipples appeared quite startled by this.

'A double gin,' Mrs Waterman said firmly.

'Ice?'

'Please.'

'Tonic?'

'Not even the suggestion of it.'

She was one of those women I always expect to hear say dreamily 'how sweet the moonlight sleeps upon the Chase Manhattan Bank'. They can be seen at openings: tapestries, paintings, ethnic wood carvings, even tarted up displays of pioneer cooking utensils (she was the first woman in Reeftown to get a bed with brass balls): their calm appraising eye and smile indicate that they understand nothing but embrace the lot. Mrs Waterman's cheque book was always poised to trap the *objet juste*. Its pages would obligingly flutter open and some enraptured dead-beat who had only lately begun to understand the prestige racketeering that now accompanied what roughneck peasants had crafted infinitely better centuries before would alight, as it were, on the blank paper and coax the ball-point of her patronage.

She sits now ignoring her hostess's startled nipples. They ruffled her sense of orderliness, but she keeps a benign and smiling eye upon the pool where the host, a trifle old for it but determinedly boyish, is pummelling hell out of a shiny black rubber raft.

Bosie follows her gaze.

'I do wish,' she says thoughtfully and with dreadfully careful vowels, 'that Brain would speak nicely. I do like a man to speak nicely.' Pensively she rubs the rim of Mrs Waterman's glass under one nipple.

'He seems,' Mrs Waterman says, flinching, 'perfectly adequate to me.'

'Oh, no. Really. No. No no no no. He will keep saying things like "beaut" and "lousy" – you know, like those terrible telly ads for the terribly normal man. He really is dreadfully careless. The children,' she accuses, looking hard into Mrs Waterman's eyes and then mine, 'the children – and thank goodness Bims and Chaps are away at boarding-school – tend to be influenced. I simply don't want that. I don't ever want that. It's so important for them to speak nicely.'

'Why?' Mrs Waterman asks brutally. Her eyes are riveted on her drink glass.

'My dear! Their friends! The people they'll meet!'

'And see,' Mrs Waterman adds. 'Very much "and see". All, all makes its mark.'

Mr Waterman, who rarely attended parties, wrote the cryptic

crosswords for half a dozen papers and magazines. The results of living with his preoccupation had given him irregular attitudes to the more banal objects of life. It was impossible for him to glimpse some autumnal grove of tamarisks without his mentally tabulating 'a grateful expression mother hazards among shrubs'. Or coming upon some possibility nugget in his steady perusal of mythological material ('Wonderful source, my dear! Wonderful source!), he would classify unicorns as 'varsity problems referable to chiropodists and other fantastic creatures'. This had its slow, its steady, its heavily rhythmic effect upon Mrs Waterman, who attended more and more church hoy drives, opened fêtes, launched yachts, slapped token mortar on foundation stones, cut ribbons and, where politically possible, jerked hydro-electric levers.

Mr Waterman was, also, a foundation member of the metric society. He was the first in the district to think in millimetres of rain, kilometres of road, kilograms of body fat and the metric statistics of wanted criminals. When he and Mrs Waterman did their biennial culture junket to Europe, he took enormous pleasure in supplying details for his passport. 'One point eight five four three metres,' he wrote against 'height'; 'eyes' – 'blue'. He would chide his wife mildly. 'No, dear. No, no. You are one point six four one two metres.' Against 'colour of eyes' she wrote 'glazed'.

She says now to Bosie, 'I like men to *think* nicely.' Her italics remain proper. 'You haven't forgotten my drink, have you?'

She kept remembering something he had said last night.

'It's possible, my dear, really possible to reduce time to units of ten. Let's take the decade, say. That means this year, 1976, one thousand nine hundred and seventy-six years after the birth of our saviour, could be expressed as AD 1976.'

'I thought Christ was born in 5 BC.'

He ignored her.

'Now if we take the decade' – he was really warming to it – 'as embracing the span of one hundred and twenty months, then it should be possible to gather not only the month of the year but – let's see . . .' He began mumbling and scribbling a great deal. 'Yes – even the day of the week as a fraction of seven times four eighty. So let's see – if we continue to regard Sunday as the first day of the week, then Thursday, say, would be . . . no, wait a minute. Let's take the *days* per month. That's it! The *days*.' His whole face was illuminated. '*So*. The third Thursday in this March would be the twenty-seventh part of thirty-one of the third of one hundred and twenty. Or . . . to put it more simply –'

Mrs Waterman had left the room.

'I mean think *simply*,' she adds as Bosie turns away. 'One might even say – normally.'

'Oh there's nothing queer about Brain.' (He spells it Brian.) 'Nothing at all. He's so – so normal. Coarsely normal, you might say.'

'You might indeed.'

'Really!' Bosie's face goes blunt. 'I'll get your gin.'

'Oh, my dear,' Mrs Waterman assures her, 'of course I meant nothing like that!'

Yoicking and cat-calls rocket from the pool. 'Hey, c'mon in! *C'mon!* In! In!' There are guggle sounds.

I fetch my own drink and on the way back to our shadowy corner dole out an absolutionary sprinkle to two boyish girl nudes who pluck at me.

'All these bodies! These bodies!' Mrs Waterman is sipping once more.

'Uh-huh!' I agree. Listless. 'But why don't we get some *women* in to liven things up?'

Mrs Waterman is a yummy forty-five. Her cool and beautiful face gazes appraisingly at me from beneath a dense simplicity of dark hair and she smiles with a terrible slowness, her ladylike fingers delicately holding her gin glass like a question mark.

Beyond the pool, feverish under light, the saffron curtain of guinea vine dangled banners of enormous and dynamic promise. Gorgeous flowers swung – rollicked would be a better word – between trees, and if there were a slightly unpleasant stench from their pannicles no-one seemed to notice. The gin helped, too, Mrs Waterman appeared to be finding, as she watched flowers and her more personally quiet manias swing in space with the blossom.

'Do you swim?'

'Only to frighten people.' I patted my bogus leg.

She laughed vigorously somewhere below middle C. Bosie was back again, hovering on our edges; but Mrs Waterman raised her glass, drank deeply this time and laughed again.

'And *do* you?'

'Only the weak-minded.'

'Then come on in.'

The pool was a fury of horse-play. Chlorinated water sloshed about our feet with spilt beer. The hi-fi belted into the night.

'*C'mon!* A voice woofed from the raft. 'Get y'gear off!'

'There. You see what I mean,' Bosie whimpered, pained. 'You do see what I mean about Brain?'

Mrs Waterman seemed to be tracking the spoor of some unsolved problem. Her eyes fixed thoughtfully on the rocking surface of the pool while one manicured hand patted my arm absently.

'I think,' she stated judgmentally, 'that I will.'

Without speed, with a kind of deft but leisurely sacrificial motion, Mrs Waterman got her gear off.

Deliberately she stepped forward into the pool-side light, her body impressively sumptuous and white. For a full minute she stood smiling abstractedly while the guests goggled and the hi-fi blared solo, then she dived, to emerge near the raft on which her host lay sprawled with two of the girls. When she turned I saw she was smiling her fête-opener's smile at them.

Something seemed to have clamped our host's tongue as she pulled herself neatly onto the raft beside him where, propped Récamier on one elbow, she contemplated the stilled waters.

'Delicious!' she commented. We could hear her at the edge. 'It really is absolutely delicious in.'

Her host was staring at her as if he'd been whacked.

'God!' he said. 'God! You're all right!'

Mrs Waterman smiled. 'There's really nothing like getting rid of the trappings is there?' she asked and ran her hands over a frightful silkiness of skin.

Brain kept dragging soaked hair back off his forehead nervously. Admiration reduced him to stammer.

'It's your cool! Your bloody cool! Your . . .' He fought around for it for a bit. 'Your elegance.'

'Thank you,' Mrs Waterman said simply.

Her host kept staring.

'In fact,' he said loudly, to our fascination, 'you're the only one here with any tits at all.'

'Oh, my God, Brain,' his wife cried, 'there you go again!'

'Not at all,' Mrs Waterman replied, disclaiming all credit with a modesty that was marvellous to see. 'Oh, truly, not at all.' She glanced down her body, the length of her legs, to feet still quite delicious, and flexed her toes. Her eyes took on a preoccupied glaze.

The noise smashed back then. Catharsis. That was it. Catharsis.

I didn't mention, did I, that it was a largely young party – business trendies from Reeftown, a sprinkling of rent-a-car girls? Yet it wasn't a scramble or a plunge now into the baptismal properties of the pool, but rather an out-of-it sidle as people came dripping along the scootway feigning a need to dry out as they slid on a this or that; a yearning for liquor, as they fumbled towels or shirts over bare flesh, until in a short while most of the guests were at least half dressed and some were making time-to-be-going noises over which Bosie quacked with a kind of unhinged bounty.

Alone with her host on the raft, Mrs Waterman observed this, smiled gently then swam gracefully to the side where she dried herself lingeringly and thoroughly on a borrowed towel. Clothed once more, she turned elegantly to her hostess.

'Now,' she commanded firmly, 'I think I will have another gin.'

Has it happened?

Here we are and it's the same party and not the same party and only the dregs of us are left having a bash at the fish nibbles and the cheese. Brain heads off to the tape-deck and whacks in another cassette and swamped by sax we attempt normal things like riffling the polls prospects, swapping tax laments, until at twelve past one – I can swear to this precisely – I heard behind me the words, 'That Johnny Hodges sure is petals from blown roses on the grass.'

In the wide light of this statement I punctured my bubble of recluse snugness straight onto the mulch of cane-grass matting, leaning back as I was from the fag-snaffling ploys of some Pucci-clad rent-a-girl. ('I don't smoke,' I say, blowing smoke on her.) And I was straining to catch more of this unexpected rupture.

So I hear these words and I swing about and it's Brain all right, almost pulverised by grog, trying a few dance steps with Mrs Waterman. We're all pulverised except Mrs Waterman.

Brain staggers a little, his wife does keep plucking so, and scatters my whisky. 'Forgive,' he pleads drunkenly. 'Forgive for Johnny Hodges's sake. Listen! Oh my God, will you listen a that!' Reeling with hand cocked to ear, catching the nightingale.

I've got a ton of absolution for this too, and, granting the benedictus with an unsteady cross, I lug Miss Pucci from her chair and dump Brain into it. Mrs Waterman composes herself on a lilo by his side.

I must tell you about Brain. He is one of nature's dazzling failures, so injected with the fraudulent potency of his wild-cat schemes he is always on the verge of financial bliss or ruin. The only number he knows is 'millions.' He likes saying it. He has tried exporting goats to Arabia, pineapples to Hawaii, crayfish to Noumea. One project that worked was the buying up of railway tracks between two abandoned townships west of here. He carved the rails into telegraph-pole lengths and sold them to a council with a big white-ant problem. Fired by his non-organic success, he developed a process for spraying the contents of waterless dunny pans with a plastic hardener that set like cement. 'A clear protective film,' he described it, 'that keeps down the flies.' Since the deposits also set like concrete in aspic, the problem was to find people prepared to dig them out.

After this failure he had a rage to die.

For two dreadful years he kept trying to kill himself. The first time he'd lain across the tracks of the Sunlander due to leave in five minutes. But there was a lightning strike he didn't know about and after three hours of waiting he was driven home by mosquitoes. The next time he tried it he slipped briskly over the side of his hired out-board at a nasty spot past the bay entrance and was picked up almost immediately by a prawn trawler coming unexpectedly from the north. 'God damn you to hell!' he was reported to have snarled as he dripped despairingly onto their decks. You see, his trouble was he wanted to go out with a roar of machismo. Not for him the pill bottle, the gas oven. 'Women's stuff!' he snapped. 'Bloody women's stuff!' He drove at trees. Only the car was wrecked. He jumped from buildings. There was none high enough in Reeftown. He tried throwing himself beneath the hooves of Queensland mounted police. The horses shied. Then two aunts he'd forgotten about died and left him a small legacy. He snapped out of his death-wish in a flash and here we are meeting while he's still on his high.

'Alfred,' he says, 'the Mouth, Tennyson.' He toasts something and tries out some others. 'Cootie Tennyson. Hey! How d'you like it? Cootie! Hotlips! Sweets!' He leans heavily across Mrs Waterman. 'Hotlips Tennyson. I like that. Jesus, I like it. Do you like it?'

'Very much.'

'And I like you very much. I like you for liking it.' He begins a boozy conducting to the tape-deck. 'I like ole Hotlips Tennyson and I like Alfred Fatha Hodges even more.'

'I like Alfred Fatha Hodges too,' I say. 'Be-bop that gentlier on the spirit lies.'

'Listen,' he says. 'Listen. I'm really onto something this time, pal.' He has an arm round Mrs Waterman but is holding me with his mariner's eye. Bosie is sitting on the lap of one of the gate-crashers from the lugger who won't go home. 'I've got this committee going, see? Top brass, mate. Politicos. Academics. But the tops! It's a wonderful, it's a huge concept.' He nods it into shape.

'For what?'

'Oh, my God! For what? he asks. For what! To stop the brain-drain, that's for what. Keep the old genius located right here in the sunburnt country. Let it drop the old fruit here, see, not some ruddy foreign country that is forever England.'

'You put that rather prettily,' says Mrs Waterman.

'I do put it prettily, don't I?' He gave her a spacious hug, pushed out his juicy lower lip. Suddenly he thumped me on the good leg. 'Keithy, baby, this is an enormous concept. You gotta bloody believe me. I tell you, mate, I've been in touch with the lot and confidentially' – he went confidential – 'confidentially, the government has come to the party. Yes. They've come to the party all right. They've promised me half a million. Imagine that. Half a bloody million!'

'Brain!' Bosie cries petulantly. 'Brain, *please!*'

He didn't even hear and I could sense the dream-power taking over. Johnny Hodges and his sax have soared right out of space.

It's rather difficult getting money from the government, isn't it? Mrs Waterman has brought the gin bottle over to the table and is serving herself generously. She is monstrously sober.

'Listen, sweetie,' Brain says, 'I have the Ministry of Science interested, the leader of the Country Party, the vice-chancellors of three universities' – he is up and away – 'several judges. Oh God, yes! *They* see, I mean they really see the magnitude of the thing. It's going to save the country millions. Millions.' He wets his lip on the word. 'Could you, my dear, hotlips, spare me one of those fags? Thank you. This, pals, is going to be a tremendous, an absolutely bloody tremendous undertaking.'

Mrs Waterman blows a perfect smoke circle that fits one of her host's eyes like a monocle.

'A little vague, isn't it?'

His head wags sadly. He's hurt. He tells us again that he's formed this committee and maybe he's right after all: we're a great country for the maunderings of indirect action. His eyes see chains of committees and sub-formations of the sub-committees, stretching into the wide brown distances, and his voice, enriched with the vibrations of delusion, comes across the cultural void along with his salesman hand that smacks mine enthusiastically and then flees to Mrs Waterman's thigh.

'That Johnny Hodges!' he sighs, groping for her fingers and then his glass.

Look at him! Can you see those doggy eyes, deeply, romantically brown? The tousled boy hair (he's only thirty-five, give or take those suicides)? The glossy failure of him? It's all fantasy, this heroic taradiddle that gushes out, and I catch Mrs Waterman's eye and know she has discovered this as well. He's one huge monument of failure sustained by phoney dreams and it's sad, sad as his enthusiastic mug.

But he's bombing us with earlier ventures, and his figures sport dangling necklaces of zeros. 'Now that's doing well. Bloody well.' There's the word 'millions' again, the noughts drifting about us with the nebulous quality of snow, gathering, flake upon flake, about the committee and throwing darkness over the countries of his mind.

For a while I stop listening and think of another like him, a job changer of distinction, who's moved from computers to audits to insurance to pineapples and has buggered three crops. He tries again. His avocados get worm. He tries again, conventionally, and pushes pen for a tobacco company. He hates it. He tries again and is one of the middle-aged flower-people throwing pots on a home-made wheel. He makes one basic pot but in six sizes. He has one glaze. 'There is only one potter in this country,' he assures me with his soft nervous uh-uh that is meant to describe a circle of charming diffidence about a core of Jahveh-like ego. He means himself, of course, and this too is very sad, hearing his voice fade in inverse ratio to the crescendo of his fantasy. I bend to absorb each lie. 'Uh-uh they're ringing me from down south now for orders uh-uh – Perth even uh-uh.'

(My subject is self-delusion and the pity of self-delusion. Sorry, Wilf!)

I keep gazing into my glass, finding its concentricity both simple and delusory, the bubble-slice of something so fragile its moment keeps glancing off from me, out of reach, out of hearing. The other guests who have been swimming steadily downwards through transparent waves of claret are now seen through this circular translucence to fluctuate, shrinking and expanding like underwater creatures whose gesturings become the fin movement of infinite sluggishness, whose yowls scream silently through wall upon wall of glass. Miss Rent-a-girl has ousted Bosie from one luggerman's lap and is making sorties on the other, while Bosie, drunkenly disconsolate, wavers towards us.

'Brain,' she is pleading, 'Brain. Sing us something.'

This is a new Brain all right. I hadn't heard about this.

'You sing, do you?' Mrs Waterman asks.

'Me? Not really. Not for years.'

'Oh, but he does!' Bosie says. 'Ever so nicely. He was in opera once, you know.'

'Chorus,' says Brain. 'One season.'

'The naughty thing wouldn't practise, would you, Brain?'

'Jesus!' says Brain.

'Really?' Mrs Waterman asks, perking up. 'Really?'

'Back row of *Boris Godounov*.'

'Oh, do sing for us. Do.'

The luggermen start in then. 'C'mon mate! Give us a tune. C'mon, feller!'

Roars. The limp smacking of hands. Brain staggers to his feet and begins divesting again. He tosses his shirt to his wife and does elbow circlings, mockingly, and takes in funny-man deep breaths. The tanned and hairy chest expands like a cartoon strong man's, while above him the patio fans describe slow fixed circles, centring our shambles.

Someone starts a slow thumping and the urging breaks out again; so reluctantly, grinning at Mrs Waterman, Brain stops his fooling, reaches over and takes her hand, raising it in a stage-pro gesture as he half-profiles to the noise and the yap.

'"Lindy,"' he begins softly, '"did yo hear dat mockin' bird sing las' night?"'

He increases the volume and bends the full force of his stupid failed eyes on Mrs Waterman. '"Lordy, it was singin' so sweet in de pale moonlight!"'

His voice is so rich, so naturally beautiful, the yappers are stilled. But Brain isn't aware of its beauty, I know it, for once again he's grinning like a goat, sending himself up as he does mammy gestures. "'Roun' dat ole magnolia tree,'" he sings, "'sang so sweet to you an' me ...'" On he sings. On. On. He misses a phrase now and then. We prompt the words. Once he almost loses the tune. But the voice! The depth! The resonance! Here it is – the one thing he can do and never talks about. He just doesn't know.

Petals from blown roses all over the drunken pool-way and the fans stir them; they settle, and I look across to Mrs Waterman who is kneeling, I swear, at his feet and bending, yes, bending, in the simple curve of devotion.

'ABCDEFGHIJKLM
NOPQRSTUVWXYZ'

1972

I select from these letters, pressing my fingers down. The letter (or an image of it) appears on the sheet of paper. It signifies little or nothing, I have to add more. Other letters are placed alongside until a 'word' is formed. And it is not always the word WORD.

The word matches either my memory of its appearance, or a picture of the object the word denotes. TREE: I see the shape of a tree at mid-distance, and green.

I am writing a story.

Here, the trouble begins.

The word 'dog', as William James pointed out, does not bite; and my story begins with a weeping woman. She sat at the kitchen table one afternoon and wept uncontrollably. How can words, particularly 'wept uncontrollably', convey her sadness (her self-pity)? Philosophers other than myself have discussed the inadequacy of words. 'Woman' covers women of every shape and size, whereas the one I have in mind is red-haired, has soft arms, plain face, high-heeled shoes with shining straps.

And she was weeping.

Her name, let us say, is Kathy Pridham.

For the past two years she has worked as a librarian for the British Council in Karachi. She, of all the British community there, was one of the few who took the trouble to learn Urdu, the local language. She could speak it, not read it: those calligraphic loops and dots meant nothing to her, except that 'it was a language'. Speaking it was enough. The local staff at the Council, shopkeepers and even the cream of Karachi society (who cultivated European manners), felt that she knew them as they themselves did.

At this point, consider the word 'Karachi'. Not having been there myself I see clusters of white-cube buildings with the edge of a port to the left, a general slowness, a shaded veranda-ed suburb for the Burrasahibs. Perhaps, eventually, boredom – or disgust with noises and smells not understood. Kathy, who was at first lonely and disturbed, quickly settled in. She became fully occupied and happy; insofar as that word has any meaning. There was a surplus of men in Karachi: young English bachelors sent out from head office, and pale appraising types who work at the embassies; but the ones who fell over themselves to be near her were Pakistanis. They were young and lazy. With her they were ardent and gay.

Already the words Kathy and Karachi are becoming inextricably linked.

It was not long before she too was rolling her head in slow motion during conversations, and clicking her tongue, as they did, to signify 'no'. Her bungalow in the European quarter with its own lawn, veranda, two archaic servants, became a sort of *salon*, especially at the Sunday lunches where Kathy reigned, supervising, flitting from one group to the next. Those afternoons never seemed to end. No-one wanted to leave. Sometimes she had musicians perform. And there was always plenty of liquor (imported), with wide dishes of hot food. Kathy spoke instantly and volubly on the country's problems, its complicated politics, yet in London if she had an opinion she rarely expressed it.

When Kathy thought of London she often saw 'London' – the six letters arranged in recognisable order. Then parts of an endless construction appeared, much of it badly blurred. There was the thick stone. Concentrating, she could recall a familiar bus stop, the interior of a building where she had last worked. Her street invariably appeared, strangely dead. Some men in overcoats. It was all so far away she sometimes thought it existed only when she was there. Her best friends had been two women, one a schoolteacher, the other married to a taciturn engineer. With them she went to Scotland for holidays, to the concerts at Albert Hall. Karachi was different. The word stands for something else.

The woman weeping at the kitchen table is Kathy Pridham. It is somewhere in London (there are virtually no kitchen tables in Karachi).

After a year or so Kathy noticed at a party a man standing apart from the others, watching her. His face was bony and fierce, and he had a thin moustache. Kathy, of course, turned away, yet at the same time tilted her chin and began acting over-earnest in conversation. For she pictured her appearance: seeing it (she thought) from his eyes.

She noticed him at other parties, and at one where she knew the host well enough, casually asked, 'Tell me. Who is that over there?'

They both looked at the man watching her.

'If you mean him, that's Syed Masood. Not your cup of tea, Kathy. What you would call a wild man.' The host was a successful journalist and drew in on his cigarette. 'Perhaps he is our best painter. I don't know; I have my doubts.'

Kathy lowered her eyes, confused.

When she looked up, the man called Syed Masood had gone.

Over the next few days, she went to the galleries around town and asked to see the paintings of Syed Masood. She was interested in local arts and crafts, and had decided that if she saw something of his she liked she would buy it. These gallery owners threw up their hands. 'He has released nothing for two years now. What has got into him I don't know.'

Somehow this made Kathy smile.

Ten or eleven days pass – in words that take only seconds to put down, even less to absorb (the discrepancy between Time and Language). It is one of her Sunday lunches. Kathy is only half-listening to conversations and when she breaks into laughter it is a fraction too loud. She has invited this man Masood and has one eye on the door. He arrives late. Perhaps he too is nervous.

Their opening conversation (aural) went something like this (visual).

'Do come in. I don't think we've met. My name is Kathy Pridham.'

'Why do you mix with these shits?' he replied, looking around the room.

Just then an alarm wristlet watch on one of the young men began ringing. Everyone laughed, slapping each other, except Masood.

'I'll get you something,' said Kathy quietly. 'You're probably hungry.'

She felt hot and awkward, although now that they were together he seemed to take no notice of her. Several of the European men came over, but Masood didn't say much and they drifted back. She watched him eat and drink: the bones of his face working.

He finally turned to her. 'You come from – where?'

'London.'

'Then why have you come here?'

She told him.

'And these?' he asked, meaning the crowd reclining on cushions.

'My friends. They're people I've met here.'

Suddenly she felt like crying.

But he took her by the shoulders. 'What is this? You speak Urdu? And not at all bad? Say something more, please.'

Before she could think of anything he said in a voice that disturbed her, 'You are something extraordinary.' He was so close she could feel his breath. 'Do you know that? Of course. But do you know how extraordinary? Let me tell you something, although another man might put it differently. It begins here' – for a second one of his many hands touched her breasts; Kathy jumped – 'and it *emanates*. Your volume fills the room. Certainly! So you are quite vast, but beautiful.'

Then he added, watching her, 'If you see what I mean.'

He was standing close to her, but when he spoke again she saw him grinning. 'Now repeat what I have just said in Urdu.'

He made her laugh.

Here – now – an interruption. While considering the change in Kathy's personality I remember an incident from last Thursday, the 12th. This is an intrusion but from 'real life'. The words in the following paragraph reconstruct the event as remembered. As accurately as possible, of course.

A beggar came up to me in a Soho bar and asked (a hoarse whisper) if I wished to see photographs of funerals. I immediately pictured a rectangular hole, sky, men and women in coats. Without waiting for my reply he fished out from an inside pocket the wad of photographs, postcard size, each one of a burial. They were dog-eared and he had dirty fingernails. 'Did you know these dead people?' He shook his head. 'Not even their names?' He shook his head. 'That one,' he said, not taking his eyes off the photographs, was dug yesterday. That one, in 1969.' There was little difference. Both showed men and women standing around a dark rectangle, perplexed. I felt a sharp tap on my wrist. The beggar had his hand out. Yes, I gave him a shilling. The barman spoke: 'Odd way to earn a living. He's been doing that for years.'

Kathy soon saw Masood again. He arrived one night with his shirt hanging out while she was entertaining the senior British Council representative, Mr L., and his wife. They were a cautious experienced pair, years in the service, yet Mrs L. began talking loudly and hastily, a sign of indignation, when Masood sat away from the table, silently watching them. Mr L. cleared his throat several times – another sign. It was a hot night with both ceiling fans hardly altering the sedentary air. Masood suddenly spoke to Kathy in his own language. She nodded and poured him another coffee. Mrs L. caught her husband's eye, and when they left shortly afterwards, Kathy and Masood leaned back and laughed.

'You can spell my name four different ways,' Masood declared in the morning, 'but I am still the one person! Ah,' he said laughing. 'I am in a good mood. This is an auspicious day.'

'I have to go to work,' said Kathy.

'Look up "auspicious" when you get to the library. See what it says in one of your English dictionaries.'

She bent over to fit her brassiere. Her body was marmoreal, the opposite to his: bony and nervy.

'Instead of thinking of me during the day,' he went on, 'think of an exclamation mark! It amounts to the same thing. I would see you, I think, as a colour. Yes, I think more than likely pink, or something soft like yellow.'

'You can talk,' said Kathy laughing.

But she liked hearing him talk. Perhaps there'll be further examples of why she enjoyed hearing him talk.

That night Masood took her to his studio. It was in the inner part of the city where Europeans rarely ventured, and as Masood strode ahead Kathy avoided, but not always successfully, the stares of women in doorways, the fingers of beggars, and rows of sleeping bodies. She noticed how some men deliberately dawdled or bumped into her; striding ahead, Masood seemed to enjoy having her there. In an alleyway he unbolted a powder-blue door as a curious crowd gathered. He suddenly clapped his hands to move them. Then Kathy was inside: a fluorescent room, dirty white-washed walls. In the corner was a wooden bed called a 'charpoy', some clothes over a chair. There were brushes in jars, and tins of paint.

'Syed, are these your pictures?'

'Leave them,' he said sharply. 'Come here. I would like to see you.'

Through the door she could feel the crowd in the alleyway. She was perspiring still and now he was undoing her blouse.

'Syed, let's go?'

He stepped back.

'What is the matter? The natives are too dirty tonight. Is that it? Yes, the walls; the disgusting size of the place. All this stench. It must be affecting your nostrils? Rub your nose in it. Lie in my shit and muck. If you wait around you might see a rat. You could dirty your Mem-sahib's hands for a change.' Then he kicked his foot through one of the canvases by the door. 'The pretty paintings you came to see.'

As she began crying she wondered why. (He was only a person who used certain words.)

I will continue with further words.

Kathy made room for Masood in her house, in her bed as well as the spare room which she made his studio. Her friends noticed a change. At work, they heard the pronoun 'we' constantly. She told them of parties they went to, the trips they planned to take, how she supervised his meals; she even confessed (laughing) he snored and possessed a violent temper. At parties, she took to sitting on the floor. She began wearing 'kurtas' instead of 'blouses', 'lungis' rather than 'dresses', even though with her large body she looked clumsy. To the Europeans she somehow became, or seemed, untidy. They no longer understood her, and so they felt sorry for her. It was about then that Kathy's luncheon parties stopped, and she and Masood, who were always together, went out less frequently. Most people saw Masood behind this – he had never disguised his contempt for her friends – but others connected it with an incident at the office. Kathy arrived one morning wearing a sari and was told by the Chief Librarian it was inappropriate; she couldn't serve at the counter wearing that. Then Mr L. himself, rapidly consulting his wife, spoke to her. He spelt out the *British* Council's function in Karachi, underlining the word British. 'Kathy, are you happy?' he suddenly asked. Like others, he was concerned. He wanted to say, 'Do you know what you are doing?' 'Oh, yes,' Kathy replied. 'With this chap, I mean,' he said, waving his hand. And Kathy left the room.

People's distrust of Masood seemed to centre around his unconventional appearance and (perhaps more than anything) his rude silences. Nobody could say they knew him, although just about everybody said he drank too much. Stories began circulating. 'A surly bugger,' he was called behind his back. That was common now. There were times when he cursed Kathy in public. Strange, though, the wives and other women were more ready to accept the affair. There was something about

Masood, his face and manner. And they recognised the tenacity with which Kathy kept living with him. They understood her quick defence of him, often silent but always there, even when she came late to work, puff-eyed from crying and once, her cheek bruised.

Here, the life of Kathy draws rapidly to a close.

It was now obvious to everyone that Masood was drinking too much. At the few parties they attended he usually made a scene of some sort; and Kathy would take him home. Think of swear words. She was arriving late for work and missed whole days. Then she disappeared for a week. They had argued one night and Kathy screamed at him to leave. He replied by hitting her across the mouth. She moved into a cheap hotel, but within the week he found her. 'Syed spent all day, every day, looking for me,' was how she later put it. 'He needs someone.' When she was reprimanded for her disappearance and general conduct, she burst into tears.

In London, the woman with elbows on the table is Kathy Pridham. She has unwrapped a parcel from Karachi. Imagine: coarse screwed-up paper and string lie on the table. Masood has sent a self-portrait, oil on canvas, quite a striking resemblance. His vanity, pride and troubles are enormous. His face, leaning against the teapot, stares across at Kathy weeping.

She cannot help thinking of him; of his appearance.

Words. These marks on paper, and so on.

THE POWERFUL OWL

1 9 9 4

Louise was born on a Monday; she was married on a Monday, and her cat was eaten by an owl on a Monday.

At first, Louise and Paul thought it might be an eagle.

'It can't be,' said Paul. 'It's the middle of the night.'

They were up at their beach house sitting on the sofa watching television when they simultaneously, so they discovered later, experienced the spooky sensation of being watched. In fact, they had both already glanced through the glass doors, just in case, but there was nothing there. Neither of them thought to look up at the long, thin triangular wedge of glass which lay between the ceiling and the doors. It wasn't until Paul got up to make a cup of coffee that he happened to see the brooding shape perched on the pergola.

'Christ!'

'What?' Louise turned, followed his gaze, and could not believe her eyes. For there, staring into the room and gazing directly at them, was a huge bird.

'Is it an eagle?' said Louise, squinting up at the towering shape.

'It can't be,' said Paul. 'It's the middle of the night.'

When they had arrived for this particular weekend at their beach house, which was perched on top of a hill backing onto a national park, they were laden down with their usual mountain of stuff – the cat and the dog, the computer, the backpacks and the groceries. Before the dog came into their lives it was not quite so crowded, it was just Paul, Louise and the cat.

Apart, that is, from the several months, which they do not even mention any more, when it was just Louise and the cat, or just Paul, because of the sudden and very surprising news that Paul had been having an affair for some months with a mousey acquaintance of theirs who was a regular partner in their Sunday morning tennis game on the weekends they were in town. This news had led swiftly to what their counsellor had called a 'trial' separation, although while Louise was undertaking the trial it felt as if her world had come to an abrupt and permanent end.

Paul had been put out when Louise had insisted on remaining in the Sunday tennis game.

'But that means I can't play,' he said at the time, sounding almost whiney, she thought.

'You and your friend can play somewhere else,' Louise said, with what she thought was considerable restraint.

'I haven't got any friends since I left you.'

Louise felt a surge of triumph. 'Well,' she said magnanimously, 'I suppose you can play this weekend. I'm going to the coast anyway.'

'Oh.' He looked crestfallen. 'You didn't mention to me you were going.'

What was it he thought he was up to, Louise had wondered to herself as she pattered around the shack with her pathetic single-person grocery bags. Even the raucous parrots living in the spotted gum outside their living room window managed a monogamous relationship. The magpies, Mr Hole-in-the-Head and Mrs Hole, had raised one noisy and ravenous offspring a few years back and were so evidently worn to a frazzle that they seemed to be practising some form of contraception because no other jangly baby Hole had made its presence felt. Mr and Mrs Hole seemed relieved, and rather plumper since they had given up raising babies. They were obviously happy together. Some days, Louise and Paul had noted in the past, Mr Hole-in-the-Head, having unearthed a plump grub, would offer his wife some of it. On other occasions, on one of their off-days, perhaps, he would keep it to himself while she scolded him noisily. Still, they were a couple, there was no doubt about that. They chased other magpies off their territory *immediately*.

'I can't believe I didn't chase *her* off,' said Louise, on one of her lonely visits, scooping up the cat and cuddling her close for yet another crying bout. Everywhere in the shack were reminders of her years with Paul, from the romance of a faded holiday snap to the more prosaic evidence of sandy bathers and shaving cream. But of all the things she hated most to see it was the recent painting of a Powerful Owl, which Paul had dashed off the day after the visitation. She had rarely seen him so fired up, and she'd got caught up too, searching through bird books for information; helping him mix his paints. At the end of the day she'd almost felt as if she'd painted the picture; she had thought to herself, 'This is one of those experiences that we'll talk about when we're old. We'll say, Do you remember the Powerful Owl?'

At the time this nocturnal visit from a bird with such an extraordinary name seemed fortuitous. Almost, Paul and Louise said over breakfast the next morning, as if their house had been blessed in a pantheistic ritual. They had looked it up in the bird book the night before, and there was no doubt it was a Powerful Owl, *Ninox strenua*.

'It inhabits mountainous forests and scrubs,' Louise read out loud while Paul scribbled notes – the painting already talked about, already hanging in the air, only needing to be coaxed into existence. 'My God! You wouldn't believe what it eats – its main diet is possums and gliders – we're talking some owl here.'

Paul pointed to Molly, curled up in her favourite armchair. 'She'd better watch out then, she's smaller than a possum.'

Louise was shocked. 'Don't even mention it,' she said. 'What a horrible thought.'

It was Molly who kept her company through the endless nights of their separation. Molly who sat on her chest, purring away, delighted that the house rules had suddenly been broken and she was allowed in the bedroom. It was Molly who would decide when Louise needed entertaining, launching herself into an acrobatic routine at the drop of a whisker, her tail fluffed up and her paws beating an irate piaffe on the slate floor. It was Molly, too, who, distressed at being locked out of their bedroom when the separation was over – when Louise had won (thank God she had won) – developed an extraordinary habit.

The first time Louise felt Molly land on her chest, she sat straight up in bed. 'How the bloody hell did she get in?' she muttered to Paul – except that Paul was sleeping soundly beside her, and there was no cat in the room, let alone on the bed. Louise didn't bother to mention it to Paul, it was so obvious it was just her imagination, but as the months passed and Molly's daily activities became abruptly curtailed by the puppy, she took to regular flying visits. It became so commonplace that Louise would occasionally get out of bed and open the door, and there would be Molly, primly sitting with her paws together, a baleful stare in her amber eyes. 'You stop that, do you hear,' Louise would whisper. 'I know exactly what you're doing and you can't come in.' Nevertheless she felt guilty that Molly was reduced to spiritual naughtiness in order to get her quota of attention. It seemed unfair.

In the beginning Louise never asked about the other woman. She did not want to jinx her and Paul's passionate reconciliation. But the questions ran around her head, all day, all night. Why had Paul found the mousey woman attractive? What was she like in bed? Was she funny? Paul always said he loved Louise's sense of humour. Did the mousey one have a sense of humour? If so, she hid it well. What did they do with their time together? Where did they go? Worst of all, the unaskable question – was he happy with her? And if he was happy with her did that mean he wasn't happy with Louise, and if he wasn't happy with Louise, why had he come back to her? Had he really come back, or would he leave again? If he left again would it be for the same mousey woman or a different one? Sometimes, not often, she would voice her fears and he always reassured her: 'It's over, it's all right, we're together and that's what counts.' What she wanted to know was how could he be so sure when she felt so unsure. It seemed the most grotesque irony that he should be the one to leave and come home so cheerfully optimistic, while she – who had been labouring under the delusion they were happy together – was left with this rattling insecurity which was quite unknown to her.

But the thing that bothered Louise most was the reason Paul had given for leaving during one of their vitriolic sessions with the counsellor.

'She writes about me,' he had said, not even looking her in the eye. 'It's like living with Woody Allen. I feel like everything I say or do is being noted for some future book.'

'But that's not true!' Louise could hardly believe her ears. 'I've always been a writer. He knew that when we met, and anyway, it's fiction.'

Paul laughed. 'Fiction, shmiction.'

The counsellor held up a warning finger. 'Here we go again,' she said, 'not listening to each other.'

Louise took no notice. 'And what about him?' she said. 'What about his paintings? Don't think I haven't noticed who he's been using as a model.'

The night that Molly went, the night she was eaten, Louise and Paul had decided to sleep separately. He wanted to finish a painting, and on such nights it might be two in the morning before he would leave his studio and come up to the house. Louise opted to sleep on her own, but before she turned in for the night, she plucked up enough courage to ask Paul her question.

'Are you happy with me?' she asked.

'Of course I am,' he said. 'We got married, didn't we? I love you, you know that.' He came and put his hands on her shoulders. 'Let it go, love,' he said. 'It really is time to let it go.' After he had gone to the studio, Louise sat outside for a while and Molly came too. The dog was shut up safe and sound in the laundry, hidden from the marauders who had been hanging around their house of late.

'We'll have to get that dog desexed immediately,' Louise told Molly. 'I think she's on heat.' Even as she spoke she could see the glowing eyes and scruffy coat of the labrador-cross from next door. 'Shoo,' she said crossly. 'Piss off.'

Powerful Owls, said the bird book, *are shy birds; they live in pairs and are strongly territorial. They roost in various tall trees – and not always together, in order to protect their territory. They eat birds and small mammals, gliders, sugar gliders, bush possums, rats, rabbits, kookaburras and magpies. They tear their prey apart and eat it piece by piece. Sometimes they take the rear end back to their roost, place it carefully on a branch and hold it all day in their talons before eating it when they leave the roost the next night. They nest at least fifteen metres above ground, using a hollow tree; the female lays two dull white eggs, and while she is nesting the male makes no attempt to guard the nest. They eat everything and regurgitate pellets.*

As Louise was cleaning her teeth she heard a familiar noise, the sound of miaowing from the roof. She stomped outside in her nightdress, put the chair on the veranda and reached up for the cat. 'Come here then, stupid,' she said, and hauled her down by the scruff of the neck. Molly followed her inside, and sat on the kitchen table looking out into the darkness.

Louise can never, no matter how hard she tries, rewind the film of that night. She can never hear again those pitiful miaows in the night and, this time, make the decision to get up – as she had done a hundred times before – and get the cat off the roof. Instead, when Molly's cries woke her, she shut out the noise, buried her head under the pillow and pretended she couldn't hear. Finally the miaowing and pacing stopped. But then, not long after, and still in the dead of night, there was a huge thump, as if a large branch had fallen on the roof. At the same time a shaft of pure white terror screeched through Louise's body – Louise felt the pain of the talons in her flesh and at that moment she and Molly became one. Louise lay in the dark and knew without a shadow of a doubt that her cat had been taken off the roof by an owl, by *Ninox strenua*.

Looking back on it, Louise wondered how she ever got to sleep, how she managed to delude herself into believing that the cat was all right. But in a way it was easy, it was simply a matter of pretending to herself that nothing was wrong – that it had, in fact, been a branch landing on the roof. In the end she had slept until the dawn broke, when she started up with the strange sensation of some forgotten disaster. She immediately went out to look for the cat, but she was nowhere to be seen. She knocked on Paul's door, tears streaming down her face.

'Molly's gone,' she said. 'She's been taken by an owl.'

He was sleepy, surprised and sceptical all at once. 'She's probably just hiding in a cupboard,' he said. 'You know how she is.' He helped her look inside the house, and then he sat on the veranda watching as she walked through the bush, calling and calling. 'Do you want to stay here?' he said. 'She'll probably come back.'

'No, she won't,' Louise said. 'There's no point in staying, she's never coming back.'

They drove back to the city quickly, with Louise snuffling into a hankie. When they stopped at the local garage, Paul got out to do the petrol.

'How are you today?' asked the attendant.

'Not so good,' Paul said. 'My wife thinks our cat's been taken by an owl.' He injected the words with a kind of male camaraderie, a sort of 'you-know-how-they-are' kind of sound.

'Bastards, those owls,' said the attendant. 'Our cat had a run-in with one, but he got away.'

Paul got back into the car looking white.

Why does she mourn so long and hard for Molly? She was, after all, only a cat. It is partly the manner of her going – as if she and Paul had prompted it all those months ago when they had seen the Powerful Owl on the pergola and Paul had remarked: 'She'd better watch out, she's smaller than a possum.' It is partly because Molly is a symbol of the relationship she and Paul shared before the mousey woman came on the scene. They had bought her in the early days when they first moved in together, and as it had become increasingly obvious there might not be children from their marriage, there was no doubt that Molly had somehow taken the place of family.

But there is something else which niggles away at Louise, something she does not understand at all, and that is that she has been finding it hard to write since Molly was taken. It is almost as if her familiar has left her; she has even been finding it hard to wreak a fictional vengeance on the mousey woman. It is as if her life is only pretending to be normal. It is as if there is something going on, something Louise should know about and does not know. Sometimes she wonders if it is because there was no corpse, no visible sign of death. Occasionally she likes to recite 'The Owl and the Pussycat' to herself; she likes to pretend that perhaps the owl took sympathy on the cat, and they are living out their lives somewhere with their little green boat on the edge of the sand.

Louise has a friend who is psychic. She talks easily about spirits and angels and devils as if these are everyday realities and not part of the unknown. The friend, who has had her name changed by deed poll to Venus, has often offered Louise a reading but Louise has always refused. Then, one day, over lunch, Louise finds herself talking about Molly, about her habit of astrally projecting herself onto the bed, and that night Venus rings her up.

'I've got my medicine cards here,' she says. 'Did you know that owl medicine is associated with clairvoyance, astral projection and black and white magic?'

Louise feels a shiver running through her body. 'Really?' she says. She thinks of Molly's neat black and white body sitting primly outside the bedroom door.

'Remember your Greek myths,' says Venus, who certainly does. 'Do you remember Athene?'

Louise thinks. 'She's the one who jumped out of Zeus's head isn't she?'

Venus laughs. 'She is, but also her emblem is the owl. She has an owl on her shoulder, and the owl is the revealer of unseen truths – it lights up her blind side, and enables her to speak the whole truth. Right way up this card is about Owl befriending you and bringing you messages through dreams and meditation, wrong way up and it means that deception has been practised, by or against you. Owl tells you to keep an eye on your property and loved ones. Remember that Owl is always asking, "Who?"' She pauses. 'Louise? Does that make sense?'

Louise would like to say no but she would be lying. 'Yes,' she says. 'It makes sense.'

Louise puts the phone down, sits on the sofa and buries her head in her hands. For now she knows what she has suspected for some time – that Paul is still seeing the mousey woman, indeed, is not going to stop seeing the mousey woman and that Louise's marriage is well and truly over.

'How did you know?' asks Paul ingenuously.

'I knew. That's all.' She has only one question left to ask her husband. 'Why?'

He puts his hand behind his back, as if distancing himself from her. 'Because I want children.'

'I see.' Louise feels strangely cold and divorced from her own body. She is cat, owl and mouse all at once. 'So you persuaded me not to have children because you didn't want any and now that you do, you're leaving me for someone who is young enough to have them. I see.'

Paul looks up at her. 'I still can't understand why you're throwing me out now. Why can't we talk about this in the morning?'

That night Molly visits Louise for the first time since her death. When Louise feels the familiar sudden weight on the bedclothes, she is un-alarmed and content. She strokes the imaginary outline, seeing the black head under her hand, the white chest and socks, the small silver rings on the tail. 'I don't know why you had to leave me, Molly,' she whispers. 'But I promise you one thing – this is something I'll never write about.'

But even as Louise speaks the words she knows she is lying. Even as it had happened to the cat, even as she had felt the talons in her back, she knew she would write about it. Just as one day she will write about Paul again, and the mousey woman, and anything else that ever happens to her, because she is Owl and she must eat everything, regurgitating the pellets of her memories, endlessly.

Marjorie Barnard

THE PERSIMMON TREE

1943

I saw the spring come once and I won't forget it. Only once. I had
been ill all the winter and I was recovering. There was no more pain,
no more treatments or visits to the doctor. The face that looked back
at me from my old silver mirror was the face of a woman who had
escaped. I had only to build up my strength. For that I wanted to be
alone, an old and natural impulse. I had been out of things for quite a
long time and the effort of returning was still too great. My mind was
transparent and as tender as new skin. Everything that happened, even
the commonest things, seemed to be happening for the first time, and
had a delicate hollow ring like music played in an empty auditorium.

I took a flat in a quiet, blind street, lined with English trees. It was
one large room, high ceilinged with pale walls, chaste as a cell in a
honey comb, and furnished with the passionless, standardised grace of
a fashionable interior decorator. It had the afternoon sun which I prefer
because I like my mornings shadowy and cool, the relaxed end of the
night prolonged as far as possible. When I arrived the trees were bare
and still against the lilac dusk. There was a block of flats opposite,
discreet, well tended, with a wide entrance. At night it lifted its oblongs
of rose and golden light far up into the sky. One of its windows was
immediately opposite mine. I noticed that it was always shut against
the air. The street was wide but because it was so quiet the window
seemed near. I was glad to see it always shut because I spend a good
deal of time at my window and it was the only one that might have
overlooked me and flawed my privacy.

I liked the room from the first. It was a shell that fitted without
touching me. The afternoon sun threw the shadow of a tree on my
light wall and it was in the shadow that I first noticed that the bare
twigs were beginning to swell with buds. A water colour, pretty and
innocuous, hung on that wall. One day I asked the silent woman who

serviced me to take it down. After that the shadow of the tree had the wall to itself and I felt cleared and tranquil as if I had expelled the last fragment of grit from my mind.

I grew familiar with all the people in the street. They came and went with a surprising regularity and they all, somehow, seemed to be cut to a very correct pattern. They were part of the mise en scene, hardly real at all and I never felt the faintest desire to become acquainted with any of them. There was one woman I noticed, about my own age. She lived over the way. She had been beautiful I thought, and was still handsome with a fine tall figure. She always wore dark clothes, tailor made, and there was reserve in her every movement. Coming and going she was always alone, but you felt that that was by her own choice, that everything she did was by her own steady choice. She walked up the steps so firmly, and vanished so resolutely into the discreet muteness of the building opposite, that I felt a faint, a very faint, envy of anyone who appeared to have her life so perfectly under control.

There was a day much warmer than anything we had had, a still, warm, milky day. I saw as soon as I got up that the window opposite was open a few inches. 'Spring comes even to the careful heart,' I thought. And the next morning not only was the window open but there was a row of persimmons set out carefully and precisely on the sill, to ripen in the sun. Shaped like a young woman's breasts, their deep, rich, golden-orange colour seemed just the highlight that the morning's spring tranquillity needed. It was almost a shock to me to see them there. I remembered at home when I was a child there was a grove of persimmon trees down one side of the house. In the autumn they had blazed deep red, taking your breath away. They cast a rosy light into rooms on that side of the house as if a fire were burning outside. Then the leaves fell and left the pointed dark gold fruit cling-ing to the bare branches. They never lost their strangeness – magical, Hesperidean trees. When I saw the Fire Bird danced my heart moved painfully because I remembered the persimmon trees in the early morning against the dark windbreak of the loquats. Why did I always think of autumn in springtime?

Persimmons belong to autumn and this was spring. I went to the window to look again. Yes, they were there, they were real. I had not imagined them, autumn fruit warming to a ripe transparency in the spring sunshine. They must have come, expensively packed in sawdust, from California or have lain all winter in storage. Fruit out of season.

It was later in the day when the sun had left the sill that I saw the window opened and a hand come out to gather the persimmons. I saw a woman's figure against the curtains. *She* lived there. It was her window opposite mine.

Often now the window was open. That in itself was like the breaking of a bud. A bowl of thick cream pottery, shaped like a boat, appeared on the sill. It was planted, I think, with bulbs. She used to water it with one of those tiny, long-spouted, hand-painted cans that you use for refilling vases, and I saw her gingerly loosening the earth with a silver table fork. She didn't look up or across the street. Not once.

Sometimes on my leisurely walks I passed her in the street. I knew her quite well now, the texture of her skin, her hands, the set of her clothes, her movements. The way you know people when you are sure you will never be put to the test of speaking to them. I could have found out her name quite easily. I had only to walk into the vestibule of her block and read it in the list of tenants, or consult the visiting card on her door. I never did.

She was a lonely woman and so was I. That was a barrier, not a link. Lonely women have something to guard. I was not exactly lonely. I had stood my life on a shelf, that was all. I could have had a dozen friends round me all day long. But there wasn't a friend that I loved and trusted above all the others, no lover, secret or declared. She had, I suppose, some nutrient hinterland on which she drew.

The bulbs in her bowl were shooting. I could see the pale new-green spears standing out of the dark loam. I was quite interested in them, wondered what they would be. I expected tulips, I don't know why. Her window was open all day long now, very fine thin curtains hung in front of it and these were never parted. Sometimes they moved but it was only in the breeze.

The trees in the street showed green now, thick with budded leaves. The shadow pattern on my wall was intricate and rich. It was no longer an austere winter pattern as it had been at first. Even the movement of the branches in the wind seemed different. I used to lie looking at the shadow when I rested in the afternoon. I was always tired then and so more permeable to impressions. I'd think about the buds, how pale and tender they were, but how implacable. The way an unborn child is implacable. If man's world were in ashes the spring would still come. I watched the moving pattern and my heart stirred with it in frail, half-sweet melancholy.

One afternoon I looked out instead of in. It was growing late and the sun would soon be gone, but it was warm. There was gold dust in the air, the sunlight had thickened. The shadows of trees and buildings fell, as they sometimes do on a fortunate day, with dramatic grace. *She* was standing there just behind the curtains, in a long dark wrap, as if she had come from her bath and was going to dress, early, for the evening. She stood so long and so still, staring out – at the budding trees, I thought – that tension began to accumulate in my mind. My blood ticked like a clock. Very slowly she raised her arms and the gown fell from her. She stood there naked, behind the veil of the curtains, the scarcely distinguishable but unmistakable form of a woman whose face was in shadow.

I turned away. The shadow of the burgeoning bough was on the white wall. I thought my heart would break.

Barbara Baynton

SQUEAKER'S MATE
1902

The woman carried the bag with the axe and maul and wedges; the man had the billy and clean tucker-bags; the cross-cut saw linked them. She was taller than the man, and the equability of her body, contrasting with his indolent slouch, accentuated the difference. 'Squeaker's mate', the men called her, and these agreed that she was the best long-haired mate that ever stepped in petticoats. The selectors' wives pretended to challenge her right to womanly garments, but if she knew what they said, it neither turned nor troubled Squeaker's mate.

Nine prospective posts and maybe sixteen rails – she calculated this yellow gum would yield. 'Come on,' she encouraged the man; 'let's tackle it.'

From the bag she took the axe, and ring-barked a preparatory circle, while he looked for a shady spot for the billy and tucker-bags.

'Come on.' She was waiting with the greased saw. He came. The saw rasped through a few inches, then he stopped and looked at the sun.

'It's nigh tucker-time,' he said, and when she dissented, he exclaimed, with sudden energy, 'There's another bee! Wait, you go on with the axe, an' I'll track 'im.'

As they came, they had already followed one and located the nest. She could not see the bee he spoke of, though her grey eyes were as keen as a black's. However, she knew the man, and her tolerance was of the mysteries.

She drew out the saw, spat on her hands, and with the axe began weakening the inclining side of the tree.

Long and steadily and in secret the worm had been busy in the heart. Suddenly the axe blade sank softly, the tree's wounded edges closed on it like a vice. There was a 'settling' quiver on its top branches, which the woman heard and understood. The man, encouraged by the

55

sounds of the axe, had returned with an armful of sticks for the billy. He shouted gleefully, 'It's fallin', look out.'

But she waited to free the axe.

With a shivering groan the tree fell, and as she sprang aside, a thick worm-eaten branch snapped at a joint and silently she went down under it.

'I tole yer t' look out,' he reminded her, as with a crowbar, and grunting earnestly, he forced it up. 'Now get out quick.'

She tried moving her arms and the upper part of her body. Do this, do that, he directed, but she made no movement after the first.

He was impatient, because for once he had actually to use his strength. His share of a heavy lift usually consisted of a make-believe grunt, delivered at a critical moment. Yet he hardly cared to let it again fall on her, though he told her he would, if she 'didn't shift'.

Near him lay a piece broken short; with his foot he drew it nearer, then gradually worked it into a position, till it acted as a stay to the lever.

He laid her on her back when he drew her out, and waited expecting some acknowledgment of his exertions, but she was silent, and as she did not notice that the axe she had tried to save lay with the fallen trunk across it, he told her. She cared almost tenderly for all their possessions and treated them as friends. But the half-buried broken axe did not affect her. He wondered a little, for only last week she had patiently chipped out the old broken head, and put in a new handle.

'Feel bad?' he inquired at length.

'Pipe,' she replied with slack lips.

Both pipes lay in the fork of a near tree. He took his, shook out the ashes, filled it, picked up a coal and puffed till it was alight – then he filled hers. Taking a small firestick he handed her the pipe. The hand she raised shook and closed in an uncertain hold, but she managed by a great effort to get it to her mouth. He lost patience with the swaying hand that tried to take the light.

'Quick,' he said, 'quick, that damn dog's at the tucker.'

He thrust it into her hand that dropped helplessly across her chest. The lighted stick, falling between her bare arm and the dress, slowly roasted the flesh and smouldered the clothes.

He rescued their dinner, pelted his dog out of sight – hers was lying near her head – put on the billy, then came back to her.

The pipe had fallen from her lips; there was blood on the stem.

'Did yer jam yer tongue?' he asked.

She always ignored trifles, he knew, therefore he passed her silence.

He told her that her dress was on fire. She took no heed. He put it out, and looked at the burnt arm, then with intentness at her.

Her eyes were turned unblinkingly to the heavens, her lips were grimly apart, and a strange greyness was upon her face, and the sweat-beads were mixing.

'Like a drink er tea? Asleep?'

He broke a green branch from the fallen tree and swished from his face the multitudes of flies that had descended with it.

In a heavy way he wondered why did she sweat, when she was not working? Why did she not keep the flies out of her mouth and eyes? She'd have bungy eyes, if she didn't. If she was asleep, why did she not close them?

But asleep or awake, as the billy began to boil, he left her, made the tea, and ate his dinner. His dog had disappeared, and as it did not come to his whistle, he threw the pieces to hers, that would not leave her head to reach them.

He whistled tunelessly his one air, beating his own time with a stick on the toe of his blucher, then looked overhead at the sun and calculated that she must have been lying like that for 'close up an hour'. He noticed that the axe handle was broken in two places, and speculated a little as to whether she would again pick out the back-broken handle or burn it out in his method, which was less trouble, if it did spoil the temper of the blade. He examined the wormdust in the stump and limbs of the newly fallen tree, mounted it and looked round the plain. The sheep were straggling in a manner that meant walking work to round them, and he supposed he would have to yard them tonight, if she didn't liven up. He looked down at unenlivened her. This changed his 'chune' to a call for his hiding dog.

'Come on, ole feller,' he commanded her dog. 'Fetch 'em back'. He whistled further instructions, slapping his thigh and pointing to the sheep.

But a brace of wrinkles either side the brute's closed mouth demonstrated determined disobedience. The dog would go if she told him, and by and by she would.

He lighted his pipe and killed half an hour smoking. With the frugality that hard graft begets, his mate limited both his and her own tobacco, so he must not smoke all afternoon. There was no work to shirk, so time began to drag. Then a 'goanner' crawling up a tree attracted him. He gathered various missiles and tried vainly to hit the seemingly grinning reptile. He came back and sneaked a fill of her tobacco, and while he was smoking, the white tilt of a cart caught his eye. He jumped up. 'There's Red Bob goin' t' our place fur th' 'oney,' he said. 'I'll go an' weigh it an' get the gonz' (money).

He ran for the cart, and kept looking back as if fearing she would follow and thwart him.

Red Bob the dealer was, in a business way, greatly concerned, when he found that Squeaker's mate was "avin' a sleep out there 'cos a tree fell on her'. She was the best honey-strainer and boiler that he dealt with. She was straight and square too. There was no water in her honey whether boiled or merely strained, and in every kerosene-tin the weight of honey was to an ounce as she said. Besides he was suspicious and diffident of paying the indecently eager Squeaker before he saw the woman. So reluctantly Squeaker led to where she lay. With many fierce oaths Red Bob sent her lawful protector for help, and compassionately poured a little from his flask down her throat, then swished away the flies from her till help came.

Together these men stripped a sheet of bark, and laying her with pathetic tenderness upon it, carried her to her hut. Squeaker followed in the rear with the billy and tucker.

Red Bob took his horse from the cart, and went to town for the doctor. Late that night at the back of the old hut (there were two) he and others who had heard that she was hurt, squatted with unlighted pipes in their mouths, waiting to hear the doctor's verdict. After he had given it and gone, they discussed in whispers, and with a look seen only on bush faces, the hard luck of that woman who alone had hard-grafted with the best of them for every acre and hoof on that selection. Squeaker would go through it in no time. Why she had allowed it to be taken up in his name, when the money had been her own, was also for them among the mysteries.

Him they called 'a nole woman', not because he was hanging round the honey-tins, but after man's fashion to eliminate all virtue. They beckoned him, and explaining his mate's injury, cautioned him to keep from her the knowledge that she would be for ever a cripple.

'Jus' th' same, now, then fur 'im,' pointing to Red Bob, 't' pay me, I'll 'ev t' go t' town.'

They told him in whispers what they thought of him, and with a cowardly look towards where she lay, but without a word of parting, like shadows these men made for their homes.

Next day the women came. Squeaker's mate was not a favourite with them – a woman with no leisure for yarning was not likely to be. After the first day they left her severely alone, their plea to their husbands, her uncompromising independence. It is in the ordering of things that by degrees most husbands accept their wives' views of other women.

The flour bespattering Squeaker's now neglected clothes spoke eloquently of his clumsy efforts at damper making. The women gave him many a feed, agreeing that it must be miserable for him.

If it were miserable and lonely for his mate, she did not complain; for her the long, long days would give place to longer nights – those nights with the pregnant bush silence suddenly cleft by a bush voice. However, she was not fanciful, and being a bush scholar knew 'twas a dingo, when a long whine came from the scrub on the skirts of which lay the axe under the worm-eaten tree. That quivering wail from the billabong lying murkily mystic towards the East was only the cry of the fearing curlew.

Always her dog – wakeful and watchful as she – patiently waiting for her to be up and about again. That would be soon, she told her complaining mate.

'Yer won't. Yer back's broke,' said Squeaker laconically. 'That's wot's wrong er yer; injoory t' th' spine. Doctor says that means back's broke, and yer won't never walk no more. No good not t' tell yer, cos I can't be doin' everythin'.'

A wild look grew on her face, and she tried to sit up.

'Erh,' said he, 'see! yer carnt, yer jes' ther same as a snake w'en ees back's broke, on'y yer don't bite yerself like a snake does w'en 'e carnt crawl. Yer did bite yer tongue w'en yer fell.'

She gasped, and he could hear her heart beating when she let her head fall back a few moments; though she wiped her wet forehead with the back of her hand, and still said that was the doctor's mistake. But day after day she tested her strength, and whatever the result, was silent, though white witnesses, halo-wise, gradually circled her brow and temples.

"Tisn't as if yer was agoin' t' get better t'morrer, the doctor says yer won't never work no more, an' I can't be cookin' an' workin' an' doin' everythin'!'

He muttered something about 'sellin' out', but she firmly refused to think of such a monstrous proposal.

He went into town one Saturday afternoon soon after, and did not return till Monday.

Her supplies, a billy of tea and scraps of salt beef and damper (her dog got the beef), gave out the first day, though that was as nothing to her compared with the bleat of the penned sheep, for it was summer and droughty, and her dog could not unpen them.

Of them and her dog only she spoke when he returned. He d—d him, and d—d her, and told her to 'double up yer ole broke back an' bite yerself.' He threw things about, made a long-range feint of kicking her threatening dog, then sat outside in the shade of the old hut, nursing his head till he slept.

She, for many reasons, had when necessary made these trips into town, walking both ways, leading a pack-horse for supplies. She never failed to indulge him in a half pint – a pipe was her luxury.

The sheep waited till next day, so did she.

For a few days he worked a little in her sight; not much – he never did. It was she who always lifted the heavy end of the log, and carried the tools; he – the billy and tucker.

She wearily watched him idling his time; reminded him that the wire lying near the fence would rust, one could run the wire through easily, and when she got up in a day or so, she would help strain and fasten it. At first he pretended he had done it, later said he wasn't goin' t' go wirin' or nothin' else by 'imself if every other man on the place did.

She spoke of many other things that could be done by one, reserving the great till she was well. Sometimes he whistled while she spoke, often swore, generally went out, and when this was inconvenient, dull as he was, he found the 'Go and bite yerself like a snake,' would instantly silence her.

At last the work worry ceased to exercise her, and for night to bring him home was a rare thing.

Her dog rounded and yarded the sheep when the sun went down and there was no sign of him, and together they kept watch on their movements till dawn. She was mindful not to speak of this care to him, knowing he would have left it for them to do constantly, and she noticed that what little interest he seemed to share went to the sheep. Why, was soon demonstrated.

Through the cracks her ever watchful eyes one day saw the dust rise out of the plain. Nearer it came till she saw him and a man on horseback rounding and driving the sheep into the yard, and later both left in charge of a little mob. Their 'Baa-baas' to her were cries for help; many had been pets. So he was selling her sheep to the town butchers.

In the middle of the next week he came from town with a fresh horse, new saddle and bridle. He wore a flash red shirt, and round his neck a silk handkerchief. On the next occasion she smelt scent, and though he did not try to display the dandy meerschaum, she saw it, and heard the squeak of the new boots, not bluchers. However he was kinder to her this time, offering a fill of his cut tobacco; he had long ceased to keep her supplied. Several of the men who sometimes in passing took a look in, would have made up her loss had they known, but no word of complaint passed her lips.

She looked at Squeaker as he filled his pipe from his pouch, but he would not meet her eyes, and, seemingly dreading something, slipped out.

She heard him hammering in the old hut at the back, which served for tools and other things which sunlight and rain did not hurt. Quite briskly he went in and out. She could see him through the cracks carrying a narrow strip of bark, and understood, he was making a bunk. When it was finished he had a smoke, then came to her and fidgeted about; he said this hut was too cold, and that she would never get well in it. She did not feel cold, but, submitting to his mood, allowed him to make a fire that would roast a sheep. He took off his hat, and, fanning himself, said he was roastin', wasn't she? She was.

He offered to carry her into the other; he would put a new roof on it in a day or two, and it would be better than this one, and she would be up in no time. He stood to say this where she could not see him.

His eagerness had tripped him.

There were months to run before all the Government conditions of residence, et cetera, in connection with the selection, would be fulfilled, still she thought perhaps he was trying to sell out, and she would not go.

He was away four days that time, and when he returned slept in the new bunk.

She compromised. Would he put a bunk there for himself, keep out of town, and not sell the place? He promised instantly with additions.

'Try could yer crawl yerself?' he coaxed, looking at her bulk.

Her nostrils quivered with her suppressed breathing, and her lips tightened, but she did not attempt to move.

It was evident some great purpose actuated him. After attempts to carry and drag her, he rolled her on the sheet of bark that had brought her home, and laboriously drew her round.

She asked for a drink, he placed her billy and tin pint besides the bunk, and left her, gasping and dazed, to her sympathetic dog.

She saw him run up and yard his horse, and though she called him, he would not answer nor come.

When he rode swiftly towards the town, her dog leaped on the bunk, and joined a refrain to her lamentation, but the cat took to the bush.

He came back at dusk next day in a spring cart – not alone – he had another mate. She saw her though he came a roundabout way, trying to keep in front of the new hut.

There were noises of moving many things from the cart to the hut. Finally he came to a crack near where she lay, and whispered the promise of many good things to her if she kept quiet, and that he would set her hut afire if she didn't. She was quiet, he need not have feared, for that time she was past it, she was stunned.

The released horse came stumbling round to the old hut, and thrust its head in the door in a domesticated fashion. Her dog promptly resented this straggler mistaking their hut for a stable. And the dog's angry dissent, together with the shod clatter of the rapidly disappearing intruder, seemed to have a disturbing effect on the pair in the new hut. The settling sounds suddenly ceased, and the cripple heard the stranger close the door, despite Squeaker's assurances that the woman in the old hut could not move from her bunk to save her life, and that her dog would not leave her.

Food, more and better, was placed near her – but, dumb and motionless, she lay with her face turned to the wall, and her dog growled menacingly at the stranger. The new woman was uneasy, and told Squeaker what people might say and do if she died.

He scared at the 'do', went into the bush and waited.

She went to the door, not the crack, the face was turned that way, and said she had come to cook and take care of her.

The disabled woman, turning her head slowly, looked steadily at her. She was not much to look at. Her red hair hung in an uncurled bang over her forehead, the lower part of her face had robbed the upper, and her figure evinced imminent motherhood, though it is doubtful if the barren woman, noting this, knew by calculation the paternity was not Squeaker's. She was not learned in these matters, though she understood all about a ewe and lamb.

One circumstance was apparent – ah! bitterest of all bitterness to women – she was younger.

The thick hair that fell from the brow of the woman on the bunk was white now.

Bread and butter the woman brought. The cripple looked at it, at her dog, at the woman. Bread and butter for a dog! but the stranger did not understand till she saw it offered to the dog. The bread and butter was not for the dog. She brought meat.

All next day the man kept hidden. The cripple saw his dog, and knew he was about.

But there was an end of this pretence when at dusk he came back with a show of haste, and a finger of his right hand bound and ostentatiously prominent. His entrance caused great excitement to his new mate. The old mate, who knew this snake-bite trick from its inception, maybe, realised how useless were the terrified stranger's efforts to rouse the snoring man after an empty pint bottle had been flung on the outside heap.

However, what the sick woman thought was not definite, for she kept silent always. Neither was it clear how much she ate, and how much she gave to her dog, though the new mate said to Squeaker one day that she believed that the dog would not take a bite more than its share.

The cripple's silence told on the stranger, especially when alone. She would rather have abuse. Eagerly she counted the days past and to pass. Then back to the town. She told no word of that hope to Squeaker, he had no place in her plans for the future. So if he spoke of what they would do by and by when his time would be up, and he able to sell out, she listened in uninterested silence.

She did tell him she was afraid of 'her', and after the first day would not go within reach, but every morning made a billy of tea, which with bread and beef Squeaker carried to her.

The rubbish heap was adorned, for the first time, with jam and fish tins from the table in the new hut. It seemed to be understood that neither woman nor dog in the old hut required them.

Squeaker's dog sniffed and barked joyfully around them till his licking efforts to bottom a salmon tin sent him careering in a muzzled frenzy, that caused the younger woman's thick lips to part grinningly till he came too close.

The remaining sheep were regularly yarded. His old mate heard him whistle as he did it. Squeaker began to work about a little burning-off. So that now, added to the other bush voices, was the call from some untimely falling giant. There is no sound so human as that from the riven souls of these tree people, or the trembling sighs of their upright neighbours whose hands in time will meet over the victim's fallen body.

There was no bunk on the side of the hut to which her eyes turned, but her dog filled that space, and the flash that passed between this back-broken woman and her dog might have been the spirit of these slain tree folk, it was so wondrous ghostly. Still, at times, the practical in her would be dominant, for in a mind so free of fancies, backed by bodily strength, hope died slowly, and forgetful of self she would almost call to Squeaker her fears that certain bees' nests were in danger.

He went into town one day and returned, as he had promised, long before sundown, and next day a clothes-line bridged the space between two trees near the back of the old hut; and – an equally rare occurrence – Squeaker placed across his shoulders the yoke that his old mate had fashioned for herself, with two kerosene-tins attached, and brought them filled with water from the distant creek; but both only partly filled the tub, a new purchase. With utter disregard of the heat and Squeaker's sweating brow, his new mate said, even after another trip, two more now for the blue water. Under her commands he brought them, though sullenly, perhaps contrasting the old mate's methods with the new.

His old mate had periodically carried their washing to the creek, and his mole-skins had been as white as snow without aid of blue.

Towards noon, on the clothes-line many strange garments fluttered, suggestive of a taunt to the barren woman. When the sun went down she could have seen the assiduous Squeaker lower the new prop-sticks and considerately stoop to gather the pegs his inconsiderate new mate had dropped. However, after one load of water next morning, on hearing her estimate that three more would put her own things through, Squeaker struck. Nothing he could urge would induce the stranger to trudge to the creek, where thirst-slaked snakes lay waiting for someone to bite. She sulked and pretended to pack up, till a bright idea struck Squeaker. He fastened a cask on a sledge and, harnessing the new horse, hitched him to it, and, under the approving eyes of his new mate, led off to the creek, though, when she went inside, he bestrode the spiritless brute.

He had various mishaps, any one of which would have served as an excuse to his old mate, but even babes soon know on whom to impose. With an energy new to him he persevered and filled the cask, but the old horse repudiated such a burden even under Squeaker's unmerciful welts. Almost half was sorrowfully baled out, and under a rain of whacks the horse shifted it a few paces, but the cask tilted and the thirsty earth got its contents. All Squeaker's adjectives over his wasted labour were as unavailing as the cure for spilt milk.

It took skill and patience to rig the cask again. He partly filled it, and, just as success seemed probable, the rusty wire fastening the cask to the sledge snapped with the strain, and, springing free, coiled affectionately round the terrified horse's hocks. Despite the sledge (the cask had been soon disposed of) that old town horse's pace then was his record. Hours after, on the plain that met the horizon, loomed two specks: the distance between them might be gauged, for the larger was Squeaker.

Anticipating a plentiful supply and lacking in bush caution, the new mate used the half-bucket of water to boil the salt mutton. Towards noon she laid this joint and bread on the rough table, then watched anxiously in the wrong direction for Squeaker.

She had drained the new teapot earlier, but she placed the spout to her thirsty mouth again.

She continued looking for him for hours.

Had he sneaked off to town, thinking she had not used that water, or not caring whether or no? She did not trust him; another had left her. Besides she judged Squeaker by his treatment of the woman who was lying in there with wide-open eyes. Anyhow no use to cry with only that silent woman to hear her.

Had she drunk all hers?

She tried to see at long range through the cracks, but the hanging bedclothes hid the billy. She went to the door and, avoiding the bunk, looked at the billy.

It was half full.

Instinctively she knew that the eyes of the woman were upon her. She turned away, and hoped and waited for thirsty minutes that seemed hours.

Desperation drove her back to the door. Dared she? No, she couldn't.

Getting a long forked prop-stick, she tried to reach it from the door, but the dog sprang at the stick. She dropped it and ran.

A scraggy growth fringed the edge of the plain. There was the creek. How far? she wondered. Oh, very far, she knew, and besides there were only a few holes where water was, and the snakes; for Squeaker, with a desire to shine in her eyes, was continually telling her of snakes – vicious and many – that daily he did battle with.

She recalled the evening he came from hiding in the scrub with a string round one finger, and said a snake had bitten him. He had drunk the pint of brandy she had brought for her sickness, and then slept till morning. True, although next day he had to dig for the string round the blue swollen finger, he was not worse than the many she had seen at the Shearer's Rest suffering a recovery. There was no brandy to cure her if she were bitten.

She cried a little in self-pity, then withdrew her eyes, that were getting red, from the outlying creek, and went again to the door. She of the bunk lay with closed eyes.

Was she asleep? The stranger's heart leapt, yet she was hardly in earnest as she tiptoed billy-wards. The dog, crouching with head between two paws, eyed her steadily, but showed no opposition. She made dumb show. 'I want to be friends with you, and won't hurt her.' Abruptly she looked at her, then at the dog. He was motionless and emotionless. Besides if that dog – certainly watching her – wanted to bite her (her dry mouth opened) it could get her any time.

She rated this dog's intelligence almost human, from many of its actions in omission and commission in connexion with this woman.

She regretted the pole, no dog would stand that.

Two more steps.

Now just one more; then, by bending and stretching her arm, she would reach it. Could she now? She tried to encourage herself by remembering how close on the first day she had been to the woman, and how delicious a few mouthfuls would be – swallowing dry mouthfuls.

She measured the space between where she had first stood and the billy. Could she get anything to draw it to her? No, the dog would not stand that, and besides the handle would rattle, and she might hear and open her eyes.

The thought of those sunken eyes suddenly opening made her heart bound. Oh! she must breathe – deep, loud breaths. Her throat clicked noisily. Looking back fearfully, she went swiftly out.

She did not look for Squeaker this time, she had given him up.

While she waited for her breath to steady, to her relief and surprise the dog came out. She made a rush to the new hut, but he passed seemingly oblivious of her, and, bounding across the plain, began rounding the sheep. Then he must know Squeaker had gone to town.

Stay! Her heart beat violently; was it because she on the bunk slept and did not want him?

She waited till her heart quieted, and again crept to the door.

The head of the woman on the bunk had fallen towards the wall as in deep sleep; it was turned from the billy, to which she must creep so softly.

Slower, from caution and deadly earnestness, she entered.

She was not so advanced as before, and felt fairly secure, for the woman's eyes were still turned to the wall, and so tightly closed she could not possibly see where she was.

She would bend right down, and try and reach it from where she was.

She bent.

It was so swift and sudden, that she had not time to scream when those bony fingers had gripped the hand that she prematurely reached for the billy. She was frozen with horror for a moment, then her screams were piercing. Panting with victory, the prostrate one held her with a hold that the other did not attempt to free herself from.

Down, down she drew her.

Her lips had drawn back from her teeth, and her breath almost scorched the face that she held so close for the staring eyes to gloat over. Her exultation was so great that she could only gloat and gasp, and hold with a tension that had stopped the victim's circulation.

As a wounded, robbed tigress might hold and look, she held and looked.

Neither heard the swift steps of the man, and if the tigress saw him enter, she was not daunted. 'Take me from her,' shrieked the terrified one. 'Quick, take me from her,' she repeated it again, nothing else. 'Take me from her.'

He hastily fastened the door and said something that the shrieks drowned, then picked up the pole. It fell with a thud across the arms which the tightening sinews had turned into steel. Once, twice, thrice. Then the one that got the fullest force bent; that side of the victim was free.

The pole had snapped. Another blow with a broken end freed the other side.

Still shrieking 'Take me from her, take me from her,' she beat on the closed door till Squeaker opened it.

Then he had to face and reckon with his old mate's maddened dog, that the closed door had baffled.

The dog suffered the shrieking woman to pass, but though Squeaker, in bitten agony, broke the stick across the dog, he was forced to give the savage brute best.

'Call 'im orf, Mary, 'e's eatin' me,' he implored. 'Oh corl 'im orf.'

But with stony face the woman lay motionless.

'Sool 'im on t' 'er.' He indicated his new mate who, as though all the plain led to the desired town, still ran in unreasoning terror.

'It's orl er doin',' he pleaded, springing on the bunk beside his old mate. But when, to rouse her sympathy, he would have laid his hand on her, the dog's teeth fastened in it and pulled him back.

Jean Bedford

COUNTRY GIRL AGAIN
1979

At last it was spring. The paddocks in front of the house were still sodden from the months of rain and until midday, when the sun was directly above the farm, the grass was covered in fine overnight cobwebs, sparkling with drops of heavy dew. Pale clear sunshine lay like moss on the flat fields which stretched from the house to the road.

When she went walking with the baby down the potholed track Anne could see the white nubs of new mushrooms all through the long grass. They would sit on the little wooden bridge over the creek while the baby threw in rocks and bits of bark, chuckling when they splashed. Then they would walk on to where the cows grazed next to the path and the little girl would try to pat them, stumbling and sinking in the clods of cow-trodden turf.

Anne watched her in a detached way. Her mind was still numb from the cold winter and what she saw as the gradual failure of her marriage. They had been saying, for the second year now, that it would all be better in spring. When they didn't have to get up at six and chop the kindling in the frost and shiver in the smoky kitchen until the fire caught . . . 'It'll be good then. We'll go on picnics and get baskets of apples from the old trees near the creek.' Terry was always the optimist. 'People will come and stay, you'll see. As soon as the weather is better.'

But she sensed that he was being held back by her reluctance and lethargy. His council job was routine, nine-to-five, with occasional stints in the hills. He would have liked to pack up his gear and set off for months at a time – really get into trees as he put it. They joked about it – she said 'Why couldn't you have stayed a maths teacher? Why wouldn't you settle for lunches at the pub and evenings at the theatre? What more has life to offer really?' and he'd grin his Peter Pan grin and say 'Yes, you've saddled yourself with Melbourne's answer to Gauguin – but at least I let you come too.'

Now she was pregnant again. She hadn't told Terry, she still hadn't decided not to get rid of it. Looking at the baby now, sitting happily in the reeds and muck she thought of a pun to tell Terry. Katherine of all the rushes. She grinned, she always laughed at her own jokes. She felt a bit better.

'Kathy. Come on. Time for yum.' She hugged the plump child to her. Fierce, fierce, she thought, is my love for you. I'd live my life in grief at the thought of killing off another Kathy. But in her head she was circling, crying – How? How? Can I be tied down by another one? I'd never be able to break free then. She'd have to make the decision herself. If she told Terry he wouldn't leave her any option. He often claimed he wanted six or seven children. He wouldn't make her have another child, but he'd never forgive her for getting rid of one.

Putting the little girl to bed after lunch she was suddenly overcome by the sheer physical effort of looking after babies. Kathy was still in nappies, she'd hardly be out of them when this one was due. I couldn't bear it, she thought angrily. Bound hand and foot by nappies and cot sheets and wet woollies. The ridiculous metaphor pleased her. God, I'm getting like my mother – making a joke of everything so she didn't have to scream.

She put the wet clothes into the trough and hung out the morning's washing, tripping over the rope of the sheep they had tethered there to crop the grass. She found herself drifting into fantasies of what she'd do if they owned this house. The farmer kept hinting that he wanted to sell. She sat on the garden wall muttering to herself. 'I'd have a kitchen garden here. With borders of marjoram and oregano and a hedge of rosemary.' A part of her these days wanted strongly to settle down. At times like this, with the baby asleep, the lamb bleating softly against her hand, the warm green grass rippling all around, it seemed a fine idea to buy a farmhouse and put down roots. 'We could make a lawn and the children could play here . . .' She stopped herself. No, no, no. She wasn't going to be drawn in like that. She went inside to make tea.

She sat in the cold kitchen and thought of her old plans to live by herself with the baby. Nothing had come of them – she didn't like living here and her relationship with Terry was obviously deteriorating, but she was too apathetic to change, too overwhelmed by tiredness and routine.

That night friends came round. A painter who lived up the valley and his wife. They had no children and although they were a good ten years older than Anne and Terry, she always thought they seemed younger and more dashing. They grew their own dope and sometimes appeared with large plastic bags of it, recently cut down. Tonight they brought wine. Alec had just sold a painting and they were celebrating.

Sometimes Anne had fantasies of fucking Alec, although she didn't know him very well – he was a romantic figure to hang her dreams of freedom on. She never did anything about it. Since her affair with Nick she had been completely faithful to Terry. One drunken night she had told him about it and been appalled at the depth of his hurt and bewilderment. She had always assumed he knew what was going on. Now they had an understanding that they would talk it out before anything like that happened again. In fact now she had become the jealous one, afraid of the possibility of losing Terry while still wishing to escape herself.

That night they drank two flagons of red wine and argued loudly and hilariously about anarchy and revolution. Alec was blatantly anti-intellectual, furious and aggressive in his contempt for wishy-washy liberals, of whom he said Terry was a prime example. Terry withdrew into his charming complaisance, letting the others argue it out. If it was like this more often, Anne thought, I could contemplate it. But she knew this surge of energy and engagement was fleeting, dependent on new and stimulating people.

She went in to make coffee and Alec followed her. Terry was talking to Carol about horses, her obsession.

'I'd like to learn to ride,' he said. 'Is it very difficult?'

Anne made a sour face. The country was really getting into him, or was it Carol?

In the kitchen Alec was amorous. She stood stiffly when he put his arms around her.

'What's the matter?'

'Nothing's the matter. Are you usually so irresistible?'

'I thought I had perceived the odd signal that you might not be exactly averse . . .' He spoke in a parody of a drunk's careful enunciation.

'Oh, well, of course I'm not averse.' She grinned. 'It isn't possible, that's all.'

'Well all right. Okay. That's fine. Enough said. Sorry I asked!' He put the cups out on a tray. She was tempted to say more, explain it in detail, but it wasn't relevant. There was a tension between them now which was rather pleasant.

While Alec went to piss she took the tray in and stood quietly for a moment outside the door listening. She was fluttering with suspicion and the wish to be proved right. But when she opened the door Carol was asleep on the couch and Terry was changing the record. She put the tray down. Of course it was silly to suspect Terry, he'd come out with it if there was anything going on.

After they had left, the still sulky Alec half dragging Carol to the car, she said, 'I've never seen her get animated about anything except her bloody horses.'

'Yeah. It's interesting though. She's going to take me riding tomorrow. That's okay isn't it?' he said, picking up her reaction. 'I'll look after the bub in the morning and you can get a rest. She's not calling for me until two.'

'Yes, of course it's all right. I hope you don't break your neck that's all.'

She brooded over it until she went to sleep and all the next morning while Terry took the baby shopping in the town. When she came down to it she didn't really care if he wanted to fuck Carol or not, she resented his freedom to even spend time with her. But I want to *own* him, she thought with a shock. This has really got to stop.

When he came back with Carol in the late afternoon, bruised and shaken from a fall, it was obvious that neither of them had any ulterior motives. Carol was rather irritable with him, she obviously thought he was hopeless. Still, even that sort of crossness can turn into sexual energy, Anne thought. She couldn't shake herself out of it. Every gesture, every word they uttered was sifted through the fine net of her jealousy until she finally had to relax and accept that there was nothing there. When Carol left, leading Terry's horse, muttering that she hoped it wasn't lamed by his carelessness, he gave an exaggerated sigh of relief.

'Jesus. Never again. I'm going to take lessons from the riding academy where they won't be so bad-tempered.'

So her last doubt was settled. She couldn't believe he was anything but genuine. Now the reaction set in. All afternoon, mulling over her jealousy, she'd been thinking of her pregnancy as her secret weapon.

If she thought she was losing Terry she would tell him. Another baby would bind him to her with iron chains. Now she felt flat, cold, even let down. Her thoughts of the last twenty-four hours had been painful and frightening, but titillating in their way. I'll have to think it through again, she told herself.

During the next week she started to feel sick in the morning. Feeding Kathy her breakfast sludge made her retch. She'd have to make a decision soon or Terry would notice. One afternoon while the baby slept she went for a walk along the creek to where it joined the river. She sat down on a lichen-covered trunk and watched the swirling water. Frog spawn rimmed the pool and little purple grassflowers were starting to poke out here and there. Everything seemed to be budding, flowering, gravid. Anne could feel the hormonal effects of pregnancy on her own mind. It would be so easy to give in to this longing to be part of the natural cycle, to be sucked in to the seasonal fertility. Oh God, she thought. There'll be baby lambs soon and then I won't have a chance.

One night Terry said, 'You're looking very down. What's the matter?'

'Nothing,' she said. 'Springtime depression. New life all around – and in here,' she pointed to her head, 'nothing new at all.'

'Why don't you go to town for a weekend? I'll mind the girl. Have a couple of nights out, get drunk, catch up on all the gossip. Go on.'

'Yes. I might,' she said, thinking, He's a kind man, I'd like to tell him and watch his pleasure. But she couldn't. She thought she'd put it off until she'd been away. She might talk to her friend Liz about it.

In the pub on Friday night it could have been a different universe. Anne felt tense among all the shouting laughing crowding people, some nof them her friends. She saw Liz and pushed her way over to her. They kissed and talked and drank. By the time they left for a party she was fairly drunk. She hadn't said anything to Liz about being pregnant.

Much later, finding herself in bed with a man she'd known and lusted after years ago she started crying. He was alarmed and tender but she wouldn't talk about it. As much as anything it was the clumsiness of being with someone else after Terry. Different contours, different textures, new body habits to be learnt. It was very sad, but very fine, she thought drunkenly as she fell asleep.

In the morning he said, 'Can you come up to town very often?'

'As often as I like, I guess. I'll have to tell Terry why though.'

'What will he do?'

'I don't know,' she said. 'I really don't know. Does it matter?'

She went round to see Liz and collect her gear and make her arrangements. Then she rang Terry.

'How's it going?'

'All right. Listen Tez, I want to stay over till Monday night. Is that possible?'

'Sure. I'll take the day off. Having a good time? Drink? Drugs? Sex-crazed Carlton heavies?'

'All that.'

'How're you feeling physically? You looked very tired when you left.'

'I feel okay. I'm pretty sure I'll be better by Monday,' she said. 'I think it's one of those three-day wogs.'

She said hello to Kathy and sent him her love over the wires and then she went to meet her new lover for lunch. He was pleased to hear they'd have an extra night. He suggested that he could also take Monday off. 'We could have a picnic in the Gardens.'

'No,' she said. 'I've got an appointment on Monday morning. And after that I don't think I'll feel like doing anything much.'

Carmel Bird

THE GOLDEN MOMENT
1990

The story of the golden moment is a story about suburban Australia in the nineteen fifties. The street in which the story takes place is often called 'the golden mile' because so many wealthy bankers and barristers and surgeons have for generations lived there in grandeur and comfort with their beautiful wives and happy families. Almost all of these families have very white skins indeed, and are by religion Christians (of the Protestant kind). The rare Jewish or Roman Catholic family is treated with superb tolerance and charity, but it is understood that such families are darkened by a blight too powerful and mysterious to name.

The houses themselves bear the names they were given by the original owners, and some of these names reflect a nostalgia for places far away, others expressing a hope in the youthful country of Australia. So a house named 'Winterbourne' stands between 'La Maison Blanche' and 'Lenna'. The style of architecture is labelled 'Federation' in recognition of the modern birth of the country itself. The trees and flowers are by and large European, and the branches of the oaks and elms that line the street on one side almost touch those on the other, so that in summer a magical green tunnel arches above the traffic, and people from less beautiful suburbs drive along here just to wonder at the beauty of the golden mile. Even ordinary traffic seems to move sedately along the grandest section of the road.

A golden moment is that time of the afternoon photographers love, when the light of the day bathes the world in one last glow of radiance, when Paradise is promised, when everything stands still at the instant between the darkness and the light, when fairies and goblins and other spirits good and bad may be revealed.

The golden moment on the golden mile is one of nature's marvels.

On the veranda of a large old house called 'The Lilacs' in this prosperous part of this Australian city there sits a woman. She wears a grandmotherly floral dress and is reclining on a cane lounge. The time is peace-time, in the middle of the nineteen fifties. There is of course a *cold* war, but in the warmth of the summer sun in the late afternoon, this cold war casts no shadow, drops no snowflake on the veranda of 'The Lilacs'.

Paths, flowerbeds, shrubs, trees, vines, a wall – these divide the land on which this house is built from the land on which the next house, called 'Santa Fe', stands. The foreign and exotic name of 'Santa Fe' alerts visitors and strangers to the fact that there is a certain difference here.

So, in this story, the sun shines and the bees drone, butterflies flit. A haze of dreamy happiness drifts across the garden of 'The Lilacs'. The woman on the veranda drinks weak gin, lime and soda, reads a book, a romance.

Ploc! Ploc! This is the sound of young men and women playing tennis on the court in the garden of 'Santa Fe'. Laughter, shouts. Ploc! Ploc! A rhododendron bush, unimaginably large, with pearly pink florets, frilled and abundant, grows between 'Santa Fe' and 'The Lilacs'. It is possible that sometimes through the spaces that thread between the leaves, a flash of white pleated skirt might dart, flick, distract.

In the romance being read by the lilac woman, men and women stare into each other's eyes. They kiss and they swim, and they dance on terraces at twilight, at dawn.

Click! Someone has taken a photograph of some of the girls and some of the boys as they sit in the shade beside the tennis court at 'Santa Fe'. The woman on her veranda is unable to hear the sound of the camera, such a small sound to travel across the distance between her and the tennis players. And all such sounds are masked by the noise of parrots in one of the gum trees. Hundreds of green birds with rosy cheeks that feed with vigour and raucous intensity, decorating the branches like little bright stuffed birds on a Christmas tree. The sound they make as they squawk and twitter all together has a peculiar quality; it seems to be able to enter the ear and invade the brain and fill the head. If Lilac shuts her eyes she can experience the absence of her brain, as her cranial cavity is inhabited by the collective cry of pleasure, competition and greed. The green and rosy joy of living.

Possibly this is Paradise. Perhaps the tennis players have just taken a picture of Paradise where the sun shines, birds sing, bees buzz, flowers bloom, woman reads, hero and heroine embrace, boys and girls in white play tennis.

The woman finishes reading, closes the book as sunset glows on the fiction of a golden beach. For a few moments the woman hovers in a corridor between the sunset on the beach and the sunlight that falls in dappled patches on the veranda. Then the hero and the heroine and the beach fade, and the woman hears Ploc! as the ball hits the racquet. The woman begins to think about the girls who are playing tennis, who live behind the hedges of 'Santa Fe'.

A white cat stalks in the shadows of 'The Lilacs'; a black dog watches the tennis at 'Santa Fe'. Each garden has a goldfish pond and a display of roses.

The woman on the veranda thinks about the girls from 'Santa Fe' – Rose, Veronica, Marion, Clare and Aurora Blackwood. Aurora, the youngest, was born without fingers. She is home from her convent boarding school for the holidays. Local rumour says she will take the veil, renounce the world, enter.

Just before the war, in 1938, Aurora was born. A kind of portent, and astonishment, a perfect picture of a baby girl with the oddest little triangles for hands and the sweetest disposition. She had intellect and a charming singing voice. She wore little mittens, always, made from fine crochet, or softest leather, or silk, or velvet. She waved her paws around like lavender bags. Ten toes, perfect. Teeth. Long golden curls. Memory like an elephant. Manners, beautiful. She was a swift and elegant swimmer.

Everybody said how did this happen, why did this happen. Was it something in the water, the food, the medicines, the air. Was it cat fur, dog hair. Lack of sunlight, exercise, vitamins. Was it the result of bad thoughts. Or the sight of a fishmonger's mittens at just the wrong moment. Radio waves. The stars. The moon. A shock, a sudden and terrible noise. Mathematics or geology. Electricity. Witchcraft. A tremor shook the earth beneath 'Santa Fe' and 'The Lilacs' and all the other houses round about *just* when the hands were forming. Or was it an insect. The war. Naturally people thought, sometimes murmured, about the possibility of heredity. But this was an idea that was quickly dismissed. Four perfect girls – and *then* the dropping off of fingers?

There was nothing whatsoever like that in the background of Handsome Mr Blackwood and his Beautiful Wife. Strange things happen. It's fate, the stars, the planets, the insects, the wars.

A friend of Mr Blackwood, a doctor, very gifted and visionary, said that if this kind of thing happened in the future it would probably be possible to reconstruct, fabricate, borrow, graft, grow the fingers. He said some really terrible and astounding things – growing fingers from culture in glass dishes – or, if another baby died, supposing, then that baby's fingers could, in time to come, he imagined, be grafted like the cuttings of a fruit tree onto the little hands of a baby such as Aurora. Imagine. A miracle.

So in one sense Aurora Blackwood was born too soon. Or was that just in time? Later in the century she could have had the knuckles, cartilage, bones, joints, sinews, muscles, blood vessels and any other material that goes to make up the hands of the dead baby of a concert violinist. Aurora's own skin would be needed, I believe. Smooth as a baby's bottom, take the silky satin from Aurora's bottom and make for her a pair of gloves. These remarkable gloves, ladies and gentlemen, were made from the skin of a baby's bottom, and will fold up and fit into the shell of a walnut. Fold up, roll up, double up with mirth. See also the miracle of the little violinist. Her hands play the sonata while her mind wanders at will. See the fattest woman in the western world, the tallest man, the dance of the seven veils, the facts of life covered by a bunch of feathers. Everything happens here under the big top. The miracle of the little violinist. Roll up.

They took Aurora to Lourdes. The whole family went. Apparently it is not unheard of for fingers, arms, legs, noses, ears to grow in the miraculous waters. But nothing happened in this case. The family did a short tour of the continent. War was coming. Visited French relatives. (Celeste Blackwood, the mother, is half French. Was it something French that caused the baby's hands to stop short just before the fingers?) They climbed the Eiffel Tower, lit candles in Notre Dame, prayed fervently in the basilica of Sacre Coeur. Papal audience. Bridge of Sighs. Gondola. First ship home. War.

When Aurora went to kindergarten she learned to do fantastic things with plasticene, and all the other children were very kind. She was a dancer and a singer. It was in the days before finger painting had been invented. She was good with crayons, bending her little paw to make marvellous marks on paper. All the colours of the rainbow and some nice thick shiny black. As she grew older, art became her thing. She drew and painted – watercolour, oil, pastel, charcoal. Aurora did pictures of houses along the golden mile and sold the pictures to the owners of the houses. Many a study wall is graced by a picture titled 'Our House by Aurora Blackwood'. She also made pots, and embroidered cloths. You should have seen the speed and skill with which she could braid her hair.

The woman on the veranda of 'The Lilacs' more or less thinks all this as she looks up from her book and hears the young people playing tennis. She hears a mixture of sounds – through the noise of the birds in the gum tree she can sometimes get the ploc of the ball on the racquet, the tink of laughter, the chink of ice in her glass, the rustle of a nearby lizard in the dry leaves, the hop of a bird, a breath of wind. Peace and goodwill and it will soon be Christmas. The telephone is ringing in the hall. The book of romance falls to the floor as the woman – her dress is green and violet and her sandals are white – gets up from the cane lounge, brushes her hair from her forehead, and goes to the hall where she answers the telephone. The caller is a neighbour from a house called 'Waratah' across the street. This neighbour has just returned from travels overseas.

'I must come over soon and tell you all about it. The hotel you suggested in London was quite wonderful, and I met a Chelsea Pensioner in full scarlet regalia as he was walking past.'

'Come over now. I'm making tea, and there's half a banana cake from yesterday.'

'Don't go to any trouble.'

'No trouble at all. Do come over. I'm keen to hear all about it, and welcome home.'

The Waratah woman sits on the veranda with the Lilac woman and they exchange views and reminiscences of the British Isles and France.

'I went to the Louvre and saw the Mona Lisa. Shopping in the rue St Honoré. Couldn't get a decent cup of tea for love or money. Brought you a small gift from Scotland.'

She hands the Lilac woman a blood-red cairngorm brooch.

'How very kind, my favourite.'

'Rhododendrons in Scotland, but nothing like the size of yours.'

'Nearly finished for the season. The Blackwood girls have people in for tennis.'

In the garden of 'Santa Fe' they have taken many photographs of this happy afternoon. Aurora is home and there are visitors, boys and girls in white with sunburnt faces and shiny hair. The black dog catches the tennis ball in his mouth. Another ball is tossed, and Ploc! The game goes on.

Milk and sugar and banana cake.

'Well, Lilac my dear, I have a tale to tell you. Think of this. Something happened. I bring a strange piece of news, a sort of revelation, all the way from Paris. You won't believe this. I could scarcely believe my own eyes and ears.'

'It was cold. Rugged up I was, and wouldn't normally go just wandering into churches. But I was looking for a post office – it's almost impossible to find them – and as I said, it was cold, bitterly cold. I was in the rue du Bac, and there was a big old church. Now I know this sounds peculiar, but it – I mean the church – it seemed to beckon to me somehow, seemed to suggest to me that I should push open the door and go inside. As you know, we're C of E, and a person doesn't normally just feel beckoned to go into a foreign RC church – well not unless it's St Marks or something in Venice – and go in out of the cold. Not normally. I can't explain it, but I went in, pushed open these great old wooden doors and went in.

'The walls were painted blue, rather pretty really, and stars on the ceiling, and a charming mural in what I always think of as a very English style. It was just the Virgin Mary and some angels, but quite attractive in its way. There were candles burning, hundreds of candles in little holders. And it was much, much warmer than outside. People were kneeling and praying, and one woman was stretched out on the floor. Very exaggerated. But there were some other tourists there just looking.

'It's a church of miracles, you see. That's it. The mural was about a magic medal that was given to a saint. So I sat down with my parcels – of course I never found the post office – and I got out my guidebook to look up information about the church. A little old nun came in and sat down beside me. She was incredibly French and all in black and I thought she looked like a witch in a fairy tale. There was a kind of sweet perfume about her. It was embarrassing, her kneeling there in prayer so close to me with my parcels and guidebook, just sitting there staring around and trying to get warm and her talking to God or praying to the Virgin Mary. I shifted along and then she lifted her head, turned to me, and looked me in the eye.

'I hope you don't think I'm making this up. She had such clear blue eyes, shining. She looked very wrinkled and wise and knowing, exactly like a witch, as I said, with her arms folded religiously in her sleeves. And then she spoke. I nearly died, I was so embarrassed. I'm not really used to talking in church. And she spoke in English with hardly any accent at all. You are a visitor, she said. And I said yes, and she welcomed me to Paris and said was I enjoying it and where did I come from, and I told her. And then – you won't believe this – then she said would I by any chance know of her niece Celeste Blackwood. I simply couldn't believe my ears. Yes, I said as if in a dream, yes, I live across the street. And the old witch said what a coincidence, but she didn't seem to be surprised. Would I be so good, she said, as to pass on to her niece her best love and blessings. Knock me down with a feather. I said I would. But now we come to the terrible part.

'I don't know if I can pass anything on to Celeste at all.'

The shadows of the afternoon are lengthening and the breeze that lifts the leaves of the vine around the veranda is cool. The white cat has gone into the house for food and comfort. The florets of the rhododendron have lost their glow. The raucous song of the birds in the gum tree has fallen still, and a silence has settled on the garden in 'Santa Fe'. Then a young woman's voice is heard calling 'Everybody stand over here for just one last shot. It's perfect. The golden moment.'

Briefly the scene is bathed with incandescence as one final burst of daylight marks the arrival of the dusk. The sharp loud click of the shutter and the final picture is taken.

The Waratah woman continues: 'And the terrible part is this, I swear it's true. I gathered up my parcels and said goodbye to the nun. She stood up to go. And she took her hands out of the sleeves of her habit. And Lilac my dear, she had no trace of any fingers at all. Hands exactly like poor Aurora's. Exactly. Clearly, Lilac, the thing runs in the family. Their fingers drop off for some reason and they put them, I mean the girls, into convents in foreign countries in an attempt to put a stop to the thing. But of course you can't. There'll always be a throwback. It's so tragic.'

Lilac's eyes fly open in surprise, and she catches her breath.

'I can't believe it. I simply can't believe it. Pardon me, but are you sure you didn't dream this thing. So far-fetched. Travel broadens the mind, and surely plays strange tricks in the light and air of foreign lands.'

'I saw it all with my own eyes, as sure as I'm sitting here.'

'Then you'll have to tell Celeste, give her the message. Sort of pretend you saw nothing, that the nun never took her hands out of her sleeves. You must just pass on the message, the blessing, the love. Forget what you saw. Imagine you imagined it.'

'How can I? And how can I pass on the message with a straight face, knowing what I know? It's on Celeste's side of the family. I can't look her in the eye. She'll *know* I know – doesn't matter what I say. It was a million to one chance I went into that church. Why did I have to do it?'

Lilac is silent. She has no answer to this question. An anguish has twisted its way into the conversation on the veranda.

The light has gone, the golden moment has passed. One last shot of the players in the garden has been registered on the film in the camera, lit by the last magic splash of light. Final exposure. The women on the veranda pack up the cups and saucers and go into the house, as a darkness, like the soft web of a spider, weaves its way through the gardens, linking 'The Lilacs' and 'Santa Fe' in the drifting pall of night.

James   Bradley

THE   TURTLES'   GRAVEYARD
1998

It has been fifteen hours since the boat left Koh Tao. Not long perhaps, in the greater scheme of things, but long enough. Long enough for the sun to wheel across the cerulean immensity of the sky. Long enough for the massing light of the constellations to rise and begin the long arc of their nightly motion. Long enough for this water, once warm as blood, to turn cool, then cold against my body. Long enough for my arms to tire, fall motionless to my side. Long enough for my skin to swell and pucker.

Have you ever raised your head, gazed upwards into rain? Seen that strange perspectiveless world of cloud and tumbling water? If you have you will know there is a moment, as the world recedes, when the rain will seem to pause in its descent, like the motion of a stone's parabola at apogee. I say a moment, but that is not quite the word, for time itself becomes elastic, slowing finally to a point, before it begins again, and there is reversal, slow at first, but hastening like the stone falling earthwards and all of a sudden the rain is no longer falling, it is you who is falling, or rather rising, upwards, against gravity, like flight, like breathing.

I fly like that now. Once this was water, but now I float in stars. Far beneath me the plankton darts and burns, phosphor bright, cold meteors against the dark. Around me the light from the stars dapples the water's surface, motes of light that move with the water like leaves across the limpid surface of a lake. And all the while I am rising into the sky, falling upwards into the ancient deep of night, the stars passing me like rain as I rise.

Beneath the water's surface my watch's face floats, ghostly green. One hand on three, the other at four: 3.20 a.m. Eight hours since Jenny left, swimming steadily away across the shimmering water, growing smaller and smaller until her body vanished into the haze of light and all I could hear was the faint sound of her stroke, growing fainter, and fainter. Then nothing. Only the fire of the setting sun on the lapping sea.

At first I wondered whether I should have gone with her, tried swimming for the shore, but I saw how low the sun had fallen, and knew, despite Jenny's protestations, that once it set we would no longer know which way to swim across the featureless sea. I cannot read the stars, nor can she. There are no stars in the city of light. And besides, I still hoped that someone might realise we were missing, seek Gerhard or Chas out in their cluttered office and demand to know who had counted the heads when they climbed back on board. That Gerhard and Chas would feel the yawning space of their error open within them as they glanced one to the other, realising what they had done, and come racing for the boat. For us.

But Jenny was frightened, too scared and angry to hear these possibilities. She knew we would not last the night, and wanted to swim for the shore. When I refused she swore and wept and then finally kissed me, her lips cold with the seawater, so I knew at the end she did not mean her words of anger.

I wonder where she is. Perhaps she can see the land, almost hear the music from the beachside discos as it echoes across the water. Maybe it is not stars that play around her but the reflected neon of the tow, slithering silkily across the waves. Or maybe she is lost like me, floating somewhere in the vastness of the night, too far from land to see the faint glow of the lights, needing the dawn and the sun to gauge which way to swim now. Or maybe she is dead, pulled beneath the surface by a shark, or just drowned, her corpse already puffy and bloating.

I know it is morbid to think like this. But I am not frightened. Instead I feel a strange calmness, almost a euphoria, which has grown in me as the night has passed. This is not how it was at the beginning, when the two of us broke the surface, excitedly laughing and talking one over the other as we pulled at our regulators, eager to share the delights we had just witnessed. Our first reef dive. The culmination of two weeks of training in that grass-walled hut with Gerhard and Chas, all for this. Not realising at first, as we turned slowly, looking for the boat, that they were gone, not quite believing our eyes as we turned once more, faster this time, only to see that it was no deception, no trick of the light, but that they had gone without us, back to the island, to the bars and lights and restaurants, leaving us out here. Alone.

Then, all of a sudden, we saw them, a receding speck in the immense blueness of sea, and although we knew it was futile we screamed and waved, using our fins to propel our bodies upwards, launching ourselves out of the water like dolphins performing in some wretched show, hoping that someone might turn and see us. But it was too late. Then, for a time, we waited here, telling each other that someone would notice, that they would realise there were too few of them, that some of the equipment was missing, that we had not been seen since they weighed anchor, but as the long day wore on that possibility receded too, and we were left, just waiting. Alone.

How strange that this should happen now. After Jenny and I saved and planned for this holiday, lured by the falling baht, by the promise of the beaches and the discos. For weeks we spent our lunchtimes planning where we would go, what we would do, until I could think of little else, my excitement as consuming as a child's. I do not remember when the diving course became part of our plans, but once it appeared it lodged, like a burr, and everything else receded, the discos of Koh Samui replaced by the more austere pleasures of Koh Tao, the sightseeing by depth charts and equipment tests. Nor do I remember whose idea it was. I would like to think that it was Jenny's but it might just as well have been mine. Not that it matters now.

This holiday was special to me. I'm sure it was special to Jenny as well, but for her it did not carry the weight of symbolism. Instead it was just another holiday, three weeks of sun and drinking and sex. Sex. Even now it makes me laugh to think of Jenny and sex. The men she took to her bed, without shame or guilt. I cannot do that, not yet, although I hoped that tonight, maybe Peter and I, we could have done it, high on beer and sun and maybe just enough grass to make me feel loose and distant from my stern, lonely flesh. For it frightens me, the idea of it, of a man I do not know taking his member and placing it into me. Would it have been like Roger? His face, pale and cruel and somehow earnest as he hammered away on top of me. I think it was the earnestness I hated most, more even than his cruelty, which was real, particularly since that afternoon at the doctor's. More even than his hypocrisy; his false tenderness before, the way he would roll off without a word when he was done. I am not even sure how other people, *normal* people actually do it. I saw a movie, at a party that Jenny took me to. I remember the way she grinned at the way I stared at it, open-mouthed, but I was surprised, there's no sense denying it. The size of his cock, the things those two women did with it. However joyless it seemed I could not help but be startled by the inventiveness of their frenzied panting. The joylessness I have experience in, the inventiveness I will have to improvise. Or would have.

I wonder where Roger is now. I imagine he is asleep, alone in that bed we shared for six years. I can almost hear his breath, the choking rattle of his snore. It will be dawn there soon, and he will wake to the alarm, shower, dress for church. It is a while since I've been, but I imagine the services are still at six each weekday, seven on Sundays. I wonder whether he has met someone else yet. Maybe Hanny Crawford, or that new girl from Perth. He's not bad looking, not like most of the creeps in the church, so he shouldn't have too much trouble. I ran into his brother Mikey on George Street a month ago, and he told me the Elders had annulled our marriage because of my Godlessness, that they had absolved him of all blame. I think he thought I would be ashamed, but I only laughed, told him that I was pleased, maybe now Roger would get a new girlfriend and stop driving past my flat in the middle of the night. He didn't like that much, but I didn't care. Mikey's a jerk.

Roger blamed my job, said if I had never gone to work in the city I would never have met Jenny or Bill or Jodie, and I suppose he is right, at least partly. It was strange, my days spent with people who were not in the Church, men and women with lives that revolved around things other than prayer. People who fornicated, who smoked and drank and took drugs, men who loved other men, like Bill. Sweet, gentle Bill. Sinners, Roger called them. And worse things.

But it wasn't Jenny or Bill or Jodie. Nor even was it Roger. It was God. That afternoon in the doctor's office, when the doctor told me the infection had affected something within me, that I would never conceive. And Roger, white faced, his sweaty palm wrapped around mine, so tight my hand turned white, then blue. That can't be, he kept saying, You're wrong, but the doctor just looked at him over his glasses, his fat face exuding sorrow, although in his eyes you could see he was bored, bored with us, with all these desperate women and men, bored with everything. I'm afraid not, he said, The tests are conclusive, and then he looked at me and said, There's always in vitro, and I said,

What? and he said it again, In vitro, and Roger looked from him to me and said, No, we can't, it's against our beliefs, and I remember thinking, Our beliefs? I don't remember believing babies were wrong.

And afterwards, in the car, as the miles and miles of suburbs passed by outside, I remember thinking that this couldn't be right, not in the way that Roger thought it couldn't be right, but that it couldn't be right at all, not if God was in the world, not if God truly loved us. I had done everything I could, I had been good, and now God took away my right to bear a child, and then forbade me to conceive one outside my body. How could He be so cruel?

For a month I carried these thoughts with me, too afraid to tell anyone. And then there was the night of Jenny's party. Roger didn't want to go, but I made him, and grudgingly, he went. We parked in the street at 8.00, winding our way up the stairs to Jenny's apartment, only to find ourselves the first ones there. Roger wouldn't take a drink, his eyes black as murder when I sipped at the beer that Jenny put in my hand. I didn't miss the way she watched his face as she closed my fingers around the cold glass of the stubbie. Then later, Roger grabbing me in front of everyone, telling me I had to come, he was leaving, his voice booming out into sudden silence, everyone turning. Now, he was saying, pulling at me, Now! and then Bill was there, between us, and Jenny was pulling me back, her arms around me. I thought Roger would strike Bill, as he did me, as he had that night after the doctor's, but he didn't, he didn't do anything, just turned and walked away without a word.

I saw him a week later, and he told me I was a whore in the eyes of God, then begged me to come back, and I said no, so he called me a whore again, and seeing the way his fist was tightening I looked him in the eye and told him that if he hit me I'd have a restraining order put on him. Jenny had told me to say it, and it worked, he went quiet. I love you, he said, and I shrugged. Don't you love me? he asked and I shrugged again. Is this about you and children? he asked, and I nodded, although I knew he didn't understand how it all connected.

On my wrist my watch still glows, the silent gleam of the hands reminding me that dawn is still two hours away. I seem weightless, as if I have slipped free of all that bound me, as if my life has no weight. As if I am become light, and I fall through the water in shafts. This morning, when we made the first dive, I saw the fish dancing, their myriad quicksilvered bodies rising as one in a spinning cylinder of bodies, upwards, through a column of light. Back in the boat between dives I told Peter what I had seen, and he just smiled, told me it was like birds in flocks, that strange unity of movements, the way their motion flickers and changes as if they were one creature in many bodies. I didn't understand, and he said it was all a matter of maths, the fish keeping a certain distance between themselves and any other fish, so that when one moves they all move, but in unison. Nothing is truly random, he said, It's all a matter of discerning deeper patterns, and I said What? like God? and as soon as it was said I regretted the sharpness of my tone, but Peter only smiled and shook his head. I don't believe in God, he said, but I do believe the world has shape and meaning if you only know where to look.

And then he told me about flowers which have sums in the structure of their petals and patterns in smoke and the way the spots of a leopard can be drawn by a computer, and while he was talking I thought I understood what he was saying, although afterwards, when I tried to explain it to Jenny, all I could remember were the sums in the petals and the flocking birds. It seemed strange to hear a mathematician talk this way, but somehow, when I listened to him, and when I thought of those fish, I felt less alone, less adrift.

We were diving here so we could see the turtles' graveyard. A hole in the coral ten metres deep, five metres round, the sand at the bottom gleaming white. Swimming downwards the water grew colder, darker, until scattered across its bottom like some primeval ossuary we saw them; the bones of the turtles. Their great bony heads and jaws half swallowed by the sand, surrounded by the protruding serrations of their ribs and shells, the folded knuckles of their fins, all picked clean and white by the darting coral fish, the tiny chomping plankton.

Gerhard told us that no-one knows what draws turtles to these holes, what invisible lines of force guide them onwards, but somehow they feel it when their time arrives, an impulse in their blood that pulls them here, and so they swim, sometimes thousands of kilometres, steady, determined, unwavering, their heavy bodies graceful against the shifting light of the surface, like great birds across a sapphire sky. Maybe that is where my bones will settle, deep amongst theirs, my flesh devoured by the fish and crabs. Will I know that then, will I remember me? As my body passes outwards, through the teeth and bellies of the fish, will I be like the schooling mackerel, one mind in many bodies? My matter part of some greater fertility, some greater whole.

On the horizon I think I see a light, the fading dark before the dawn. Maybe a boat will come, maybe not, but either way it will be too late. Am I sky? Or am I water? I no longer know. Maybe this is how the turtles feel it, the coming of their time. Maybe they too feel it like a waking, like breathing.

Like flight.

David Brooks

JOHN GILBERT'S DOG
1985

I

William Hovell, John Septimus Roe, Paul Edmund ('The Count') de Strzelecki, Louis de Torres, Charles Throsby, John Claus Voss, de Freycinet, Cristovao de Mendonca, Nicholas Kostas, Wommai, Lieutenant Tobias Furneaux: almost exclusively, the real history of my country has been the history of its exploration. The name of its discoverers, fêted in the court of Portugal, or lost in the Great Sandy Desert, echoed in the schools of my childhood and were taken home as projects to be researched in the encyclopaedia or, more actively, in a series of explorations long before begun in the furthest corners of the yard and soon extended to daring, morning-long ascents of the mountain that began at the end of the street. Even now, what I most remember from my early summers are the days of discovery, afternoons when the heat in the houses would drive us out to picnics in Westbourne Woods or the Cotter Reserve, or down to Lennox Crossing, now so many fathoms beneath the surface of a man-made lake. In the one it was the world of endless pine-trunks, the thick carpet of dry needles that could be scraped into ships or fortresses; in the others it was the vast forest of bullrushes with the beaten, trodden places that we made our camps, or the world of the rocks and water, the thick tea-tree that, on nights at Scout camps years later, would fill with real torches, real staves, real raiding-parties.

Later, in school holidays, it would be the dunes of Huskisson. Alone or with others, I would press further and further down the three-mile beach toward Vincentia before turning abruptly inward, grabbing for clump-grass, pulling myself up through sliding sand toward the moment when the reliable familiarity of the ocean side gave way to the unpredictable. One day it was to find dense and impenetrable scrub, another a stagnant lagoon, another the yard of a dilapidated shack, another, to my great confusion, only the back fence and chook-pen of our summer landlady. Now, decades later, when I sit down to what I sometimes think of as realer matters, each paragraph, each set of images that might begin a poem or a story, can become a track through bullrushes, a path through tea-tree, a sliding climb through clump-grass that might lead, yes, into the street I am living on, but also, as it sometimes does, into a place I had never imagined – as if one were to climb into the familiar ash tree in one's own backyard, only to find that it now continued, that its boughs joined other boughs, its leafy arcades others, until there were systems, tree-scapes, countries that had been inconceivable before.

One kind of exploration ends, another – if the myths, the traditions, the childhoods are strong – begins. Of history, as of the parched, dust-covered men on exhausted horses, a linear progression ceases and the lateral, the vertical take over. The lines on the charts, once straight and simple, begin to turn back on themselves, to buckle and convolute as more and more is known, until the maps resemble less a primitive rock painting than the surface of a brain.

II

In one of the drawings of a German artist whose work I have long admired, files of human figures are moving in opposite directions on a staircase. If we follow either line – the one going up, or the one going down – we find that, although the figures never reverse direction, and although the stairway continues to rise in front of the one set and descend before the other, the head of each line meets its tail, the four turns in the stairway having formed a square in which, although there is a strictly limited number of steps, there is one flight perpetually rising, another forever going down. Both flights are the same flight. We call this an Optical Illusion, which is our way of denying that somewhere this place, this same set of stairs, exists.

This denial, this shutting of the gates, is perhaps just as well, for if it were possible that this staircase existed in space, it would have – since all ascents and descents take some period to accomplish – to exist in time also. It would then be possible that, just as the figures perpetually climb or descend, yet perpetually meet the tail of their own line, so time passes and yet never advances, and that, as it both advances and fails to advance – as it moves forward only to repeat itself – so there is alongside it a time scale that perpetually 'regresses', perpetually repeats itself, another temporal zone, moving in a direction opposite to our own.

In Canada, working on a thesis through the steaming summer, I would turn from a dull passage in some academic text, and look out from my second-storey window, and there would be the leaves of the chestnut, with the tunnels along the branches, the secret passages. Then, as sometimes even now, I would imagine myself entering, penetrating even further than before. And what if, now, today, I should do that, should go down one of the corridors, follow it through all the turnings and the bough-lanes? Would I find myself, my earlier self, the young child in his ash world, or the student in a hot Toronto Summer? Would he know me? Would he understand me? Would I believe what he had to say?

Is this inconceivable? I don't think so, for surely human life itself is so to any other creature, its extravagance and its wonder so great that few of us ever get out, or wish to, from under its perplexing shadow, but instead spend all our days numb to its true dimensions, so afraid of the hugeness, the strangeness revealed by every wayward step, that we have long ceased to take such steps and in preference pass the time until our end in the drawing of closer barriers, the erection of walls, as if each new word were a wolf, each strange thought or angle of perception a barbarian on a thunderous horse, bearing down upon us, his spear already launched.

No. Nothing is inconceivable. Life itself is so unlikely that our very presence denies the privilege of denial. If our time is a thing that moves 'forward', if 'distance' is a thing that separates, if 'reality' is distinguishable from 'dream', if human consciousness is, as I sometimes suspect, a flickering circle of light about a dark, bewildered centre, these are only our terms, our language, the small salvage of the bewildered from the incomprehensible, and may, as yet, be like the myths that supposed primitives have evolved to explain their universe: that the moon is an ancient hag chasing her wayward son, that the stars are the sand flung up to blind her. And who is to say that the very extravagance of the human imagination, pedestrian as it might seem to a greater eye, is not another 'reality' beckoning, as a child lures a pony with sugar, or a dog is thrown scraps from a table? An explorer's dog – John Gilbert's, say or Watkin Tench's – gnawing at the shin-bone of a beast he's never seen before.

III

This early evening there is a cool breeze through the coral-trees. I can detect the faint, almost-imperceptible scent of the jacaranda that at the end of the yard is coating the gravel with its lilac blooms, and from behind me there comes the drier earthen smell of potatoes baking. I am sipping hot tea and thinking of the beauty of objects in this cool grey light that has in it the first faint touch of darkness. It is the artist's light, the light of still life. From my balcony every shade of the leaves' green is discrete and the trees are wholly at home in their bodies, as if they, too, need the first hint of death in their senses to live truly. In my small flat, with my busyness, my debts, I would call this moment one of luxury, my balcony in its green cathedral, the smell of the potatoes baking, the birds beginning to sing – three different sounds already – and every object distinct.

A man is whistling as he zig-zags up the stairs of the building opposite, and an Indian woman in a red top and bright orange sari pauses on the landing to call to someone I cannot see. She is a splash of rich colour through the leaves. Moments like these – so particular, and yet almost without identity – seem as if suspended between worlds. One could be nowhere but here, and yet here could be anywhere: in Australia, in Brazil, in California, in India. The woman standing on the stair is unaware that she is poised upon a border, that she has just stepped very nearly out of time and place, that this moment, as she goes as usual to buy milk at Constantino's, she has stepped into composition, that she has entered a page, a frame, and is at once devoid of identity and, in a sense, more full of her identity than she has ever been.

John Bryson

CHILDREN AREN'T SUPPOSED TO BE HERE AT ALL
1979

Our apartment has the best view in Sydney.

Father tells us often. A panorama wall-to-wall. Two hundred feet above the harbour, and every foot a thousand dollars. How much is that in metres, Troilus asked and walked away before his father could think of it. Troilus is six.

We look out over our pier. It stands on piles, a path over the water, whitewashed thumbs for holding Owner's Craft Only from washing away with the tide. Troilus thinks we should have a boat. A boat, his father said, is a risk, how do you realise an investment that is sunk? Troilus crooked his finger into a boat-hook, you fish it up again. Boats, father sucked his teeth dry, boats will not hold their value.

Troilus squinted though his windscreen, twenty-two storeys high, there is no salt on it.

My parents' friends visit the Apartment most nights. The living room fills with stories above the music, the brushing together of autumn mohair from Scandinavia, we're all into texture this year, lacquered fingernails wave away the smoke. Mother keeps the drapes open to air the view.

She likes us to mix around before we go to bed. It's not so bad for me, I'm twelve, but it's an effort for Troilus. He sleeps in the next morning. Particularly, he doesn't like meeting their new friends. Neither do I. Introduce yourselves now, and my mother moves off swirling her caftan to drink with another group, purposefully not looking back. Hullo, this is my brother Troilus and I am Cassandra. If they are trying not to laugh, I laugh first and then they're sorry about that. It works okay.

Troilus hates to be made to stay too long. He will say a few unconnected things to confuse them, and after a short silence or two we can go. Troilus, you will get us both into trouble.

It's a rule of the household, individually for everyone, so we all have separate rooms. My father is an architect and into real estate now, he is keen on individuality. And that's why I am so successful, success is getting what you set out to get, my father explains it to Troilus. They explain all the longer words, it's a rule of the household, we don't talk down to the children.

For the last month, Troilus has been going to bed early. He says he reads a lot. I doubt that, but couldn't begin to guess what he does. He sings late at night. A pale sound, thin as the first strands of mist. I can never catch the tune.

The Apartment takes the whole of the twenty-second floor. Above us is the roofgarden, and swaying potted shrubs crisp on one side, and a ruffled blue pool. My father told me the pool is on the roof because it gets the sun. That sounded all right to me, I had asked the question. But Troilus pulled his jacket tightly closed. That's stupid, it's too windy. His father answered him slowly, you can't have everything. What have we got, Troilus said, if we can't use it?

We are allowed onto the roofgarden, but only with someone. Mother is afraid we might climb about and fall off. People fall off tall buildings, she said as we looked down. I asked how many. She didn't understand. How many people in the one year fall off tall buildings in Sydney? She leaned over the concrete rampart and did not answer immediately. Wearing a pale blue slacksuit made for her by Fiorucci in Milan, her legs looked very long, though her knees are beginning to turn in. I know she thinks her legs are her best feature. She used to be a top model, a super-thin. The wind was blowing her hair untidy, a thing she hates, I could see grey seeping up the roots. I don't know exactly, she said, dozens. The cars in the lot looked smaller than in a dream.

Then some people must mean to fall off, Troilus shouted suddenly next to her, the ends of his words whipped away with the wind, he was so far over. She took us downstairs. Mother is right, I don't know what we can do with him either.

You are going to be a looker too, my mother will tell me, if you care for your complexion and keep brushing your hair. Yes, I do. You can be a top earner, she will say, I was a top earner. Mother owns a small model agency, she will laugh, not for small models. She is, she laughs, far too past her prime to get work herself, her hand angled onto the bump of her hip. She has photographs pinned to the walls of

her en suite she calls it, her dressing-room, Troilus. From *Harpers &*
Queen, *Vogue*, circulations in the hundreds of thousands, father will
tell us. Fifty shots to one print for some of them. Photographers just
burn film if they like you, she will say, and I will go into the routine,
headup, click, chin to shoulder, click, hands to knee, click, pout, click.
Good she will say, very good, you'll make it okay, look after your
complexion, yes I do mother, and she will sit slack on her regency
stool gazing into the gilded mirror while I am silent. She has a way of
opening her mouth instead of smiling that does not crack her make-
up. I can do that already but I don't tell her.

Troilus never goes into her dressing-room. He likes her best, he
says, when she first gets up in the morning.

He will not kiss her when she arrives home at night. She is never
later than six, but her face is brittle and she still smells of a heavy
lunch and perfumed gin from the crystal decanter in the dining room.
She is slow, and irritable if we are loud, I'm sorry I'm just tired, and
she orders our dinner from the restaurant on the ground floor. Father
doesn't like her doing that, it costs a fortune, iniquitous. He sent us to
the TV room while they talked about that again. I turned the TV up,
over the faltering gusts of their voices, but Troilus leaned his head
against the door and I could not pull him away. What are latchkey
children? I don't know, I've never seen one. We were quiet until we
could go to bed.

The Apartment is on strata title, my father will tell new friends but
never before the third drink, and cost the mint. But it's a hedge against
inflation, good property is never a bad buy, prime position yields a
prime return, if he is forced to sell. To sell, Troilus hates to hear him
say it. The threat buffets his face and his eyes sting. I have seen that.

Don't you like living with us? Father made himself incredulous. He
waited for Troilus to answer. Yes, softly. Troilus had made a periscope
to look into the apartment below. An empty wine-box, the best bulk
red in the Hunter Valley, my father met the vintner, and a mirror, and
a long string. We just lower it down and see what's there. He sat side-
saddle on the windowsill. The wind took the box like a kite, out and
up, until the yards of hanging string began to belly, and the box
dropped. Troilus leaned out reefing in the slack hand over hand, frantic
as a fisherman. The line tightened. It pulled into his fingers like gut. I
caught Troilus by the sweater and tumbled him back into the room.

There was an explosion from below. I looked over the sill. Shattered glass sparkled like sleet in the wind.

Troilus's face was the grey of watching himself fall.

Father made him stand up. You don't want to live with someone else? His mother was in her bedroom. No, I like it here, please. It was patently a lie, but inevitable. Father sucked his teeth dry, children aren't supposed to be here at all, you know that. We did both know that, but it didn't seem so serious before. No children, no pets. Father was inexorable, if it doesn't work out we will have to sell up. Troilus sucked his knuckles white, what will this desirable four-bedroom family bring on the open market, he could hear it, the only true value is market value. Troilus didn't say anything. It wasn't my fault, I said, and turned away.

Father noticed the balcony had become a colony for early morning gulls, bobbing along the parapet, pearly grey heads glaring through the glass one red eye at a time. Father scraped away from the breakfast table, and fluttered them off, waving his arms overhead with the distress of a signalling survivor. Pets are not allowed, if we encourage those birds they could be construed to be our pets in a court of law, constructive ownership, he said, and they dirty the balcony with their business. Troilus poked at the crusts on the side of his plate, they've got to shit somewhere, he said, and father made him leave the table.

Troilus made straight for his room after school every day. He had his dinner there. I heard him singing at night.

Father left on a hunting trip by light aircraft to shoot camels and brumbies in the Northern Territory. He had bought a rifle especially, feel the action, two walnut stocks carved by the craftsmen of Munich to the Aga Khan's personal specification, two, this is the other one, a steal. Father stacked his gear into the lift, rucksack with a super-lite frame, saffron silk hiking tent, Katmandu sleeping-bag with hood. The rifle was slung over his shoulder. He waved.

You could, Troilus shouted but only as the doors were closing, ride them out to shoot the camels and kill the horses afterwards. Mother pulled him away.

We had a party here the next night. It was catered by the restaurant on the ground floor. Mother was still dancing with Mister Broderick when I got up, I didn't know he could dance. The room smelled of cigarette butts and spilled claret. They danced very slowly, as if they were asleep together. He is my father's friend and in real estate, he often laughs, I wouldn't let my best friend beat me to any deal. They were surprised it was morning. He said again I was going to be as pretty as mother, stroking my hair.

Troilus was up late and went straight to school.

Walking home, he wouldn't talk and I was irritated with him, he was drawing out his hurt, sucking the white bones of his knuckles. Mother won't let him suck his thumb. I lifted Troilus up, he pushed the main-door buzzer, and through the speaker said who it was, the door clicked and we pushed it open. If this is such a great area, Troilus said, I don't know why we take all this care. Old Gyngell mumbled into the foyer still pulling on his blue coat, and turned the lift key. Again Troilus went to his room.

Facing across the harbour, I brushed my hair, I do, mother, curls tumbling over my chest, good, very Sassoon, make it bounce.

Troilus sat down beside me, gentle, and although he had not been alone long, had the softness of half-sleep about him. We gazed through the glass wall, the harbour a warm blue, three ships dark at the naval dock, chunky green ferries, a yacht ballooning a yellow sunburst with opals in its wake. The best view in Sydney, panorama wall-to-wall, a thousand dollars a foot.

All that view, Troilus said, locks us in.

A quick noise behind us, as sudden as the wings of a fast bird. The sound flutters from a redwood panel built around the air-conditioner. The noise changes, to the turntable sound of a pick-up scraping a record, to a sharp grinding of tin. It stops. No longer a slithering of air from the ducting the apartment is silent.

The air-conditioner, it's stuck. Troilus does not move. Turn it off, he whispers. No need, it's done that itself. His eyes narrow to the pupils, turn it off now. I climb onto the bench to reach the thermostat. It's silly to get upset, it couldn't be our fault. Two switches click to off, one is marked Fan. The fan, I tell him, and climb down. Troilus is not in the room at all.

I don't know why something is so wrong. Troilus. They will know it is not our fault, I call a little higher, walking towards his bedroom, feet slapping cold on the tiles.

The side of Troilus's room is against the wall of the air-conditioner. I call, you can't fix it from there. Troilus is a tinkerer, god knows why she says, your father does nothing at home, and toys are to stay in your room or I'll throw them out. Parts of his grandfather's crystal wireless-set he called it, the speedometer from a 1940 Buick swapped at school for a postcard mother sent him of New York but he never told her, not much but everything a prize, a cardboard box he had wound around with shining wire and mother caught him jamming into the electricity outlet, it's a radiator, he said, I'm cold.

Troilus has his back to me. His legs and elbows are smudged the lavender grey of old dust, the air-conditioning duct is an empty square in the skirting board, the grate lies face down on the floor. You couldn't believe he'd got in there it's so small.

Troilus, I say and softly. His face is tiny, his eyes squeeze tightly closed, left cheek freckled, a dark red soaks across the front of his velour sweater, mother will kill us.

He is holding a cat.

His fingers are wet gloves with its blood. It's not my fault, he says, I didn't know she would. I can see the edge of a saucer inside the duct.

The cat is not moving. Let me see please. Troilus half turns away. He makes his mouth work, she's hurt. His eyes are mirrors. The cat's head is shapeless where the ginger fur has clotted and the brown nose tilts like a suede button. It's hurt all right.

Troilus blinks to clear his eyes. Get the cat ambulance, he whispers. There's no cat ambulance I tell him, and reach for the cat. Get the cat ambulance, and he squeezes the cat with his effort. I have never heard him scream in the Apartment before. The room shimmers with his words after his mouth has closed.

The telephone book is under a phone in the study. There is no cat ambulance. I get it under Pet. Hampton Park Pet Hospital and Ambulance Service. Give Your Pet The Royal Treatment. She takes my name and address before she will listen. What authority do you have, and I tell her it is an emergency. She doesn't answer, I tell her Bankcard. We don't take dead animals, but I don't understand what she means. Is it breathing she asks, and I tell Troilus they don't take animals that, who, are dead and not breathing.

She's breathing, she's breathing, and he squeezes the cat to his chest so its throat honks like a duck, and I say you can hear that, it's breathing, and she sends one in a minute.

We are down into the foyer and old Gyngell is pulling on his coat. He looks at the cat and puts a thin hand down to Troilus's shoulder. I tell old Gyngell about the pet ambulance and we wait inside the sliding doors and watch the driveway. He doesn't ask more about the cat. Troilus's head is leaning on the bone of his old thigh. Animals aren't supposed to be here at all, I say.

Old Gyngell doesn't answer that for a minute. He and Troilus are looking at me. There is no expression on their faces at all. A white van pulls up in the drive, and old Gyngell opens the sliding doors. Say she is your parents' cat, I catch as I pass him.

The driver is breezy, in white overalls and a handpainted cream tie. He looks at the cat but does not move to take it. His moustache runs down the sides of his chin. I remember my mother's younger brother who stroked his moustache with his fingers a lot and sold used sports cars from home on weekends. He's dead now.

The driver hands me a clipboard and ball-pen. Sign for the ambulance, and he takes a white towel from inside the rear door. He drapes it over his hands so that only their shapes show through. Here, he says to Troilus, I'll see if it's alive. Troilus drops his head to the cat. It's breathing, he whispers.

The cat is panting. Its eyes are still closed, the fur tufted over them, but its mouth is open, the tiny tongue a pink camellia petal fluttering in its breath.

Oxygen, he takes the clipboard and makes a mark, sign here. As I sign, Troilus says yes, it's a very good cat, sign for oxygen.

Three in the front, the van has a hard ride. The driver wheels it fast between the traffic. I think of the cat in a hissing perspex box in the back, the sides of the box clear as oxygen. The driver turns the radio up very loud. Troilus has a white towel the driver gave him for his hands, he hugs it to the stain on his chest. I have no idea where we are. Mother ought to be home at six. She will have a drink before she looks in our rooms. We stop at a set of traffic lights, I have not been smart enough to leave a note, mother will kill us.

The sign on the gate says it is the hospital though it looks like a very large home and we drive past cars parked in the driveway. The front garden is green, many of the trees have white scaled trunks and weeping boughs. It looks English. As we pass the trees, the gardens open to a lawn the size of a bowling green, white posts with iron rings stand in a square: I expect to see people walking dogs or cats, but there is no-one. Yes, we pass a lady in black and white polkadots sitting on the grass. She looks very old. She feeds a Dalmatian with pieces from a wicker basket. She looks at us, and gets up onto one knee only with the help of a crutch that looks like a narrow stool. I can't see anything wrong with the dog.

We back into a vehicular entrance at the side of the house and stop, the rear of the van flush with the brick wall. The driver turns off the radio and looks at me. Here we are, you go in there, and there is a lead-glass door marked Reception. Before I open the cabin door, he marks the clipboard and hands it across Troilus to me. The sheet is as narrow as a laundry ticket from room-service in the Apartments. Sign for the towels.

A battleship-grey limousine stands under the white-painted sign, Clients' Cars Only, a chauffeur's cap on the scuttle behind the windscreen. I look in. Glass divides the front from the rear. There are no seats in the back at all, the floor is a long cushion upholstered in diamond patterns bulging between the studs. A basket-weave of black tape hangs slack from the rear ledge like an empty parachute harness, and it takes a second to realise it is the safety-belt for a dog.

Reception is a regency lounge room. In a corner at the far end sits a lady at an oak dining-room table used as a desk. Come over here, dear. Hullo, this is my brother Troilus and I am Cassandra. I will take your particulars. My particulars are my father's name and address, but he's away hunting, and his occupation, architect. What authority do you have? Mother pays for things by Bankcard, she will come and pick us up, I would like to use the phone. But it is my parents' cat, I say.

She writes on a clipboard. A short white coat over her day frock. She is not like anyone I know. Though perhaps The Spinster Aunt my mother called her, who used to babysit for us, not a real aunt, a friend of father's mother, she worked in an accountant's office for forty years and never married. In the winter knitting children's cardigans for the Sisters of Charity, let me try it against you for size, do stand still. She had a baby once, my mother told me, but never say. What is the cat's name?

What is the cat's name, she asks me. The cat is a vacuum, the name is a hole in the sheet. It is my parents' cat, old Gyngell will tell you it is, my mother will come and pick us up. She will know, she will not know the cat's name, she will not use her Bankcard to fill the blank, old Gyngell has not seen the hole.

The cat's name, says Troilus, is Batcat.

The telephone in the Apartment gives me an engaged burr. I will not know what to tell her, and put it down quickly. Thank you for letting me try, I will ring again later. The spinster hands me the clipboard. Sign at the bottom for admission, she gives me the pen, and this is the schedule of charges, let me try it against you for size, eighty dollars per day intensive care, recuperation days fifty, surgery per hour at a hundred dollars plus anaesthetic and extras. She marks them off. It is upside-down for her but her pen ticks quickly, she makes no mistakes. Do stand still. She expects me to be business-like, not a child.

Yes father, we can say it, a fortune, but we didn't know how much, they didn't tell us, it's not my fault. I turn up the ends of my smile and look directly at the bridge of the spinster's nose, honesty will charm her. Yes, I understand that, thank you.

The spinster leaves the room, opening the door to the barking and yelping of dogs, and is back quickly. They are doing what they can for, she looks at her clipboard, Batcat, but it is very sick, the skull is fractured and there is some brain damage. She hands me the clipboard. Sign here for the anaesthetic and surgery.

She leaves us sitting on the striped sofa, and chokes off the call of the dogs with the door. Troilus still has the towel and I should take it away, it looks very childish. I don't think I can. Over the mantelpiece, the picture of a white dog listens to an old phonograph speaker. There are thirteen other pictures, of horses and dogs and cats, each with the caption Royal Pets Through The Ages. They all look very fit. Why isn't anyone else in here?

I didn't notice him when we came in: a man sitting close to the door, the chauffeur, still as a grey shadow in his uniform. He doesn't look at us, his eyelids are peaked, the twin gables of old attic windows, no movement behind them as if he stays well back.

Troilus leans against my arm. The magazines on the coffee table are business journals and *Vogue*. I have seen the *Vogues*, mother has them delivered. I should ring her again, but I will wait. Colour brochures: your pet its health and beauty, Pet Holiday Apartments by-the-sea, early morning swimming and rub-down, we immunise your pet against home-sickness, unusual dietary habits catered for and piped music, and

Pet Park Cemetery the largest in the southern hemisphere, through life and after life you care, by association with Hampton Park Monumental Masons in immortal stone. There is a yelping of dogs.

One, two men come in through the door, both in white coats. I sit up straight, no that is wrong, and I stand. Troilus only looks up. Is she all right, he whispers to them through a handful of stained towel. Is my parents' cat all right, I ask?

The two look very alike. A little early to tell, the one says looking at his clipboard, about the feline patient Batcat. We hope it will not become, he looks at the other, Requiescat. They laugh backwards and forwards. We have reconstructed the skull as best we could. One and one quarter hours at surgery rates plus anaesthetic, he hands the clipboard to me, sign for surgery and anaesthetic. Their heads lean together in sympathy. The one says it needs time, and the other nods, it has cardiac insufficiency. I do not understand him. The one explains, the heart is not pumping properly. The heart is a tired muscle and needs help. I shake my hair so it bounces, click, smile, click, yes I understand that, a heart would. The other nods again, cardiac support, he says. And pulmonary embolism, and the lungs are not clear. Oh, a hand over my perceptibly open mouth, click. Cardiac and respiratory support until we can gauge the extent of brain damage. Heart and lung machines, what do you want to do?

Troilus holds his towel in his lap. Will that fix the cat? She is valuable, my father likes that cat, and he looks toward me, not crying but his eyes are melting ice and his voice high. The one and the other both smile. They are Mister Broderick, father's friend and real estate, never beaten to a deal, masks at his New Year party, house right on the water, cost the mint today my father says, private jetty and tie your boat up to the party, a movie later only for adults, both stroking my hair. Their screaming masks hung against my wall into the new year, take them away mother, I can't stand it.

Troilus hugs the towel to his chest with brown fingers cracked by old blood, his face the grey of watching himself fall.

I wish mother were here. I did not know I had said it aloud, but Troilus's mouth is ragged, what good is she, he says, she's drunk. It is a pale cry, lonely as songs in his empty room.

I turn toward him, how dare you talk like that, learn to be more responsible, do sit up. Children aren't supposed to be here at all.

I sign. One and one quarter hours surgery per hour at a hundred dollars, anaesthetic ninety-five, ambulance sixty, oxygen hissing into his saffron tent, cardiac and respiratory support pumping blood and air my father knew the vintner, at seventy litres a minute, how much is that in metres and walk away before he thinks of it, surgical hoses bulging into a row of beads, how do you realise its value, the mask reconstructed as best we could, you can shoot them later, it wasn't my fault.

Thank you, Doctor. I hand back the clipboard. Headup, click, pout, click, squeezing his damp fingers with my lacquered nails. Do what you can. And my mother's smile parts without creasing my cheeks.

Thank you, we will wait.

Janine Burke

THE CRUELTY OF MERMAIDS
1990

We had quit the beach house due to my melancholy attachment to seaweed.

I festooned the furniture with it before Ralphie, nostrils seized with distaste, dumped it on the patio, where, in an ecstasy of nostalgia, I would roll to cast my bosom on the dying kelp. It was too much for a man like Ralphie. Twenty-five years in the same job and a gold watch to show for it.

So we packed up, taking Ralphie's collection of Hawaiian shirts and the harpoon that was my cupid. I used the harpoon as a stick when, in the evenings, I would wheel myself to the water, hoist myself from the chair, and dive. Flirtatious waves caressed my belly and a sweet southerly smelling of seals filled the air. This was the place I had met my saviour.

Ralphie was a widower, a soft white mollusc of sadness, clinging to the rocks at sunset. Howling. It is not often a man takes my fancy but, like the whales and the dolphins, I, too, am dependent upon the barbarians. The dolphins are worst: curious and cynical, they've become showgirls for the tourists. The whales, before they heave five fathoms to laugh, tell dirty jokes marine biologists compute in terms of human intelligence.

We're a dying race. It's not only the oil spills and the radiation sickness, it is also our innocence. I am not the first to have abandoned man's imagination to come crawling into his arms. It is cold on the ocean floor, cold and heavy, an asylum whose keepers are glum fish with lights in their heads and disapproving lips.

Ralphie had decided to finish himself off. He was heading for the horizon in that clumsy and endearing fashion in which humans approach death by drowning. They are always surprised to find themselves in over their heads. Follows the thrashing and the gulping. I felt such pity, I nearly let him go through with it, but I glided up as he passed out and carried him slowly back to shore. There I squeezed him, and water sprang from his mouth.

As we lay entangled, I remembered the sailor of the Java Seas who went for my breasts with a cleaver. I remembered the ones who'd bound and gagged me, penetrated me with sharp instruments, hauled me up and weighed me, ogled me and fed me eggs. Was Ralphie one of these? Or did he possess a liquid soul?

He came to, crying 'Esme, I meant to join you!' as I slid under the surf.

Ralphie became fascinated by the site of his rescue. He no longer roamed the shore with the cries of the dugong in his throat. He'd gained a purpose in life, an attitude towards survival. Each evening he would return to sit cross-legged in contemplation. I left gifts for him: lustrous mother-of-pearl, iridescent abalone shells, a tiger cowrie, a pink conch, some strands of purple seaweed. These I would arrange in such a way their arrival seemed fortuitous, and Ralphie would fall on them with delight.

Revealing myself is always the tricky part. Ralphie didn't come down at night and night is a better stage for me. I appear less remarkable. There was no choice but to assume the full frontal at dusk, comb in one hand, mirror in the other, singing a tune such as sends ships into sandbars. But I'd forgotten my smell, which is perfume on the waves but high as rotting fish on land.

It hit him first. Seagulls swooped and cawed. Ralphie ducked behind a rock.

'Lovely evening,' I remarked. His head bobbed up, then disappeared again. 'I consider the sunsets here quite magical.' The head came up and stayed. His eyes didn't falter at my tail but ploughed on, veering off at the fins. Which twitched.

'Who are you?' he breathed.

'Your destiny, in a manner of speaking.'

He sighed. 'So I am not alone.'

We made a tryst each night at six, unless the beach was taken over by the huffing and puffing ones in shorts. The sky was a radiant wave of light breaking over our heads, the air swarmed with pacific gulls, treasure was on the sands.

Ralphie poured out his heart. Esme was his grief, she of the violet eyes and the lamingtons. Men have one story to tell which they shape and polish until it's sharp as a blade. Ralphie dug Esme in so her senile dementia, which took her wandering to the water's edge once too often, pricked my heart. 'She was a game girl,' Ralphie said sorrowfully. I offered to make a search – the ocean floor is littered with dentures, bones and wedding rings – but he didn't want back even a bit of her.

After Ralphie had exhausted himself, we played a game with the harpoon. I'd slide from the rocks as though a wave had taken me and Ralphie would swing the harpoon and haul me in. Never damaged a scale. 'Abandon the sea,' Ralphie would cry, 'abandon the sea and be my wife.'

I don't tease, I'm no coquette but the land is strange to me. I am used to underneath, the cool and slippery all below. The mountains I've crossed are encrusted with coral. My vistas are drowned. I have lived in sunken cities with seaweed-curtained windows and lobsters strolling the avenues. In that green silence, skeletons embrace and gold buys no passage save to some further, buried existence.

I couldn't show Ralphie my domain. His wrangle with the deep had made him loath to even paddle.

I said I'd try to live out of water.

You see, there have been other men and other promises. But it turned out badly, apart from the Arab. There was a price for wriggling into the mundane, for the men as much as for me. As yet I had not quit the ocean proper for my love. Tanks, yes. Swimming pools, of course. But the lounge room, the video recorder and the Sunday roast?

Ralphie's proudest moment came when he taxied me through the supermarket in a wheelchair. My tail was wrapped in a mohair rug, a straw hat hid my green-gold hair and my skin was coated with talcum powder to extinguish my aroma and to make my cheeks less blue. I wore an old beaded cardigan of Esme's and my broad shoulders seemed a little more feminine under its influence.

We would buy up big and then go home to gorge. There is no breakfast, lunch and dinner in the depths. It is catch as catch can and regulated eating times made me rather faint until Ralphie installed a freezer, stuffed full of fish, that I could chew to my heart's content.

There is a level where the sea turns purple and a mermaid's buoyancy meets the weight of the ocean. It is like being held in a vast embrace, nearly painful, but having something so marvellously firm about it, that it's utterly soothing. You have to go down a long way to find just the right mixture of trench and plateau where few bothersome currents will interrupt your pleasure. You can almost hear it coming, the balance.

Lying in bed next to Ralphie, I would quietly moan, dreaming of the thrust of the deep.

On bad nights, I'd crawl to the veranda and deck myself with kelp. The odour had a tranquillising effect but Ralphie was horrified that a neighbour might see me reclining on my hairy mattress. 'And then where would I be!'

It was concerns of this nature that provoked Ralphie to consider city living.

He felt if we were away from the sea's continual tug, I might be more of a woman and he more of a man.

Enough drooling over waves and sunsets! Enough wandering along fatal shores!

Let us go to the suburbs, the freeways, the shopping plazas. Let us remember what it means to be ordinary.

That is how we came to live in the house near the highway. Ralphie thought we should have a view and I became adept at picking the difference between a Holden Commodore and a Ford Fairlane.

'Ralphie,' I said one lazy afternoon, 'Ralphie, let's play princess and pirate.'

In the early days of our courtship, we'd had fun with costumes. Ralphie had been shy about his collection of Hawaiian shirts but I'd encouraged him to drag them out, even to stock up on more. I like a bit of colour on a man.

'Eh?' said Ralphie. The television was on. Two men punched each other in the face until blood ran into their eyes. 'A game,' he muttered.

'Yes, my love.'

'It's not right.'

'Then what about Antony and Cleopatra? We can use the couch as her boat. You were always fond of that.'

One of the men fell insensible to the ground, the other raised his arms in a victory salute and a crowd booed.

He gazed at me and clutched my fingers tightly. 'Shouldn't we think about consecrating our union? You know what I mean, girl. In the eyes of God.'

I was downcast. We'd gone to the place of chanting where old women knelt before a little tortured plaster victim. I had pointed out He'd not done much for Esme but Ralphie opined it was all God's will. Even me, apparently. I was caught in the same net. 'I'm not sure I'm up to it,' I said in a low voice.

He raised my hand to his lips and, holding his breath, kissed it.

I noticed that the talcum powder gave my skin a pearly glow such as the dead have, a few days on.

Marriage did wonders for Ralphie. He whistled around the house, becoming a regular little handyman. With a refreshed sense of purpose, he offered to build me a pool in the living room.

Since the wedding he'd grown touchy about my appearance. When his sister-in-law began to ask pointed questions about exactly where I came from, I laughingly replied Ralphie had picked me up on the beach. From the set of her mouth, it was not the sort of answer she was looking for.

The mother of the Arab tried to poison me. The daughter of one amorous old salt dragged me from the boat's cabin by my green-gold locks. A sailor's wife set the dog on me, and when that didn't work, the cat. I am unsurprised by the violence of women. They cannot afford to be sisterly, they have too much to lose. There is greater companionship to be found among dwarves and hunchbacks, though the circus, as a way of life, does not suit me.

Ralphie painted the walls blue and decorated them with plastic fish cut from a shower curtain. Then he dragged in a fibreglass pool and filled it with tap water, which I abhor.

Not wishing to crush his enthusiasm, I ventured to suggest salt water might be more accurate. Ralphie used to make model aircraft so he appreciates the value of details.

'Of course,' says he, and emptied the salt cellar into the water. He drew the blinds so the man who came to read the gasometer would be in no danger of dying of fright and he welcomed me to wet my fins.

'You know, Ralphie,' I said, as I flipped and dipped and did the tricks that made him smile, 'it would be awfully nice to go to the beach.'

'You've got all the ocean you want right here,' Ralphie said, settling down with the evening paper.

It was the hour when the traffic was the loudest, when the irregular grumbles and beeps turned to a roar as motorists fled the city for the coast, for that was where the highway led, straight to the sea.

I must have slipped because a sudden splash drenched Ralphie's paper. He enjoyed nothing more than his paper and the can of beer that accompanied it, and when he knocked over the beer while putting aside the sodden newsprint, he said phrases of the kind that are favoured by sailors.

For myself, I began to hum the haunting melody that had lured Ralphie in our courting days, but it had the reverse effect and he left the room.

In the morning I was alarmed to find my wheelchair in pieces on the back veranda. Ralphie said he was fixing it and that I would have to stay in the pool until it was done.

In a small voice, I asked Ralphie how long he thought that would be.

He said it was hard to tell. He was waiting on a part. He did not raise his eyes as he spoke but stared intently at the array of bolts and screws.

I crawled back inside.

The traffic seemed closer that day as if, just outside the blinds, the semitrailers revved.

At night on the sea, the world turns silver. The moon journeys across the sky, marking a path on the water, and the flying fish leap. Many who rarely broke the surface came up to play, creatures with claws and breasts and beards and perpendicular eyes. We would find a deserted cove, some sanctuary for our revels where the dawn would find us, the company of the deep.

That was how I met the Arab. I had lingered too long at the mouth of the cave and the tide went out, leaving me stranded. He was the first man who wasn't startled at the sight of me and who addressed me, not as a freak of nature, but a woman of feeling.

He clung to my neck and I took him far, far out to sea. He whispered he came from the desert and that these blue wastes were similar in their beauty and their loneliness. I brought him to my favourite shore where we feasted on abalone and lay together on the midnight sand.

He was a fisherman and I his woman. I made him rich, and the moon tattoo above my heart, I wear for him.

Once he held his breath until his lungs nearly burst and I dragged him up for air, proud, terrified and amazed a man would die to chart my depths.

Our living-room beach had one major flaw. There was no sand and without sand how could I truly believe, as Ralphie so earnestly desired, that I had the ocean here at home?

I suggested this to Ralphie and he was stumped. 'Good quality,' I said. 'None of that inferior rubbish. It must be pale gold, gritty but not pebbly, shot through with shells and certainly free of ice-cream wrappers. The odd tendril of seaweed would not go astray.'

I could see the logic of this idea working on Ralphie and he would stare at the living-room floor, considering just what quantity he would need.

He didn't mention the wheelchair. He did the shopping alone. In fact, I never left the house.

A week passed before he asked me where the best variety of sand could be found and another before he linked the trailer to the car. When he returned to the kitchen to make himself some sandwiches, I slid down the back steps, rolled across the lawn and dived into the trailer. I was planning to give Ralphie a surprise, you see.

I could smell the sea long before we reached it. It made me quite dizzy but that may have been the effects of dehydration.

He pulled up at the car park facing the beach and decided, dear predictable Ralphie, to partake of food before beginning his task. I used the opportunity to slide from beneath the tarpaulin and wriggle under the car.

The sun was setting as he shovelled the last load of sand into the trailer. He didn't notice me in the dying light but just as I gasped my first lungful of pure sea water, I heard him cry my name.

I turned and waved him on, and when he was in knee deep, I grasped him.

'Come, Ralphie,' I said, 'come my love.' It was ages since we'd played our games. I had the pent-up energy of a child. He tried to swim, I took him under, each time a little deeper, each time a little slower to surface. He was excited. He tried to tell me so but there were too many bubbles coming out of his mouth. I held him closer. He went quite wild and then quite limp as I drew him tenderly to the cave of eternal embrace.

There is a level where the sea turns purple and a mermaid's buoyancy meets the weight of the ocean. It is sweet hurt to ride the currents until bliss comes like a wave, dissolving memory. I have remained there, time out of time, washed clean of dreams. There is nothing to fear. No ships, no submarines, just the moving pressures of the wide, dark sea.

Keith Butler

SODASI
1998

During the Indian monsoon of June 1857, my great-grandfather, James Shepherd, wrote in his diary, '. . . *lotus flowers, leaves of brinjals and bits of goat flesh are being passed from sepoy to sepoy in the Cawnpore regiment . . . expecting trouble . . .*' Scribbled on the door of his Commissariat office was '*Sab lal hogea hai*' which he knew meant 'Soon all will be red'. Amulets promising protection were being sold in their hundreds at the Cawnpore bazaar. The commanding officer Major Bunty Marks refused to believe that the Cawnpore Ninth would ever mutiny – it could happen elsewhere but not with his *babalogues*, his babies.

The sepoys first rebelled in faraway Barrackpore, refusing to use the pork or beef fat greased cartridges in their Enfield rifles. They thought it was a plot to make them lose their caste and Christianise them; but the start of the rebellion went largely unnoticed. I too missed my daughter's soft mutinies. Or were they wars of independence?

Seven days later, Big Da, as my grandfather was known, wrote:

> 7 June . . . we were seated in a corner . . . Ellen had Nancy
> in her arms answering her innocent smile when a bullet hit
> the pillar and rebounding through the arch struck the baby
> under the ear and sliding between skin and skull was thereof
> retained . . .

Big Da was incarcerated with Nanna Ellen and two daughters in the siege of Cawnpore. Outside the small barracks the sepoys swirled, pounding the entrenchment with grapeshot, chain and cannon. Inside, soldiers and civilians huddled. Food and water were fast running out. Spying the small band of besieged picking over garbage for food scraps the sepoys filled a cannon with sweetmeats so that the juice dripped out of the rear, tied a goat to the muzzle mouth and lit the fuse.

After one hundred days of confinement, Big Da, fortified with arrack, dressed in the ungurkha coat of a cook and calling himself Budhloo the *Bubbochee* walked out of the camp, hoping to reach a British Garrison for help. He was instantly apprehended in his drunken state and flung into jail by the sepoys because he had cooked for the British.

Eventually General Havelock raised the siege and Big Da was reunited with Nanna Ellen, but by then she had eyes of clouds. Big Da could not look into them. The children had not survived. Their bodies had been thrown into a well. This much Big Da gleaned from other survivors, but from Nanna Ellen there was only silence. She sat in the corner of the parlour and the clouds in her eyes moved over the dusting, the cooking and her husband. Big Da spent the rest of his life imagining the course of events in that compound. Every night he created new mutinies in his head; the sepoys would march on the barracks, the residents scurried into the shelters, the mutineers charged and just before something conclusive happened Big Da arrested the action, to start again.

Big Da's diary is like the Indian sweetmeat, Lady Canning's Ball; it has an empty centre. He filled the pages with juicy reports of other mutinies, Delhi, Lucknow, Calcutta; of soft hair embedded in sword cuts on walls of the Bibighur; of the discovery of rows of children's shoes with left-over warm ankles in them at Savada House; of the opening of a pregnant woman's stomach at Sateechaura Ghat; but of the fate of his own children he knew nothing. When he returned home and saw the tombstone face of his wife, his mind tingled, puffs of smoke rose from his fingertips and he went to his desk before dinner.

The remarkable thing about Big Da's diary is his use of hyphens; they were everywhere. I think he felt most comfortable with the hyphen because his life was like one; he was an Anglo-Indian and a half-caste according to the mores of the time. He, like the hyphen, was used to living in a gap and he probably felt he had no right to a history; Big Da was used to blankness but I do not know how he handled the lacuna of his daughters' history.

Like Big Da, my daughter Sodasi, perfect maiden of sixteen, has a blankness about her and I fill in the gaps. One day she left our home; one day she came back. Why did she leave? What happened to her during those forty-two days when she lived in foster care in nearby

Lavender Crescent? And I had the freedom to move anywhere but contact her. Eventually she returned but Sodasi had changed. Her eyes are calculating, moving explanations around me. Her counsellor wearing neutral colour sandals tells me '. . . it's the confidentiality thing . . . I need her permission to release that information . . .' and I venture '. . . You're a father, why can't you just tell me . . .' but the man-to-man thing has no currency. So I deal with Meccano theories, build, demolish, start again.

Our lives are divided into Before and After. I often go into Before, searching like Big Da, mine-sweeping for understanding; bleeding suspicion into the colour of past family photographs, sleep-overs, lateness, birthday parties, rock concerts. Once upon a time Before had been a happy sock.

Sodasi was put under Community care on August 18, 1994. When she left I was under siege. Government forces swirled around me, pens poised, the courteous war began.

Where were you born? India.

Are you Hindu? No.

When were you converted? I was born a Roman Catholic.

Have you changed your name? No.

But your name is not an Indian one. I am Anglo-Indian.

What was the native name of the family? The native name is Shepherd.

Where did you learn to speak English? Dum-Dum.

Is your daughter a Roman Catholic? No, she is sixteen . . .

Your daughter has applied to be removed from your care. She says she is unhappy and the Department of Social Welfare has the power to remove her because she is at risk.

Risk from what? I ask.

At this stage we cannot say, they said.

I now realise that when I left India in 1972 I packed the war of 1857 into my suitcase. The Empress follows me. After 1858 the rule of India passed away from the East India Company and directly to Maharanee Victoria. My daughter was removed from my house by the State of Victoria. No family contact was allowed. She was put into foster care in a house in Lavender Street. That is when I conducted my siege. My car tyres encircled the house where she stayed. At night I would buy another bottle of milk to put along the row of bottles in the fridge, and I would sit outside the residence in Lavender St, to watch the light whilst the milk went warm. Like Big Da sitting in that nearby jail in Cawnpore all those years ago, my daughter was within reach but I was unable to see her.

After the mutiny, as a reward, Da was given the village of Jummunneah which he renamed Elgingaur, in honour of the viceroy. He and Nanna Ellen would sit in the parlour under the punkah fan and at precisely eleven past ten in the morning every day Nanna Ellen would say, 'Why is the baby puling?' No more words passed between them. Later in the evening Nanna Ellen would draw Nanna Dhoondopunt, again and again, bug-eyed, pearls dangling from his turban, fleshy faced, and a dagger stuck in his waistband. She had seen the face in an English newspaper, little knowing that the visage touted as the Beast of Cawnpore, and Ravager of the Angels of Albion, was in fact the countenance of an ally, a merchant trader called Jottee Pershad. The real Dhoondopunt looked like a restaurateur who was his own best customer. Evil often looks domestic. Big Da had more trouble coping with the peace than with the war.

I think about liberation. In the forty-two days that Sodasi was under foster care I was finally allowed to visit her; took her to lunch; she wore red taffeta, and balanced on new stilettos as we went for 'Eat-as-much-as-you-can spaghetti for $9.99'. I escorted her to a party and she stood in the corner wearing a handkerchief dress and the youth with the swept-back long hair wanted her address. We went to the op shop for her Grunge outfit and I saw the angel wings of her shoulder blades. Her collarbone was a hanger on which hung skin. Her backbone, like her life, was a journey of bony full stops.

Sodasi's living agreement with the Department of Community Services was for six weeks. The counsellor persuaded her to return home; '. . . just put your toe in the water and see what it's like' she was told. The house was divided into spaces; hers, mine, cigarette-smoking. Every evening when I returned there was a drawing. Sometimes in pencil, sometimes in pastel. One was of a head, a snaggle tooth, sunken-cheeked face, one eye closed, and the other open with the iris dangling perpendicularly, like an exclamation mark in the eyeball. She said it was a portrait hanging inside the wall of her head. Another was of a razor blade, with the edge smudged with red ink.

That was when she started to cut herself, first the inside of her arms, making skin bangles, then under the jeans above her knees. At night I kept her door ajar by placing a slipper in her doorway. Sometimes the drawings changed. Blue pastel colours washed over tulips, the tendrils flowing past the frame of the page. She asked for artist's supplies. Pots of greens, violet and lilac were transformed into shapes that looked like spiralling flowers or starfish or jelly cannonballs. The background was of heavy dark colours, thickly applied. She attended night classes for jewellery making. She made a ring of minute thorns and wore it. After school she wore sliced black stockings over her fair legs so that at a distance Sodasi looked feral.

I attended parenting classes and armed myself with the words of peace; I was offered a gleaming vocabulary. Compromise. Concessions. Negotiations. Boundaries. Consequences. Ownership. All lying side by side as if packed in a munitions box. The smell of tallow hung in the air. I learned how to press out treaties, to retreat gracefully, to give way and not give in, to avoid paternalism. We sat in the church hall in circles and shared; about rebelliousness, wars of independence and freedom. We learned the dangers of colonising the future of our children. One day the counsellor asked, 'What do you most fear and where does it come from?' I wonder if they understood about that mutiny in my suitcase, and about Anglo-Indian maleness.

Every day Sodasi changed. She wore black lipstick and dark clothes, her hair done in two bangs with a middle part. Her mouth looked like it had a bat hanging on it. When we were shopping it was I who sometimes pretended not to be with her. Once we sat at a table in Chadstone Food Court. Sodasi saw a school friend who was a model, all lightness and freshness. I watched as Sodasi talked to her. The friend shifted her designer jeans in the plastic seat and did not introduce the boyfriend. The conversation finished and Sodasi headed back to me whilst the friend leaned across to whisper to her companion.

Later that night I pulled her drunk out of a taxi. She mumbled, 'Why did you call me the perfect maiden of sixteen?'

She does not know about the time when she went into the City Square and I disappeared into the crowd after altering the jaw-line of the middle-aged pony-tailed man with her.

Nanna Ellen jumped when the washerman hit the clothes on a stone at the side of a pond. When Big Da was late Nanna Ellen wound the handle of the gramophone and listened to 'The Relief of Cawnpore Grand March'. Da returned in the evening to a cold house and the skirl of bagpipes. I would come home to the lyrics of Kurt Cobain. Sodasi sought her Nirvana from a plastic CD. Then Cobain went 'slightly numb to regain his enthusiasm' as he put it in his suicide note, and became a secondary God to the fans.

I wrote closures; a half eulogy in my head respecting Sodasi's wish to lie in Sherbrooke forest; a treaty with God, as I walked Akbar-like, around her bed three times bargaining for her life.

I am to blame for missing the signs of an impending insurrection, the thinning hair, the weight loss, the Reader's Digest medical manual, the Sylvia Plath writings; *mea culpa* . . . the rebel is too good for me.

Then Sodasi decided to live. She split into two. One Sodasi slipped away, back to the photographs on the mantelpiece, standing in the front row of the Year 9 Catholic College photograph, then giggling into the Year 8 concert, rushing back now with long hair into the first year of secondary school, then hands folded, veiled and white, bobbed hair, first holy communion, Bride of Christ, a quick change, wearing Small Fashion Denim for kindergarten, the birth, all that black hair, the warm womb, back into me, and I, catherine-wheeling, returned to Big Da and 1857.

The other Sodasi went forward on high heels and a bent back.

I started to write beginnings.

When friends ask where Sodasi is, I do not say she has left home but that she is living independently. She brings her washing and I make her curries. I am getting used to not being told what happened to her. I now fear knowing. Sometimes capsules of information leak out to me; they look suspiciously like greased cartridges. I met her foster family. Sam and Helen. The caregivers. At Sodasi's wedding. They were busy explaining to a guest that Sodasi went to them when she had to have time-out from us.

The guest told us this.

Not for me to write about her life. Sodasi must write her own history. I still cannot look at her eyes. I put glass between us. I visit her on birthdays and watch her through the lens. I saw her wedding through a video camera. I converse with her with my spectacles on. I love Sodasi through glass.

Ada Cambridge

ARRIVING IN MELBOURNE
1903

I suppose it was about nine o'clock when we dropped anchor. All we could see of the near city was a three-quarter ring of lights dividing dark water from dark sky – just what I see now every night when I come upstairs to bed, before I draw the blinds down. We watched them, fascinated, and – still more fascinating – the boats that presently found their way to us, bringing welcoming friends and relatives to those passengers who possessed them. We, strangers in a strange land, sat apart and watched these favoured ones – listened to their callings back and forth over the ship's side, beheld their embraces at the gangway, their excited interviews in the cuddy, their gay departures into the night and the unknown, which in nearly every case swallowed them for ever as far as we were concerned. Three only of the whole company have we set eyes on since – excepting the friend who became our brother – and one of these three renewed acquaintance with us but a year or two ago. Another I saw once across a hotel dinner-table. The third was the clergyman who had been so kindly foisted on us – or we on him – before we left England; and it was enough for us to see him afar off at such few diocesan functions as we afterwards attended together; we dropped closer relations as soon as there was room to drop them. However, he was a useful and respected member of his profession, and much valued by his own parish, from which death removed him many a year ago. Quite a deputation of church members came off to welcome him on that night of his return from his English holiday, and to tell him of the things his *locum tenens* had been doing in his absence. He was furious at learning that this person – at the present moment the head of the Church of England in this state – had had the presumption to replace an old organ – *his* old organ – with a new one. In the deputation were ladies with votive bouquets for his wife; the perfume of spring violets in the saloon deepened the sense of exile and solitude that crept upon us when their boat and the rest had vanished from view, leaving but the few friendless ones to the hospitality of the ship for a last night's lodging.

However, in the morning, we had our turn. It was the loveliest morning, a sample of the really matchless climate (which we had been informed was exactly like that of the palm-houses at Kew), clear as crystal, full of sunshine and freshness; and when we awoke amid strange noises, and looked out of our porthole, we saw that not sea but wooden planks lay under it – Port Melbourne railway pier, exactly as it is now, only that its name was then Sandridge and its old piles thirty years stouter where salt water and barnacles gnawed them.

With what joy as well as confidence did we don our best clerical coat and our best purple petticoat and immaculate black gown (the skirt pulled up out of harm's way through a stout elastic waist-cord, over which it hung behind in a soft, unobtrusive bag, for street wear), and lay out our Peter Robinson jacket and bonnet, and gloves from the hermetically sealed bottle, upon the bare bunk! And the breakfast we then went to is a memory to gloat upon – the succulent steak, the fresh butter and cream, the shore-baked rolls, the piled fruits and salads; nothing ever surpassed it except the midday meal following, with its juicy sirloin and such spring vegetables as I had never seen. This also I battened on, with my splendidly prepared appetite, though G. did not. The bishop's representative – our first Australian friend, whose fine and kindly face is little changed in all these years, and which I never look upon without recalling that moment, my first and just impression of it and him – appeared in our cabin doorway early in the morning; and it was deemed expedient that G. should go with him to report himself at headquarters, and return for me when that business was done. So I spent some hours alone, watching the railway station at the head of the pier through my strong glasses. In the afternoon I too landed, and was driven to lodgings that had been secured for us in East Melbourne, where we at once dressed for dinner at the house of our newest friend, and for one of the most charming social evenings that I ever spent. The feature of it that I best remember was a vivid literary discussion based upon *Lothair*, which was the new book of the hour, and from which our host read excruciating extracts. How brightly every detail of those first hours in Australia stands out in the mind's records of the past – the refined little dinner (I could name every dish on the dainty table), the beautiful and adored invalid hostess, who died not long afterwards, and whom those who knew her still speak of as 'too good for this world'; the refreshment of intellectual talk after the banalities of the ship; the warm kindness of everybody, even our landlady, who was really a lady, and like a mother to me; the comfort of the sweet and clean shore life – I shall never cease to glow at the recollection of these things. The beautiful weather enhanced the charm of all, and – still more – the fact that, although at first I staggered with the weakness left by such long seasickness, I not only recovered as soon as my foot touched land, but enjoyed the best health of my life for a full year afterwards.

The second day was a Saturday, and we were taken out to see the sights. No description that we had read or heard of, even from our fellow-passengers whose homes were there, had prepared us for the wonder that Melbourne was to us. As I remember our metropolis then, and see it now, I am not conscious of any striking general change, although of course, the changes in detail are innumerable. It was a greater city for its age thirty years ago than it is today, great as it is today. I lately read in some English magazine the statement that tree-stumps – likewise, if I mistake not, kangaroos – were features of Collins Street 'twenty-five years ago'. I can answer for it that in 1870 it was excellently paved and macadamised, thronged with its wagonette-cabs, omnibuses, and private carriages – a perfectly good and proper street, except for its open drainage gutters. The nearest kangaroo hopped in the Zoological Gardens at Royal Park. In 1870, also – although the theatrical proceedings of the Kelly gang took place later – bushranging was virtually a thing of the past. So was the Bret Harte mining-camp. We are credited still, I believe, with those romantic institutions, and our local storywriters love to pander to the delusion of some folks that Australia is made up of them; I can only say – and I ought to know – that in Victoria, at any rate, they have not existed in my time. Had they existed in the other colonies, I must have heard of it. The last real bushranger came to his inevitable bad end shortly before we arrived. The cowardly Kellys, murderers, and brigands as they were, and costlier than all their predecessors to hunt down, always seemed to me but imitation bushrangers. Mining has been a sober pursuit, weighted with expensive machinery. Indeed, we have been quite steady and respectable, so far as I know. In the way of public rowdyism I can recall nothing worth mentioning – unless it be the great strike of 1890.

We went to see the Town Hall – the present one, lacking only its present portico; and the splendid Public Library, as it was until a few years ago, when a wing was added; and the Melbourne Hospital, as it stands today; and the University, housed as it is now, and beginning to gather its family of colleges about it. We were taken a-walking in the Fitzroy Gardens – saw the same fern gully, the same plaster statues, that still adorn it; and to the Botanical Gardens, already furnished with their lakes and swans, and rustic bridges, and all the rest of it. And how beautiful we thought it all! As I have said, it was springtime, and the weather glorious. There had been excessive rains, and were soon to be more – rains which caused 1870 to be marked in history as 'the year of the great floods' – but the loveliness of the weather as we first knew it I shall never forget.

We finished the week in the suburban parish that included Pentridge, the great prison of the State – an awesome pile of dressed granite then as now. The incumbent was not well, and G. was sent to help him with his Sunday duty. The first early function was at the gaol, from which they brought back an exquisitely designed programme of the music and order of service, which I still keep amongst my mementoes of those days. It was done by a prisoner, who supplied one, and always a different one, to the chaplain each Sunday.

At his house – where again we were surprised to find all the refinements we had supposed ourselves to have left in England, for he and his wife were exceptionally cultivated persons – we slept on the ground floor for the first time in our lives, all mixed up with drawing-room and garden, which felt very strange and public, and almost improper. Now I prefer the bungalow arrangement to any other; I like to feel the house all round me, close and cosy, and to be able to slip from my bed into the open air when I like, and not to be cut off from folks when I am ill. For more than twenty years I was accustomed to it, sleeping with open windows and unlocked doors, like any Bedouin in his tent, unmolested in the loneliest localities by night-prowling man or beast. I miss this now, when I live in town and have to climb stairs and isolate myself – or sleep with shut windows (which I never will) in a ground-floor fortress, made burglar-proof at every point.

Bishop and Mrs Perry had a dinner-party for us on Monday. That day was otherwise given to our particular ship friend (of whom I shall say more presently); with him, a stranger in the land like ourselves, we had adventures and excursions 'on our own', eluding the many kind folk who would have liked to play courier. We lunched plentifully at an excellent restaurant – I cannot identify it now, but it fixed our impression that we had indeed come to a land of milk and honey – and then rambled at large. The evening was very pleasant. Whether as host or guest, the first Bishop of Melbourne was always perfect, and we met some interesting people at his board. Others came in after dinner, amongst them two of the 'sweetly pretty daughters', of whom we had heard in England, and who did not quite come up to our expectations. They are hoary-headed maiden ladies now – the youngest as white as the muslin of the frock she wore that night.

We did many things during the remainder of the week, which was full of business, pleasure, and hospitalities, very little of our time being spent in privacy. The shops were surprisingly well furnished and tempting, and we acted upon our supposition that we should find none to speak of in the Bush. We made careful little purchases from day to day. The very first of them, I think, was Professor Halford's snake-bite cure. We had an idea that, once out of the city, our lives would not be safe without it for a day. It was a hypodermic syringe and bottle of stuff, done up in a neat pocket-case. That case did cumber pockets for a time, but it was never opened, and eventually went astray and was no more seen – or missed. Yet snakes were quite common objects of the country then. I used to get weary of the monotony of sitting my horse and holding G.'s, while at every mile or so he stopped to kill one, during our Bush-rides in warm weather. English readers should know that in the bush it has ever been a point of honour, by no means to be evaded, to kill every snake you see, if possible, no matter how difficult the job, nor how great your impatience to be after other jobs. That probably is why they are so infrequent now that any chance appearance of the creature is chronicled in the papers as news.

Another early purchase was a couple of large pineapples, at threepence apiece. We each ate one (surreptitiously, in a retired spot), and realised one of the ambitions of our lives – to get enough of that delicacy for once.

On Saturday the 24th, the eighth day from our arrival, we turned our backs upon all this wild dissipation and our faces towards stern duty. We left Melbourne for the Bush.

Peter Carey

THE LAST DAYS OF A FAMOUS MIME
1974

1

The Mime arrived on Alitalia with very little luggage: a brown paper parcel and what looked like a woman's handbag.

Asked the contents of the brown paper parcel he said, 'String.'

Asked what the string was for he replied: 'Tying up bigger parcels.'

It had not been intended as a joke, but the Mime was pleased when the reporters laughed. Inducing laughter was not his forte. He was famous for terror.

Although his state of despair was famous throughout Europe, few guessed at his hope for the future. 'The string,' he explained, 'is a prayer that I am always praying.'

Reluctantly he untied his parcel and showed them the string. It was blue and when extended measured exactly fifty-three metres.

The Mime and the string appeared on the front pages of the evening papers.

2

The first audiences panicked easily. They had not been prepared for his ability to mime terror. They fled their seats continually. Only to return again.

Like snorkel divers they appeared at the doors outside the concert hall with red faces and were puzzled to find the world as they had left it.

3

Books had been written about him. He was the subject of an award-winning film. But in his first morning in a provincial town he was distressed to find that his performance had not been liked by the one newspaper's one critic.

'I cannot see,' the critic wrote, 'the use of invoking terror in an audience.'

The Mime sat on his bed, pondering ways to make his performance more light-hearted.

4

As usual he attracted women who wished to still the raging storms of his heart.

They attended his bed like highly paid surgeons operating on a difficult case. They were both passionate and intelligent. They did not suffer defeat lightly.

5

Wrongly accused of merely miming love in his private life he was somewhat surprised to be confronted with hatred.

'Surely,' he said, 'if you now hate me, it was you who were imitating love, not I.'

'You always were a slimy bastard,' she said. 'What's in that parcel?'

'I told you before,' he said helplessly, 'string.'

'You're a liar,' she said.

But later when he untied the parcel he found that she had opened it to check on his story. Her understanding of the string had been perfect. She had cut it into small pieces like spaghetti in a lousy restaurant.

6

Against the advice of the tour organisers he devoted two concerts entirely to love and laughter. They were disasters. It was felt that love and laughter were not, in his case, as instructive as terror.

The next performance was quickly announced.

TWO HOURS OF REGRET.

Tickets sold quickly. He began with a brief interpretation of love using it merely as a prelude to regret which he elaborated on in a complex and moving performance which left the audience pale and shaken. In a final flourish he passed from regret to loneliness to terror. The audience devoured the terror like brave tourists eating the hottest curry in an Indian restaurant.

7

'What you are doing,' she said, 'is capitalising on your neuroses. Personally I find it disgusting, like someone exhibiting their club foot, or Turkish beggars with strange deformities.'

He said nothing. He was mildly annoyed at her presumption: that he had not thought this many, many times before.

With perfect misunderstanding she interpreted his passivity as disdain.

Wishing to hurt him, she slapped his face.

Wishing to hurt her, he smiled brilliantly.

8

The story of the blue string touched the public imagination. Small brown paper packages were sold at the doors of his concerts.

Standing on stage he could hear the packages being noisily unwrapped. He thought of American matrons buying Muslim prayer rugs.

9

Exhausted and weakened by the heavy schedule he fell prey to the doubts that had pricked at him insistently for years. He lost all sense of direction and spent many listless hours by himself, sitting in a motel room listening to the air-conditioner.

He had lost confidence in the social uses of controlled terror. He no longer understood the audience's need to experience the very things he so desperately wished to escape from.

He emptied the ashtrays fastidiously.

He opened the brown paper parcel and threw the small pieces of string down the cistern. When the torrent of white water subsided they remained floating there like flotsam from a disaster at sea.

10

The Mime called a press conference to announce that there would be no more concerts. He seemed small and foreign and smelt of garlic. The press regarded him without enthusiasm. He watched their hovering pens anxiously, unsuccessfully willing them to write down his words.

Briefly he announced that he wished to throw his talent open to broader influences. His skills would be at the disposal of the people, who would be free to request his services for any purpose at any time.

His skin seemed sallow but his eyes seemed as bright as those on a nodding fur mascot on the back window ledge of an American car.

11

Asked to describe death he busied himself taking Polaroid photographs of his questioners.

12

Asked to describe marriage he handed out small cheap mirrors with MADE IN TUNISIA written on the back.

13

His popularity declined. It was felt that he had become obscure and beyond the understanding of ordinary people. In response he requested easier questions. He held back nothing of himself in his effort to please his audience.

14

Asked to describe an aeroplane he flew three times around the city, only injuring himself slightly on landing.

15

Asked to describe a river, he drowned himself.

16

It is unfortunate that this, his last and least typical performance, is the only one which has been recorded on film.

There is a small crowd by the riverbank, no more than thirty people. A small, neat man dressed in a grey suit picks his way through some children who seem more interested in the large plastic toy dog they are playing with.

He steps into the river, which, at the bank, is already quite deep. His head is only visible above the water for a second or two. And then he is gone.

A policeman looks expectantly over the edge, as if waiting for him to appear. Then the film stops.

Watching this last performance it is difficult to imagine how this man stirred such emotions in the hearts of those who saw him.

Gavin Casey

DUST

1 9 3 6

A feathery tower of dust was dancing over the housetops towards the hospital buildings, swaying and leaning, and scurrying across open spaces so fast that it sometimes left its top trailing away behind it. After the manner of inland willy-willies, it picked up light things that lay in its path and tossed them high, swooped through open doors, leaving a red trail wherever it went.

From the laboratory veranda a dozen men watched its erratic progress and eventual dissolution as they waited.

The red, honest dirt of the surface soil that was swept about by the wind, thought Parker, visible and avoidable, quite unlike the stale, still, malicious menace that polluted the atmosphere of far underground.

'Marvellous what them things'll shift if they git right under it,' said Big Joe.

'I seen one take the roof off my front veranda an' land it in th' chookyard at the back,' said old Penberthy, who was squarely built and had inherited thick, strong limbs from many generations of mining ancestors.

The morning was bright and warm, and normally Parker and the others would have been far below the sunlight, underground. Parker wished he was. He leaned, with his elbows on the rail, smoking and watching the dumps away on the other side of the town.

His breathing was heavy, sometimes catching and whistling softly in some mysterious passage behind his chest. He felt tired and listless. The long row of glittering, curtainless windows of the laboratory depressed him, because he always thought of the 'tickets' that were made out, signed, recorded and filed away behind them as 'death warrants'. The ordeal of waiting for the doctors to open the doors, and then for his turn to go in and be subjected to the tests and examinations that might mean the end of everything, shattered his nerves, as it always did.

'Y' git miner's complaint jist as easy on th' surface as y' do down below,' someone was saying. "Specially in th' mill.'

'We all git it at the office every third an' seventeenth,' came the voice of young Pope. 'Not enough money!'

Parker shivered.

It was a hell of a subject to joke about, he thought indignantly. The kid was too young to know any better, had probably never seen a man with 'dust'. But old Penberthy and Big Joe – they should know.

Pictures out of the past floated on the heat haze that shimmered over the red earth in front of Parker. His old dad, just before he passed out, when Parker himself was just a little shaver. Still on the right side of fifty the old boy had been, but there had been only nine stone left of his original fourteen. The lungs rotted out of him, so that every movement was heavy labour. Bleached, papery claws of hands that had seemed natural enough to the boy. Now he could well imagine the kind of fists the old man had had before the dust got him. He looked at his own big, hard paws, clutching the rail in the sunshine.

Of course things had changed, he tried to reassure himself. In his dad's time a man had just kept going in ill-ventilated depths until he could work no longer, and then it had been too late to do much for him. To avoid that sort of thing was the purpose of the laboratory, the periodical examination of all mine employees, the whole system of first tickets and second tickets and pensions. Venturis down below and water everywhere to keep the dust down.

But some men still went out. Give it time enough to do its work and the dust still defied science.

When the big doors at last clashed open the pumping of Parker's heart and lungs forced a wheezy whistle between his teeth that terrified him.

Treading the jarrah boards heavily, Big Joe went in, and Parker glimpsed a dancing muscle behind the giant's jaw that seemed to tell of nervous tenseness. Even in Pope's eyes there seemed to be the shadow of a vague, unspoken fear. Parker felt for a moment very much one with his comrades, held together by fear and hatred of the life they lived.

Why had he given all those years since the war to toil in the deep levels? Why must he continue there, breathing stagnant death? Why could he laugh at risks to life and limb in the months that fled between each laboratory inspection, and yet inevitably find himself quailing before the memory of his old dad, in agony and fear each time the day for his examination drew closer? Was he all his life to tremble at the after-effects of a stubborn cold, imagining a warning of disease in every speck of phlegm?

By the time Big Joe came tramping out and young Pope went in Parker felt elated and wanted to laugh at them both. The dust would get them sooner or later. It was only a matter of time.

But he, Parker, was stepping out of it all, just like that. Right now he was going to set out for town with Big Joe, have a drink and say goodbye to the mines for ever. Chuckles bubbled in his throat and then there whistled through them a tiny, sobbing intake of breath, sucked through some obstruction by labouring lungs. Parker put down the hat he had grabbed and stayed where he was.

'Well, that's that!' said Big Joe, tightening his belt. 'Y' don't look too good, Tom.'

'I'm all right,' Parker managed. 'Got a bit of a cold.'

When the other had gone he prayed wordlessly as he leaned against the veranda rail in the sunshine. He would leave the mines, but first he must know, be sure that the wheezing in his lungs was only the aftermath of the cold that had gripped him earlier in the year. He could not go now. He must have the verdict, and then he would be through with underground.

When his turn came he tensed himself to go through with it. To the X-ray operator he even tried to voice the customary jocular comment on the coldness of the plate against his bare chest, but it stuck in his throat. The doctors he knew from many previous visits, and he wanted to ask questions, but dared not.

'You're heavier,' announced the last of them amiably as Parker dressed himself. 'Six-seven pounds on since the last card was filled in.'

Parker took courage from the fact.

'When'll a man know if he's come through all right?' He tried to make his tones unconcerned and casual, though blood seemed to be pumping hard against his eardrums.

'I won't see the plates for a day or two,' said the doctor, 'but I'd bet on you without seeing them. You're as fit as a fiddle, Parker, and we certainly won't be using any ink making out a ticket for you this time.'

His surroundings turned momentarily black. Light-hearted and faint with relief he scrambled into his clothes, and when he reached the sun-warmed outer air he sucked it in in appreciative gulps. Bright skies looked good, and the subdued thunder of the mines was a pleasant drone that sang of toil and prosperity.

'Well,' he said to old Penberthy, 'that's over for another six months! I'll hang around until they're through with you and we'll have one at th' corner.'

'If they're ever through,' grumbled Penberthy irritably. 'They muck about enough, don't they? Doesn't matter t' these wages fellers t' miss half a shift, but you an' me ought t' be pushin' th' winze down right now, Tom. They ought t' let a man make a time fer this that suits him.'

'Aw, we should worry,' said Parker gaily. 'It'll be a good pay fer us without this mornin', anyway. An' Doolan was tellin' me that when we got her finished he wants one on th' Fifteen. We can make a bit down there.'

'Th' Fifteen?' said Penberthy. ''S unhealthy on th' Fifteen. Dunno as I altogether like th' Fifteen.'

'Aw, bunk!' said Parker. 'The unhealthy places is where th' money is.'

Brian   Castro

SONATINA
1994

When he finally came down from the mountain the sun was winking through cloud like a twenty-watt bulb. Then a light rain fell, with its freight of ash, smudging the windscreen of his old Ford, and he was thinking of the correspondence between music and water, of dissonance as polyphony, of the C-major triad, the wipers squelching as he wrenched the heavy car over the lip of Lapstone Pass, pulling over into the ruts to view the plains below.

Shit, he thought, his life was a mess.

A stale mist scoured the fields, lined the river with steam and was pushing upwards where the heat was strongest, thunderheads forming along the miles of treeless estates near the freeway. He felt an empty melancholy come over him and knew this was the territory from which he had to draw his music.

For months he had been wrestling with a kind of unspaced test, a solid line of note which would deliver up music without partitioning for breath, for art, for life. No rests, no time signatures, no bars, leaving a stream of intensity which abandoned the artificially romantic for the unstoppable. But something was missing. So far it had been nothing save a possibility, that little object of desire which made ordinary living perverse.

And now his friend had died at forty. Elizabeth had believed in him, fought for him, got him the teaching post at the university, even went through the charade of interviewing a dozen or so applicants and all the time she had been in love with him and he wasn't aware of it, not even at the last moment when she collapsed and was diagnosed with cancer, when he held her hand in the hospital. They hadn't renegotiated his contract and he thought her little squeezes of his hand were reassurances, marvelling at how very brave she was right up until the end. Even had he known that she loved him, he would not have contemplated anything further. Two broken marriages had been enough. He thought of the noise, the clashing wills, other people's children. But now Elizabeth was dead and he was coming down for her funeral, feeling a little shabby at the way he had kept everything on a professional level. He thought it was cowardly for him to have been so reserved in these matters, thinking of her smile, the attractive dimple in her chin and of the long hours they had spent arranging and transcribing his music when the national orchestra took it abroad, establishing him, in a way, as promising.

That was when he turned his back on everything, refused to consolidate. Regressed. He didn't care. He would learn to scrounge again. He had a gift for improvidence. Wanted to end the struggle, to sing while others stored. Yes, to be foolish, impenetrable. To begin again, and to begin again until he grew tired of living with his mistakes, finally making that one bold entry into the vacancy.

He released the handbrake and the Ford lurched out of the ruts, a recalcitrant wheel fluttering and slapping, spinning the car sideways so it scraped a tree, tearing off a piece of side trim. On the freeway it made a rhythmic drumming, syncopated, depending on the speed at which he drove. He accelerated and decelerated, annoying everybody. He was trying to figure out where to turn off for Pine Grove Cemetery.

When he swung off into the exit ramp he narrowly missed a motorcycle cruising through on the inside lane, not realising at all until the fellow rode up and kicked at his door and then thundered away. He remembered the full beard and the dark glasses and the arm like an orang-outang's with eloquent fingers perched on the raised handlebar. The heat intensified. An ambulance rushed the opposite way, siren beating through unmoving traffic, jumping the median strip and bouncing away on the wrong side. At the wide intersection superintended by four service stations the lights turned red. He let the car idle and noticed the engine racing. The choke was stuck. The meathead next to him responded by gunning his panel van in time to his radio and there was this symphony of exhausts and waves of aggression like a blast, like a loud cracker or backfire, but there was something altogether different to that, a disturbing resonance which made the meathead turn down his sound system. There it was again, louder, and almost simultaneously a pelting of stones against the car and when he turned he saw a young woman running through the lanes of traffic, her shoes in one hand and in the other, some clothes over her nakedness. She was crouching, he thought, modestly, and was rather taken with this until he saw another puff of smoke and when he looked again the woman was wrenching his door open and crawling over him onto the floor behind, his back window frosting and then shattering.

'Go!' she shouted. 'Go, for Chrissake!'

He jerked the Ford into a wheel-spin and speared into cross-traffic, weaving round the back of a semitrailer until he gained the open road. His heart was pounding. He couldn't see behind him.

'Jesus!' the woman said from the floor. She was picking glass out of her hair and trying to dress at the same time. Jesus. She looked nice. He adjusted the mirror. Saw that her left leg was bleeding. Saw that she could have been no more than eighteen.

'You've been hit,' he said and was automatically heading towards Nepean hospital. 'Hit? Hell no. It's your bloody car; I caught myself on something sharp.'

He passed her his handkerchief and presently heard her moaning. He noticed the trim was no longer thrumming. He drove fast, skidded into Casualty and the orderlies stared at him thinking that some people just loved drama.

In Outpatients they were efficient. They put in half a dozen stitches and gave her tetanus shots.

'They're always fast when there's a bit of blood,' she grinned.

He liked her grin and couldn't understand why the way she looked, the sensitivity there, seemed completely out of place. He found it attractive, but dismissed it, putting it down to the trauma she had come through and the distortion of the moment. He was even more puzzled when the policeman who came to interview her seemed to know her. She calmly answered the questions with a twinkle in her eye and that ironic grin reserved especially for himself he was thinking. The policeman was taken by her too, he could see, by the story of her life; how she was trying to make a go of it without her lunatic ex-husband, how she had a restraining order on him. She said she had enrolled in a course at the university. What was she doing then at the Crossroads near Pine Grove? the policeman was asking. Well, she had to make some money, she said, quite seriously, and named a few names and the policeman was quite impressed and patted her arm as he left,

saying they would take care of things from now on and telling her not
to worry.

She pulled out a little box of powder.

'Want some?'

'No thanks.'

She sniffed a pinch up each nostril.

He was more than a little unsettled, feeling a mixture of curiosity,
desire and duty, as though he were entering a dream which exacted
its own rituals and it was only these rituals which could keep things
together. A psychiatrist friend had called it *cognitive dissonance*. What
about love, though? he had responded. Don't you cross the boundary
between reality and dream when you fall in love? His friend had nodded
in a way which said love too was psychologically suspect.

He had taken that aboard, and now at the first sign of chaos, he
looked for order. You didn't make mistakes that way, he was thinking,
as he cruised the corridors of the hospital for information, a sign which
would point him in one direction or another. He found an orderly
wheeling a bed. There was a woman on it, wired up with tubes with a
basin of blood under her. He walked. The orderly said:

'This your wife?'

'No.'

'They took out half her stomach. Don't worry. She can't hear us.
You a relative?'

'No. Just want some information.'

'Information? Doctors tell you nothing.'

'No. I mean. I don't know this area.'

'You don't?'

'What happens at the Crossroads near Pine Grove?'

'Crossroads? It's a pick-up place.'

'For what?'

'Prostitutes, pal!'

The old guy was chuckling.

He went back to Outpatients and waited until they said she could
go and then offered to drive her home. He was surprised by her ac-
quiescence and continued to be so and felt good to have her holding
onto his arm as he walked her to the car, looking at her sideways,
liking the sound of her voice, the way she made a joke of everything.
But in his heart, he knew this was her bedside manner. It was exactly

the same way he treated women who he sensed liked him, and for the first time in several hours, he thought of Elizabeth's funeral. He had missed it entirely and felt badly and drove in silence for a while. I've inherited indifference instead of character, he was thinking.

Tina was sensitive to this disturbance. Yes, Tina; that was her name. She was telling him about her ex-husband, an asshole, she said, using the Americanism which didn't mine much bitterness even though he'd sought her out and fired a shotgun at her, gunning his Harley between lines of cars and aiming low from a distance. They had been married four months.

'He only meant to scare me,' she said. 'They'll put him away for a while and when he comes out he'll have so many stories some other poor woman'll fall for him.'

'But he meant to harm you.'

'He was only using rat-shot,' she grinned. 'I'm sorry about your windscreen. You want some money for it?

'No.'

At her place by the river, a large, untidy house she shared with two friends, she suddenly collapsed, for real he thought, and he carried her inside. It had all been too much, he remarked, making her some soup.

'Saves embarrassment over an invitation,' she said, smiling sadly between mouthfuls.

He left at dusk when her flatmates came home and drove solemnly up the mountain filled with a bittersweet emotion. Loss tugged on one side and on the other, the looming shadow of his own solitude. He knew that he would probably begin a composition that night and could already hear the peculiar music of that passerine summer; late nestings of notes. This was as much as he could possibly say at the moment about his happiness . . . that it was inspired by her.

He came down from the mountain regularly after that, and resolved to call on her. Each time he did something else instead, but returned with more ideas for his music. Then one day he got drunk at midday and rang her to ask her to dinner. Mustering great discipline, he was formal and polite and awkward. She didn't allow any gaps to embarrass him, sounding pleased and flattered, leaving at the same time the impression there was no ornamentation necessary for such a simple invitation.

At dinner he decided to find out as much as possible about her. She had left school early . . . she said with that fierceness which was startling and intriguing . . . out of rebellion more than anything else. She had worked her way through a number of jobs and then left home and began studying again. The latter was always on and off. Institutions of learning gave off an air of hopelessness. Her father was violent and sought her out and she moved house three or four times a year. Then began the drinking and the drugs, but all the time she was recording and documenting secretly and managed good grades and suddenly had this urge to study criminology. Then everything was in abeyance because she got married, because that was the thing you did, she said. He was a wild guy with tattoos on his eyelids and under his fingernails and she got close, she said, she got very close to the hub of the real. And now . . . now she wanted to straighten out her life.

They ate in silence for a while. She was now enrolled in a music composition course, she finally said. She wanted to get a proper job.

He took her out to dinner a few more times and on each occasion saw her to the door. Their conversation had been helpful, she said. Although physical intimacy was what he most desired, he knew he was hearing a different music, the continuum of which he could not break.

He composed feverishly. He cut the top off the Ford, leaving only the windscreen, had a bigger engine installed and by night drove fast through the western suburbs feeling the heat sear past, hearing the backwash of pleasure which came after the pain and weight of depression, sounding like surf in his ears. Once or twice a carload of youths pulled alongside, radios blaring, and tried to throw beer bottles at him. He outpaced them, cornering at high speed, enjoying it immensely. Then one day the university rang and he was asked if he would like to apply for his old position.

On the third or fourth occasion that they met, he opened up his own life a little. They were sitting in a booth, the restaurant was crowded, and he was a little drunk. He began by saying that men expressing themselves to men have a long tradition of nobility, but a man expressing himself to a woman always bears the innuendo of a kind of sordidness: the gigolo factor, he called it. She thought his opinion entirely irrelevant, though she couldn't have known he was talking about music . . . that it didn't help with composition to be sentimental or to court display.

'You need,' she said suddenly, 'to come down from your mountain and into the dark forest with me.'

This was entirely unexpected.

'I will show you things, lives, you have only read about. You won't like it. You may not be able to take it at all. If you come out the other side . . . and I cannot guarantee you that . . . you'll know what expression is, even if you've needle marks in your arms and you're ready to walk in front of a train or hang yourself. But you need to be *of* it, to *be* it, in order to know.'

She was biting a corner of her napkin.

'I tried to work undercover once,' she said. 'There's no such thing, believe me. To be lost . . . you have to be lost to hear the music. Listen. I can introduce you to people; people for whom nothing means anything, for whom there is no reason for continuing. But then . . . it may not be like that at all for you.'

He looked at the menu, at the waitresses, at the piano player hunching over the keys fellating the microphone with a leer on his face that pretended much pain; looked at the expensive décor, the mock sophistication, at the food, the carpet, and then he looked back at her and saw that she was staring straight into his eyes with a clinical curiosity he had mistaken for desire.

'You know,' she said, 'we're all the same in the darkness. There it is,' she grinned. 'You can come with me. It's yours if you want it. I'm not precious about these things. But if you want to be happy, that's a different question.'

He explained that it wasn't a question of happiness. He could have said that his heroism depended on seclusion. But he didn't need to say it. She was already smiling in a different way.

Then she looked around and shifted to the far end of the booth.

'I want you to know something.'

'Okay.'

'You have to close your eyes.'

'Fine.'

He closed his eyes. The pianist was playing 'Memories'. He felt he was losing her.

'All right. Open.'

He saw that she had lifted up her top. Above her left breast there was a blue and yellow tattoo of an ancient Egyptian goddess, a cat-headed woman holding a kind of shield or cymbal.

'That's very nice,' he said.

He didn't know what else to say. He didn't raise his eyes in case he saw others looking.

'It's Bast. The goddess of music. Done by the best tats man in Australia.' She was grinning again. 'It's for you.'

When he drove home alone that night he passed the performing arts centre, believing he could hear strains of music leaking, now baroque, now atonal, without being able to identify the specific instruments. He turned off his lights and drifted. A motorcycle roared ahead picking out the pass with its beam and on the bends, swept the unspaced trees. The music intensified. He urged the Ford up a gear; accelerated, and suddenly he could see the piece he was composing ... saw himself driving through its frame and realised immediately that it was in that interstice that he was dying. He swerved to the left, pulled the car around, clattered over the median strip and drove back.

After a while he saw the glittering plains below and turned on his lights, knowing, as he watched over the city while easing and floating into the bends, that whenever anyone talked about love, the world was also listening and watching and waiting ...

John Clark

JOHNNY CAKE DAYS

1993

I hitchhiked down the Princes Highway and walked along the back road that leads to the mission. It's a lonely road and you don't often get a ride so I jumped the barbed-wire fence and cut across the paddocks. I came at last to the riverbank and looked across at the mission on the other side. Granny Alice's house is a little wooden one with a red tin roof and I can make out the toilet and chookshed, the bungalow and wrecked car by the woodheap. I crossed the river at the place we set the eel net. You can make your tracks between scrubby bracken and ferns, past the boxthorn bushes and into Granny's backyard. Aunty Faye is hanging out a line of clothes.

'Ah Johnny boy, back already?' she says with a peg between her teeth.

Dogs and cats are gathered at the back door as well as chooks and ducks, all waiting for a chance to get inside. I slip smartly in, shut the door and there's a rooster on the table, a cat on the chair and two pups asleep at the foot of the big wood stove. The kitchen is warm and smells like there's a damper in the oven. Granny's in the front room by the fire with a cup of tea. My cousin Mouse and the kids are watching television as I settle down by the fire with Granny and we yarn for a while.

A lot can happen on the mission in a short time. Uncle Donny went mad with the chainsaw again. Speedy is on the booze in town somewhere. Charlie's locked up for fighting coppers and some racist idiots have been driving down the mission shouting out 'Dirty Abos' and shit like that. Aunty Faye grabs the broom and together with a lot of swearing and cursing they hunt all the animals outside.

I cut wood till dark and looked at the stars for a while. Granny told me the stars are the camp fires of our ancestors. Our ancestors must look down on the lights of the mission and wonder how it came down to this. Once the proud owners of this country, now a few thousand acres to call home. The moon is up now. Somewhere a dog is barking and I can hear the Hopkins River rumbling over the falls as it winds its way to the sea.

I woke up in the rusty red and yellow bus-bungalow and heard the magpies yodelling in the wattles outside. The sound of a car approaching, bumping along the wet mission road, draws a mob of dogs out to greet it, yelping and playfully biting the tyres. A horn toots and voices. It's Aunty Violet. She wants to know if we want some tea or sugar from the store about four miles up the road. Someone calls out 'Book it up till pension day.' The car pulls away amid a chorus of barking dogs and then all is quiet except for old Billy, the goat, who calls out between mouthfuls of Granny's creeping roses. On my way into the house I pick up a handful of bark and sticks to light the stove. Granny is out in the backyard scattering bread and grain to a sea of squabbling hens, roosters, ducks, drakes and two white geese hissing and honking.

Inside, little David, Bernadette and Conny are eating porridge while Aunty Faye fixes their school lunches. She threatens to flog little David if he doesn't hurry up and get dressed. This is the story on most mornings, as little David likes to push his luck and stretch after him as he bolts out the door and down the road. Aunty Faye stops breathless and laughs, he's already halfway to school clutching his tomato sauce sandwiches.

I had grilled eel and damper for breakfast and I made a cup of tea for cousin Mouse. Mouse is still in bed breastfeeding her twins Ivy and Heather. They look up at me wide-eyed and blinking like baby mopokes. These two little darlings played up last night and Mouse is red-eyed and worn out. In comes Aunty Faye, 'Come on Mousie, help me clean up this place.' Mouse mumbles something about 'In a minute' as Aunty Faye collects Ivy and Heather and sets them down in the front room where they play in the sunlight streaming in through the windows.

Aunty Faye is mopping the floor now, humming along with Hank Williams on the radio. *Hey good lookin', what you got cookin', how's about cooking something up with me.* Granny comes in the kitchen with some eggs wrapped up in her cardigan and I tell her I'm going shooting.

'I'll take the dogs for a run, Gran,' I say.

'Take the useless rotters and throw 'em in the river.' Granny is wild with the dogs because a fox has been snatching the chickens.

I felt for the rifle under Granny's mattress and pulled out an old .22 bolt action. That's where we hide the guns away from drunks – under the mattress. The bolt for the rifle was put in another safe place and nobody knew where. It took me some time to find it inside an empty jam tin along with six bullets and a pocketknife that needs a sharpen. I ask Aunty Faye, 'You know where the file is?' She's peeling potatoes at the sink and says, 'The kids had it last.' When you hear that the kids have had something last, you know that it is lost forever.

. . . Take these chains from my heart and set me free.

Granny stared hard through the window (she doesn't see too well nowadays). Old Billy the goat was chewing up Gran's white daisies. Old Billy has fiendish yellow eyes, a twisted pair of horns and with his long whiskers he roams about the mission butting the kids and smelling awful. I have seen him lift his leg and drink his own piss. Old Billy is under the kitchen window chomping away on white marguerites when he looks up and puts his evil eye on Granny. Granny screws her face up, 'I'll kill that mangy old bastard,' she says as she shuffles outside, 'fetch the broom Faye.'

I slung the rifle over my shoulder and stepped out into the backyard. When the dogs see the gun they get excited, jumping up and down, carrying on like two-bob watches. The rifle is unreliable as it sometimes misfires so I'll take a post hole shovel to dig the *bad habits* from their burrows. The dogs and I make tracks through the chook shit and pass by the front garden where Granny and Aunty Faye have exhausted themselves trying to chase the goat away with sticks and stones. Even the sharp end of the broom doesn't deter him. The women are flustered. They really don't want to harm old Billy, it's just that he's so wooden headed. I said I'd be back by dark and left them there swearing, throwing buckets of water on Billy as he started in on the sweet peas.

Uncle Percy lives just a stone's throw along the road from Granny.

His little weatherboard house is painted blue and surrounded by leafy trees and garden. The dogs follow me through the gate, which is really a rusty old bed-end, past the woodpile and round to the back door where I leave the shovel and step inside.

'You home, Uncle?' I call and blink my eyes in the cool darkness of the hallway.

'Who's that there?' I hear him ask.

'Just me, Uncle Percy,' I call coming into the kitchen. Uncle Percy is propped in front of the stove toasting a thick slab of bread on the end of a long wire fork. The embers glow brightly in the dimness. A little ginger cat is coiled on Uncle Percy's shoulder, purring loudly into his ear. Uncle Percy is a true gentleman who hasn't changed much over the years, although he is a little greyer and thinner lately. He still favours dark pin-stripe suits and hats. When he's dressed up and smoking his cherry wood pipe at the races he looks as flash as a rat with a gold tooth.

'Hot water in the kettle if you want a cup of tea, Jack,' he says.

Uncle Percy calls everyone Jack. So I stood the rifle in the corner and pulled a chair up close to the heat of the old black stove. We drank tea and talked about racehorses and bad luck while the 'Turf Talk' show babbled on over the radio. The warmth and familiar feel of this old place sets me thinking of when I was a little boy running about with my cousins when they lived here. It was a house full of people then but they moved to a commission house in town. There were lots of people on the mission then and always something happening. I could go to anyone's house and be cared for.

'You Rita's boy?' someone might ask and that's all they'd need to know.

I remember small dim houses in candle light. Mysterious black uncles and aunties telling ghost stories around the fireplace. 'So you kids don't go down the bridge or the headless man will get youse.' Drunks mad on red wine, 'Now stay away from Uncle Norman, he'll fall on yas.'

Things aren't the same on the mission. The magic of this haunted old place is gone, gone with the old people back to the dreaming. Uncle Percy shifts in his chair and turns a page of his newspaper. The cat purrs on. A plum tree scratches at the window and the ticking of the clock on the mantelpiece winds my mind back again.

We kids would make sleds from sheets of corrugated iron and slide down the steep riverbanks crashing through the tall bracken. Spotlighting was fun. We'd all race to be the first to stun the rabbits with our waddies. Spearing eels at the bottom of the falls in daylight or at night with a torch was always a good time. There were only about twenty of us kids went to our one-room schoolhouse. The teacher lived next door to the school and he would put on a do for Christmas. I remember someone playing guitar while he played bass on a piece of string tied to a broomstick and a wooden tea chest turned upside down. He'd thump away on it singing 'King of the Road' and 'Kingston Town'.

Only five or six kids go to the mission school now. They say they're going to close it down soon as the weatherboards are falling off and the windows are broken. The little green shelter shed under the pines is falling down. We'd play kick the tin in the shelter shed where you could peep through the cracks and see where the other kids were hiding. Now there's more weeds and thistles than boys and girls in the playground and I wonder where all my cousins have gone.

I am roused from my daydreams by the loud snapping and snarling of dogs outside. Uncle Percy is marking down the scratchings on his racing guide, 'What the bloody hell's going on, Jack?' The cat arched his back, spat and leapt to the floor, leaving a patch of orange fur on Uncle Percy's antique coat.

'It's them silly dogs. I'll round 'em up and get going,' I said, taking up the rifle. 'I'll save a rabbit for you, Uncle Percy.'

No doubt Uncle Percy will get a ride to town soon, park himself at the bar and bet on horses. He is a keen punter and when he backs a winner he's as happy as a witchetty grub in a wooden leg.

'Watch out for snakes, Jack,' he says but I can hardly hear him for another violent outburst at the back door.

Sure enough, it's a dogfight. My motley crew have Uncle Percy's red kelpie bailed up in a corner. One of my hunters, Woofy, a big bandy-legged mongrel, has the kelpie by the throat. I fear the eyes of the red dog will pop out as he howls in pain and fear. The rest of the pack snap at him mercilessly. The riot stops the instant I appear with the gun. As if struck by a magic wand the mangy mob turn and follow me onto the road.

The thin blue-metal road twists around and down to the bridge spanning the river. Cypress trees line one side of the road and from the odd patches of boxthorn I hear the chattering of willy wagtails and wrens. The dogs string out ahead of me. Dark woollen clouds, drifting in from the south-west, are slowly breaking up and huge rays of sunshine seep through the cracks to sweep across the land like big friendly laser beams. Winter is almost over and the magpies will soon be collecting twigs for the nests and sharpening their beaks on branches high in the gum trees. The gold will fall from the wattles and little grey joeys will wriggle from the warmth of mother's pouch to feed in the sanctuary of the bushland at the top of the mission. Like the kangaroos, my people have found refuge here. A place where the scattered children of Bunjil can regroup, grow and gain strength in the knowledge that we have survived as refugees in our own country.

Uncle Russell's shack overlooks the road and across to the riverbanks. Puffs of smoke spill from the sandstone chimney and I can see him standing in the doorway. He waves and I wave back. Already his lot of dogs are tearing out to meet us. The shack and cow-trodden yard are surrounded by a huge boxthorn hedge entangled with pink rambling roses. There is hardly a trace of the dairy that gave milk to the mission years ago. I remember as a boy, the fresh cream and jam and damper every morning. No trace of the pigsties but the old car bodies are still here, lying rusted and bullet ridden under the pines. We kids used to play in the cars and *gammon* we were Bonnie and Clyde. It seems like yesterday but it was long ago.

The dogs prowl about the doorstep, growing, circling each other with tails up like question marks. Uncle Russell's little dog Minnie is crouched low to the ground and whimpering as Woofy sniffs her intently up and down. He could swallow her with no trouble but obviously he has other ideas. Uncle Russ appears with the teapot in his hand. He slings the contents over the animals, 'Garn, get out of it ya silly bastards.'

'Good day Uncle, you look crook,' I say. I heard he was on the grog yesterday.

'Aw, I'm feeling all right now bud,' he says in his gravelly voice.

He's wearing a red headband, a green shirt with one sleeve, baggy trousers and no shoes. I follow him inside.

'Drink of tea, bud?' he says as he places the kettle on the flames.

'Yes, Uncle, thanks,' I say as I settle into a three-legged armchair. 'Don't chuck it at me though.' He throws his curly head back and laughs at that.

'How's your mum and dad going in that place down yonder?'

'They settled in okay, it's not bad for a commission house.' He nods his head as he spreads golden syrup on a johnny cake and hands it to me. The black iron kettle bubbles and spits. Uncle Russ makes tea and pours it into a battered mug for me.

'No, I don't like that powdered milk,' I say. 'Here, Granny gave me your tobacco ya lost yesterday.'

'Oh yeah, I was lookin' everywhere this morning for that.' He starts rolling one up. He'd dropped his tobacco beside the road yesterday where he fell down and smashed his flagon. He's often found sleeping in the grass, drunk, his dogs huddled close around him like huskies around an eskimo. He lights his skinny smoke with a stick from the fire and says, 'Did you know Devil bit Mary the other day?' Mary is my great-grandmother. A proud religious woman.

'Yeah,' I say. 'I heard about that.' Great Granny Mary is ninety-nine if she's a day and she hobbles about the mission preaching the evils of the demon alcohol. She can talk the lingo too.

'Yeah,' I say, 'she went in to see Aunty Elsie and that mad one, Devil's, took a piece of her ankle.'

'Ain't he chained up?' asks Uncle Russ.

'He is now. The ambulance came out and took Gran to town to get stitches.'

'Ah well, she won't be walking about the place for a while then,' says Uncle Russ, with a hint of satisfaction.

Uncle Russell picks up a boomerang he has cut from a blackwood tree. He's heating a piece of fencing wire to burn designs on his latest weapon. He will probably sell this one in the pub or give it to someone as a gift. I watch him working away while I sip black tea. Sparks crackle and jump from the fire. Wood shavings lie scattered on the floor with dog-food cans and empty flagons. A hessian-bag curtain flaps in the breeze. At the dark end of the room is his bed, blankets tossed about, magazines and cowboy stories beside the kero lamp. It strikes me that I've never known Uncle Russ to have a steady woman. He's a loner like Uncle Percy. Uncle Russell coughs and splutters, spits in the fire and curses his wicked headache.

'I'll get goin', Uncle,' I say. 'I'll send one of the kids down with a rabbit for ya tomorrow probably.'

'Good, bud, see ya after,' he says as he hot-wires the boomerang, squinting his eyes from the smoke.

By the time I reached the steep slopes of the riverbank I was almost doubled over with a stitch. I rested, leaning on the shovel and cursed myself for eating too many johnny cakes. Below, the dogs have fanned out, sniffing and nosing their way about in the dense dark green fernery. The river has cut a wide arc here and formed a small bay with a sandy shore. I remember when groups of mission folk would light a fire on the sand and fish for eels in the cool of evening.

Recovered from my johnny cake attack, I make my way along the trail, down through the bracken to the old mission swimming hole and crossing place. Here the water looks cool and golden, streaming across pink and grey stones, running into deeper pools, swirling and twisting, tugging at overhanging tea-tree and wattles.

I pick my way across the stones and the dogs follow, one by one.

Ringo, the old fellow with one yellow tooth jutting from his jaw; Sandy, the greyhound, stretching from rock to rock like a caterpillar. Next, little Tommy Blackballs with his tail up high. Now silly Browny, his fox-like coat thick with burrs. Big Woofy crashes out from the scrub and leaps for the first stone only to lose his back legs and sweep downstream in the current. Snorting like a water-logged hippo he casually paddles to the bank where he emerges and shakes himself, flinging water all about.

Yips of excitement as Ringo and Tommy flush a rabbit from the grassy embankment. There's a short chase with Sandy making up good ground but the rabbit reaches the safety of the boxthorns. We move on following the course of the river upstream. Treading carefully through tall spindly grasses and tussocks in swampy areas and on through a rocky gully littered with huge boulders tumbled down from above. Every now and then a cloud is swept across the face of the sun and the scene is in twilight for brief periods. The wind is picking up a little. Up ahead I hear the pack barking in the heat of the chase but the *bad habits* have the advantage in the blackberry brambles and nettles.

A rabbit appears in front of me lower down on the flat. Sitting up-right in the swaying grass he makes a set shot. I slowly lower the shovel to the ground and slip the rifle from my shoulder. I take aim, hold my breath and squeeze the trigger. A short crack as the echo is carried away on the wind. The rabbit flicked his ears and looked around. A gang of cockatoos, startled, cast themselves from their perch screaming in a flurry of white frenzy. I swear and select another bullet. The rabbit tucks his ears in and squats. Aiming at the eye I pull the trigger only to hear a dull click. Cock the bolt again, aim, squeeze . . . click. Cursing under my breath I try again. Cock, aim, squeeze, crack.

The sound rings loud and true in my ear but the bullet strays. The rabbit flicks his ears and looks around. Again the cockatoos rise.

Screaming blue murder they circle and re-form to settle like a shroud of snow upon the limbs of a dead gum tree. In silent rage and frustration I consider throwing the gun at the rabbit but he is gone.

Ringo and Tommy Blackballs have returned to investigate the shooting. They sniff about and look up at me as if to say 'What, no rabbits?' They turn their tails to me and I follow them. The river runs deep and wide here, drifting through a shady avenue of knotty red gums. Shy blue waterhens dart from thickets of reeds squawking in alarm. A pair of wild ducks depart in a flap creating rings of crystal on the mirrored surface. Metallic green dragonflies skim across reflections of the sky. The clouds are ganging up and the breeze is getting cheeky as I fight my way through sword grass and blackberry bushes to a clearing where the dogs are intently scraping at a couple of burrows.

A bunny springs from a pophole and Sandy snatches it by the hind legs. The bunny squeals and Browny clamps his teeth on the neck and pulls. The two dogs are effectively skinning their prey when Woofy, wild-eyed and crazed, rushes in and plunges his yellow fangs into the soft pink flesh of the rabbit's mid-section. Bones crack as the rodent is split three ways. Tommy and Ringo have their heads inside the burrows. Snorting, snarling and pawing madly at the soil. This is a good sign. I collect some sizable rocks and block most of the exits. 'Okay Tommy, look out now.' I start to dig, following the small tunnel until I have exposed a good deal of the tiny chambers. Pausing now and then to allow Ringo or Tommy to poke their trusty noses into the hole.

Tommy Blackballs is a small dog, black as tar and beady-eyed. He has his head down in the burrow, his hindquarters skyward. This is how he got his name, for his namesakes are exposed and displayed in comic fashion. Old Ringo looks on patiently. Tommy shows signs of desperation. Howling and scratching frantically at the small opening. I drag him back and feed a slender stick of bracken into the burrow. Sure enough, I feel soft flesh and movement. On the jagged end of the stick are fine slivers of fur. Kneeling down I reach into the chamber and grip the powerful hind legs of a full-grown buck rabbit. I break its neck immediately and slit the stomach. I throw the warm bloodied contents to the dogs, making sure that Tommy and Ringo enjoy the liver and heart. While the jackals feed I pull out three more pop-eyed rabbits.

Homeward bound as shades of evening creep round the river valley.

The wind bites cold and sends a shiver down the glassy face of the river. The reeds and rushes sway in harmony with the trees. Clouds mill about like angry black bulls waiting to stampede. At the crossing place a mob of sheep take shelter in some low scrub. As we draw near they nervously disperse and this excites Browny and Woofy who launch into the round-up like old hands. I am reminded of the latest mission gossip about sheep being savaged by stray dogs and local farmers up in arms. I roar at the two marauders, throwing stones and cursing wildly. Ringo, Tommy and Sandy take heed of my threats and stay behind. Woofy changed course when a stone bounced off his ribs. He took to the river, swam across and headed home. Browny had a change of heart too. When I approached he flopped to the ground and rolled onto his back pleading for mercy. As no damage has been done I let him be, although I imagine Browny and Woofy transformed into wolflike creatures under a full moon; thirsting for the blood of the sheep.

We haul into Granny's backyard as darkness falls. The back door cracks open and light and sound spill out on the back porch. Little David steps out for a piss. He doesn't see me in the outer darkness so I sneak up close and say loudly, 'I didn't mean to scare you mate.'

His little body jolts in fright. Fumbling with his trousers and flashing wide eyes at me he swallows a gulp and says, 'How many you got, Uncle Johnny?'

'I got four, buddy, here, take 'em inside for me.' He drags the corpses inside and I put the shovel in the pine tree for safekeeping.

In the warmth of the kitchen I stand at the sink pulling skin from the rabbits. A green-eyed ginger tom cat waits at my feet. Music and laughter escape from the lounge as Mouse comes in.

'Hey Johnny boy, they nice big rabbits.' She collects three blue cans from the fridge.

'Yeah, took me a while to get 'em.' I replied.

'Uncle Percy and Donny and Brenda in here,' she motions to the lounge. 'Mum said there's stew on the stove and come and have a drink.'

'Okay, I'll just have a wash and a feed first.'

In the lounge Aunty Faye is in charge of the record player.

Selecting scratchy old favourites and playing requests. Slim Dusty sings something about driving a truck but the lights coming over the hill are blinding him. Granny has baby Heather cradled in one arm.

Gently rocking in her chair, she hums softly into Heather's ear as she has done for countless other children. Including myself. In the fire-light a glass of beer glows golden amber on the floor by her feet. Uncle Percy sips from his glass and takes a pull on his pipe. He pushes his hat back and looks into the fire tapping his foot to the music. A nervous red kelpie waits faithfully by his knee.

Aunty Faye shouts, 'This one's for you Donny.' Uncle Donny, his left hand bandaged from a fight with a drunken fish tank, untangles his long legs and swings into his Elvis impersonation. With his jet-black hair brushed back he dances about can in hand, miming and making faces till his ankles collide and he stumbles.

'Sit down, Don, sit down before ya fall down,' warns Aunty Brenda.

'Play it again, Faye, I'm just warmin' up.'

Aunty Brenda pulls black Elvis down into his chair.

Little David, Bernadette and Connie roll about on the couch in fits of laughter at Uncle Donny's antics. Aunty Faye reminds them. 'School in the morning you kids, get to bed now, it's getting late.' She herds the reluctant children from the room and Mouse collects her sleeping babes and takes them to bed.

Uncle Percy refills my glass. In the break between records we hear the sound of light rain on the roof. After a while the music is louder, the drinks flow faster and everyone talks at once. From what I can gather the dog catchers came out today and took Devil away for biting Great Granny Mary. Two fat coppers escorted the dog catchers while they picked up Devil and other dogs who chased the divvy van up the road.

'Just as well Ringo and Tommy went with you budda boy,' said Granny. She had a soft spot for her two hunters.

'They all lucky they didn't get pinched,' says Aunty Brenda. We all agree on this and fill our glasses.

I stare into the fire and think of what could have happened. I have a vision of Ringo, Tommy Blackballs, Sandy, Browny and Woofy peering misty-eyed through the bars of their cold cells. Old Ringo plays 'Swing Low Sweet Chariot' on the mouth organ, while Devil is led away to be strapped into an electric chair.

The rain is heavier now, drumming on the rooftop. Another log is reduced to ashes and the cold wind slips under the door. Granny wants to hear 'Me and Bobby McGee'.

'That's the one, tidda girl. Turn it up a bit.' Uncle Percy is telling us how he picked the daily double today. Uncle Donny reckons he was waiting on the results of a photo finish to win the Quadrella, but by the time his horse got there it was too dark to take the picture. I'm almost too tired to laugh. Again my eyes are drawn into the glow of the coals and I dream my dreams only to see them go up the chimney in smoke. I say goodnight to all and step out into the darkness.

... *Freedom's just another word for nothing left to lose and nothing ain't worth nothing but it's free* ...

The words are carried on the wind as I cross the muddy yard to the bungalow.

I light up the lamp and flop my weary frame on the bed. The wind kicks up a storm now and the crack and rumble of thunder splits the sky. The bulls are stampeding. Hailstones sweep across the settlement in sheets of ice. The mission is lit up in electric flashes of lightning or is it Bunjil taking photographs? The driving rain is deafening on the bungalow. Uncle Russell must hear the same sound on his roof. I imagine his dogs gathered round his bed in the darkness, pricking their ears up at the sound of thunder. I wonder what Uncle Russell dreams of. Rain, rain, rain. What's that song Granny sings? It starts off ... *there's a rainbow round the dear old Hopkins River* ...

B e r n a r d   C o h e n

LIFE IN PIECES
1 9 9 6

1

Nothing about him is new. All is the affectation of art. He takes his smile from Goya. He takes his benevolent eyes from the old school principal. He is engineered impeccably. He is Sir Robert frozen in thought, heavy black shadows, thin highlights across his forehead, his lips flexing to the left. He is Sir Robert, frozen in time: the image of him poses with the scissor blades open, the ceremonial ribbon between, the thrusting-chinned dignitaries around him hoping to share with him the cameras' blown kisses. He is Sir Robert frozen in space, à la Cartier-Bresson: he is leaping over a puddle of oil. In the background is Flinders Street Railway Station. The sky is ridged with white against heavy greys. Here he remains, in the archives.

2

His parents predeceased him. In dying they acted out a child's endless abandonments. He has forgotten them. He has done it all on his own. The world provides him with enough material for any project of which he can conceive. He has produced national monuments from Venetian glass, antelope hide, ice, titanium foil and advertising billboards, a permanent sound tape singing the national songs. A nation provides him with the capital to make anything he wants. He makes a continent-size screen to hide his lost parents.

3

The politician is always under suspicion. Menzies insists he did nothing wrong. He was an honest man. He took no payment; he did no favours. He never enriched himself. The public servants were safe. He never commented on your astonishing breasts.

4

The language, if one allows it to do its work, produces anguish. His words come back to him in the melancholy voices of newsreaders and historians, actors and political analysts. He never repeated anything and yet his words echo and echo. He is the prime minister, and the succession of new policy contexts permutated anything that might have sounded similar. He is the prime minister? Time has moved past him, subtly shading everything he said.

5

He is pissed as anything, waiting for a bus. His identity is lost. He is hanging onto the bus stop pole, swinging like a dunny door. He is a very old man. His life was ordinary, but he loves Australia, full of places called Nuriootpa and at every moment people are oiling squeaky gates. The bus pulls up and the driver, not recognising him, nonetheless comes from behind the wheel to help him up the steps.

6

Hate him, hate him, spit on his memory, scowl at the mention of his name. He doesn't care, he'll never deign to hate you. He has so many friends whom he may treat with disdain. And this is all he needs in the manner of pleasure: the sharpness of his tongue, his quick wit immortalised in the diaries of its victims.

7

He also offers flexibility. He smiles without implications, waiting for you to add political meaning. He is so readable. He's like an overwritten poem, full of its reader's agonies. Never mind that the half-moon of his presence is hollowing; away from you he is as if self-contained.

8

Once there was a child who would grow up to be him and then to die. That is it. That is all there is. Beyond this, life is too complicated to narrate. He could tell you epic stories, huge, many-chaptered accounts of his time. He can speak all night without a note. He can read you encyclopaedias of his national achievements. But, in the pauses and hesitations, in the drawings of breath, behind every syllable and phatic exhalation, is silence.

9

The nameless department stores in Melbourne appear organic, not merely quoted from similar stores in London, New York and Toronto. In the menswear sections, he is given preferential treatment: 'May I measure you, sir? May I decorate your midriff with my cool palms?'

He clothes himself with the freshest colours, the most brilliant ties, the most comforting jackets. He wears his hat straight and without irony. He wears it as a necessity, this unquestionable headwear.

His adornment is in the public interest. He dresses as a public service. He is bejewelled with fine speeches. He has no identifiable or censoriously traceable past. His clothing hangs from his assertive shoulders as purposefully as monologues.

10

Imagine if he was to begin explaining himself and then, halfway through his explanation, suddenly went out of fashion. He doubts you would wait around till the end of his story. He doubts it very much. You'd be out of hearing range so fast the Doppler effect wouldn't touch you.

11

When people bring Menzies to mind, do they also think of his mother? Perhaps they wonder what she taught him, which of his gestures are hers, if his posture was her posture, how she spoke to him as he grew up – whether she deepened her voice to match his deepening voice, what of her ideas he made his own and then formed into policy, whether his taste in art was a reflection of hers. Perhaps she read everything he said in public, sometimes in draft, sometimes in the newspapers. When he said something she felt reflected poorly on his family, on motherhood, or on his upbringing and by extension on her, she probably telephoned him, sobbing, 'Robert, Robert, how could you?'

12

These days he is depressed all the time. All the work he did to build the nation is expressed in colourful T-shirts, department store window displays, advertising signs on the sides of government buses, the deep pits of building sites, the shapes of new cars, the attentions of fathers to their little children, the rhythm of the cicadas, the sports pages. He is filled with great sadness at what could have been or what would have been even had he never lived. He pauses at 'Men Working' signs and ponders as the car engine hums: had it not been for him, would the roads have come so far?

13

For him, unchangeability is infinitely preferable and more elusive. Once, on the hottest day of summer, he lay on the floor for hours trying not to perspire. When the southerly came through that night at nine-fifteen, the temperature dropped suddenly. He opened all the doors and windows and the house filled with wind. When the change came through, he stalked around the house finding eddies everywhere.

14

The other politicians think public opinion is slightly amusing, but to be avoided. And yet, public opinion is what he keeps coming back to. Is he loved? Is this the issue? May God protect his psyche from the newspapers!

15

He *is* loved. The wind hisses his name. In rainstorms, the thunder cracks his name across the low clouds. The traffic is his mantra. The developing industries chant after him. This is suprahuman emotion. No mere person is capable of such devotions. The slamming doors love him: why else do they make such a commotion?

16

He has: a residence, a holiday house, a pastoral property, two cars, the use of a government car with driver, some very fine furniture, a bed in each bedroom, china, silver cutlery, a television, a wireless with good speakers, the opportunity to travel with his wife, an aging cat . . .
  It's not enough. What he wants is his youth.

17

In his dreams there is a beautiful woman. In her hands is a secret elixir which must destroy them both. In his dreams, he has never seen into her eyes. She is a secret woman. This is the woman whom he is always approaching but never touching. She teases his dreams. When she speaks, it is his voice he hears. When she moves, it is with his gait. When this woman smiles, though her eyes are closed, he sees his teeth in her mouth. He is this woman who tears himself to shreds.

18

He once gave a speech to the Country Women's Association of NSW. To women, he spoke with charm and poise, though he always felt he was speaking across an unbridgeable gap. 'Women, ladies', he would say, never hiding behind the sort of camaraderie men expected of him, never pretending he was spontaneous or mouthing other than approximations of what he had been advised they might wish to hear.

In exchange, the women were permitted to own him. He permitted them. He consented. He is theirs.

19

A very close friend, also in politics, once told him there was no-one else who took all the criticism so much to heart as Menzies did.

'Tell yourself it is not personal,' the friend advised. 'Chant this to yourself until you believe it one hundred per cent. It's not really directed at you. If you were someone else, you'd cop just as much.'

Menzies doubted that. Who else had ever been accused of carelessness, scruffiness, unpreparedness, rudeness, submissiveness, being on the leash of various pastoralists, industrialists and ideas mobs, overcaution, ignorance, poor education, elitism, plagiarism, improvisation, and so on (even hypersensitivity) (these all quotes from said columns). His voters were also denigrated: cap-wearing, subcultural, unBritish, Pacific Islander, dependent, naive, foolhardy, Antipodean, pre-industrial, et cetera (also direct from columns).

Well, he thought, nothing to lose, I'll try this self-inflation thing. Immediate results: opinion columns complained of his new-found arrogance, his impermeability to criticism, his blank looks in parliament. The polls fell eight points. He changed back.

This brief period of insensitivity was the only time during his long service when he did not suffer, when it did not hurt to adhere to his strong views.

20

They write that he is not a great prime minister, not a great leader.

Perhaps not. But look at their examples. Compare him with David Lloyd George, Robespierre. Consider George I of England. Remember old Russians, Prussians or Ottomans. Think of Jesus or Moses or St Paul. Line him up against Augustine and Eric the Red and Aethelred the Unrede. Put in your mind George Washington or Gustavus II of Sweden. All of them are so old. Most wouldn't know how to switch on a microphone or knot a tie. In their places and centuries he would be more than adequate. He would be startlingly successful.

<h2 style="text-align:center">21</h2>

Why is he a politician and others mere citizens? In a room full of mosquitoes, he is as likely to be bitten as the next man. That is all he will say in defence of the others. He is careful not to attack those less politically endowed but, still, it is necessary to be firm. He is a leader, with the stuff of leadership. Others are not.

<h2 style="text-align:center">22</h2>

If he were not criticised for his leadership, for determination, courage and sense of purpose, he might not feel compelled to point out that what he is called upon to defend is something supposedly highly valued. This is what he argues: leadership is only valued in the abstract. Those who praise the abstract quality of leadership frown upon its concrete and real practice.

<h2 style="text-align:center">23</h2>

Ah, but then there are his satellites. His wife, his deputy. These are people who understand quality. In the presence of his wife and his deputy, he realises how minute is this life, and how like microscopic parasites on the backs of insects are his critics. His deputy and his wife have no enemies; enemies gravitate to him. Menzies negotiates with foreign leaders. He vacillates, fluctuates, backs down, loses face. His wife and his deputy need not compromise. Their good manners suffice.

<h2 style="text-align:center">24</h2>

From time to time, he thinks about the bodies of women . . . For the remainder, most imagine the politician as a figure in history. But he is different. There are no previous politicians like him. He sees people differently. When he thinks of people, he thinks of everything imaginable;

he thinks of all the beings in the universe, all the gestures, all the shifts in scale and form. He loves people because they embody possibility.

25

For Menzies, the technique of living is drawn from the ocean, the earth and the atmosphere. We are like the sea, constructed of multitudes of amplitudes and frequencies. We are like a rock in wearing down by force of repetition. Every breath one draws is of a different length and composition. We are like air in filling all imaginable spaces with the sense of volume.

26

After his election to parliament, he went to dinner with close friends to celebrate what he considered a temporary and minor career move. It was not yet his style to throw lavish and sumptuous banquets for people he didn't know. He was not a presumptuous young man.

Amongst the happy and usual banter, it occurred to him that he knew these people no better than newly acquired supporters he shook hands with in the street. It could have been anyone sitting around this table making droll and knowing comments about the shrinking empire. And yet, it was a modestly happy time, and provided a feeling he would always choose to feel, if he were able. Sitting there, contented, he decided to lead the nation.

27

What he would say to his siblings: 'Stop talking to me about the goddamned weather. Its apparent randomness is no concern of mine'. He doesn't believe the change of seasons indicates anything at all. These clouds shifting around might be exactly the same ones as yesterday. He didn't see them move off. How does he know they've blown away into the future? Stop talking to him about your new technological instruments. He doesn't want explanation. Life is chance, whether the winning ticket was sold by God or spawned by frogs. This is what he told his siblings down by the creek collecting tadpoles in round, yellow ice-cream containers, as they punched holes in the lids so the tadpoles could breathe until they died.

The sky today is so beautiful, a pale, pale European blue between grey-edged clouds. Eucalypts break the horizon in a dozen places.

Currawongs insist on territory. If he were to walk fifty steps into the forest, he would discover an identical creek to the childhood creek he carries in his mind.

28

In the old days, every word he spoke during the day – policy and wisdom – was recorded and transcribed, carried to his department and the other ministries, interpreted, and elucidated into national imperatives. His words were like uranium, with a long half-life and the promise of prosperity. When Menzies spoke, the air textured and beaded.

A politician's job is to make everything he or she touches political. It is to create issues from anecdotes and hearsay. In this sense, even once he retired from politics, he remained a politician. No longer. Nowadays when he makes a statement or gives an interview, the journalists' reports leak sympathy and sentiment. No matter how forthrightly he speaks, no matter how extreme or crucial his point, he is forced to read of the dampness around his eyes, his lapses in concentration.

But the words he speaks at night are different. They are words that carry a different potency, the potency of secrets. Nothing will be published. Nothing will have effects. His nightwords are pure potential power, seductive as the confidences of gods.

29

What is he waiting for when he waits? The fruit trees produce fruit and men pick it and pack it and transport it to market where greengrocers argue about falling demand and growers give business-like laughs and advise them of the importance of designing effective displays. The fruit turns up in his bowl, stewed into unrecognisable shapes. Calves are dragged into the world while their mothers bellow. The calves grow, and produce milk and more calves, all in the time it takes him to call for his glasses. Parrots pick the nut trees bare before he can blink. Millions of plastic pegs fall into plastic bags and are mechanically heat-sealed. Corporations lodge applications for patents.

People expected so much of him and then they stopped. There is no-one left to frustrate except himself.

30

To be him now is to conjure his image from the page, to re-read his speeches and reconstitute the person who chose that sequence for those words. It is to stare at photographs and newsreel footage, to read the accounts of journalists and biographers, the interviews with associates, friends and family. These people have not found him. Perhaps they are too fearful to want him truly. Perhaps he can no longer exist. To find him is to wake up at odd hours through the night and to feel his body aching. It is to move his saliva around with his tongue and to put off the swallowing because of the pain. It is to lean on his stick and move across the room slowly, hurting every step of the way.

31

He will make a new start just as soon as he finishes with his life to date. If he had his life to live again, he would hold on to it so tightly. He would fill it again and again. There is no such thing as a minute wasted.

THE JEWELLER'S SHOP
1905

During the dreary winter of '70, Fred Schlapp and Antoine Dubois had the one decent claim in the vicinity of the Native Cat. And they deserved such luck, if only for the spirit which had prompted each to select a racial enemy as his working mate. For there was a principle underlying their partnership. At a time when Socialism presented itself to the average mind as a crude and personal fad, rather than as an evolutionary National policy, these men were Socialists; and happy where no Rhenish trumpet sung, they purposely made their fellowship an object-lesson to the society of the Native Cat.

They lived in the hut nearest mine, and we were intimate, though I was, in the most literal sense, an Individualist. Abe Spoker – last of my three mates – had cleared out, leaving me sole owner of the four men's ground registered as No. 309. Not being able to work a forty-foot shaft of my own, I just baled a bucket of water every morning, by way of complying with the labour conditions, and spent the rest of my time partly in fossicking for half-tucker, and partly in futile negotiations for renewal of tick at the store. I still believed in No. 309 as firmly as any Orangeman believes in the Number of the Beast.

Returning to my hut one evening, I picked up one of the Melbourne weeklies, which somebody had dropped; and, reading as I went along, I found the announcement of the Franco-German War. Thinking that the news might have some interest for my European friends, I looked into their hut as I passed, and gave them half the paper. It might have been fifteen or twenty minutes afterward – at all events, I had just roused up the fire and put my last three spuds in the embers to roast – when I heard something like an altercation next door. I went outside, and listened –

'*Sacré cochon de tête carrée! il y a longtemps que nous vous avons donné une brûlée, cette fois-ci nous allons vous etouiller!*'

'Du bist ein meserabler Froschfresser, und ein verdammter Constan-
tinopoliander-schustergeselle! Das nextema wen ir euth am Rhein shen,
lasst dan werden wir eith eure rote Hosen apziehen und den erseufen!'

Jupiter! Had it come to this? Yes, and worse; for there was a sound
of trampling and scuffling, followed by a clatter of tin table service on
the floor, and more confusion of tongues. I darted across, to act as
referee, but the door was fastened inside, and I could only watch the
misunderstanding through a crack in the wall. The candle was out, but
the bright firelight showed my two friends dragging, pushing, swaying
over the littered floor; not in body-holts, but each with his hands
woven in the other's hair. No blows were struck; it was purely a question of the respective root-hold of Gallic and Teutonic thatch. Both
varieties of roofing material gave way at the same time, and each
combatant glanced round for a weapon. Antoine secured a long vinegar
bottle, and Fred a short-handled frying pan.

At the next onslaught the bottle smashed on the edge of the pan,
and Antoine, now weaponless, made a tactical movement, head-
foremost, through the calico window beside him.

But man is not constructed for sliding swiftly across narrow sills;
and before Antoine's hands touched the ground outside, Fred pinned
his feet against the wall inside, and fell furiously on his unprotected
rear with the flat of the frying pan – smote him hip and thigh, as the
Scripture bluntly puts it.

I kicked at the door, demanding fair play, British or foreign, but
Fred still spanked and spared not. At last I ran round to the window;
but by this time Antoine had managed to kick loose and clear himself.
Then he disappeared in the darkness, and I returned to my hut.

I had finished my three spuds, and was wondering where the next
three would come from, when Antoine entered, and sat down by the
fire, with danger in his eye. He sat there all night, declining to take
the spare bunk, with one of my two blankets. The frying pan had
entered into his soul.

In the morning he went to the store, and presently brought back
such a quantity of eatables as made me resolve to neither borrow nor
lend. After breakfast, he accompanied me to Hungry Gully, where I
had left my tub and tools. We worked and yarned together all day, and
cleaned up at sundown for seven or eight grains of dull, water-worn
gold.

After supper, leaving Antoine in my hut, I went across and had a long, friendly conversation with Fred. My friends' claim was about worked out, and I wanted them to join me in unearthing the half-ton of gold located just where the rainbow met the ground in No. 309. My proposal was that they should buy into the claim for a couple of notes each – and I wanted ten shillings of the money *down*.

Next day, Antoine and I shifted the fossicking plant, and tried the Mosquito, panning out a pinch of sharp, bright reef-gold – again about seven or eight grains. Antoine was disgusted; yet this was good compared with the average of the district – bar the solitary sluicing claim from which my two friends had taken sixty ounces in three months. Antoine forgot to give me our two days' gold, but that was neither here nor there; he had given me ten times its value in stores.

Fred, Antoine and I spent the evening together over a half-gallon of villainous ale from the shanty, and arranged to give No. 309 a fair trial in the morning, leaving the premium for after consideration. The tiff between the two mates was smoothed over by this time. Blessed are the peacemakers.

After an easy forenoon's baling of the accumulated water, I lowered Fred and Antoine down the shaft with some tools; then pegged the windlass – with the bucket just off the bottom – and followed by the rope. Fred was panning off a prospect in a pool of water up the north drive, while Antoine held the candle. I had barely time to see a fine show of gold in the dish, when Antoine caught sight of me over Fred's shoulder, and sharply ordered me to keep away. I returned up the rope, and waited.

Half an hour afterward, I pulled up the tools and the prospectors. On reaching the surface, Fred – who was the most deeply scientific man I ever knew – stepped aside to examine privately and minutely, by the sunlight, the prospects which he had collected in a bit of paper. Whilst doing so, an involuntary exclamation broke from him, and he glanced furtively round; but I was occupied in detailing, and Antoine in hearing, how the claim had been wrecked through the pigheadedness of my former mates.

My friends kept together, and avoided me, for the rest of the day; but the next morning, before daylight, Antoine came into my hut and woke me quietly –

'Ve vill vash damfine prospec' in you clem,' said he impressively.

'Olt Sauerkraut he vant grab de lot. Dat iss de Sherman go alvays time. Shoke me off; shoke me off. Ver vell. I haf vat you call 'settle-me-up' vit him. You vill qvick, qvick sell him you clem. Tventee note – no less – cash dan on de top of de nell. Tventee note, mind!' and Antoine slipped out as quietly as he had entered.

Early in the forenoon of the same day he packed his swag, bade goodbye to Fred and me, took the track toward Spring Creek; and the Native Cat knew him no more.

As Antoine disappeared across the hill, Fred, in casual conversation, depreciated No. 309 till my heart was in my boots. But he was a good sort. He would give me ten shillings to face the road with, and take the claim off my hands. Here was a change! However, remembering Antoine's counsel, I carelessly remarked that I should like to see some of the Gluepot fellows first. I could tell them something about the claim that would set them tumbling over each other in the race for shares. And I turned away toward the Gluepot.

Fred, starting afresh from that base, sprung to £2; then to £5; then little by little, to £10; then, more slowly still, to an anguish-laden £20; and we closed the bargain. By his desire, we set off at once for the Mining Registrar's Office, which was on the Golconda, about a mile distant.

Now it happened that I had never been able to run a Miner's Right. The few pounds I had embezzled on leaving home had been thrown away to the last penny in the greenhorn purchase of a fourth share in No. 309, from the original holder, who, according to custom, had merely handed me his paper, endorsed:

> To the mineing register Pleas transfer this Share too Thomas
> Collins and oblige yours truely
> JOHN MILTOM

But the transfer couldn't take place till I produced a Miner's Right; and you might as well have asked me to produce a patent of nobility. Of course, I held the other three shares on the same fragile tenure.

So, as we walked on together, I explained to Fred that he would have to advance me six shillings – the price of a Miner's Right – in order to bridge the gap between the original holders and himself. He readily consented; but shortly afterward found that he had forgotten his purse in the hurry. This meant postponement of the business till next day. Being, however, so far on the way, he thought he would go on to the Golconda, to see a man he knew. I therefore returned alone to the Native Cat.

I lay on my bunk for the rest of the afternoon; reflecting that the claim might be no good after all; and investing my £20 in twenty different ways. In the evening, going out for firewood, I noticed four blue documents tacked on the uprights of the windlass. A closer inspection showed these to be formal applications by Frederick Schlapp, for the four men's ground registered as No. 309, and now abandoned by the original holders. The claim was jumped.

Hungry as I was for satisfaction, I perceived that a subterranean policy would suit me best. I still held the ground by prior occupation, and until Fred's application was confirmed there was no law to prevent me putting improvements on the claim. I proposed beginning with the face of the south drive, where a leaking, dripping wall of five feet thick held back the mass of water which filled the old workings of the original Native Cat. These extended half a mile, shallowing up to the surface, and tapping no end of perennial springs.

To keep Fred out of the way, I interviewed him through a crack in his hut, to such effect that, for some weeks to come, he would certainly avoid all places favourable to ambuscade.

Powder, fuse, paper and pitch being inedible, I had the material for one good earthquaking cartridge. I lowered a gad-hammer, two drills and a tamping bar into the shaft; then followed down the rope, carrying my cartridge and candle. At the face of the south drive I threw off the corn-sack tunic with which poverty had made me acquainted, and got to work. Some time after midnight I set the fuse going, and lit out for the shaft, leaving my tunic and tools to puzzle antiquarians of future ages. Before I got halfway to the surface, the explosion came off, nearly smothering me with powder-smoke. But I heard the churning of the water as it came in with a forty-foot head, and returned to my hut filled with a great, silent peace. I am of Irish extraction.

The claim was granted to Fred. He hired a cheap man and began baling.

Next day he rigged twenty-gallon hide buckets and hired two more cheap men.

A few days later, he sacked his men and hired a portable engine, with pumping plant.

After a week's continuous working, he sacked the engine and, with incredible pertinacity, set to work taking levels for a tunnel. This would give him nearly two hundred yards of nasty slate to go through, but he tackled it single-handed; evidently determined to run the claim as a one-man enterprise. At last I began to pit his infatuation, and called round on him while he was putting in his second set.

'You're doing a foolish thing, Fred,' said I. 'I'm not interested in the claim now, and I know her for what she is; she's worse than a duffer; she's a stringer. She'd ruin Money Miller.'

'Der vogs mit der sour greps!' sneered Fred. 'Unt you schall der vater svamp mit – eh?'

'Yes; I put a bit of a shot in her before I left.'

'I veesh you will progue (broke) you neg mit. Bot der Gott schall pe ver goot. You pelong notteen mo you svag mit; unt minezelluf I pelong dot glaim mit der yeweller's yop.'

'Jeweller's shop!' I repeated in dismay.

'Yoos so. Dot knog you – eh? I vill esplen: Vhen dwo rons golt come altogedder mit, unt after von py hezelluf, dhere schall pe der yeweller's yop – eh?'

'Yes, that's the theory, Fred.'

'Teory pe plo! – I haf on Pallarat vorg (work). Now you schall see – mit hanse off, py yimgo!'

He produced a match-box, and from this, a prospect, enfolded in ply after ply of paper; then with a splinter of wood he separated the prospect into two fairly equal parts. One portion consisted of a few bits of dull, water-worn gold; the other of sharp, bright reef-gold; and there might have been a third of a dwt. in each lot.

'Dhere!' he continued, in ungenerous triumph. 'Minezelluf I schall dot brobec' in der vorgins (workings) vash yoos vhere I plattivell (bloody well) blease, mit der nort' drife, unt mit der sout' drife. Dwo roms golt dhere – eh? Vot pig yackass dot Yermance vos! Youzelluf you schall dhree monse vorg mit dot yewleller's yop you nose onter, semple ass der A P C. Go vay unt posh you het in von pag!'

I could find no rejoinder. Like a ragged fossicker in a dream I stood hazily contemplating the two samples – each so different from the smooth, scaly gold with which No. 309 had lured her former victims to ruin. But had I seen those two diverse prospects before – under other conditions, or in some former state of existence? Or was it merely a case of unconscious cerebration? Or was it my brain softening under the cares of the world and the deceitfulness of riches?

'Minezelluf,' continued Fred, repacking his prospect, 'I schall pe mit von yare der yentlemans, mit der golt vatch unt der belldopper, unt you schall youzelluf mit plattivel zbite on der gom-tree hang. Soolim!'

Matthew   Condon

THE SANDFLY MAN
1 9 9 5

I am curled up on a canvas bunk in my parents' summer holiday tent and I can hear him coming, the Sandfly Man.

I don't know then, aged five, that he will be my personal ghost for the rest of my life, a figure that hisses and walks through mist, never fully formed, perpetually coming towards me, coming for me, but never quite catching me. I don't want to look at him but like all the five-year-olds I cannot help myself. Through the gauze of the tent window I see him. He walks in slow motion. He wears a sort of space suit with an eye slit, gloves, boots, and carries a tank on his back. In one hand he has a long steel rod that is attached to the tank. From the end of the rod he sprays glittering clouds of pesticide. The Sandfly Man. Stalking down the laneways of the caravan park. Out to kill the blood-sucking, disease-carrying dipterous fly of the genus *Phlebotomus* or *Calicoidus*. The spray whorls around him in tendrils that catch the late afternoon sun. He is coming for me through the mist. He hisses like steam. I hide under an eiderdown on the bunk and pray the ghost will go away.

Our family lived in Brisbane. Father worked in a finance company. Mother spent some time in a butcher shop, cutting carcasses alongside men without the full complement of fingers. (She once saw a colleague slice three fingers clean off, and swore one of the fingers jumped around on the cool tiled floor.) My twin sister and I went to school. She played piano, I played football. We were all Catholics, went to mass, had confirmation medals and pictures of Jesus, knew prayers off by heart, went to confession and begged forgiveness for not eating our brussels sprouts. Our family was just like thousands of others in Brisbane, Queensland.

Every summer, too, we were just like other families. There were two options. You either went to the North Coast for the holidays, or you went south to the Gold Coast. You either stayed in a caravan or you stayed in a tent. We always had a decent tent, perhaps because father was once an accomplished boy scout. And we always stayed at Tallebudgera Creek Caravan Park on the Gold Coast. Not far away at Burleigh Heads Caravan Park, my father's parents had an annual caravan site. They were close but far enough away. This, I see now, is what it is like in Queensland. Families near each other but just out of sight. Relatives living in the same streets or a few blocks away in the same suburb. Families packing up for the summer holidays and still within each others' orbit.

It was the same with the caravan parks. The same people on the same sites, year in year out. You'd see everyone grow up, get older, turn grey, grow taller, fatter or thinner. It is the peculiar nature of summer caravan park life that the effects of time passing become so much more real. If you see somebody only once a year, their ageing is shockingly apparent, their lines and greyness so marked, the changes so stark. Some years someone would be missing. An elderly man, an elderly woman, a child. Small holes appeared in the fabric of the park. There would be discreet talk about this amongst the adults. Tragedies. Deaths. Infidelities. Cancer, they'd say, riddled with it. Electrocuted, they'd say, in his garden shed. Ran off with the postman, can you believe that? All manner of intricate matters that would lead back into the missing year between summers, that lost block of time where anything could happen. There would be quiet discussion across annexe ropes, in the shower blocks with arms full of towels and soaps and toothbrushes in plastic containers. Whispering as quiet as the passage of a sandfly.

Yet the languorous life of the caravan park would go on. It struck me that this was a whole 'other' world with its own consistent shape, its own rules and regulations and borders that appeared in December and disappeared in January. It was a little Queensland within the low white fence of the park. Tiny homes away from home complete with flower pots and gas lanterns and tables and chairs and doormats and bedrooms and kitchens. With scuffs and thongs in rows outside the tent and portable dishwashing tubs on legs and stoves and mini pantries. It was our whole world writ small. Our lives pared down to the essentials, as simple as a child's drawings.

During the day we swam or slept, fished or slept, went to the picture theatre or slept, then had dinner and slept. Sometimes we would visit my grandparents across the bluff and sally through the cool evenings to the Burleigh Heads Ambulance Headquarters where they had, on the driveway, a lucky wheel. My grandparents had a passion for this wheel and would buy ticket after ticket and watch it spin round, hypnotised by the star in the centre and the blur of the numbers. I always remember the clack of that wheel and see it now not just as a piece of rubber striking dozens of metal prongs, but as the summer ebbing away, perhaps life itself, starting off with great energy then hitting a rhythm then slowing and slowing until, finally, it stops.

On other nights we would see from our bunks inside the dark tent our parents and their friends playing cards under the annexe. Their laughing faces in the glow of the gas lantern. Their concentration. All of them leaning in towards the light, towards the hiss of the lantern. If I closed my eyes I could see the Sandfly Man, coming for me through that swirling mist, moving slowly forward, his boots crunching on the dirt laneways. As I grew older and when I left Queensland he became much more. He was my fear of the church, the government, God, the devil all rolled into one. And he was summer, too. We would wake in our bunks with bite marks on our arms and legs and I knew the Sandfly Man would be coming again the next afternoon.

There were many other things that made those summers so precious, so unique and so peculiarly Queensland. There was the daily trip to the Miami Ice Factory, the blocks picked up by the icemen with pincers and taken away by my father in hessian sacks. There were the ouija board sessions under the stars and fingertips on an upturned glass. I don't remember now if it told the future or not. There is the family legend that my aunty discovered the name of her future husband. That was before I was born, but in the same caravan park, at the same site, at the same fold-out card table. There were the early evening showers in the shower blocks with soapy water from the other people's bodies roaring down the communal drain, a small milky river flashing past, and steam, always steam, like the mist that shrouded my ghost the Sandfly Man.

Later, in adolescence, this whole world began to shift. The girls on the beach became more significant. The summer heat itself changed meaning, became charged with sexuality, with longing not yet understood. Wet hair, hair still carrying the sea, became interesting. Moments alone on the basalt boulders at the end of Burleigh Heads beach became more frequent. And still our parents played canasta with their friends in the glow of the lantern, and our grandparents went to the lucky wheel, and the wheel ticked away.

At some point – it's impossible now to identify it exactly – we stopped going to the caravan park at Tallebudgera. My sister married and had her own children. I went to Sydney, and spent my first summer away from Queensland in a rented terrace in Surry Hills. On Christmas morning I sat alone on the floor of the lounge room with a glass of orange juice and some ham my mother had sent me, and watched the religious services on television. I wondered what they were doing back home. Whether they had arrived at the beach yet, erected the umbrellas, spread out the towels. Whether father had his rods and creel prepared. Whether mother had packed a hamper. Whether my sister was there with her own children. Whether the Sandfly Man was filling his tanks, checking the mechanics of his spray apparatus, slipping on his space suit and boots.

Now my sister and her family have their own annual caravan park site, this time on the North Coast. They play cards with their own friends around the gas lantern when their children are asleep, or pretending to sleep. They, too, open all their presents on Christmas Day in the cool of the annexe, then head for the ocean and swim and kick footballs and sleep in the shade of the pandanus trees. My sister has returned to it after a gap of several years. She is back inside our past, inside family, in the heart of Queensland in summer.

And still I haven't found my way back. Maybe I have to have my own children to get back there. It still exists. It's still all there. Something, though, is stopping me, and most of the time I blame him – the Sandfly Man. If I close my eyes he's there, this dark figure coming towards me, this ghost from the past, pushing through rolling clouds, reaching out for me.

Peter Corris

TIE-BREAKER
1989

'It's the only way,' Grafton told me.

'Then there's no way,' I said. 'Because I'm not going to do it.'

'You *have* to do it, George, otherwise you'll go inside for a long, long time. You'll improve your chess and your ping pong and probably change your sex habits, but you can forget about your tennis career. What'll you be in, say, ten years – thirty-three?'

'Thirty-four,' I said. 'I lied about my age to get an edge on the other kids in the juniors.'

'So you always were a crook.' Detective Sergeant Neil Grafton let out his belt a notch. I could smell the beer on him along with the expensive aftershave. 'I'm giving you a chance to rehabilitate yourself.'

We were sitting in a small, cold room off the Customs Hall at Sydney airport. My bags were on the floor; I was jet-lagged and my palms were wet. 'You're giving me a chance to be dead.'

'Drugs'll kill you anyway, George.'

'I know guys on the circuit who've been doing drugs for ten years. Still winning.'

Grafton smiled, which meant that his fat, white face creased up a bit. 'You wear the wire and talk to the man. Otherwise, it's all over the papers that "Jumping" George Trent, the number seven ranked tennis player in the world, takes cocaine and is depraved enough to import it into the country that is so proud of him.'

'A quarter of a thimble-full,' I said.

'If that, but there you are'.

'And it wasn't even mine.'

'It was in your bag, that's what counts. Well George, it's the fifth set, you're down four five and thirty forty on your serve. What's it going to be?'

What could I say? I was just back from the US Open where I'd lost

in the quarters – not so bad because I hate those cement courts like
poison. Colin Crawford and me had made the doubles final which
meant a lot to Colin, money- and ranking-wise. So he did some coke
before the match and we lost and the coke ended up in my bag somehow. I *don't* know any coke-taking winners; that was just sounding
tough for Grafton who'd been summoned by the customs officer after
inspecting my bag.

I was supposed to have a meet with a man, promise him access to
the coke-heads on the tour, and so keep a clean sheet. What a joke!

'Okay, I'll do it,' I said. 'Now let me get out of here. I'm bushed and
I'm supposed to be playing tomorrow.'

'It's only a New South Wales indoors,' Grafton said. 'You've won it
before, you'll probably win again if you keep a clear head.'

'Very funny. D'you know how important peace of mind is to an
athlete?'

'You shouldn't keep bad company, George. I'll be in touch.'

Grafton knocked and a customs officer opened the door. They had
a quick conference. The official said, 'You can go, Mr Trent,' and I was
out with my bags and racquets and problems. Grafton even knew about
Colin it seemed, so dobbing wouldn't be any use, even if I could've
brought myself to do it. There was only one thing to do – tell everything
to Roger Landy. I booked into the Hyatt Kingsgate, phoned Roger and
had him knocking on my door within thirty minutes. Roger is an
Australian and the number one security man, minder and arse-kicker
on the pro tennis tour. I was seeded number one for a Grand Prix
tournament: naturally he'd help.

'Shit,' Roger said after I'd told him the story.

'No, coke,' I said.

'You always were a smart-arse, George. And your backhand crumbled
under pressure against Olafsen.' Roger got up and started pacing the
room. He's a tall, thin character, dark and desperate-looking. They
say he gets a lot of sex on the tour but he also gets a lot of problems.
He bailed Bjorn Borg out of something crazy in Madrid in 1982, and
absolutely saved the life of one of the women (whom I won't name)
in Paris a few years later. He plays a reasonable sort of game himself
and can put a few past you until you get warmed up.

'Well, I need to practise, don't I? Which means I need good karma.
I don't need to be running around playing cops 'n' robbers.'

'Let me think. Yeah, well, it's not so different from what happened to you-know-who in San Francisco.'

'Who?' I said.

'Better lobber than you, sport. All right, here's what you do. First you have to meet this Grafton socially.'

'Why?'

'I'll play my game, you play yours.'

The NSW indoors was being held at the Entertainment Centre. That's fine for guys like Cash and McEnroe who play the guitar, but it feels a bit strange for me to be hitting balls on the very spot where I saw Mark Knopfler do 'Sultans of Swing'. Not that the two businesses are all that different – there's a lot of drugs in tennis, sexual power plays and when the gamblers get a grip on a player some pretty strange results can come up, even in the big events.

I had no trouble in the early rounds. Then I got a call from Grafton.

'Your place,' I said.

'Come on. I'll buy you dinner.'

'Your place, Grafton. You know all about me. I want to know a bit about you. I'm trusting you with my career, at least you can show me that you don't live in a sewer.'

It's one of the advantages of being a celebrity; people are happy to see you and ecstatic to feed you. He turned out to live in a suburban monstrosity in Ryde with a neat blonde wife named Peggy and a plump fifteen-year-old daughter name Gigi. Surprise, surprise, both of Fatty Grafton's women were tennis fans. I'd just beaten Emilio Gomez, a sneaky Argentinian, in the round of sixteen, so I treated it as a night out. Peggy and Gigi lapped up the glamour, the stories about Martina and all; I lapped up some of Grafton's good red. It was a great night. At the end of it, standing out by my rented Mazda, Grafton said, 'The next call you get from me will be all about business. Did you bring it?'

He'd asked me to bring along one of my racquets. I handed it over and he took it. 'Don't you want it autographed for Gigi?'

Grafton glared at me. He'd doubled my intake of the red and it was showing in the whites of his eyes. 'Don't be too smart, George. You've got Boris tomorrow.'

That was true. Boris was on the skids and didn't know it. It's funny, but I still think that an American college education is the best preparation for a pro tennis career. I left Sydney Boys' High after Year 10, but managed five semesters at the University of Arkansas on a tennis scholarship. I majored in English Literature, because I could read the novels and poems in the locker room. It gives you a poise that these raw kids who play in the French Open at fifteen don't get. Mind you, they get a lot of French. I reported on my social evening chez Grafton in minute detail to Roger Landy.

'Good,' Roger said.

'Good? When do I get off the hook?'

'You're not on the hook yet. You can't get off till you've been on. Worry about Boris.'

As it happened, I didn't have to worry about Boris. He dived for a forehand volley in the first set, jarred his elbow and knee, and couldn't get his big shots to work properly after that. I lobbed him to death and won in two. In the semi, I played Pierre Pascal. He held match point at 5–4 up and serving in the third set tie-breaker. His arm 'turned to jello' as my old coach at the U of Ark used to say. Double fault; 5 all. I served, rushed the net and hit a volley at his nuts which he deflected. 6–5, Trent. I served a fast kicker to his backhand and he had to jump and couldn't get any stick on it. I put the volley into the corner and was in the final.

The next day was the women's final so I had some time to worry about playing Christian Dart, a 198-centimetre South African left-hander. Dart was ranked eleven; if he beat me he'd get into the top ten. Apart from his serve, the worst thing about playing him was the prayers he muttered on the changes. They'd got my goat both times we'd played. Head to head, we stood 1–1. As it happened, I didn't get time to worry about Dart because Grafton rang in the afternoon while I was watching the women's match on TV.

'Tomorrow morning,' he said. 'Ten o'clock.'

'I'm playing in the afternoon.'

'All the better. You'll be keen to get this little matter behind you, eh? Here's what you do.' He told me where the man would be standing and what he'd be wearing. He told me to wear a tracksuit and carry a tennis bag. I was to be sure to collect the racquet he'd borrowed the other night, from the desk at the hotel, and to press the button on the bottom of the handle when I put it in the bag.

'What do I say?'

'I've seen you acting on the court, Georgie. You'd rather fake out an umpire than hit a smash. You'll think of something; just be sure he makes you a clear offer. Only a nice, clean tape does you any good.'

Landy was at the match. I left a message for him and paced my room until he arrived. I told him about the meet.

'That's tight,' he said. 'Still, it could be all right.'

'Could be, Roger? Could be? You said you had a plan.'

'I do. It depends on how things go tonight.'

'What things?'

'You don't want to know. How do you feel about Dart?'

'Like forfeiting and flying to London.'

He laughed. 'What's the prize money?'

'I don't give a shit.'

'Don't be like that, George. Go for a swim, have a sauna. Go to the movies. Have you seen *Rambo III*?'

I stared at him and felt the beginning of a cramp in my leg.

'Trust me,' Roger said. 'I'll see you around nine in the morning, God willing.'

'You sound like Dart with that God stuff.'

'It works for him.'

I had a practice session late in the afternoon and was lousy. I didn't sleep much. I was in great shape for the final. At nine o'clock Roger arrived; he was all smiles although the skin around his eyes was dark and he was sensitive to light and sound.

'Christ, what have you been doing?' I said.

He handed me an envelope. 'Working. Give this to Grafton after the meet. Don't look at it now, you'll spoil the fun.'

'Fun! What the fuck do I say to the pusher?'

'Nothing. Talk tennis.'

It was a beautiful Sydney early spring morning. Sunday, in my home town. Very quiet. A few church bells. Not many.

Dart would probably be in church praying to play his best. I walked from the hotel to Woolloomooloo carrying the tennis bag. I'd collected the racquet and pressed the button, but I hadn't worn the tracksuit. Fuck Grafton. I was wearing a T-shirt, jeans and sneakers. I didn't want to get shot dead in a tracksuit. Not classy.

A night breeze had cleared away the week's smog and some rain had flushed the bay. The water by the finger wharf looked clean and smelled like the ocean. I tried to remember the good sea-going writer the professor had talked about. Conrad. That's right. Maybe I could buy a Conrad novel and read it on the changes. The game's half psychology; maybe my reading Conrad would freak out Christian Dart.

I walked past the eye hospital and the Domain car park and up the footpath beside the Cahill Expressway as per instructions. He was standing on the dividing strip about a tennis court's length from the entrance to the tunnel. He fitted Grafton's description – fair hair, stoutish, grey suit. I heard a car cruise up behind me and stop. The man crossed the road, opened the rear door of the blue Commodore and spoke to me over the top of the car. 'Get in, George.'

I slung my bag on to the back seat and climbed in. The bag sat between us. The Commodore picked up and we went into the tunnel. The driver wore heavy wrap-around sunglasses and drove as if he'd started doing it in primary school.

The stout guy lit a cigarette and wound down his window a little. The tyres made a whipping sound as we drove through the tunnel, under the lights.

'Well, George, what's on your mind?'

'Tennis,' I said.

He smiled and didn't say anything until we were in the second tunnel.

'How's that again?'

'I'm playing in the final today. Guy's got a wicked serve.'

Out of the tunnel and along beside the mini-skyscrapers. He looked at me but didn't say anything until we were under the arch of the bridge. The water and air were as blue and clear as they are in the cigarette commercials.

'I don't give a shit about tennis. I thought we were here to talk business.'

'Tennis *is* my business. I made three-quarters of a million last year, but you wouldn't believe the expenses. And the agent's fees, Jesus! Still, there's always the endorsements. Tax is a problem, too.'

Over the bridge and my companion tapped the driver on the shoulder. Sunglasses nodded and took the Lavender Street exit. We went down to Luna Park, turned left and came up through Milson's Point.

'Nice spot,' I said. My knees were shaking but you get used to that in tennis. It doesn't mean you can't win the next point. 'Be good to have a flat here, don't you think?'

No reply until we were on the bridge. I handed him a dollar and he swore and threw it and his cigarette out the window. 'I'll give it one more try, arsehole. I don't know what bloody game you're playing, but you better start talking sense.'

The driver dropped his coin in the basket and we kept left for the Expressway exit. I looked down at the Quay; a ferry was pulling out, churning up the water. 'Reminds me of Monte Carlo,' I said. 'Would you like to hear how I took Edberg in three at Monte?'

We did the rest of the drive in silence – down the ramp, through the tunnel and on past the Botanic Gardens. The Commodore stopped at Cowper Wharf and the man-who-didn't-like-tennis jerked his thumb at me. 'Out,' he said.

I got out. 'Oops, nearly forgot my bag.' I grabbed it and slammed the door as the Commodore pulled away.

I wandered down Bourke Street admiring the renovated terraces, and Grafton appeared from nowhere. 'Well?' he said.

I spoke out of the corner of my mouth. 'Not here. We might be observed. Let's go to the high ground.'

Grafton's breath was coming in short, wheezy gasps by the time we reached Art Gallery Road. He gripped the rail of the bridge across the Expressway. I mimed an intense survey of the area. 'All clear,' I said.

He seized the bag, took out the racquet and unscrewed its handle. A cylindrical mechanism slid out into his hand. Grafton smiled. His face was paler than Roger Landy's had been, but it wore the same traces of excess of everything except sleep. 'Where did you go?'

'Straight into the tunnel and over the bridge and back. He only spoke when we were in the tunnels and under the arch.'

Grafton snorted. 'Old trick. Used to work – fuck up the reception. But not with this baby. It filters out everything.' He fiddled with some switches and pressed a tiny red button. My voice came through loud and clear: 'I'm playing in the final today. Guy's got a wicked serve.'

Grafton listened to the rest of the dialogue. A vein throbbed in his forehead. 'You're finished,' he said when the tape of the silence and road noise stopped. He depressed a little green button on his device.

I handed him the envelope Landy had given me. 'Present for you, Neil.'

'What's this?'

'Take a look.'

I was curious myself. He opened the envelope and six glossy, postcard size photographs fanned out in his hand. They all showed pretty much the same thing – Grafton naked, and several other men in the same condition. They were all admiring each other's genitals. Some of the admiration was gastronomic.

'Oh, poor Peggy,' I said. 'And what will Gigi think?'

The face Grafton turned to me was ghastly. 'These are fakes.'

I shook my head and improvised. 'I've got the negs, Fatty.' I prodded him in the chest and felt the flab. Sweat dampened his shirt where my finger touched it. 'You should pick your men a little better, professionally and socially.'

I retrieved the hollowed-out racquet and walked away, but I took a look back. Grafton was leaning over the rail tearing up the photographs. The pieces floated down over the Cahill Expressway.

Raimondo Cortese

THE PREACHER IN THE TOWER
1998

I remember it clearly, although I was only five at the time. We visited him as he stood on the stone ramparts of his tower, right in the middle of the lake. His lean figure strutted this way and that, and with his left hand he stroked his waxed moustache, some would say nervously, as though even then he could detect any wavering in our scrupulous attention, without so much as a glance in our direction. An awestruck silence would sweep over the entire assembly. Only then did the preacher turn to address us. And what an unforgettable experience it was.

Preaching was certainly not his occupation. He never tried to earn any money from it, nor did he ever make an effort to encourage anyone to come and hear him talk. Nobody can recall how and when it all started. All we knew was that he was old, poor and lived in seclusion, and that his real name and title was the Marquis Alfonse d'Albiac-Perri.

Longobardic stonemasons built the tower in the eleventh century. It had passed down through the noble family of Albiac, of which the preacher was a direct descendant. Originally the tower was a central turret for an entire castle, which in turn was surrounded by inner and outer defensive walls. These in turn were surrounded by an intricate moat system. For centuries the castle had repelled attackers: heretical Cathars, Muslim infidels, anti-royalist usurpers, royalists (after the Albiacs signed a treaty with the usurpers, then entrenched on the throne), pro-Spanish pretenders, pro-Spanish anti-royalist usurpers, pro-royalist anti-Spanish pretenders (after the usurping, anti-royalist Spaniard Sonia of Aragon married Raymond Pierre d'Albiac in secrecy). Such were the shifting sands of medieval fealty.

But politics played only a minor role in the castle's demise. Four hundred years after its construction, the outer wall of the castle collapsed overnight, prompting the Albiacs to enter into connubial arrangements with the less noble but supremely wealthy Perri mercantile clan to overcome a cash-flow shortage. The web of natural canals beneath the castle, which sustained the moat and provided the inhabitants with clean water, had seeped into the foundations. Soon the inner wall followed and disappeared into the moat (by this stage we can think of it in terms of a lake), killing several family members and servants.

What remained of the castle had become too dangerous to inhabit. The best engineers were consulted and they all came to one conclusion: the only course of action was to relocate. This the family did, across the Atlantic to the newly discovered Americas in pursuit of the yellow metal, leaving behind a handful of staunch family traditionalists who hid themselves within their stone confines, preferring a merciless existence and premature death to being severed from the castle that had become synonymous with their dignified name.

It is to these traditionalists that the preacher's rather eccentric behaviour can be traced; despite everything, he steadfastly refused to leave, even when it was too late. Even now, as I look out across the lake, it is easy to immerse oneself in the history of those ancient stones.

Every Sunday, the local families gathered on the lake's edge, divided themselves among the various skiffs, and rowed to the tower. When everybody had converged and the oars were rested inside the boats, our eyes would rise, beseeching the preacher to commence his sermon. Sometimes a faint whisper could be heard from one of the children, too young to appreciate the solemnity of the occasion. The adults knew how off-putting this might be for the preacher, but somehow the child would suddenly go quiet, and all that could be heard was the water lapping against the stones.

The preacher then gave his characteristic hand motion that signalled his readiness. Dressed in a tight-fitting waistcoat that covered a faded white shirt, black trousers and pince-nez, he eulogised on various topics, most of which were totally beyond us. It was he who for the first and last time opened my modest ears to such mysteries as metaphysical enantiomorphism, Assyrian astronomy, hydroponic maintenance of Himalayan flora, the atavistic beliefs of the Gonads, and the procedure known as shirring (a method of baking eggs).

While it is true that we comprehended almost nothing of what the preacher had to offer, and that his phrasing was far too sophisticated for his humble audience, this neglects to account for the special way we appreciated and understood him. The subtleties in his performance method – I shall resist calling it a style – always kept us spellbound. What's more, this method was thoroughly innate, making it all the more captivating.

The sheer resolution in the preacher's voice was enough to engross his audience until long after he had concluded. Some insisted that he had once sung in the great opera houses of Europe. These rumours were never substantiated, and I personally doubt whether the preacher would ever have availed himself of an art form that people of his status regarded as decadent. Besides, as far as I know, the preacher had never sung. I'm not saying that he wouldn't have been extraordinary if he tried, but the fact is no-one ever heard him sing the shortest of melodies, not even from within the walls of the tower.

No, he always spoke with measured tones. His vowels and consonants were precisely enunciated and without a trace of indulgence. Even the crowds gathered on the lake's perimeter could hear him perfectly, and he never raised his voice. If he whispered, you could be sure we always heard him without straining a muscle.

To do him justice, however, it is not appropriate to isolate one element of his performance from another. His posture was equally impressive. Legs a strict pace apart with spine rigorously straight and a prominent chin, he conveyed the kind of natural authority that only centuries of discipline could produce. I have already alluded to the simple but effective feature he used to begin sermons. I should add that he also made this gesture, a simple loop of the forefinger, while he spoke, as though to punctuate important passages. Sometimes he used other gestures that were no less remarkable, but were never called upon again, like the way he once drew two fingers together and brushed them across his cheek quite unexpectedly. The impact on that occasion was so profound that a huge moan erupted from the crowd.

It would be impossible to describe all these delicate manoeuvrings to someone who never experienced them at first hand, but even a hint will help one to appreciate the devastating consequences of what began to happen to the tower.

As the years unfolded – I must have been about ten when I first heard about it – the tower began to grow. I mean it literally grew right out of the lake. The process began so slowly that we almost didn't notice. But some of the children had taken to counting the bricks.

'Hey, there's seventeen!' one of them cried.

'Shh!' came the response from the adults. But, sure enough, there were three extra layers. And the following week a fresh row of bricks poked out just above the water line.

There was no doubt about it, the tower was ascending.

We continued with our weekly pilgrimage, but it became impossible to ignore the fact that the preacher was not adapting well to the changes. As the distance between us and him increased, his speeches began to lose their magic. While his voice seemed to harness the same assurance as before, a handful of us began to detect the stress in his tone. His delivery would waver, something quite unheard of in the past, and every so often he'd gesticulate frantically, making it difficult to catch what he was saying.

It was about this time that some of the locals began to stay home on Sundays. Of course the preacher must have been aware of their absence and no doubt suffered greatly for it. To make matters worse, the tower was growing faster then ever, compounding his acoustic problems. He decided to deal with this by incorporating a bizarre mix of foot signals into his performance. Unfortunately, the result resembled a kind of insane dance.

Back at the town hall, the locals debated whether or not to communicate our feelings to the preacher. The decision was unanimous and, when Sunday came round, our appointed spokesman rowed ahead of us, dressed in a cotton shirt and an elegant bow tie. The man, who was chosen for his sense of decorum, stood up in his skiff and did the unthinkable. At the time, the preacher was in the midst of a discourse on clam dichotomies, a popular topic among the lakeside inhabitants.

'Excuse me, sir, we've brought you something which we think might help,' interjected our unenviable spokesman, holding up a megaphone and visibly shaking.

The preacher stopped mid-sentence, stared blankly for a few seconds, then abruptly turned and vanished within the tower.

The next Sunday barely half the village turned up. The tower grew faster than ever. In less than two months it had doubled in size. To make matters worse, the preacher had a new competitor, one of the locals returned from his travels with a brown box he called a radio. Every night his friends crowded round in awe while it emitted strange sounds from afar. Within two months, radios whined incessantly from every home in the lake's vicinity.

The preacher became completely inaudible. His sermons were reduced to wild gesticulations, which he employed, I suspect, in a desperate and pitiful bid to curb the steady depreciation of his audience. Some of the younger generation came along just to have a laugh. Tourists turned up to witness the spectacle before it disappeared forever. Couples could be seen amiably rowing back and forth with their portable gramophones belting out the latest in jazz. On Sundays canoe enthusiasts came from distant cities and competed feverishly around the tower.

Only a few of us still treated the preacher with the respect he deserved. The tower grew higher still. We could barely see him and had to resort to binoculars. His magnified face was shadowed by sadness. Sometimes he stood there perfectly still, looking down in silence for hours on end, or he neglected to make an appearance at all.

Before long even his most ardent supporters gave up on him entirely and spent their Sundays swimming or listening to the radio or gramophone. The tower eventually grew as high as the clouds and took the preacher with it. Some say it took him as far as the moon. At any rate, he disappeared for eternity.

Now as I look out across the lake, nothing remains of the tower bar a shabby ruin, squatting a few feet above the water. Even it too, I suspect, will disappear before long.

THE VOICE

1964

The staffroom was warm. He closed the door on the wind that seemed concentrated along the corridor as if it had blown nowhere else. He crossed to the fire in the glass-fronted fireplace, one pane of glass missing, so that beyond the small cube the flames held a sudden reality, before he saw that she was sitting in the easy chair by the long window.

He had thought he might have, briefly, the room to himself, like some respite from the endless impact of personalities, from the words that must be found, the demand of faces.

He said, 'Cold enough. Still.'

'Yes. This room is warm, though.'

He looked up quickly from the fire. He saw her every day, without particular note. Quite a time ago she had deepened her hair colour to black. Before that he seemed to remember indeterminate shades, neutral, in keeping with her rather broad, quiet face, that her glasses with their emphasised rims seemed to guard. It was a face that revealed little, he thought, except a rather determined pleasantness, and he was aware suddenly how slight had been his curiosity or his interest. And nothing that he saw as he looked at her now would have changed his feeling. But her voice was so altered that for a moment it seemed grotesque, as if some joke had been played on him.

She smiled faintly, as if she read his thought.

'Laryngitis. Isn't it stupid? I'm helpless in class.'

'Yes,' he said. Her voice had ordinarily been different, a little high-pitched, with something of a childish quality. Now it seemed to hold authority, and something that eluded him. He could have laughed at a certain wariness in himself, afraid still this might be some trick.

'I'm going home last period. I've no class then.'

'It's the only thing to do,' he said. 'I remember a headmaster once, more noted for his voice than any minor qualities such as intelligence, saying to me when I'd had the flu, "You're pretty helpless without a voice." It was the nearest I ever saw him come to self-revelation. And to smiling.'

He realised as he spoke that his joke was not communicable and he was irritated with himself for having placed the pointless words between them. But she smiled and said, 'That wouldn't have been Pete?'

'Yes. Did you know him?'

'He terrified me. When I was just out of training college. I can still hear his voice booming down corridors.'

'Always.' He laughed. 'It's a few years since I knew him. He retired quite a while back.'

She nodded. He thought probably she did not want to talk, but he would have liked to hear her voice. The change intrigued him, its tone somehow intrigued him, its tone somehow provocative, what one might have called, he thought suddenly, suggestive. He almost smiled. It was exaggerated, a bit stagy, as if she were acting in some not very competent theatrical. He looked at her quiet, rather serious face that he had always felt to be too plainly reserved, prim, and he thought how incongruous the voice was. But her eyes met his and she might somehow have shared his amusement, so that he was suddenly uncertain.

'I've nothing to read,' she said. 'You haven't a good thriller, something light?'

'I don't know – I don't think so. Not here. What would you like?'

'As long as it's not serious I don't care. I've finished all the exam marking and I just want to relax. And with this throat on top of it all I'm a bit fed up.'

'As are we all,' he said. 'I'll see what I can find in the library.'

'I've looked.'

'Oh. Nothing?'

'Not that I haven't read. It doesn't matter. It was only for tonight.'

She stretched herself, her arms lifting, and then let her hands fall suddenly, her fingers spread, her palms upturned towards him. He looked down at the fire.

'I'm getting lazy here.'

'Why not?' he said.

'In this hive? It must be the fire.'

'I could get you a couple of books,' he said. 'I think I've some would do.'

'It doesn't matter.'

'It's no trouble. I could run them round to you.'

Once or twice, after late staff meetings, he had taken her home, with two other teachers who lived in the direction of his own suburb.

'Do you think you could?'

'Yes. I've a games practice after school, I may be a bit late –'

'After tea,' she said. 'There's no hurry. It's good of you –'

The bell broke the classrooms to sound and deliberate disorder. He looked up towards the window and the rain was moving greyly across the buildings and the black quadrangle.

The flat was on the ground floor of a small block of four. As the door opened and she stood beneath the light of the small entrance hall he felt a surprise that he realised she perhaps perceived. He had expected some evidence of the invalid. Heavy clothes. A thick sweater, perhaps. Even a scarf about her throat. Now that he thought of it, a bandage would have been possible. It would not have been out of keeping with the practicality he had always associated with her nature. Just as in winter she wore a shapeless grey raincoat like a man's. And heavy flat shoes.

'Come in,' she said. Her voice was deep, faintly strained. He had wanted to hear it again. But as he followed her into the room he had not been prepared for the white blouse, short sleeved, the thin brown skirt that suggested so plainly her hips and thighs. He could no longer remember the anonymity of the clothes she wore to the school. She looked quickly at him, perhaps aware of his comparison.

'My voice is strained,' she said. 'It's not the flu or anything like that. I'm not really an invalid.' She smiled. 'It was good of you to bother with these.'

He handed her the books.

'You said something light –'

'Thank you. These look just what I wanted. Sit down, Max.'

There was a heater near the fireplace. She went across to the corner of the room and turned on the television. He looked at the meaningless images that steadied to a pattern he did not bother to encompass.

'Mother is out,' she said. 'She plays bridge on Tuesdays.'

He looked about the room that seemed crowded with small pieces of furniture that achieved no particular balance, and he wondered if the personalities of herself and her mother had somehow reached a stalemate in the furnishings of this main room of the flat. It might have been that the furnishings of two different periods found an uneasy common ground, the old, ornately carved china cabinet and the clear, rather sharp lines of the low coffee table, the wide, high-backed settee and the chrome television chairs, contrasts so obvious as to seem deliberate. He had never met her mother.

She asked him about one of the books he had brought, and they discussed the writer, neither of them, he realised, interested, the words giving them excuse. About her wrist she wore two thin silver bracelets that slipped along her arm, they drew his gaze, for he could not remember her affecting any such adornment at the school.

He said suddenly, 'We've both been round at the school quite a time.'

She laughed, seeming not to find his remark unexpected.

'I suppose so. I was going to get a transfer about a year ago, but nothing came of it.'

'I'm used to the place,' he said. 'Probably I'll stay until I'm moved perforce.'

'That doesn't sound very cheerful.'

'Well – you know yourself, there are enough times it seems an insane asylum, and the warders the least sane.'

'Oh yes.'

He shrugged, 'Somehow one stays.'

'Perhaps we're afraid to go outside,' she said.

He looked at her quickly, but she was watching the television. Her fingers moved the thin bracelets back along her arm. For a time they allowed the shadows that moved in the diminutive world to hold them. Once or twice he noticed her lift her hand to her throat, and he wondered if her voice was painful to use, despite her denial. But it seemed to him that the evening had somehow broken, deriding them, as if it had offered some promise now withdrawn. Or perhaps, he thought, promise that had existed only in his own mind, unformed and now unlikely to find form. There was the beginning of uneasiness between them. He could find no words that might confirm their own reality, that after all this time they should be here, in the room of her flat, and she met his few obvious commonplaces too quickly. As the inanity of advertising filled the small screen before them, she stood up, smoothing briefly her thin skirt.

'I'll make some coffee. I won't be a moment.'

While she was out of the room he went across to the bookshelf and looked at the neat, even lines of the books. There was one strong section of travel, perhaps her mother's, he thought, but the rest held a queer neutrality almost like some disguise of a personality, the books perhaps expected of a teacher, of one who had been educated. As she came in he turned away.

She said, 'Nothing very much there.'

He stood close to her, taking the cup from the small tray. Her features were attractive, he thought in faint surprise, no longer marked with the air of rather conscientious worry she had always seemed to affect, and which he had found irritating. She smiled at him suddenly, and he had again the sense that his feeling must have been obvious, but the restraint between them seemed to have passed, and they talked without awkwardness, content to allow pauses to lengthen between them while they looked idly at the film, which reflected some of the tinsel of another age.

When again advertising without subtlety broke upon the screen as if to cancel all that had existed before it, he said, 'I must go. I've kept you late, and with your throat like that – you must be tired –'

'Oh no.' She rose with him. 'Those old films are curious – to think we felt like that – accepted all that as valid –'

He laughed. 'And the same will happen to today's.'

'Yes.'

He said, 'Your voice – I'd like you to go on talking –'

'My voice –' She laughed.

He was standing close to her, touching her arms and she looked up at him. He thought she seemed without coquetry or evasion as she was without the forced jollity, the careful good fellowship he had associated with her.

'It's not yours, really, I suppose.'

'Isn't it? How do you know?'

The television screen was suddenly blank, and she smiled, moving to turn it off.

He said, 'I didn't know it was as late as that.'

'It's not really.'

He said, 'If someone – suddenly isn't that person –'

She began to laugh and he said, 'It's very confusing.'

'It must be. How could it happen, Max?'

'I'm not sure.'

They heard the front door of the flat open, and he thought that for a moment she looked startled, and her mother came quietly into the room.

'Hullo,' she said. She looked at them as they stood near the television set. 'I wondered how you were. We finished early, so I came straight home to make sure you were all right. And meet Mr Webster. Evelyn said you would lend her some books. It was good of you.'

As they spoke, and he made his excuses for leaving, he looked at the small woman, whose quiet manner held something of authority. There was a certain fussiness about her, as though she did not like things disturbed, or to be unexpected, a suggestion of the fixity of routine that was perhaps also in the younger woman who came to the door with him, thanking him again for the books.

She did not come to school the next day. He had thought of ringing to ask how she was, but in the haste of activity that seemed so often meaningless he did not get to the phone. The following day, just before morning break, he came into the staffroom and she was standing by the window, talking to the history teacher. He went towards them and she looked up. As soon as she spoke he knew that the kind of strain, the depth, the faint suggestiveness her voice had seemed to hold was gone.

He said, 'You're better.'

Her smile had a briskness. 'Oh yes. A day home worked wonders.'

'Something we could all do with more often.' The history teacher laughed at his own commonplace.

As he looked at them she seemed so much as he had always known her that he thought perhaps his feeling had been imagination, that he had somehow, on the verge of making a humiliating revelation, been reprieved. Or, as he listened to her laugh which echoed only an impersonal gesture, he thought it might have been a mask had been replaced, the revelation not his alone, and he would suddenly have spoken to her. But she was offering some triteness to match that of the history teacher, the mask would perhaps not slip again. He turned away as the bell rang for the morning break.

Eleanor Dark

SERPENTS
1959

It would be pleasant to believe that Science, when it grouped snakes under the name of Squamata, was indulging in a spot of imaginative whimsy, for the most conspicuous thing about these creatures is their manner of locomotion, and for this no more aptly descriptive term than squamatous could possibly be invented. But imaginative whimsy would, of course, be a very improper thing for Science to indulge in, so we must regretfully accept the fact that the word refers to their scales, and not to their movements.

All the same, it is the erroneous interpretation which will probably linger in our minds, for the attitude of most people to snakes is less scientific than emotional – an attitude which, we suggest, dates from the very earliest recorded association of man and reptile. We do not wish to harp unduly upon the Garden of Eden, but it naturally keeps on popping up, for the events which took place there set the pattern for much that goes on in the Lane, including the uneasy relationship between ourselves and representatives of the order Squamata.

It will be remembered that when sentence was passed upon Adam and Eve, the Serpent also did not escape uncursed. Indeed, grim as were the words which condemned our first parents to swink for ever among thorns and thistles, they seem almost mild when compared with those which so terrifyingly pronounced doom upon the Serpent. UPON THY BELLY SHALT THOU GO, AND DUST SHALT THOU EAT. Appalling! The mere sound of it is enough to chill the blood – and that, apparently, is exactly what it did. When there is added the further decree of perpetual enmity between men and snakes – the former neglecting no opportunity of bruising the latter's head, and the latter making a dead set at the former's heel – no mystery remains in the fact that the generally prevailing good-neighbour policy in the Lane here comes up against a formidable psychological obstacle.

It is true that the sons of Adam are inclined to be tolerant of carpet snakes, and when they see one basking in the sun, spread out along the tops of the pineapple plants, they will usually allow it to slide away with its head unbruised. But the daughters of Eve, on their own ground, are less forbearing. 'I know it's harmless,' they will say, gazing with distaste at eight feet of richly patterned reptile squaming indolently across the veranda, 'but I just don't *like* snakes, and I *will not* have them in the house, so you just get a stick while I watch it.'

What makes the gentle sex so savage is precisely this habit snakes have of entering houses. The women allow them to be a fair enough hazard out of doors, but resent finding them in the bath, or lying along the kitchen mantelpiece behind the tea and sugar. And who can blame them? It was surely not unreasonable of Myra to be riled when a copper snake fell out of Aub's shirt as she picked it up? And when Marge, having found a four-foot Black crawling into the top drawer of her dressing table, seized a broom and violently pushed the drawer shut upon it, can we fairly censure her for gazing in sombre triumph at the corpse which Bruce presently extracted, and flung out the window? As she said indignantly: 'I was just going to get a pair of socks, and I might have put my *hand* on it!'

Note the form of this protest. She does not complain that it might have bitten her; she merely has the horrors because she might have touched it. Had it been a carpet snake, Bruce would undoubtedly have made the asinine, and typically masculine reply that it wouldn't have hurt her if she had; but this point of view is totally irrelevant, for what women feel towards snakes is far less fear than an aversion.

Consider, too, the illuminating lament of Heather Arnold when she perceived a sinuous shape stealing across her bedroom windowsill, which is at least ten feet from the ground. 'I can never,' she cried passionately, 'get used to the way they *climb*!' This is the very voice of evicted Eve. In the time of innocence before the Fall, she must often have watched, with admiration and pleasure, the Serpent elegantly weaving its way through the top-most branches of the Tree of Knowledge – but now her deepest instincts are outraged by the sight of a snake climbing anything. They clamour that the wretched thing should stay on its belly in the dust, for thanks to its machinations she was landed with domesticity, and if she must work out her sentence, should it not do likewise? Insult, she feels, is added to injury when it assumes the perpendicular for the purpose of invading her own exclusive domain.

So snakes of any kind are for it once they cross the threshold or the windowsill, and the poisoners are for it anywhere, unless they can make a fast getaway. Not that they don't have a good run for their money indoors, where there are so many things for them to retreat behind, or beneath, and one cannot swipe at them so freely. The one that got under Amy's wardrobe stood siege for nearly an hour, defying the united efforts of the family to eject it. But Biddy effected what is unanimously allowed to be the neatest capture in the history of our community, and she did it all by herself, too, for Tim had gone to Rothwell, and she was alone in the house, except for the children. Admittedly, the snake played right into her hands by entering the fridge when she had it open for defrosting; but she slammed it shut like lightning, and turned on the current, so presently hibernation set in, and when Tim came home the creature was too drowsy to know what hit it. This execution – so clean and simple – was in marked contrast to the bloody massacre which took place under the Dawsons' bed. That invader was a really big Black, and when Aub and Myra came in and switched on the light, it decided to make itself inconspic-uous by stretching out under the bed, close up against the skirting-board. This was not a bad idea at all, and would have been successful if it had not passed between the wall and one leg of the bed, leaving its tail protruding. The tail was not noticed however, though Myra must have almost trodden on it when she arranged her pillow; the discovery was made only because Aub stood on one foot while he removed his shoe from the other (a thing which Myra is always telling him he is no longer young enough, or slim enough to do), lost his balance, and bumped the foot of the bed, thus pushing its head hard against the wall. In such circumstances even the most stoical snake must have betrayed its presence by a convulsive movement.

For once there was no question of you-watch-it-while-I-get-a-stick. The thing was caught, and the only problem was how to hit it. If you have ever tried to hit a snake which is pressing itself closely into the angle of floor and wall underneath a low double bed, you will under-stand why Aub's efforts merely made him very hot, breathless and profane. At one stage he even advocated pulling the bed away, and letting the ruddy so-and-so escape, because at this rate it would be time to rise before they got to sleep. But Myra vehemently opposed this suggestion, and in the end they both crawled under the bed, and Myra pinned its head against the wall while Aub cut its throat with the bread-knife.

The harmless snakes are pretty safe out of doors, though. (Of course the word 'harmless' is rather ambiguous, and the affair in the Griffiths' fowlyard shows that there are limits to the indulgence of the menfolk.) Packing-sheds are, by tradition, sanctuary for carpet snakes, and Biddy just has to put up with the one that lives in theirs. She tries to find consolation in Tim's assurance that it saves him pounds a year by eating the rats which would otherwise eat his wheat and laying-mash; but all the same, when she is packing pines she keeps a wary and hostile eye on the squamiferous coils looped round the rafter above her head.

Sue Griffith used to be the weak spot in the women's united front, for she is by temperament disposed to love all creatures – even snakes. This may have been all right, perhaps, for St Francis of Assisi, but it is an extremely difficult stance for farmers to maintain. We are surrounded by so many creatures, nearly all of which seem to exist for the purpose of impeding or frustrating our efforts to make a living. We may manage, with a good deal of determination, to subdue our feeling of malevolence towards Brother Leech, for he merely sucks our blood, and we can spare a little of that without actual damage to our bank accounts. We can forgive the Brother Tick who confines his attentions to ourselves, but we are implacably hostile to the one who attacks our cattle. And it calls for a greater degree of Christian forbearance than even Sue can command, to love Brother Borer, Brother Fruit-fly, and a host of other brethren whose activities contribute so largely to our financially depressed condition. It is also discouraging to observe that while we strive conscientiously to love as many creatures as possible, they make no attempt to love each other. Sue frequently finds herself troubled and embarrassed by Brother Snake's penchant for devouring Brother Frog, and by the rapacious appetite of Brother Hawk for little Sister Chicken.

Nevertheless, she used to insist – before the episode in the fowlyard – that she quite liked snakes. There is reason to suspect that she has deliberately taken her eyes off some which Henry has bidden her watch while he fetched a weapon, thus conniving at their escape;

and she always used to speak heatedly about the wickedness of slaying poor, inoffensive carpet snakes. She declared indignantly that no snake had any real wish to intrude, and, when it accidentally did so, was only too anxious to withdraw without causing any trouble. No-one argued about this, but the other women said it was not the point; when she ganged up with the men about carpet snakes, and even sabotaged operations against more dangerous Squamata, they took the view that she was letting the side down.

But all that is changed now, and we shall tell you why.

One evening, when Tony and Aunt Isabelle, escorted by Jake, had gone to a birthday party at the Bells', Sue and Henry settled down for a nice, peaceful evening. Henry went to sleep in his chair with an open book on his knee, and Sue went to sleep in hers with some knitting on her lap, and the nine o'clock voice of the ABC composedly reporting the sensations and disasters of the past twelve hours fell upon two pairs of happily deaf ears. But although tidings of floods, tornadoes, revolutions, murders, juvenile delinquencies and exploding H-bombs failed to disturb their little nap, an ominous outburst of noise from their own backyard brought them both to their feet in a split second.

Seizing a torch, Henry dived out the kitchen door, with Sue close upon his heels. It happened to be one of those quite abnormal occasions when neither moon nor stars glorified our sky, and the night was inky black. From the henhouse came the kind of hysterical clamour which only panic-stricken poultry can emit. The ray of the torch, sweeping to and fro, came dramatically to rest upon a long, dark, shining, gliding shape. 'Holy smoke!' exclaimed Henry. 'What a whopper!'

At the same moment, the whopper (which was next morning found to be, by Bruce Kennedy's precise measurement, twelve feet two and a half inches long) realised that escape rather than banqueting must now be its aim, and, doubling swiftly back upon itself, sought egress from the fowlyard by the same hole in the wire netting which had allowed its entry. Perhaps it takes some time for the rear end of so long a snake to grasp what its front end is up to; at all events, there was a brief, but fatal hitch in its execution of this manoeuvre, owing to the fact that it found the hole still plugged by about three feet of its own tail. This seemed to confuse it a little, and Henry, summing up the situation in a trice, called out to Sue: 'Grab it while I get a stick!'

Much may happen in the human mind during a second or two of crisis; indeed, almost the only thing which does not seem to have occurred to Sue was the advisability of retorting: '*You* grab it while *I* get a stick.' Instead, she apparently condensed into one tick of the clock enough anguished spiritual indecision to have kept Hamlet going for a year. To grab, or not to grab? That was the question. On the one hand were her Franciscan principles – for not only was this a poor, inoffensive carpet snake, but it was doing everything in its power to demonstrate the truth of her contention that Squamata in general only want to get away. To grab, therefore, would be shocking. On the other hand, she was, as custodian of the chooks, aware that her egg-money would be gravely jeopardised if poor, inoffensive carpet snakes were to consume her hens whenever they felt so disposed. Not to grab, therefore, would be silly.

And yet – quite apart from Franciscan benevolence – she hesitated. For although she is always handling such things as frogs, mice, spiders, crickets, worms and lizards, the only snakes she had so far handled had been dead ones, and she was now astonished to discover in herself a strong, emotional disinclination to obey Henry's command.

Meanwhile, Brother Snake had got his problem worked out, and his head was posted beside his tail, superintending its withdrawal from the hole; a bare two feet now remained outside the wire. Henry, rummaging about on the woodheap for a suitable weapon, was holding the torch in such a manner that its light played only dimly and fitfully over these proceedings, and the smoothly flowing movement, half-seen, of dark and shining coils filled Sue with a sudden abhorrence which brought her vacillations to an end. She perceived that if she did not stop the tail from going in, the head would speedily come out, and for more reasons than one, this was clearly undesirable. So she took a deep breath, jumped forward, and grabbed. It was comforting to know that Henry was just behind her, and, presumably, now armed.

'Oh, blast,' said his voice in a tone of mild annoyance, 'this stick's rotten. I'd better go and get the brush-hook.'

And with these words he departed, taking the torch with him.

Darkness closed about Sue and the Thing which she was grasping. Perhaps, since it wrapped itself so fiercely about her wrists, we might say with equal exactitude, that it was grasping her. At all events, they were joined together in a struggle as fearful and implacable as man's struggle with sin. There was a terrible sound of thudding and threshing; the earth vibrated, the fence-posts creaked; something splintered. The wire netting strained outward under the writhing weight hurled desperately upon it; then it strained inward as Sue, dragged forward, lost her footing and fell against it on her knees. Awful thoughts jostled each other in her mind. It was very old netting. It probably had other holes in it. There might be one quite near. It could give way anywhere. She might suddenly feel great, cold, powerful coils encircling her. She scrambled to her feet, dug her heels into the ground, and pulled with the strength of terror. The Thing in her hands – the hard, chilly, muscular, squamiferous Thing – leapt and wrenched and dragged against her. She could hear its other extremity banging against the bit of corrugated iron on the gate. Perhaps it could get under the gate . . . ?

She screamed.

'What's wrong?' called Henry from the packing-shed.

'What's *wrong*?' shrieked Sue between gasps of panic and exertion. 'Have I got to stand here all night hanging on to a bloody snake's tail?'

'Calm down, old girl,' said Henry rebukingly. 'It's only a carpet – it's harmless. Tony must have left the brush-hook out somewhere, damn it. Don't let go, will you?'

'I *can't* let go!' yelled Sue furiously. 'I *daren't* let go! It might be coming out under the gate! How do I know where its other end is? Oh! Oh, Heavens! *Hurry up . . .* !'

The last words were a squeal of despair for the Poor Inoffensive had changed its tactics. It had now anchored itself firmly to a post of the fowlhouse, and was settling down to a really serious tug-of-war. Sue lifted her voice in frantic appeal.

'Quick! Oh, Henry – *quick*! It's pulling!'

'Good grief,' cried Henry disgustedly, 'what do you expect? I'll be there as soon as I find this ruddy brush-hook. All you've got to do is hold it.'

Sue's plight was now dire indeed. She gave ground inch by inch. Her hands, dragged down and down, touched the earth, scraped along it, and came up against the wire. In darkness atavistic memories stir, and ancient evils breed. Never, since the first day of the Creation, had there been a darker darkness than this. She was no longer grappling with a mere marauding reptile, but with a monstrous and malevolent force out of the time when time itself was young, and innocence was first imperilled . . .

Well, it is remarkable what powers of exorcism may reside in a four-and-ninepenny Woolworth torch. 'Hullo,' said Henry, approaching behind a blessed beam of golden light, 'got you down, has it? Never mind, just hang on a few minutes more – I've got the brush-hook.'

When the execution had been accomplished, and the still writhing remains flung upon the woodheap, Sue stumbled up to the house on legs which wobbled slightly.

'What's the matter?' inquired Henry when he saw her in a good light. 'I thought you liked snakes?'

Sue has not told us what she replied to this, nor have we asked. There are moments in every marriage when husbands must expect to hear, in precise and forceful terms, just what their wives think of them.

Sue is still kind to spiders, and goofy about frogs. She still pleads for mice, and declines to tread on scorpions. But she no longer rushes to intervene when there is a scurry out of doors, and someone calls for a stick. To her, nowadays, as to all true daughters of Eve, every snake is The Serpent.

Luke Davies

THE MIND OF HOWARD HUGHES
1998

The XF-II. A magnificent machine. There is not a lot of difference
between the front projection techniques I developed in my early films
(in *Wings*, for example, or *Hell's Angels*) and the view through the
windscreen on the XF-II. A sense of the unreal, a break with the open
perspectives of sight. A screen. I'm talking not just of the rush of the
wind, but of speed itself.

I've flown in open biplanes. But that's entirely different. In an open
cockpit what becomes apparent is an immediate relationship with the
massive machineries of flight: an immersion in engine and wind. The
great noise of a laborious metallic effort to break the bonds of gravity
and land. In the XF-II, surrounded by exquisite technology and a
plexiglass curve, you can look at the screen and enjoy the movie.

On July 7, 1946, as the XF-II lazily smashed through trees in the
streets of Beverly Hills, I was struck by the unreality of that view
unfolding. When the windscreen shatters, you realise how fast you are
going. Then I caught fire.

It was horrible but magnificent. As I sat on the footpath in the
midday sun my flying leathers were melted into my skin and I thirsted
for morphine like a man lost in the desert would yearn for water. A
whirring noise in my ears, but everything silent and still all around
me. The plane in pieces, along the street, in yards, in trees.

From out of the smoke a man emerged, running towards me like a
silhouette from Bedlam.

'Are you all right?' he hissed.

It was then I knew I was a god. Or godlike. From behind the
horrified face which loomed over me the sun drilled into my retinas
and in slow motion on the open sky the frenzied patterns of my blood
vessels danced.

That is how I knew I must remove myself from the company of men.

Four times I have been in a plane crash, so I bathe in that perfumed glow. The XF-II in Beverly Hills in '46 was the worst. And yet with each crash an anointing occurs. The greases and oils of predestination, more holy than any musk or myrrh.

Everything had gone silent, despite the gargantuan whining of the engines. But when the windscreen broke I heard a rush of air, and then the gates of hell broke open.

To pass through those last seconds before impact in such elongated terror. And they say I'm unhinged. Who would not be? I've seen the streets of Beverly Hills in ways unique to me. Finally I felt still and serene as trees, telegraph poles, houses, roads, stood up one after the other to smack me in the nose.

Oh my planes. My beautiful toys. In Texas as a boy I knew a profound solitude in the woods with my tin toys. Then aeroplanes allowed me to take my solitude into the air, into space. To take my solitude with me into spaciousness. At night I tried to masturbate, but often could not focus on the image that would make me come. This was in the cockpit, mind you! Falling upwards into the atmosphere utterly private. Encased in the freedom my money could buy, that dazzling horizon always unfolding, that beckoning horizon – a finger hooked deep in the chest – beyond which could be anything: good, evil, anything.

In 1938 I circled the globe. Speed is the rite that initiates us into emptiness. I circled the globe in a Cyclone.

The Lockheed Cyclone. Most reliable of aeroplanes. I flew around the world in an endless arc. I left five days ago and in my end is my beginning. The power of the circle and my own immense power. Not just New York, great city of beginnings. But Floyd Bennett field, in New York, which has changed only in time while I circled away. Everything still here. The same airfield. I taxi the Cyclone into the same hangar. The same wheelblocks in the same place. I am the master of Time.

There I was in the flow and the smoothness of power and speed. There were no angles on this record-breaking flight. I flew a straight line, nothing but a straight line through curved space. More or less.

I stared for hours; you would think the horizon doesn't change. But I moved east, across the Atlantic, away from the sun, with the spin of the planet, so darkness falls early.

Mid-Atlantic, in the middle of the night, I switched off the control-panel lights. In a blackness I had never known I felt the fear that freedom brings.

Suddenly I was aware of the ceaseless drone of the giant Lockheed engines. The brutal magic of the stainless steel that pushed me through the brittle air. For many hours this deafening comfort had lodged in the back of my mind. Now, with the light cut, my senses clung to noise. It seemed an intruder in the blackness, the blood through my temples noise enough.

Could I cut the engines? Did I have the courage? Could I cut the engines and would they start again? To crash in the ocean. A death without form and location, unnoticed by all who watch my every move. The one who is known by everybody in the world: that is fame. To be in a place that is neither true south, nor true north, but true nowhere: that is the trick. For death to be uncertain.

So I cut the engines.

Not silence but something close as the engines wound down. And the soothing rush of the wind on steel, high in the air in the middle of the night. I put my hand in front of my face. I could see nothing. Looked all around me, to the roof, to my feet, to where the windscreen was. Nothing. I saw more light when I closed my eyes than in all that open space.

I said, I am Howard. Howard, How-ard. Howard Hughes.

I could hear the words come out of my mouth, my own clear voice for the first time since dawn.

I could not tell if in any way I could feel the descent of the plane. Not yet. I hoped my sense of time stayed true. Eight thousand feet, strong tailwind: I calculated I could give myself one hundred seconds of darkness and silence, allowing a huge margin of safety.

A kind of bloodrush. A kind of unconsciousness. The blackness crushes you. You feel it in the thighs. You feel so hot. It's the cunt of the goddess of the night. The plane descending. Squeezing your tiny thighs. My tiny thighs. The thighs of Howard Hughes, so frail beneath the haunches of the night. The haunches of the night descending on my cock.

I needed to come. I wanted to come in that black silence of descent.

I switched on the engines and control lights. The cockpit glowed. The engines shuddered and took. Climbing towards twelve thousand feet, I licked my right hand and began to masturbate. The normal images. Women I'd known. Or men. Jean Harlow going down on me. A mass of blonde hair, a silver sequinned gown. Elma Rane at high school in Houston, the girl beyond attainment. How I longed to stroke her knees, untie the ribbons in her rigid hair.

Several times in the climb I came close to coming. Then I'd stop for a moment to let it subside. Or open my eyes to check the instrument panel. For seven thousand feet I drifted in and out of this languorous state as the plane strained and hauled through the air.

Then for the second time, I cut the engines and lights. Instantly the bright fantasies of submissive girls disappeared. The plane began to angle downwards. Dark gales howled inside my head, whose boundaries expanded wider than the cockpit and wider than the Atlantic. Down there my body and legs and my cock connected to my right hand.

I dreamed – did I dream? – that a giant, a goddess, had straddled me, was fucking me. I am most worthy I said. Fuck me fuck me. My head rolled back. That fierce wind, the wind of sex. More saliva. A huge woman. The rolls of fat. Her thighs. My thighs. The fatness of the night.

She had a face, but it was galaxies away. It did not matter. I buried my expanded head in her breasts. I was not this small tin thing crawling through the air like an ant across a football field. I began to moan. The cosmic push of her belly on mine was the deep satisfaction that death must be. The smell of the goddess: diesel and grease. I could fuck you forever oh goddess of diesel and grease. I could fuck you forever.

I slipped into the final stage, the long slide into coming when you're powerless to stop. I was beside myself with a pleasure matched only by morphine. Crystal patterns broke and reformed in front of my eyes. With my left hand I pushed the joystick forward. The plane dived steeply. I spread my legs. Inside my boots my toes arched backwards. My spine pressed hard into the seat. In vertical descent the plane reached terminal velocity. The ocean down there in the darkness, heading straight towards me. I had no way of knowing how much time was left. My hand was hot, the only hand in the world. No, goddess, the only goddess. My hand a vehicle of the goddess. Instrument of the will of the goddess of sex and death. Or was that night and day? I could not think straight, pinned to the seat and facing the rolling Atlantic at lethal speed. If I was to die it was important that I came first. I imagined the ocean smashing my eyeballs back through their sockets. My head awash with death and salt.

But the goddess lets us have our cake and eat it too. I came. She pushed down hard upon me. I felt her pelvis grind on mine. I tilted my head and frowned. My left hand splayed in front of me, palm open, as if saying, to everything in the world, 'Wait. Wait.' Wait for what? I was in the middle of it, suddenly hot on the web of my hand between my thumb and index finger, hot on my belly and my undershirt.

I tried to gain my breath. The metal screeched. My temples throbbed. I heard the wind louder and louder. Terminal velocity. Where was I? Jesus! I pulled the joystick back, straining at first. The plane pulled into a curve as if it was set on a toboggan run. I flicked the switch. The engines cut back in, stuttered, then roared. Gradually the Lockheed pulled level. It might have been that nothing had happened, nothing at all for thousands of feet in the infinite night. I switched on the lights and felt the deep sadness that so often came after coming.

I was dangerously low: eleven hundred feet. I took it slowly back up to eight thousand feet, wiping myself with a rag, and lumbered on into the dawn.

Hours later, at 4.00 a.m., somewhere above the Azores, I find myself crying. I am in the cockpit and suddenly I am in the knowledge that I have everything and nothing and that this is the end of the world. The glow of the control panel is both profound and distressing. In the intimacy of an airplane adrift on the sky I could shout hosanna. I could put the barrel of this flare gun inside my mouth and scatter my head into phosphorus and flame. Then eventually the Cyclone would fall out of the sky.

But I know that with daylight will come Paris.

And they'll be waiting, with bulbs flashing, to connect me back to the world of light. Then I will be me again. I am Howard. Howard Hughes. Desired by all.

The planet spun, the night rolled into dawn. I ate a stale sandwich, drank some water, pissed. The horizon began to glow pink. Above and below that line of light the sky and the ocean were equally dark. After about twenty minutes I could begin to make out the soft shapes of clouds in the distance.

Finally the sun began to emerge, scattering light through every scratch and fragment on the windscreen. I was shivering by now: the coldest time of night. The sun was welcome. The cockpit glowed a warm orange. I closed my eyes. I hadn't slept for nearly twenty-four hours. I must have dozed for a minute or two.

I woke with a start, thinking the Lockheed was engulfed in flames. Just the sun.

Soon I'd see the coast of France, then track north to St Nazaire and inland to Paris. I stamped, stretched, cracked my knuckles, shouted, drank some coffee, swallowed some amphetamines. The morning took shape and there in the distance was the clear coast of France.

In a couple of hours I would land, the very angel of glamour. Howard Hughes, descending from the clouds, arrayed in silver.

The outskirts of Paris at last. I lowered the flaps and began the descent towards the field.

The Lockheed bumped to a halt amid the cheering throng. I cut the engines for the third time since New York. If only they knew. I could feel my body vibrate – a humming in the bones – as I climbed down from the cockpit. God's pitchfork, Howard Hughes, the biggest and the first. The clear sound of the future. He has come through the ether like a light wave.

Félicitations, Monsieur Hughes.

Toute la France vous souhaite la bienvenue!

Vous êtes fatigué?

My ears rang as the propellers died. The bulbs snapped. I was blind among my subjects.

Already the day was hot. Through all the human activity I could hear the whole field thick with the buzzing of insects. Perhaps the whole of Paris that day, July 11, 1938, was a hive of nectar and pistil and stamen and flowering, of all the bees sucking the life from the buds. A juicy kind of day. Perhaps the whole of France was awash with the drone of cicadas.

I walked towards the hangar thinking of bees and childhood. A translator had found me. I whispered in his ear.

Mr Hughes will have four hours' rest, he said.

Frank Dalby Davison

THE WOMAN AT THE MILL
1940

In the kitchen of the dwelling at the mill the little yellow-faced alarm-clock, ticking loudly on the shelf above the stove recess, marked the hour at noon. At the table, Irene Lawrence, in a wine-red dress that looked rather inappropriate to the hour and place, was sitting staring straight before her. In her ears were ringing the sound of a horse's hoof-beats, receding at a canter, dwindling into silence along the track leading to the township.

The mill was unwontedly quiet. Generally it was a noisy little mill, its saw splitting the air every few seconds with a hungry shriek as it tore its way through the green cypress-pine logs and loosed the scent of their sap on the air. At other times there would be heard the clatter of planks being stacked for seasoning, the shouts of Dick Skinner, and the cracking of his whip, as his team drew a load of logs in from the bush, muffled trampling of hooves, the thud of logs being let slip from the chains, and the jingle of shaken harness.

Today there were none of these sounds. Mat Lawrence, the owner of the mill, was in Wilgatown, arranging the disposal of sawn timber; Skinner had taken the day off to attend to some jobs on his selection, and Eric, the youth who helped Mat on the saw-bench, was with him.

Irene, Mat's wife, had spent the morning awaiting the arrival of Bert Caswell. She had heard that he had returned from the droving trip that had taken him out beyond Cunnamulla, and that he was staying with his relations, the Warburtons, in the township.

Her reasons for supposing that he might come were that he would be almost sure to know of Lawrence's departure on the Wilgatown train and being, she hoped, as eager to see her as she was to see him, he would ride out toward the mill. Its inactivity would surely draw him to complete the journey.

Her suppositions were not in themselves of great strength, but they were supported in her mind by her urgent wish toward their fulfilment. Since hearing of Caswell's return to the settlement, three days ago, she had lived in a secret welter of doubts and longings, resolutions and their immediate retractions. She had thought of seeking a meeting with him in the township under cover of a visit to the store, but had been deterred by two considerations. First, the fear of observing eyes – people were quick to put two and two together, particularly if the total promised a scandal; second, the torturing conviction that for proof that what had happened between them meant the same thing to them both she must wait upon his seeking her.

Mat had gone off with the children in the old sulky in which they travelled between home and school. As soon as he was well on his way she had begun making preparations for Caswell's coming; tidying up the house, and changing her dress. The speed of her movements had varied. At one moment she hurried as if his arrival were imminent, at another she lingered over brushing down the stove, or smoothing a coverlet, as if hope ceased temporarily to sustain her, or she feared running out of occupations with which to fill the time of waiting. Impossibly soon after Mat's departure – it took three-quarters of an hour to reach the railhead – she fancied she heard the mutter of approaching hooves. More than once, as if wishing conjured up a picture, she had glanced, in passing the kitchen door, to where the track appeared through the grass, on the ridge, under the solitary silver-leafed ironbark.

She had put on an afternoon frock, old enough that wearing it of a morning seemed justifiable, and long enough in temporary disuse that it had regained freshness in her own eyes. Its colour, wine-red, was the same as that she had worn the night she danced with Caswell. Its hue supported her gipsyish colouring.

While changing, before taking the frock down from its hanger, she had stood with bare arms before her mirror, taking stock of herself, fortifying herself with a brief survey of her charms. Full-figured in youth, the grossness that seemed likely to be her portion in later life had begun to overtake her at thirty-five. The almost waistless body, the large loose bust and thick shoulders, could scarcely have been overlooked except by eyes filled to satisfaction with her more attractive qualities. It was on these that her attention was concentrated.

The fine texture and creamy-whiteness of her skin was a consolation for the increasing quantity of flesh it covered. A well-shaped mouth, large dark eyes under a broad, smooth forehead, and brows that arched naturally, compensated for crow's-feet, sunburn, cheeks that were no longer firm, and a throat that had begun to sag. To further the love she made to herself, she put her hands to her head and shook out her dark mane. It fell about her shoulders, giving a gleam to their whiteness, and framed her face, seeming to focus attention on its good features. The act was one that Bert Caswell might be imagined performing. She clung to the thought a moment, embarrassed by it, yet tasting its sweetness. With a few swift strokes she brushed out her hair and re-coiled it, studying her reflection appreciatively the while.

Her toilet was completed when she produced a stick of carmine from the back of the dressing-table drawer and applied it to her lips. She had used it before only experimentally, briefly and in secret. The shrewd look she believed the sight of it would have brought to Mat's eyes would have embarrassed her. She had her doubts about Mat, when he was in Wilgatown. There were those girls at the Western Star. But Mat wasn't one to tolerate any romantic longings in a wife – and he would have taken the lipstick as a sure advertisement. Not that he seemed to mind the sight of it on other men's wives. She was slightly tremulous now, in using it; and exultant, too. On her unaccustomed lips she found its effect pleasingly dramatic. It heightened the tone values of natural colouring.

She returned to the kitchen, experiencing a quickening of her heart-beats when she saw that the clock, at a quarter past ten, confirmed her thoughts that Bert might possibly now be on his way. She glanced at the little blistered mirror on the wall by the roller-towel, then stood for a while by the window, looking out along the track.

She had no qualms – scarcely even a thought – about the part she was playing toward Mat, with his compact nuggety body; his gingery head, round and hard like quandong nut; his green eyes, flecked with brown, bright but opaque, like glass marbles, and the little hard bulge in his cheek where he carried his chew of tobacco. For more years than she could accurately number she had cherished a grudge against him, a quiet secret grudge.

There were times when she remembered with exasperation the girl she thought she must have been when she married him. She couldn't recall her motive. Good nature, simplicity, and no clear idea of what she was committing herself to, was how she explained it to herself. Hers, as she remembered it, had been a singularly vacant girlhood. The mentality of childhood seemed to have carried over into adolescence, and that of adolescence into maturity. She couldn't recall a wide-awake state of being such as she observed – or seemed to observe – and envied in so many of the young girls she now saw about her.

Mat was a cattle dealer at that time, and a fairly frequent caller at her father's farm on the Darling Downs. She had a – nowadays – displeasing recollection of him, on Sundays and holidays, flashily dressed and driving in a polished and twinkling sulky behind a smart-stepping pony. He was five years her senior. She had a feeling that in spirit, if not in fact, she had been part of a deal arranged between Mat and her father; a feeling that Mat had led her from her father's farm as he might have led a well-grown and promising heifer. It angered her to recall that she had once been pleased and flattered to go driving with him in his twinkling sulky.

He had got three children by her. That was how she thought of it – in terms of the paddock. The first was the child of her complete inexperience; the bearing of the second and third she had faced with the accommodating good humour with which she met circumstances she felt incapable of combating. Three, Mat had decided, would do. Toward them she was affectionate, but not with any depths of tenderness; a good humour came in again here. They didn't expect a great deal from her beyond feeding and clothing. They were tough like Mat; as toddlers they had looked upon the world with his eyes.

Awakening – maturity of outlook – seemed to have begun between the coming of the first and second child. It gained with the years. Generally she was able to get a twisted humour out of the contemplation of her lot; but from it fell a fine accumulating sediment of resentment. On this her thoughts fed during those times when cheerfulness failed her. She thought about things over the cooking stove and the sewing-machine, over the wash-tubs, lying beside Mat, and even in moments of greater intimacy.

She suspected herself of being a fool, in the sense of having capacity to feel, to experience, without being able to wrest from these things an ability to cope with life. Mat made her feel like that. His mentality was the dominant one; it undermined her, making her feel that in secret he estimated her exactly, marked her limitations, and valued her for what she was worth to him; that he thought of her, behind those unrevealing eyes, as a man might think of a docile and profitable cow. It wasn't quite like that really, but that was how, in her discontent, she dramatised it.

She turned from the window with a deep-drawn sigh. Its prospect was not absorbing for long. There was just a partial view of the iron roof of the mill, silent now, and of the track running up the slope between the tall yellow grass to where, under a solitary, leaning silver-leaf ironbark, it sidled over the low ridge; above these a blue void.

From a shelf she lifted an armful of old magazines, weeklies and department-store catalogues, and flopped them on the table. Seating herself, she drew them to her one by one – as she had done a hundred times before in leaden-footed hours – and turned the pages, glancing at the illustrations with inattentive eyes.

Bert Caswell was not the first man who had engaged her notice. Since she first suspected that she had started married life on the wrong foot she had, without fully acknowledging it to herself, been keeping covert watch for someone with whom she might find consolation. She had no clear idea of what she would do with such a person when found; it was just a groping for something with which to ease a dis-satisfaction.

During the years a changing acquaintanceship had brought a num-ber of candidates into view, but fastidiousness, caution, and points of principle had caused each to be rejected, often without their knowing they had been objects of consideration. There had been Larry Matheson, a distant relation of Mat's, who used to stay with them sometimes. She had been friendly with Larry, big, slow and kindly, but she had never become unaware of his neglected teeth and warty hands. There had been Alec Withers, with whom Mat had been in partnership for a short while in a carrying business in Toowoomba. She liked looking at Alec, but that was as far as it got. Other things aside, she feared Mat's sharp-ness. Then there had been Tom Wallace, a stock and station agent. Here had arisen the consideration of her friendly regard for his wife; though *he* had been willing enough – unexpectedly, embarrassingly so, on one occasion.

On the new settlement, before Bert Caswell's arrival, and just after the establishment of the police station, she had found herself thinking sometimes of the sergeant of police. At dances and bush races, and when he called at the mill on patrol, she was able, by a special show of friendliness, to gain his attention. The sergeant was interested, and the consideration of going back on a fellow-woman didn't arise here, for she and Mrs Fitzpatrick were unfriendly; but there was the counter-consideration that the unfriendliness was rooted in Mrs Fitzpatrick's sense of social superiority. In the circumstances wouldn't Irene be degrading herself? While these matters were under review by her the affair slipped from her hands. By a subtle change of behaviour the sergeant indicated that his capacity as a gallant, his moral or immoral predilections, his sense of marital fidelity – or sense of caution or whatever it was – must all remain for ever unriddled beneath the cloak of his official dignity.

Within ten minutes of meeting Bert Caswell she was happy in the thought that none of these previous fancies had come to flower. They met at the Murdochs', whose homestead lay just a hundred yards through the bush at the back of the township. They were friends of hers and also of the Warburtons, who had offered him, following the death of his parents, the right to make their home his during the intervals of his bush wanderings. Two of the younger Warburtons had brought him to the Murdochs' on the afternoon of her call.

In his late twenties, upstanding, jauntily confident of himself, friendly facing the world, and with a ready laugh, he had filled her eyes at once. It had been no more than a polite social occasion, but they had exchanged a little one-to-one cross-room conversation, and she had found it easy to catch his eye between times. She had driven home thinking about him, and had continued to do so during the two days that elapsed before they met again. Thought of him fed a glow within her. Two things caused her a pang each time they came to mind. He was six or seven years her junior and he was – she thought – better-looking than any man had a right to be. The first she assuaged by the thought that sometimes such differences didn't matter, the second was cancelled out as often as it cropped up by the reflection that she wouldn't have him any different if she could.

At the end of two days she had driven into the township armed with a list of errands sufficient to keep her there for the afternoon. Whether she was making the journey really to do errands or in hope of seeing Bert she would decide on the drive home, in the light of whether she ran into him or not.

As if in answer to her anxious hope, Bert had come from the store just as she drove up to it. Before he went on his way, and before she entered the store to begin a list of errands whose nature had miraculously changed from dubious to gladsome, they had a short but pregnant conversation under the store veranda. She had almost gulped when he, obviously daring a little, had called her Irene, but she was glad of it and instantly called him Bert.

They didn't meet again till the night of the dance.

As the evening wore on there had been a certain amount of coming and going between the Murdochs' – where wraps and sleeping children were left – and the School of Arts. They met on the track in the darkness under the boughs.

'It's you, is it?'

'Yes.'

And a little later at the sound of approaching voices:

'There's someone coming.'

They withdrew among the trees to one side, and there she had both encouraged and yielded to Caswell's ardour. She wasn't sure whether she was doing the best thing. She felt she hadn't meant to come so quickly to this part of it, but she couldn't bring herself to say no to him, and she wanted to herself, anyway.

On the next morning but one Caswell left for the job for which he had engaged, at Charleville.

For a while, afterwards, Irene was lost in her feelings between being something aghast at what she had done, and taking pride in that she had gone, daring worthily, where most women ventured only in guarded excursions of the imagination.

From her thoughts of the future relationship of herself and Caswell she was not able to draw comfort. During the months he was away she lived over and over again, in smallest detail, every memory she had of him, from the first moment she had seen him, finding a significance in the recollection of a look, a gesture, a movement of his head, the readiness or unreadiness of a reply to something she had said to him.

From those that were pleasing to recall she built a happy dwelling-place for her spirit. While the mood of optimism was on her it sufficed her need. She didn't begrudge him his absence – he had his living to earn. Even the lack of a letter was immaterial – he was unhandy with the pen; he feared making trouble for her. There had been the consolation of a message contained in a single scrawled page to the Warburtons, 'Remember me especially to Mrs Lawrence.' She had built a lot around that.

But there were times when doubt tortured her; when she felt she had nothing of his in her keeping. She had given too much and too readily. From so many of the remembered things there might be drawn a disturbing significance. Perhaps in finding assurance in her memories, she was deluding herself. There was the word he might have given, but hadn't; the touch she might have had but didn't receive. He had scarcely thought of her since he went away! In the pain of it she built a hell for herself. She could have hated him – with a hate that would have melted at the sight of him.

Looking always at the same set of facts she would swing, like that, from one extreme of feeling to another. She was being foolish in hoping that there was some lasting bond between them. Heaven was witness to the strength of their attachment. He hadn't given her another thought. He was being careful out of fear for her. She would never see him again. When he came he would take her away with him. Perhaps, at the last, she wouldn't be able to leave the children. But there must be some way past all difficulties for feeling such as theirs.

Through these alternating fears and hopes she passed in quick succession as she sat turning the pages of the magazines. At one moment warming to the thought of his nearness. At worst he was no further away than the township. At another moment cold in the stomach and shaking in the limbs. He had returned three days ago! He should have come to her, if only to give her the comfort of a word. He wasn't coming.

At the sound of hooves on the track she went paper-white. For a few seconds she couldn't move, feared she was going to faint; then she raised herself and looked through the window.

It was he. He had dropped his horse's reins at the edge of the grass and was coming toward the house.

'Good day!' His tall figure was in the doorway, blocking the light.

'Hullo, Bert . . . Come in and sit down.'

She was standing by the table. Her colour had returned. Her heart was thumping so violently that it pained her. Her eyes were idolatrous.

Caswell did as he was bidden, taking a seat on the bench by the wall. She – physically lost to consciousness of herself – remained standing. They were both nervous, uncertain of their ground.

'You're back again, Bert!'

'Yes, Irene. For a little while.'

'Why?' In his reply there had been an inflection of voice that she didn't understand and which gave her a stab of fear. 'You're not going away again soon?' It seemed incredible to her that he should come to her talking of going away.

'I might.' The question – it seemed – had touched the quick of his pride of calling. He swung one leg across the other. 'There's a man after me now to go with him to pick up a mob of cattle out from Quilpie. Never have much trouble about getting a job!'

She caught the note of vainglory, and a short laugh that was almost a sob expressed the relief to her feelings. Men, Bert included, were just like big boys. She saw how it was; because Bert was just as nervous as herself. Their opening exchanges had taken on an unfortunate turn, run off into an irrelevancy. She could see now, by the way he was smiling, that that was how it was.

They went on to talk of the trip he had just finished. She inquiring and he replying. Their talk continued for some time.

But this was only conversation. They were looking at each other all the time with questioning eyes.

Caswell rose and came over to her. He was thinking how nice she looked, and was wondering how soon he could come to the point. His uncertainty vanished when he went to take her in his arms and found with what eagerness she accepted.

The yellow-faced alarm-clock had the room to itself for an hour before the door leading to the rest of the house opened and Bert and Irene re-entered the kitchen. He took a cigarette from his pocket and stood tapping the end on the back of his hand.

'I'll put the kettle on for a cup of tea.' Irene went to the stove, shook up the embers and put fresh wood on.

Caswell glanced at her back, then walked across the room and sat down on the bench. He was uneasy again, not nervously, this time, but thoughtfully.

He had ridden out from the township in some doubt as to his reception. What had taken place between them had been a good deal in his thoughts during his months on the stock route. He felt genuinely attracted to Irene. When he had called her by her name that day under the store veranda it had been a spontaneous act, an act of momentary daring. It had gratified him, quite innocently, when she responded. He had been a rather surprised as well as a much elated young man, that night of the dance, when he had found his amorous advances being welcomed. Hitherto his experiences had been confined to the girls at fourth-rate country pubs; housemaids whose employers expected them not to be above entertaining guests on terms to be arranged between them. This matter of his encounter with a very desirable married woman was in a different class. Life was opening out! At the same time their contact with each other had been so brief as to be rather insubstantial in recollection. By the camp fires of the west a doubt as to the probable reception awaiting him when he next saw Irene had, in consequence, developed in him. He needed the reassurance of repetition.

Events since coming to the mill had set his mind at rest in that connection, but something fresh had come to his notice. He had become aware of a difference between himself and her; a difference of intention. She didn't want just occasional adventure. She wanted all of him. Things she had said, questions she had asked him while they were in the bedroom, had apprised him of that. He had concealed the effect on him, but it had come as a bit of a jolt. She had possessed his body with a passion that exceeded his own, a soft abandonment that at once gratified and daunted him.

Irene was setting out the cups and saucers. Though she had yielded to his request as if will were a thing apart from herself, and having yielded had done so without reserve, she had been, for a moment, a little hurt that he should have come at her so soon after his arrival. However, that moment of regret was past now; its memory deeply overlaid by the memory of their intimacy; the memory of the joy of yielding without an inward core of resentment against her partner. She recalled the directness of his approach that night under the trees; perhaps it was part of his nature. She didn't mind if it was; so long as he had other feelings for her. They had touched on these while in the bedroom, but she hoped to hear more fully. A good part of the day – before he need go – was still before them. She wasn't quite reassured as yet, but she had enough warrant for belief, for – as now – imagining his tenderness when she told him how much she had thought of him while he was away.

Caswell was looking out the door as if he was concerned about his horse. He was thinking how, by half-truths, evasions and direct lies, by both feigning to answer, and stifling questions with caresses, he had misled her in the bedroom. But what else could he have done? He didn't mean to be unkind – you couldn't think unkindly of a woman who had taken you to bed with her – but she really was a bit of a mug!

'I'll have to be getting along as soon as we've drunk our tea,' he said. He had one thought now – escape.

'Not right away?' she asked.

His ear caught the expected note of surprise and pain in her voice, and from the tail of his eye he saw her movements cease.

'Yes, I'll have to be pushing along.'

'I thought you'd stay awhile with me, Bert.' She spoke with a tremor.

He was still pretending to concentrate on the scene outside, and was intensely conscious of her watching him. She had a right to expect that he would stay awhile, he knew that. He wasn't treating her with even common politeness. But he couldn't help that; couldn't bring himself to meet what he felt sure would come if he waited.

She had come a few paces toward him, and was standing there with the teapot in her hand. Just standing there. Why didn't she put the teapot down?

'I thought you'd want us to have a nice long talk together,' she was saying. 'We could. We've got all day.'

He could no longer avoid looking at her. Their eyes met and held; his like one trapped, hers bright with pain.

'You see, Irene,' he explained, 'I've got to see that man about lifting those cattle. I wouldn't like to miss that job.'

Her eyes searched his. Why had the matter suddenly become urgent?

He smiled defensively as he returned her glance, but his eyes were hard.

'I've got to see that man,' he repeated.

She searched his face for a little while, her own pale, and showing the full tally of her years. She realised now the extent of her past pretences; her house of make-belief had vanished. Neither in the months of his absence nor in the recent hour of their clipped bodies had they shared a thought. What to her had been a blind groping for something of which life had cheated her had been for him just a cheap sexual success, something to bolster his conceit of himself.

Her mind told her this, but she couldn't quite bring her feelings to acquiesce. There was still a little hope. She would go and sit beside him and tell her story. At least he would sympathise and understand. She put the teapot down and took a step toward him, but that was as far as she got. She saw him flinch, and move as if he were about to get up. He was afraid of a scene. Well, she'd spare him that.

She had sunk into the chair by the table, scarcely aware of having moved. She had a feeling that she wasn't a fool any more, but that it was going to be a long time before she could bring herself to accept this sudden accretion of wisdom. There was a long silence in which the ticking of the clock sounded like a gong.

'When do you think you'll be back this way, Bert?' Her voice was scarcely above a whisper. There was something guilty about her question, as if the words were torn out of her by her feelings, against the command of her mind.

He knew instinctively that she was clutching at straws. 'Not for some time, I suppose, Irene,' he answered firmly. 'We're taking cattle out to Windorah and then I understand there's a chance of picking up another mob at Bedourie.'

Again silence fell. He saw that she had forgotten about the tea. He might be able to get away.

He scuffled uncertainly in the doorway.

'Well, so-long, Irene.'

'Goodbye, Bert,' she answered, 'and the best of luck!' She looked up at him in speaking and smiled. She must appear to take what had happened between them in the spirit in which he had intended – at any rate until he was gone.

For a moment his eyes were held unwillingly by hers. He saw in them pain, and resignation to pain that was yet to be endured; he caught a glimpse of reaches of human feeling that he hadn't known to exist. He looked away hurriedly. He was half-angry that this light enterprise should have brought him to this.

He went down the steps. With his foot in the stirrup he looked back at the house; then swung into the saddle and moved off. The sooner he saw that man about the cattle the better.

Liam Davison

THE SHIPWRECK PARTY

1989

Captain Youl was a man in control of his ship. He stood with his hand firmly on the brass lever at his side, looking out to sea. When he pushed it forward a message was sent through a wire which ran like a nerve through the body of the ship. It went through the two crowded upper decks, through the Mezzanine to the bar where drinks were being served, down through the four-inch steel plates of the bulkheads and along the 310-foot length of the ship. At the engine room a little bell was rung. Men responded to the bell. They opened furnace doors, adjusted valves, sweated, and the 1410 tons of steel moved a fraction faster through the water.

To John Bannister, who watched from the balcony of the Grand Hotel, the change in speed was barely noticeable. Later, he would say that things seemed to be running as normal, but then he wasn't an expert on ships. He'd watched the *Hydra* make three round trips to the point on the opposite side of the bay, not so much out of interest but because he enjoyed the sun. From the balcony, he looked out over a calm sea. Even along the shore it had given up throwing itself at the sand and lay there, flat and exhausted, waiting for the day to end. Children wet their feet without interest. Men and women sat talking on the lawns in front of the hotel or else walked slowly along the esplanade in pairs or out to the end of the pier for something to do. In the rotunda, a little way round to the right, musicians were packing away their instruments. All afternoon, music had floated up through the heat to the balcony and out across the bay.

Beyond all this, the *Hydra* created only a small disturbance in the water. John Bannister took little notice of its moving back and forth. Each time he looked out to sea and caught it in the periphery of his vision, it seemed to be in exactly the same spot as the time before, so it might not have been moving at all. That's why at first he couldn't quite tell what had happened. There was no noise, no obvious sign of disturbance, but something, something important had changed.

Eventually he noticed that the *Hydra* had stopped. It tilted slightly to one side like a picture that had slipped on its nail. Everything else was the same but the sight of the crooked ship disconcerted him. He looked back to the straight pier, the people on the esplanade, the musicians in the rotunda, trying to avoid it. But, as usual, the one blemish on the scene, small as it was, kept catching his eye. The *Hydra* was sinking.

By late afternoon it was listing badly and a flotilla of small craft had converged on the ship. Men who would normally never have taken to the sea took off their coats, rolled up their sleeves and rowed out to look for themselves. The children, happy that something had finally happened, ran round to the point for a closer look. Even the ladies craned their necks from the end of the pier.

The passengers were removed safely from the ship. Ladders were lowered over the sides to the small boats waiting below and, as each one was filled, it made its way slowly to the end of the pier. Some of the ladies wet their feet and one, unsettled at being part of a shipwreck, dropped her parasol into the water. It floated for a while like a cotton jellyfish then sank slowly down to the bottom.

As more boats came in, word came back to the hotel that Captain Youl was firmly in control. His name was passed from person to person, each time with some new reference to the way he was handling things: Captain Youl continued giving orders from the bridge, Captain Youl had saved a man from drowning, Captain Youl was the last to leave the ship. So by the time John Bannister heard his name it had already established a reputation.

It was with this reputation that the captain himself finally arrived at the Grand Hotel. He seemed unperturbed by the day's events, happy even with the interest he'd created in the town. A cable had been sent to Melbourne informing the company directors of what had happened. Questions were asked about how a ship could simply run aground like that. People spoke of an inquiry. Negligence was mentioned more than once. Captain Youl made light of the situation, speaking of far worse calamities he'd seen at sea.

'There's not much can come of a shipwreck the likes of this,' he said. 'Hardly a shipwreck at all when you think of things.'

From the hotel the *Hydra* looked like she was sinking further into the sea as the tide came in. Her great wheel was little more than a hump in the water at her side, and her twin funnels pointed obliquely like guns at the sky. Others commented too on the nature of the sinking. 'There should be more to a shipwreck than this,' they said, 'more noise and confusion.' Shipwrecks, they knew, shouldn't be tidy affairs.

Captain Youl glanced only occasionally at the sea and seemed unperturbed at the prospect of an inquiry. Even ashore he was in control of things. People turned to him to see what would happen next or else they spread rumours about his colourful past so his reputation grew beyond belief. When he announced the party it was as if that was what people had been waiting for. Even the least adventurous were excited by the idea of a party on board a sinking ship. There was talk of irresponsibility of course, and questions of safety. Some argued about the likelihood of the ship taking more water and tilting further on its side or the possibility of it turning completely over, but all of this only attracted more interest to the idea of the party. John Bannister watched with reservations as the preparations were made.

Crates of Pimms and glasses were carried to the end of the pier and loaded into the same small boats which had, only hours before, brought the passengers ashore. The captain himself directed the loading. He wore full uniform with his cap sitting straight on his head as if he knew it might soon be gone. Four crates of poultry, a pheasant under glass, boxes of fruit and two round cheeses all found their way from the hotel kitchens into the waiting boats. A case of wine was brought for the captain's table along with a dozen crayfish all pink and whistling with steam. One by one the hotel's kitchen staff filed into the boats to be rowed precariously out to the ship. 'There's nothing to worry about,' the captain reassured. 'Nothing to worry about at all.' Finally the musicians from the rotunda were crowded into the last of the boats. They huddled over their instruments, anxious about the water, and a gold tuba sprouted like a funnel from the back of the boat.

John Bannister was one of the last to leave for the ship, except for those who weren't invited or were too afraid to go. Strings of lights had been roped between the funnels and around the decks so it looked like a floating palace. The musicians had already started playing their music and it floated out across the still, black water. On board,

everything was tilted to one side. The guests gripped tightly to railings
to stop them from slipping into the water which they were surprised
to find beside them instead of beneath their feet. It was as if they were
already drunk even before they'd had enough to drink. Women fell
willingly into men's arms and wondered whether the ship was moving.
The decks, awash with spilt drinks, sloped dangerously away.

The captain welcomed John Bannister aboard, his strong arms lifting
him up the last few steps of the ladder and his face smiling out from
beneath the cap. 'Welcome aboard the *Hydra*,' he said. 'We thought the
last had arrived.'

John Bannister felt the ship slipping away beneath his feet. 'I hadn't
planned to come,' he said, 'but then . . .'

'You don't like ships, Mr Bannister? Or parties?'

'I don't mind either,' he said, 'but perhaps not the two together. I
don't like sinking ships.'

'The *Hydra* is quite safe as she is. She's grounded on rock,' said the
captain. 'Can I get you a drink, or introduce you to someone perhaps.'

'I was wondering, Captain Youl, with a vessel the size of the *Hydra*,'
he looked along her polished deck and up to the crowded promenade,
'how can a ship just sink like this?'

'You're not experienced with the sea, Mr Bannister?'

'I watch it from the shore,' he said. 'It seemed harmless enough
today.'

'Things aren't always what they seem, Mr Bannister, especially not
the sea. You'll learn that if you stay by it long enough.'

'But there must be charts? Navigational aids? It doesn't change that
much.'

'The sea has many variables, Mr Bannister. And I have many guests.
If you'll excuse me, you'll find drinks being served in the bar.'

The captain returned to the foredeck where a group of ladies waited
patiently for his return. They stood close by him, attracted by the uniform and hanging on every word he spoke. Some of the younger men,
anxious to make themselves known, stood back waiting for an
introduction. John Bannister made his unsteady way towards the mid-
deck doorways. Some of the guests had started a game, seeing who
could walk the length of the ship without slipping or clutching for
support. They filed past him, arms out like tightrope walkers, laughing
and calling to him to join their fun. Inside, the crowd leaned against

each other marvelling at the idea of the party on board this ship.

John Bannister stood by the open doors watching as they grew louder and more excited trying to serve themselves food from the sloping table. A woman, making for the doorway, careered into him, spilling her drink onto her shoes and laughing at her poor coordination. She trailed another man behind her as a sort of balancing device.

'Are you a friend of the captain's?' she asked.

John Bannister guessed she was talking to him. 'I've only met him the once. In fact . . .'

'Then you're staying at the hotel,' she said. 'Yes you look like you'd be staying at the hotel. Then you must let me show you the ship.' She let go of the other man and leaned heavily against John Bannister's arm.

'I'm sorry . . .'

'What Miss Martin means, Sir,' said the other man, 'is that everyone staying at the hotel was invited aboard.'

'You must let me show you. We're going below the decks.'

'Below the decks?'

'There's a group of us. We're going to open the hatches. It will be fun don't you think?'

John Bannister looked to the other man for an answer.

'It can't do any harm,' he said. 'A few drinks. The damage is already done.'

'But the captain.'

'You don't know the captain, Mr . . . ?'

'Bannister. No, I don't know him, but surely he wouldn't approve.'

'The captain is a man who believes in taking risks. That's how we come to be where we are.' He took a cigarette from his pocket and lit it. 'Have you any idea how much the captain lost today?'

He felt Miss Martin's body leaning close to his own.

'On the crossing, Mr Bannister. You're not a gambling man? There's not much excitement in Sunday excursions for a man like Captain Youl. So, a little money changes hands. The *Hydra* is a fast ship for its size. People are prepared to bet on it.'

'What sort of people?'

'Business people, Mr Bannister. Syndicates. Their names might come out in the inquiry. But then again . . . It had to happen of course, given time. You can only get so close to the reef on a lowish tide, even with Youl at the helm.'

Outside, the band was starting another tune and people were trying to dance on the sloping boards. Miss Martin still held John Bannister's arm. She called out across the room something about opening the hatches and spilt more of her drink on the floor.

'But why give a party?'

'The captain's a man of style, Mr Bannister. I mean, you've only got to look at him to see. Even when he's losing he does it right and, when it's all said and done, there's no real harm resulted. No-one's been hurt. People are enjoying themselves. That's the function of a party.'

Miss Martin drew him away towards the hatches, her arm linked through his. 'No-one will know,' she said. 'There's only a few of us. We've found some lights.'

At the rear of the ship, two metal hatches were set tight in the decking. A man, already clumsy with drink, was trying unsuccessfully to prise one of them open while two women and another man stood watching, offering advice and giggling with anticipation. 'Get your fingers underneath it and it should lift straight up,' the man said. 'There's nothing to stop it.'

John Bannister looked back towards the rest of the party. Miss Martin drew him on. 'They say there's passages,' she whispered, 'leading right through to the front of the ship, and they won't all be filled with water. Imagine,' she said, 'if we all came up from nowhere through that hatch at the front of the ship. Wouldn't that be a surprise? Wouldn't that just stop the party?' The others nodded and laughed their approval. John Bannister stood looking down at the hatches.

'Do you think it's really wise?'

'Of course it's not wise,' Miss Martin laughed. 'It's fun. Where's your sense of adventure?'

The man giving advice thrust a light into John Bannister's hand and bent down to open the hatch himself. It lifted heavily outwards revealing a dark square hole in the deck. The sound of lapping water came out of it and strange echoes from deep inside the ship. There was an iron ladder disappearing into it.

'Shine the light inside.'

John Bannister did as he was told. The light showed the hole opening into the hold of the ship. Water dripped from the metal beams and lay in great dark puddles on the lower side of the ship. Miss Martin undid the straps of her shoes and set them neatly by the hatch.

'I'll go first,' she said. 'I'll lead the expedition.'

'Perhaps someone with a light should lead the way,' said the other man. They looked at John Bannister.

'It should be a man,' said one of the other women. 'It should be a man with a light.'

John Bannister removed his shoes and placed them beside Miss Martin's. 'I'll wait at the bottom then to give some light,' he said. 'I really don't know about going further.'

Inside the ship, the light reflected strangely off the water, throwing distorted illuminations up onto the steel walls. All around he could hear the dripping of water and the hollow booms of things nudging against each other further inside the ship. There was a passage leading forward from the hold. Miss Martin edged him towards it. 'That will lead to the cabins,' she said. 'You go first.'

They moved warily along the passage, leaning against the lower wall and moving their feet through water. The ship creaked and strained, and every now and then they heard a louder bang like something heavy falling far away as one of the steel plates shifted or buckled under the weight of water. There was a machine noise too, a regular humming of the generators used to light the decks, and further on they could see that some of the passageways were lit irregularly with weak yellow lights.

They moved past great chambers opening off the passageways, steel compartments half-filled with water. Further inside, the water rose almost to their knees and was filled with floating things, bits of wood and personal belongings. John Bannister felt them brushing past his legs as he moved deeper into the ship.

'The crew's quarters will be further forward,' said Miss Martin. 'Then there should be stairways leading up.'

They passed metal ladders leading further down into the body of the ship, into the engine rooms where dark shapes rose out of the water, and somewhere beneath it all, the steel plates had been rent apart exposing the black rock of the reef. Above them, they could hear the muffled sounds of the party, the music coming down through a maze of openings and corridors and mingling with the ever-present sound of water. John Bannister imagined he could hear the captain's voice. The passage they were in turned sharply to the left, towards the list of the ship so the water rose even higher up their legs.

'I think perhaps we might have come far enough,' John Bannister said. He could hear Miss Martin's breathing close behind him and the sounds of the others pushing though water. 'We'll have to go back.'

'We can't go back,' she said. 'We're almost there. Listen, you can hear them.' The others laughed and splashed behind them, showing no intention of turning back.

The passage turned again towards the bow of the ship and was filled with moving light which reflected off the water up onto the walls and ceiling. They passed a number of doors, all shut tight with water, with the names of crew members stencilled onto them. John Bannister shone his light through the round window in each of them and saw mattresses, broken chairs, bits of paper, all floating in the murky water. In the last window his light shone into a small chamber with the body of a man floating face-down inside it. Its swollen arms bumped against the bottom of the window and John Bannister could see other things floating beside it – a small chest, two books and the back of a chair – but his eyes came back to the body. Floating like that inside the steel room, it hardly seemed human at all, more like some strange creature glimpsed from outside a dark aquarium. The name on the door was Hughes.

The others followed John Bannister along the passage, unknowingly past Mr Hughes's quiet door, and into the stairwells which took them up, out of the water, back towards the surface. Miss Martin and her friends giggled with excitement as they appeared, dripping with water, from the body of the ship. She stumbled away, screeching with delight as she went. 'You'll never believe,' she squealed. 'Such an adventure. The whole length of the ship.'

John Bannister let them go, feeling conscious of his wet trousers and the party going on around him. Few people noticed their arrival.

On the foredeck he found the captain. He looked remarkably at ease on the sloping deck, unaware of what floated at the heart of his ship. Even his cap sat straight on his head. John Bannister caught his eye.

'Captain Youl,' he said. 'If you'll excuse me for a moment. There's something I think you should know about your ship.'

Marele Day

EMBROIDERY
1999

Flicker flicker flicker gold and blue and an orange one with black here
they come again and there are no trees or places for them to settle just
flicker flicker in from both sides then out fluttering up an invisible
scent trail and fading away their legs and antennae are thin as pieces
of cotton little wisps you snip snip off when you've finished sewing
and you gather them all up into a tiny nest and throw them away into
the bin or the compost heap and bury them and they could be there
when the butterflies come out of the cocoons and need their little
cotton legs.

'Mum?'

Mum mum mum mum mum.

'I've brought some soup. Potato and leek. Your favourite.'

Something warm in her mouth, warm and white, and some of it
goes down in the swallow and some dribbles out and makes the chin
furry and cold. It's a long way to Tipperary.

'Where's Graham?'

'He's coming this afternoon. When you've finished the soup.'

Karen looked up from the embroidery. Late afternoon sun filled the
room, motes of dust dancing in the yellow light. It reminded her of
the fake snowflakes that flurried about in the glass mound when you
turned it upside down. The glass mound which trapped a tiny house
with Santa Claus standing outside, harnessing his reindeer, the sleigh
already laden with the presents he would deliver to all the children in
the world in one night. It was magical. She got it the Christmas she
was five. Years later, in Europe, she was surprised how crunchy snow
was underfoot. Not like the snow in the glass mound at all. Back in
this house, her mind often landed on childhood things.

She concentrated on the needle and thread, the precision of the stitches, the fabric firm under the embroidery hoop. In and out, in and out, piercing the fabric, bringing the needle towards herself, doing this again and again until the long thin thread turned into the petal of a rose. She passed the pad of her finger over it, felt its soft silky smoothness. It was pleasing to the touch. The look of it was less important. Nevertheless Karen had worked the threads so that the deeper reds were in the folds.

She heard a car pull up and the muted slam of the door. Two doors. Graham had brought Lydia with him. She folded the work away. Graham had a key but knocked on the door like a visitor, not like someone who'd spent half his life in this house.

'It's Graham, Mum. I'm just going to go and let him in. Won't be a minute.'

Draughty air back of the head and the butterflies start up again they do that they ride the air currents like birds and in some areas they are protected species and they always return to the same place every year, not the same ones several generations removed but it's in their genes did you know that dear and sometimes if the wind is strong they are blown off course and they end up in Africa and they don't know where they are they fly over the big blue and then there are trees and they alight.

This was the first time Lydia had seen Grandma since she was sick. Dad had told her that Grandma was different, she did not talk properly but that she'd be really pleased to see her, even if it didn't look like it. Her head was flopped over to one shoulder and she was staring, as if trying to look up Lydia's nose.

'Hi,' said Lydia, pulling her mouth back into a smile. She stood there looking at Grandma's hands, inert in her lap, at the pretty rings on her bumpy fingers, the shiny nails. Though Grandma didn't talk or even move, she was big in the room. There was lots of space around her but it was as if she was connected to strings that reached into every corner.

Dad kissed Grandma on the forehead. 'They keeping you busy?' he asked in a jolly way.

'Yep, pretty busy,' said Aunty Karen. She said it in the same jolly way but she looked at Dad as if something was his fault. It made Lydia think of when she was real little and grown-ups would talk about her as if she wasn't there. This was the opposite, they were talking through Grandma to each other, as if Grandma was the phone or something.

Lydia took a step closer and put her hand on the edge of the wheelchair, gingerly, wary that one of Grandma's hands might spring out and pull her down into the wheelchair with her.

'Show Grandma your painting,' said Dad.

Lydia slipped her backpack off, pulled out the painting and held it up. 'That's the fish we caught off the wharf last weekend,' explained Lydia. 'See, it's got the hook in the mouth and that's the line,' she filled the silence. She edged it towards Grandma, placing it in her lap. It slipped onto the floor in front of her. Lydia bent down to retrieve it. There was a bad smell, like a baby had just dirtied its nappy.

'Let's put the painting on the fridge door, shall we?' said Dad.

Under the brown leaves the earth is dank and foetid and in the rich dark earth nestle cocoons some butterflies live for only one day some spend years in the ground and fly up for their day when they are ready the monarchs are an endangered species bright flakes of colour in the garden dipping from flower to flower and what a sight in the season when there are clusters of them in cold weather their limbs are stiff and Father carefully picks one up opens his mouth blows warm breath on it to make it supple it flies away.

They were gone. Graham could never stay long. Karen would have liked the excuse of a business meeting to go to, a drama class to pick Lydia up from. There were days she couldn't look at her mother, couldn't bear to be in the same room. The mother had become the baby, and the child the mother looking after her. But who looked after Karen? 'There are options,' the doctor had advised. 'They're well looked after you know.' 'She'd prefer to be here. At home,' Karen had said. But where was her mother – in that waxy body in the wheelchair?

She took up the embroidery once again. It was pleasant to work with the colours, think of the layout, to make the tiny perforation and pull the thread through. Here at least she felt she was making progress.

A leaf came to rest in Karen's lap. There were brown leaves all over the lawn, the rose bushes were scraggy. The garden had been her mother's joy. One childhood afternoon Karen had come home from school to find her mother cutting away dead branches. She turned to greet Karen, ask her what she'd done today at school. The movement must have disturbed a couple of butterflies because they darted straight up out of her hair. Her mother slowly raised herself from her kneeling position, following the movement of the butterflies so smoothly Karen half-expected her mother to float up into the sky as well. 'What?' asked her mother. 'Nothing. Butterflies flew out of your hair.' Smiling, her mother snapped shut the secateurs, picked up the rose prunings and placed them in the compost heap. She took off the gardening gloves to reveal much smaller hands inside.

There was a noise from inside, a soft kind of grunt. Karen put aside the embroidery and went in. Her mother stared in that naked vacant way, head flopped to the left. There was the smell of dirty nappies again. How could she do so much when she was hardly eating anything? 'Baby want to do poo-poo?' No response of course. 'Baby already done poo-poo?'

Karen opened the window and stood in the fresh air. Her mother could sit in her own dirt for a while, what difference did it make. Maybe if Karen just left the window open permanently. She could catch pneumonia and die. Her mother would prefer that. She always said, if I get like that, you know, where I don't know which way is up, pour a bottle of whisky into me, point me in the direction of New Zealand and tell me to start swimming. Karen could push the wheelchair out-side, through the gate, onto the footpath and let it freewheel down the hill, cross the main road and if in the extraordinary event that it didn't collide with a car, watch it plunge into the harbour.

She hated the feeding, the changing of the underwear and the bedsheets. Her mother had become a baby. When it started happening Karen wanted to clutch at the air, but of course air is nothing to hold onto. She remembered a time at the beach when she waded into the water, wading in after her mother who was swimming further out. She remembered when she couldn't touch the bottom and she'd lost sight of her mother. She started screaming and thrashing her arms. She hadn't realised that she was actually treading water and quite afloat on her own. She wanted her mother to rescue her. Her mother had come back, she was probably only a few metres away but it was forever for Karen. 'It's all right, darling,' her mother had said. 'Look, you're keeping your head above water all by yourself.' But that was only how it looked on the surface.

Abruptly Karen went into the hallway. She picked up the phone and jabbed at the numbers like a bird pecking seed. He was in a meeting of course. 'Tell him it's his sister. A matter of life and death.'

'Graham, it's me. Do it.'

She took a slow deep breath in and out then went back to attend to her mother.

Cold damp swampy ground that's better breathe warmth onto me dry me and keep me warm put me in the sun, hold me in your mouth and breathe warm air so that I can fly.

A plate with a red smear of spaghetti sauce and a lonely fork sat on the coffee table. The TV was on for some background noise, low enough so that she could hear any noises in her mother's room through the intercom. Karen needed a thicker texture, something for hair.

Karen went up to her bedroom, the room she'd been sleeping in again since she'd moved back to care for her mother. When she'd arrived, the room had been a museum of her childhood. The pyjama dog in its traditional place on the pillow. A photo of her age five, off to school for the first time. All neat as a pin. Now the bed remained unmade and the floor was strewn with clothes. Karen's own private revolt.

She reached into the top section of the cupboard, final resting place of dolls, and felt the cold metal of the money box. It was the bust of a Negro, his hand in front. If you laid a coin in the open palm, pressed a lever at the back, the hand came up to the mouth which swallowed the coin. Karen curved her hand around his curly head, fitting it cosy as a cap. She always like doing that and was very fond of the black man even though the world had changed since Karen's childhood and they thought it better that they hid him in the cupboard.

Behind him she felt the softness of the raggedy doll, a little moth-eaten despite the camphor. She pulled a thread from a loose stitch. Ideal for hair. The whole thing would unravel if she kept doing it, pulling and pulling at the thread, making the doll turn in a slow motion dance. Round and round the doll turned till its woollen skin was off and its grey stuffing, compacted with the years, exposed.

She looked in as she passed her mother's room. She appeared to be peaceful, but it was hard to tell.

When she had bought the cloth, the silk thread and the needles, the woman in the shop had shown her some pieces with the design already stencilled onto it – flowers, dolls, chickens and other cute animals. 'Ideal for beginners,' she said. But Karen wanted to see what came out of her own mind. Creative doodling. It was something she had started to keep her hands and mind busy, when she sat with her mother in the awful stillness. There was no reason why she should limit herself to silk thread, she could use wool, sew on pieces of fabric, pearls if she wanted. Despite the busyness of her mind, when she did the embroidery she sat very still, like a woman in a painting.

When the therapist came, she poked and prodded, lifted her mother's eyelids, took her head in her hands, turned it this way and that, gave Karen instructions. She never wanted any of Karen's offers of help so Karen went back to her embroidery. 'Wow, that's really something,' the therapist commented. 'A wall hanging?' 'No,' said Karen. The therapist waited for more but Karen had said all she was going to say. She became absorbed in the work under her hand. 'Well, I guess that's it for today,' said the therapist, packing up her things. Karen felt suddenly in league with her mother. She cast her a sly grin.

They classify and label and put them in boxes and stick pins in and use chemicals to preserve the beautiful transitory wings they're grubs they're larva and then beautiful winged creatures who live for so little time.

The therapist was there when Graham rang. Tomorrow. They could take her tomorrow. Karen stood staring at the wall, regret much greater than relief. 'Everything all right?' asked the therapist, wanting to know. 'Yes, thanks.'

Radiant blue and the flicker shimmer deep orange velvet and white spots around the frilly edge of wings their bodies soft and furry like minks up they go like confetti and fill the sky so much sky and they make noises soft fluttering noises and the sheen is like peacock wings and they whisper and sigh and their tiny cotton legs and antennae write messages in the sky and the butterflies are flying to their winter palaces.

Karen worked late into the night on the embroidery. What had started as something to pass the time, to occupy her hands and her mind, had assumed a shape and a purpose. Added to this was an urgency, to have it ready in time for her mother to take with her.

She had just finished stitching the last wing when she heard the dawn birds call. She made a cup of tea and watched the grey pale into blue. It would be a fine day. She got out the iron and ironed the embroidery smooth. It was done.

Even though the room was still darkened, Karen knew. She stood in the doorway reluctant to take the first step in, hanging onto the mad thought that perhaps if she came back later everything would be different. She made her way to the bed, the recently ironed embroidery still warm under her hands.

It wasn't a bottle of whisky and a swim to New Zealand but her mother had chosen her moment all the same. Though there was no sign of life the spirit still seemed to be here, waiting in a corner for Karen to come. As if the death had occurred only minutes ago, and there was a shadow of life playing itself out.

Karen spread the embroidery on the bed, tucked it right up to her mother's face so that she could feel it. Then Karen sat on the bed and whispered to her mother the story that the embroidery told. 'This is the rose garden with the big crimson roses, and here are the butterflies that flew out of your hair that day when I came home from school. This is your wedding dress, feel the pearls, and Dad's shiny bow tie. Here is your daughter in her pram and your son beside it, wheeling it proudly. This is the rag doll you knitted and I took to bed every night and here . . .' Karen could no longer speak. Tears rolled down her cheeks onto the wings of an embroidered butterfly. She stared at the glistening wings, watching more drops fall.

Then she remembered something from a long time ago, something her mother had told her. That in cold weather if you hold butterflies to your mouth and breathe warm air onto them they can fly. She bent down close to the body, took up the story once more, breathing the words into her mother's ears, her nose, her mouth. Warming the spirit so it could lift and soar on its journey.

Robert Dessaix

SACRED HEART
1 9 9 6

Toc-toc, toc-toc, toc-toc. Brass and polished rosewood. A twist or two
of the tiny gold key and it sprang alive – tocking, tocking – and Sister
Mary Francis would tap at the music with her long, thin pointer.
Squinting, I'd press my lips together and we'd be off.

The metronome was magic, but above it on the greenish wall hung
something quite astounding. It was a picture of a pallid young man
with flowing fair hair and full pink lips, gleaming moistly. In an opening
in his ruby and emerald robes hovered a rosy heart. Ringed with thorns,
it had thick tongues of yellowish flame curling out of the top of it, like
an advertisement for a bedside asthma lamp. Jesus himself, I remember,
looked gracefully unmoved by the experience – indeed, beyond responding to anything that had ever happened or might one day happen, neither
forgiving nor unforgiving, just delicately vacant. Even at six I knew
sensitive indifference when I saw it. Why this expression so often evokes
slavish devotion remains a mystery to me.

Somehow or other, as I stumbled through my scales and *Für Elise*
and *Rondo alla Turca* and all the other things Sister Mary Francis
thought I might be ready to give pleasure with when called upon, the
Sacred Heart (plucked from its cavity) fused with the beat of the
metronome's rod (once the rosewood cover had been eased from its
slot) to instil in me a lifelong fascination with removable panels,
especially during a performance. I hope against hope to seize upon the
very heart of some magic.

Pianolas, of course: slide back the doors with a snap and there it all
is, exquisitely disappointing, wheezing and soulless, just as we thought,
but brilliant in its artifice, pounding out genius. Puppet theatres appeal
as well – not all this modern tomfoolery, but the old-fashioned pull-
back-the-curtains enchanted-world-in-a-box stuff. Breech-clouts and
codpieces have a certain charm as well. Even replacing the batteries in

a transistor radio is mildly exciting at the front – Beethoven or a voice speaking live from Moscow; at the back (press and slide upwards) – just a plastic hollow with a couple of inert capsules in it. Deliciously disenchanting.

I'm not sure at this distance what it was that Sister Mary Francis, girlishly strict and swathed in hot black, meant to teach me on that windowed veranda at the Convent of Mercy. How to imitate a mystery, perhaps. How a particular kind of beauty or even sacred sorcery worked and how to master the rules. How to open a door and glimpse the living heart of something. All this we'd have called simply 'learning the piano'. Yet, oddly, the desire those afternoons fed was less to be touched by Beauty than to slide back the panel and catch the mystery out – in all its banality, with its dead cogs and levers and empty corners. The only consolation in this chase after disillusionment is that there is always one more panel to slide back . . . the mind that dreamt up the pianola, the mind that made the music . . . Perhaps behind the very last one . . .

When I was very small (and this is *à propos*), whenever I went visiting with my parents, I'd look around once I was inside the front door to see if there was a piano anywhere. A house without a piano was an empty house, a house with no spiritual hearth, literally soulless. Pop-up toasters, electric stoves, hot-water systems, night-and-day beds, refrigerators, inside toilets – all things we didn't have – were intriguing but patently dead. A piano glowed with life. Not that I could work any miracles with it, but there was wizardry and light secreted in a piano, under the satin finish, which could give those hours of childish tedium and embarrassment in a strange house a sharp focus of pleasure. I don't recall the moment the magic of a piano's presence faded, but I do remember in my teenage years looking for something much more mechanical as I came in the front door: the television set. In fact, before we had our own set, I used to gaze in awe from the footpath, as I walked the dog at dusk, at the eerie blue light glowing behind the venetians of certain houses on certain streets. These houses seemed possessed of a kind of magnetism, they seemed peculiarly blessed. By a box with wires in it.

Apart from schooling me in disenchantment – and, of course, the mechanics of piano-playing – those afternoons with Sister Mary Francis, the Sacred Heart of Jesus and the metronome taught me something else they didn't mean to, something precious. They taught me that I wasn't *going anywhere*. Needless to say, it was all set up to teach me the opposite: First Grade, Second Grade, examinations, eisteddfods, practice, improvement, 'much better', 'needs more work' ... Even the Sacred Heart of Jesus promised some sort of reward for my travails, a point to suffering, a reward for faithfulness, an elevation. But no, in fact *that was it*. Things *are* often just it. Yet no less worthwhile. For years as a schoolboy I felt a failed pianist. When I came home from school I'd feel the piano, to the right just inside the front door, reproaching me, silent and filmed with dust. But why must a Sunday painter be a failed master?

Nowadays all I can play on a piano is a few arpeggios, a stirring hymn or two and a few bars from *Oklahoma*. It doesn't matter. Those warm half-hours with Sister Mary Francis, the rosewood metronome, the sickly Sacred Heart of Jesus, the Chopin preludes ... they were all steps in the zig-zag, shards in the kaleidoscope, tangles in the skein, leaven in the lump – in a word, time beautifully spent.

And at the other end of my life, when I go visiting I look around again, once inside the front door, for the soft sheen of a piano somewhere in the house. It's like a sign or a talisman. I can be alone again in a room with a piano and still feel someone is there.

Barry Dickins

REAL GOOD SLIDE NIGHT
1991

Great is the hero worship for my God, my Dad; myself but old. He hops up like the freckled brown bunny rabbits on that high hill adorned with the Lord's loathed last least flower, the prickle, that crowns our town with dreamy purple hearts and spikey *gotcha!* petals of death. My father rises alarm clockwise at 4 a.m. and Army toes sail into yawning socks. The hernia belt on and teeth in, the same teeth with DEPARTMENT OF DEFENCE stamped indelibly into upper and lower plate. Mum, out like a light and dreaming, I hope, of the time she sang for the troops at Melbourne Town Hall: she too must rise at the Army's hour of unconsciousness and bend her sleepy head in sublime worship position over the All Bran.

Military knifefuls of Golden Syrup aswim upon ashen toast, dead as a dodo, stewed tea by the birdbath, he is off in the rain on the bike, to his new printing premises and we are still there. Death by breakfast. Mummified in Milo. Still asleep, Mum makes date sandwiches and my young brother Chris gives Arnold, our turtle, a cheeseburger. It kills him. We find him upside down in a blue plastic dish in the morning. We never had been good with pets.

MUM:

Gee, look at Arnold. Dead!

CHRIS:

I didn't know what to feed it.

MUM:

Lucky he got anything, I suppose.

And the notes that came down from the sky were gloomy; they were from the Baptist Church congregation down the buttock rather than bottom of our road. Mum and Dad forced us to attend their dispiriting gatherings as solemn as squeezed lemon in your eye Sunday School mournings. Going irreligiously to these lessons is downright sadism; it made me the miserable bastard I am today; I have no doubt of it. The Reverend Gordon W. Stephens was Boss. We bowed our spun out of sunlight heads and were bad as the Reverend Gordon W. Stephens sunk the blasphemous boot in. We burnt for badness and pined for Imaginary Christ to forgive us, and give us a kick of the footy on the open road. It was not to be. Mrs Loftus played the original sin organ, and we cried. Tears were life; Christ was Dead: it was our ten-year-old fault. Let me take you into Mr Stephens' holy heart. Now, he prays for you: the curtain is up on our downtroddenness.

THE REVEREND GORDON W. STEPHENS

We are bad and we are very bad; I have no doubt of that, Flock, for you are *Flock*! Sheep is what you *are*! You sin and call it a living; well, you are very wrong, Flock! Our town is very slow receiving sewerage; that is a pressure we must confront and learn to love. Our town is very slow to adapt to Christ's sparkling teachings. Some of you younger flock are quick to seize upon this desperate and some might say deliberate slowness. The songs we sing are not designed to give us hope; they are written for us to plummet, and die.

The attendances in Sunday School are well down; they could, of course, be worse if no-one turned up. But you will, of course, always turn up and harken to the tune of gorgeous disappointment; the voice of the True Christ. Optimism and the Barn Dance go one way; parables and prayers of the Reservoir Baptist Church go the other. It is never enough to bow your heads and weep; even if you weep tears of blood that is never enough, flock. My Flock! What *is* enough is that the lesson comes through to you that suffering is enlightenment. This is why Reservoir is a Dry Area. *Got that?* Soon our spies tell us that not far off in the land of Sodom and Gomorrah, in other words Thomastown, there is to be a hotel built. A hotel built that will celebrate the seven-ounce glass of beer and the ten-ounce glass of beer: where will it all end. It will end in the jug of beer and you, my flock, will be awash with sin and sudsy slops of the breweries' work which, of course, is the work of the Devil. It is a hard fight and a fight we will win with weekend cricket and definitely basketball; for women, as well as men.

Save up your Sunday School cards; the cards I hand out as invitations to the greatest prize of all. The perfect recollection of the Old Testament! Memorise the psalms, Flock, memorise them. And you will not fear

the Devil in the dark, nor the vicious Death Adder of temptation. The
boys and girls who learn them best will win a packet of Willow Mints.
Can you ask fairer than that. You cannot ask fairer than that, Flock.
Amen. We must build up the town, our town, your town and my town.
That way we will not come a thud when He searches us out. We will
now turn to the Book of Job. [*GREAT SIGHING COMES NOW: ENORMOUS
SIGHING; PATIENCE AND REDEMPTION AND PUBERTY*]

I politely observe the football calves of Mrs Dot Loftus pump up on
the gloomloving foot pedals of the Reservoir Baptist Church organ. She
is not delicate, in keeping with the perfect image of a simple Messiah;
she strikes those wooden pedals with all the loneliness in her. Her
power is metaphysical; the spiritual never give in will come later as
she sits in with lessons from the Reverend Gordon W. Stephens, our
cut-price Christ. My infantile eyes stare hot and dead blank at all the
drowning lettering of the tortured syntax of sorriness. I sing it and
realise I am bad with every breath I breathe here.

We trickle to our sad classes at the Reservoir Baptist Church. I have
Mr Tansey to teach me love unending. He is a short and precise man
who unrolls a scroll depicting Jesus holding a model aeroplane. Christ
is sitting melancholy enough with various differently coloured kids of
the whole world. Everyone is Baptist friendly. They are green and red
and Chinese and Mongoloid. We are all mates under Keith Tansey.

It is Eastertime and Mr Keith Tansey places the felt cutout angels
and enemies of Christ on a blackboard for us to see the spirit better. I
fidget and Mr Keith Tansey knocks me rotten. What a Baptist backhander!
MR TANSEY:
Don't you want to hear the word of Jesus, Dickins?
MYSELF:
Are you Jesus, Mr Tansey? You look different.
Keith Tansey lifts his fist up to do me. And that is the end of the lesson
in goodness, mercy and forgiveness. But not quite. It transpires I have
won the Willow Mint award. I have recited The Lord's Prayer, Psalm
Forty-Eight and I have Job off by heart, so he can get stuffed. I accept
the prize of Willow Mints and drift into the toilet, where Graeme
Blundell is fondling a girl's Baptist bosoms.
GRAEME BLUNDELL:
Everything all right, Dig?

I blush.

John and me run home to Dad and Mum and Nan, whose poor name is Gert. Gert is the boss of the wash, and there is no gainsaying Gert. Mum is expecting a visit from Uncle Len, of Uncle Len's milk bar. There are scones baking and chocolate crackle mix awaiting starved us. Uncle Len and Auntie Marg perch behind the flywire door and wait and wait. Our family is going for their lives on the fluffy, scrumptious, hot scones and jam and cream. Uncle Len blinks through the flywire door. And blinks and blinks. My father eventually goes over to his face and says:

DAD:

You're probably wondering why I'm not invitin' ya in are ya?

UNCLE LEN:

Yeah.

[*DISSOLVE TO BLACKNESS*]

A few nights later we are the lucky recipients of a visit by our Uncle Ted, who has been to America. Uncle Ted does slide nights. Our family has never been to even Albury and Uncle Ted shows us insanely clear Kodachromes of the USA. Uncle Ted purchased a projector in California and lords it over us that the wife and he have stayed in plush rooms of Burbank. They have been nodded to by Cecil B. de Mille, he'd have us believe. My Dad is a monument to patience as Uncle Ted lights up.

[*PROJECTOR EFFECT: DARKNESS: UNCLE TED WITH FIFTY-CENT CIGAR*]

UNCLE TED:

This is the El Dorado Room in LA.

DAD:

[*UNDER HIS BREATH*] So what?

UNCLE TED:

And this is an expensive suite of rooms in Tokyo. You can see the room we stayed in because there's an orange towel hangin' out the window.

DAD:

[*UNDER HIS BREATH*] Big deal for the Abos.

After ten thousand perfectly crystal clear slides of his nowhere tour of the globe, Uncle Ted expires under the influence of a Canadian Club whisky. Mum makes tea for us all. We boys laugh behind our boyhood as Dad winks at us and indicates boozed success Uncle Ted, flaked out and nowhere on our never-pay-it-off carpet.

DAD:

As Pop says: 'You're better off carrying the hod.' The hod is an instrument for carting roofing tiles; an honest but difficult living at the very best of times.

Eventually Uncle Ted departs, his arrogant slides with him in a bundle; and Auntie Jean and he stumble towards their never-give-it-a-rest brand-spanking-new '56 Holden, with its idiotic burgundy seats and real flash extractors. Mum, always the good scout, kisses Uncle Ted and Auntie Long Suffering Jean, and we have cups of tea and a slice of inedible fruitcake before the homely fireplace. I am suddenly a socialist. Mum has taught me the only thing worthwhile in all life. Don't lie. It's best to be honest, even if the snobs do put it on you.

Mr Wilson is my nemesis at school and his enormous bullying head terrifies me even now, as I put bile to paper. Never bad, but a boy full of life, and the life of blood, it is Mr Wilson who makes me an artist. I never once gave him cheek. He always assumed I was bad because I was alive: I assume he was a member of the Reservoir Baptist Church Assembly. He had a way of making me feel guilty, especially if I did nothing. My drawings good, he made them bad. My life good, he made it seem worthless. I was simply spirited, a sensation not tolerated in our town. I often kicked and fought and acted up to play the wag; but if you didn't play the wag you were a suck; and I was no suck. Anything but.

MR WILSON:

I now sadly will cane your arse, Dickins.

He caned my unfortunate arse, and I fainted. Sixteen strikes of the wooden ruler, and you are supposed to lose faith. My pants pulled down, class clown I, it hurt but I would not show it. I merely fainted. An old device I know, but a good one. Actor!!

To my amazement, Mr Wilson wasn't too good the next day. I seemed to think his depression had something to do with the violent caning he delivered to me. But no. It was the fact that my steadfast cobber, Lionel Bullock, inserted a large Pontiac Potato up Mr Wilson's Holden exhaust pipe. It blew right up. Totally up.

Mr Hall was our unforgiving headmaster, and no-one crueller ever strode the globe since Adolf Hitler gave the game away. It was our difficult duty to deliver to Mr Hall a perfect recital of *The Man From Ironbark*. If you were no good, Adios.

MR HALL:

Do you know in full *The Man From Ironbark* without hesitancy?

MYSELF:

No, Sir.

MR HALL:

Bend over, Sir. I'll give you hesitancy!

Mr Hall would then extract his horsehair strap from the secret compartment of his desk and have into you. There was an enormous horsehair which appeared to grow from the middle of the strap; it cracked something shocking when Mr Hall had into you. He was a Rodeo Man.

[*SOUND EFFECT OF SIX BELTS OF THE STRAP*]

MR HALL:

Now do you know *The Man From Ironbark*, Dickins?

MYSELF:

No, Sir.

Six more swipes of the strap. Raw arse. More boys. No-one knows anything about Australian poetry. Mr Hall has strapped it all out of 'em.

AMATEUR HOUR

1 9 8 6

Sometimes they sounded like poets. I was new there, and they wanted me to understand, and sometimes their words lodged in my head like songs.

On the morning of the tragedy, Evert took me to map a slope of Black Mountain. Tobias followed us, carrying our equipment upon his shoulder and collecting wood for his fire. We worked through the day, and late in the afternoon we climbed to the top of the mountain to see the view, to see how tiny our camp was at the base, and, while Tobias squatted and smoked a cigarette at a seemly distance from us, Evert explained things to me, because I was new there, and an *Engelsman*.

A lucky soaking of spring rain in that part of the desert always brought on a brief, famed crop of wildflowers, he said. They grew almost overnight; along the dunes, between the claypans, around the eroded hills. People came from everywhere to see them. Last year a BBC television crew filmed them, he said. *National Geographic* did a story. He motioned with his hand and said 'Picture it.'

I looked out, to the edges of the desert. In Springbok and Pofadder the tourists stop the mail drivers and shopping farmers ask, 'Is this the best time?' They drive ninety kilometres for a Sunday picnic at the favoured spot, the veldt near Black Mountain, skimming over the corrugations that otherwise would rattle their bones, speeding back at the end of the day in time for Evening Prayers.

'Those TV boys got bogged in the sand,' said Evert.

Had they been covering the necklace killings, the evictions, the bulldozings? They have time to spare and fly to Springbok and hire a car. They joke with the farmer, who has given them permission to use his access road, that they are after a bit of local colour. They speak slowly, clearly, for the fellow is an Afrikaner. English tangles his tongue.

Families snug at home turn on their TV sets. A reporter is gesturing at Black Mountain and the wildflower carpet behind him. Sunlight glints on the strap of his wristwatch. He announces that this is a land of great beauty and . . . But what can he say next? And great extremes, he says.

'Everyone gets hayfever then,' said Evert.

In the mornings the geologists and field hands lie in bed, tapping their knuckles against the fibro-cement walls of their huts, waiting for the first aching sneeze. They walk to the mess and kick the petals unfolding in the sun.

'Mr Weeramantry sells hayfever pills,' said Evert, and he told me the story of Wikkie Roux, the man who had this job before me. Wikkie Roux races in from the veldt at knock-off time on Saturday afternoons, sneezing his head off in the dust and pollen swirling around in the Land Rover's cabin. He pauses at the Coloureds' Compound just long enough for Tobias to jump out, and then whooh! man, flat out to Weeramantry's trading store to buy six bottles of Carling beer and a packet of hayfever pills. The combination is fatal. He tilts back his chair in the mess, thumps his fist, roars out sentimental songs of the Republic, a bit touchy, a little violent, on the subjects of kaffirs, wildflowers and low camp morale, and then, more than likely, he passes out, and some poor bloody coloured, like our cook boy, Willem Pretorius, has to drag him out.

'Good story, ay?' Evert said.

The wind blew in from the South Atlantic. It was very cold. I watched Tobias draw on the cigarette cupped between his palms. He had pulled his woollen cap down over his ears, and he wore his coat inside out to show the satin lining. I drew my coat closed at the neck. Only Evert seemed unaffected. He was in a mood to be sentimental, in his shorts and thin shirt and unbuttoned anorak, as though his flanks were not veined and bumpy in the wind, his skin not stretched tight to tearing point over his shin bones.

'Hell of a cold, ay?' he said. He grinned and told me to wait a few weeks, for the sunshine and the spring rains, when the red and yellow and blue wildflowers would spill along the canyons and spread over the veldt and gather at the base of the stony peaks.

His words were like a song, but the cold wind blew and the desert looked endless, wrung out and inconvenient. Here and there wheel tracks scribbled over the sand. Clouds scudded across the sky, their shadows creeping like stains over the dunes and the camp huts. Some-one had tied down the helicopter. The windsock pointed in the wind like a finger. Sand drifts were obscuring the black letters on the laboratory roof: 'Zuurwater' and 'Kendell Copper Tucson'. No-one was walking around down there.

I identified my hut among the other tiny corrugated iron roofs on the far side of the airstrip. I knew it was mine, because it had no garden and I would have to plant one soon. Our engineer and his wife lived in the hut next to me. They had two extra rooms, a carport for their station wagon, a garden and a trellis vine. Every day two maids came up from the Coloureds' Compound, a hessian and tin town never seen by any Tucson executive. After lunch Marion Reed liked to open the tailgate of the station wagon, bundle the maids in and drive the one kilometre to Mr Weeramantry's to do the shopping, in the manner of a housewife in a suburb.

Then I remembered. Nothing ever happened here, the trouble was elsewhere, but I had heard a man's resolute shout in the darkness one night as I lay trying to sleep: 'Get away from here, you black bugger.'

There was a moment of heatless sunlight. It flared on the red dunes and brightened the distant hills. We were drenched in it. Evert stood up and swept round in a circle, stretching his arms, suddenly on top of the world. 'London,' he shouted, offering his left hand, 'Antarctica,' unfolding his right. And the border where he had been a conscript halting the terrorists, the blind gully where Boers had trapped British soldiers, the Orange River and baboons and crocodiles and diamonds. And Cape Town, the Sea Point guesthouses, compared and dreamed over in the mess hut every evening.

'Time to go back,' Evert said. '*Kom*, Tobias.'

Tobias stubbed out his cigarette on a rock and put the butt into a paper bag in his pocket.

'*Yirra*,' said Evert.

Far below us a police Land Rover was pitching about on the track leading out of the wadi by the Coloureds' Compound. It reached the Springbok road and gained speed, sliding on the corners and raising a dust cloud.

'Tobias,' said Evert. 'What is the trouble, hey?'

'I don't know, my boss.'

He was climbing down ahead of us, a tripod upon his shoulder, firewood under his arm. Evert muttered, '*Ag*, I don't like it, man.' He nodded at Tobias clambering over the treacherous round stones. 'Your coloured out here is a peaceful fellow, isn't it. He hasn't got his head filled with ideas.' He clicked his tongue.

We hurried down. At the bottom of the mountain Tobias loaded the Land Rover and Evert took him back to the Compound. I walked through the camp and across the airstrip to my hut. There was a note under the door 'Pop in for a drink after work, before the *braaivleis*. Marion Reed.'

Marion handed me a clay mug and said, 'This will warm you up.'

I held the mug with both hands, feeling the heat coming through from the fluid inside it. I put my nose to the rising steam. A rush of hot, spiced claret fumes filled my head. My eyes watered.

Everyone laughed. '*Gluhwein*,' said Don Reed. 'Marion made it to take to the *braaivleis* tonight.'

They smiled at me. Two small girls, home from their boarding school, sprawled on a hide rug at my feet. I looked around the room. The Reeds had moved from continent to continent, mining camp to mining camp. They had ricepaper fans, jade idols, Texan hats, boomerangs, shields, ivory elephants. We sipped our drinks and I had the sensation that the Reed family was waiting for a moment when they might declare me theirs.

'Something I wanted to ask you,' Marion said. 'I edit the camp newspaper. Would you like to write something for us? About impressions, anything like that.'

She handed me a sheaf of roneod pages stapled together along one edge. 'You see, camp morale's at an all-time low, and we're trying to do something about it.'

'The men are depressed by the food and the early starts and the cold weather,' Don said. 'Arguments, fights. You probably haven't noticed it yet.'

'It's sad,' said Marion. 'They just live for their next week off at Sea Point and don't care about anything else.'

'Hence the newspaper and the *braaivleis*. And we're having an Amateur Hour concert soon.'

The two little girls sat on the arms of my chair and turned the roneod pages with me while their parents talked. They stopped me at *Don's Diary:* 'Last month's film was the best we've had in a long time. It must have been; the coloureds enjoyed it – pow! boof! crash!'

'If there's anything you're good at,' Don said, 'any special interest, just let us know. Can you shoot?'

I looked at him. He leaned forward and said, 'I thought I'd start a gun club.'

He stood up and walked out of the room. Marion said, 'The police were at the Compound today. I suppose you heard.'

Don returned carrying a small wooden case. Inside it were two handguns resting in moulded foam. 'I'll use these,' he said. 'I'll use them if I have to, make no mistake about that. If they want to creep around here at night they can learn what to expect.'

Marion laughed. She steadied him with her hand on his arm and she gave me a look as if to say: What am I going to do with this man?

'A wife and two daughters,' Don said.

The kitchen staff had set the mess chairs upon the blighted patch of lawn near the main office. Willem Pretorius cooked steaks and chops for us on iron grilling plates and we leaned towards the burning logs, paper plates on our knees. We talked. They drank to my health.

Clouds blocked the stars and the moon, the fire lost its heat and the firelight was meagre, but the plan had worked, Marion and Don had a right to beam. They nodded to Willem and his men, thank you, go home now, threw logs onto the coals, and called us to bring our chairs closer. Marion's *gluhwein* kept us warm and crack-brained, we stamped our feet, we sang 'Zulu Warrior, Zulu Chief'.

Later, when the generator was turned off, we could hear the wind between the huts. People drifted off to bed, but some of us remained, staring into the coals. Evert produced a bottle of brandy. Sunday tomorrow, we said.

At one point we saw headlights and heard a vehicle, far out on the black veldt. It approached the camp but turned away and disappeared behind Black Mountain. The passengers were singing, whoever they were. Evert laughed. 'Sunday tomorrow.'

I said, 'Did you find out what the police wanted?'

'Just a patrol,' he said. Then he slapped his thigh. 'Tobias is hell of a lucky kaffir he was with us today. They saw his bakkie in the

Compound and told his wife to get it registered. Did she give him hell. Whooh!'

There were five of us left. We looked into the coals, nursing the last of the brandy, telling each other that we had stamina. We dreamed. 'Stay at the Carnaby,' Evert said, 'for your week off. Ay, kaffir,' he said, 'what do you want in this place?'

Tobias came shyly into the light of the fire, grinning, holding his woollen cap, looking around at someone behind him and back at Evert again, unable to suppress a little snorting laugh.

'Please, the boss he is give me a drink?'

Evert waved him away. 'Cheeky kaffir. I gave you five rands last week and now you want me to give you a drink.'

Tobias giggled again and moved back into the dark with his friends.

The incident woke us up. We climbed onto the back of a Land Rover and Evert drove us to the Reeds' house, where we parked and roared: 'We love you Marion, oh yes we do.' The Reeds ignored us yet they were awake, I think; I could feel them listening. But it was late and too cold and we soon fell silent. I jumped out and said goodnight.

I walked across to my hut, where I lit a lantern, feeling too alert to sleep. I sat and thought, re-read a love letter, moved things around. Tobias knocked on my door.

'Please boss, you are give me a drink?' he said. 'I must have a drink for my head.'

'Go home to bed, Tobias,' I said. 'It's late. It's cold.'

'Tomorrow we are not working, isn't it?' he said. 'Tonight I am have a party, my boss, same like always. You are give me a drink please?'

'I haven't got any,' I said.

'Oh.' He drew back. He looked at my room, at my rucksack in the corner by the rickety wardrobe.

'The boss he is come from America?'

'No,' I said.

He said 'Oh' again, but then he whirled round and crouched, his feet wide apart, his hand quick-drawing a gun from the holster on his hip, his smoking finger drilling me through the heart. I jumped in fright and laughed.

'John Wayne,' said Tobias, delighted. He put his thumb behind his satin lapel as though there were a badge pinned to it. 'Sheriff,' he said.

He shrugged off the role and looked moodily at the walls, the spindly furniture, his shadow swooping in the lamplight. 'The boss is give me five rands?' he said. 'For to buy petrol for my bakkie to go to church tomorrow.'

I gave him the money. He said, 'You is believe in Jesus Christ, my boss?'

I thought, and replied, 'No.'

I could have said yes. In that little room, in the dislocating darkness of the hour, I had distressed him. He held his hands together. He said that he would pray for me.

He left and I went to bed.

It is clear to me now that Tobias set off to see who else might be awake, and that his head would not let him alone. He negotiated the precise rows of white-painted stones that defined the Reeds' yard, and he passed among the wires and stakes in their garden beds, but he was snarled by two new garbage bins, specials from Weeramantry's I heard, almost at once, Don Reed cry out and then shoot him.

He shot twice more while I was running from my hut, and he was still shooting when I came upon him, firing shot after shot into the ground as though he could not make the gun stop, crying out, 'Oh don't, oh don't.' He threw the gun away, aghast.

Marion stepped out of the house, a gas lantern in her hand. She put her arm around her husband and led him inside. 'Poor old boy,' she said. 'Poor old boy.'

In the mornings I walked along the beach at Sea Point, returning in time for lunch in the Carnaby's dining room, and in the afternoons I went into the centre of Cape Town, where I saw films or paid to join the half-day bus tours of the area. I had my ticket home and I was waiting for the day. I went in to pick up my pay cheque from the company's Cape Town office. The man there frowned: over the years he had grown sick and tired of fellows who wouldn't stay on – didn't we get paid top rates? They had photographs hanging on their walls: the camp, springbok and bat-eared foxes among the wildflowers, secretary birds, Black Mountain, all in gaudy colours and with the company logo in one corner. Once, I saw our technician on the beach; in Sea Point to begin his week off, I suppose. He stared at me and I at him, and, at the moment we drew alongside one another, he looked up at the guesthouses on the beach front and I looked out at the sea.

But the thing is, one afternoon when the days were dragging I happened to stand by my window at the Carnaby and look down at a woman lying drunk on her side in the alley across the street, lying with her head on her arm, her feet in men's shoes neatly together, and as I watched her she rolled on her hip and put her hand under her dress, she pulled down her pants until they stretched like a web across her knees, and she fell back slowly in relief as her urine poured along the ground. I thought how sharp it would smell, and how her thighs would rub together and irritate the damp skin, and as I watched a maid from the Carnaby ran across the street to her. The maid leaned down and tugged at the woman's arm. The woman was too heavy. The maid looked around helplessly, sensed me and looked up. The thing is, I didn't move from the window, I continued to watch, even as the maid stood holding her dress out from me, her face turned away from me, overcome by shame, and it was only when two policemen threw the woman into a van and drove away that I turned away from the window. It was that look on the maid's face that dislodged anything else I might have been thinking.

Sara Dowse

THE CHOICE FOR CARLOS MENENDEZ
1997

Throughout life we are encouraged to make choices. This is the sign, is it not, of a cultivated human being? An animal is limited in its choices. It lives according to instinct, whereas a human being, he chooses, according to constantly refined principles of sensibility and taste.

This is how it was for Carlos Menendez as he stood at my window, gazing wistfully at an article of furniture that might have gone unnoticed by any other passerby. It was, simply put, a sofa, but as Carlos was only too aware, such things are never so simple. Sofa: now this is a word of affectation; it marks its user as a lower kind of person, anxious to emulate his superiors. Whereas, couch, this is even more complicated. To say couch, for those who know, is like uttering a secret password, but for those who don't, only makes one seem common.

So. The couch in question was a glossy, plump, brown leather Chesterfield, and he could just make it out through the glare of the sun on the window and the fronds of the Alexandra palm set tastefully by its side. The shop was filled with new items that season – love seats, armoires, recliners – but none of these were of interest. It was the Chesterfield that moved him, that transported him through a panoply of dreams, that made his nostrils swell with the aroma of leather and his teeth ache with longing. Such yearning might make another person sneak back at night, heave a brick through the window and lift the Chesterfield through it, but such an action would be inconceivable for Carlos. Even if it entered his head he would never have had – how can I say – the diligence to carry it off. And another thing, he would have had to find someone to help him.

How do I know all this? Well, things get around, and it is, for anyone who knows it, a very sad story. You may accuse me of embellishment if you like but I am sure that this is how it was, and, besides, he told me. At least some of it. For three days he came to the shop, staring in that hopeless, disconsolate fashion through the window and, finally, I set aside my scruples for any embarrassment I might cause and invited him in. Of course, he said he did not expect this: how could he realise that I'd been watching him, when he was so accustomed to nobody watching – that was his method, he would come to tell me, to sink into the background, that was the way he held onto a certain power. But all this was gone by the time he started hanging around outside the shop, to ogle that Chesterfield.

He came with me because of this, following me through the shop door as if his absorption had left him without a will of his own, and was scarcely attending when, standing before it, I asked: 'Would you care to try it?'

Abruptly awakened, he stammered. 'Uh, no . . . No, I was only . . .'

His dark eyes flitted about the showroom, frantic for some other object – any other object – on which to settle. But age and experience have emboldened me. 'Go on,' I importuned. 'It came with our most recent shipment, we've only just unpacked it. We need to find out what potential customers think.'

He blushed. Yes, blushed. And at first he only ventured to lower his bottom to the edge and he sat there, like an anxious schoolboy, until I gestured for him to move further into it, so that his back was flush against the smooth, quilted leather, and his right arm was elevated, draped on the curve that formed the armrest. His fingers stroked the piping at the front, in a timid, slow, circular movement, but then he became conscious of it, and stopped, looking up and smiling at me as he did. His hand was raised then, as though it had been arrested in mid-motion, or it might have been a gesture of culpability, as though he'd been caught in some mildly reprehensible act. He shrugged, still smiling, and brought the hand down. I watched his every gesture and the smile that went with them, until I was sure.

'Well,' I said, as casual as I could make it, glancing at my watch, 'it's been quite a day and it's time for tea for me. You can stay there for longer if you like but it would please me very much, if you were to join me.'

Those dark liquid eyes flashed again, moving over the showroom rather than meet my gaze; then they clouded over, and I noticed a little shudder go through him. But I had chosen my words carefully and continued to look at him and in the end he was forced to look back. The expression of resignation that now marched across his features was so abject, so pitiful, that I began to feel angry with him. He was gaunt, there were greenish hollows under those deep dark eyes, and pimples on his skin – was he stupid with it as well? I took a slow breath and said: 'Come, you have nothing to lose, and nothing to worry about either.'

Naturally, I tried to draw him out. I told him about the shop, how I got into it, what kind of merchandise we sold, not really antiques, though we liked to think so, and we did insist on quality. I'd prattled on in this vein for a while, careful not to injure his sense of privacy but hopeful that my openness would encourage him. I would like to think that my motives were pure in this, but whose ever are? At what point, I have often asked myself, did I abandon any notion that this encounter would lead where such encounters often lead, and I honestly can't say. All I know is that suddenly I was conscious that what I wanted from him, more than anything, was his reason for being so attracted by the couch. I'd been watching him, I said, for three days – not that I'm in the habit of spying on people, I assured him, but how could I help but notice? 'It's a finely crafted piece of furniture, I grant you that, and I do appreciate your taste,' I told him. 'But I can't afford to give it to you, you know, though I certainly wish I could and with Chesterfields becoming fashionable again, it's not as though it's the only one of its kind.'

He was as famished as I thought he was. Perhaps he had forgotten about his hunger and other longings had begun to take its place. Fortunately, I am as considered in what I eat as I am everything else. The little kitchen at the back was chock-a-block. Lovely fresh olive bread, green pepper pâté, Bulgarian fetta, Spanish salami – I even had some rocket for a salad. He fell on it all, scarcely listening, not caring a fig about how he appeared, but eating greedily, hardly taking time to savour the feast. But then, suddenly, he slowed down. He seemed to have trouble swallowing; breathing; and almost without thinking nudged his plate forward. After a few minutes I gently removed it and handed him a cup of tea. His hands were shaking but he took it, as he did the sugar. And it was while he was stirring it, slowly, with a gesture not unlike his earlier stroking of the leather piping, that he began to talk.

And was surprisingly forthcoming. He stirred the sugar in his teacup, thoughtfully as I've said, and then with a leap he was into the story. And, as it so happened there was a couch, just like the one in the window, in a flat he had stayed in only recently. Well, the one in the flat was crimson. He had made love on it many times, he said, and had come to know it intimately, the pattern of tufts on the leather, the many minute scratches that seemed to intensify the pungency of its odour, mingled as it was with those of manly sweat and sex. At times, too, he watched his own tears soak the leather and that had its own aroma. Tears? He didn't know why, or found it too difficult to say.

I asked him then if he wanted to rest and, again, there was a moment when I risked being misunderstood or, to be honest, when I poised on the edge of an understanding, ready to go either way. Whether he was thinking of the couch in the showroom, making the most of the pathos of his tale, I cannot say, but he shook his head as if to say that there were things that he needed to say but he had to do so gradually, step by step, in his own time.

And he really didn't want to rest. Like chunks of ice on the point of melting, the story rushed forth, becoming more turbulent and heated as he continued. It was his story, but there's only one story, is there not? Each of us with his desires, seeking pleasure, seeking love. And love, is it not a trap? His lover, with his scuffed crimson Chesterfield, had been nice, had been kind, had been his benefactor. 'How often,' I nodded in sympathy, 'this is the case.' Carlos didn't say where they'd met but I suspect it was further downtown, but possibly not at a bar, more likely in one of the theatres. At any rate, Carlos knew the places, and probably worked them, but that much he wasn't going to tell. The point is that what was so good about this man was that he liked Carlos, as a person. 'He made me feel special', 'He appreciated my talents', 'He loved me for myself' – and so forth. He discovered that Carlos played basketball, and went to the games to watch, and for the first time in a long time Carlos wasn't self-conscious or uneasy about someone showing this kind of interest. But there were scenes over small infidelities – meaningless encounters – and because it was a question of money, well, presto! Carlos found he had a benefactor and, for the first time, again, in a long time, he didn't have to worry.

But habit dies hard. And what is habit, I ask you, but ritualised self-destruction? Certain flowers bloom in the dark, their perfumes are muskier, their hues are intensified; stronger, seductive. For this kind of truth Carlos had few words. He shrugged that characteristic shrug and, for one brief moment, his dark eyes swam with arrested tears. There comes a time, for some late in life, for some early on, when a man comes to know himself and the darkness within. The shrug, the eyes: this is what this look of his said. And he gave himself up to it. Late at night or early the following morning, when his key would turn in the lock and, all in silence, the heavy door to the flat would click open, springy as his step, a light would come on in the dark, and there would be his lover, his mouth pursed in disappointment, his arms wrapped tight across his chest: a father, *the* father, what did it matter? – a man he would always flee from, and always go back to in fear.

He stood up, shaking more than he would wish, and, extending his hand, thanked me for the food. Then I took him back through the showroom, past the Chesterfield, all brown and gleaming like some well-fed stallion in the soft light creeping from the street lamps. I unlocked the glass door to let him out, and watched him walk up the footpath a bit, pause, and turn on his heel so as to catch one more glimpse of me and wave. At twilight his smile was all the more endearing and charming.

Did he ever return? Well, this is the choice he had. And did I not tell you that it is by the choices a man makes that we know him as a human being?

H . Drake-Brockman

FEAR

1933

The woman stood in the doorway of her wood-and-iron house and looked across to the big shed. If anything, the shed appeared rather better finished than the house. But they were neither of them much; the buildings had only been there a year or two – set back a little from the creek, where the river-gums, as befitted the only trees for miles, smirked at their reflections in a dark pool – set back right on the edge of the ranges, on the very rim of civilisation.

The slanting afternoon sun made the spiky, prickly tufts of spinifex grass look soft, luxurious; then spent its golden virtue in a riot of rainbow colour over on the ironstone ridge. And the dry, aromatic smell of an uninhabited land rose fragrant to the nostrils.

Behind the house, in the brush lean-to serving as kitchen – it was cooler that way and kept the flies from the house – the woman could hear Edie and Sam at play with pots and cans. She would have to stop them – too costly and difficult to get if small hands should do damage. And they'd be getting into the store-cupboard next – Sam was a terror for sugar, just like the natives! Baby would be awake in a few minutes, too; he was regular as a clock for his feed.

Yet she continued to stand there, staring across at the shed. She was feeling restless; had she not been a woman of great sense and fortitude, she would have called herself nervous.

The sunlight streamed without mercy on her well-worn print dress with its boned bodice and yards of skirt; but it caressed lightly a young face long since drained of colour, tanned to a golden brown. The light had drawn early lines round a pair of blue eyes, too; she was for ever running out, hatless, into the glare after the children.

All round about the few scattered buildings roamed her blue eyes. Except for little noises from the children, and the caw-cawing of crows sailing over the killing pen, an unearthly silence wrapped the place.

Not a native in sight. The kitchen gins had padded off to their noon camp the moment washing-up was over. Most afternoons she could stand and listen to the tapping of sticks or a drowsy corroboree chant. But today everything was silent. She imagined it must have been the silence that had brought her out.

Where were little Johnnie, and that Lloyd?

She didn't like Lloyd. She had told John so, many a time. But her husband just said men were difficult to get; Lloyd was all right, a good stockman and all that. But she didn't trust the fellow; he was altogether too rough on the natives. John himself could be brutal enough at times, but he was always just; the boys respected the boss, liked him – his kind of brutality was their own, and seen only when the isolation of the place rendered a firm hand advisable. But that Lloyd! She could never forget seeing him set the dogs on to the gins one day, so the poor wretches ran screaming to the trees and scaled them like cats. Horrible, it had been. And Lloyd had laughed fit to kill himself. Pity he hadn't! She had told John. That time he had spoken to the man, said such a thing must not happen again. And it hadn't.

All the same, she did wish it had not been necessary for John to go into the port to meet their first mob of sheep, to leave her like this, alone with the children and Lloyd.

The man she was thinking about came suddenly round the shed, little Johnnie at his heels. The small boy staggered along under the weight of a saddle; the man carried a knot of twine. The mother's anger rose. Just like him! There they had seated themselves, backs to the shed, and Lloyd was proceeding to mend a rent in the leather. She would call Johnnie, she decided, get him to mind the others. She hated the way he was for ever trailing after Lloyd. But what could you expect? A little fellow of seven loved to be out with the men, and the sooner a child learned to fend for himself in this country the better.

Her lips parted for a shout which congealed to a strangled intake of breath.

Once again round the corner came a figure, a painted buck. Red and yellow ochre and a white lime pattern on his body made him look like a walking skeleton. Quicker than thought the long shaft of the spear already quivering in his woomera flew out. It missed the little boy by inches and buried itself, still quivering, in the man's outstretched arm. Before ever Lloyd yelled, the native was gone.

The woman ran across the hard earth, her tanned face livid, yellow. The child flew to meet her. The man lay picking at the spear hanging from his arm. His eyes twisted, terrified.

But there was nothing to see. Everything was silent, except for the short sobs of the boy and the cawing of the crows.

She left the four children with Lloyd in the front room while she went alone to the kitchen for hot water. Johnnie seemed calm enough now, only interested, like the others, in the barb stuck in Lloyd's arm, and keen to watch the blood oozing out. 'It was Billycan, that was,' the boy kept repeating excitedly. 'Why ever should old Billy do that?'

Lloyd said nothing. He was white and trembling. The woman, as she fetched the water, decided she would have to give him a little of the whisky she kept, hidden, just in case. Her eyes raked the plain and slid along the creek-bed. She wanted to keep her mind busy with observation, but there was nothing worth observing. Still only the silent countryside. She could sweep the horizon right round and see nothing. She found herself thinking that the gins wouldn't be coming up now – probably the camp was deserted; they had cleared to the hills. She couldn't expect John for another couple of days, either. Hastily she dragged her mind from such thoughts and ran back to the house.

She had already broken the shaft from the barb – only about a foot stuck out of Lloyd's arm now.

'It'll hurt,' she said to him. 'I'll have to cut it out.'

He whined.

'I'll give you something first,' she said and, going to the bedroom, came back with a tot in an old pannikin. 'There'll be another when it's over,' she said.

She sent the children away – told them to keep baby quiet; he was wide awake now and would begin fretting soon. Then she ripped up a sheet.

She hated touching the man. And he shrank beneath her gentle hands, whined again, begged more whisky. His beady dark eyes, set in a face dirty with half-grown beard, grew scared and shifty.

The woman said: 'It's got to be done, Lloyd. Don't be a fool.' And she did it. A bloody job. But at last it was finished, the wound bound, most of the mess cleared away. Lloyd had another tot. Then demanded the lot. Said he needed it.

'No,' she said.

'Yes, missus. You make no mistake about it. I'm having that whisky and then – well, I'm scooting.'

'Scooting?' she repeated blankly, her mind with the children.

'Scooting. Going. Clearing out. That's plain, ain't it? I'm not stopping here for no more blanky niggers to run spears through me! I'm off into the town, I am. The boss left one moke in the horse-yard, and that's mine. Or soon will be. I'm off. I'll tell 'em to hurry on out here, if you like.'

She flared. 'Thank you! Call yourself a man, do you?'

'Hell to you! I'm going. Anyway, you're all right, missus. The abos ain't no call to touch you. Didn't you reckon they would all be gone?'

'Yes. But if it *was* all right, they would still be here. They mean trouble when they go.'

'Well, I tell you I'm not staying, anyhow.'

She noticed he was still trembling. 'Go, then,' she flung at him. 'You're no use as you are!' So that he would not discover her fear, she turned aside.

Too late she realised he was banging the door behind him and that the whisky bottle was under his arm. Like a fool she had let him take it!

She fought down her fears, and with a smiling face went in to the children. But Edie said, as she was pushed aside from the baby, 'Oh, Mum, how cold your hands are!'

Johnnie immediately wanted to go outside, but she forbade him. They had to stay and play quietly while she nursed baby. And as she sat there, on the low chair her husband had made, her mind flew back and forth like one of the ever-hovering crows.

Presently the beat of a horse's hoofs hammered the silence.

'Mum,' cried Johnnie from the window, 'where's Lloyd going?'

'Just a message for me,' she answered tranquilly; but, sharp and bitter, her mind recalled the chance-heard remark of another man, an epithet applied to Lloyd. 'It's right, too,' she thought. '"Not got the pluck of a louse," he said. That's just what Lloyd is – vermin. No good in him.'

All the afternoon nothing stirred outside. The children grumbled at having to stay with their mother; they wanted to go down to the camp and play with the blacks. At sundown the woman fed them well, and put on what warm clothes they possessed. The nights grew cold outside.

Then she made up a packet of food and filled three waterbags. She went into the bedroom, returned wearing a coat; in the secrecy of her pocket her fingers closed on the butt of a revolver her husband had given her when first they sailed north.

Already it had grown murky outside, with the swift falling of the Australian night.

'Come, children,' she said, 'we're going walkabout tonight. It will be fun to camp out in the spinifex.'

She could not repress a shudder. Often enough she had groaned over her rough little home. Yet how cosy it looked now, and safe! Filled with things she had herself fashioned from bits and ends, just to make it bright. She lit the lamp, set it on the table, and drew the curtains.

She picked up the baby. As she went out, followed by the children carrying the waterbags, she wondered if she was being a fool – subjecting them to unnecessary exposure. Well, in that case they could return in the morning. But she felt she couldn't risk the night; the natives might come after Lloyd again; they might come after the stores; that one act of violence might have gone to their heads. She did not want to think the childlike people she had so often looked after would set out to harm her children or herself; but she had to remember that two years ago they had not ever seen a white man.

She did not make the children walk far: if the worst befell they would have many miles to go. Just a little way on towards the distant settlement she took them; then, hiding snug behind an outcrop of rocks, she settled them down. Even though it was pitch-black by now, she knew that she was still within sight of the homestead.

Sam and Edie fell asleep. 'Mum,' whispered Johnnie, 'are you frightened of the Abos? Don't be scared, Mum, I'll look after you. Why did old Billycan do that to Lloyd, Mum?'

'I'm not frightened,' she replied. How frightened she was! 'But I think they might go a bit mad tonight . . . Lloyd was a rough, bad man, son, that's why.'

An age she crouched there, it seemed to the woman. Even Johnnie prattled himself to sleep. She began to call herself a silly, nervous creature.

A tongue of flame leapt up in the darkness. To the woman it seemed to leap through her own veins. The shed! They had fired the shed!

Instantly with the light came sounds. The sharp, staccato barking of dogs, shrill native voices, yells, bursts of song. As the light gained she could distinguish figures leaping like black imps in the blaze of a second fire. That was the house! She knew now that the storeroom had been raided; she could see black naked figures posturing about, throwing things to each other.

The noise increased. She shook the children. Time to move. As long as the natives feasted and played with the fire she was safe; she still did not want to think they would hurt her – but they had burned her home. Guilty consciences wrought terrible crimes. They could track her so easily had they a mind.

She looked at the heavens, took a bearing south by the Cross and the cold sparkling Pointers, and stumbled off, the sleepy children dragging at her heels. There would be a moon later, she remembered with thankfulness, after Sam had been picked up and the place kissed five times – she had to take his waterbag, along with the baby, then. Yet she stumbled on, resolute, cheerful with the children.

At last the moon rose, but its fading brilliance only unleashed her long-held fear. The country lay spread about like a desert peopled with terror, a void filled by shadows having no substance. Cold, cruel, impersonal, rejecting the soft alien woman and her brood.

The baby wakened, began to kick and struggle. Her whispers and the thin cries of the children seemed to reverberate like a laugh echoing beneath a church dome. She offered no comfort when Sam and Edie started to complain. She was sharp now. She gave the baby to Johnnie, and he staggered along as best he might, while the mother took Sam pick-a-back. She found the child's weight did nothing to deaden the nausea threatening to engulf her, the sickness of fear.

At length the keen edge of sensation dulled. She no longer looked at every shadow with a cold thrill of rigid expectancy; she no longer strained her ears for fancied footfalls.

She grew harsh with the children. A slave-driver. Even Johnnie sobbed at her rough words. And he was being so good! 'Don't fret, Mum,' he kept on saying. 'They wouldn't hurt us. Billycan's a mate of mine – they wouldn't hurt us.'

The night was without end; the country without end. Did there exist, anywhere in this grey and silver emptiness, human creatures other than black devils: were there houses, helping hands?

Dawn at last – and an unbearable radiance in the skies. A hard, rough land; and a sun gaining hourly in strength. A short sleep for the children. A drink of water and a piece of bread. Then up and on.

The woman felt safe from the natives now. She could reckon they would not attack until night fell again, if they were after her. That was what the men always said, anyhow. But if John were not already on the way out! The ghastly sickness swept back – they would all perish long before little legs could reach the settlement.

She was too tired to think for long. It took all her energy to watch. Up and on, then; up and on; through heat, with flies clinging and children crying. Hotter and hotter and hotter.

They had come on to the track – faint wheel-marks across the baked earth – soon after sunrise. It was Johnnie who spotted his father. The woman was trudging along with her eyes on the ground; she was carrying both Sam and the baby now. Breathing burnt her chest. Yet not until she looked into her husband's face did she realise *how* she must look. Haggard, livid, fallen-in, his face was. He had been riding, with two others, most of the night. That miserable Lloyd must have passed them, after all!

'Anna,' was all her husband could say for a bit. 'My God! Anna!'

The evil wrought by Lloyd was over, the woman told herself; but as she sobbed out her tale she knew it had only just begun. The other men were petting and soothing the children; Johnnie was boasting of all he'd done, telling them Billycan was a mate of his. Her husband's hand on her wrist felt safe, firm, tender.

'We'll take you into town, dearest,' he said. 'Then we'll come back and teach those black devils a lesson.'

'Lloyd!' she murmured.

'He'll have to leave the North, I reckon,' struck in one of the men.

'It was all his fault,' she repeated. But she knew it was no use arguing. The work of years had been destroyed; probably half their cattle had been speared now, too. What devils fear made of men, whether black or white – an hour ago she had been inhuman herself! But now, as she lifted heavy eyes to her husband's grim mask, she felt sorry for the natives.

Robert Drewe

RADIANT HEAT

1989

My mother heard it on the radio. They found the boy's body at 4.30 when they were packing up the picnic things, in a metre of water where the bottom of the lagoon shelved suddenly. In the panic it took them twenty minutes to think of counting heads. Then they discovered that another little boy was missing.

The second underwater search in thirty minutes. One child drowned, then another. It's too affecting a beginning, too much to accept. I feel uncomfortable ordering it so definitely. Wise after the event as usual. Full of selective certainties. But I know the second boy was a year younger than the first. Aged six. Lawrence Barker. I forget the first boy's name but obviously I remember Lawrence's. The compounded tragedy, the coincidences of the same name, age and place – Big Heron Lagoon – even their attending the same holiday child-care centre, saw to that. And my mother's reaction when she heard the news.

I'd told her that it was Peter's and Jenna's week with me. I know I'd said they were staying with Lucy and me down at the coast. They were not with Ellen, not spending their holidays at the child-care centre as usual, they were with me. (Somehow my mother's generation has trouble linking the ideas of 'father' and 'children'.) And 'Lawrence' hardly sounds like 'Peter'. But in the drama of a news bulletin enough connections could be made. I could see her making the leaps of imagination and despair. She knew we'd borrowed a friend's cottage at Bundeena, and Bundeena abuts the Royal National Park where the boys had died. So she had plenty to go on. For a long half-hour she was convinced that her grandson had drowned at a badly supervised children's picnic. When she finally reached me on the phone, I had to repeat to her, 'Mother, I can see Peter from here. He's watching "Inspector Gadget". I'll call him to the phone if you like.'

I never called her Mother but I was terse with her. She didn't believe me. She was babbling. Actually, my hand was trembling on the phone. I felt stunned. Peter was sitting cross-legged on the floor in his pyjamas watching television, and yet this evening there was a drowned boy named Barker, aged six.

Another layer of coincidence was making my hands shake. Only the day before, Lucy and I had taken the kids into the park for a picnic by the same lagoon. While my mother sighed and tutted I was replaying the day in my mind like a film, and recalling every frame. I remembered exactly the way the bottom of the shallow lagoon fell away suddenly in the middle. The water was a quieter, creamier green where the fresh creek met the salty white sand of the ocean beach – where, in winter, the higher tides burst through into the lagoon. I could feel the sandy bottom falling away right then, shifting and oozing around my ankles, the cooler currents around my shins, and I kicked away from the water-filled silence. And while my mother gradually calmed down and I turned the conversation around to Christmas plans, it struck me that my supervision of the children had been less than total. Certainly I watched them while they played in the water, but I read a magazine at the same time. I felt warm and lazy. The sun was bright and heavy on my eyelids; I couldn't swear that I didn't close them once or twice. And when I eventually dived in, the water was so bracing after the thick air that I stretched out and swam for several minutes, around a bend and temporarily out of sight.

Frankly, at the time I knew the risk. It occurred to me and I swam on. Worse, I anticipated *something*.

I looked at Peter and Jenna, absorbed by the cartoon, amusement flickering on their cheeks. I stared at them. Peter's hair was wet and spiky from his bath; a trickle ran down his neck behind his ear. Now and then he hummed the 'Inspector Gadget' theme. Despite his dead boy's particulars he moved, he spoke. I went over and stroked his head. To keep things fair, I reached over and patted Jenna's too. They didn't notice. A little later I began feeling guilty. Waves of guilt swept over me. But I couldn't dwell on the other parents, on what those families were doing right then. I could imagine, but I tried to put them out of my mind. And I succeeded. I was ruthless. I erased their anguish. I burned it out of the air.

Both my children are good swimmers now. That summer we had them coached, and they still train regularly. Swimming is Peter's only sporting interest. When adults ask his hobbies, he's apt to say, 'My hobby is imagination.' He's one of those sort of ten-year-olds. A sci-fi reader. A dreamy monster-lover. He moons through school classes but knows twenty ancient instruments of torture. He's a 'Dungeons and Dragons' buff. He likes those adventure books where the reader is the hero, and gets to decide which plot strand to follow. Already Peter wants to channel his fate, if only to choose the sword-fight with the skeleton ahead of the possible mauling by the werewolf.

Lucy and I moved to the coast ourselves last year, north rather than south, escaping from city real estate prices as much as other tensions. We bought a cottage at Springstone, a renovated weekender whose high position on Blackwall Hill we believed would compensate for its drawbacks. The views of the bay even made up for the mosquitoes and sandflies which rose from the reeds and mangrove flats at low tide and settled on the house. 'Citronella Heights,' I joked. Lucy is a member of the post-pesticide generation, an advocate of citronella oil as an insect repellent. Last summer we'd spray ourselves before drinks in the garden, before going to the beach, even – especially – before bed. The pungent citronella oil soaked into our clothes, sheets, furnishings, car upholstery. I didn't mind it; the fragrance was nostalgic. It brought back serene times, patchouli oil and incense and women in caftans. But everyone entering our house or car would ask, 'What *is* that smell?'

The children had no faith in citronella. They liked the way pesticides *annihilated* mosquitoes. One Saturday Peter woke with a badly bitten forehead and puffy eyelids. He was struck with awe and admiration for the face in the mirror ('I look like a halfling, a demi-human. I told you that stuff didn't work.'). But his ogre's demeanour had lapsed by bedtime. The first mosquito whine made him frantic. 'They're coming for me!' he yelled. We allowed him dispensation: he was permitted the old poison.

Destruction can be enjoyable, especially with right on your side. It's hard to put more than the broadest Buddhist case for the mosquito. A day I remember from last spring, the Monday of a holiday long-weekend: the arrow on the gauge outside town pointed to Extreme Fire Danger; in the way of city people I was heeding the warning and clearing the bush around the house. What I was doing was really more drastic than clearing. I was hacking into the lantana and scrub with the new Japanese brush-cutter. I was razing things flush to the earth. My blade screamed. Insects flew from the din and lizards scuttled in panic. In the trees above me, lines of kookaburras conspired patiently to swoop on newly exposed centipedes. I was righteous in my destruction: the lantana is an introduced pest, the centipede's bite is painful and poisonous, and so on. I stomped through the scrub wielding the cutter. Rock shards bounced off my heavy-plastic protective glasses, branches snapped underfoot. 'You look like "The Terminator",' Peter said. He approved. He was swinging a scythe. It was too big for him but he swung it anyway. The Grim Reaper, of course, and pleased to be him.

This was the month of unseasonal heat when people in shops and at bus stops first began talking about the Greenhouse Effect. Arsonists were lighting fires in the national parks, and an infestation of Bogong moths, blown by the north-westerlies, descended on the city and coast. The moths had become disoriented on their migration south from Queensland to the alpine country. They turned up in every building. They crawled into cupboards and kettles and shoes, into the luggage lockers in aircraft cabins and the more sinuous wind instruments of orchestras. They flew hundreds of miles out to sea before dropping in the waves. Some made it to New Zealand. Cats and dogs got fat and bored with eating them. (They were big and calorific; on windscreens they splattered into yellow grease.) Everyone had moths, and those places where bottlebrush trees were flowering for spring – the moths' favourite food was bottlebrush nectar – had a hundred times more.

In the hot wind the moths rose in a flurry from our bottlebrushes and showered red pollen on my son's head. Lucy and Jenna had left us to our mayhem. We cut and slashed and raked, but eventually stopped to have a drink. Peter was still charged with an edgy friskiness. While I drank a beer he entertained me with his repertoire of murderous noises and death scenes. He mimed axes in skulls and arrows in throats. He did blow-pipes and bazookas. He lurched about with his red-tinged hair, grunting and gurgling. He switched roles from killer to victim. Bullets ricocheted off rocks, scimitars flashed. He could crumple to the ground a dozen ways, holding his entrails in.

The air on our hill was yellow and smoky. Against the blurry horizon he filled me in on monsters. His favourites were the Undead – zombies, ghouls, wights, wraiths, mummies and skeletons. 'They're *chaotic*,' he said. What he liked about them, and gave him the creeps, was their potential for anarchy. Their evil was disorderly. Despite his patient explanations he lost me after that. The bushfires were on my mind and 'Dungeons and Dragons' is a complex game. But I've flipped through his guidebook, wondering at the attraction. 'A wraith looks like a shadow which flies, and *drains levels* as a wight. A mummy does not drain levels.' I'm none the wiser. I notice they all seem impervious to heroics. 'Ghouls are immune to *sleep and charm spells*. They are hideous beast-like humans who will attack any living thing. Any hit from a ghoul will paralyse any creature of ogre-size or smaller (except elves) . . .'

I knew zombies from those comedy-duo films of the fifties where they chased Abbott and Costello and Martin and Lewis. I knew Malcolm Rydge. This is an easy joke now that I can safely glance out of restaurant windows and not catch him looking in. I can walk the streets and not see him jog past, averting his eyes. I can leave my house suddenly without his car accelerating away. I can return the children to my old house, to Ellen, and not hear his excitable gabble in the kitchen, my name ringing in the air, the abrupt hush, the scramble for the back door.

There was finally a moment, a Friday lunch, when I looked down from the New Hellas, randomly, between mouthfuls of souvlakia, into Elizabeth Street. Malcolm was standing across the road in Hyde Park staring up at my window seat, my regular table. Our eyes met and held this time, in some sort of recognition. There is always someone who thinks you know the secret. Any secret. The secret of knowing Ellen first. The secret of the window table. Ellen had just thrown him out, he told me on my way out. He was waiting for me. It occurred to me later that he could have had a gun, a knife, in that shoulder bag he always wore. He slipped up in his running shoes and shook my hand as if he liked me. His eyes were distracted. His skin was damp and flickery. She had someone else. The voodoo was over, at least for me.

Lucy doesn't scoff at unquiet spirits. Ellen shuts them all out. She drops the portcullis. Her father went for a walk after lunch when she was twelve and never came back. From the veranda she saw him disappear into the treeline, swinging his stick and eating a Granny Smith apple. No-one ever found anything. Before it was called Alzheimer's Disease, my mother's mother was always trudging into town to hand in her own belongings to the police. 'I found this handbag in Myer's,' she would say. 'Some lass *will* be in a state.' She basked in her honesty as the cops drove her home again. My mother used to examine her own behaviour for early signs. Now that she doesn't any longer, I do.

Is it a sign that she gets younger every year? That since her sixtieth birthday she's been in reverse gear, hurrying backwards from the end? In the nine years since, she's shed twelve – lopping them off like old branches. Soon she'll pass me coming the other way. And this fifty-seven-year-old Elizabeth (who must have given birth to me at fourteen!) has lately turned into Bettina, having arrived there via Betty and Beth. Doesn't she remember the big party, the guests, the witnesses to her turning sixty? That I gave a speech? That we made a fuss of her? 'What's up with Bet?' her old friends wonder. What can I say? Her old friends look seventy. 'Bettina' looks, well, a cagey fifty-eight. She began getting younger in the 1970s with everyone else. In the 1980s, when everyone else started ageing again, she wilfully stayed behind. Is this a sign? The chin lift? The capped teeth? The bag removals? Lots of purple and gold? Sudden yellow hair? Leopard-skin materials? 'Ocelot,' she says firmly. 'Not leopard, ocelot.' What's the difference? It's not as if it's real skin, animal fur. It's only fabric, cotton blend stretch or something. 'It's what leopard skin *stands for*,' my North Shore sister grumbles. 'She's no chicken.'

Why does Penny always bring our father into it, even into the question of the ocelot-print stretch pants, even nine years later? Because our mother began getting younger as soon as he died? Well, she looked old for a month or two, for appearances' sake, then she started going backwards. 'I just know what Dad would say,' Penny says. But she never says what he'd say. ('I'd prefer not to see those pants on you, Betty.') 'Maybe he'll let us know,' I could say to Penny. In one of his posthumous letters with the yellow stamps shaped like bananas and a Tonga postmark.

That afternoon the wind carried the sound of fire sirens from the expressway to the coast. They closed the expressway to traffic when the fire jumped the six lanes and surged eastward. From our hill the western sky was a thick bruised cloud fading to yellow. The eucalypts around the house suddenly began to peel. The hot winds had dried and cracked their bark and given the trees a strange mottled look, as if they'd pulled on camouflage uniforms. Now the bloodwoods and peppermints and angophoras were peeling and shedding fast in the wind, dropping sheets of bark all around us, changing their colour and shape before our eyes. Some trees revealed themselves as orange, others were pink, yellow, even purple underneath. All of them seemed moist and vulnerable, membrane instead of wood. They looked as if they'd shiver if you touched them.

All the bushfire-warning literature talks about 'radiant heat'. I'd read that radiant heat was the killer factor in bushfires and I wondered if the trees peeling was some sensitive early-warning system, an early stage of radiant heat. People can't survive more than a few kilowatts of radiant heat touching them. I read that to stand in front of a fire only sixty metres wide was like being exposed to the entire electrical output of the State of Victoria at peak load. Every single metre of this sixty metres beams out the heat of thirty-three thousand household radiators! And now it seemed to be getting hotter even as the sun got lower.

Wary of Peter's vivid imagination, I kept quiet about radiant heat. With the growing clouds of smoke, the trees changing, his eyes were already skittish. 'What holiday is it supposed to be today?' he asked me. Labor Day? I couldn't remember. On rare days things come together: heat, a moth plague, fires, crowds of people. When random factors combine you anticipate more things happening. The drowning tragedy on the news. Maybe the arrival of a letter, mailed from some dozy South Pacific port six months before, from a father five months dead. ('I think the cruise has done me the world of good.') Peter made poison darts fizz through the air, *phht, phht, phht*. 'Let's get out of here,' he said.

In Australia people always run to the coast. Maybe the myth of the bush is a myth. In the car we had less than a kilometre to travel. The heat and the closed windows had activated the citronella oil in the upholstery. It felt like breathing citronella into one lung and smoke into the other.

At the beach we found Lucy and Jenna in the crowd by the rock pool. Everyone seemed to have the same idea. People brushed away moths as they laughed nervously about the smoky wind. Dead moths littered the high-tide line, moths and bluebottles that had been washed ashore. The bluebottles' floats, electric-blue and still full of air, were sharp and erect as puppies' penises. There was a rotting smell from a pile of dead shags. The force of the westerly had flattened the surf; the waves were low and snapping and plumes of spindrift shot away from the beach. People had put up windbreaks and lounged behind them, facing the sea and drinking beer. One group was drinking champagne and giggling.

'What's that red stuff in Peter's hair?' Jenna said.

'Pollen,' I said. 'From the moths.'

'It'll wash off in the sea,' Lucy said.

At sunset the wind dropped suddenly and by the time we needed to leave for the city the expressway was open again. It was early evening. Jenna and Peter had to return to school the next day, back to Ellen's. I was sorry the expressway had reopened. It would have been an excuse to keep them for a while. Maybe they'd have been stuck with me for days, with the road closed, the lines down. We would have been safe enough. We could always run into the sea.

Lucy kissed us goodbye. The narrow road out of Springstone was clogged with cars, everyone leaving at the same time. On the approach to the expressway the service stations all had fire trucks pulled into the back. Dirty fire-fighters slumped around the trucks, drinking from cans. One man was sitting on the ground trickling water from a hose over his head.

I pulled into the Shell station and filled the tank. I went inside and paid, and bought the kids some drinks. When I came out I noticed how badly the smoky wind and squashed moths had smeared the windscreen. I began to clean it. Just then a small Nissan truck came in fast and braked hard next to our car. A man in his late twenties jumped out of the driver's seat a few metres from me and headed around to the passenger side where a woman was screaming.

The woman was holding a boy of three or four on her lap. She was screaming in his face. 'You're going to die! Do you hear me? Die! Die!'

For a moment the man stood indecisively at the woman's window. He had wavy blond hair and he ran his hands through it and muttered something to the woman, something mild and self-conscious in tone, but she continued to scream at the child that he was going to die. The child looked stunned, as if he had just woken. I was standing there transfixed, with the squeegee in one hand and a wiper blade in the other. The man saw me looking and gave a wink. He took a couple of steps in my direction. 'Sorry, mate,' he said.

I didn't say anything. Through the windscreen I saw Peter's and

Jenna's faces staring at the truck cabin. They both had shocked, embarrassed smiles. The man turned to go into the service station office, but the woman began screaming louder and hurling obscenities and he turned back to the truck.

It was no place to be. I was hurrying to finish the windscreen, but – isn't it always the way? – those splattered moths were stuck fast. I seemed to be working in slow motion. Although I was making brisk, fussy dabs at the glass nothing much was improving. I had a sudden inkling the woman was doing something cruel to the boy that the man and I couldn't see. She was dark-haired, dark-eyed, the man's age or a bit older, and the wide spaces between her front teeth showed when she screamed. The boy had her looks and colouring. It's odd hearing a woman calling a man a cunt, over and over. Peter and Jenna weren't smiling any more. Jenna was pale and cupped her hands over her ears. She was near tears, whereas Peter's expression was confused and distant. He looked straight ahead, blinked, tried a silly scowl. His face was off-centre.

'Die, die, die!' the woman screamed again, and began to smack the little boy's face. He started to scream, too. The reaction of the blond man to her onslaught was so mild and understated as he leaned in the cabin window that two thoughts struck me: *that's not his child* and *what did he do or say to her just before this*?

'Please don't do that, you're hurting him,' he said as she continued to hit the boy's face. 'You're making him cry.'

I wanted the man to do something. I wanted him to stop shuffling on the driveway and take over. Do whatever's necessary, I willed him. Get tough with her. By now other motorists were pulling in and staring across at the disruption as they filled their tanks. Two teenagers sauntered past, snickering. I could see the lone service station employee peering out from behind the cash register. There was just enough room in the truck cabin for the woman to swing at the boy while she was holding him on her lap, and she began to punch his head.

'Hey!' I yelled. As if he'd been waiting for a complaint from the general public, the man leaned through the window and tried to grab her arm. She hit him with a flurry of punches, and her screeches and abuse rose in pitch. The boy screamed higher. The man stepped back from the truck and ran his fingers through his hair. 'I'm going for those cigarettes,' he announced, and walked inside the service station.

The woman stopped yelling and began rocking the boy on her lap. She stroked his cheeks, murmuring to him, and pulled his head down on her chest. Gradually, he stopped crying. I put the bucket and squeegee back beside the pumps. As I got back in the car she looked up and shot me a defiant glance. She was still glaring at me, muttering something, as we drove off.

Neither the children nor I said anything. My stomach felt queasy. While I was trying to think of something to say my stomach was turning over. Suddenly I couldn't bear the sickly smell of citronella in the car, the way the air-conditioner re-circulated and revived it. I opened my window to get some air. 'Open your windows,' I said. The smell of fire immediately came into the car. Little specks of ash floated in. Trees were smouldering on both sides of the expressway. Even the grass on the median strip was charred and off to the left flames glowed in a gully.

'Look down there!' I said. I was enthusiastic. I welcomed the diversion of the fire. 'It burned right through here, jumped the highway, and there it is now!'

'Wow,' said Peter, in a low voice. In the heavy traffic we were driving in the inside slow lane, well under the limit, peering out at the fire. The firemen had driven it up against a treeless sandstone bridge. It was fading fast without the wind behind it. But then light burst beside us and there was a roar. For an instant I thought *fire!* but it was the Nissan truck accelerating past us on the inside, on the narrow asphalt shoulder, showering us with loose stones. I saw the three profiles as they passed: the man driving with a cigarette in his mouth, the woman with the boy on her knees. The truck swung back on to the road, swerved around three or four other cars, shot into the outside lane and out of sight.

After I took the children home I drove to my mother's flat. Sometimes I stay overnight with her and head back to the coast first thing in the morning. She has a spare bedroom I've been using for emergencies ever since she moved into the flat after Dad died. I was there for a month when Ellen and I broke up. It was after eleven when I got there this time. I was so drained I could hardly think.

She was in her red tracksuit and gold slippers eating toast. She had face cream on her forehead and cheeks. 'Oh, dear,' she said when she saw me. She extracted a tissue from her tracksuit pocket and wiped her face. 'How are you, dear?'

I quickly said I was fine. Often these days she asks me questions and doesn't listen to the answers. I've just begun to answer and she's on to another question. Sometimes I have to say, 'Do you want to hear this or not? It's all the same to me. I'm just answering you.'

'I'm fine, Mum,' I said. 'I just need a brandy and I'll be fine.' I poured us both a drink and carried them into the living room. It's a small room; I sat next to her on the sofa. 'I was thinking of you watching the news,' I said. 'I hoped you wouldn't worry. The fires didn't get near us. Anyway, Peter and I cleared away all the scrub. No need to worry about fires reaching us.'

'What fires?' she said. 'I've been out. I went to see that Meryl Streep film. I thought she looked a bit horsey.'

'You always say she looks horsey!' I said. 'She's gorgeous. What do you mean, anyway, horsey?'

'You know, angular. Aquiline features or whatever they are. Equine.'

'Meryl Streep's beautiful! Can't you see that? She's the best film actress in the world.'

'Well, she's not my cup of tea,' my mother said. 'She was playing a booze artist, some Skid Row type.' She sipped her drink daintily. She still drinks alcohol in company like a guilty teenager, as if she's new to it, but there are always a couple of empty Remy Martin bottles when I take her garbage out.

'She was *acting*, Mum.'

'What's this about fires?' she said.

'It doesn't matter.' I took a big sip of brandy and swallowed it. 'The whole central coast nearly went up in flames. But it's under control now.'

'Oh, dear,' she said.

'It was weird. All our trees were cracking and peeling. Hot ash was flying everywhere. We escaped to the beach.'

'You must be careful, living up there.' She got up frowning and padded into the kitchen to make me more toast. 'It's the smoke you die from, not the flames,' she said.

'It's the radiant heat,' I said.

I could hear her out in the kitchen muttering something about smoke. 'Don't worry,' I called out. She was making familiar kitchen noises. I listened for her tutting sound, the anxious clicks her tongue made on her teeth when she did things for us. Things would come back to her: events, feelings, memories as organised as snapshots. When she brought me the toast she would lightly touch me on my head or shoulder. A little pat or squeeze. I was a war baby. He was away fighting in the Solomons. For two years it was just me and her. I sank back into the sofa and called out again, 'You really don't need to worry!'

Nick Earls

THE GOATFLAP BROTHERS
AND THE HOUSE OF NAMES
1995

It wasn't easy becoming Cleveland Goatflap. And who would have thought it could lead to the discovery of a brother?

I had tired of many things and determined that I could change few. So much in life, I realised, is fixed.

But I could change my name. I could change my name and from this straightforward but fundamental change I could then make others, as time permitted. Of course, this should not be a change to just any name. It should be a name with flourish, a name with which to embark on a new journey. A name with boldness, a name from which there could be no retreat. And change could then proceed, perhaps in small measures, perhaps at a charge. And perhaps the speed depended on the name itself. So the business of the name was clearly the most important of choices.

This took thought. Weeks, months of thought, list after list of names, and suddenly my life was filled with possibility. And I pinned the lists to my noticeboard at home, then Blu-Tacked them to the walls when the noticeboard was full. On my computer at work I alphabetised them and cut and pasted and printed in seven point so I could fit more to a page.

At home my walls filled till I lived in a house of names, where every conceivable surface was clad in Reflex 80 A4 paper, each sheet crammed to bursting with delightful proper and improper nouns. Names under my bare feet when I walked, names on the ceiling when I lay in bed, sheets of names crinkling attractively as I pulled my doona up over me. Comfortable soft noises like whispering voices as I rolled over in my bed filled with balled-up lists of names.

And I lived with the windows shut all this time, fearing that the slightest breeze would blow down my walls. But this was not a time for fear. There was no turning back, barely a thought of the old name my parents had given me, and which I would never speak again.

I lay awake most nights in the silent airless house. The Blu-Tack held. No pages fell.

I pressed on and I experimented with all kinds of things that might be names fit for journeying, old names and new names, the names of objects and countries and American states and unexpected species of flower and insect. I had a list of actual words so that I could, if I chose, compose names that would never be picked up by a computer spell checker: Cliff Carpenter, Dane Tailor and the concise but elusive Book Smith.

But in the end there was no name that rolled off the tongue with quite the finesse of Cleveland Goatflap.

I was ready.

In my lunch hour I left work, work where they still called me by the name I was now forgetting, the name I found it harder and harder to remember to answer to. And when I returned I would be informing them I would answer to it no more. But for now, in the interests of safety, I feigned purposelessness, and I headed in the wrong direction. I walked into an arcade and bought a hat and walked out of the other end of the arcade wearing it. I bought very dark glasses and a ferocious tie at Crazy Clark's, and I put them on. I walked the streets and no-one knew me. And already I walked with a more deliberate stride, the stride of a man who was going places.

The security guard watched me pass as I walked into the building, but he said nothing. I expect he could recognise I was involved in something of importance. I took the lift to the appropriate floor, took a number, filled in my form, checked the proof of identity documentation that bore the name I was about to cast off like an old skin. And I waited.

Around me others were doing the same, carrying proof of something, holding papers to carry out some act of registration.

My number was called.

I explained my purpose to the man behind the counter. He looked at my form, looked at me, looked at my passport with its photo of a younger, less distinguished man than someone who was almost Cleveland Goatflap.

He said to me *I might have to see you without the hat and glasses.*

But I wear them now, I told him, and he thought about it for a while and said *Righto*, but not with any certainty.

He read my form again. He looked up.

Might be a problem with the name, sir.

I told him I couldn't see it.

Some people might think it was frivolous.

I told him I found the very notion offensive. He apologised. I told him they were old family names, both of them, that my mother's mother had been a Cleveland and my father's grandmother a Goatflap. But here I outwitted him. I told him that the word he might presently be reading as Goatflap, an obvious choice for which I could forgive him, was actually a very old and distinguished French name and should be pronounced Gofla. I told him that when I was very young my father's grandmother, to whom I had been close, had suggested it derived from a Basque name, from a family who made terracotta roof tiles and moved to Toulouse in the twelfth century, and that there had most certainly been Goflas on the French side during the Hundred Years' War and that they had, sir, served with distinction.

He told me he would have a word with his supervisor.

He was gone for several minutes and he returned with an older man who studied me carefully as he approached.

Never heard of this Goatflap, sir, he said. *Heard of a lot of French names in my time, but never Goatflap.*

It's pronounced Gofla, I told him, and it may have been curiously translated from the Basque.

I was becoming concerned. Becoming concerned and starting to sweat more than a little. Clearly this man was an expert in the business of names and would not easily be bluffed with bluster and stories of roof tiles. But I had put months into this name. I couldn't imagine living a moment longer without living as Cleveland Goatflap.

Excuse me, a voice said beside me. *Excuse me.*

It was a voice of very individual intonation. A voice that spoke perhaps the way a chicken would speak if it could speak actual words. A chicken's voice, if chickens had lips.

I can confirm that, Gofla, he said, with such a flourish that his head snapped back, *is in fact a very old French name, very old indeed. And I can confirm this*, he went on sternly to the supervisor, *for I, monsieur, am this man's brother. I too carry the blood of Goflas in my veins.*

And with this he rolled up a sleeve and shook his fist around till the veins stood out like ropes and he pointed to them as proof positive of his Goatflap origins.

We embraced, despite his problem with personal hygiene, and I felt tears well in my eyes for my parents had always told me I was their only son.

He slapped his form defiantly down on the counter and I could see he had crossed out his previous choice of a new name and replaced it with Eleanor Goatflap in bold black capitals.

He pushed the form to the more junior officer who read it and looked up at him.

So you, sir, are at present Eduardo Saliva, wishing to change your name to Eleanor Gofla.

That's correct.

You've been here before, haven't you, sir?

Too bloody right.

The Eleanor, sir. Are you aware that that is a woman's name?

Sounds like discrimination to me son.

And I liked Eleanor already. I liked his feistiness. He was a good man to have on your team.

The supervisor interrupted and said *Geoff, I don't think the department would like to see itself standing in the way of a family reunion.*

And the junior officer smiled and said *No, Stan, I guess not.*

So we left the building arm in arm as brothers, my eyes still misting over periodically as we walked through the mall.

Let's have a drink, young Cleveland, Eleanor said. *To family, and to the great days of France.*

So Eleanor took me to a pub where he asked if they had French beer so we could celebrate appropriately. They told him they were all out of French beer and he said *Not to worry. Vive le bloody Fourex, eh?*

So we drank toast after toast in Fourex. We toasted the family and the great days of France. We swapped sides and toasted Blenheim, Ramillies, Oudenarde and Malplaquet. We even toasted Waterloo, though as Eleanor said, it's not really our time.

And suddenly all the changes I could ever need were mine.

We went home to my house, the House of Names, and Eleanor said *It looks like bloody heaven to me, a place like this. You've done well for yourself, young Cleveland. All these names. All these possibilities.*

And I felt proud. Proud as he spent hours just reading my walls, exploring all my surfaces, marking his favourites with a highlighter.

We enrolled in French classes together and practised all our spare time.

I even took him along to confront the parents who had abandoned him years before, though he was quite hesitant about such a meeting and could barely remember them. I parked outside their house and we spoke in the car and he said he was a bit tense but I told him he'd be fine.

He took a deep breath and hugged my father and addressed him as *mon père.*

And the last words I recall my father saying were him shouting after us *This is madness* as we left. *He's bloody older than I am.*

But we talked in the car and decided we would let no-one come between us. And my parents can make their own choices. I told Eleanor that, and I told him not to worry. I said we'd be okay.

So we live in the same house now, our house, the House of Names. We speak only French there. We pal around. We share the same dreams, Eleanor and I.

Delia Falconer

THE WATER POETS
1994

> The Water Poets are an innocent tribe and deserve all the
> encouragement I can give them. It would be barbarous to treat
> those writers with bitterness who never write out of season and
> whose works are *useful* with the waters.
>
> — STEELE, *The Guardian* No 174 (1713)

The farmer's boy points his sled down the hill towards the valley and
we begin to gather speed. And as is my habit, I, Treat, resident of Bath,
attendant at the baths and hitcher of lifts, with the wind entering
through my mouth and whistling through my bumgut, cling to the
side surrounded by divers vegetables and give thanks to God that I am
not a Water Poet.

About my feet, potatoes and carrots, the regenerative organs of the
earth, tremble and agitate at our descent back to the humid centre of
the world. And, as a man, with the seeds of infinite possibility in my
volatile blood, which vegetable shall I become today? In faith, that is
too easy. You may envisage Treat as an old and coruscated strawberry
with open pores, fattened upon the excretions of mankind, who also
quivers with increasing rapidity as the sleigh skids towards the vaporous
kettle of his natural home. This sink. This stew.

My first task is to scrape the cowl of scum from the surface of the
King's bath. The bowels of the earth ferment a strong hops, the head of
which proves too strong for invalid skins which rash and blister at its
touch. Next, I assemble my instruments: my pumps for anal and vaginal
injection, my pails for bucketing. I arrange flowers for the moister,
warmer sex on japanned trays. These little prows they arm with nose-
gays and unguents and attach to their breasts, inhaling a sentimental
mist less aggressive to tender noses than the sulphuric vapours of the
bath, and more sweetening to the odour of their own eructations.

The winds blow the stars from the heavens and the sun begins to warm the east. In my archway I wait for the bodies to arrive, those timid sponges which it is my duty to pry from their sedan chairs and drape in linen, to open and expose, by gentleness or force, to the healing liquids of the baths.

What is a body? It is a host of currents, an orb of celestial tempers. It is tides and shores which mark the airy passage of the spheres. It is a perfect sop steeped in the hopes and liquors of the world.

The first treatment I ever gave, before my beard grew, was to a woman of beauty who came to Bath in search of an heir. After I had removed her clothes and lowered the yellow gown over her arms, we paused at a corner of the baths, where the strong currents wedged us, and I felt my sex bobbing like a fish. As I led her up the steps to my archway I held her cool hand in my own. Gently, while she lay on her back, I introduced the pump. To my shame, I dissolved into scalding cream and tears, she into laughter.

Nine months later I had word of a son, born in a rush of acrid water, who floated without fear in the christening font. In the last months of her confinement her husband scoured the county to satisfy her womb's strange hunger for strawberries.

Once, years later, I braced the thin shoulders of a scholar as he strained over the planks, voiding his gravel and calling my name.

Are these fit subjects for Water Poetry?

In the Grove, Water Poems are pinned to the trees, impaled upon the smaller branches: it is like a massacre of the innocents in miniature. Although it provides some sport for the invalids and is well watered by their lachrymal secretions, the Grove is a dismal place, blasted by the sighs of melancholy lungs and bowels. From such saline soil there is but one sort of fruit which grows and that is Love. It is a copious and lustrous crop without odour or taste or seeds. It is my great amusement to see it swell in the Season, wither in autumn, and drop from the branches by winter.

Each Poet seeks to plot the course of Love, as if he were measuring out a field. He counts its instances like heads of wheat. Among the chief subjects of the Poets – Love inflamed by the waters; death by

Love; the callous nymph who ignores her sweetheart's pain – feeling is plucked from the body's innards and distilled. Fence lines are drawn, weeds eradicated. There is a lot of anxious threshing.

In the Grove, Love is valued by the pound.

What is a body? It is a climate of whirlpools and eddies searching for their source. It seeks the liquid balance of its earliest months. It is a promise of mixture, a constant alchemy of shit and gold.

If Water Poetry bears a relation to the baths it is a sort of evaporation. It is a cheap purgative for uncorsetted livers, a drain for the dropsied organ. It is a quack's physic which rids one of the embarrassment of seeing one's tailor at the baths, who also has a body which burns and bleeds. I pity those poor shivering sponges squeezed of all humours, fixed to the trees, and hung out to dry. There is a well-worn track from the planks to the Grove. I am shamed by such simplicity.

There are as many forms of faithlessness as romance. I knew a woman married to a glutton who deserted her each night at his club for a side of lamb. I had charge once of a gouty earl whose wife pined throughout his cure for her cat, left in the care of her housemaid, and each day by coach she sent back Bath waters to improve its coat. I have been paid by a cleric to let him place his head in the impression of a lady's water-gate, left upon her chair, and doused a wet nurse who, each time she gave suck, dreamed of the father of the child.

Are there poems for that?

This season I have devoted myself to an old boat caught between the wind and water too many times, so that now she is afire and cold pumpings fail to ease her scalds. She is a leaky vessel. As swiftly as she drinks water runs from her. There is a nest of towels beneath her skirt.

It is so long since I was touched by hands, she says, that my body no longer resembles a living person. It is swollen out of proportion. Indeed, she has painted her face with the image of a young girl, but crudely, with hands that have forgotten how the young flesh sat.

I will map you, I promise her, unwinding long white hair and coiling it beneath her cap. My fingers brush the frail mountain on her back.

She enters so heartily into the seething dance floor that it breaks my heart. Ignoring the jeers of the crowded gallery, I steer her about with her head upon my heart. I feel the bones loosen in her flesh, her body supple in my arms, her hungry hips tight against my own. She finds recognition in my loins and forgiveness in my face.

I know a woman took a tripe bath in Paris, I tell her, as we dance, and she got a calf from it.

I took a playwright in London, she replies, and I got the clap from it, which is more than he received for any performance.

In my fleshy palm I still the twitching of her hands.

She cries to leave the waters and feel about her the air which now exacts an unfair toll upon her life. Her body once had days and seasons, now it is all droughts and inundations like a cursed land. The smell of pain taints her breath. It has been my great delight to rekindle for a moment her body's girlishness.

I stroke her cheek to make it real for her. My own guts are cruelly mixed. One day, soon, her breath will quicken and life will pour out through her mouth and thighs, and she will lose herself entirely in my arms. Treat will pack her tenderly in damp sheets, fold her arms and legs in her sedan chair, kiss her lips and send her on her way. I shall write no poems for her – I will burn her towels in the fire.

What is a body? What paths should it take?

The waters are thick with turns and crossings.

I feel their rhythms within my veins and tune my steps to each body's dance. I perform the syphilitic quadrille, the promenade of green sickness, the jig to release the stale fart, the march which tightens a promiscuous bladder. How I laugh when these motions are repeated, in silk and lace, in the mirrored dance halls across the way.

It is a busy morning. In the corner a flushed cleric romances a crusty beau. A crummy maid and a pale virgin engage in furtive buttocking. A petticoat pensioner fingers his wife's old pouter beneath her tray.

Teeth fall into the water like cannon fire. Some days it is like the Spanish Armada, and England is losing.

An old libertine sniffs her perfumed handkerchief and licks her gums, inching closer to her prey. He endures his cure with the knowledge that he will have wrapped himself about a pheasant by noon. Yet in the Grove, if she can supply him with quill and paper, she may yet get her nose back.

How long must I hang here by these rings? he calls. Until your eggs are boiled, sir, snaps Treat, retiring to his cave.

In the Grove there is but one sex – paper.

The body of love which haunts the groves is a sick thing: its spermatical parts dried up, veins turned to ink, deprived of stools and fed on sighs, its arse-end sealed from the outside world.

You would think Love had four corners and no apertures.

Whereas I, Treat, have seen where Love starts. Its means and points of infection are numerous. The schoolmaster with wens on his fingers, the libertine with cheeks full of snail tracks, the widow playing at a fleshy lozenge on her tongue, the duellist whose trousers are heavy with leaking grapes, have not escaped my eyes.

There is a Water Poet here today. He cuts a fine figure at the Gaming Tables and observes the ladies with the melancholy aspect of a newt nibbling at a toadstool until they blush, at least those without rashes who still may. Yet this poet, who is stricken by the bloat and shits smaller than a mouse, is faithful only to his bowels. He dotes upon the enema and lusts after the planks. Between the pool and his lodgings, sunk in the fetid winds of his sedan chair, he transfers his gripes into Love, and hangs his Poems from the trees. This rescues him from the inconvenience of denying roast beef and pudding and expelling his tripe by other means.

I think, by the logic of Love, he may yet make a fine match out of it.

There was a young girl put into my care with the faintest shadow on her moss-rose and a green tint to her lips, whose strength was weakened and whose eyes had dulled from too many bleedings. When I carried her about the baths in my arms she was as light as steam drifting across the water's surface. For weeks I lived to feel the pale hint of breath in the hollow of my collarbone, and our linen shrouds entwine. She was my Little Death and I bore her tenderly, yet she seemed no more conscious of my presence than the stars fleeing from us in the firmament. Each dawn I bucketed her while her small hand idly fingered my bauble. I held glasses for her to piss in and sniffed them like wine.

One day she pissed clear and defied the physician. It was a fine cellar-age. I raised the glass to my lips and moaned.

The soldier overlain by his horse had a strong shoulder that fitted well beneath my arm. I will be your mount, I said, and galloped him through the baths. If *you* overlaid me, Treat, I should not mind, he whispered in my ear. Beneath his breeches his legs were as dry and withered as the Sunday joint, yet in the waters they unfurled, and when they tongued him, he spent like a rich man against my thigh.

Were these affairs? Why render an account with Water Poetry?

I have heard it said that what the water reveals, the pen must conceal, and indeed this is the Philosophy of the Water Poets.

Are your bowels dried up? Purge them with Poetry. Is your cream-stick gone sour? Write about Love. Do your buttocks ache from being tabered by a regiment? Become a Water Poet. This is Treat's advice.

What is Treat's body, how would I describe it? I am a joyful, shifting orb, a moist creature with bowels loose, belches unchecked, sound of chest, and mixed of feeling. I continue to entertain in my blood the struggle between life and death. I am plant, animal, vegetable, wind, water and fire united, and I tune the heavens to my body, rooting my toes in the gaseous emanations of the earth.

In an hour I shall dry my crotch, put away my instruments, and begin the long climb to my hearth, gulping at the air. I shall pass through the grove, laugh and spit heartily, and continue on my way, keeping, as ordained to man, a constant forward motion. The air which directs the stars and blows the ships about will cross back and forth across the porous surface of my skin and I, Treat, glad that I am not a Water Poet, may yet wake to find myself tomorrow the Angel or the wise man of Bath, my natural home, this sink, this stew.

Beverley Farmer

A MAN IN THE LAUNDRETTE
1985

She never wants to disturb him but she has to sometimes, as this room in which he studies and writes and reads is the only way in and out of his apartment. Now that he has got up to make coffee in the kitchen, though, she can put on her boots and coat and rummage in the wardrobe for the glossy black garbage bag where they keep their dirty clothes, and not be disturbing him. 'I'll only be an hour or two,' she says quickly when he comes back in. She holds up the bag to show why.

'Are you sure?' His eyebrows lift. 'It must be my turn by now.' They were scrupulous about such matters when she first moved in.

'I'm sure. I must get out more. Meet the people.' She shrugs at his stare. 'I want to see what I can of life in the States, after all.'

'Not to be with me.'

She smiles. 'Of course to be with you. You know that.'

'I thought you had a story you wanted to finish.'

'I had. It's finished. You know you don't have time to go, and I like going.'

He stands there unsmiling, holding the two mugs. 'I made you a coffee,' he says.

'Thanks.' She perches on the bed and drinks little scalding sips while, turned in his chair, he stares out at the sky.

His window is above the street and on brighter afternoons than this it catches the whole heavy sun as it goes down. He always works in front of the window but facing the wall, a dark profile.

He says, 'Look how dark it's getting.'

'It's just clouds,' she says. 'It's only a little after three.'

'Still. Why today? Saturday.'

'Why not? That's your last shirt.'

'It's mostly my clothes, I suppose.' It always is. She washes hers in

285

the bathroom basin and hangs them on the pipes. He has never said that this bothers him; but then she has never asked. He shrugs. 'You don't know your way around too well. That's all.'

'I do! Enough for the laundrette.'

'Well. Okay. You've got Fred's number?'

She nods. Fred, who lives on the floor above, has the only telephone in the building and is sick of having to fetch his neighbours to take calls. She rang Fred's number once. She gets up without finishing her coffee.

'Okay. Take care.' He settles at the table with his back to her and to the door and to his bed in which she sleeps at night even now, lying with the arm that shades her eyes chilled and stiff, sallowed by the lamp, while he works late. Sighing, he switches this lamp on now and holds his coffee up to it in both hands, watching the steam fray.

Quietly she shuts the door.

The apartment houses have lamps on already under their green awnings. They are old three-storey brick mansions, red ivy shawling them. Old elms all the way along his street are golden-leaved and full of quick squirrels: the air is bright with leaves falling. The few clumps that were left this morning of the first snow of the season have all dripped away now. As she comes down the stoop a cold wind throws leaves over her, drops of rain as sharp as snow prickle her face. The wind shuffles her and her clumsy bag around the corner, under the viaduct, down block after weedy block of the patched bare roadway. The laundrette seems further away than it should be. Has she lost her way? No, there it is at last on the next corner: DK's Bar and Laundrette. With a shudder, slamming the glass door behind her, she seals herself in the warm steam and rumble, and looks round.

There are more people here than ever before. Saturday would be a busy day, she should have known that. Everywhere solemn grey-haired black couples are sitting in silence side by side, their hands folded. Four small black girls with pigtails and ribbons erect on their furrowed scalps give her gap-toothed smiles. A scowling fat white woman is the only other white. All the washers are going. Worse, the coins in her pocket turn out not to be quarters but Australian coins, useless. All she has in US currency is a couple of dollar notes. There is a hatch for change with a buzzer in one wall, opening, she remembers, into a back room of the bar, but no-one answers it when she presses the buzzer.

Too shy to ask anyone there for the change, she hurries out to ask in DK's Bar instead. In the dark room into which she falters, wind-whipped, her own head meets her afloat among lamps in mirrors. Eyes in smoky booths turn and stare. She waits, fingering her dollar notes, but no-one goes behind the bar. She creeps out again. The wind shoves her into the laundrette.

This time she keeps on pressing and pressing the buzzer until a voice bawls, 'Aw, *shit*,' and the hatch thuds open on the usual surly old Irishman in his grey hat.

'Hullo!' Her voice sounds too bright. 'I thought you weren't *here!*' She hands him her two dollars.

'Always here.' He flicks his cigarette. 'Big fight's on cable.' A roar from the TV set and he jerks away, slapping down her eight quarters, slamming the hatch.

She is in luck. A washer has just been emptied and no-one else is claiming it. Redfaced, she tips her clothes in. Once she has got the washer churning she sits on a chair nearby with her garbage bag, fumbling in it for her writing pad and pen. She always writes in the laundrette.

She never wants to disturb him, she scrawls on a new page, *but she has to sometimes, as this room in which he studies and writes and reads is the only way in and out of his apartment.*

A side door opens for a moment on to the layered smoke of the bar. A young black man, hefty in a padded jacket, lurches out almost on top of her and stands swaying. His white jeans come closer each time to her bent head. She edges away.

Now that he has got up to make coffee in the kitchen, though, she can put on her boots and coat and rummage in the wardrobe for the glossy black garbage bag where they keep their dirty clothes, and not be disturbing him.

'Pretty handwriting,' purrs a voice in her ear. When she looks up, he smiles. Under his moustache he has front teeth missing, and one eyetooth is a furred brown stump. 'What's *that* say?' A pale fingernail taps her pad.

'Uh, nothing.'

'*Show* me.' He flaps the pad over. Its cover is a photograph of the white-hooded Opera House. 'Sydney, Australia,' he spells out. 'You from Australia?'

'Yes.'

'Stayin' long?'

'Just visiting.'

'I *said* are you stayin' *long*?'

'No.'

'Don' like the U-nited States.'

She shrugs. 'It's time I went home.'

'Home to Australia. Well now. My teacher were from Australia, my music teacher. She were a nice Australian lady. She got me into the Yale School of Music.' He waits.

'That's good.' She gives him a brief smile, hunching over her writing pad.

'I'll only be an hour or two,' she says quickly when he comes back in. She holds up the bag to show why.

'Are you sure?' His eyebrows lift. 'It must be my turn by now.'

'What you writin'?'

'A story.'

'Story, huh? I write songs. I'm a musician. I was four years at the Yale School of Music. That's *good*, is it?' He thrusts his face close to hers and she smells rotting teeth and fumes of something – bourbon, perhaps, or rum. So that's what it is: he is drunk. He has a bunched brown paper bag with a bottle in it, which he unscrews with difficulty and wags at her. 'Have some.' She shakes her head. Shrugging, he throws his head back to swallow, chokes and splutters on the floor. He wipes his lips on the back of his hand, glaring round. Everyone is carefully not looking. One small black girl snorts and they all fall into giggles. He bows to them.

'I work in a piana bar, you listenin', hey *you*, I ain' talkin' to myself.' She looks up. 'That's *bet*ter. My mother and father own it so you wanna hear me sing I get you in for free. Hey, you wanna hear me sing or don't you?' She nods. 'All *right*.' What he sings in a slow, hoarse tremolo sounds like a spiritual, though the few words she picks up make no sense. The black girls writhe. The couples sitting in front of the dryers exchange an unwilling smile and shake of the head.

'You like that, huh?' She nods. 'She *like* that. Now I sing you all another little number I wrote, I write all my own numbers and I call this little number Calypso Blues.' Then he sings more, as far as she can tell, of the same song.

They were scrupulous about such matters when she first moved in.

'I'm sure. I must get out more. Meet the people.' She shrugs at his stare. 'I want to see what I can of life in the States, after all.'

'Like that one? My mother and father – *hey* – they real rich peoples, ain' just the piana bar, they got three houses. Trucks. Boats too. I don' go along with that shit. Ownin' things, makin' money, that's all shit. What you say your name was? Hey, *you*. You hear me talkin' to you?'

'Uh, Anne,' she lies, her head bowed.

'Pretty.' He leans over to finger her hair. 'Long yeller hair. Real . . . pretty.'

'Don't.'

'"I want to see what I can of life in the States after" – after *what?*'

'*All.*' She crams the pad into her garbage bag.

'You sha' or somethin'?'

'What?'

'You sha'? You deaf or somethin'? You *shacked?*'

'Oh! Shacked? Shacked – yes, I am. Yes.' She keeps glancing at the door. The first few times that it was her turn to do the laundry he came along anyway after a while, smiling self-consciously, whispering, 'I missed you.' But not today, she knows. She stares at somebody's clothes flapping and soaring in a dryer. She could take hers home wet, though they would be heavy: but then this man might follow her home.

'So where you live?'

'Never mind,' she mutters.

'What's that?'

'I don't *know*. Oh, down the road.'

'Well, you can tell me.'

'No, I'd – I don't *know* its name.'

'I just wanna talk to you – *Anne*. I just wanna be friends. You don' wanna be friends, that what you sayin'? You think I got somethin' nasty in my mind, well I think *you* do.' He snorts. 'My lady she a white lady like you an' let me tell *you* you ain' nothin' alongside of her. *You ain' nothin'.*'

She stares down. He prods her arm. 'Don't,' she says.

'Don' what?'

'Just don't.'

'Hear me, bitch?'

'Don't talk to me like that.'

'Oh, don' talk to you like that? I wanna talk to you, I talk to you how I like, don't you order *me* roun' tell me how I can talk to you.' He jabs his fist at her shoulder then holds it against her ear. 'Go on, look out the door. Expectin' somebody?'

'My friend's coming.'

'Huh. She expectin' her *friend*.' The couples look back gravely. 'My brothers they all gangsters,' he shouts, 'an' one word from me gets anybody I *want* killed. We gonna kill them *all*.' He is sweaty and shaking now. 'We gonna kill them and dig them up and kill them all *over* again. Trouble with you, Miss Australia, you don' like the black peoples, that's trouble with you. Well we gonna kill you *all*.' He drinks and gasps, licking his lips.

The door opens. She jumps up. With a whoop the wind pushes in two Puerto Rican couples with garbage bags. Leaves and papers come rattling over the floor to her feet. One of the Puerto Ricans buzzes and knocks at the hatch for change, but no-one opens it; in the end they pool what quarters they find in their pockets, start their washers and sit in a quiet row on a table. Her machine has stopped now. There is a dryer free. She throws the tangled clothes in, twists two quarters in the slot and sits hunched on another chair to wait.

He has lost her. He spits into the corner, staggering, wiping his sweat with a sleeve, then begs a cigarette from the sullen white woman, who turns scornfully away without a word. 'Bitch,' he growls: a jet of spit just misses her boot. One of the Puerto Ricans offers him an open pack. Mumbling, he picks one, gets it lit, splutters it out and squats shakily to pick it up out of his splash of spit. He sucks smoke in, sighs it out. Staring round, he finds her again and stumbles over. 'Where you get to?' He coughs smoke in her face. His bottle is empty: not a drop comes out when he tips it up over his mouth. 'Go*dam*,' he wails, and lets it drop on the floor, where it smashes. 'Goddam mothers, you all givin' me *shit*!'

'No-one doin' that,' mutters a wrinkled black man.

He has swaggered up close, his fly almost touching her forehead. '*Don't*,' she says despairingly.

'Don't, don't. Why not? I like you, Miss Australia.' He gives a wide grin. 'Gotta go next door for a minute. Wanna come? No? Okay. Don' nobody bother her now. Don't nobody interfere. She *my* lady.'

He stumbles to the side door and opens it on a darkness slashed with red mirrors. Once the door shuts the black couples slump and sigh. One old woman hustles the little black girls out on to the street. An old man leans forward and says, 'He your friend, miss?'

'No! I've never seen him before.'

The old man and his wife roll their eyes, their faces netting with anxious wrinkles. 'You better watch out,' he says.

'What if he follows me home?'

They nod. 'He a load of trouble, that boy. Oh, his poor mother.'

'Maybe he'll stay in there and won't come back?' she says.

'Best thing is you call a cab, go on home. They got a pay phone here.'

'Oh, *where?*'

'In the bar.'

'*Where!*'

The side door slams open, then shut, and they all sit back guiltily. She huddles, not looking round. Her clothes float down in the dryer, so she opens it and stoops into the hot dark barrel to pick them out, tangled still and clinging to each other. Suddenly he is bending over her, his hands braced on the wall above the dryer, his belly thrust hard against her back. She twists angrily out from under him, clutching hot shirts.

'Now stop that! That's enough!'

'Not for me it ain', not yet.'

'Leave me alone!'

'I wanna talk. Wanna talk to you.'

'No! Go away!' She crams the clothes into her garbage bag.

'Hey, you not well, man,' mumbles the old black. 'Better go on home now. Go on home.'

'Who you, man, you gonna tell *me* what to do?' He throws a wide punch and falls to the floor. With a shriek of rage and terror the old woman runs to the side door and pounds on it. It slaps open, just missing her, and two white men tumble in.

'Okay,' one grunts. 'What's trouble here?'

'Where you *been*? You supposed to keep *order!*' she wails, and the old man hushes her. The young man is on his knees, shaking his frizzy head with both his hands.

With gestures of horrified embarrassment to everyone she sees watching her, she swings the glass door open on to the dim street. A man has followed her: one of the two Puerto Ricans. 'Is okay. I see you safe home,' he says, and slings her bag over his shoulder.

'Oh, thank you! But your wife's still in there.'

'My brother is there.' He takes her arm, almost dragging her away.

'He was so drunk,' she says. 'What made him act like that. I mean, why me?'

His fine black hair flaps in the wind. 'You didn't handle him right,' he says.

'What's *right*?'

'You dunno. Everybody see that. Just whatever you did, you got the guy mad, you know?'

They are far enough away to risk looking back. He is out on the road, his body arched, yelling at three white men: the old Irishman in the hat has joined the other two and they are barring his way at the door of the laundrette. There is something of forbearance, even of compunction, in their stance. 'They'll leave him alone, won't they?' she asks.

He nods. 'Looks like they know him.'

He has seen her all the way to the corner before she can persuade him, thanking him fervently, that she can look after herself from here on. He stands guard in the wind, his white face uneasily smiling whenever she turns to grin and wave him on. The wind thrashes her along their street. In the west the clouds are fraying, letting a glint of light through, but the streetlamps are coming on already with a milky fluttering, bluish-white, among the gold tossings of the elms.

A squirrel on their fence fixes one black resentful eye on her: it whirls and stands erect, its hands folded and its muzzle twitching, until abruptly it darts away, stops once to look back, and the silver spray of its tail follows it up an elm.

The lamp is on in his window – none of the windows in these streets has curtains – and he is still in front of it, a shadow. She fumbles with her key. Rushing in, she disturbs him.

'Am I late? Sorry! There was this terrible man in the laundrette.' Panting, she leans against the dim wall to tell him the story. Halfway through she sees that his face is stiff and grey.

'You're thinking I brought it on myself.'

'Didn't you?'

'By going out, you mean? By not wanting to be rude?'

He stares. 'No, you wouldn't.'

'What did I do that was wrong?'

'A man can always tell if a woman fancies him.'

'Infallibly?' He shrugs. 'I led him on, is that what you mean?'

'Didn't you?'

'Why would I?'

'You can't seem to help it.'

'Why do you think that?'

'I've seen you in action.'

'*When?*'

'Whenever you talk to a man, it's there'

'This is sick,' she says. He shakes his head. 'Well, *what's* there?' But he turns back without a word to the lamplit papers on his table.

Shivering, she folds his shirts on the wooden settle in the passage, hangs up his trousers, pairs his socks. Her few things she drops into her suitcase, open on the floor of the wardrobe; she has never properly unpacked. Now she never will. There is no light in this passage, at one end of which is his hood of yellow lamplight and at the other the twin yellow bubbles of hers, wastefully left on while she was out. The tall windows behind her lamps are nailed shut. A crack in one glitters like a blade. Wasps dying of the cold have nested in the shaggy corners. In the panes, as in those of his window, only a greyness like still water is left of the day.

But set at eye level in the wall of the passage where she is standing with her garbage bag is a strip of window overgrown with ivy, one small casement of which she creeps up at night from his bed to prise open, and he later to close: and here a slant of sun strikes. Leaves all the colours of fire flicker and tap the glass.

'Look. You'd think it was stained glass, wouldn't you? Look,' she is suddenly saying aloud. 'I'll never forget this window.'

He could be a statue or the shadow of one, a hard edge to the lamplight. He gives no sign of having heard.

Wasps are slithering, whining over her window panes. One comes bumbling in hesitant orbits round her head. It has yellow legs and rasps across her papers jerking its long ringed belly. She slaps it with a newspaper and sweeps it on to the floor, afraid to touch it in case a dead wasp can still sting, if you touch the sting. Then she sits down at the table under the lamps with her writing pad and pen and scrawls on, though her hand, she sees, is shaking.

'Not to be with me.'

She smiles. 'Of course to be with you. You know that.'

'I thought you had a story you wanted to finish.'

'I had. It's finished.'

Helen Garner

THE LIFE OF ART

1985

My friend and I went walking the dog in the cemetery. It was a Melbourne autumn: mild breezes, soft air, gentle sun. The dog trotted in front of us between the graves. I had a pair of scissors in my pocket in case we came across a rose bush on a forgotten tomb.

'I don't like roses,' said my friend. 'I despise them for having thorns.'

The dog entered a patch of ivy and posed there. We pranced past the Elvis Presley memorial.

'What would you like to have written on your grave,' said my friend, 'as a tribute?'

I thought for a long time. Then I said, '*Owner of two hundred pairs of boots.*'

When we had recovered, my friend pointed out a headstone which said, *She lived only for others.* 'Poor thing,' said my friend. 'On *my* grave I want you to write, *She lived only for herself.*'

We went stumbling along the overgrown paths.

My friend and I had known each other for twenty years, but we had never lived in the same house. She came back from Europe at the perfect moment to take over a room in the house I rented. It became empty because the man – but that's another story.

My friend has certain beliefs which I have always secretly categorised as *batty*. Sometimes I have thought, 'My friend is what used to be called "a dizzy dame".' My friend believes in reincarnation: not that this in itself is unacceptable to me. Sometimes she would write me long letters from wherever she was in the world, letters in her lovely, graceful, sweeping hand, full of tales from one or other of her previous lives, tales to explain her psychological make-up and behaviour in her present incarnation. My eye would fly along the lines, sped by embarrassment.

My friend is a painter.

When I first met my friend she was engaged. She was wearing an antique sapphire ring and Italian boots. Next time I saw her, in Myer's, her hand was bare. I never asked. We were students then. We went dancing in a club in South Yarra. The boys in the band were students too. We fancied them, but at twenty-two we felt ourselves to be older women, already fading, almost predatory. We read *The Roman Spring of Mrs Stone*. This was in 1965; before feminism.

My friend came off the plane with her suitcase. 'Have you ever noticed,' she said, 'how Australian men, even in their forties, dress like small boys? They wear shorts and thongs and little stripy T-shirts.'

A cat was asleep under a bush in our backyard each morning when we opened the door. We took him in. My friend and I fought over whose lap he would lie in while we watched TV.

My friend is tone deaf. But she once sang 'Blue Moon', verses and chorus, in a talking, tuneless voice in the back of the car going up the Punt Road hill and down again and over the river, travelling north; and she did not care.

My friend lived as a student in a house near the university. Her bed was right under the window in the front room downstairs. One afternoon her father came to visit. He tapped on the door. When no-one answered he looked through the window. What he saw caused him to stagger back into the fence. It was a kind of heart attack, my friend said.

My friend went walking in the afternoons near our house. She came out of lanes behind armfuls of greenery. She found vases in my dusty cupboards. The arrangements she made with the leaves were stylish and generous-handed.

Before either of us married, I went to my friend's house to help her paint the bathroom. The paint was orange, and so was the cotton dress I was wearing. She laughed because all she could see of me when I stood in the bathroom were my limbs and my head. Later, when it got dark, we sat at her kitchen table and she rolled a joint. It was the first dope I had ever seen or smoked. I was afraid that a detective might look through the kitchen window. I could not understand why my friend did not pull the curtain across. We walked up to Genevieve in the warm night and ate two bowls of spaghetti. It seemed to me that I could feel every strand.

My friend's father died when she was in a distant country.

'So now,' she said to me, 'I know what grief is.'

'What is it?' I said.

'Sometimes,' said my friend, 'it is what you expect. And sometimes it is nothing more than bad temper.'

When my friend's father died, his affairs were not in order and he had no money.

My friend was the first person I ever saw break the taboo against wearing striped and floral patterns together. She stood on the steps of the Shrine of Remembrance and held a black umbrella over her head. This was in the 1960s.

My friend came back from Europe and found a job. On the days when she was not painting theatre sets for money she went to her cold and dirty studio in the city and painted for the other thing, whatever that is. She wore cheap shoes and pinned her hair into a roll on her neck.

My friend babysat, as a student, for a well-known woman in her forties who worked at night.

'What is she like?' I said.

'She took me upstairs,' said my friend, 'and showed me her bedroom. It was full of flowers. We stood at the door looking in. She said, "Sex is not a problem for me." '

When the person . . . the man whose room my friend had taken came to dinner, my friend and he would talk for hours after everyone else had left the table about different modes of perception and understanding. My friend spoke slowly, in long, convoluted sentences and mixed metaphors, and often laughed. The man, a scientist, spoke in a light, rapid voice, but he sat still. They seemed to listen to each other.

'I don't mean a god in the Christian sense,' said my friend.

'It is egotism,' said the man, 'that makes people want their lives to have meaning beyond themselves.'

My friend and I worked one summer in the men's underwear department of a big store in Footscray. We wore our little cotton dresses, our blue sandals. We were happy there, selling, wrapping, running up and down the ladder, clinging the register, going to the park for lunch with the boys from the shop. *I* was happy. The youngest boy looked at us and sighed and said, 'I don't know which one of youse I love the most.' One day my friend was serving a thin-faced woman at the specials box. There was a cry. I looked up. My friend was dashing for the door. She was sobbing. We all stood still, in attitudes of drama. The woman spread her hands. She spoke to the frozen shop at large.

'I never said a thing,' she said. 'It's got nothing to do with *me*.'

I left my customer and ran after my friend. She was halfway down the street, looking in a shop window. She had stopped crying. She began to tell me about . . . but it doesn't matter now. This was in the 1960s; before feminism.

My friend came home from her studio some nights in a calm bliss. 'What we need in work,' she said, 'are those moments of abandon, when the real stuff runs down our arm without obstruction.'

My friend cut lemons into chunks and dropped them into the water jug when there was no money for wine.

My friend came out of the surgery. I ran to take her arm but she pushed past me and bent over the gutter. I gave her my hanky. Through the open sides of the tram the summer wind blew freely. We stood up and held on to the leather straps. 'I can't sit down,' said my friend. 'He put a great bolt of gauze up me.' This was in the 1960s; before feminism. The tram rolled past the deep gardens. My friend was smiling.

My friend and her husband came to visit me and my husband. We heard their car and looked out the upstairs window. We could hear his voice haranguing her, and hers raised in sobs and wails. I ran down to open the door. They were standing on the mat, looking ordinary. We went to Royal Park and flew a kite that her husband had made. The nickname he had for her was one he had picked up from her father. They both loved her, of course. This was in the 1960s.

My friend was lonely.

My friend sold some of her paintings. I went to look at them in her studio before they were taken away. The smell of the oil paint was a shock to me: a smell I would have thought of as masculine. This was in the 1980s; after feminism. The paintings were big. I did not 'understand' them; but then again perhaps I did, for they made me feel like fainting, her weird plants and creatures streaming back towards a source of irresistible yellow light.

'When happiness comes,' said my friend, 'it's so thick and smooth and uneventful, it's like nothing at all.'

My friend picked up a fresh chicken at the market. 'Oh,' she said. 'Feel this.' I took it from her. Its flesh was pimpled and tender, and moved on its bones like the flesh of a very young baby.

I went into my friend's room while she was out. On the wall was stuck a sheet of paper on which she had written: 'Henry James to a friend in trouble: "throw yourself on the *alternative* life . . . which is what I mean by the life of art, and which religiously invoked and handsomely understood, je vous le garantis, never fails the sincere invoker – sees him through everything, and reveals to him the secrets of and for doing so." '

I was sick. My friend served me pretty snacks at sensitive intervals. I sat up on my pillows and strummed softly the five chords I had learnt on my ukulele. My friend sat on the edge of a chair, with her bony hands folded round a cup, and talked. She uttered great streams of words. Her gaze skimmed my shoulder and vanished into the clouds outside the window. She was like a machine made to talk on and on forever. She talked about how much money she would have to spend on paint and stretchers, about the lightness, the optimism, the femaleness of her work, about what she was going to paint next, about how much tougher and more violent her pictures would have to be in order to attract proper attention from critics, about what the men in her field were doing now, about how she must find this out before she began her next lot of pictures.

'Listen,' I said. 'You don't have to think about any of that. Your work is *terrific*.'

'My work is terrific,' said my friend on a high note, 'but *I'm not*.' Her mouth fell down her chin and opened. She began to sob. 'I'm forty,' said my friend, 'and I've got *no money*.'

I played the chords G, A and C.

'I'm lonely,' said my friend. Tears were running down her cheeks. Her mouth was too low in her face. 'I want a man.'

'You could have one,' I said.

'I don't want just any man,' said my friend. 'And I don't want a boy. I want a man who's not going to think my ideas are crazy. I want a man who'll see the part of me that no-one ever sees. I want a man who'll look after me and love me. I want a grown-up.'

I thought, If I could play better, I could turn what she has just said into a song.

'Women like us,' I said to my friend, 'don't have men like that. Why should you expect to find a man like that?'

'Why shouldn't I?' said my friend.

'Because men won't do those things for women like us. We've done something to ourselves so that men won't do it. Well – there are men who will. But we despise them.'

My friend stopped crying.

I played the ukulele. My friend drank from the cup.

Kerryn   Goldsworthy

14TH OCTOBER 1843
1994

The history of the pianoforte and the history of the social status
of women can be interpreted in terms of one another . . . Being
'accomplished' generally was judged to render a girl a more
valuable prize in the marriage gamble; her little singing and
piano playing was not only an amorous lure . . . it was also a
way of confirming her family's gentility.

> ARTHUR LOESSER, *Men, Women and Pianos: A Social History*

There is every reason to think, in fact, that pianos meant more
to Australians precisely because of their own distance in time
and space from Europe . . . Middle-class values have rarely expressed themselves with more touching gallantry and tenacity
than in the sacrifices and discomforts endured by countless
families in order to bring this cumbersome symbol of higher
values to their chosen home in small, unstable ships and on
grinding bullock drays.

> ROGER COVELL, *Australia's Music*

14th October 1843
Six Days South of Adelaide

Writing, perhaps, will order my thoughts – I cannot see what else
might do it – Mr Honeywell would tell me that Prayer would be more
appropriate than writing in my Journal & perhaps he would be right –
but he is safe at home in Yorkshire & if here in this tent without the
comforts of the Vicarage might find himself less certain, of himself &
me, & perhaps even of God. A little while ago I watched the Sun set
& all that I could think of was Jerusalem the Golden – yet in this
country God seems very far away.

The children are asleep after much protesting & unrest & I do not think I should be using up this candle for who knows when we will get more? The boys & my dear Husband are still out searching but must return soon for it is almost completely dark.

I can hear the Children – Breathing – but feel I am the only person in the world –

I try to think where she might be but all I can see in my mind is what I began to think of even while I watched as the Explosion of the Piano. Perhaps watched is the wrong word – heard? felt?

I will write it down. After tea Louisa went out to get some bark & branches for the fire, & she did not come back.

This morning as we were packing up, one of the ropes restraining the piano broke – we think it must have been rubbing & fraying on a sharp corner of one of the boxes, all this time, with the jolting of the waggon, & that the agitation of this morning's packing snapped it at last. As it gave way so did another which could not sustain the sudden Weight & the piano fell – slid – off the waggon. To our astonishment it landed upright among the stones but its travelling-case was all smashed to bits down one side & Robert's hand was crushed as he tried to catch & steady it from where he was standing near – with a great splinter of wood driven straight into one of his fingers. This is not the first time the piano has hurt one of the boys. I see I am writing about it as though it were a kind of Wild Animal –

Robert said he would not take it another mile – not another *step* – that for his part he did not play or sing & did not want to learn – that the strumming & banging of the children on the instrument drove him wild – that if Louisa could not pass for a Lady without sitting down & playing the 'Last Rose of Summer' then perhaps she should learn to behave more Ladylike in other ways – whereupon my dear Husband intervened & Robert was forced to apologise to his Sister for his rudeness.

But he could not be persuaded to pack up the Piano once more & Richard supported him very loyally in a Brotherly way at which I could not but be glad, tho' secretly – for I could not be seen to support them in their disobedience – & tho' my heart ached for Louisa who even when very young would sit at the piano for hours at a time – playing her little airs over & over, so patient & earnest, a bar at a time – her fingers so small she must stretch & strive for an Octave, & weep when she could not reach it – & when older would storm at the keys in a way that drove her Father out of doors – he said it was like an Atmospheric Disturbance – even tho' she was so much sought after for dances & balls, & for musical evenings everywhere. She would offer always to play for other people to dance – tho' herself pretty & never in want of a partner she preferred to be at the piano, where she could see the dance – & *order* it to her liking. I sometimes think she wanted not to be looked at – but to direct what was there to be seen, the spectacle of dancing. But people's eyes were drawn to her – I think precisely *because* she was so remote & so removed – as tho' she preferred the company of the Piano. Which she did. She did.

I wish that she would not fight so with the boys. It is not ladylike. She is quite *passionate* about her music & this too is unladylike yet to *play* is very proper though at present her beautiful Hands are cracked & scratched for she will insist on helping with ropes & horses & the digging of innumerable Holes which seems to be part of this Gipsy life – that is one of the things she fights with the Boys about – they tease her about her blistered hands & her face which is positively *tanned* & she flies at them like a wild Cat.

Left behind us in the dust & the afternoon sun, the Piano looked a ridiculous object but also very beautiful. Louisa let out a strange *sob* – Oh I cannot bear it she said we cannot leave it there like a child in the street – push it over the cliff & Drown it –

The edge of the cliff crumbled a little as they pushed it over & so there was no clean moment, just a sort of tilt & then a bang as it went over the side. The children rushed to the edge to watch & I was so afraid they would follow it over & so determined they would not that I did not look at the Piano till just before it struck an outcrop of rock about twenty feet below us, turning a sort of slow cartwheel in the air & then – *bursting* –

There was a great roaring as the strings snapped & it flew apart & keys & splinters soared in every direction – it disturbed a large number of Sea Birds & they all rose up screaming in the air, it is a miracle they were not struck as all the Piano Fragments bounced & bounced again on the great rocks strewn down the cliffside & planted in the sand. It had stopped being a Thing – the beach below us was covered in debris of all kinds, all looking like meaningless rubbish except for the Keys – still recognisable but all in chaos – I thought for the first time how all the Keys were only *themselves* when in relation to each other – & how tightly & neatly they fit together – & how much is latent in them – how much a piano can, when properly played, *set free* – but an A-flat key that one knows intimately when in its proper place, on the keyboard, or at the heart of a chord, does not look, when lying on the beach, like anything at all – only a dead black *stick* –

In Adelaide they told us that hundreds of pianos were arriving in Australia every year, for people who have them in England do not want them left behind – & all the stories are so different about what we will find when we arrive that no-one can be certain but that they might never touch a keyboard again. So they – we – bring them from home & carry them all over the country, lumbering like snails. One story we heard at dinner concerned a ship in trouble at sea whose Captain ordered the thirteen pianos on board with much of the other cargo to be thrown into the sea – & there was almost a Riot on the ship as the owners tried to prevent him & were shouted down by the other passengers, fearing for their lives.

I think that it is to do with the idea of order. Outside the new cities the country is so wild that it sends people Mad – there are no hedges or fences or roads or tracks & there are no maps – whereas the thing about a piano is that it is so *precise*. It is astonishing how important this orderliness becomes when you are in a place with no names or directions & it seems no Rules – & the piano becomes a way of telling yourself & other people where & who you are. I fear that ours had got sadly out of tune. But when a piano is in tune then the distance between the pitch of any two notes lying side by side is the same as any other two & you can sing them – you know where you are in the scale, & on the keyboard, just by looking – & the pattern of notes is repeated every octave – only in black & white & in straight, straight lines. You can come to both ends of a piano by moving nothing but your Hands, as if the whole world of the Instrument – a kind of Infinity – were ordered & within your grasp.

I am exceedingly glad that Mr Honeywell cannot see what I have written here about Infinity for he would think it Blasphemous – but I think that it is true.

How many other people, I wonder, have been forced to do what we have done? Perhaps all over this terrifying country there are Dead Pianos – left on beaches – abandoned on tracks – pushed over cliffs – rotting in ruined huts & cabins – making peculiar Homes for birds &

mice & spiders playing witches' music among the strings & fretwork, & the silk all gone to rags.

We were warned in Adelaide that this far south there are wild Blacks & that even if we can see no trace of them it does not mean they are not there. I think this is very likely true & yet it is not what I fear most for Louisa. It sounds very strange – almost *mad* – to say I would rather they were there than not. But if there are none, then the thing I cannot imagine is *where she might be*. In this countryside *we* are the only Place there is – for all the terrible space that stretches out on every side but the coast, it is as if there is nowhere else for her to *be*, if not with us. What makes a Place a Place after all – if not having People in it? In this tent – here – now – with the children asleep & everything in order & no – endless – *voices talking* – I feel as though the Bush were organised around us & we knew the name of every Animal – as though the pull of the Moon on the Tide were to do with us, as if it were towards us. But without a small place of safety – without a Fire or a Family – I cannot see how my darling can *be* – how she can fail to *fly apart* –

I have just looked across the tent at her work-basket – there is the petticoat she has been making for Breta from my old white muslin blouse, that she was working on at tea-time. The needle is threaded & woven through the seam as she left it & sits ready for her to continue – it speaks eloquently of her presence rather than of her absence, which I cannot, I think, much longer endure. When I looked at the needle sitting where she has so precisely left it in the middle of her Task & saw her hands as clear as if they had truly been there – I thought of some words that I remember from the night in Adelaide that we all went to the Play – I do love nothing in the world so well as you, is not that strange?

It is n

I can hear *voices* – but only those of Men –

Peter Goldsworthy

THE LIST OF ALL ANSWERS
1986

1

Again the child plucked at his mother's sleeve. 'Why do onions make my eyes water?' He demanded to know. 'Why?'

She shook her arm free and continued chopping the slippery, soapish segments, trying to ignore him. But there was no escape.

'Mummy, Mummy, why do . . . ?'

At precisely that moment the idea first came to her.

'Three,' she said.

'Three?'

'Three,' she repeated, not exactly sure what she meant herself. 'The answer to your question is – three.'

Silence descended while the child puzzled at this.

'What's three mean?' he shortly came out with.

His father, slicing tomatoes at the other end of the bench, intervened: 'One of Mummy's little jokes. *Another* of Mummy's little jokes.'

He glanced severely at his wife, she smiled steadily back. How else was she to cope? Battling away in a classroom full of Year 5s all day, then home to this. A second classroom, she was beginning to think it. No, worse: a second front.

'The head is like a pressure-cooker,' she began to explain, speaking in the direction of her son, but actually through him to his father. 'It can only hold so much.'

She paused, and glanced at her husband. He sliced a tomato clinically, pretending to ignore her. She turned back to the boy: 'If a joke doesn't emerge from the mouth, steam will shoot out the ears . . .'

'Or worse,' the husband added, also talking through the medium of their child.

'I still don't get it,' the boy said. 'What's number three?'

She still didn't get it herself completely: a half-formed notion, the tip of a berg she could barely sense beneath the surface.

'Number three,' she told him, 'on the list.'

'What list?'

'I'll show you after dinner.'

'What's for dinner?'

She bit her tongue. These endless chains of question and response – once begun there was no ending them. From the moment she collected the child from the creche to the moment he finally succumbed to sleep some hours later – his chatter ceasing suddenly, his neck muscles giving out, head plopping softly onto the pillow mid-sentence – he never stopped plucking sleeves, turning up that insistent face, repeating his endless interrogations. *Why, Mummy? Why?*

'The list,' he remembered as he helped the two of them clear the table after dinner. 'The list! The list!'

'Yes, the list,' his father echoed, teasing, but with a harder edge to his voice. 'Show us the list.'

She retreated to the study and tucked a sheet of quarto into the typewriter. The list took some time to emerge, it was little more than an idea, after all. A vague shape. As for her typing – search and destroy, her husband liked to mock it.

The List Of All Possible Answers, she typed across the top of the page, patiently seeking out each key, and destroying. That accomplished, she moved down the page in a vertical column.

#1: No.

#2: Maybe.

#3: . . .

Here she paused. Three? She was tired, the thoughts refused to flow . . . *Because*, she finally improvised, then tugged her handiwork from the carriage and returned to the kitchen.

As she taped the list to the fridge door, her husband peered over her shoulder.

'"Because",' he muttered. 'What kind of answer is that? "Because" what?'

'"Because" nothing. Just "because".'

'Sounds like a cop-out to me.'

'It's not a definitive list,' she defended herself. 'Feel free to add to it.'

He opened the fridge door and unzipped a can of beer.

'Because that's the way God made it,' he suggested, sipping. 'Because that's the way God meant it to be.'

She laughed out loud: 'Who was accusing whom of a cop-out?'

She yanked open the kitchen oddments drawer, scrabbled among the odds and ends, and emerged with a pen. *Because that's the way things are*, she added to the list, landing the full-stop with an audible thump.

'It's still a cop-out,' he insisted. 'You want a beer?'

'Four,' she said.

'You want *four* beers?'

She shook her head: 'The answer to your question is four.'

He glanced again at the list.

'I don't see any number four.'

She yawned: 'Ask me tomorrow. I'm going to bed.'

2

She watched with interest as he plucked his first can from the fridge the next evening after work.

#4: he read. *Ask me again tomorrow.*

'Your list of all answers,' he told her, 'is beginning to look like a list of all evasions.'

'Congratulations,' she said. 'You just caught on.'

The list grew quickly in the days that followed. *#5: What Do You Think?* was pencilled in the following night, and *#6: Because I said so* added the night after that. Towards the end of the week, however, the rate in increase seemed to slow. After *#7: You're too young to understand* there were no further additions for several days.

'Finished, have we?' her husband, who had been pretending to ignore it all, couldn't prevent himself from asking. 'Finished our little list?'

'No,' she said.

'How many more?'

She paused, considering.

'A finite number,' she guessed. 'Maybe ten.' She paused, pleased with the roundness, the rightness of the figure. 'Yes, ten should just about cover everything.'

'What's "finite" mean, Mummy?'

Her husband's gaze caught hers; he waited, challenging. She thought for a moment, then reached for her pen:

#8: she wrote. *Look it up in the Britannica.*

She smiled back at her husband, smugly: 'Maybe not even ten. Maybe eight will cover everything.'

For a time it seemed that she was right. For several days she successfully deflected the child's questions, glancing up from lesson preparations, or from housework, to snap *Three* or *Seven* or *Four* – and especially, repeatedly, *One.*

The child kept pressing, as if trying to test the limits of the list, to push beyond, break its shackles. His questions seemed to become more difficult to field, more abstract. In church the following Sunday he finally seemed to find the theme he had been looking for: some garbled naive version of things he had heard in the sermon, or overheard as he scribbled in his colouring book, and which he began to hark on as soon as the benediction was over.

'Where is heaven, Mummy? Were we in heaven before we were born?'

They walked home in dazzling sunshine, holding hands: two parents with their small child between them, all in Sunday-best. The rituals of church, the singing, the drone of prayers, usually soothed her at the end of a hard school week, but not today. She could sense her husband waiting for her answers, ready to pounce.

'Shall we stop at the playground?' she suggested.

'Is Grandma in heaven? Will you go to heaven? Will we see God in heaven?'

'The answer to that could be nine,' her husband intervened – aid from an unexpected quarter.

'Nine?' the child wondered.

'Ask Mummy when she's in a better mood,' he said. 'Ask Mummy when she's learnt a little patience.'

They turned in at their gate, and entered the house. He took a red felt-tip pen from the oddments drawer and added the words in inch-high letters at the bottom of the list. *#9: ASK MUMMY WHEN SHE'S IN A BETTER MOOD.*

'Enough is enough,' he said. 'The joke has gone too far.'

3

The blank facade of the fridge struck him the moment he entered the kitchen the following night. Once again, she was watching carefully.

'Where's the list?' he asked.

'Where's the list?' their child, trotting behind, echoed.

'You were right,' she said. 'The list had gone too far.'

Her husband smiled, relieved, but the child's lower lip began to tremble.

'I want my list,' he stammered. 'I want my answer list.'

His father bent to comfort him: 'The list has gone. It was a silly list.'

The child would not be comforted. 'No,' he shouted, twisting away. 'No! I want my list.'

As he ran from the room, his mother was already sifting through the kitchen wastebasket. She found the crumpled sheet, smoothed it between hand and bench, and began to tape it back onto the fridge.

'Please,' her husband said. 'No.'

'Yes,' she insisted.

'How much longer?'

'I don't know,' she admitted. 'I honestly don't know.'

He took a pen from his pocket.

#10: he wrote. *I don't know. I honestly don't know.*

He ruled a thick line across the page beneath his words. If nothing else, there would surely be no need for further entries.

K a t e   G r e n v i l l e

D R O P P I N G   D A N C E
1 9 8 5

When Louise thought about her life, at night, the pillow became slimy. Why does no-one want me, she cried. What have I done to deserve this? In the morning she put on scorn with her clothes and turned the pillow over before she left for work.

I am alone, she said to herself and shredded her bus ticket. I am alone. Why me? When the inspector climbed on the bus she saw how his lips were mauve with effort, and how he was panting. She smiled a great deal so he would not be cross about her shredded ticket. *There is a fine*, he said, but she saw his sad mauve lips and knew that this was a sick man who would never fine a smiling face. He waited for the bus to stop completely before he climbed down, and she heard a grunt as if he had been struck when his foot touched the kerb.

At the office she smiled at Myra the silly receptionist who got every-thing wrong, but it was not the same as the smile she had given the bus inspector. *Mr Trink is waiting for you*, Myra said, and Louise prepared a smile for Mr Trink.

I am sending you to Italy, Mr Trink said. For a moment she wanted to jump up and touch the ceiling, but then she remembered that she was all alone. Even Italy is not much fun alone, she thought, but remembered the way her mother always said, *you never know who you might meet*. Mr Trink did not care if she had no boyfriend or twenty of them, although at the Christmas party, after the third or fourth glass, he had held her against him as they danced and told her she was a fine figure of a woman. Mr Trink lit the stub of his cigar and puffed blue smoke as he spoke, and she had to concentrate hard on what he was saying. The brown smell of his cigar made her remember how she had not always been all alone. The way the smoke gave a soft edge to Mr Trink's face and desk made her remember that she had had a happy childhood, full of cigar smoke and the steam of threepences being boiled. Everything in the kitchen had become dewy and friendly when the threepences were being boiled. The steam had billowed up from the pot and everyone's face had smiled through steam, because everyone had enjoyed the business of boiling the threepences. Something went wrong, she thought as Mr Trink talked about Italy. What went wrong? Mr Trink was handing her a plane ticket, maps, brochures. *It is some new ski place*, he said, *in that place that is like a disease, Dolomites*. He puffed, coughed, and said, *Or perhaps Dolomites is the cure*. She smiled her Mr Trink smile, the professional smile that said, You are right to rely on me. *It will be a little while away for you*, Mr Trink said, *and you will write them a good piece. You have been looking peaky*. She felt a tear swell in each eye and thought of how she would like to say, oh yes, I am peaky, I have been left all alone again, I am very peaky indeed, but in spite of the cigar, and the way it made everything look sympathetic, she knew that Mr Trink did not want to hear why she was peaky. *And no scorn*, he said as she was opening the door to leave. *None of that scorn like in the piece about Isles of the Aegean, understand?*

When they arrived at the village where people were going to come for the skiing, many people were waiting for them, and Louise smiled at them all but thought, there is no-one for me here, although most of them were from her own country, and tried not to scorn. There was a fat man and his thin wife, who ran the hotel where the skiers would stay. *We have given you the best room*, the fat man shouted, *so you better write a good piece about us*, and his thin wife shouted too: *We will make sure you have a fine time*. A man called Scotty was not a Scot, but was going to teach the people how to ski, and was joking now, and doing knee-bends, as if getting in practice. *I am that hungry*, he told Louise, *I could eat the crotch out of a low-flying duck*. Everyone laughed and Louise laughed too, but falsely, feeling her face ache. I am showing too many teeth, she thought, and closed her mouth. Now perhaps I am looking glum, she thought, and hoped the fat man or his thin wife would suggest she go to her room to unpack. *He is the clown of the place*, the travel man said to her. *That Scotty is a laugh a minute*. Marigold was a pretty girl with glossy hair and a fine bosom. *I'm that excited* she told Louise. *Never been out of Thin Ridge before and I've made that many friends already*. She joined Scotty in knee-bends so they looked like a pair of things on springs, but giggled from her red mouth and had to be grabbed by Scotty when she lost her balance. Franco tried to grab her but he was too slow and had to smile out of his square face while Marigold clung to Scotty. Franco had a flat face like a rock with small crevices for the mouth and eyes. *I am the guide of the mountains,* he told Louise. *That is a fine profession,* Louise said, looking at the slab of his face. She could imagine him beckoning the mountains. They were all around them, but she had tried not to look at them until now because they made her feel as if nothing much mattered. But she looked while Franco told her about them and tried not to think about nothing mattering. The mountains were jagged like pages ripped out of a book, and were moving steadily against the sky towards them. There was a little early snow on the peaks, but not much. Franco told Louise what each mountain was called but could not stop watching the way the last rays of sun made Marigold's hair look like something good to drink.

I am more alone than ever, Louise thought in her room, and watched herself in the mirror. The more people there are, the more I am alone. She sat with her face in her fists, staring at herself in the mirror. She tried to pretend that the reflection was not herself, but someone else, and had almost succeeded when there was a sneeze behind the reflection. She got up quickly in case the mirror disappeared and she would have to look at pretty Marigold, leaning into the mirror plucking her eyebrows and sneezing.

What did the parson say to the choirboy? Scotty shouted down the table at dinner, and everyone laughed. *Why did the elephant cross the road?* he yelled, and everyone laughed again. The fat man and the thin woman were kept busy filling everyone's plates and glasses. *What's red and blue and collects stamps?* The laughter beat back from the walls. Marigold looked as if she would wet herself laughing. Her bra was made of black lace and could be seen through her blouse. Louise was shrivelled and lonely against the wall, and the wine sat cold in her stomach like unhappiness. *Why did the dago have his head up a bull's bum?* Scotty cried, and had to add, *No offence intended Franco and none taken I'm sure.* Louise was sick of laughing and the bald travel man's close-set eyes were making her queasy. I am miserable, she told herself, and not understood by anyone. It seemed that no-one could come to her rescue.

Next day Franco took them up a mountain. In the beginning it was easy and Louise kicked through drifts of dead leaves and watched how the top of the mountain hung weightless in the morning sun. I am alive and well, although alone, she told herself, and at present climbing a mountain, and heard with scorn the fat man panting behind her. But the path became steeper and steeper and soon she could not hear the fat man's panting, but only her own. Ahead of her and always further up, Franco walked on and on in his square boots and she began to hate the way his feet came down one after the other without stopping. I hate this, she began to think, and had to remind herself, this is not a plot. When the path stopped being a path and became a stony place where water must rush down in spring, she thought Franco might stop. If she had not been aware of the fat man grunting behind her as he laboured up behind her, she would have sat down on a rock until her blood cooled and her chest stopped burning. It came to her that she was not sufficiently alone at this particular moment.

Marigold was just behind Franco, and began to squeal so that he looked around at last and everyone was allowed to rest. The top of the mountain did not hang in the air any more, but loomed over them. It was not weightless now, but ponderous and unfriendly. There were no trees up here, only prickly bushes and tussocks of grass, and there was nowhere much to sit, and only the grey stone of the mountain to look at.

After they had rested as long as Franco let them, they went on and the path became more difficult. Louise had to grasp at rocks and sharp grass to pull herself up, and felt the stones roll out from under her feet. Her ankles were tired from so much twisting on the loose rocks, and her neck ached from looking up for the next place to step. There were patches of snow, iced-over and hard, that her shoes slithered over, and a long steep slope of chips of stone that was like dandruff on the shoulders of the mountain. Nature is vile, she was beginning to think, when she saw that Franco had stopped and was staggering with Marigold in his arms around a cairn of stones. They were at the top, it seemed, although mountains still surrounded them.

Scotty shouted to hear his voice vanish into the air, and rolled stones down the slope for a while, to see how gravity snatched them, and the fat man lay on his back and wheezed. The thin woman put a stone on the top of the cairn and spat on it: *Instead of champers*, she shouted. Her spit dried quickly on the stone so it seemed that it had never been there. The thin woman looked around at the empty sky and the mountains, and began to wind her watch. There was too much air up here to fill, and too much mountain to look at. When everyone stopped talking at the same moment they could all hear the thin woman's watch being wound.

Louise had taken off her shoe to get out a stone when Franco shouted *Down!* and everyone began to leap down the slope after him. Louise got the stone out of her shoe and was comforted by the hot rising smell of her sock. I am not completely alone, she thought, no-one is completely alone who has the smell of their socks. When she had put the sock and shoe back on she stood up and was suddenly dizzy. The mountain was so silent it deafened her. Silence roared at her. It surged into her ears and made her want to hide but the mountain was grey in the shadows now, and there was nowhere to go. Suddenly she was not sure which way was the way down, and she could see two valleys both full of the same dark green trees. She could not be sure which way the others had gone, and could not hear anything except the silence in her ears.

Sunlight was sliding off the peaks around her. She watched as it slid like water up a rock and left darkness behind. *Help*, she tried to say, but had to cough. *Help!* she tried again, but the silence was like a waterfall in her ears. *Help me!* she shrieked, and a bird made a creaking sound with its wings as it flew along below her. I have been abandoned, she thought, and tried again: *Help!*

She began to pick her way down one of the slopes, but her ankles would not hold her up and her shoes twisted and slipped on the steep rocks at every step. She sat down and began to cry. She wanted her white pillow and her quiet room more than she had ever wanted anything, but had only sharp chips of grey rock to cry on, and they were quickly becoming cold. *You swine*, she began to screech, *you pigs*. Her voice cracked but she went on shouting. *You rotten lumpish buggers, you vile toads!* She stopped and listened, but could only hear silence ebbing and flowing in her head. *Rescue me*, she called, and heard her tears break up the words. *Save me*. She waited a long time, but no-one came.

When she had waited a long time she began to go down again. She limped and whimpered and made small moans of distress. *You don't care and you don't give a damn*, she whispered and her feet slipped and twisted. *You bastards have left me here alone to die*. Dusk was deepening and she had to look hard to see where she was going. I could break my leg, she thought, or my neck, and she ran a few steps down the slope. I am asking for trouble, running, she thought, but she kept running and jumping down from rock to rock. She hoped she would fall and break something, and when the search party found her they would have to carry her down carefully on a stretcher, and give her brandy to drink, and wrap her in warm blankets, and keep up her spirits with jokes all the way down the mountain.

The mountain was flying past under the feet like something flowing, and the air rushed up against her face. She opened her mouth so the air could come into her mouth and she could hear the music of air and speed in her head. Under her feet the grey stones were a blur and out of the corner of her eye she saw white banks of snow pouring past. Around her the whitening sky filled with mountain, as she ran further down into the valley. *There, there, there, there*, she began to shout as each foot landed and sprang and she felt her hair blow out behind her. Stones that were loosened by her feet kept her company, rolling down after her, but they could not keep up. Faster and faster she swallowed the mountainside. Like a bird, she thought, I am like a bird now. Free as a bird. Her arms made arabesques in the air around her as she sprang down. She felt as though she had invented a language and was writing it on the air. I am a bird, she thought, or the wind. I could run like this all the way down every hill to the sea.

When she reached the hut at the bottom where everyone was, she stopped, but did not want to go in. The windows of the hut were filled with yellow light and she could hear everyone talking and laughing, and a tinkle of glasses. Someone threw a log on a fire and sparks leapt red out of the top of the chimney. She did not want to go in and be with other people, but would have liked to go on running and watching the sky that was slowly turning into night.

The fat man came to the door of the hut with a big pot between his hands. *You are there*, he said. *We were wondering*. Silhouetted in the doorway, his size was stupendous and he was wrapped in a halo of lamplight. He stood there with the pot in his hand, staring up at the mountain she had just danced down. *I have always been afraid of heights*, the fat man said suddenly, and began to drain water from the spaghetti in the pot. The steam gushed up suddenly and swirled around him as he bent over it, concentrating. The shape of his body was made soft and luminous by so much steam lapping around him. He finished draining the water and stood looking at the sky between the treetops. *This is my first mountain*, he said, and Louise could hear that he was smiling. *My first mountain*, he repeated, and the rising steam enveloped his head as if it would carry it away into the night.

Marion Halligan

THE EGO IN ARCADIA

1986

I

Your French window is the best kind of window there is. I don't mean what the English call a french window, I mean the sort of window you get in France. It folds inwards, absolutely disengaging its frame, so that what you have is an opening on to the landscape with no let, a rectangular space in the wall of the house, shaping a fragment of the outside.

In Australia our windows push upwards or outwards, or slide across one another, but always, however impressively large they are as sheets of glass, they are there, in the frame, you can't get rid of them. And as well there is the obscuration of the flyscreen, the fussy metal mesh that keeping out insects muddies the view.

Your French window may allow insects to pass, but that's irrelevant. It exists to be a hole in the wall; the view is untrammelled, the eye is untrammelled. So I say this is an essence of windowness, to be perfectly absent, not there.

On the other hand, sometimes the window is shut, and then it is very palpably there, divided by upright and crossbars into six panes of elegant but not equal proportions, and the old glass having a mind of its own. You see with the window's own eyes, age giving a most delicate warp, a faint watery wander. In comparison, modern mechanical accurate glass is very dull, not spirited like the old glass.

You can sit in the room, in this chair or that, and let it show you different pictures. From here, for instance, you can see tall pearly towers, distant in the misty fold of the valley, magically sunlit but veiled by the myriad bare twigs of the hundred-year oak in this garden. And veiled too by a faint thickening of the air, which might suggest that they exist only in the imagination, but is more likely to be the effect of atmospheric pollution. They are actually blocks of cheap high-rise housing, out in the suburbs, with attendant swimming-pools and sports centres and supermarkets to stop people going out of their minds in them. But not through this window, which can choose how it sees things, how it shows them.

II

There is a picture in a room high up in one of the towers. A portrait in a gilt frame with a large rose at each corner and trails of cornflowers and roses along each edge; even the strand of wire that holds these trails together is faithfully moulded in gilded plaster. It is of a young woman, whose clothes and hair were fashionable a century and a half ago. She's holding a posy of roses and cornflowers; they and her bracelet, the ribbons on her sleeves, and her eyes, are of the same intense blue, while her lips and necklace and ear-rings are coral.

She is a plain young woman. Her ears protrude beneath the smooth brown hair, her eyes are large and flat, her nose and her whole face are too long, and her mouth is rather prim over what are almost certainly protuberant teeth. But she looks directly at you with a hint of amusement in those large flat eyes, in the faintly lifted corners of the prim little mouth. As a portrait, plain though the young woman is, it is perfectly charming.

It's done in pastel, very fresh and lively, so it's under glass. There are faint watery flaws in this glass too, and sometimes the light falls across it in such a way that you can't see the picture at all but a reflection of the Norman cupboard on the other side of the room, with its carving of flowers and billing doves: a marriage cupboard to keep the wedding linen in.

III

I forgot to mention that a good French window has an embryonic balcony effect. The sill is low, at knee level, and very wide, the thickness of the house walls, and you are prevented from falling out, or at least made to feel secure, by an ornamental band. Here it is a coarse trellis, with embossed knobs, and ivy winding across it, green iron ivy leaves. In summer the walls are thick with fleshy windblown replicas which cluster round the mysterious hole of the window, vigorous, browning, dying and returning to the earth. They mingle with the tendrils of metal ivy permanently trailing, everlastingly green.

Other houses have different patterns. There are stiff little posies, and acanthus ferns, heraldic arabesques, or simple square grilles. Even the baluster blossom of the wild pomegranate. I imagine that when you built your house you chose from a pattern book. There must have been lots of designs. Round here they are all different.

IV

I have discovered that the English word 'window' means 'the eye of the wind'. From the old Norse, *vindir*, and *auga*. It was probably a draughty hole.

And the eye is the window of the soul. Or the mind, if you prefer. But when we talk about the windows of heaven opening, we only mean that it is pouring with rain. As though some great celestial slop bucket were being emptied over us. *Gardy loo!* Whereas the French don't talk about the windows of heaven but the cataracts of the firmament, which involves no theological judgments. And the cataracts of man, his elegant artificial ones, have their eyes too: that is the name for the opening through which the water of a fountain wells. The unexpected sadness of ornamental waters.

Nomenclature stinks of mortality. It is smugly sublunary. God may have made the world, but it is hard to believe that he named it, unless in pre-Babel days. But no, that was Adam, already the seeds of his fall in him. And now, since the disastrous tower divided us, each country writes off the objectionable on some other language. There's the English, the French, the Dutch disease, for instance, no-one accepting for a minute that the clap could have anything to do with his own country. Or the tit-for-tat of a condom's being a french letter or a *capote anglais*. Sex and disease: the same old smell of mortality.

The French don't have french windows, the English do, so since they aren't disgusting they must find them in some way exotic or bizarre or perhaps just glamorous. English french windows serve for exits and entrances, as the French name, *porte-fenêtre*, door window, indicates. Not at all the sort of thing for someone who wants to stay undisturbed inside and look out at a world made work of art by a frame. The world as a picture.

There is a right word in English – a satisfactory language, it rarely lets you down, hardly ever leaves you tongue-tied, wishing for an exact term for what you want to say – a good Keatsian word, and that is casement. A poetic word, of course, but that is what you want, for these are poetic windows. Though the French name for them, *fenêtre croisée*, is prickly and clumsy and has no such connotations. My French windows, the windows I look through, are casements, casements opening on those faery towers forlorn. And perilous.

But these are words, and words aren't stories, to most people.

V

Once upon a time there was a handsome old lady – but that's now. Once upon a time there was a plain young woman, who had been a plain child, but charming. She had a pale long face and large flat eyes, and it was hard to see where the charm lay, though it was undeniable. Perhaps she simply looked rather highly bred, the result of a long history of carefully selected unions between the right families.

Anyway, the plain young woman married a count, a quite minor count, and the title in theory of no account since they lived in a republic, actually something of a nuisance, they claimed with pride. More useful was his family's ownership of a bank, but even that did not last; in his middle age the bank was nationalised, and though he was director still or president or by whatever name the head of it, it wasn't the same as owning it.

They lived in two pleasant establishments, an apartment in the city in the sixteenth *arrondissement*, and a small chateau, or manor house, in the country. Each had large beautiful rooms with high ceilings decorated with plaster wedding-cake work, and tall narrow windows elaborately banded in ornamental iron – one was a cornucopia pattern – and life paced very smoothly in them.

The young woman and the count had five children, being patriotic, four daughters and a son. The son was killed at the age of eighteen in a road accident, along with some twelve thousand people in France that year. His death grieved them dynastically as well as personally, because whatever they said about the title, they cared about the family name. The four daughters did what they chose: two married, one well, into a good family; one badly, to a young man she fell in love with at university, whose father was a waiter in Nantes; one lived with a man she had no intention of marrying, and the fourth went to America. None of them was particularly plain, but then girls aren't these days; they are works of art and the expression is irrelevant.

The second daughter, who married beneath herself, found a portrait in the attic when looking for things to furnish a flat. There was not much hope of the waiter's providing anything, though he surprised them with a fine old linen cupboard. Her own papa said that if she wanted to make her own life by all means go ahead. The portrait was a pastel of a young woman holding a posy of roses and cornflowers, with a gilt frame to match. She wiped the dust off the old glass and exclaimed that her mother should have a portrait of herself as a young girl and such a charming thing too, stuck away in the attic. Her mother, very dry, pointed out that it had been drawn before the middle of the nineteenth century. So the daughter, even more pleased to have found a picture of an ancestor so like her mother, cleaned it up and hung it over the marble fireplace that was the only beauty of their small flat. One of the corner roses had been broken off, and there were some chips in the gilt, nothing a restorer couldn't have fixed, but they never had it done. And the old glass with its idiosyncrasies was also very shiny and it was difficult to find a place to view it where you could see the portrait and not a reflection of the room.

There are two small ironies in this story; one is that the plain young woman of its beginning had grown into a very handsome spare old lady and was not aware of it, and the other is that the resurrection of the portrait (for she had put it away in the attic because of its resemblance to her) made her wonder whether her husband had married her for love at all, or because she was a good person to mate with.

VI

The eye of the wind: it doesn't conjure up a hole in the wall but swift movement. A great sweep of rushing wind and the eye at its head seeing, leading it on its courses round the world. Or what about the viewless wings of poesy? Not blind, but invisible, perhaps too vast to be seen, but the eye seeing, far above, sharp as a hawk.

The train seems to rush, but not at all like the wind. Far too controlled. Tied to heavy metal tracks. Constantly stopping on its way from the far-flung suburbs to the city. Its speed is not swooping, looping, free like the wind seen in the curve of a kite-string; it's a bad simile. And the train windows frame nothing, they fragment the world outside. They are dirty and runnelled as with tears; trying to observe the lives of the houses, the lives in the houses, that closely line the track, you have to allow for this patched and grubby view, always fleeing. And every now and then is a tunnel, and the window becomes a mirror, and you see your own reflection, disturbing as always when you haven't put on the face you use for viewing yourself in mirrors. But let's not get started on mirrors. They need a story to themselves.

Instead you can look at their lives in the faces of others. They have tales to tell.

Opposite is a young woman. The second daughter, who married neither richly nor elegantly, but for love, who hung the plain girl's portrait in a tiny flat, and took it with her when they moved into another much larger and really quite pleasant apartment in one of those perilous towers of economical housing. By that time they had two small girls and needed the space.

One day she left the little girls, who were called Aurélie and Elodie, alone in the flat on the tenth floor while she dashed down to buy the bread. She would only be a minute and she didn't want to have to wrap them up and take them out in the cold, especially as Aurélie, the three-year-old, had a touch of bronchitis. The children stood on chairs and watched through the window as their mother crossed the courtyard between the towers. They called and waved but she didn't hear so they opened the window, not a casement but a kind that opens outwards and upwards by winding a handle, and called and still she didn't hear and called and leaned out further and fell. Both of them. One after the other. Fell ten storeys. Not quite at her feet. But near enough.

So much for the eye of the wind. How could even the wind see it, and let it happen? It howls and wails and moans about the towers, but mourning is no help.

The young woman sits and stares with unmoving eyes. If eyes are the windows of the soul what can you see in hers? She sits staring out at the land passing by, flashing dark and light against her face but never catching her attention. Her head is turned at an angle, so you can see the profile of her eyes and the clear thickness of the green iris, and only imagine the soul. A green glass soul hard as a marble with a mandala in it. The whorled dark shape of a mandala endlessly turning upon itself.

VII

The murderous towers in the fold of the valley are still very beautiful. They are veiled by the gently breeze-stirred twigs of the oak tree. And the magical polluted mist. Soon they will be hidden altogether, for it is already beginning spring. The crocuses are in flower, and so are the snowdrops, the *perce-neiges* with no more snow to pierce. The prunus is fragile with blossom, the lilac pregnant with buds. The three-legged cat from next door makes skittish progress across the flower-weeded lawn. The birds are gobbling the bread put out for them on the low table made by the trunk of the cut-down lime: it was diseased, alas. There are sparrows, and a robin redbreast, blackbirds, and some starlings that could be done without. The tree-creepers do not care for bread.

You have to make the most of looking at the houses, caught in glimpses anyway, spread up and down the slope of the hill: at the dormered attics, and the particular pattern of cast-iron that balconies the windows, and the beauty of the old terracotta tiles on their roofs. Terracotta tiles reward contemplation. Soon all this will disappear in the foliage, when the poplars and the sycamores and the oak are in leaf. The season demands it. I remember this winter when the oak was covered in ice, each branch, thick or slender, each tiny twig, encased in ice, the whole thing an enormous fragile structure of frozen water. After the freeze the sun shone, and the whole tree glittered with shards of light. The beauty of summer is a matter of light too, but a thick embosomed green light, of flesh, not glass.

The window will still frame it, still give it shape, whatever the season.

Barbara   Hanrahan

SISTERS

1991

1

You are funny looking. You are so small. You are a grown-up but you
dress like a child.

Always, in the photographs, you are lost in shadow. The brim of
your hat cuts off your eyes; when you sit by the fig tree it hides your
face completely. Again and again your body is swallowed up. Or you
are lost in white light – the snapshot is dazzled away.

There is a photo of you with your arm round Barbara, who is a baby
leaning against you on a table, and your chin is tucked in, important.
And there is a photo of you sitting beside Barbara. She is the small one
who looks away; you, Reece, are the big one who stares stolidly on.
Your glasses slip down and cast a shadow that makes your face look
as if it's tattooed.

It was your house then, too – your sister, Iris, who was Barbara's
grandmother, was in charge. You swept the floor and set the table and
boiled the hankies in the saucepan and did the ironing and wiped when
your sister washed up. At night the wireless voices talked while your
knitting needles clicked till you said it was time for bunko.

And it was your garden then, too. There was the fig tree, the apricot
tree, the quince tree. You emptied the tea-leaves on the red and white
geraniums by the tap. You took Barbara for walks down the path –
past the agapanthus and the lavatory to the shed by the back fence.
You'd go out the front and hang over the gate and wait for her to come
home from kindergarten.

But Barbara kept growing till she was taller than you. She turned
into someone who could make you cry. When you cried you couldn't
help it. You were not safe. There was an awful trembling.

The songs came into your head for comfort. Granma songs, Granpa
songs. 'Down the River of Golden Dreams', 'Two Little Girls in Blue'.

You woke early and had a sing-song: 'Daisy' and 'K-K-K-Katy'.

You had a celluloid doll with a big head who looked something like you, but her name was Peggy. You had a canary and then a budgerigar called Tony. You had a pencil-sharpener like a globe of the world, and you knitted face-washers and bed-socks in plain stitch, and you coloured in with your Lakeland coloured pencils, and you kept licking your finger to turn over the pages of old *Women's Weekly*s that you held upside down.

Barbara tried to make you read but you couldn't. 'You are stupid, Reece,' she said. 'Your eyes are like a Jap spy's,' she said. 'Wash up my arms, Reece,' she said, so you went into the bathroom and rubbed with Lux soap till Barbara had long soapy gloves.

When it's morning tea you put two teaspoons of Amgoorie in the teapot and there is CPS cheese and the small brown malt loaf Iris brings home from Balfour's when she goes to town. Or Letitia cake with the crumbly top or rockies, queen cakes, butterfly cakes. For lunch there is cold meat with Rosella tomato sauce, and you both dip your Golden Crust bread in the red sauce puddle. Your mother used to say to chew every mouthful forty times, but you can't count so you always eat slow. 'Reece is a slow eater,' Barbara says; and your belly rattles, you cannot help it. 'Pardon,' you say, though Barbara says it should be 'I beg your pardon'.

But you know things. Aunty Peggy on 5AD has adopted an Indian boy. Uncle Dick Moore and Uncle Bob Fricker and Uncle Ron Sullivan are 5AD, too. Bob Dyer is *Pick-a-Box*, Jack Davey says, 'Hi Ho, everybody!' and there is *When a Girl Marries* after tea, and *Dr Paul* is on the wireless at lunchtime. Five o'clock means *Superman*. *Hymns We Remember* is on Sunday, and you can do a sing-along then.

In winter you get dressed in bed. Your clothes feel cosy because they've been under the eiderdown all night. They are clothes for doing jobs in: old grey pinafore and jumper with a stain. You wear them till afternoon-tea time when Aunty Peggy's gone from the wireless. Then you go to have your wash and put on your good clothes and powder your face. You are grown up; you even have brassieres for best. You are Iris's sister. When she is talking to Mrs O'Brien over the fence you go out and stand beside her. Barbara reckons you shouldn't always follow after your sister. But the people she talks to are your friends, too.

At night, sometimes, in summer, you and Iris go for walks together. Down the street, past Mrs Newton's mulberry tree. You hear the hoses in gardens, and people call out in the dark. They say, 'Hello, Mrs Goodridge. Hello, Reece.'

It seemed that house and that garden would be there for ever, but they went, just like the mother and father you had once. You moved away to a new suburb where there were new houses with new gardens, and though you stayed the same, Barbara grew and grew into somebody who disappeared to England, but she sent you a postcard every week. When Postie blew his whistle, Iris brought your card in with her blue letter. You got Queenie and the Palace and a red London bus and a puppy dog ... And every birthday and Christmas the card is bigger and Barbara sends you lily of the valley powder, carnation powder, sweet pea powder.

2

Suddenly, one night – steam still clouding the mirror, a footprint framed in talcum on the floor – Iris fell down. You were waiting with your nightie to have the bathwater next. It only took an instant, and that animal cry in the throat.

But then they took her from the bed for ever. She didn't come back and with her went your splintered glimpses of the past. For that day your case was packed, and all the faces changed.

3

Growing old has made you even smaller, Reece.

You stoop when you sit in your chair; you keep very still. But you came to life once when it was Easter and they tried to take the chocolate egg from you. You kicked and fought and squealed, and then you crammed all the chocolate in your mouth. Afterwards you were sick. It is a nice place, where you live now, Reece. There is a drive lined with Moreton Bay fig trees and the old part looks like a castle. You live in the new part. Ladies and Gentlemen are separate. Some people say Girls and Boys, even though Lottie is eighty-four and Edward not much younger. There is a billiard table on the Boys' veranda, and their boots are lined up by the wall after work in the vegetable garden. When visitors come Edward says, 'Excuse me, have you ever been kidnapped?'

On the Girls' veranda there is a line of sewing-boxes and knitting-bags on a bench. You keep your slippers under the bench and when it is time for tea you change into them. There is a budgie in a cage and a guinea-pig. You have afternoon tea on the veranda. When tea is over people go to the lavatory in pairs.

Joy walks with one leg stiff from her stroke. She is forty-six but she looks older; she has thin grey hair and a pale grey face. Lottie has lived in the Girls' part since she was seven. June is a lot younger, and wears lipstick and has a boyfriend. He is one of the boys on the other veranda and he gave her a rolled gold bangle. And June has treasures safety-pinned to the strap of her petticoat. She pulls back her dress to show you: a plastic heart that says BE MY VALENTINE, a brooch shaped like an elephant, an opal ring. June is always showing you a birthday card, too, and saying it's her birthday. 'It's not,' says Milly scornfully. 'You don't even know when your birthday is.'

Milly can't stop talking, and there is something wrong with her eyes – they are a cloudy blue, and soon she must have an operation. Ada has teeth that stick out; Susan has scabs on her lips. One of the old ones has blue cloth stumps instead of legs: she was born without legs. Another has legs so skinny it seems her ankles will snap when she walks. She has white hair and wrinkles and carries a doll with her everywhere.

Frieda is your special friend. She is a little shrivelled-up thing with gingery hair and droopy shoulders and a hearing-aid. She likes doing housework and keeps a folded tea towel in her sewing-box; and she knits tea-cosies and asks visitors for their bus tickets so she can write her name on them. Frieda takes you to the lavatory, and undoes your shoes and puts your feet into your slippers when it's afternoon-tea time.

There is a Sick Bay. You were taken there when you went all funny. You fell over and couldn't help it and above you they said, 'It is her heart.' You lay in a bed with silver bars round the edge. You did wee-wee in bed, but it didn't matter because there was a rubber sheet. You felt strange – it was the pills and the needle they stuck in your arm. You went red in the face and started to talk again – but in a secret language no-one could understand. There was a scab on your face, and you laughed to yourself about it, but it sounded as if you were crying. You hid under the sheet and when Nurse leaned over the bars you hit her head. But the scab dropped off, and you got better, and ate ice-cream and jelly and watched TV. In the TV-room were people who lived in the Sick Bay all the time. Some were twisted like snakes and wore Onkaparinga dressing-gowns. They never left their chairs and the nurses had to feed them, and the ones that were boys were pushed along in a line to be shaved.

It stops being quiet on the veranda when the new girl comes. She is eighteen and has short hair like a boy's; she wears shorts and has a skipping-rope and skips up and down. 'Go away, go away,' Milly cries. 'Be quiet.' Susan hides behind June when the new girl comes past, because Ada said the new girl bites.

One by one they go inside – even Frieda – till you and the new girl are the only ones left. She stops in front of you and smiles and then starts laughing and skipping again, up and down the veranda.

MY FATHER AND THE JEWS
1980

My father held a high opinion of Jews.

He often said that all the great intellectual achievements of the human race were due to Jews (no rhyme intended).

My father lived by a series of assertions: 'There's no such thing as a good war or a bad strike.' 'The worst enemies of the workers are the press and the pulpit.' And his favourite assertion was that the three greatest men of our time were Marx, Freud and Einstein. So far as I know, he'd never read one word written by any of these men, but he attributed some of his favourite aphorisms to one or other of them. He was fond of pointing out to my mother that Sigmund Freud himself had said that religion was the opium of the people.

I remember one winter's night in Benson's Valley during the Depression, my father leaning on the mantelpiece sounding off about Karl, Sigmund and Albert.

'And what nationality were these great men?' he challenged.

'German!' my brother Michael said. He'd joined the Campion Society and had learned a lot of finer points about religion and politics.

'They were Jews, smart alec,' my father replied. 'It's that bastard Hitler who's a German – and he burned their books.'

'Hitler's an Austrian, Toss,' Michael persisted. He was the only one in the household who stood up to my father – that's if you didn't count my mother. We all called my father Toss, for reasons now forgotten, but probably because, in his signature, he abbreviated his first name, Thomas, to read Thos.

The only other people Toss had much time for were Lenin and Henry Lawson. He claimed that Lenin was a Jew, though, as usual, he adduced no evidence for his assertion. He never even claimed membership of the Chosen Race for Lawson. He couldn't very well because Henry wrote a few anti-Semitic poems – but, of course, my father didn't know that, not having read even his Gentile poems!

'They were Germans,' Michael went on, risking a clout over the earhole by a hand as hard as a piece of four by two (no racist rhyming slang intended) – to wit by my father's right hand. 'The Jews are not a nationality.'

'Not a nationality?' my father repeated. 'All right, then, they're a race.'

'They're not a race either, they're a religion.'

'Those bloody Jesuits have been corrupting your mind,' Toss said, always abusive when having an argument.

'The Jews killed Jesus Christ,' my mother ventured.

'Jesus Christ was a Jew himself, so how the hell could the Jews kill him? I mean, if they did, it's a non-event.'

'Because the Jews are a religion and they killed the leader of another religion.'

'Jesus Christ was a bloody Jew and never you forget it,' my father asserted and went to bed with the sulks.

Michael said to me, 'The old man's all talk.'

'Don't speak about your father like that,' my mother admonished. She was extremely loyal to him most of the time and they loved each other so far as love is possible between an Irish Catholic and a Welsh atheist.

Michael got his Irish name because he was born during a period when my mother was winning the Holy War in our household; she had her way most of the time, really, judging by the fact that six of her eight children had Irish Catholic names. The other two were my only sister, who was called Rachel, and my eldest brother, who was called Solomon. Sol changed his name by deed poll to Patrick after Dad died because he couldn't get a job in the Public Service because the Christians in charge there thought he was a Jew.

My father had all his seven sons circumcised, even those with the Irish names. I thought this was a religious or racial victory over my mother (until years later I heard him assert in the local pub that 'It's harder to pick up the pox if you're circumcised'). My mother had her share of victories. All the children went to Catholic First Communion, even the two Jews. My father said, 'No worries, it's just like a Bar Mitzvah, or that ceremony the blackfellas have. All bloody superstitions, but, if it makes Maureen happy . . .'

The Holy War sometimes took the form of the removal of portraits from the walls of our living room. My father, when angry or pissed, removed pictures of the Sacred Heart, the Virgin Mary and the Pope; my mother when upset would remove the pictures of Marx, Freud and Einstein. When they eventually made up, the pictures would all be restored and the anxiety of the children subside for a while. The only pictures that were never removed from our walls were those of Ned Kelly, the Australian bushranger, and James Connelly, the Irish revolutionary: they were martyrs for both sides in the Holy War.

There were hints that my father had been a member of the IWW – the Wobblies, so-called, the Industrial Workers of the World. My brother, Michael, reckoned that's where he must have fallen under the influence of the Jews – a kind of Wobbly-Jewish Conspiracy. My father never ever actually admitted membership, though he was fond of quoting One Big Union slogans and even defended the rule of Bryant and May (referring to the fines the Wobblies set in Sydney in 1916) and told uproarious stories of their vain attempts to deflate the Australian currency by distributing forged £5 notes. And he could have worked for them when he was on his trips away from home working or looking for work. He never denied that, even when Michael said that no doubt the only work he ever did for the IWW was to distribute crook £5 notes for them.

My mother defended him against this charge. 'Your father did every kind of hard work all his life and always brought what money he earned home. If he'd have handled any of those fivers, some of them would have come into this house.' She had the tinted view of the Irish of what constituted criminal behaviour and wouldn't have baulked at a few fivers, just because they might have been forged by the IWW.

'You couldn't have picked one of them from a real fiver,' my father asserted ambivalently.

As I grew to my teens, impressed with my father's political wisdom, I became his favourite son, and he occasionally took me on his forays into politics: like interjecting at both Conservative and Labor election meetings. He viewed the major parties as Tweedledee and Tweedledum, with Labor the worst by default: the boneheaded workers knew where they stood with the Conservatives. 'Acourse the bastards don't call 'emselves Conservatives, they call 'emselves Liberals.' It was that great Jewish thinker Vladimir Lenin himself who said, and I quote, 'The parties in Australia have got the wrong names: the Labor Party is really a Liberal Party and the Liberals are really fucking Conservatives.'

During the Depression in the 1930s, my father took a particular interest in combating the activities of fascists and anti-Semites; and had a dead-set hatred for Eric Butler, who was already then, as a young man, preaching anti-Semitism and Douglas Credit and selling *The Protocols of the Ancients of Zion.*

My father would occasionally journey to Melbourne to heckle Butler's meetings. On the first such occasion, he took me with him. This entailed a thirty-mile journey on a milk truck and a seven-mile walk from the Sunshine railway gates to the city.

We arrived to find a hall full of men: well-dressed clerks, shopkeepers and thugs, and shabby unemployed men seeking any answer to the questions one would read in their despairing eyes. And the answer Butler gave was that the Jewish bankers had conspired to bring about the world economic crisis. Indeed, the Jewish bankers had, in some unexplained way, conspired with the Communists in this dastardly aim.

I had painful memories of being thrown out of various meetings with my father, and sensed that the pain here would be multiplied. I secretly prayed that my father wouldn't speak – but, of course, he did. Immediately Butler had finished, Toss was on his feet to be first in for question time. He struck an imposing figure with his snow-white hair and black eyebrows, in his dark suit and celluloid collar. The effect was somewhat spoiled by the sleeves of his coat being too short, scarcely below his elbows (this as a result of his scissoring the frays off the cuffs for nearly twenty years). He launched into a speech as a preface to his question: that mongrel Hitler, the workers' greatest enemy, had invented the idea of the Jewish-Communist conspiracy which was a load of rusty rabbit traps; everyone knew that *The Protocols of the Ancients of Zion* was a forgery . . .

At this point, the chairman, a man with expressionless eyes, a toothbrush moustache and military bearing, advised my father that the League of Rights had ways and means of dealing with Communist agitators, and that he should confine himself to asking a question.

'Well, all right,' my father said, displaying his usual foolhardy (no pun intended) courage. 'I'll ask a question and it's this: Is the speaker aware that there are no Jewish bankers in Australia?' (Uproar in the hall from Butler's sturdy, edgy supporters.) 'It's a fact,' Toss went on – and I watched the thugs cluster around us. 'I'll read here from the Melbourne *Herald* of April 1931, a list of directors of the major Australian banks . . .'

The fascists closed in but my father managed to read from a press cutting the names of the owners of one of the banks. The names were all Scottish, like McPherson and Robinson. But he was grabbed by six fascists and dragged towards the door before he could continue. He was a powerful man, had been a champion footballer in his youth and had studied the art of fisticuffs, as he called it, and he resisted violently. I was not powerful, was not a champion footballer and had not studied the art of fisticuffs but, as always, I tried to go to his aid out of some queer twist of filial loyalty.

At the door, he managed to free himself momentarily from the monsters bent on maiming him and turned to the aghast shabby part of the audience. 'Don't listen to Butler. The bankers of Australia are all bloody Scotchmen. Would you blame a Scotchman for all your troubles? No, well don't blame a Jew either, because the Jews are interested in great ideas. Men like Marx, and Freud and Einstein, all bloody Jews. Truth is, it's not the Scotchmen or the Jews, or any other race – it's the rotten system of capitalistic exploitation . . .'

At this point, his edifying remarks were slightly brought to a sudden end: to wit, he was seized violently by about eight fascists and hurled down the steps onto the footpath outside. One of them grabbed me by the ear and dragged me after him – and I ended up in the gutter beside Toss. A fascist was kicking him in the stomach; I protested and got a kick in the ribs for my trouble.

After he lay still for a while (pretending to be dead so they wouldn't kick him any more, he explained later), Toss got to his feet and helped me to mine.

He wiped a trickle of blood from the corner of his mouth. 'You all right, son? Well, I got it in: I got the fucking message in!'

'Yeh, you got it in, Dad,' I managed to reply, holding my sore ribs.

'Come on, lad, we better hurry, or we'll miss the milk truck back to the Valley.'

Soon afterwards, my father decided to tackle an even more elevated centre of capitalistic reaction: the Sunday Night Debate, held weekly on radio station 3DB. He saw an advertisement in the

Melbourne *Herald* for a debate on Marxism, and the public was invited.

Again we journeyed forth by milk truck and shoe leather to find seats at the rear of the studio in the *Herald* building in Flinders Street. A fat chairman sat in front of three fat microphones, flanked by two lean and learned-looking academics.

As I recall, both speakers in the debate were anti-Marxist and so was the chairman. This agitated my father, who was quickly on his feet, arm upraised, seeking the chairman's eye. I waited for him to speak, wondering how he could possibly combat such learned arguments against the theories of one of his favourite Jews.

A microphone on a long handle was held under his nose by a young man wearing a pair of headphones.

'Mr Chairman, I wish to ask a question of both speakers,' he began. 'Are the speakers aware that Karl Marx rewrote the German language?'

Faced with this extraordinary assertion with a question mark after it, the two speakers went into a troubled huddle behind the back of the chairman while he read an advertisement for Akubra hats.

The speakers then whispered to the chairman, who said to my father, 'Sir, each of the speakers is only too well aware that Marx rewrote the German language and have asked me to state that, in criticising his atheistic, violent theories, they did not wish to deny his intellectual ability.'

My father always viewed that night as his finest hour. And I don't blame him – because in thirty-five years since as a student of Marx and an associate of Marxists, I have never discovered one tittle of evidence that the old Karl ever rewrote, or in any way tampered with, the German language; nor have I ever met one of his supporters who gave any credence whatever to the assertion. My father lived to see the foundation of the Jewish state of Israel in 1948. I mentioned the news to him, expecting it to receive his approbation.

However, he said thoughtfully (and I remember disagreeing with him at the time), 'Well, I don't know. I think they're making a mistake. Acourse, every race is entitled to a state if they want it. But, you know what I reckon? The Jews are the world's greatest thinkers – because they haven't had a state. They don't give a stuff about kings or queens or politicians, or generals or any other bureaucratic bastard; they don't give a stuff for patriotism or any of that crap, so they think for themselves. And another thing, they live in different countries and take in all the best ideas from each country. They're great readers and read all the best books of every nation. And they write the best books. They're the best fucking fiddle players, the best philosophers, the best composers . . .'

My brother Michael said, 'And the best moneylenders.'

Pausing, with his right forefinger in mid-air, my father snarled sarcastically, 'Trust you to say that, those fucking Jesuits have turned your mind into a tin of worms. A few Jews became bankers and merchants – because they were forced off the land all over Europe. But you don't mention Marx, Freud or Einstein, oh no.'

He turned to me again. 'Maybe they'll become farmers again, now those settlers in Palestine have formed a state – but, wishing them no harm, I think they might fuck themselves up, and start declaring wars and having public holidays for religious and military anniversaries like we do in this bone-headed country; but acourse, we've got no Karls or Sigmunds or Alberts here, mate.'

My brother (Paddy, *né* Solomon) and I had joined the Communist Party, under the influence of my father's ideas, of course; but in his own perverse way, he had strong reservations, especially when the Party supported the war, after Hitler invaded Russia in 1941.

'There's no such thing as a good war or a bad strike,' he told us in the Benson's Valley hotel at the time. Then he announced to the shocked drinkers (some were in uniform like myself, and most of the rest were patriotic veterans from the First World War), 'I'm a fifth columnist – and what's more, I'm fucking proud of it.'

My father died a lingering, painful death of cancer – in a Catholic old men's home. He went to the Catholic home unwillingly, guessing my mother hoped to convert him to Catholicism in his days of doom. In fact, he did receive the Catholic last rites – but Solomon (Paddy) reckoned he was unconscious before they got at him.

We went to visit him before he died. On the way to the home in a cable tram, we agreed that the Jews we had met in the Communist Party were intelligent, warm-hearted people. 'He was right, just once more, when he said that the Jews were the greatest people on earth,' Paddy said. 'Wonder where he met them?'

We puzzled over this question for a while (no Jews had dwelt in Benson's Valley or the other towns in which we had lived before coming to Melbourne). We finally decided he must have met Jews during his frequent travels away from home in his younger days.

At the home hospital (a sort of hospice for the dying) we found he was sinking fast. A skin cancer on his face, long neglected and treated with ointments borrowed from neighbours and friends, had invaded his system savagely, reducing his powerful body to mere skin and bone and withering the right side of his face.

After an awkward session beside the bed, during which we took bets from him for the horse races to be run next day, the results of which he was not to live to hear, I mentioned our new Jewish friends and asked how he came to know the Jews so intimately.

'Well,' he said, speaking with difficulty through the side of his twisted mouth, 'I can't rightly say I ever met one. But they are the greatest thinkers on earth . . . Marx . . . Freud . . . Einstein . . .'

Elizabeth Harrower

THE COST OF THINGS

1974

Dan Freeman shut the white-painted garage doors and went across the paved courtyard to the house which was painted a glossy white, too. *A lovely home.* Visitors always used these words to describe it and Dan always looked intent and curious when they did, as if he suspected them of irony. But the house did impress him for all that he wasn't fond of it.

When the Freemans bought the place they said apologetically to their friends that they couldn't afford it *but* ... People just looked unfriendly and didn't smile back. Then came the grind, the worry, fear, boredom, paring down, the sacrifices large and small of material and, it really did seem, spiritual comforts, the eternal use of the negative, habitual meanness, harassment. And it wasn't paid for yet, not *yet.* They had been careful, he and Mary, though, to see that the children hadn't – to use Mary's phrase – gone without.

Lately Dan had begun to think it mightn't have done any harm if Bill and Laura *had* been a bit deprived. They might now be applying themselves to their books occasionally, and thinking about scholarships. But, oh no! They had no doubt their requirements would all be supplied just for the wanting. Marvellous! The amount of work they did, it would be a miracle if either of them matriculated.

'Hullo. You're late. Dinner's ready,' Mary called as the back door closed.

Leaning round into the kitchen, he looked at her seriously and sniffed the air. 'What is it?'

'Iced soup. Your special steak. Salad with –'

He rolled his eyes. 'There's the paper. Five minutes to get cleaned up and I'm with you.'

Mary was an excellent cook. The Freemans had always eaten well, but since Dan had come home from his six months' interstate transfer,

338

she had outdone herself. 'I experimented while you were away,' she explained, producing dinners nightly that would have earned their house several stars in the *Guide Michelin* had it ever been examined in this light.

'Experimented!' Dan laughed in an unreal, very nearly guilty, way the first time she said this, because he was listening to another voice in his head reply smartly, 'So did I! So did I!'

Feeling the way he felt or, rather, remembering the name Clea, he was shocked at the gleeful fellow in him who could treat that name simply as something secret from Mary. And he thought *I am ashamed* although he did not *feel* ashamed to find himself taking pride in the sombre and splendid addition to his past that the name represented. Clea, he thought, as if it were some expensive collectors' item he had picked up, not without personal risk, for which it was not unnatural to accept credit. At the sound of that guilty laugh or the puffing of vanity, Dan mentally groaned and muttered, 'I'm sorry. I'm sorry.'

For the first weeks after his return to Melbourne, he had blocked all memories of those Sydney months since he could not guarantee the behaviour of his mind, and if to remember in such ways was to dishonour, he had emerged out of a state of careful non-consideration with the impression that to remember truly might not be wise. But lately, lately ... He realised that lately when he was alone he sat for hours visualising his own hand reaching to grasp hers. And each time he produced this scene its significance had to be considered afresh, without words, through timeless periods of silence. Or he pictured her walking away from him as he had once seen her do. An occasion of no significance at all. She had merely been a few steps in front of him. And he pictured her arms rising. For hours, weeks, he had watched her walk away. Then for nights, days and weeks he had looked at the movement of her arms.

He could not see her face.

Wrenching his mind back with all his energy and concentration, he set about tracking down her face, methodically collecting her features and firmly assembling them. The results were static portraits of no-one in particular, faded and distant as cathedral paintings of angels and martyrs. These faces were curiously, painfully undisturbing, as meaningless as the dots on a radar screen to an untrained observer.

In their elaborate dining room, he and Mary sat at the long table dipping spoons into chilled soup.

'Where are the kids?'

'Bill's playing squash with Philip, and Laura's over at Rachel's. They're all going on to a birthday party together.'

'At this time of night?'

'They have to go through some records.'

'What about their work? I thought they agreed to put in three hours a night till the end of term?'

'You can't keep them home from a party, Dan. All the others are going.'

'All the others don't want to be physicists! Or they've got wealthy fathers and don't have to win scholarships. These two'll end up in a factory if they're not careful.'

Mary looked at him. 'You *are* in a bad mood. Did something go wrong at the office?'

'They're irresponsible. If they knew what a depression was like, or a war –'

'Now don't spoil your dinner. How do you like the soup? At the last minute I discovered I didn't have any parsley and I had to use mint. What do you think? Is it awful?'

She hadn't altered her hairstyle since they were married. She still chose dresses that would have suited her when she was twenty and wore size ten. Her face was bare of make-up except for a rim of lipstick round the edge of her mouth. And there was something in the total of all this indifference that amounted to a crime.

How easily she had divested herself of the girl with the interests and pleasant ways. And what contempt she had felt for him and shown him, for having been so easily deceived, when she was sure of her home, her children. She had transformed herself before his eyes, laughing.

Anyway, he gave in when she wanted this house, which was pretentious and impossible for them, really. But he even thought he might find it a sort of hobby, a bulwark, himself. You have to have something.

'What are you looking at? Dan? Is it the mint? Is it awful?' She was really anxious. He lifted another spoonful from his plate and tasted it. Mary waited. He felt he ought to say something. 'Mary . . .' What had they been discussing? 'It's – extra good,' he said very suddenly.

'*Extra* good.' She gave a little scoffing laugh. 'You sound like Bill.'

Not raising his eyes, he asked, 'What sort of a day have you had?' and Mary began to tell him while the creamy soup slid weirdly down his throat, seeming to freeze him to the marrow. He shivered. It was a warm summer night. Crickets were creaking in the garden outside.

'– and Bill wants to start golf soon. He asked me to sound you out about a set of clubs. And while I'm at it, Laura's hinting she'd like that French course on records. She says it'd be a help with the accent.'

'*Mary*,' he protested bitterly and paused, forgetting. 'For God's sake!' he added on the strength of his remembered feeling, gaining time. Then again, as before, the weight descended – the facts he knew, the emotions. 'What are you trying to do? You encourage them to want – impossible things. Why? To turn me into a villain when I refuse? You know how we stand. Your attitude baffles me.' Mary's expression was rather blank but also rather triumphant. He went on, and stammered slightly, 'I want them to have – everything. I grudge them nothing. But these grown-up toys – it can't be done. If Laura would stay home and work at her French – and Bill already has so many strings to his bow he can't hold a sensible conversation about anything. They'll end up bus conductors if they're not careful.'

Mary looked at him sharply. 'Have you been drinking, Dan?'

'Two beers.'

'I thought so! . . . Really, if I have to hear you complain about the cost of their education for the next six years, I don't think it would be worth it. Not to them either, I'm sure.'

He said nothing.

'*We* aren't going without anything. We've got the house and car. And the garden at weekends. It isn't as if we were young.' Mary waved an arm. 'But if you feel like this, ask them to re-pay you when they've qualified. They won't want to be indebted to you.'

He stared at her heavily, lifted his formal-looking squarish face with its blue eyes and stared at her, saying nothing. Mary breathed through her nose at him, then collected his plate and hers and went away to the kitchen.

'Clea . . .' It was a groan. Tears came to his eyes. It was the night he had thought to go away with her. They could *not* be parted. How could he explain? It was against nature, could not *be*. He would sell everything and leave all but a small essential amount with Mary and the children. Then he and Clea would go – far away. And great liners trailing music and streamers sailed from Sydney daily for all the world's ports. Now that he'd found Clea, he would find the circumstances he had always expected, with their tests that would ask more of him than perseverance, resignation. They would live – somewhere, and be – very happy.

Commonsense had cabled him at this point: this would all be quite charming except for one minor problem that springs to mind.

What would they live on? A glorified clerk, his sole value as a worker lay in his memory of a thousand details relating to television films bought by the corporation. Away from the department he had no special knowledge, no money-raising skills. Could he begin to acquire a profession at forty-five? Living on what, in the meantime?

'There. At least there's nothing wrong with the steak.' Mary looked at him expectantly, and he looked at the platter of food for some seconds. 'It's – done to a turn.'

'*Overdone?*'

'No.' He thought of saying to her pleased face, 'I thought of deserting you, Mary.' And he had, oh, he had. 'What? . . . Yes, everything's fine.' The only trouble was that unfortunately, unfortunately, he was beginning to feel sick.

'Dan, I forgot to mention this since you got back. You're never here with all this extra work –'

'Yes?' Here it came: the proof that he had been right to return, that he and Mary *did* have a life in common. How often had he pleaded with Clea in those last days, 'You can't walk out on twenty years of memories.' (Not that she had ever asked or expected him to.)

'It's the roof. The tiles. There was a landslide into the azaleas while you were away. I thought you'd notice the broken bushes.'

'Oh.'

'So do you think I should get someone to look over the whole roof?'

'Yes, I suppose so.'

'Well, it's important to get it fixed before we start springing leaks.'

'Yes. All right. Ring Harvey. Get him to give us an estimate.'

'Dan? Where are you going? You haven't touched your dinner!'

'I'm sorry. I've got to get some air. No, stay there. Eat your dinner.'

'Aren't you well?' She half-rose from her chair, but he warded her off and compelled her to sink back to the table with a large forbidding movement of his arm. Mary shrugged, gave a tiny snort of boredom and disdain, and resumed eating.

Sydney ... At the end of a week he had begun to look forward to getting back to Mary's cooking. The department wasn't lavish with away-from-home expenses for officers on his grade, and he had the usual accounts flying in from Melbourne by every post, in addition to an exorbitant hotel bill for the very ordinary room he occupied near the office. The hotel served a 'continental' breakfast and no other meals. At lunchtime he and Alan Parker leapt out for beer and a sandwich which cost next to nothing, then by six o'clock he was famished. Somehow surreptitiously, he started to treat himself to substantial and well-cooked dinners in restaurants all over the city. In Melbourne he only patronised places like these once a year for a birthday or anniversary. He felt rather ill-at-ease eating, so to speak, Mary's new dress or the children's holidays, and he was putting on flesh. But – everything was hopeless. You had to have something. But money harassed him. He felt a kind of anguished dullness at the thought of it. It made him dwell on the place where it was cheaper and less worrying to be: home.

As the representative of his department, he was invited one Friday evening to an official cocktail party. A woman entered the building as he did, and together they ran for the row of automatic lifts, entered one, were shot up to some height between the fourth and fifth floors and imprisoned there for over half an hour. Clea.

Dan's first thought was that she looked a bit flashy. Everything about her looked a fraction more colourful than was quite seemly: the peacock-blue dress, and blonde hair – not natural, the make-up, and, in another sense, the drawling low-pitched voice. (This would certainly have been Mary's view.)

Then while the alarm bell rang and caretakers and electricians shouted instructions at one another, they stood exchanging words and Dan looked into her eyes with the usual polite, rather stuffy, slightly patronising expression.

He was surprised. Under gold-painted lids, her blue eyes glanced up and actually saw him, with a look that twenty years, fifteen years, ago he had met daily in his mirror. It was as familiar as that. She *wasn't young*. It wasn't a young look. It was alarmingly straight. It was the look by which he had once identified his friends.

At the party when they were finally released, however, Clea treated him with wonderful reserve, recognising nothing about him. She remained steadfastly with the group least likely to succeed in charming the person Dan imagined her to be, smiling a lazy gallant smile, bestowing gestures and phrases on their sturdy senses. Showing pretty teeth, laughing huskily, she stood near them and *was*. When Dan approached, though, that all appeared to have been illusory. She was merely quiet, watchful, sceptical, an onlooker.

Ah, well! He put her from him. He expected nothing. It had been a momentary interest, and this wasn't the first time, after all, that circumstances had separated him from someone whom he would in some way always know.

But he met her one day in the street accidentally. (Though Sydney is two million strong, people who live there can never lose touch, eager though they might be to do so.) He remembered they said something about the party, and something else about the lift, and then they said goodbye and parted. It wasn't till he had gone some eight or nine steps that Dan realised he had walked backwards away from her.

The following Saturday night they met at another inter-departmental party and after that there were no backward steps till this inevitable, irrevocable return to hearth and home.

Clea had a flat – kitchen, bathroom, bed-sitting room – in a converted habourside mansion, and a minor executive job with a film unit that paid rent and food and clothing bills. Once she had been an art student but at the end of four years she stopped attending classes and took a job.

'You were too critical of yourself,' Dan said. 'Your standards were too high.'

She smiled.

In her spare time she had continued to paint, she told Dan, and he had an impression of fierceness and energy and he felt he knew how she must have looked. So she had painted. And it was why she was sane. And why people who knew nothing whatever about her liked to be near her. But ages ago, and permanently, she had laid it aside. That is, laid aside the doing, but not the looking, not the thinking, not finally herself.

Dan insisted on being shown the few pieces of work that she hadn't destroyed, and he examined them solemnly, and felt this discarded talent of Clea's was a thing to respect. In addition (and less respectably, he knew) he saw it as a decoration to her personality not unflattering to himself. From talk of art, which he invariably started, he would find he had led the way back to that perennially sustaining subject – their first meeting.

'At the party that night, why were you so – cold?'

'For good reasons. Which you know. How many times do you think I can survive this sort of thing?'

They were in Clea's room on an old blue sofa by the fire. Dan turned his head away, saying nothing. She said, 'It's no fun. You get tired. Like a bird on the wing, and no land. It's – no fun. You feel trapped and hunted at the same time. And the weather seems menacing. (No, I don't mean now. But there have been times.) And in the long run, it's so much less effort to stay where your belongings are ... Wives shouldn't worry too much. And even other women shouldn't. By the time they find themselves listening to remorseful remembrances of things past they're too – killed to care. And they find they can prompt their loved one with considerable detachment when he reels off the well-known items – old clothes and family illnesses, holidays and food and friends ... Make me stop talking.'

It mattered very little to them where they went, but they walked a lot and saw a few plays. They went to some art galleries. And once they had a picnic.

'It's winter, but the sun never goes in,' he said.

'Except now and then at night. Sydney's like that.'

In the evenings Clea sometimes read aloud to Dan at his suggestion. And he would think: *The fire is burning. I am watching her face and listening to her voice.* And he felt he knew something eternal that he had always wanted to know. One night Clea read the passage in which Yury Zhivago, receiving a letter from his wife after their long and tragic separation, falls unconscious.

Because Clea existed and he was in her presence, Dan felt himself resurrected and so, though what she read was beautiful and he thought so, he laughed with a kind of senseless joy as at something irrelevant when she stopped.

'All right, darling, I suppose it is wonderful. That Russian intensity. If *I* could ever totter to a sofa and collapse with sheer strength of feeling, I'd think: "Congratulations, Freeman! You're really living."'

Clea laughed, too, but said, 'Ah, don't laugh. Because if you can laugh, you make it impossible . . .'

One thing Clea could not do was cook. It took Dan some weeks to accept this, because she wasn't indifferent to food. If they ate in a restaurant, she enjoyed a well-chosen meal as much as he did. But when he discovered that she could tackle any sort of diet with much the same enthusiasm, he was depressed.

'What do you live on when I'm not around?' he demanded, a little disgruntled.

She thought. 'Coffee.'

He was proud of her. He even liked her a lot. But he couldn't help saying, 'I get hungry.'

She looked abstracted. 'Dan, I – You're *hungry*. Oh . . . We had steak?'

'Yes, but no – no *trimmings*,' he tried to joke. 'No art.'

'Dan –'

'I take it back about no art.'

'I'll – tomorrow –'

'I take it back about no art.'

'I will do better.' And after this she tried to cook what she thought were complicated meals for him, and he didn't discourage her.

It was the night they came back from their picnic in the mountains that he had the brilliant idea of asking her why she had never married.

She laughed.

'You wouldn't have had any trouble,' he insisted, trying to see her face.

Still smiling, she said, 'The candidates came at the wrong time or they were too young for me when I was young.' She looked at him, raising her brows. 'How old were you? When you married.'

'Twenty-one.'

'I wouldn't have liked you then.'

'You'd have been right. But *you* – tell me.'

She moved restlessly on the sofa, and spread her arms along the back. He felt it was cruel to question her, but knew he would never stop. She said, 'Oh . . . I met someone, and bang went five years. Then some time rolled by while I picked myself up. Then I met – someone else who was married. Names don't matter.'

He looked at her.

'All right, they do. But not now . . . So, by the time you look round after that, you're well into your thirties. And a few of the boys have turned into men, but they're married to girls who preferred them – quite young.'

'Are you saying this to blame me? You are, aren't you?' He heard the rhetorical note in his voice. He knew he had asked her.

Clea seemed to examine the stitches of the black hand-knitted sweater he was wearing. She jumped up quickly and out in the kitchen poured whisky into two glasses, carrying one back to him.

'I can only say, Clea – if things were different – things would be different . . . All right, it sounds lame. But I *mean* it. What do you *want* me to do?'

'And what would you *like* me to say? You'll go back to Mary. Do you want me to plead with you?'

He could see that it was neither reasonable nor honourable in him to want that, but in her it would have been more *natural*, he felt. He said so.

Clea was biting the fingernails of her left hand, cagily. He saw again that it was cruel to talk to her like this, but he knew he would never stop.

She glanced at him over her hand. 'You're beginning to think about your old clothes and family holidays just as I said. And why shouldn't you? These intimate little things are what count in the end, aren't they?'

And she disposed of her hand, wrapping it round her glass as she lifted it from the floor to drink. She rolled a sardonic blue eye at Dan and he gave the impression of having blushed without a change in colour, and frowned and drank, too. Because of course his mind *had* turned lately in that direction. He *had* begun to remember the existence of all that infinitely boring, engulfing domesticity, and his vital but unimportant part in it. It was all *there*, and his. What could he do about it?

Clea knew too much, drank too much, was nervy, pushed herself to excess, bit her fingernails. She was the least conditioned human being he had ever encountered. She was like a mirror held up to his soul. She was intelligent, feeling and witty. He loved her.

'Many thanks.' But she wouldn't meet his eyes.

'Marriage,' he said, harking back suddenly. 'When I think of it! And you're so independent. What could it give you? Really? No, don't smile.'

Still, she did smile faintly, saying nothing, then said irritatingly, 'Someone to – set mouse traps and dispose of the bodies.'

He brushed this away. 'You hate the office. Why?'

'Dan.' She was patient.

'Why do you hate the office?' He did feel vaguely that he was torturing her. 'Why?'

'I don't see the sun. I lose the daylight hours. The routine's exacting, but the work doesn't matter. It takes all my time from me and I see nothing beautiful.'

'And just what would you do with this time?' he asked, somehow scientifically. He would prove to her how much better off . . .

With her left hand, distracted, she seemed to consider the length and texture of the hair that fell over her ear. 'Oh. Look about. Exist.'

Dan thought of Mary. 'Some wives are busy all day long.' He was positive that Mary would be in no way flattered if it were ever suggested that *she* had had time to practise as a student of life. 'In fact,' he went on, 'though cultivation is supposed to be the prerogative of the leisured classes, I think women in your position form a sort of non-wealthy aristocracy all to themselves.'

'Do you?' Clea shifted the dinner plate from her lap and went over to the deal table where she had a lot of paraphernalia brought home from the office spread out. At random she picked up a pencil and tested its point against the cushion of her forefinger saying, 'That's an observation!'

'No, don't be angry.' He turned eagerly to explain to her over the back of the sofa. 'What I mean is that however busy you are from nine till five, you have all the remaining hours of the day and night to concentrate on yourself – your care, cultivation, understanding, amusement . . .'

She smiled at him. 'Don't eat that if you can't bear it. I'll make something else.'

He said, 'Forgive me.'

They quarrelled once, one Thursday evening when he passed on Alan and Joyce Parker's invitation to drive out into the country the following Sunday.

Alan Parker was a tall mild man of fifty, who clerked with dedication among the television films of the library. His wife, whom both Clea and Dan had met at official parties, was friendly and chatty. The Parkers knew Dan was married, and they knew that (as they put it) Dan and Clea had a thing about each other. But they liked Dan because he wasn't disagreeably ambitious though he was younger than and senior to Alan, and they implied a fondness for Clea. Dan guessed that they would be the subject of Joyce's conversation for a week after the trip, but he couldn't find it in his heart to dislike anyone to whom he could mention Clea's name.

But she said swiftly, 'Oh no, I couldn't go with them.'

He paused, amazed, in the act of kicking a piece of wood back into the fire. 'What do you mean? Why not?'

'No, I just couldn't go,' she said definitely, beginning to look for her place in the book she was holding.

'But *why*?' Dan fixed the fire, buffed some ash from his hands and turned to sit beside her on the sofa. He took the book from her, thrust it behind his back, and forced her to lift her head.

Her look daunted him. He said in parenthesis, 'I'm addicted to that eye-shadow.' He said reasonably, 'Only last week you talked about getting out of town.'

'I'd be bored, Dan.'

'Bored? I'd be there!' he rallied her, smiling in a teasing way. 'And Joyce's going to produce a real French picnic lunch.'

There was a smile in her that he sensed and resented.

She said, 'I'm sorry.'

'And *I'm* sorry if the fact that I like to eat one meal a day is offensive to you.'

'Darling. Please go, if you'd like to. No recriminations. Truly.'

Mondays to Fridays he didn't see her all day. He couldn't have borne to lose hours of her company. Six months, he'd had, just days ago. Now there were ten weeks.

He said unpleasantly, 'You do set yourself up with your nerves and your fine sensibility, Clea. When you begin to feel that a day in the company of nice easy-going people like the Parkers would be unbearably boring, *I* begin to feel you're carrying affectation too far. If you pander to yourself much more you'll find you're unfit to live in the world at all!'

She didn't answer that, or appear to react. Instead she caught his wrist in her right hand and smoothed her thumb against the suede of his watch-strap. 'In their car, Dan, I'd feel imprisoned. I have to be able to get away. I'd be bored, Dan.' She said, 'I don't love them.'

He stared, jerked his arm away, gave a short incredulous laugh and stood up. 'Don't *love* them!'

She added, 'As things are.'

Throwing on his coat he went to the door still uttering sarcastic laughs. 'Don't *love* them! Well – *good – night – Clea!*'

In ten minutes he returned. And the ten weeks passed.

'Dan? How are you now?' Mary peered down at him, then glanced abruptly right and left, bringing her chin parallel with each of her shoulders in turn. It was dark on the balcony. 'Do you still want your dinner? It'll be ruined, but it's there if you want it . . . Dan!' She leant over him.

'What?'

'Well, for heaven's sake, you can still answer when I speak to you! I thought you'd had a stroke or something, sitting there like an image.' She bridled with relief and exasperation.

'No.'

In a brisk admonitory voice she said, 'Well, I think you'd better get yourself along to Dr Barnes in the morning. It's all this extra work. And you're not eating. Sometimes I think you don't even know you're home again.'

He said something she couldn't catch.

'What? Where's *what*? . . . Your dinner's in the oven.' Mary waited for him to speak again. 'Smell the garden, Dan . . . We'd better get ready, then. Jack and Freda'll be over soon.'

'What?' He stirred cautiously in the padded bamboo chair. He felt like someone who has had the top of his head blown off, but is still, astonishingly, alive, and must learn to cope with the light, the light, and all it illuminated.

'I told you this morning,' Mary accused him. 'You hadn't forgotten?'

Carefully he hauled himself up by the balcony railing. 'I'll be bored,' he said.

In the soft black night, Mary went to stand in front of him, tilting her face to look at him. 'Bored, Dan?' she sounded nervous. 'You know Jack and Freda,' she appealed to him, touching his shirt-sleeve.

'I don't care for them,' he complained gently, not to her. And added, 'As things are.'

'Oh, Dan!' Mary swallowed. Tears sprang to her eyes. She caught his arm and walked him through the front door, and down the carpeted hall to their bedroom. 'Lie down, Dan. Just lie there.'

He heard her going to the telephone. She rang the doctor. Then she rang Freda and Jack to apologise and ask them not to come. He heard her crying a little with fright as she repeated his uncanny remark in explanation.

And Dan took a deep breath, and looked at the ceiling, and smiled.

Gwen Harwood

THE GLASS BOY
1982

My friend Alice and I were forbidden to go anywhere near the creek, but we had taken some lollies saved for a secret feast to one of our caves in the lantana, where God could not see us through the tangles. Our refuge was near a grassy hollow overhung by the creek bank, sometimes flooded but now dry. We heard voices, and looked down, unseen. What we saw astonished us.

One of our Sunday School teachers was squashing Poor Myrtle. He was lying right on top of her and kissing her plump dollface. He must have been tickling her to make her giggle so much. No doubt we would have watched to see what they did next, but Alice sneezed. Fearful of discovery we scuttled back through the lantana tunnels, past the chow's cabbage field, and in through my back fence to the orange orchard. There we lay on the grass and played at squashing, giving one another kisses flavoured with Jersey toffee. We were giggling so much we did not hear my grandmother approaching.

'Get up, you naughty rude little girls. You'll have to be put back to First Babies. How dare you play such silly games!'

She gave us both a good smacking. Alice began to whinge. 'I'll tell my mother you smacked me.'

'When you are left for me to mind, I'll smack you when you need it.'

I was enchanted by the rhythm of this, so like 'Speak roughly to your little boy, and beat him when he sneezes'. Were there special smacking poems? Blubbering Alice gave away our secret. 'We saw Harold Rubin lying on top of Poor Myrtle.'

Where had we seen this? We got another smack for going near the creek but Granny seemed more worried than cross. The day was turning melancholy. She spoke to my father, who was chopping wood for the stove. He put down his axe and went indoors. My mother came out of the house and took Alice to be brushed and tidied and returned home. I was given my tea early and put to bed with another scolding.

That night there was a kind of meeting at our house. It was not an evening, with music and cards. Without understanding, I heard that Myrtle was four months already and that there were five or six of them. They ought to be in jail. But they were only boys, a voice said. 'If they can do *that* they're not boys,' my grandmother said.

What was *that*? The big boys teased poor simple Myrtle continually. They would give her presents and surprises which turned out, when she unwrapped them, to be a dog's turd, a fish head, a skinned frog. Myrtle was unteachable. It was because her father had been killed in the war, right at the beginning before she was even born. The shock had been too much.

She ought to go to Wooloowin, a voice said. But my grandmother cried. 'No, no, no. Why should the Micks have her? It's not her fault. The misery of that place would kill her.' I had heard about Holy Cross. Had even, on my naughty days, been threatened with it and with what the Sisters of Mercy would do to teach me better behaviour.

One of the big girls at school said that Holy Cross had thirteen windows across the front, the Devil's number, and a pit where the nuns buried their babies in quicklime. The voices went on as I drifted into sleep. Myrtle would stay at home with a lock on the gate. My mother said she could have the clothes Little Joe had grown out of. Veronica had her midwifery and would be there when she was needed.

Veronica was everyone's favourite. She was a nurse who lived with her old great-aunt. Every morning she got up very early, washed and dressed Aunty, and put her out in the sun with her breakfast and her two sticks 'to watch the world go by'. Only the odd horse and cart went by along our dusty road, but the neighbours would look in on Aunty while Veronica was at work in a private hospital. Aunty always spoke her mind, which was sharp and savage. She told everyone that Myrtle was far better off at home than working in the steam laundry for the bloody Pats.

Veronica was beautiful, kind and sweet-smelling. One morning she came in on her way to work and said that Myrtle had a lovely boy, the finest she had ever seen. An easy birth, a perfect child. Then Veronica asked a favour. She had a special friend, and she would like to ask him down to Mitchelton on her next day off, but we knew how cantankerous

Aunty was. Aunty didn't like her friend, whom Veronica had met while she was nursing his dying mother. He was clever and handsome. She hoped they would get engaged. Handsome is as handsome does, said Granny, but she invited Veronica to bring him for dinner. Big Joe would be taking my mother and Little Joe out in the sulky for a picnic. What a choice! I decided to stay with Granny and meet Veronica's friend, who was an accountant and had a University degree.

'I hear you are going to entertain Mr I Always,' said the old great-aunt next morning. What a curious name, I thought. Was his name Isaac Always? Ivan Always? Isaiah Always? 'I've told her,' continued Aunty, 'she won't get the house if she marries him. He's a mother's boy. He wants another mother.'

When the day came I helped Granny prepare the chook for Mr Always. We set the table in the sitting room instead of on the back veranda. Veronica met Mr Always at the station and brought him up our front stairs to be introduced. His name was Mr Cecil Stitt. How could Aunty have made such a mistake? We sat on the front veranda with glasses of mandarin juice. I wanted to read to Veronica from my *Children's Encyclopaedia*, but she said it would be rude, and we must make conversation. When she and Granny went in to the kitchen I made conversation with Mr Stitt.

'Dinner will soon be ready.'

'You mean lunch.'

'Did you have a pleasant journey down on the train?'

'No. I always say trains are a dirty way to travel.'

'Do you have any little girls?'

'Certainly not.'

'Any little boys?'

'Certainly not. I am not married.'

'God gave Myrtle a little boy and she's not married.'

'I always say children shouldn't speak until they are spoken to.'

'Do you keep chooks?'

'Certainly not.'

I did not think him handsome. His face was stern and tight. I began to give him my grandmother's lecture on poultry. They were good company. They gave you eggs and a nice dinner when they were too old to lay. And feather pillows. You could use them all except the head and the claws. I knew where the heart was. And the lights. And the gizzard.

Dinner was served. Granny carved some white meat for Veronica and was beginning to put dark meat on Mr Stitt's plate when he said, 'I should like some breast, please. I always prefer the breast.' I saw Granny's lips compress, but she carved him some breast. White meat for the ladies, dark meat for the gentlemen, and drumsticks for the children. Had nobody taught him? I ate carefully with my big knife and fork and saw that Mr Stitt was mashing up his dinner as if it were being prepared for Little Joe. He mashed peas into the gravy and potato into the peas and stuffing into everything. I would not have dared to do it in company. He left a lot of good food on his plate, and did not say it was delicious. When the ladies went out to wash up I resumed my lecture.

He barked at me, 'I always say having children at the table makes them bold.'

I replied boldly, 'Only babies mash their dinner.'

He insisted on leaving far too early for the train and made Veronica go.

'He hates fowls,' I told Granny.

'Sometimes education cuts people off,' she said.

Veronica married him quietly. The great-aunt spoke her mind finally by dying just before the wedding and leaving her house to a great-nephew who sold it and gambled the money away. Myrtle's boy continued to thrive. I heard Veronica telling Granny on one of her now rare visits that Myrtle treated him like a doll and often forgot about him. Myrtle's mother reared him as she had reared Myrtle, on milk arrowroot biscuits and condensed milk. Veronica seemed thinner and sadder, though she was as beautiful and kind as ever.

Granny told my parents that Veronica was far from happy. He would not let her go to work. He made her account for every penny. He worked at home and expected her to be there when he was. Nobody called him Cecil, or Mr Stitt. It was always he, like Jehovah.

One day Granny and I were invited to dinner, which Veronica now called lunch, at her home in Ascot. The house was huge, dark and gloomy. It smelt unfriendly. Veronica had the table set for four, but he came in and asked for lunch in his study. He did not bother to talk to the visitors. I found a water-closet which fascinated me utterly, and was repeatedly pulling the handle, which had the word PULL embossed in black letters on ivory, when he appeared and said, 'I always say children should be left at home.'

A maid took away our luncheon dishes and brought us tea, and we began to talk about old times. He appeared again and asked us to talk outside, so we took our tea onto the shady veranda. I tried to roll on the lawn, but the buffalo grass was too scratchy, so I found a corner where I could hear what Veronica was telling my grandmother. She felt like a prisoner. There was nothing to do. She had an ice-chest and the laundry went out to Holy Cross and came back so starchy you had to tear it apart. He had kept his mother's house exactly as it was, and kept his mother's cranky, bossy maid, who put things back if Veronica tried to arrange them. 'Well, my dear,' said Granny, 'it is for better or worse. You know you're always welcome with us. You might have a child.'

'He doesn't want one. He can't abide children.'

Time passed as usual at Mitchelton, until something terrible happened. Myrtle's mother left the gate unlocked and Myrtle wandered off with her little boy. She took him down to the creek and forgot all about him. He rolled into the water and drowned. Veronica came down for the funeral, and afterwards sat with my grandmother. I was in my darkened room. That evening I was to be allowed up to listen to a new crystal set my father had built, so I had to lie down for a horrible enforced afternoon rest. I heard Veronica telling Granny how she had tried for one last time to get things right. 'We took a shack at Humpybong for a few days. I thought we might talk things out by ourselves, but he didn't want to listen. I borrowed a dinghy and went out fishing, and got a bream, not very big but enough for tea, and found a beach with lovely polished stones. I felt like a child again, and thought of that poem you taught Gwennie:

> White foam on the sea-top
> Green leaves on the tree-top
> The wind blows gay,
> Sing ho! sing hey!

'I found one stone like a heart, and one with a face, and a brown one like a perfect egg. And in the seaweed a glass buoy covered in rope. I felt it was a sort of sign that things would be better, and put everything in the fishing bucket and rowed back. But when I got to our beach he was waiting, angry because his tea was late and he'd had enough of the seaside. He said the fish was too small, and tipped everything out of the bucket. I cried and cried. I felt like a helpless child.'

She cried again. No wonder, with such treasures lost. An egg, a face and a heart. And the wonderful glass boy. I saw him, translucent green, the colour of the marbles we used to stop the jam sticking to the kettle; he had his ropes taken off and was set on the windowsill to catch the morning light. Granny was getting four o'clock, and I went in to cuddle Veronica.

'The glass boy, were his arms joined to his sides, or did they move like a doll's? Was he a baby boy or a grown-up boy? Could you stand him up like an ornament? Was he hollow or glass all through?'

'Not that kind of boy,' she said. 'Bring me your book of words.' I brought the book, and she wrote down BUOY. 'It's something that keeps you afloat in the water. Or tells you there are dangers, like rocks underneath. This one was a ball of glass, hollow inside; not a doll, my darling.'

My friend Alice was brought in that night to hear the wireless. We sat in our nightgowns with one headphone each.

'What can you hear?' asked my father.

'A piano playing. Ladies singing.'

'What are they singing?'

Alice did not know, though we had learnt the song at school. Her family was not musical.

My father said wireless would change the world.

> Over the rolling waters go,
> Come from the dying moon and blow,
> Blow him again to me –

I mourned for the green glass boy, born of a mistake in my head, floating on the waves in his net cradle as I lay before sleep listening to the stone-curlews. But I did not grieve for Myrtle's baby.

Our street was full of boys. It was nature's way of making up for the Great War.

Shirley Hazzard

THE PICNIC
1962

It was like Nettie, Clem thought, to wear a dress like that to a picnic
and to spill something on it. His wife, May, was wearing shorts and a
plaid shirt, and here was Nettie in a dress that showed her white arms
and shoulders – and, as she bent over the wine stain, her bosom; a
dress with a green design of grapes and vine leaves. He could tell, too,
that she had been to the hairdresser yesterday, or even this morning
before setting out to visit them. She hadn't changed at all. Unrealistic,
that was the word for Nettie . . . But the word, suggesting laughter and
extravagance, unexpectedly gave him pleasure. Feeling as though Nettie
herself had cheated him of his judgment, he turned away from her and
glanced down the hillside to where May was playing catch with Ivor,
their youngest boy.

If May had left them alone deliberately, as he assumed she had –
and he honoured that generosity in her – she was mistaken in thinking they had anything to say to one another. They had been sitting
for some minutes in complete silence, Nettie repacking the remains
of the lunch into the picnic basket or, since the accident with the
wine, fiddling with her dress. But what could two people talk about
after ten years (for it must be getting on to that)? Nettie, though
quite chatty throughout lunch, certainly hadn't said much since.
Perhaps she expected him to mention all that business; it would fit
in with her sentimental ideas. Naturally, he had no intention of
doing anything of the kind – why bring up something that happened
at least ten years ago and made all three of them miserable enough,
God knows, at the time? Yes, that would be Nettie all over, wanting
to be told that he had often thought about her, had never forgotten
her, never would – although whole months passed sometimes when
Nettie never entered his head, and he was sure it must be the same
way for her; at least, he presumed so. Even then, he would remember

her only because someone else – May, perhaps – spoke of her.

In fact, it was because someone else brought her to his attention that the thing had come about in the first place. He had not, in the beginning, thought her attractive – a young cousin of May's who came to the house for weekends in the summer. He had scarcely noticed her until a casual visitor, the wife of one of his partners, spoke about her. A beautiful woman, she had called her – the phrase struck him all the more because he or May would have said, at most, a pretty girl. And Nettie, that day, had been dressed in a crumpled yellow cotton, he remembered – not at her best *at* all. Later, he had reflected that his whole life had been jeopardised because someone thoughtlessly said: 'She is beautiful.'

Now Nettie looked up at him, drawing her hair away from her face with the back of her hand. Still they did not speak, and to make the silence more natural by seeming at his ease Clem stretched on his elbow among the ferns. Nettie released the loop of hair and poured a little water from a thermos onto the mark on her dress. Her earrings swung; her dress shifted along one shoulder. Her head lowered intently – he supposed that she had become short-sighted and refused to wear glasses.

He could hardly recall how it had developed, what had first been said between them, whether either of them resisted the idea. His memories of Nettie were like a pile of snapshots never arranged according to date. He could see her quite clearly, though, sitting in a garden chair, and in a car, and, of all things, riding a bicycle; and facing him across a table – in a restaurant, he thought – looking profoundly sad and enjoying herself hugely.

If, he told himself, I were to say now that I've thought of her (just because it would please her – and they would probably never meet again), she might simply get emotional. Not having thought of it for years, she might seize the opportunity to have a good cry. Or perhaps she doesn't really want to discuss the past; perhaps she's as uncomfortable as I ... All the same, she looked quite composed. He might almost have said a little satirical, as though she found his life quite dull and could rejoice that, after all, she had not shared it. (He saw himself, for an instant, with what he imagined to be her eyes. What a pity she had come just now – he had worked hard last winter, and he thought it had told on him.)

It was true, of course, that he had responsibilities, couldn't be rushing about the world pleasing himself, as she could. But no man, he assured himself irritably, could be entirely satisfied with what had happened to him. There must always be the things one had chosen not to do. One couldn't explore every possibility – one didn't have a thousand years. In the end, what was important? One's experience, one's ideas, what one read; some taste, understanding. He had his three sons, his work, his friends, this house. There was Matt, his eldest boy, who was so promising. (Then he recalled that during lunch today he had spoken sharply to Matt over something or other, and Nettie had laughed. She had made a flippant remark about impatience; that he hadn't changed at all, was that it? Some such silly, proprietary thing – which he had answered, briefly, with dignity. He knew himself to be extremely patient.)

Yes, Nettie could be quite tiresome, he remembered – almost with relief, having feared, for a moment, his own sentimentality. She made excessive demands on people; her talk was full of exaggerations. She had no sense of proportion, none whatever – and wasn't that exactly the thing one looked for in a woman? And she took a positive pride in condoning certain kinds of conduct, because they demonstrated weaknesses similar to her own. She was not fastidious, as May was.

That was it, of course. He had in his marriage the thing they would never have managed together, Nettie and he – a sort of perseverance, a persistent understanding. Where would Nettie have found strength for the unremitting concessions of daily life? She was precipitated from delight to lamentation without logical sequence, as though life were too short; she must cram everything in and perhaps sort it out later. (He rather imagined, from the look of things, that the sorting process had been postponed indefinitely.) For her, all experience was dramatic, every love eternal. Whereas he could only look on a love affair, now, as a displacement, not just of his habits – though that, too – but of his intelligence. Of the mind itself. Being in love was, like pain, an indignity, a reducing thing. So nearly did it seem in retrospect a form of insanity, the odd thing to him was that it should be considered normal.

Not that it wasn't exciting in its own way, Nettie's ardour, her very irresponsibility. It was what had fascinated him at the time, no doubt. And she was easily amused – though that was one of her drawbacks; she laughed at men, and naturally they felt it. Even when she had been, so to speak, in love with him, he had sometimes felt she had laughed at him, too.

In all events, his marriage had survived Nettie's attractions, whatever they were. It was not easy, of course. In contrast to Nettie, May assumed too many burdens. Where Nettie was impetuous and inconsiderate, May was scrupulous and methodical. He was often concerned about May. She worried, almost with passion (he surprised himself with the word), over human untidiness, civic affairs, the international situation. He was willing to bet that the international situation never crossed Nettie's mind. May had a horror of disorder – 'Let's get organised,' she would say, faced with a picnic, a dinner party; faced with life itself. If his marriage lacked romance, which would scarcely be astonishing after twenty years, it was more securely established on respect and affection. There were times, he knew, when May still needed him intensely, but their relations were so carefully balanced that he was finding it more and more difficult to detect the moment of appeal.

He felt a sudden hatred for Nettie, and for this silence of hers that prejudiced one's affections and one's principles. She tried – he could feel it; it was to salve her own pride – to make him consider himself fettered, diminished, a shore from which the wave of life receded. And what had *she* achieved, after all, that she should question the purpose of his existence? He didn't know much about her life these past few years – which alone showed there couldn't be much to learn. A brief, impossible marriage, a lot of trips, and some flighty jobs. What did she have to show for all this time – without children, no longer young, sitting there preoccupied with a stain on her dress? She couldn't suggest that he was to blame for the turn her life had taken – she wasn't all *that* unjust. She had suffered at the time, no doubt, but it was so long ago. They couldn't begin now to accuse or vindicate one another. That was why it was much better not to open the subject at all, actually. He glanced severely at her, restraining her recriminations. But she had lost her mocking, judicial air. She was still looking down, though less attentively. Her hands were folded over her knee.

Well, she *was* beautiful; he would have noticed it even if it had never been pointed out to him . . . All at once he wanted to say 'I have often thought of you' (for it was true, he realised now; he thought of her every day). Abruptly, he looked away. At the foot of the hill, May had stopped playing with the children and was sitting on a rock. It is my own decision, he reminded himself, that Nettie isn't mine, that I haven't seen her in all these years. And the knowledge, though not completely gratifying, gave him a sense of integrity and self-denial, so that when he looked at her again it was without desire, and he told himself, I have grown.

He has aged, Nettie thought. Just now, looking into his face – which was, curiously, more familiar to her than anyone else's – she had found nothing to stir her. One might say that he was faded, as one would say it of a woman. He would soon be fifty. He had a fretful, touchy air about him. During lunch, when she had laughed at his impatience, he had replied primly (here in her mind she pulled a long, solemn, comic face): 'I have my faults, I suppose, like everyone else.' And like everyone else, she noted, he was willing to admit the general probability so long as no specific instance was brought to his attention. He made little announcements about himself, too, protesting his tolerance, his sincerity. 'I am a sensitive person,' he had declared, absolutely out of the blue (something, anyway, that no truly sensitive person would say). He was so cautious – anyone would think he had a thousand years to live and didn't need to invite experience. And while, of course, any marriage must involve compromise (and who, indeed, would know that better than she?), that was no reason for Clem and May to behave toward one another like a couple of . . . civil servants.

She could acknowledge his intelligence. And he had always been a very competent person. Wrecked on a desert island, for instance (one of her favourite criteria), he would have known what to do. But life demanded more, after all, than the ability to build a fire without matches, or recognise the breadfruit tree on sight. And one could hardly choose to be wrecked simply in order to have an opportunity for demonstrating such accomplishments.

Strange that he should have aged like this in so short a time – it would be precisely eight years in June since they parted. It was still a thing she couldn't bring herself to think of, the sort of thing people had in mind when they said, not quite laughing, that they wouldn't want their youth over again. Oddly enough, it was the beginning, not the end, that didn't bear thinking about. One weekend, they had stopped at a bar, in the country, on the way to this house. It was summer, and their drinks came with long plastic sticks in them. Clem had picked up one of the sticks and traced the outline of her fingers, lying flat on the Formica tabletop. They had not said anything at all, then, but she had known simply because he did that. Even now, the thought of his drawing that ridiculous plastic stick around her fingers was inexpressibly touching.

Naturally, she didn't imagine poor old Clem had planned an affair in advance, but even at the time she had felt he was ready for something of the kind – that she was the first person he happened to notice. For the fact was that they were not really suited to one another, which he would have discovered if he had ever tried to understand her properly. He had no idea of what she was like, none whatever. To this day, she was sure, he thought her trivial, almost frivolous. (And she was actually an acutely sensitive person.) No wonder they found nothing to say to one another now.

It *was* a strain, however, their being alone like this. And how like May to have arranged it this way, how ostentatiously forbearing. Magnanimous, Clem would have called it (solemn again), but May had a way, Nettie felt, of being magnanimous, as it were, at one's expense. Still, what did it matter? Since they had invited her, after she had run into May in a shop one afternoon, she could hardly have refused to come. In an hour or two it would be over; she need never come again.

It did matter. It wouldn't be over, really. Her life was associated with Clem's, however little he might mean to her now, and she must always be different because she had known him. She wasn't saying that he was responsible for the pattern of her life – she wasn't that unjust. It was, rather, that he cropped up, uninvited, in her thoughts almost every day. She found herself wondering over and over again what he would think of things that happened to her, or wanting to tell him a story that would amuse him. And surely that is the sense, she thought, in which one might say that love is eternal. She was pleased when people spoke well of him in her hearing – and yet resentful, because she had no part, now, in his good qualities. And when she heard small accusations against him, she worried whether she should contest them. But, for all she knew, they might be justified. That was the trouble with experience; it taught you that most people were capable of any-thing, so that loyalty was never quite on firm ground – or, rather, became a matter of pardoning offences instead of denying their existence.

She sympathised with his attitude. It was tempting to confine oneself to what one could cope with. And one couldn't cope with love. (In her experience, at any rate, it had always got out of hand.) But, after all, it was the only state in which one could consider oneself normal; which engaged all one's capacities, rather than just those developed by necessity – or shipwreck. One never realised how much was lacking until one fell in love again, because love – like pain, actually – couldn't be properly remembered or conveyed.

How sad it was. Looking into his face just now, finding nothing of interest, she had been so pierced by sadness that tears filled her eyes and she had to bend over the stain on her dress to hide her face. It was absurd that they should face each other this way – antagonistically, in silence – simply because they had once been so close. She would have done anything for him. Even though she no longer cared for him, saw his weakness quite clearly, still she would do anything for him. She cared for him, now, less than for any man she knew, and yet she would have done anything ... It *was* a pity about her dress, though – wine was absolutely the worst thing; it would never come out.

Upright on her rock, May gave a short, exhausted sigh. She closed her eyes for a moment, to clear them, and Ivor called out to her that she must watch him, watch the game. She looked back at him without smiling. On either side, her palms were pressed hard against the stone.

X a v i e r   H e r b e r t

KAIJEK THE SONGMAN
1 9 4 1

Kaijek the Songman and his lubra Ninyul came up the river, picking their way through wind-stricken cane-grass and palm-leaves and splintered limbs and boughs that littered the pad they were following. It was a still and misty morning, after a night of one of those violent south-east blows which clean up the wet monsoon. Mist hid the tops of the tall river timber and completely hid the swirling yellow stream. The day had dawned clear and cool; but now it was warming up again.

Sweat was trickling down Kaijek's broad gaunt face and through his curly raven beard, and down his long thin naked body from his armpits. He wore nothing but a loin-clout, a strip of dirty calico torn from a flour-bag and rigged on a waist-belt of woven hair. On his right shoulder he carried three spears and a woomera; and from his left hung a long bag of banyan-cord containing his big painted didgeridoo and music-sticks. Fat little Ninyul, puffing at his heels, bore the bulk of their belongings – swag balanced on her curly head, big grass dillybag hanging from a brow-strap down her back, tommy-axe and yam-sticks in a sugar bag slung on her left shoulder, and fire-stick and billy in her right hand. She wore a sarong made from an ancient blue silk dress.

Ninyul sniffed at the strong effluvium of her man. Not that she objected to it. Indeed, she was as proud of it as of his talent, of which she considered it an expression. As her wide fleshy nostrils dilated, she thought of how lesser songmen always came to him during corroborees to have him rub them with his sweat. And she glowed in recollection of the great success he had made at the last gathering they had attended – amongst the Marrawudda people on the coast – with his latest song, 'The Pine Creek Races'. Apart from the classics, corroboree-crowds liked nothing better than a good skit in song on the ways of the white man. But this pleasant recollection lasted only for a moment.

Ninyul became aware again of her man's drooped shoulders and his frenzied gait; and her anxiety for him in his struggle with his muse returned. At full moon they were due to attend a great initiation gathering amongst the Marratheil of the Paperbarks. The moon was nearly full already; and they were getting further from the Paperbarks every day; and still Kaijek had not composed the song that would be expected of him.

Kaijek was the most famous songman in the land. His songs were known from the red mountains of the Kimberley to the salt arms of the Gulf. Wherever they went, Kaijek and Ninyul, who was always with him, were warmly welcomed; for, though Kaijek's songs always travelled ahead of him, he never failed to come to a gathering with a new one. Not that Kaijek found composing easy. Far from it! Often his muse would elude him for moons. And so wretched would he become in his impotence, and so ashamed, that – pursued by Ninyul – he would fly from the faces of his fellows, to range the wilderness like one of those solitary ramping devil-doctors called the Moombas.

He was in the throes of that impotence now, while he went crashing up the river through the tangle of wrecked grass and trees. So he and Ninyul went on and on, travelling at great speed, but heading nowhere. Wallabies heard them coming and fled crashing and thudding from them. White cockatoos in the river timber dropped down to pry at them, and wheeled back shrieking into the mist. And on and on – till suddenly they were stopped in their tracks by a burst of uproarious dog-barking in the mist ahead.

Kaijek, staring ahead, heard the click of Ninyul's tongue, and turned to her. She gave the sign 'white man', then pointed with her lips to the left. Kaijek looked and saw the stumps of a couple of saplings of size such as no blackfellow ever would fell to make a camp. Ninyul was already aware of the likelihood of a white man's presence in the neighbourhood, because some little distance back she had observed fresh prints of shod horses, and just before the dog barked had fancied she heard a horse-bell. Kaijek had seen and heard nothing consciously for miles. He turned and looked ahead again.

Then the dog appeared, a little red kelpie. When he saw them he yelped, turned tail and disappeared, yapping shrilly. They heard a white man yell at him. Still he yapped. They judged the distance. For a moment they stood. Ninyul glanced into the mist to the left, thinking of wheeling round that way to avoid what lay ahead. Then Kaijek turned to her again and hissed, 'Inta jah – tobacca!'

She nodded. They had been without tobacco for a long while. Kaijek had often moaned in his despair that if he had only a finger of tobacco he might find his song.

They went ahead cautiously. A score of paces brought them into dim view of a camp. There was a tent, a bark-roofed skillion, a bark-covered fireplace, a springcart, and pieces of mining gear. Kaijek and Ninyul knew what the gear was for, because they had often worked for prospectors. There was only one white man, and no sign of blacks. The white man was sitting on a box in the skillion, kneading a damper in a prospecting-dish between his feet, and looking into the mist in their direction. His dog was crouched before him, silent now, but tense.

Kaijek gave his spears and bag to Ninyul, but retained the woomera. Ninyul slipped behind a tree. Kaijek went on slowly. The white man soon saw him, stared hard at him with bulging blue eyes that bade him anything but welcome. Kaijek stopped at the fireplace. He knew the man slightly. He had seen him working a tin show in the Kingarri country, and had heard blacks describe him as a moody and often violent fellow. He was Andy Gant, a man of fifty or so, stout and stocky, with a big red bristly face and sandy greying hair and a long gingery unkempt moustache.

Andy Gant was in a particularly bad mood just then. The heavy humidity had upset his liver and brought out his prickly heat; which was why he was doing camp chores at that time of day, instead of digging gravel from the bench behind the camp and lumping it down to the sluice-box. To slave at digging that hard-packed gravel and washing out the lousy bit of gold it yielded was heart-breaking at any time, and too much to bear with a lumpy liver and fiery itch. He had slaved at that mean bench-placer throughout the wet, and had not won enough gold from it to pay for tucker, although the indications were that there was rich gold thereabouts. And most of the time he had been alone, deserted by the couple of blacks he had brought with him. He was just about ready now to shoot any nigger on sight.

Kaijek spat in the fire to show his friendliness, then grinned and said, 'Goottay, boss!' And he stroked his beard and lifted his right foot and placed it against his left thigh just above the knee, and propped himself up with the woomera.

For answer Andy raised a broken lip and showed big yellow teeth. Then he gave attention to his damper.

Kaijek coughed, spat again, then said, 'Eh, boss – me wuk longa you, eh?'

Andy's face darkened. He kneaded vigorously.

A pause, during which Kaijek coveted the pipe and plug of tobacco on the sapling-legged table at Andy's back. Then Kaijek said, 'Me prop'ly goot wukker, boss. Get up be-fore deelight, wuk like plutty-ell –'

Andy could contain himself no longer. With eyes ablaze he leapt to his feet and roared, 'Git to jiggery out of it, you stinkin' rottin' black sumpen, before I put a bullet through you.'

And his dog joined in with him, yapping furiously and dancing about.

'Wha' nim?' cried Kaijek, dropping his leg.

Andy grabbed a pick-handle with a doughy hand, and shouted, 'I'll show you what name, you beggin' son of a sheeter – I'll show you what name – the ghost I will!' And he rushed.

'Eh, look out!' yelled Kaijek, and turned and fled back to Ninyul with the dog snapping at his heels. Ninyul bowled the dog over with a stick. Then together they snatched up their belongings and bolted back along the track.

They stopped at the sapling stumps. 'Marjidi naijil!' grunted Kaijek, and spat over his shoulder to show his contempt. Then he pointed with lips to the left, and set off in that direction. But though they were not seen as they skirted the camp, and though they went warily, their going was followed every step of the way in imagination by Andy's dog yapping at his master's side.

They had gone no more than fifty paces past the camp, and were still at the foot of the flood-bench, when they came upon a rivergum that had been uprooted in the night. Kaijek paused to look among the broken roots for bardies, and saw gold gleaming in a lump of quartzy gravel. He knew gold well, but had no more idea of its value than any average bush blackfellow. He gave his spears to Ninyul, and fished out the lump of gravel and freed the gold. It was a nugget of about two ounces on a piece of quartz. Kaijek picked it clean, spat on it, rubbed it on his thigh, weighed it, then looked at Ninyul and said with a grin, 'Kudjing-gah – tobacca!'

They turned back, heading straight for the camp. The dog knew they were coming, and barked blue murder. Andy, now at the fireplace setting his damper in the camp-oven, rose up and peered into the mist again; and when Kaijek appeared he let out a stream of invective and grabbed up the pick-handle and rushed.

'No more – no more!' yelled Kaijek, and held out the nugget in his palm.

Andy had the handle raised to hurl it at him. He saw the gold. But his dog was flying at Kaijek.

'Goold – goold!' yelled Kaijek, and flung it at Andy's feet, and made a swing at the dog with his woomera.

Andy snatched up the nugget, goggled at it, then looked up at Kaijek fighting with the dog, and rushed in with the handle to put the dog to flight. 'Where – where'd you find it?' he gasped.

Kaijek pointed with his lips and replied, 'Close-up behind.'

'Then show me,' gasped Andy. 'Show me!' And his voice rose shrill. 'Quick – where is it? Show me!'

Kaijek knew the symptoms of the fever. He turned and led the way with a rush.

Andy fairly flung himself at the roots. In a moment he had another nugget of an ounce or more, and then found one as big as a goose-egg. He turned his jerking face to Kaijek and cried, 'Go longa camp. Gettim pick an' shovel. An' the axe. Quick, quick!'

Kaijek moved to obey, then turned and said, 'Me hungry longa tobacca, boss.'

'Tobacca there longa camp.'

'No-more gottim pipe, boss.'

'Pipe there, too,' yelled Andy. 'Take it. Take anything you like. But be quick!'

Kaijek flew. Ninyul, in the background, set down the belongings and followed him. It was she who took the things to Andy. Kaijek stopped in the camp to chop up tobacco and fill Andy's pipe; and when he went to the fireplace to light the pipe he swigged a quart of cold stewed tea he found there. Then he strolled back to the tree, puffing luxuriously.

Andy now had a good dozen ounces of gold on a rock beside him, and was chopping off roots with the energy of a raving madman. And it was the eyes of a madman he turned on Kaijek when at length he paused for breath. He lowered the axe, and stepped up to Kaijek, and laid a great wet hairy hand on his slim black shoulder, and gurgled lovingly in his face, 'Thank you, brother, thank you! It's what I've been lookin' for all me flamin' life. An' I owe it all to you. Yes, to you who I nearly druv away.' He shook Kaijek till he rocked. 'I won't forget it,' he went on; and now he was near to tears. 'My oath I won't! I'll look after you, brother, don't you worry. I'll pay you the biggest wages a nigger ever got. I'll pay you bigger'n white man's wages. Oh, ghost, I love you! I'll buy you everything you ever want. Gawd bless you!' And with that he flung himself back at the roots.

For a while Kaijek watched him. Then he said, 'Eh, boss, me two-fella lubra hungry longa tucker.'

Andy stopped chopping and gasped at him, 'Plenty tucker longa camp. Take the lot. Take the rintin' jiggerin' lot! And when you're comin' back bring another pick an' shovel, an' a dish. There's damper in the oven. Eat it! Eat anything you flamin' well want to, brother. Everything I got is yours!'

Kaijek turned away, and signed to Ninyul, who picked up the belongings and followed him to the camp.

They sat by the fireplace, gorging bully-beef and hot damper and treacle, and swilling syrupy tea, while the racket of Andy's joyous labouring went on in the distance. Then they sat taking turn about with the pipe. Twice Andy yelled to them to come see fresh treasures he had unearthed. The first call Kaijek answered. Ninyul answered the second, because Kaijek, the artist, staring fixedly at the fire and humming to himself, did not hear it. Then suddenly Kaijek leapt up and smacked his rump and danced a few steps and began to sing:

> O munnijurra karjin jai, ee minni kinni goold,
> Wah narra akinyinya koori, mungawaddi yu . . .

He swung on Ninyul, whose eyes were shining and lips aquiver. For a moment he stared at her. Then he began to clap his hands and stamp a foot.

Kaijek stopped, turned panting to Ninyul. She leapt and cried joyously, 'Yakkarai!'

Then Andy's voice rang out through the thinning mist, 'Eh, brother – come here! Come quick! Come quick an' see what the angels've planted for you an' me. O Gawd!' He ended with a sob.

Kaijek looked towards him for a while. Then he turned back to Ninyul and made a sign. She went to their belongings. He followed her, and gathered up his stuff and shouldered it, then led the way down the river again, heading full speed for the gathering in the Paperbarks.

Dorothy Hewett

NULLARBOR HONEYMOON

1996

I am running down George Street with a northerly blowing grit in my face, one and a half hours late for my wedding. I can see Chris on the corner, furious with heat and waiting.

'Where the hell have you been?'

'I walked the wrong way, towards the Quay instead of the railway.'

'For Christ's sake how many years did you live in this city?'

'I wasn't thinking, but look, I bought a new blouse in Farmers.' And I'd almost stolen a new pair of shoes but I was too honest or too scared. I can still see them floating, high heeled, pale beige, Italian leather. I twirl in front of him.

'Get fucked,' he says and strides off through the maze of streets, rolling a little on the balls of his feet from the remembered motion of the sea.

We walk up the hill by the park on opposite sides of the road. He is wearing thongs and a crumpled yellow shirt with a frayed collar. He might have changed into something decent.

Outside the Registry Office our two witnesses are waiting, Englishmen, dressed up to the nines with white carnations in their buttonholes. The registrar is confused, his eyes searching for the bridegroom. Chris steps forward. He probably thinks I've picked up some derro in the park, I think bitterly.

Now we are in the nearest pub, one of those typical Sydney pubs, dirty green tiles, stinking of Tooheys Old. Reg is ordering half a bottle of champagne. 'I'll shout you a wedding breakfast,' he says magnanimously. 'What's on the menu?'

'Poi'n'peas,' mumbles the adenoidal barmaid.

When we come out again into the glare of the streets Reg puts his arm around me. A cockney who has pulled himself up by his bootstraps in Australia, he is used to taking charge.

'Well,' he says, 'Em can come home with us . . . And Chris . . .' He leaves the sentence hanging. He doesn't care where Chris goes. Chris bristles. 'Emily's coming with me.'

Together we walk away down the hill, smiling. I have no idea where we are going.

Chris takes me to the little terrace in Redfern where he always stays with a folkie friend when he pays off a ship.

'This is my room,' he says. I look around. The walls are splotched and peeling with damp. There isn't a stick of furniture.

'But where do we sleep?'

'On the floor. I've got a blanket in my kit.'

'I will not,' I say indignantly, 'sleep on the bare floor on my wedding night.'

We buy a double mattress, pillows and unbleached sheets from Grace Brothers. The day is coming to a close, so we order steak and salad in a greasy cafe on the corner of Crown and Cleveland, but the steak is off so Chris sends it back to the kitchen. The cafe owner stands belligerently by our table.

'The steak is good.' Chris shoves a forkful of dubious meat in his face.

'You eat it then.' The Greek eats it.

When we walk back to the terrace house we are still hungry but too tired to do anything about it. The room is full of shadows. Riffling through his friend's record collection I discover a copy of *The White-haired Girl*. 'Listen to this,' I say, as the strange, heart-breaking wail fills the little room.

I am sitting with Len in a crowded Peking cinema. The only Europeans among the mass of Mao-suited Chinese. We are entranced by the music, the story of the tragic outcast singing on the mountainside.

'Turn that fucking caterwauling thing off.'

I stare at Chris in horror. 'But it's *The White-haired Girl*!'

'I don't care who it is. Turn it off.'

'It's a great modern Chinese opera.'

'If you don't turn it off I will!'

He lunges across the room and switches it off. 'I can't live with you!

I'm going,' I say bitterly. 'You're a philistine – I've got nothing in common with you.'

I storm out and begin to pack up my things. I'll go back. It's been in my mind like a temptation ever since we flew into Sydney. *The White-haired Girl* has done it. It is the straw in the wind. I see myself catching the train at Central, getting off at Rockdale, lugging my case across the overpass. Will he still be there with his head full of voices, his only companion the lop-eared, brindle dog he found on the tip?

'Well goodbye, I'm going.'

'That didn't last long,' Chris is lying full length on the sofa with his eyes half closed. 'Would you like a cup of coffee before you go?'

'Okay.'

When he gets up to put the coffee on I catch at his sleeve.

'Chris?'

We look at each other and laugh. Nine years of life with the madman in the house above the railway cutting go up in smoke. How could I ever have imagined I could go back. No, for better or worse, I'm married now to this big man with the sleepy eyes and the sense of humour who hates *The White-haired Girl*.

Afterwards she lay beside him in the airless bedroom listening to the love cries of Redfern, the crunch of fist on bone.

'Y'knocked me down y'fucken cunt what'd y' do that for?'

'I only pushed y'.'

Her wedding night hadn't been much of a success. She was still bleeding and Chris had a fixed primitive belief that a menstruating woman would give him the clap. The abortion had been her idea. She couldn't bear the thought of a shotgun wedding and anyway she wasn't sure that he wanted to marry her. He was one of those old-fashioned militants who believed that marriage destroyed your usefulness in the working-class struggle. Of course she wanted him to say, 'Don't worry, we'll have the baby,' but he didn't. He was always good at those fatal silences that decided so much without a word being spoken. So with her legs in stirrups and a drip in her arm she'd had a painful curette in a surgery in the Cross. The toilet was strewn with bloodstained napkins and cotton-balls. She'd fainted twice in the taxi and Chris had to carry her in a fireman's lift through a roomful of people.

The abortion had made a big hole in his money.

'I'll have to ship out again,' he said.

She remembered how relieved he looked, excited even, when he told her he'd picked up for the Brisbane run sailing tomorrow. He had already left her.

She stared at him horrified. 'But you said you loved me.'

'It's all right,' he said. 'It's not the end of the world.'

'It is, it is,' she sobbed. 'I'll never see you again.'

'I'll come across to the West sometime.'

'Sometime,' she said bitterly, 'no you won't, you'll forget about me.'

He looked at her helplessly. 'Well then, we'd better get married.'

But she was worried about Chris's politics. The Party was calling him a Revisionist and had failed to reissue his Party card. Worldwide the Communists were in turmoil. Kruschev had given his speech on Stalin's crimes, the Russians had destroyed the Hungarian revolution, the intellectuals had been expelled or resigned in droves. When Emily joined the Communist Party she had been told you could never resign, it was a lifetime commitment and she was still a good Party girl. She made an appointment to see Eddie Maher, the Secretary of the Trade Union Committee.

'What do you want to know?' he asked her.

'Is it all right to marry him?'

He looked across his desk, smiling at the small, serious woman with the naive eyes.

'Chris is okay,' he said, 'he's like a lot of our waterfront comrades, they keep on butting their heads against a brick wall until the blood flows. They're anarchists. They never give up and they never get any-where. But go ahead and marry him if you want to. He's a good bloke and you might tone him down a bit.'

In the Left Bookshop in Market Street the manager thrust his long furtive face across the counter.

'You've been seen around with that Chris Ryder. I'm warning you, he's in bad odour with the Party.'

'Too late,' she laughed, 'I married him yesterday.'

Next morning, Chris goes off to retrieve his Matador truck. It has been driven all over Sydney while he was at sea. We are full of hope, we will confound the sceptics, we will drive back across the Nullarbor to the little city where my children are waiting and my mother's friends are darkly predicting: 'You won't see hide nor hair of her again.'

Under the tarp Chris has rigged over the roll bars we have stowed the double mattress, drums of water, a spirit stove, camp-oven, kerosene tin, frying pan and billy can. Looking back on that epic journey we made, the Matador trundling along with a top speed of 85 ks, the tarp flapping in the wind, it seems to me like the journey of an ant crawling across the vast map of Australia. Past rivers and towns, salt lakes and farms, rumbling over cattle grids we moved in a cloud of dust pulled inexorably towards the magnet of the great saltbush plains. Occasionally we camped in a caravan park or a showground where we could have a cold shower, but mostly I washed in the kerosene tin, heating the water up on the spirit stove. Sometimes we ordered steak and eggs from a road-side cafe while I fumed at Chris flirting with the waitress. At night, wrapped in blankets in the back of the truck, we slept under a multitude of stars. I have stopped bleeding. I am dying for Chris to make love to me again. Parked above the beach at Port Augusta I search frantically through my port for my diaphragm but it's disappeared.

'Have you got any French letters?' But of course he hasn't.

'Couldn't you get some from the chemist?'

'What, at this hour? Have a heart. We'll fix something up in the morning.'

I sit moodily on the tail of the truck.

'You don't even care. Well, you don't do you? You never have cared.'

'Shut up and go to sleep,' he says.

Down on the beach a party of young folkies are playing their guitars, singing Australian bush ballads.

'Don't just lie there, say something.' But he only turns over and sighs while I nurse my dangerous rage.

'Okay,' I tell him. 'I've had enough of this. I'm going.'

'Going where?' he mutters.

'I'll hook a lift back to Sydney with one of the truckies.'

'Suit yourself,' he says.

Pride drives me on. I can't turn back now.

'Better take some dough then.' He gropes for his wallet.

'Half each. That's fair.'

I take the notes and pick up my port. The light from the folkies' camp fire frames the ring of faces, the clink of bottles, the laughter.

I walk away from the Matador towards the distant town. Only once I turn back, seeing it hunched under a great wheel of stars, the only secure signpost in all this immensity. I sit on my port on the highway, watching the semis like great lighted ships sailing down on me, shaking the earth. What am I doing here? Running away again, and what will happen to the children? *You won't see hide nor hair of her*, but there is nowhere left to run to – only the madman's house above the railway cutting and I'm finished with that kind of love, the kind that risks everything and always fails. Wandering along I am lonely, maybe I can join the folkies and sing all night around their campfire. They are drunk now, singing the most racist song in their repertoire:

> O don't you remember Sweet Alice Ben Bolt,
> Sweet Alice so dusky and dark,
> the Warrego gin with a straw through her nose,
> and teeth like a Moreton Bay shark.

When I reach the Matador I get undressed and climb in, lying close against Chris, groping for his hand.

'Em,' he mutters, 'Em.' He turns towards me and I take him into me, so warm, the slow rolling movement like the endless enveloping motion of the sea. I can hear the Gulf water brushing against the sand.

> The terrible sheepwash tobacco she smoked
> in her gunya down there by the lake . . .

Huge shadows roll down the Flinders Ranges, semis shudder towards us like mirages floating on water, drawing us dangerously close in the wind of their passing.

Early morning in Ceduna, white limestone on the Bight, smell of dust and salt, last touch of civilisation, last reliable water.

Chris fills the drums in the pub yard. An Aborigine in a limp felt hat is chopping wood, his axe strokes thudding in the frosty air. Penong, low scrubby hills, and an old cowboy flogging a country and western tape. He's written a song about his dead son, killed in a Queensland rodeo.

The border, a busted tyre and an empty oil drum, WELCOME TO

WESTERN AUSTRALIA; Eucla, a silent nervous woman pulling petrol among the sand-dunes; a cold beer and a hot shower at Madura. Two old photographs have survived from that time; one of Emily, desolate, dressed in black with a couple of mongrel dogs nosing around her skirts. Another, dead tired, dusty, barefoot, slumped on the running board of the Matador drinking a mug of tea.

They are out in the desert now, on a corrugated dirt road, potholed with bulldust, the carcasses of dead bush animals or a wrecked car chassis on the verge; an occasional water tank dark on the skyline, no trees, only the endless grey monotony of the saltbush plains.

Chris is singing tunelessly:

> I was a canecutter but now I'm at sea,
> stool it and top it and load it up high,
> once cane killed Abel but it won't kill me . . .

'I'll take you to the canefields for a season,' he says. 'We can live in the cane-barracks.'

Emily imagined a shed lined with single stretchers, singleted men coming in exhausted, black from the burn-off, the cane rustling outside.

'Where would we sleep?'

'We could hang up a blanket.'

'But the children. How would the children go to school?'

'You could teach them.'

'I can't, I can't. I have other things to do, books to write.'

'Or we can take a tent,' Chris says, 'and camp out in the big scrubs. It's always cool up there with the mists falling.'

That's better. She can imagine the romance of it. But what irony, to live under that great canopy while Chris cuts it down. Of course she knows what he wants. He wants her to share his wild, wandering, footloose life. But how can she when she wants him to share hers? She remembers waiting for him in Melbourne under a huge oak tree in the Botanical Gardens. He'd come straight out of the stokehold in his greasy overalls with his poems in his pocket. She'd read them, thinking, 'These are a bit rough but they've got something.'

'Why don't you come to Western Australia?' she asked him.

'What would I do there?'

'Don't you want to learn how to write poetry?'

He stared at her amazed. He thought he knew already. When he does come, she buys a pink, candy-striped cotton dress for the occasion and watches him kissing a redhead goodbye on the interstate platform.

'We're going home, Chris,' she says. He is reciting Will Ogilvie:

> On the crimson breast of the sunset the grey selections lie,
> And their lonely grief-stained faces are turned to a pitiless
> sky . . .

Then the generator burns out and the Matador gives up the ghost.

They could have stayed there for days but they were lucky. A few hours later a big semi gives Chris a lift into Cocklebiddy.

'Won't be long,' he tells her. 'I'll ring through to Kalgoorlie and get them to send out the new part. You'd better stay with the gear. They reckon they come in out of the desert and strip an unattended vehicle clean.'

She watches him disappear, waving, in clouds of dust. The silence rolls in. Far away on the horizon the willy-willies dance, bowing and scraping. Is this the Dead Heart, the Great Australian Loneliness?

I am a desert God. Find me if you can. Is there anything out there at all? She takes out Simone de Beauvoir's *The Mandarins* and begins to read. Later she makes herself a cup of tea. When the first streaks appear in the sky the wind springs up, the saltbush rustles and a flock of galahs screeches out of the sunset, flashing the pink underside of their wings. It will be night soon. She shivers. The abrupt changes of temperature in the desert always astonish her. The air is full of a tiny ticking she can't identify, a creep, a whir, a sudden cry. She remembers all the gruesome stories she's read about women raped and murdered in lonely places. She switches on the headlights. Don't panic she tells herself, he'll be back soon. He won't leave me here in the dark alone.

From a long way off she picks up the sound of the approaching car coming from the wrong direction. Feeling suddenly vulnerable she switches the lights off again, but when the car pulls over there are children, a Methodist minister in a dog collar, with a thin, weary wife. Unpacking the car, spreading blankets in the scrub, the wife insists she join them for the evening meal. Grateful for the company she helps the woman lay out the plates on the white tablecloth while the children run around gathering up little sticks for the fire. The parson is on his knees praying by a patch of saltbush. When the semi comes back from Cocklebiddy bringing Chris and the two young truckies with it, how delighted Emily is to see him – even when he tells her he hasn't been able to get through to Kalgoorlie.

'I'm Keith and this is Billy,' says the truckie with the cheeky grin. Billy, wrapped in his own morose thoughts, says nothing. He has lost his holiday pay digging the semi out of a sand-drift on the other side of Eucla.

'I'll give you a hand,' Chris says to the parson's wife.

'You're a true Christian,' she tells him.

Drinking tea round the camp fire Chris recites Banjo Paterson and Billy finds his voice:

> Of all the things I'd like to be
> I'd like to be a sparrer,
> just sittin' on the Princess Bridge and gazin' in the Yarrer.

It's a strange little ditty he'll repeat like a homesick mantra in the days to come.

'I'm only twenty-two,' Keith says, 'but I got a wife and two kids back in Melbourne. Billy's sixteen and he's got nothin' (he giggles) 'not even his paypacket.'

When Emily woke next morning the car had gone and Chris having negotiated the longest tow in history, was knotting the rope to the towbar.

And so it began – those days and nights of eating red dust and diesel oil; Chris, red-eyed from lack of sleep, steering over potholes like a madman. When the towrope frayed and broke he used strands of wire twisted off the station fences. When they snapped and the semi lumbered on he leapt out of the cabin and fired a shot from his 303 to bring them back again. Then the wire broke for the umpteenth time and Keith said they'd had enough.

'You can leave the Matador and ride up front with us.'

'You can't do that,' Chris said. He stood there by the side of the road swaying like some weary giant but still dangerous. There was a long pause.

'That's cool mate,' Keith said, whistling between his teeth, 'let's go then.'

He was interested in Emily or anything else to break the monotony.

He wanted her to travel with him in the semi. 'Away,' he said, 'from all the dust and oil fumes,' but when he got her there he handed the driving over to Billy, and, pinned on the makeshift bed behind the driver's seat, she had to fight savagely for her virtue.

'Have y' got a jealous husband?' he taunted. Emily went thankfully back to Chris and the beleaguered Matador, but the sharp spermy smell of him stayed on her skin for days.

Sometimes she slept in the back and woke to see spindly gums crashing overhead as Chris fell asleep and veered off the road. Only once he gave up, handed over the wheel to Billy and crawled in with her. While the Matador swerved and bucked they lay locked together in a wild climax until he fell backwards to sleep like the dead. Emily lay awake under the gritty blanket, watching the Southern Cross slip down the sky.

So the grotesque cavalcade passed, rolling out of the desert down the wide, empty streets of Norseman, past the twisted gimlets, the ghost town of Coolgardie, the rabbit-proof fences. Why didn't they cut the wire for good, leave the Matador for repairs and catch the train in Kalgoorlie? They would never know. It was as if they were joined in some macabre marriage that could never be dissolved until the final end.

We reach the escarpment at dawn and look down on the city lying in its green bowl with the Swan River meandering through it. We are like the dust bowl Joads gazing down on the Californian orange groves. It's like a miracle, a mirage of the promised land. A few early-risers are out in the streets gazing after us open-mouthed. The semi is badly crippled, great gouts of diesel oil foul the air. The Matador, caked with oil and dust, drags in its wake like an injured insect. When we pull up outside my parents' house in their posh suburb above the river, the children, running out to greet us, stop aghast. Who are these strange inhuman monsters, painted black and red like demons, who have staggered out of the desert?

But life goes on, the stories are soon told, and we go home with my three children to live, as Chris always says, 'in the backyards of the bourgeoisie.'

It is literally true. My father has subdivided the block and built me a grace and favour residence on the old tennis court. Sometimes I still imagine I hear the soft thud thud of the balls, love-thirty, deuce, advantage Emily.

My mother refuses to believe we are married until Chris triumphantly produces our marriage lines. Her friends had predicted that my life was over. With three little kids to keep I would never find another husband. Well, I have found him. And we lie wrapped together in the second bedroom fucking deliriously, with a new diaphragm. (You can buy them over the counter. Small, medium, large.) But it is too late. Willow, called after Will Ogilvie, will be born in early December.

Billy and Keith, stranded in Perth with their crippled semi, are bedded down in my study. It is the least we can do.

But things are turning sour. Keith is making a big play for my sister's young housekeeper. He has also developed a habit of sneaking up behind me while I am doing the ironing. I can feel his erection through his jeans. He wants to know when Chris will be shipping out.

The inevitable always happens. Chris picks up a ship and arrives home with an ultimatum.

'I'm shipping out in half an hour and I've ordered a cab for you in fifteen minutes.'

Keith leaves with black looks and a muttered protest about ingratitude, Billy goes out the door saying:

> Of all the things I'd like to be
> I'd like to be a sparrer,
> just sittin' on the Princess Bridge
> and gazin' in the Yarrer.

I feel a bit guilty. After all they towed us under duress for over two thousand k's but I know I could never handle Keith on my own.

The women in the Union Auxiliary tell me they love being married to seamen.

'Every six weeks is another honeymoon, the kids are yours, and you're your own boss in between.'

But I hate it. I try to write but I can't. I am silent with loneliness.

So after six weeks on the Darwin run Chris pays off the *Lady Isobel* and comes home, to discover that the Matador tool box is missing.

'The bastards!' he says, and I wonder if they are still driving backwards and forwards across the Nullarbor in some other semi, ghosts of a life we might have lived.

Barry Hill

HEADLOCKS
1983

Late in the day the boy went to the front gate to look out for his father. Saturday: his father went down the road for a few drinks on Saturday, and he came home the long way; down the quarry road that gave a view of the sea two miles off, then down the hill towards the few blocks that were still paddocks. The boy met him at the same spot each week, and each week the father met the boy's expectations absolutely – listening to all that he had to say until they were indoors, were eating dinner, and drinking their tea quietly in the kitchen.

One afternoon the boy ran towards his father in the usual way, but found himself pulling up short: someone was with his father . . . When the boy wanted to withdraw like that, as he sometimes did when the man had a few too many drinks and was carelessly attentive, he thought of him as father rather than as the old man. But when things were good he was the old man, just as his father had called grandpa when he was still alive; a disrespectful term thought the relatives, though the boy knew, as his father always had, that it was not.

'Hi, Greg,' his father said. 'This is Mr Morrison, Ed Morrison.'

Greg said hello and the men went on walking.

Ed was about the same age as his father except he had more hair, with more oil on it. A tattoo covered the back of one hand while others seemed about to crawl out of his rolled-up shirt sleeves. As the men strolled along the footpath Greg walked slightly behind them, veering onto the nature strip whenever he tried to keep even. At the front gate he said to his father that the stumps were already in position in the backyard. But his father touched his shoulder and led Ed into the kitchen to meet his mother.

Once Ed had washed his hands and sat down at the table Greg brought out some of his drawings. 'Did you do all these yourself?' Ed said. 'That's good.'

The beer was poured. Greg put his collection of sinkers and hooks on the table, and Ed fiddled with the big hooks as he went on talking. Ed was telling his father about the mussels to be got from the docks at Alexandria, and his father was telling Ed that no-one could have got better mussels than they had been getting from the local piers before the Italians came.

Greg went out into the backyard and came in with his lizards. He put the wooden seed box on the floor and lifted the cellophane. The smell of the dead ones wafted up towards the steaming corn beef that his mother had just placed on the table.

'He forgets to feed them,' his father informed Ed.

'I do not.' Greg looked up by way of appeal.

'No,' the old man added, 'we have trouble with our supply of fresh insects.'

'What you need to do is this,' said Ed, snatching the air. One by one Greg lifted the man's fingers until, wriggling in his palm, the fly appeared.

Mum had made the mayonnaise salad. Onto Ed's plate she piled an eggy oniony section, then Greg was allowed to help himself. It was a hot night; the back door was open, the dog was scratching near the step, and the crickets were going silly.

Ed and the old man were still talking. Mum looked on. Now and then Ed paused to pay her special attention, but at the end of the meal she insisted on clearing the table herself and carrying the dishes to the sink while the men went into the front room. Greg followed the men and sat on the floor near the window, beside the old man's chair. From where he was he could see ginger tufts of hair in his father's ear, and the face of Ed steadily flushing. A faint breeze came in through the venetian blinds.

The Middle East was mentioned again. Greg got up and left the room. He came back with an olive-green book that had as its first picture a painting of a troopship: on the deck dozens of wounded men sat about in the sun, or were stretched in the shade of lifeboats and tarpaulins. 'Yes,' said Ed excitedly, and Greg sat beside him while they thumbed through the pages. Presently, his mother came in waving a postcard.

Two men in shorts stood on a bare stretch of sand, hands behind their backs, grinning. No shirts, only their bare chests as brown or as dirty as their legs. The one with the slouch hat was Ed; the other was Uncle Allen, his mother's brother. 'Bet you haven't seen that for a while,' his mother said to Ed.

While Ed was looking, Greg tried to get as close to the card as possible. He almost scooped it out of Ed's hand.

'Looking at the bloody gun, are yuh,' said Ed. Hanging from his uncle's belt was a large revolver. 'Stand up a tick,' Ed said.

Taking up a position near the door, Ed told Greg to run towards him. 'Come on, just come at me,' he said, leaning forward with his arms loose, as if a dog was going to leap up at his face.

Greg took a few steps. In football the old man had taught him how to mock a run and spin off on the ball of the right foot. But here there was no room and before he got anywhere, Ed had turned him around and was holding the edge of the postcard at his throat. 'You don't really need a gun, see.'

'Now stand there,' Ed said, once he had let go.

Greg waited within inhaling distance of the man's breath. He knew the old man was watching so there was no need to turn around. Ed tightened the roll of his sleeves and fixed the buckle of his belt. 'Now I'll show you some of the crucial points. Your old man might have a bit to learn as well,' he said with a wink. Just then, Greg might well have turned, but Ed was already at work with his finger.

'Here,' he said, pressing a spot on Greg's neck, 'is where they go out cold.' He grimaced as if he had pushed right in.

'Or, this way you don't have to worry about them either.' He pressed his knuckles into the boy's Adam's apple.

'Or here!' Swinging his arm up from the floor he brought his fist just short of the boy's groin. 'You might need to use some of these on the old man, one day. Never know.'

'He won't need to do anything of the sort,' Greg heard his mother say.

Ed laughed.

'I don't want anybody teaching him that sort of thing.' His mother smoked one cigarette a night and she had stubbed it out.

'I'm just giving the kid the science of the show. So he won't have to use guns.' Ed smiled and tapped his empty pockets.

'No, you're not. You're putting ideas into his head, crook ones,' his mother called.

Ed took a good look at the woman.

Greg had never seen his mother so pigheaded. She got like that when she rowed with his father. Now she sat stiff as a broomstick, while Ed shoved back the chairs.

Greg threw himself at the man's belly, butted the soft part so hard that Ed fell back with a grunt against the door. Greg dived at the floor and took hold of the man's knee, tried to bend it. Ed picked him up by the middle, turned him round and locked his wrists behind his back. Greg tried to kick his shins but they danced away.

'That's enough,' his mother snarled.

'One more, Mum.' He went limp until Ed let go.

'Now what you can't do,' Ed was saying, 'is run at someone like a Mallee bull. He'll have you down in no time, even if you're waving a knife.'

They started close, with Greg making a quick chop at the man's neck. A swipe at the other arm. Blocked again. Finally lifted his knee – but collected a hip bone. 'Now stand back and we'll do it again,' Ed said.

Greg was flushed. He didn't speak – couldn't. Catch himself in the mirror, and he'd blubber for sure; catch the old man's eye, and he was done. He got ready to go at the enemy again . . .

'Stop it now, you're upsetting him.'

But Ed took no notice of his mother.

Oh, shut up, Mum, shut up, Greg thought, and then at last he heard: 'Let them go,' and it was the old man's voice and any minute he would . . . yes, *yes*.

This time, Greg thought, if Ed blocks my knee with his hip I'll be able to get my arm over as he bends. Then I'll have him in that headlock. When his face is down and his ears are jammed I'll get him onto the floor and before he can roll, straddle him. All I need to do is get my arm over quick enough . . . He went in with his eyes open. He saw Ed's face until the last instant, right up until they went down – down, it seemed, into the pile of the carpet.

The hot night pressed green and purple into the face and brown shot through his eyes so fast that he missed the first moves beside him. But together they pinned Ed down, one to each arm, then with the old man holding the shoulders, Greg bashed the man's skull against the floor. When the face was still he hit it a few times with the glass bottom of the ashtray.

They lifted together and carried the body outside where it went straight into a sugar bag; the old man tossed it over his shoulder and up the ladder they went to the roof of the garage where they'd piled newspapers and old boxes and wood. They watched the body burn until suddenly when the rocket went off, you didn't see it at all, not until it was coming down again, rekindling in the fall while he and the old man were laughing and yelling, hooting together like mad.

Janette Turner Hospital

AFTER LONG ABSENCE
1986

For years it has branched extravagantly in dreams, but the mango tree outside the kitchen window in Brisbane is even greener than the jubilant greens of memory. I could almost believe my mother had been out there with spit and polish, buffing up each leaf for my visit. I suggest this to her and she laughs, handing me a china plate.

Her hands are a bright slippery pink from the soap suds and the fierce water, and when I take the plate it is as though I have touched the livid element of a stove. In the nick of time, I grunt something unintelligible in lieu of swearing. 'Oh heck,' I mumble, cradling the plate and my seared fingers in the tea towel. 'I'd forgotten'. And we both laugh. It is one of those family idiosyncrasies, an heirloom of sorts, passed down with the plate itself which entered family history on my grandmother's wedding day. The women in my mother's family have always believed that dishwashing water should be just on the leeside of boiling, and somehow, through sheer conviction that cleanliness is next to godliness, I suppose, their hands can calmly swim in it.

I glance at the wall above the refrigerator, and yes, the needlepoint text is still there, paler from another decade of sun, but otherwise undiminished: *He shall try you in a refiner's fire.*

'Do you still have your pieces?' my mother asks.

She means the cup, saucer, and plate from my grandmother's dinner set, which is of fine bone china, but Victorian, out of fashion. The heavy band of black and pale orange and gold leaf speaks of boundaries that cannot be questioned.

'I'd never part with it,' I say.

And I realise from the way in which she smiles and closes her eyes that she has been afraid it would be one more thing I would have jettisoned. I suppose it seems rather arbitrary to my parents, what I have rejected and what I have hung onto. My mother is suspended there, dishmop in hand, eyes closed, for several seconds. She is 'giving thanks'. I think with irritation: nothing has ever been secular in this house. Not even the tiniest thing.

'Leave this,' my mother says, before I am halfway through the sensation of annoyance. 'I'll finish. You sit outside and get some writing done.'

And I think helplessly: It's always been like this, a seesaw of frustration and tenderness. Whose childhood and adolescence could have been more stifled or more pampered?

'But I *like* doing this with you,' I assure her. 'I really do.' She smiles and 'gives thanks' again, a fleeting and exasperating and totally unconscious gesture. 'Honestly,' I add, precisely because it has suddenly become untrue, because my irritation has surged as quixotically as the Brisbane River in flood. 'It's one of . . .' but I decide not to add that it is one of the few things we can do in absolute harmony.

'You should enjoy the sun while you can,' she says. Meaning: before you go back to those unimaginable Canadian winters. 'Besides, you'll want to write your letters.' She pauses awkwardly, delicately avoiding the inexplicable fact that the others have not yet arrived. She cannot imagine a circumstance that would have taken her away, even temporarily, from her husband and children. All her instincts tell her that such action is negligent and immoral. But she will make no judgments, regardless of inner cost. 'And then,' she says valiantly, 'there's your book. You shouldn't be wasting time . . . You should get on with your book.' My book, which they fear will embarrass them again. My book which will cause them such pride and bewilderment and sorrow. 'Off with you,' she says. 'Sun's waiting.'

I've been back less than twenty-four hours and already I'm dizzy – the same old roller-coaster of anger and love. I surrender the damp linen tea towel which is stamped with the coats of arms of all the Australian states. I gather up notepad and pen, and head for the sun.

They are old comforters, the sun and the mango tree. I think I've always been pagan at heart, a sun worshipper, perhaps all Queensland children are. There was always far more solace in the upper branches of this tree than in the obligatory family Bible reading and prayers that followed dinner. I wrap my arms around the trunk, I press my cheek to the rough bark, remembering that wasteland of time, the fifth grade.

I can smell it again, sharp and bitter, see all the cruel young faces. The tree sap still stinks of it. My fingers touch scars in the trunk, the blisters of nail heads hammered in long years ago when we read somewhere that the iron improved the mangoes. The rust comes off now on my hands, a dark stain. I am falling down the endless concrete stairs, I feel the pushing again, the kicking, blood coming from some-where, I can taste that old fear.

I reach for the branch where I hid; lower now, it seems – which disturbs me. Not as inaccessibly safe as I had thought.

Each night, the pale face of my brother would float from behind the glass of his isolation ward and rise through the mango leaves like a moon. I never asked, I was afraid to ask, 'Will he die?' And the next day at school, and the next, I remember, remember: all the eyes pressed up against my life, staring, mocking, hostile, menacing.

There was a mark on me.

I try now to imagine myself as one of the others. I suppose I would simply have seen what they saw: someone dipped in death, someone trailing a shadowy cloak of contamination, someone wilfully dangerous. Why should I blame them that they had to ward me off?

This had, in any case, been foretold.

I had known we were strange from my earliest weeks in the first grade. 'The nurse has arrived with your needles,' our teacher said, and everyone seemed to know what she was talking about. 'You'll go when your name is called. It doesn't hurt.'

'It does so,' called out Patrick Murphy, and was made to stand in the corner.

'With a name like that,' said the teacher, 'I'm not surprised.'

She was busy unfurling and smoothing out the flutter of consent letters which we had all dutifully returned from home, some of us arriving with the letters safety-pinned to our pinafores. The teacher singled out one of the slips, her brow furrowed.

'I see we have our share of religious fanatics,' she said. She began to prowl between the desks, waving the white letter like a flag. 'Someone in our class,' she announced, 'is a killer.' She stopped beside my desk and I could smell her anger, musky and acrid and damp. It was something I recognised, having smelled it when our cat was playing with a bird, though I could not have said what part of the smell came from which creature. The teacher put her finger on my shoulder, a summons, and I followed to the front of the class. 'This person,' said the teacher, 'is our killer.'

And everyone, myself included, solemnly observed. I looked at my hands and feet, curious. A killer, I thought, tasting the double *l* with interest and terror, my tongue forward against the roof of my mouth.

'Irresponsible! Morally irresponsible!' The teacher's voice was like that of our own pastor when he climbed into the pulpit. She was red in the face. I waited for her, my first victim, to go up in smoke. 'Ignorant fanatics,' she said, 'you and your family. You're the kind who cause an epidemic.'

I always remembered the word, not knowing what it meant. I saw it as dark and cumulous, freighted with classroom awe, a bringer of lightning bolts. *Epidemic.* I sometimes credit that moment with the birth of my passionate interest in the pure sound of arrangements of syllables. *Epidemic.* And later, of course, in the fifth grade, *diphtheria*, a beautiful word, but deadly.

I know a lot about words, about their sensuous surfaces, the way the tongue licks at them. And about the depth charges they carry.

My mother brings tea and an Arnott's biscuit, though I have been out here scarcely an hour, and though I have not written a word. I have been sitting here crushing her ferns, my back against the mango tree, remembering Patrick Murphy: how no amount of standings-in-the-corner or of canings (I can hear the surf-like whisper of the switch against his bare calves) could put a dent in his exuberance or his self-destructive honesty.

Once, in the first grade, he retrieved my shoes from the railway tracks where Jimmy Simpson had placed them. In the fifth grade he was sometimes able to protect me, and word reached me that one of his black eyes was on my account. One day I brought him home, and my parents said later they had always believed that some Catholics would be saved, that some were among the Lord's anointed in spite of rank superstition and the idols in their churches. But I was not seriously encouraged to hope that Patrick would be in the company of this elect. When my mother offered him home-made lemonade, he told her it beat the bejesus out of the stuff you could get at the shops. He also said that most of the kids at school were full of ratshit and that only one or two sheilas made the place any better than buggery.

One morning Patrick Murphy and I woke up and it was time for high school. We went to different ones, and lost touch, though I saw him one Friday night in the heart of Brisbane, on the corner of Adelaide and Albert Streets, outside the Commonwealth Bank. The Tivoli and the Wintergarden ('dens of iniquity,' the pastor said) were emptying and he was part of that crowd, his brush-back flopping into his eyes, a girl on his arm. The girl was stunning in a sleazy kind of way: close-fitting slacks and spike heels, a tight sweater, platinum blonde hair and crimson lips. My kind of sheila, I imagined Patrick Murphy grinning, and the thought of his mouth on hers disturbed me. I rather imagined that an extra dollop of original sin came with breasts like hers. I rather hoped so.

I was praying Patrick Murphy wouldn't see me.

From my very reluctant spot in the circle, I could see that his eyes were wholly on his girl's cleavage. I moved slightly, so that my back was to the footpath, but so that I could still see him from out of the corner of my eye. Our circle, which took up two parking spaces, was bisected by the curb outside the Commonwealth Bank. There were perhaps fifteen of us ranged around a woman who sat on a folding chair and hugged a piano accordion. We all had a certain *look*, which was as identifiable in its own way as the look of Patrick Murphy's sheila. My dress was ... well, *ladylike*, I wore flat heels, I might as well have been branded. I hoped only that my face (unspoiled, as our pastor would have said, by the devil's paintbox) might blend indistinguishably with the colourless air.

At the moment of Patrick Murphy's appearance, my father had the megaphone in his hand and was offering the peace that passeth understanding to all the lost who rushed hither and thither before us, not knowing where they were going.

The theatregoers, their sense of direction thus set at nought, appeared to me incandescent with goodwill, the light of weekend in their eyes. I (for whom Friday night was the most dreaded night of a circumscribed week) watched them as a starving waif might peer through a restaurant window.

'I speak not of the pleasures of this world, which are fleeting,' my father said through the megaphone. 'Not, as the world giveth, give I unto you ...'

Patrick Murphy and his sheila had drawn level with the Common-wealth Bank. Dear God, I prayed, let the gutter swallow me up. Let the heavens open. Let not Patrick Murphy see me.

Patrick Murphy stopped dead in his tracks and a slow grin of recognition lit his face. I squirmed with mortal shame, I could feel the heat rash on my cheeks.

'Jesus,' laughed his sheila, snapping her gum. 'Will ya look at those Holy Rollers.'

'They got guts,' said Patrick Murphy. 'I always did go for guts,' and he gave me the thumbs-up sign with a wink and a grin.

At Wallace Bishop's Diamond Arcade, he turned back to blow me a kiss.

It was the last time I saw him before he hitched his motorcycle to the tailgate of a truck and got tossed under its sixteen double tyres. This happened on the Sandgate Road, near Nudgee College, and the piece in the *Courier-Mail* ran a comment by one of the priests. A bit foolhardy, perhaps, Father O'Shaughnessy said, a bit of a daredevil. Yet a brave lad, just the same; and a good one at heart. Father O'Shaughnessy could vouch for this, although he had not had the privilege, etcetera. But the lad was wearing a scapular around his neck.

Rest in peace, Patrick Murphy, I murmur, making a cross in the dust with a mango twig.

'What are you doing?' my mother asks, smelling liturgical errors.

'Doodling. Just doodling.' But certain statues in churches – the Saint Peters, the faulty impetuous saints – have always had Patrick Murphy's eyes.

A few minutes later, my mother is back. 'We've had a call from Miss Martin's niece in Melbourne. You remember Miss Martin? Her niece is worried. Miss Martin isn't answering her phone so we're going over.' They call out from the car: 'She still lives in Red Hill, we won't be long.'

Miss Martin was old when I was a child. She's ninety-eight now, part of the adopted family, a network of the elderly, the lonely, the infirm, the derelict. My parents collect them. It has always been like this, and I've lost count of how many there are: people they check in on, they visit, they sit with, they take meals to. My mother writes letters for ladies with crippled arthritic hands and mails them to distant relatives who never visit. She has a long inventory of birthdays to be celebrated, she takes little gifts and cakes with candles.

By mid-afternoon she calls. 'We're at the hospital. We got to her just in time. Do you mind getting your own dinner? I think we should stay with her, she'll be frightened when she regains consciousness.'

They keep vigil throughout the night.

At dawn the phone wakes me. 'She's gone,' my mother says. 'The Lord called her to be with Himself. Such a peaceful going home.'

The day after the funeral, my father and I drive out to the university.

'It's not easy,' he says, 'trying to get a BA at my age.'

But there is pride, just the same, in this mad scheme I have talked him into. I have always thought of him as an intellectual *manqué* whose life was interfered with by the Depression and the Gospel – (His aunts in Adelaide never recovered from the distress. 'Oh your father,' they said to me sadly, shaking their heads. 'He was led astray.' By my mother's family, they meant. 'We do wish he hadn't been taken by such a . . . We do wish he would come back to a *respectable* religion.') – and whose retirement is now interfered with by all the lives that must be succoured and sustained. 'It's hard to find time to study,' he confesses ruefully.

People will keep on dying, or otherwise needing him.

In the university library, he leafs through books like an acolyte who has at last – after a lifetime of longing – been permitted to touch the holy objects. He strokes them with work-knotted fingers. But we are simply passing through the library today, we are on our way to meet friends of mine for lunch at the staff club. I am privately apprehensive about this, though my father is delighted, curious, secretly flattered. He has never been in a *staff* club lounge.

At the table reserved for us the waiter is asking, 'Red or white, sir?' and my heart sinks. The air is full of greeting and reminiscence, but I am waiting for my father's inevitable gesture, the equivalent of the megaphone outside the Commonwealth Bank. I am bracing myself to stay calm, knowing I will be as angered by the small patronising smiles of my old friends as by my father's compulsion to 'bear witness'. He will turn his wineglass upside down at the very least; possibly he will make some mild moral comment on drink; he may offer the peace that passeth understanding to the staff club at large.

He does none of these things.

To my astonishment, he permits the waiter to fill his glass with white wine. He is bemused, I decide, by his surroundings. And yet twice during the course of the meal, he takes polite sips from his glass.

The magnitude of this gesture overwhelms me. I have to excuse myself from the table for ten minutes.

For a week I have cunningly avoided being home with my parents for dinner, but the moment of reckoning has come. We are all here, brothers and sisters-in-law and nieces and nephews, an exuberantly affectionate bunch.

The table has been cleared now, and my father has reached for the Bible. A pause. I feel like a gladiator waiting for the lions, all the expectant faces turned towards me. It is time. The visitor always chooses the Bible reading, the visitor reads; and then my father leads family prayer.

It should be a small thing. In anyone else's home I would endure it with docile politeness.

It cannot be a concession anywhere near as great as my father's two sips of wine – a costly self-damning act.

It should be a small thing for me to open the Bible and read. There is no moral principle at stake.

Yet I cannot do it.

'I am sorry,' I say quietly, hating myself.

Outside I hug the mango tree and weep for the kind of holy innocence that can inflict appalling damage; and because it is clear that they, the theologically rigid, are more forgiving than I am.

But I also move out of the shaft of light that falls from the house, knowing, with a rush of annoyance, that if they see me weeping they will discern the Holy Spirit who hovers always with his bright demanding wings.

I lean against the dark side of the mango tree and wait. A flying fox screeches in the banana clump. Gloating, the Holy Spirit whispers: *Behold the foxes, the little foxes, that spoil the vines.* One by one the savaged bananas fall, thumping softly on the grass. From the window the sweet evening voices drift out in a hymn. The flying fox, above me, arches his black gargoyle wings.

Jan   Hutchinson

EXTRA VIRGIN

1988

Our friend Janey loved butter. She tossed wedges of it onto huge platters of newly made pasta. She stirred big spoonfuls of it into pots of steaming hot rice. She put lashings of it on mashed potato, watching with delight as golden rivulets coursed down fluffy white mountainsides. She could spread the stuff thicker than anyone else we knew on her breakfast toast. And she could get ounces of it on a crumpet.

'That's what they're for,' she'd explain impatiently, 'all those holes. They're not just air spaces, you know,' she'd admonish us. 'They're there to soak up the butter. And the more you can get in the better.'

Janey had a way with French bread and fresh brie too. 'The chunk method' we called it.

'You just take the chunks and put them together,' she'd tell us. 'A chunk of bread, a chunk of butter, a chunk of cheese.'

It'd be all white and creamy and hard to see the crust through buttery yellow and the raw floury skin of the cheese. Janey would take a bite.

'Go on, try it,' she'd urge with her mouth full.

And we would.

'No, no, no, you've got it all wrong,' she would say. 'Don't slice the bread, break it off. A big piece, like you really mean it. And none of this spreading business,' she'd continue. 'Just pile it on.'

And we'd try.

'Now you're getting the hang of it,' Janey would congratulate.

'She heaps on men in much the same way,' we'd say amongst ourselves after she'd left. 'And licks her fingers clean after each one.'

And we'd laugh.

Janey was the only person we knew who had a butter curler. And used it. She'd invite us all over for afternoon tea. Before our very eyes she'd whip up batches of like-our-mothers-used-to-make scones, turn out steaming date loaves. She'd drizzle thin icing over just-out-of-the-oven orange yeast buns, cut a hot cheese damper into thick uneven wedges. She'd put on fresh coffee and make big pots of tea. She'd set out bowls of jams and conserves she'd made the night before, all glowing and transparent in the sun. Then, just when we'd think that was it, she'd whisk a big bowl of butter curls swimming in iced water out of the fridge, deftly drain and transfer them to pretty glass or thick ceramic or fine bone china depending on her mood or the weather or the numbers or whether the moon was in Scorpio.

Janey had tried all sorts of butter. Salted and unsalted. North coast and South coast. She could argue for hours about the merits of each. She'd visited the dairies, inspected the factories, investigated the additives. She knew her stuff. She refused to buy butter with no name. And she never, ever bought margarine.

'You can't begin to imagine what they put in it,' she'd say whenever she came across a plastic tub in one of our fridges.

Janey liked nothing better than to make her own butter. Once we sat in her kitchen for an entire morning while she whipped at cream with a whisk.

'If you're going to do it at all then you may as well do it right,' she said, and beat on when we suggested an electric beater. Then we de-cided against even thinking of mentioning food processors. Janey beat and beat.

'You'll get RSI, Janey,' we warned.

'They did it in the old days,' she said, 'and if it was good enough for them it's good enough for me.'

And she rinsed with cold running water and added salt, just a touch at a time, testing all the way. She patted it into wooden moulds that had been carved on the other side of the world. She smoothed off the tops and packed them in the fridge in neat rows across the top shelf.

Janey had a collection of butter moulds, of butter dishes, of butter knives. She'd overlook vast numbers of treasures on trestles at the markets. She'd peruse shelf after shelf in the op shops. She'd tip out and sort through cartons of old cutlery at clearing sales. She'd ransack the homes of ageing relatives.

'It'll all be in a museum one day, Janey,' we'd tease, not realising we were only encouraging her. 'The Janey Richardson Memorial Butter Collection.'

Janey found sachets of butter distasteful.

'It's a disgrace,' she'd say, 'the things people think they can get away with these days. And charge you for it,' she'd add loudly, in restaurants or buffet cars. More than once she'd sent back those little foil-wrapped slices and demanded butter in a tiny pot. And got it.

'So they should,' she'd say.

And we'd concentrate hard on the meals in front of us.

Janey not only knew about butter, she knew about the food to go with it. And where to buy it. She had a well-worn path round her suburb from shop to shop. She knew the best deli, the one place to buy free-range poultry. She'd only go to the fish markets late in the week.

'After the fresh catches come in,' she'd said the first time we'd asked.

And she'd winked.

Janey dragged a succession of Friday night lovers shopping with her on Saturday mornings when they'd much rather have still been in bed.

'Now just in here for the olives,' she'd murmur. And each would heave himself after her, pushing fast through crowds speaking in several languages.

'And just up the road here for the coffee,' she'd sing out. 'It's worth it. They roast their own,' she'd reassure. 'The smell, you'll love it.'

And they would.

'You don't mind, do you?' Janey'd ask.

And they wouldn't.

'You're right, Janey,' they'd say, one after the other, all the way home.

Janey swore by the butcher where they cured their own meats.

'When you gonna get married girl?' the butcher would ask, week after week, year in year out. 'Time a young girl like you settled down. Find a good bloke. Eh, what about you? You gonna marry this nice lady?'

'Nope,' Janey'd drawl as she eyed off the suspended salami and looped cabanossi not long out of the smoke room. 'I'm not the marrying type.'

'Where do you find them all?' we asked Janey once.

'Not at the supermarket, that's for sure,' she said.

Janey detested supermarkets.

'Only good for toilet paper and detergent,' she'd say. 'You'd never want to buy food at one.'

And she didn't.

If Janey had to go to a supermarket she'd find a continental one. She'd buy imported cans, imported tubes, imported packets. She'd pause every time over the shelf of olive oil in glass-stoppered bottles.

'So,' she'd pounce, 'what do you think it is?'

'What?'

'Extra virgin,' she'd say. 'And how do you get to be one?'

We'd noticed that Janey was not herself.

'What's eating you, Janey? You okay?'

'Why shouldn't I be?' she'd snapped.

'Not a man?' we pursued.

'Don't be silly.'

But Janey wasn't all right. We could tell. When she unexpectedly cancelled one of her afternoon teas, at very short notice, we knew something was up.

And we told each other.

'Something's up with Janey,' we said.

'What's got into you, Janey?' we tried again.

'Oh nothing,' she paused. 'Much.'

There! We knew. All along. It had to be a man.

Janey was the kind of person who could see the bus you wanted coming from the stop outside Farmers while you were waiting outside the County Council.

'So why can't she see what she does to herself?' we all thought. 'There's just one after the other.'

But it took a drive to the mountains and the promise of a Devonshire tea to get it out of her. On the way up in the car the tension was so smooth and yellow you could have cut it with a butter knife.

On the veranda of the tea shop it wasn't hard to miss that Janey drank her tea weak and black and she barely nibbled at her scone.

'Janey?' we coaxed her like a tired child, through white mouthfuls of dough and whipped cream run through with the shiny new red of real strawberry jam.

'I've been to a doctor,' Janey finally opened up.

'And?'

We'd stopped eating. We sat on the edge of our chairs. We waited. We listened.

We feared the worst. Janey never got sick. We knew that.

'A doctor?'

'Well, I wasn't myself.'

'We knew. All along. Didn't we?' we all agreed.

'Wanted to spend all day in bed. Alone. Asleep.'

'And?'

'So I went.' Janey drew in a quick brave breath. 'She said: "I'll have to do a few tests. I'll need to take a bit of blood." Well, you know what that means?'

'What?' We weren't too sure and not keen enough to suggest.

'Well,' she went on, 'the results came back.'

'Cholesterol levels,' Janey wailed. 'My cholesterol levels. They're up. Way beyond buggery.'

'Oh, Janey.'

It was all we could say.

'So you know what that means?'

And we did.

And we shuddered at the thought of it. For Janey, of course.

But Janey wasn't going to let a little thing like that get her down. She'd made up her mind. Overnight. She'd follow medical instructions. No red meat, no fats, no dairy. And she meant it. She was serious. She'd get by.

'I'll get by,' she said. 'It's not the end of the world.'

And of course it wasn't.

'Course it's not, Janey,' we said. 'You'll be right.'

And we hoped she would.

'You'll be okay, Janey,' we said. 'We know you will.'

We were being supportive.

'At least she didn't say no sex,' we said, reading off the scrawl she'd handed to us.

We were being encouraging.

'Nope,' she said, 'that too.'

'Whoever would have thought it,' we would say to each other later.

'Just not what you would have expected,' we would reassure each other in our surprise.

'Trust Janey to turn the tables on us like that,' we would shake our heads.

For once we'd been wrong. We found it hard to believe.

For Janey gave up men the day she gave up butter.

'But, Janey? But why?' we all asked.

We wanted to be told. We needed to know. We were her friends.

'Why, Janey?' we gave it a last go.

'Bad for the heart,' was all she said.

Susan   Johnson

SEEING

1988

The things you see, I am thinking to myself as a man goes by, his large belly a moving, writhing mass in front of him. The cotton of his T-shirt is pulled tight across it, the flesh beneath alive and rippling like sea-snakes in a bag. I read a story once about a young girl in India who ate some fertilised food and a snake hatched in her stomach: she only knew it was there because it began to chirp quietly like a baby bird or a finch. I believe there was some laborious operation to retrieve it but luckily it turned out to be the non-poisonous type, its eyes used to the wet dark of the human stomach. I watch this man's middle-aged belly, conscious of the presence of snakes. It lolls and sways, benign fat probably, untutored; totally unlike the learned belly of a belly dancer sending out fleshy waves from her ribs. His is most busy nonetheless, never completely becalmed for a second.

I take all this in with my one eye: I am listening to footsteps, my ear pressed hard to the ground, my other eye scrunched up in the dark against the towel. I lie like a star, my arms and legs spread and I sift hot sand with my fingers. I listen to the footsteps booming up through the sand, subterranean and immense, a giant's throb. The man and his animated stomach move on, I can hear the squeal of the sand.

The sun falls upon us, heavy and sweet. I turn my head and the eye that has been released from the dark is briefly entertained by a series of yellow and purple shapes: dots, circles, cartwheels, blemishes, until its pupil adjusts to the light. When I can see again my glance falls on a group of teenagers, Italian or Lebanese, their fierce upswept bodies chiacking in the sand, a ghetto blaster issuing vibrations. A girl in a white bikini, large-boned and fleshy, her murky skin still carrying the marks of her clothes, is sitting astride her boyfriend. He lies pinned to the ground beneath her, a thin strip of humanity, her long breasts wobbling gently in his face. The teenagers realise they are being photographed by a group of wandering tourists and the girl straddling the boy begins to rock back and forth upon his body, rubbing her small white bikini pants and their contents up and down his belly, leaning over to kiss his open mouth. The tourists love it and loud American voices call out *right on, honey* and *hey, baby* and she arches her back and rears her head, bouncing now in time to the music. The teenagers giggle, the photographers snap.

I look to see if Louis is watching. His head is turned away from me and I can't tell if his eyes are opened or closed. He lies spread-eagled too, the swell of his back rises and falls with his breathing, his blue Speedos cut ever so slightly into his flesh. I have watched him settle into the sand, he always wriggles slightly, looking for a comfortable place for the soft sack between his legs to fall, a gentle displacement of elements. Women do it too, for their breasts; a lovely ritual, kind of sly and private, the soft tissue spilling out at the side.

With one foot I scrape my toenail up his leg, then pinch the sliver of tendon at the back of his foot with my big toe and the next. My toes are very strong, prehensile, and when he doesn't respond I lean over him, my breasts resting on his hot back. *He-llo,* I say, speaking into his oily ear like a Dalek or a computer voice, *is anybody list-en-ing.* I peer down into his sunglasses and see that his eyes are open and he is watching something closely. I crawl over his back, resting momentarily on top of him, my body pressed into his, his bottom pushing plumply against my pubic bone, the heat rising from him like odour. I thrust into him just once, but quickly, and roll onto the towel next to him: he rolls over and cradles me, spoon-fashion, and I push my buttocks down into his hot lap. His large arms circle my head and I am locked in a small space, satisfied. I look out from between his arms and see a little girl.

She is between eight and ten but she is one of those children who carry the adult in their face. She has an intelligence in her eyes, her eyebrows are straight and black, her mouth swollen and pretty. She is naked, tanned so deeply she seems no longer Caucasian, and she wears a necklace of white shells around her dark neck. Her body is sinewy, tough; her little belly round and perky. She has black curling hair, real ringlets, and her teeth shine whitely in her head.

She walks towards us across the sand then sits down with her back to us, but close enough so I can see the soft down on her shoulders.

She swings around every now and then to pick up a shell behind her, chattering and laughing to herself. Her legs are very wide apart, each leg splayed right out on either side of her body like a ballet dancer or an athlete stretching her ligaments. The bones in her feet arch up like a spine, the crease between her buttocks is white from under-exposure. A little pile of sand nestles there, the tiniest sandcastle, which rises and falls with each shift of a buttock. She is doing something with the sand in front of her, a tunnel perhaps, or another castle, and I cannot help but wonder what she looks like from the front: her legs spread wide, the tiny lips between grazing the sand like a sea creature, its layered face nuzzling wetly into the earth.

As I watch she stands up, laughing, shaking off the sand and runs down to the water, her arms open wide, her head thrown back in the air.

Louis and I watch as the girl plunges hard into the water, dives below the waves and then runs up the beach to a woman lying face-up in the sun. The woman has the same unkempt hair; she sits on an old faded sarong, her breasts flat and wizened from child-bearing. The girl dumps more shells in her lap then quickly runs in our direction again: she begins a series of wild cartwheels, her hair frenzied and dripping, her body undulating and graceful, loose as a snake. She does a backward flip, arching her back high up in the air, and suddenly the fine line of her vagina is turned towards us: hairless, highly coloured, perfectly formed. She stays completely still for perhaps thirty seconds then moves into another cartwheel but quickly this time, so that each part of her body is no more than the whole. She is laughing wildly, she never once looks in our direction and it is impossible to tell whether she is aware of us as an audience or completely unselfconscious. The tourists have moved on, the teenagers are swimming, the beach is almost empty. I watch her closely for signs of theatre but she is diligently noncommittal: untiring, fluid as water, mesmeric.

She flips herself backwards again, exposing herself. I can feel Louis's cock begin to stiffen, almost imperceptibly at first, just the slow creep of material beneath my buttocks as his cock fills and lengthens, swelling out its plump head. Her tiny vagina lies completely open now, revealed in its little crinkled folds, frilled and gleaming. Louis breathes into my neck, his cock like a bone at my back. He swings one large arm across me now and kisses me on the shoulder, placing a warm open hand on my thigh. I turn my head to look at him, and push his fat fingers away. *I've been menstruating too long for your tastes*, I tell him angrily as I stand up, *and I don't get turned on by children*. He falls back on his towel with an exasperated click of the tongue, his cock still straining against shiny cloth.

I walk fast back along the hot sand to the car, holding my hair away from my sweaty neck with one hand. When I open the door I am hit by a blast of fevered air; I open all the doors and lay a towel across the burning upholstery so that I can sit down. When I am settled I look out and see the little girl with the woman I assume to be her mother heading in my direction, the child dressed now in blue shorts. For a moment I think they mean to speak, but they continue talking to each other and pass right in front of the car. The girl places a tiny hand on the bonnet to steady herself: I notice her nipples are pale and insubstantial on her flat chest, she is not even pubescent. She briefly looks up as she does this, running her hard little hand along the scorched surface with a child's uninformed sensuality, tough and plain. I see clearly she is only an unfettered girl in the sun at the beach, a holy child in the uncharted world of adults.

I look out and feel a sharp pain as I watch Louis still lying on sand. He rests on his back with one arm across his face, beached. There is a certain vision behind his eyes, of highly coloured folds; moist, brilliant, sensually moving. I know because I can see it too: I am thinking of snakes, the human belly and an unselfconscious girl child. I am thinking of Louis, of the things we see and the things we don't, and of vast, unnavigable distances.

MR BERRINGTON

1987

We liked our dresses very much. They were blue with little white spots. They were made by our mother's dressmaker. Our spotted frocks we called them.

'What pretty dresses,' a woman at the shop said, 'and matching too. Are you twins?' she asked.

'Our frocks are from Mr Berrington,' I said. 'And yes, we are twins,' I told her. 'I'm ten and she's nine.'

It did not seem at all strange then that Mr Berrington provided new dresses for us . . .

I thought it would be simple to write something about him, about Mr Berrington. Simple, an everyday thing like taking off clothes and stepping with a wise smile into a warm shower. Simple like that. But it is not simple.

First I must explain something about my father. He was always seeing me or other people off at the bus stop or the station.

'I'll come to the train with you,' he'd say at the last minute, just before it was time to set off. His coming to London to see off the boat-train was unexpected. Because of this habit of his it should have been expected. On that occasion Mr Berrington, after consulting his watch, said that it looked as if the train would be leaving on time. He moved his folded raincoat from one arm to the other and held open the compartment door for my mother and me to climb in. Then he shook hands with my father. He hoped, he said, that my father would have a pleasant journey back to the Midlands. It is necessary to say here that I remember clearly that long summer in Germany in 1938. I was supposed to be improving my German and my mother was pretending to be finding a suitable place in which I should study music; an ambition she retained even after the war started and even when she knew I could not sing and, after ten years of laborious piano lessons, had made only the slightest progress.

The following year, on the day war was declared, when we heard Mr Chamberlain's voice on the radio saying 'Britain is at war with Germany,' my father wept. Knowing the suffering brought about by the Great War he could not believe that there would be another one. He had spent some time then in prison for refusing to fight and had, after the war, brought home a bride from Vienna. He met my mother when he was working with the Quaker Famine Relief taking meals to schoolchildren in Austria.

'Is Mr Berrington coming?' I asked my mother while my father was praying in the front room. 'Yes,' she said, 'of course he's coming to lunch as usual.' A sense of safety and relief seemed to pass through me. It was a feeling that, in the familiar shape of Mr Berrington, everything was to be 'as usual'. I have never forgotten this. I was sixteen then.

If I write about Mr Berrington it is also necessary to add a few things about our family because he was for a very long time 'The Friend of the Family'. Perhaps it would be more accurate to say he was my mother's Friend. Looking back on the way in which she treated him towards the end, I realise that it is only when people have been very close, intimate is perhaps the word, that they can hurt each other as my mother repeatedly hurt Mr Berrington. In the face of her unkindness and anger he remained quiet and dignified. Needing, I suppose, to be near her, he smoked his one pipe after supper while she, with great noise and temper, flung open the windows on the coldest nights because, she said, the foul smell he made disgusted her. Perhaps I should explain here that my mother, having enjoyed the few last years of the Hapsburg Empire and after suffering the starvation and poverty in post-war Vienna, had looked forward to England as a romantic answer to all her desires. She had been disappointed. At times, because of her own unhappiness, she had the gift of making everyone unhappy.

Mr Berrington lived alone in a house which was bigger and better than those in the surrounding streets and he died alone. He had been dead for about a week when the police, responding to a call from a neighbour, broke into his house. Because the hedges were so high, uncut for a long time, the neighbour said she did not see Mr B. very often but it was now some days since she had clapped eyes on him and she was just wondering . . .

Shortly before his death he sent me a letter saying in his kind and rather shy way that he had heard that my little girl now had a baby brother and he hoped the children would grow up to be healthy and happy. He was enclosing, he wrote, a little present in the letter.

After his death my mother, because of my training, asked me if Mr Berrington would have suffered for a long time. Did he lie there choking and trying to call out, she wanted to know. Had he been helpless and conscious, praying that someone would come? She had not attempted to visit him when he had not come to the house as usual. Would he have died at once, she asked, in his sleep?

Yes, I told her, yes he would have just gone on sleeping. But how could I know.

The police were surprised, they said, because his bedroom door was locked. My father, who went there with them, explained that Mr Berrington belonged to an age in which people did lock their bedroom doors even when they lived alone.

Is there any point in writing an account of the life of an ordinary man who never attracted public attention for anything he did. Well, perhaps. Professor Peter Gay has recently shattered long-held images of Victorian domesticity by his account of an English teacher in a small New Hampshire College. Not that Mr Berrington was an ordinary man. He came from a long-established professional family. A barrister and a KC he must have been the envy of many of his colleagues. He was the chairman of many legal committees and was on the boards of a number of charities. He belonged to a bridge club and a tennis club and was a member of the local branch of the Conservative Party. He was a church-warden. He had never married. Up till the very last years of his life he had an elderly unmarried housekeeper who occupied the upper rooms in his house. He did not replace her when she died. My mother bought toilet rolls for him because he was shy about asking for them in a shop. The supermarket as we know it did not exist then. My father gave him copies of *Peace News*, which he always folded carefully into his breast pocket.

No-one would have guessed Mr Berrington's occupation from his appearance. The last time I saw him was from the front seat on the top deck of a Midland Red bus at the terminus behind New Street station. It was a place crowded with buses and lorries and great horse-drawn wagons. A brewer's dray does not go as fast as a motor vehicle but neither can it be stopped quickly. Suddenly I saw Mr Berrington crossing the street. He was still the same, his large head covered with short grey hair, his spectacles small on his large immobile face. Over one arm he had his folded raincoat and he was carrying his briefcase and umbrella. He walked slowly, as an old man walks, weaving in and out of the traffic as if unaware of it and unconcerned. He seemed untroubled by the noise and the dried horse dung blowing in his face. If he was troubled he did not show it. He resembled a badger. A *Wind in the Willows* badger. With that unrealistic sense of feeling that I would be able to see him at some other time I did not go down to the street. I sat there watching him, thinking that I would run down and run after him. I hesitated and did not go and quite soon, with a few grinding jerks, the bus started off and I lost sight of him straight away.

My mother taught German in evening classes and Mr Berrington attended them. He must have been attracted by the language and its literature. Later he came to our house for lessons. Sometimes she went to his house. When they sat together over a text, even if it was only a grammar, it could be said, *Galeotto fu il libro e chi lo scrisse* but it was many years before I realised this.

For as long as I can remember Mr Berrington came for Sunday lunch. My sister and I looked forward to his coming. He brought magazines for us. Every week there was a story in one of them about Quick Change Pearl. She was a detective who slipped into telephone boxes, emerging instantly in different clothes. In many disguises she solved one mystery after another. The magazines were also held underneath Mr Berrington's raincoat so we never knew, when we watched him coming down the street, whether he had remembered to buy them or not. We admired Quick Change Pearl and emulated her, stripping off our clothes in the cupboard under the stairs and putting on other things. It was dark in there and once my sister stepped into the pail of waterglass where the preserved eggs were.

'She has no opinions of her own, she is the kind of woman,' Mr Berrington was saying to my mother, 'who forms some sort of muddled thought from the latest thing she has read in the newspaper.' He was talking about Aunt Daisy and my mother, soothed and good-humoured, said never mind about the eggs . . .

Before meals Mr Berrington had a way of looking unconcerned. He seemed, in Germany too, to blunder into the dining rooms of the hotels as if a meal was not the thing he was seeking. Because Mr Berrington called the midday meal luncheon we were not allowed to say dinner though this was the acceptable middle-class term for the Sunday meal, Evensong usually starting at six-thirty. My mother wanted us to speak nicely like Mr Berrington, and to hold our knives and forks properly. 'The handle of the knife must be inside the palm of the hand,' she said, 'like this.' Firmly she pressed the knife handle into place. 'Barth,' she said, 'and parth, you must say are, barth and parth, not bath and path.'

'Don't make me laff,' I said.

My father and Mr Berrington exchanged the texts of the sermons at their respective churches during the first course and the weather forecast while the pudding was served. My mother, who was clever and charming – attracting many admirers – possessed a wonderful ability to literally look black and the outlook for any meal was stormy.

Later Mr Berrington would stand in the kitchen holding a tea towel. Only my mother could wash the dishes and the rest of us stood about waiting to dry them. And only those who knew the order of things in the cupboards could put away the plates and cups and the cutlery.

'*Wir wollen uns der Liebe freu'n*,' when Mr Berrington sang it was like a bee humming and the words could hardly be heard:

> Mann und Weib, und Weib und Mann
> Reichet an die Gottheit an . . .

we knew the words.

In this hesitant singing was Mr Berrington secretly teasing my mother, making half-hidden declarations?

On some Sundays my mother went to Mr Berrington's house for afternoon tea and German conversation. We waited, in our nightdresses, at the top of the stairs, for the two pieces of sugar bread she would bring, wrapped in a paper napkin, in her handbag. My father prowled up and down the hall. He called out at times telling us to go to bed. He was restless as on the nights of her evening classes when the train was late because of the fog.

Mr Berrington was remarkably generous. I understand now, but did not then, that his generosity enabled my mother to re-establish her own good taste which she had suppressed in order to fit in with the dreary surroundings in which she found herself. She had her own dressmaker and Mr Berrington gave the impression, without actually saying anything, that he liked to see her in good quality clothes. I do not know if my father minded. I never heard him make a critical remark. He often paid my mother compliments, perhaps putting into words the things Mr Berrington did not say. It was some time before I came to the conclusion that Mr Berrington did admire and praise her but, of course, only when other people were not there. Clytemnaestra has, at one point to remind Electra:

> But when people judge someone, they ought
> To learn the facts, and then hate, if they've reason to.

In the story 'What Men Live By' Tolstoy says, *It was not given to the mother to know what her children needed for their life.* If the words 'mother' and 'child' are exchanged another very real truth emerges. In spite of social changes the isolation and loneliness of the hidden relationship still exists.

Perhaps my first realisation that it was not usual for a family to have a friend like Mr Berrington came during the long golden summer in 1938. I resolved during that summer, after refusing to eat and speak for two days, to try to be like Mr Berrington. Quick Change Pearl's qualities belonged to childhood. I would in future be considerate and thoughtfully measured and kind always. But for how long can the ordinary person manage this?

We are on our way to Germany. In the train I am possessive and careful over my mother, pleased to have her to myself. My father, coming at the last minute to see us off, disappears as the train begins to move. I make my mother have the corner seat. I stroke her dress and tell her she looks nice. I sit close to her. I like her perfume. She gives me some, a tiny dab behind one ear. 'What is the boat-train like?' I ask her.

It is a surprise, when we reach London, to see Mr Berrington on the platform with his luggage and two porters.

'Are we taking Mr Berrington then?' I ask, indignation forcing tears.

'He's taking us,' her whisper is a hiss. 'Behave yourself!' She gives my arm a little shake. The station swims with people and noise. I can't speak. I stumble along behind the porters. We have to change stations for the boat-train.

Everybody is boarding the boat-train and luggage is being stacked in the vans. My mother and Mr Berrington have given up trying to make me reply to their remarks. I like Mr Berrington and I don't know why I can't say anything to him. I have always talked to him, especially since I have been at boarding school, and he asks my opinions about all sorts of things. I can't even look at Mr Berrington. It is not his fault.

'There's Daddy.' Suddenly I see my father making his way towards us through all the people. 'Daddy!' I call him.

'I came on the same train,' my father says, 'but not first class.' He is white-faced. 'I travelled on a platform ticket,' he says apologetically, 'and had to pay when I got to London.'

We all stand together in a little group and my father and Mr Berrington discuss the weather and decide that the crossing should be smooth. Mr Berrington checks the station clock with his watch and says it looks as if the boat-train will be leaving on time.

'Stay on deck,' my father says to me, 'and then you won't be seasick.' I remember being dreadfully seasick once all over my father. He said then it was the bad air in the overcrowded cabin. We should have stayed, he said then, on deck even though there was a storm. 'Get a sailor,' my father says to me, 'to tie you in a deck chair.'

Mr Berrington moves his folded raincoat from one arm to the other and holds open the door of the compartment for my mother and me to climb up. Before following us he shakes hands with my father and hopes he will have a pleasant journey back to the Midlands.

As the train begins to move, my father walks alongside on the platform. The train gathers speed and my father runs smiling and waving. His face, anxious and sad behind the smile, is the last thing I see.

'LIFE PROBABLY SAVED BY IMBECILE DWARF'

1992

(*Index entry in Ronald W Clarke's* Freud: The Man and the Cause, *Granada, 1982; for which exists only one slim and secretive paragraph of exposition.*)

Is the tape recorder on? Well, let me see.

It was a long time ago now of course. Vienna was still very lovely in those days, before so many cars filled up the streets with their noise and their roars, like great metal predators. There were more trees along the boulevard, the Ringstrasse. It was quieter, too, and the light was clean and more clear. Women were more beautiful, hats, red lips, men more polite, still bowing and with gloves.

I was only a junior nurse when Dr Deutsch admitted him, but I remember it well. It was some time in April, 1923. I remember the exact month because it was the very same month in which my Claus proposed marriage; I was in love, you see. Well one day in April Dr Deutsch brought in his patient Dr Freud for a biopsy. (We didn't know at that stage that he had cancer of the jaw; it seemed more likely to be benign, what we call a leukoplakia: smokers get them all the time.) One of the other nurses, I recall, came over to me and whispered, 'It is that sex doctor Freud; I'll bet he has contracted a cancer for his sins,' and she squinted her eyes and looked maliciously in his direction. I shall never forget it. Greta, her name was. For myself I was surprised at how solid and how forceful he actually appeared. He was almost sixty-seven, and you think to yourself: sixty-seven, maybe cancer: frail, shrivelled. But he was not like that at all. Those photographs you showed me – where he looks at the camera directly and rudely, so like a man – that is more like it. He was elegantly dressed, carried a cane, wore a hat, had a neatly trimmed white beard above a black satin tie, oh, and a watch chain, as was the fashion those days, hanging from his waistcoat. Gold rings on his fingers. All very bourgeois. And, would you believe it, he came to the hospital smoking a cigar like a chimney! Ach! So stupid!

Dr Freud was supposed to be admitted for a quick biopsy and then taken home. He had an appointment with Dr Hajek, a rhinologist – a nose doctor, would you believe – in the outpatient clinic. So we hadn't booked him a bed, thinking there was no need. Not foreseeable, any-way. But then later Dr Hajek came striding up the corridor towards me and said in a loud voice (he was a very loud man) 'My patient Dr Freud has lost more blood than expected. We will leave him here overnight for observation. Arrange a bed if you please.' Well, can you imagine? Arranging beds wasn't my task but I fixed it up anyway, them being men of such importance, me being young and looking up to such men. (And not knowing then the sort of things I know now.)

You said this new biography will have lots of bits and pieces that the others left out – what did you call it? – 'marginalia based'. Well let me just tell you something really good. Dr Freud had a thing, a strange thing, about numbers, a superstition, a dread. You knew that already? Ach, never mind. Anyway, with some trouble I had found him a bed in Ward 5, but he straightaway objected. 'Wrong number,' he mumbled with his hand up to his jaw. 'Wrong number.' He shook his head at me stern-like. I could see he was in pain and the bandages around his face were already soaking crimson, so I tried to be kind and settle the matter quickly. I took Dr Freud by the arm and led him to the tiny utility room, out towards the back, where we kept the dwarf. It was a room, incidentally – I remember it now – where there remained on the wall a portrait of the late emperor, Emperor Franz Josef. You used to see them everywhere in the days of my youth, in banks, in post offices, our Emperor with fluffy sideburns, but on his death in 1916 they all suddenly disappeared. But someone had retained just this single one, and hung it up regardless. It made you feel you had slipped a little backwards in time – with the old Emperor looking on, alive as ever in his picture. Anyway the room – numberless, as it happened – had only two cots and was very stuffy and dark, and not really fitted out for taking patients at all. But then the dwarf was an idiot, and didn't seem to notice. I helped Dr Freud onto the cot and then I said to Jacob –

that's the dwarf – I said 'Jacob, this man is important. He is a doctor. He is good. You look after him, Jacob.'

Let me tell you about Jacob. He was just over one metre tall and very fat for his size, in addition, that is, to being an idiot. Every now and then, when he was sick (which was often) we had him in at the hospital, staying in the utility room. We didn't put him in a ward because he tended to disturb all the other patients with his songs. Always singing was Jacob. Usually it was lullabies, but rather disjointed and hard to follow, if you know what I mean. I think he made them up. All moonlight and mothers, sometimes bits of Yiddish. Starry nights, soft winds, that sort of thing. A bit of humming, too.

Jacob – this will surprise you – had both a mother and a wife. We think of these people as alone somehow, don't we? But Jacob lived with his small family in an apartment only two doors away from my rooms: that was how I knew. His mother was a tall and willowy woman, about forty, I think. She looked like a silent movie star, very dark and pale, a lovely face with definite lips of the sort that men of my generation go for: tightly pursed, pointed, and in the shape of a heart. Grey eyes – beautiful – a remote and rather nowhere-looking gaze. Anyway, I only spoke to her once or twice, so I can't really say we were actually acquainted. But I saw her a lot, standing at the window of her apartment that fronted the street, looking straight out. She would just stand there and stare. Sometimes men paused or slowed down as they walked past, but she never seemed to notice them. She just stood looking out. Sort of desolate and thoughtful.

The daughter-in-law, I must say, was much more interesting: you must put her in your book. Bertha, her name was. She was an idiot, too. I often wondered how they got together, Jacob and Bertha, how they managed to find each other at all in such a large city, and avoid the institutions. Anyway, Bertha was normal-sized but had, poor woman, the strangest condition. She had some kind of facial palsy that fixed her face rather awkwardly in a permanent smile. It was quite disconcerting. Her head hung down to one side, and her mouth tilted upwards. I remember I first met her on my way to the subway on Karlsplatz – I was meeting my Claus after work and we were going off together to have tea with his mother. I saw, from a distance, that a man was accosting her. He was proposing obscenities and she had her face turned away from him, sad and smiling. Her cheeks were very red and her eyes brimmed with tears, but the contradicting smile must have given this fellow the wrong message. He had his hand on her breast, and there she was smiling. I rushed up to the man and struck him with my carry-bag. 'How dare you!' I said. 'How dare you take advantage!' (I was very confident for my age.) Bertha immediately recognised me as some kind of neighbour, stepped forward and clutched my arm. So I was hitting with one side and had the idiot on the other. The man immediately withdrew. Seeing my nurse's uniform perhaps he thought me an authority of some kind. Anyway, he withdrew. I took Bertha by the hand and delivered her home, forgetting entirely about my meeting with Claus and the appointment with his mother. (Later I remembered, and had to write a note of apology, on pretty coloured paper, as was the custom in those days. Mind you, it did Claus no harm at all to be left waiting and expectant.)

I actually saw Bertha quite often after that. Believe it or not we became good friends. Sometimes on Sundays we would walk down to the park together, arm in arm. On the Sundays, that is, that Jacob was in hospital. I can't for the life of me imagine what we talked about – Bertha being as she was, though not as dim as you might expect – but I recall that our short times together were pleasant. Apart from Claus, who, as a working man, worked very long hours, I didn't really know many people in the city. (My family, you see, were all back in Eisenerz.) So I enjoyed her company. When Jacob came home from the hospital we sometimes, all three, went out walking together – but not very often. I didn't mind being seen in the company of Bertha, but with the two of them together we were really very conspicuous, and attracted attention. Once in the park a little girl screamed and burst into tears when she saw us coming, all three, along the path towards her. A terrible thing. A real sweetie, too.

I forgot to mention, by the way, that Bertha was employed. Well, part-time, in fact. She was employed doing menial chores two days a week at the home of Karl Kraus – you may have heard of him – the notorious writer of nasty pamphlets. The story goes that Karl Kraus had been out walking one day – no doubt on the lookout for scandals to print and embarrass – and spied our dear Bertha. Interested, for some reason, he followed her home where he proposed to the mother a contract of employment. I have no idea – it seems so rash and irresponsible – why she accepted. They did not appear hard up, but then you never can be sure with other people, can you? And to such a man!

One day the mother came to me – it was already evening (the lamps were on) and I was just home from work – and asked me if I would go and fetch Bertha from Herr Kraus's house. It seems she was late, much, much later than usual. Why the mother didn't go herself I really don't know, though now that I think about it she hardly ever went out. Anyway, it was the very first time she had come to my rooms, and as she was a commanding and mysterious woman, I felt it must be important and so agreed to the errand. The mother handed me a piece of paper with the address printed on it in a perfectly neat hand, and I set out through the dark.

Can you imagine? I was asked to wait in the parlour while a woman went to fetch her. Very fancy it was; very bourgeois. Long mirrors, Turkish rugs, silk coverings on the furniture, two columns in the door-way with identical candlesticks, stiff chairs, Venetian glass. Before the woman returned, there was Karl Kraus himself – much kinder looking than I had imagined, and rather vulnerable, I think, behind those rimless glasses – leading Bertha by the hand and bringing her forward. He said something like: 'So you have come to fetch Bertha, Bertha the very symbol of Vienna herself: beguiling grin on the outside, crescent, conventional, covering like a mask the imbecile vacancy within.' Just like that! Those very words! And he said this, mind you, in such a friendly tone that for a moment I was not sure at all how to respond. But then I realised what he had said, how unpleasant, how uncalled for, and seized Bertha from him, turned swiftly and left, without uttering in reply a single word. Such an awful man! I shall never forget it.

But I have digressed, haven't I? It is the Freud story, isn't it, you wish to know.

Dr Freud was placed, as I said, in the utility room with Franz Josef and the idiot dwarf Jacob. He seemed settled when I left him, and I assumed he would sleep. I went on with other duties nearby, just up the corridor, and to be honest quite forgot that he was with us. But then, to my astonishment, there was Jacob running towards me in his clumsy fat-man way and shouting at the top of his head: 'The blood of doctor! The blood of doctor!' I shall never forget it. I rushed back to the room – with Jacob stumbling at my heels – to see Dr Freud lying prostrate in a mess of new blood. The bandages on his face were completely soaked, and his hands were bloody also, as though he had tried to stop the flow by clasping them to his wound. And the whole of his pillow was red and damp, a profuse haemorrhage, in short, and still streaming out. I felt suddenly guilty – knowing this man's importance, knowing he was stuck here in the utility room with the dwarf, knowing that a doctor would have to be immediately found. I settled Jacob by the bed to watch over Dr Freud, and hurried off for a physician. What a wasted effort! Dr Hajek was nowhere at all to be found; he had left after surgery. So I rushed back to the utility room without a doctor. The dwarf Jacob, thank God, was still in attendance. With one hand he held the dangling hand of poor Sigmund Freud, the other he had firmly fastened at Dr Freud's jaw, perhaps in imitation of something he had seen earlier. It was a curious sight, and might have looked, at a glance, as though Jacob had just committed some shocking crime, and was busy hushing up the screams of his victim. But in fact he was tender and firm and gentle as a child. More sensible, too, than I'd had reason to believe.

I pushed him aside and set about repair work. Pressure. New bandages. Binding. More pressure. (Until the doctor came and took over – as doctors do.) I learned later that our patient had been very close to death, and that the dwarf had certainly saved him by raising the alarm and helping to stop the blood. (No thanks to Dr Hajek who should have stuck to noses.)

When the crisis was over the patient communicated on paper – since he could now not speak at all without extreme discomfort – that he would like to remain in the utility room rather than move to a ward. This surprised us all, especially in the light of his later accusations. (You will know, of course, that Dr Freud later charged that the hospital had been deliberately negligent since its staff was jealous and resentful of the success of psychoanalysis!) Anyway, he stayed, recuperating, for a few days where he had first been put. His daughter Anna slept on a chair in the same awful room.

There is something – let me tell you – I have always remembered.

Bertha came to visit while Dr Freud was still there. She didn't often visit Jacob when he was stuck there in hospital; for some reason I think – though I'm not sure why – that the mother prohibited it. Still she came in one day, and this is how I see them. Dr Freud is propped up in bed with a heavily bandaged jaw, with the face of Emperor Franz Josef hovering alive above his head. In comes our dear Bertha – I led her in myself – who goes straight over to Jacob and gives him one of those cumbersome and slobbering embraces that such people seem invariably to have. Quite touching, really. Kisses, holding hands. Dr Freud had been observing her and beckoned with his finger for Bertha to come over to him. Which she did, smiling. Then he held her face in both hands and ran his fingers carefully over her features as though he were somehow medically appraising her odd condition. (The smile, I mean, not the idiocy.) A sort of medical appraisal. I watched him very closely and thought for just one moment, just one moment, mind you, that he was going to cry. He didn't, of course; men didn't in those days. But just for one moment I thought that he would. The famous Sigmund Freud crying; can you imagine?

No, I know nothing more of the idiot dwarf Jacob; I'm sorry to say. Except that he died of complications of pneumonia not very long after, early, I think it was, in 1924. Bertha and the mother stayed on in the apartment, though I moved out to live with my husband Claus. I heard later that they were taken away by the Nazis – two of the first to go, and her no longer by that time looking like a silent movie star with heart-shaped lips, but much, much older, and her hair gone grey as her eyes. No-one seems to know of their final fate, but one can guess, of course, where Nazis are concerned.

Really, there is nothing more I can tell you about Jacob. I know you want to write up the dwarf part of the story but I remember other things. When I think back on Jacob and the time of the biopsy, I think mostly of the women. I think of the mother at her window, so beautiful and quiet, and most of all of dear Bertha, who was always smiling and affectionate, and a friend despite all. And who that terrible man – Karl Kraus was his name – said one night was somehow the very symbol of Vienna.

John Kinsella

THE WHITE FEATHER

1988

Before he notices how large and gracious the room is he sees the white feather on the dresser. A white feather with just a dusting of sulphur. Everything he sees from that moment on is tainted by the feather. She senses something is wrong but hasn't seen the feather and even if she had would probably consider it an interesting addition to the room. Almost in character. She'd think it was something to do with the room itself, which is, by reputation, haunted by the ghost of a famous woman. She remarks on the splendour of the four-poster bed and magnificent view through the bay window. It opens out onto the escarpment, the city distantly below haloed with a blue smog. He follows her lead and forces himself to look anywhere but at the feather which she eventually remarks on, twirling it in her fingers, pricking his skin. Metaphorically one of Icarus's feathers, she jokes. He's at the bay window falling into the valley below. The sun is streaming in over the thick rose-patterned carpet, its rays dragging the ice-cold stuff of the stone house into the room. They both shiver. There is a magnificent open fireplace and a box full of wood and chips and a can of kerosene-soaked sawdust with a spoon speared into it for getting the fire started. They busy themselves doing just this and by the time darkness coats the bay window the fire is driving the ice back into the stone. At around seven they descend the broad jarrah staircase and enter the dining room. The other guests are milling around reading, chatting, having a pre-dinner drink. They mingle comfortably. He smiles wonderfully and the guests gather around him. The hosts show them to their places. The meal passes congenially, or so it seems to her. He sweats a little and then remembers the fire and excuses himself so he can check on it. The wire screen is in place, and he stares through it deep into the flames to burn the darkness out of his head. He returns and is even more amusing than before. That night they make love with the experience of twenty years' marriage and the enthusiasm of their wedding night. And it's even better because they're basically sober. She refers to the white feather shortly before turning the light out. The fire is low in the grate and the embers seethe. Light rain is stinging the bay window. The curtains are open because they want to wake at first light, to set out early in the hope of recording birdsong. A wet night will make the calls richer in timbre. It's strange, you know, I haven't seen sulphur-crested cockatoos around these parts for years. Though I do recall a flock settling on the lawn on the afternoon of our wedding. He shifts uncomfortably and the wet patch on the sheet grows bitterly cold. It's always on my side, he mumbles. What? she asks incredulously before bursting into laughter and saying, Bastard! Not so loud, he says, almost laughing. They cuddle up close and the rain drives them into each other's silence. With the morning they rug up and head outside. They're ten minutes from the house when they realise they've not put batteries in the recording machine, it was a crazy idea anyway – we'd never listen to them. Just an excuse to get outside and away from the others. But we don't need an excuse, it's hard accepting that. So they just walk down the hill, the wet foliage lashing at their trousers, soaking them to the skin. It feels so fresh. The discomfort is exhilarating. The birds are present in orchestral proportions. Their music is eclectic – one minute in perfect harmony, like a Beethoven symphony progressing towards its glory, another contrapuntal like a piece of baroque intricacy. And then thoroughly modern, like Schönberg. If they hear the sound of tapping sticks and didgeridoos they keep it close to their hearts, guilt hanging like the city's smog. Reaching the creek at the base of the hill they crouch on their haunches and stare into the crystal-clear water. It looks so clean, I'd love to take a drink. Don't, because upstream there are orchards and it's probably full of pesticide. That's the truth of it. She asks him if he enjoyed catching up with old friends last night at dinner. Friends from before their marriage. She asks him about Joel, his best man. You hardly spoke, though you seemed quite friendly. Maybe you've nothing in common now. The few remaining rain clouds are clearing away towards the east. The sun shines on their skin, just warm enough to make the cold of their legs sharp. But as the minutes pass in silence, it works its subterfuge and slowly and almost imperceptibly drives the cold away. He looks over at his wife who is watching him intently. She is almost smiling, though he can sense her unease. His face seems different to her – tired and worn by an excess that is only just catching up with him. Did you tell him we were heading out early to record the birds? Yes, I did, but only quietly. *The soft feathers of the sulphur-crested cockatoos had confettied the lawn, their raucous call splintering down over the party as they lifted as one, vanishing for a decade.* I love that house, she says softly. There's something about its stone that resists change. Last night I woke up and listened to the wind and the rain just as one is supposed to in such houses. And I felt the comfort of being close to you, and of the house. And the harder I listened the more I realised that the wind and rain were only masking the noises one should be listening for. The words and love that only stone in all its unliving hears. And do you know what the stone said to me? That a white feather is not a sign of cowardice, but beauty. It is a thank you. *The cry of cockatoos bit deep into me too.* He smiled and felt good as the deep baritone voice of the past echoed down from the house calling them to breakfast.

Terry   Lane

HICKENLOOPER'S SYNDROME
1994

Morris Major was born on 6 August 1945, the day they dropped the Bomb on Hiroshima. The coincidence of his birthday and the dropping of the atomic bomb affected Morris Major's attitude to life. He was a solemn child and a melancholy man who took the cares of the world on his shoulders.

Dolores Major, Morris's wife, was born on Christmas day 1955 and was consequently of a congenitally cheerful disposition. She had learned to live with her husband's melancholia, but she never ceased to hold the opinion that he worried too much about events over which he had no control and for which he was not responsible.

Morris was a news junkie. First thing in the morning he listened to news and current affairs on the wireless. Then he breakfasted with the newspapers – four dailies, including the financial paper. He worried about fluctuations in the value of the dollar. He was anxious about the All Ordinaries and the Nikkei and the Dow Jones.

But these were the least of his worries. He worried about Somalia. And apartheid. And atrocities and outrages in Bosnia. He worried incessantly about starving millions and Ulster and floods and earthquakes. He agonised over rape and murder and the road toll.

'Look,' he said to Dolores one morning, 'the rainforest is disappearing at the rate of two hectares a second . . .'

'Yes, dear. Perhaps you could save a few trees by cancelling some of your newspapers and magazines?'

Morris Major spent his nights watching news and current affairs programs on the television. He watched documentaries on natural disasters and man's inhumanity to man. The ozone layer and the greenhouse effect were constantly on his mind. He never missed a program about pollution and the extinction of the species.

On his birthday he was always particularly miserable. 'I see that people are still dying from the effects of the bomb,' he said to Dolores.

'Really, dear. How do they know?'

'How do they know what?'

'That people are still dying from the effects of the bomb. They could be dying of old age. It was a long time ago. Shall we go out to dinner for your birthday?'

Morris Major was a vegetarian. It was his personal contribution to saving the atmosphere from farting cattle and flatulent sheep. 'Do you have any idea how much methane is generated by farm animals every year?'

Then he read that termites and cockroaches also fart more than their fair share of methane into the atmosphere and he was despondent for days. He had pledged never to use insecticides because of their deleterious effect on birds and other living creatures so he could not for the life of him see what he could do about the termites and the cockroaches. Morris Major dreamt apocalyptic dreams about the end of the world.

The Majors had no children. That was Morris's choice. He was frantic about overpopulation and did the responsible thing. He had had a vasectomy years before it was fashionable. Dolores suffered a twinge of regret now and again.

Morris worried about Aborigines, the Middle East, the rhinoceros (black and white), drugs, AIDS, oil spills, the Liberal party leadership, gorillas (lowland and mountain), police brutality – whatever was making news that day was grist for his worry mill. Then one day, on his forty-fifth birthday, a strange thing happened. Morris Major became illiterate. He ceased to be able to read. He picked up his morning papers and he could not make head nor tail of their contents. The type might as well have been Tibetan for all the sense that it made. (He worried about Tibet.)

He held the paper out to Dolores and said: 'There's something peculiar about the papers today, dear. Look. It's all gibberish. Are the typesetters taking industrial action do you think?' Morris Major was a union man – it gave him something extra to worry about.

Dolores looked at the papers. 'They look all right to me, dear.'

'Can you actually read them?'

'Yes. It says: "Bomb Outrage in Sarajevo. 83 Killed."'

Morris looked again. Still it made no sense to him. Did he need glasses? No. What he was seeing was too radically incomprehensible for glasses to make any difference. He began to panic.

'I must be going blind!'

Dolores said: 'But you can see other things all right, can't you?'

He looked around the kitchen. Everything was as clear as it had always been, except that the brand name on the fridge which had been his constant mealtime companion for many years was indecipherable. 'What is the brand of our fridge, dear?'

'Kelvinator, of course.'

'Kelvinator . . .' He turned the word over in his mind for a moment, but the label on the fridge could not be made to match the word. 'I think I had better call on Evangeline on the way to work.'

Evangeline Cutter, the Majors' doctor, was perplexed. She thought the most likely explanation to be a tumour pressing on the part of Morris's brain that processed writing. She sent him for immediate and urgent tests. He was X-rayed and CAT-scanned that very day, but the results showed nothing.

That night Morris Major noticed something else going on in his head. The moment he turned on the television to watch the news it was as though he had been hit on the skull by an enormous hammer. The pain made him close his eyes. He ran from the room to the bathroom to take an aspirin, and the moment he could no longer see or hear the television the pain went.

When he returned to the television room he was again felled by the terrible pain in his head. The moment that he left the room the pain went. He turned on the radio to listen to the news. The same blinding flash of agony. For the first day that he could remember in his entire adult life Morris Major went to bed without hearing or reading or seeing a single item of news. He was devastated.

Morris Major believed that those who did not watch, read and listen to the news as avidly as he did were irresponsible. They should be ashamed of themselves for taking so little interest in the world. Their cheerful lack of concern for the raped, starving, bombed, treeless, polluted millions was immoral, he said. Now here he was, forced to go through an entire day without the usual grim tidings from at home and abroad. He was suffering the torments of the addict going cold turkey.

Next day he went again to Dr Evangeline Cutter. She was totally nonplussed, but seeing that there were no signs of organic malfunction she referred him urgently to a psychiatrist, Dr Hermione Hickenlooper, whose great-grandfather on her father's side had once sold tobacco to Dr Sigmund Freud in Vienna in the old days. This had set Dr Hickenlooper's destiny as surely as the Bomb had set the destiny of Morris Major.

Dr Hickenlooper was tremendously excited by Major's condition. At first she broadly categorised it as hysterical illiteracy. Then she began to make her description and diagnosis more precise and specific. She could not find such a condition described anywhere in the literature, which meant that she had been presented with the gift of which every medical specialist dreams, the chance to immortalise her name by attaching it to a syndrome. In future, she believed, the condition of hysterical illiteracy would be known to the profession as Hickenlooper's syndrome. She secretly hoped it would be common.

Dr Hickenlooper looked for a cause of Morris Major's condition in the conventional places. Did he hate his father because he wouldn't let him watch television when he was a boy? No. Was there sibling rivalry for the radio? No, he was an only child. Did he want to kill his father and make love to his mother because he wouldn't let him watch the television and she would? She drew a blank.

She tried reverse aversion therapy. She showed him an erotic video, thinking that it might be the content rather than the medium itself which was producing the extreme reaction of pain and nausea. It didn't work. Just having the television on brought on the hammering on the head. He covered his head with his hands and begged her to turn it off.

'Anyway, what does it matter?' she asked. So he couldn't read newspapers or watch the TV or listen to the wireless. Is that such a terrible loss? Dr Hickenlooper herself did none of these things. She considered them a waste of time. He was better off without them. Which made Morris Major launch into his speech about the irresponsibility and moral turpitude of those people who refuse to take their daily dose of news and to do the creative worrying about the planet without which it will not survive.

'But Mr Major,' Hickenlooper argued, 'what does it matter whether or not you know about bombs in Bosnia or starvation in Somalia or rainforests in Brazil? What can you do about them?'

A theory began to form in her mind and she imagined how she would flesh it out and argue it in her seminal article on Hickenlooper's syndrome in *Lancet*. Consider the ear.

Inside the ear there are thousands of little hairs waving around. Some are sensitive to some frequencies and some to others. When sound enters the ear as vibrations through the eardrum these little hairs are set in motion. This stimulates the auditory nerve and a message is sent to the brain. People who work in noisy environments often go deaf on the frequency of the loudest noise around them. So jackhammer operators go deaf on the frequency of the hammer and rock musicians go deaf on all frequencies, because the little hairs just lie down and refuse to take any more.

Now what if, Hickenlooper speculated, there is a moral equivalent of the hairs in the ears? What if there is a sort of anxiety overload that produces this effect in the conscience? Hickenlooper's syndrome could very well be a case of hysterical illiteracy brought on by anxiety or compassion overload. A failure of the concern nerve under constant assault.

Anyway, the good news for Morris Major was that after a week of withdrawal symptoms of gradually diminishing severity he found that he didn't care. Occasionally he wondered what was going on in the hell-holes of the world and he felt a twinge of guilt, but it never lasted more than a split second. His only real problem was that he had to give up his job as an assessor in the taxation department and get a job where illiteracy was not an impediment. He took up gardening. He loved it.

Dolores Major was at first alarmed by her husband's sudden illiteracy, but soon she did not mind in the least. She was delighted, in fact, that she no longer had to take in a daily dose of misery with her breakfast. She found that the less Morris worried about Bosnia the more he paid attention to her. For a while, deprived of calamities, Morris didn't have much to talk about, but as the months went by he discovered the joys of trivial conversation.

'Oranges are cheap,' he said. 'And big. With really big navels. Very nice.'

When the boronia was in flower at the nursery he couldn't wait to get home to Dolores with a bunch. He couldn't remember having ever smelled boronia before. Everything in the garden was, indeed, lovely.

Dr Hermione Hickenlooper lost interest in Morris Major. As his initial alarm at his condition turned to cheerful indifference she became more and more irritated. After all, what use is a happy patient to a psychiatrist? Her article appeared in *Lancet*, but so far Hickenlooper's syndrome is not a common condition.

One glorious morning when the market stalls were loaded with big, fat oranges and the perfume of boronia was everywhere, Morris Major rode his bike past a church wall which he had passed many times before on his way to and from work. Someone had sprayed a wordy graffiti on the wall. This is what it said: 'Live the life you love.' Then, on the next line: 'Pick a God you trust . . .' And under that: '. . . and don't take it all too seriously.'

Morris Major braked to a stop. He could scarcely believe what he was seeing. He could read every word on the wall. Perfectly. But when he looked around at the signs and newspaper headlines and so on they were as meaningless as ever. He looked back at the church wall and read the words with perfect comprehension.

Imagine you are in a foreign city and the signs and labels are in an alien alphabet and mean nothing to you, then, unexpectedly, through the haze of meaningless symbols you see a sign in English. It was like that.

Morris Major was not a religious man. He reckoned that there was too much misery in the world for anyone to be able to defend the idea of an omnipotent and loving god. He left Sunday School when he was eight, when the teacher couldn't answer the simple question: 'Was God on holidays when they dropped the Bomb on Hiroshima?'

The church wall became Major's shrine. His holy place. Every day, on the way to and from work, he stopped at the wall and read the words, the only words he ever saw that made sense. He would lean against his bike and wonder what the graffitist meant. 'Live the life you love . . .' Did it mean that he should live his own life and not try to live other people's lives for them? Perhaps. '. . . And don't take it all too seriously' was straightforward, if a little irresponsible. But what could he make of 'Pick a God you trust'? He would pedal off murmuring the words over and over. 'Pick a God you trust . . .'

One evening, on the way home from work, he stopped at the wall and suddenly he understood it. 'Pick a God you trust . . .' he realised, means simply that you must create your own God. Ready-made gods, handed to you by a priest or a rabbi, are worthless. Everyone should invent their own god. Your god is as personal as your toothbrush. Would you use someone else's toothbrush? Never. So why use someone else's god?

Immensely cheered he rode off, whistling 'See, the conquering hero comes', to tell Dolores about his theological revelation.

On the way home and on the spur of the moment he stopped off at the surgery of Dr Evangeline Cutter to ask her a question which had been on his mind for some time.

'Yes,' she said. 'Sometimes it can be reversed. We can but try.' Which she did. And it worked. One year later on the feast day of St Cecilia, the patron saint of music, this notice appeared in the paper:

> To Dolores and Morris, a son. Morris Minor. Welcome to a beautiful world. Deo gratias.

Henry Lawson

THE LOADED DOG

1902

Dave Regan, Jim Bently, and Andy Page were sinking a shaft at Stony Creek in search of a rich gold quartz reef which was supposed to exist in the vicinity. There is always a rich reef supposed to exist in the vicinity; the only questions are whether it is ten feet or hundreds beneath the surface, and in which direction. They had struck some pretty solid rock, also water which kept them baling. They used the old-fashioned blasting-powder and time-fuse. They'd make a sausage or cartridge of blasting-powder in a skin of strong calico or canvas, the mouth sewn and bound round the end of the fuse. They'd dip the cartridge in melted tallow to make it watertight, get the drill-hole as dry as possible, drop in the cartridge with some dry dust, and wad and ram with stiff clay and broken brick. Then they'd light the fuse and get out of the hole and wait. The result was usually an ugly pothole in the bottom of the shaft and half a barrow-load of broken rock.

There was plenty of fish in the creek, freshwater bream, cod, cat-fish, and tailers. The party were fond of fish, and Andy and Dave of fishing. Andy would fish for three hours at a stretch if encouraged by a 'nibble' or a 'bite' now and then – say once in twenty minutes. The butcher was always willing to give meat in exchange for fish when they caught more than they could eat; but now it was winter, and these fish wouldn't bite. However, the creek was low, just a chain of muddy waterholes, from the hole with a few bucketfuls in it to the sizable pool with an average depth of six or seven feet, and they could get fish by bailing out the smaller holes or muddying up the water in the larger ones till the fish rose to the surface. There was the catfish, with spikes growing out of the sides of its head, and if you got pricked you'd know it, as Dave said. Andy took off his boots, tucked up his trousers and went into a hole one day to stir up the mud with his feet, and he knew it too; his arm swelled, and the pain throbbed up into his shoulder, and down into his stomach, too, he said, like a toothache he had once, and kept him awake for two nights – only the toothache pain had a 'burred edge,' Dave said.

Dave got an idea.

'Why not blow the fish up in the big waterhole with a cartridge?' he said. 'I'll try it.'

He thought the thing out and Andy Page worked it out. Andy usually put Dave's theories into practice if they were able, or bore the blame for the failure and the chaffing of his mates if they weren't.

He made a cartridge about three times the size of those they used in the rock. Jim Bently said it was big enough to blow the bottom out of the river. The inner skin was of stout calico; Andy stuck the end of a six-foot piece of fuse well down in the powder and bound the mouth of the bag firmly to it with whipcord. The idea was to sink the cartridge in the water with the open end of the fuse attached to a float on the surface, ready for lighting. Andy dipped the cartridge in melted beeswax to make it watertight. 'We'll have to leave it some time before we light it,' said Dave, 'to give the fish time to get over their scare when we put it in, and come nosing round again; so we'll want it well watertight.'

Round the cartridge Andy, at Dave's suggestion, bound a strip of sail canvas – that they used for making waterbags – to increase the force of the explosion, and round that he pasted layers of stiff brown paper – on the plan of the sort of fireworks we called 'gun-crackers'. He let the paper dry in the sun, sewed a covering of two thicknesses of canvas over it, and bound the thing from end to end with stout fishing-line. Dave's schemes were elaborate, and he often worked his inventions out to nothing. The cartridge was rigid and solid enough now – a formidable bomb; but Andy and Dave wanted to be sure. Andy sewed on another layer of canvas, dipped the cartridge in melted tallow, twisted a length of fencing-wire round it as an afterthought, dipped it in tallow again, and stood it carefully against a tent-peg, where he'd know where to find it, and wound the fuse loosely round it. Then he went to the camp fire to try some potatoes which were boiling in their jackets in a billy, and to see about frying some chops for dinner. Dave and Jim were at work in the claim that morning.

They had a big black young retriever dog – or rather an overgrown pup, a big, foolish, four-footed mate, who was always slobbering round them and lashing their legs with his heavy tail that swung round like a stock-whip. Most of his head was usually a red, idiotic slobbering grin of appreciation of his own silliness. He seemed to take life, the world, his two-legged mates, and his own instinct as a huge joke. He'd retrieve anything; he carted back most of the camp rubbish that Andy threw away. They had a cat that died in hot weather, and Andy threw it a good distance away in the scrub; and early one morning the dog found the cat, after it had been dead a week or so, and carried it back to camp, and laid it just inside the tent-flaps, where it could best make its presence known when the mates should rise and begin to sniff suspiciously in the sickly smothering atmosphere of the summer sunrise. He used to retrieve them when they went in swimming; he'd jump in after them, and take their hands in his mouth, and try to swim out with them, and scratch their naked bodies with his paws. They loved him for his good-heartedness and his foolishness, but when they wished to enjoy a swim they had to tie him up in camp.

He watched Andy with great interest all the morning making the cartridge, and hindered him considerably, trying to help; but about noon he went off to the claim to see how Dave and Jim were getting on, and to come home to dinner with them. Andy saw them coming, and put a panful of mutton-chops on the fire. Andy was cook today; Dave and Jim stood with their backs to the fire, as bushmen do in all weathers, waiting till dinner should be ready. The retriever went nosing round after something he seemed to have missed.

Andy's brain still worked on the cartridge; his eye was caught by the glare of an empty kerosene tin lying in the bushes, and it struck him that it wouldn't be a bad idea to sink the cartridge packed with clay, sand, or stones in the tin, to increase the force of the explosion. He may have been all out, from a scientific point of view, but the notion looked all right to him. Jim Bently, by the way, wasn't interested in their 'damned silliness'. Andy noticed an empty treacle tin – the sort with the little tin neck or spout soldered on to the tap for the convenience of pouring out the treacle – and it struck him that this would have made the best kind of cartridge-case: he would only have had to pour in the powder, stick the fuse in through the neck, and cork and seal it with beeswax. He was turning to suggest this to Dave, when Dave glanced over his shoulder to see how the chops were doing – and bolted. He explained afterwards that he thought he heard the pan spluttering extra, and looked to see if the chops were burning. Jim

Bently looked behind and bolted after Dave. Andy stood stock-still, staring after them.

'Run, Andy! Run!' they shouted back at him. 'Run! Look behind you, you fool!' Andy turned slowly and looked, and there, close behind him, was the retriever with the cartridge in his mouth – wedged into his broadest and silliest grin. And that wasn't all. The dog had come round the fire to Andy, and the loose end of the fuse had trailed and waggled over the burning sticks into the blaze; Andy had slit and nicked the firing end of the fuse well, and now it was hissing and spitting properly.

Andy's legs started with a jolt; his legs started before his brain did, and he made after Dave and Jim. And the dog followed Andy.

Dave and Jim were good runners – Jim the best – for a short distance; and Andy was slow and heavy, but he had the strength and the wind and could last. The dog capered round him, delighted as a dog could be to find his mates, as he thought, on for a frolic. Dave and Jim kept shouting back, 'Don't foller us! Don't foller us, you coloured fool!' But Andy kept on, no matter how they dodged. They could never explain, any more than the dog, why they followed each other, but so they ran, Dave keeping in Jim's track in all its turnings, Andy after Dave, and the dog circling round Andy – the live fuse swishing in all directions and hissing and spluttering and stinking. Jim yelling to Dave not to follow him, Dave shouting to Andy to go in another direction – to 'spread out,' and Andy roaring at the dog to go home. Then Andy's brain began to work, stimulated by the crisis: he tried to get a running kick at the dog, but the dog dodged; he snatched up sticks and stones and threw them at the dog and ran on again. The retriever saw that he'd made a mistake about Andy, and left him and bounded after Dave. Dave, who had the presence of mind to think that the fuse's time wasn't up yet, made a dive and a grab for the dog, caught him by the tail, and as he swung round snatched the cartridge out of his mouth and flung it as far as he could; the dog immediately bounded after it and retrieved it. Dave roared and cursed at the dog, who, seeing that Dave was offended, left him and went after Jim, who was well ahead. Jim swung to a sapling and went up it like a native bear; it was a young sapling, and Jim couldn't safely get more than ten or twelve feet from the ground. The dog laid the cartridge, as carefully as if it were a kitten, at the foot of the sapling, and capered and leaped and whooped joyously round under Jim. The big pup reckoned that this was part of the lark – he was all right now – it was Jim who was out for a spree. The fuse sounded as if it were going a mile a minute. Jim tried to climb higher and the sapling bent and cracked. Jim fell on his feet and ran. The dog swooped on the cartridge and followed. It all took but a very few moments. Jim ran to a digger's hole, about ten feet deep, and dropped down into it – landing on soft mud – and was safe. The dog grinned sardonically down on him, over the edge, for a moment, as if he thought it would be a good lark to drop the cartridge down on Jim.

'Go away, Tommy,' said Jim feebly, 'go away.'

The dog bounded off after Dave, who was the only one in sight now; Andy had dropped behind a log, where he lay flat on his face, having suddenly remembered a picture of the Russo-Turkish war with a circle of Turks lying flat on their faces (as if they were ashamed) round a newly arrived shell.

There was a small hotel or shanty on the creek, on the main road, not far from the claim. Dave was desperate, the time flew much faster in his stimulated imagination than it did in reality, so he made for the shanty. There were several casual bushmen on the veranda and in the bar; Dave rushed into the bar, banging the door to behind him. 'My dog!' he gasped, in reply to the astonished stare of the publican, 'the blanky retriever – he's got a live cartridge in his mouth –'

The retriever, finding the front door shut against him, had bounded round and in by the back way, and now stood smiling in the doorway leading from the passage, the cartridge still in his mouth and the fuse spluttering. They burst out of that bar. Tommy bounded first after one and then after another, for, being a young dog, he tried to make friends with everybody.

The bushmen ran round corners, and some shut themselves in the stable. There was a new weatherboard and corrugated-iron kitchen and wash-house on piles in the backyard, with some women washing clothes inside. Dave and the publican bundled in there and shut the door – the publican cursing Dave and calling him a crimson fool, in hurried tones, and wanting to know what the hell he came here for.

The retriever went in under the kitchen, amongst the piles, but, luckily for those inside, there was a vicious yellow mongrel cattle-dog sulking and nursing his nastiness under there – a sneaking, fighting, thieving canine, whom neighbours had tried for years to shoot or poison. Tommy saw his danger – he'd had experience from this dog – and started out and across the yard, still sticking to the cartridge. Halfway across the yard the yellow dog caught him and nipped him. Tommy dropped the cartridge, gave one terrified yell, and took to the bush. The yellow dog followed him to the fence and then ran back to see what he had dropped. Nearly a dozen other dogs came from round all the corners and under the buildings – spidery, thievish, cold-blooded kangaroo dogs, mongrel sheep and cattle-dogs, vicious black and yellow dogs – that slip after you in the dark, nip your heels, and vanish without explaining – and yapping, yelping small fry. They kept at a respectable distance round the nasty yellow dog, for it was dangerous to go near him when he thought he had found something which might be good for a dog or cat. He sniffed at the cartridge, and was just taking a third cautious sniff when –

It was very good blasting-powder – a new brand that Dave recently got up from Sydney; and the cartridge had been excellently well made. Andy was very patient and painstaking in all he did, and nearly as handy as the average sailor with needles, twine, canvas and rope.

Bushmen say that that kitchen jumped off its piles and on again. When the smoke and dust cleared away, the remains of the nasty yellow dog were lying against the paling fence of the yard looking as if he had been kicked into a fire by a horse and afterwards rolled in the dust under a barrow, and finally thrown against the fence from a distance. Several saddle-horses, which had been 'hanging-up' round the veranda, were galloping wildly down the road in clouds of dust, broken bridle-reins flying; and from a circle round the outskirts, from every point of the compass in the scrub, came the yelping of dogs. Two of them went home, to the place they were born, thirty miles away, and reached it the same night and stayed there; it was not till towards evening the rest came back cautiously to make inquiries. One was trying to walk on two legs, and most of 'em looked more or less singed; and a little, singed, stumpy-tailed dog, who had been in the habit of hopping the back half of him along on one leg, had reason to be glad that he'd saved up the other leg all those years, for he needed it now. There was one old one-eyed cattle-dog round that shanty for years afterwards, who couldn't stand the smell of a gun being cleaned. He it was who had taken an interest, only second to that of the yellow dog, in the cartridge. Bushmen said that it was amusing to slip up on his blind side and stick a dirty ramrod under his nose: he wouldn't wait to bring his solitary eye to bear – he'd take to the bush and stay out all night.

For half an hour or so after the explosion there were several bushmen round behind the stable who crouched, doubled up, against the wall, or rolled gently on the dust, trying to laugh without shrieking. There were two white women in hysterics at the house, and a half-caste rushing aimlessly round with a dipper of cold water. The publican was holding his wife tight and begging her between her squawks, to 'hold up for my sake, Mary, or I'll lam the life out of ye'.

Dave decided to apologise later on, 'when things had settled a bit', and went back to camp. And the dog that had done it all, Tommy, the great, idiotic mongrel retriever, came slobbering round Dave and lashing his legs with his tail, and trotted home after him, smiling his broadest, longest, and reddest smile of amiability, and apparently satisfied for one afternoon with the fun he'd had.

Andy chained the dog up securely, and cooked some more chops, while Dave went to help Jim out of the hole.

And most of this is why, for years afterwards, lanky, easy-going bushmen, riding lazily past Dave's camp, would cry, in a lazy drawl and with just a hint of the nasal twang:

''Ello, Da-a-ve! How's the fishin' getting on, Da-a-ve!'

Joan London

NEW YEAR

1 9 8 6

1

They are in the middle of a heatwave. All across the city people are doing unusual things. Walking into fountains, sleeping on the beach, holding conversations under a sprinkler ... 'It's the heat': don't the Arabs have a wind, Rowena is trying to think of the name of it, a desert wind, so hot that a man is excused for killing his wife while it is blowing?

Harry and Rowena are having dinner with the Hutchisons. This is not unusual, since they live in the Hutchisons' house and share most meals with them: but it's New Year's Eve and here they are on the terrace, legs looped over chairs, opening their second bottle of wine. Festive yet resigned, like workers choosing to drink together after a hard day. The Hutchisons have chosen to stay home with Harry and Rowena tonight. This is what is unusual.

This is what Rowena thinks, stirring Harry's chicken stock in the kitchen. The kitchen is a glassed-in veranda three steps up from the terrace. Tonight it is a little box lit up with heat. Grease glistens in beads behind the stove. Oily fingers seem to have smeared everything, handles, cookery books, jars of herbs. Vine leaves over the terrace drape around the windows, limp and still, dropped hands.

The chicken stock is for pilau, Harry's speciality. Later Rowena, who doesn't have a speciality, will make a fruit salad. It's their turn to cook tonight.

Although Rowena likes watching stock, its slow rich bubble, she knows it does not really need stirring. She is really listening out for her baby Tom. If she can get to him quickly when he wakes – he wakes a great deal – she might be able to settle him back to sleep. Meanwhile she gives a few busy taps to the saucepan with the side of the spoon.

'The person who really needs a drink,' Hutch calls out, 'is Rowena.'

Lately Rowena has suspected a consensus in the house about her, about maternal over-commitment. Her case has been discussed, heads shaken ... coming down the kitchen steps now as this person is not quite real to her. She feels a fruitless swinging to her arms, she is breasting dark air. She sits down quickly.

'This is very civilised,' Harry is saying. He has just taken off his T-shirt and he stretches out, rubbing the fan of black hair that spouts up over his waistband.

'Hardly civilised,' Hutch says, 'taking off your clothes.' He has a way of drawing out the Australian accent that makes everything he says sound measured and judicious.

'Let's face it,' Harry says, 'we're a hedonist culture. On a night like this we ought to take off the lot.' His hand hovers for a moment over the front stud of his jeans.

'D'you hear what your husband's proposing?' Hutch turns to Rowena. She has no answer. She never has an answer for Hutch.

'Diane has more of the hedonist spirit,' says Harry. Diane is wearing a sarong hitched up and looped around her neck like a miniature toga.

'Oh for heaven's sake,' says Diane, rearranging her legs. 'It's *hot*.'

'Or is she just going with the au-naturel flow of our household?' Hutch says to Harry.

'I'll drink to that,' says Harry. Across the table his torso is white amongst the shadows of the terrace. Winter white. Like her own hands around her glass. It had stopped being winter when they first arrived here from the beach house. They had stood beside their car in the mild city air, pale, in coats, as if they had come a long way ...

'What are you looking at?' Harry's voice is low across the table.

'My hands.'

'What's *wrong* with your hands?' Harry mutters. But a steady droning is rising from the house. Their eyes lift and meet. Tom.

'Already?' Diane says. 'He's incredible.'

'He fell asleep early,' Rowena says on her way back up the steps. 'It's the heat ...' But who would understand the logic and rhythm of Tom's day? Who would want to? She takes her glass with her.

'How about some music,' Hutch is saying.

'It's your *turn*,' Diane says.

2

In that house music was kept going like a tribal fire. Whoever came home first went straight to the living room and put on music. The speakers were lugged up and down the hall on long cords, following the action. When they left again Rowena let the music die. There were many arrivals and departures. The Hutchisons were both studying part-time. They belonged to societies, separately, they went to films and rock concerts. Harry often went with them.

In the weekends they were careful to keep the sound well stoked. Music nudged away each moment, bit at the fringes of thought. Open the bedroom door and you swam wordless into it. The first nights they were here Rowena went walking. Up the empty street. Turn the corner. Drawn curtains at the end of driveways silhouetted with shrubs. Silence. Block after block of it. The beat of the music met her again on the home stretch. Their house looked party bright. She sat on the front steps and leaned her head against a column. It seemed to have caught a pulse inside it. She watched the light behind the roofs of the houses across the road. She didn't know where else to go.

Now as Tom sucks, his head seems to pump back and forward against her, in time. Their room is another piece of veranda, a partitioned cavern. Curtainless, it is dark all day, shadowed by the house next door, but at night the neighbours' bathroom light beacons through the louvres and everything, the cartons from the beach house stacked around the walls, Harry's shirt dangling from the door frame, the roundness of Tom's head, is outlined in this dull radiance.

Last night, lying like this on the mattress, she had said to Harry: 'How much longer are we going to stay here?'

Harry had just shut his book, put out the light and turned over: there was a sense of purpose about everything he did these days, even to going to sleep. He turned onto his back and unfolded one finger, two, as if they had been waiting to spring open.

'We're still paying off the bookshop.' He had to whisper. Behind the wall next to them were the Hutchisons, also in bed. 'We could never afford to live like this so close to the city.' End of point two: he closed his hand into a fist over their sheet.

'I could live in a tiny flat,' Rowena said. Whispering was provisional, it was like taking off your shoes and tiptoeing around each other. 'I could live in a room. If we were alone.'

'We're always alone,' Harry said.

Tom sucks and, elbow up, she sips her wine.

3

The light is on under the vines of the terrace but nobody is there. Moths bang against the light bulb and fall among the glasses on the table. Somebody has watered the ferns and they rustle and drip around the steps. Intermission. This happens sometimes. Everybody will suddenly desert on private missions, to read the newspaper, make a phone call, slump across a bed . . . The light is on in the kitchen too. Harry is cooking.

He looks up as Rowena comes up the steps, his chin lifted, eyes gathered together to hold in the tears. But it will do for a greeting, it is so familiar. Onions. He turns back to his chopping board. Steam rises, oil sizzles ready, his strokes are neat and sure. Harry cooks with a sense of ceremony. Step by step, a beautiful patient logic towards a known destination: no panicky improvisations, no peering at the recipe wishing it would tell you more.

He is singing, a beat behind and lower than the larger voice that fills the room beyond them.

> Still crazy,
> Still crazy,
> After all these years . . .

Harry singing, onions frying: Rowena stands for a moment in the doorway. He has always sung, to car radios, in supermarkets and restaurants, easily, knowing the words, 'Yesterday', 'O Sole Mio', 'You Are So Beautiful', as if in tune with a fellow experience.

'Want some help?'

He never says he does.

The Hutchisons' house is old, one day they are going to knock it down. Meanwhile they have hung mounted posters of things like sneakers and Coca Cola bottles on the stucco walls. Leads and aerials loop between picture railings. The mantel pieces are cluttered with jokey plunder: KEEP LEFT and NO SMOKING signs, a Chinese demon kite, a Snoopy mug half full of small change. But the rooms remain dark and sedate; tonight each is a cell of hot still air. The two visions of the house don't match, they are overlaid like illusionist sheets, demand something of you . . . a trick of wit, Rowena feels, and she would see it as a style.

The front door is open, the steps of the porch are still warm. Rowena lights a cigarette. She has taken up smoking again.

'Are these for real?' she had asked Hutch, pointing at the NO SMOKING signs.

'Why else would they be there?' Hutch said.

Why else did Rowena, finding an old packet of cigarettes in Harry's winter jacket, take one out and smoke it? The air before her lifted and shook. She took another one. This time it tasted more real, the house seemed to retreat behind the fraying coil of smoke. She bought her own packet. She enjoyed the crackle as she opened it, the neat decision of the cylinders stacked as close as bullets. She took to carrying a packet in the pouch pocket of her overalls. At odd moments, outside the house, she smoked them.

Just as she lights up now, Hutch breaks through the darkness at the side of the house, pulling a hose. In the other hand he carries his glass of wine. He doesn't seem to see her, but if she wasn't there would he stroll across the lawn like this, taking sips as he plants the sprinkler near her and turns on the tap? He suddenly sinks beside her.

'Very contemplative,' he says. 'You're always very contemplative, Rowena.'

The sprinkler's arms have corralled them against the porch. Water patters at their feet. Hutch is always setting up these little moments with her and she always comes away feeling she has failed a test.

'The madonna,' Hutch says. 'I take it that's what you want to be.'

His voice has dropped, his blond head is bowed towards her. Rowena hunches her shoulders. She will not look at him.

'Dinner,' she says, waving her arm vaguely, getting up. 'Must help Harry.' Her voice is husky, out of practice. She throws her cigarette into the garden and then remembers it is his garden and makes a little useless dive mid-air. She closes her eyes for a moment on her way back up the hall. She should have stamped the butt out at his feet, raised her eyebrows, stalked off . . . Why? Because he would have liked that? In this house value is given to performance.

Just as Harry places the big platter of yellow rice on the terrace table, Tom wakes. A loud outraged howl this time.

'Oh God,' Diane says. 'How do you bear it?'

Harry serves, and Rowena hands out plates.

'Maybe I'm just not the type,' Diane goes on. She picks up her fork with her narrow freckled hand, looks around the table. She often has this moment of animation when a plate of food is put in front of her, Rowena has noticed. 'Why do people *do* this to themselves d'you think?'

'Because they don't know what they're letting themselves in for,' Harry says.

Hutch stands up, turning and turning at the corkscrew embedded in the bottle between his legs. They all watch, wait for the triumphant Pop! 'Tight one,' Hutch says, chasing sweat across his forehead in a kind of salute.

Tom's cry is urgent. Rowena drains her glass, reaches over and takes a forkful of pilau from the platter. She won't be back for a while.

'All I know is,' Diane says, turning to her plate, 'nobody could ever make me miss my meal.'

'Go on,' Harry says to Rowena. 'We'll leave you some.'

4

One night Harry came home very late to the beach house. It was so black outside you could imagine that he might never find them again, the frail house could disappear into a shifting fold of the dunes . . . He would have phoned, if of course there was a phone . . . it was becoming bloody impossible . . . he swayed slightly above her and Tom in the bed. He'd been drinking with Hutch and his wife, he'd been thinking . . . The Hutchisons said, come and live with them, they're interested in sharing . . . No the Hutchisons have no children. But a child shouldn't make any difference, they said.

Harry seemed to have forgotten that he used to say that too.

There are photos – here, kept close beside the bed – of the time that they first brought Tom home to the beach house. In this bright darkness the black and white leap out at you as if in moonlight. They are good photos of Rowena because she has at last stopped looking at the camera. She is smiling, she can't stop smiling, looking at Tom in her arms. Her hair, which reaches to her elbows, is now tucked back out of the way. She's wearing overalls, but you can see that her breasts are enormous. In the background a tea-tree brushes against asbestos. That's the beach house.

The photos of Harry with Tom are slightly out of focus. Rowena took them. There was no-one else around to take them all together, *en famille*. The blurring gives the impression of a high wind. Harry is bending over Tom in his pram as if he's sheltering him. He is frowning in a comic-father way. The tea-tree appears to be in violent action, caught up in a storm. But you can see that the cigarette Harry holds behind him is still alight.

The bathroom of the beach house was separate, a quick dash from the back door. When one of them wanted a shower the other had to be there to feed the chip heater. The heater roared, the pipes shuddered, draughts rushed in through the warped door. Spiders rocked their cradles of dead blowflies in amongst the steam.

Bent over the heater one morning she thought she heard Harry groan.

'What's the matter?'

He stood still. He was wearing her shower cap. Water ran on and on, clung to the tip of his nose, the panels of black hair on his shoulders, his chest, above his penis, swirled about his feet. He looked straight ahead, through water.

He didn't go to the shop that morning. He went to bed. He stayed there for nine days. It wouldn't matter, nobody came anyway, he said. (Second-hand books! Out there! You must be crazy, everyone had said when he set up the shop.) He slept for twelve hours at a time.

Tom cried and cried. She walked him up and down the veranda, around the peripheries of the house. It might be after midday before she could get dressed. When he slept she lay on the couch with him in the crook of her arm, like a book.

Sand crept in under the doors. Mice scrabbled, but she could not bear to set the traps. Every living creature reminded her of Tom. The fridge went empty. From time to time she found herself before the open kitchen cupboard eating nuts and raisins fist after fist. She trod carefully past Harry's door. It seemed to take her whole being just to keep Tom alive.

When Harry was awake she sat on the end of the gritty bed, feeding Tom.

'Do something different!' Harry said, sitting up, smoking, watching her with glittering eyes. 'Is this all you ever do? Surprise me! Surprise me sometimes why don't you.'

(He didn't remember saying any of this, later on.)

A storm passed quickly on the beach front. You saw it coming, a mist wiping out the horizon ruled across the windows, whiteness on whiteness, while somewhere a blind flapped, louvres rattled, trees grew furtive. The voice outside took over, the house was hollowed into darkness, din, like a loss of consciousness: five minutes and it was over, a bird sang, the radio spoke again.

Harry got a job with the government. In the mornings the car steamed as he encouraged Tom to wave bye-bye. It would be well after dark by the time he got back from the city. He made friends with someone called Hutchison, his age, but a senior administrator in the department. He stopped taking a packed lunch. He gave up smoking.

In the late afternoon the wind dropped and Rowena and Tom went walking. Down the carefully curved roads, some still gravel, named 'Pleasant Drive' or 'Linden Way'. It was all allotments, waiting to become numbered houses in a suburb; flowers grew among scrub and hillocks, tough, close-clustered, with a medicinal perfume that scented the dunes. When she picked them she could feel the shadow of clouds moving across the sunlight on her bent back.

At this hour retired couples came out like moths and walked arm in arm towards the glow settling over the sea. The rattle of the pram echoed behind them. They turned to smile at her from their end of the road.

The beach itself was unspectacular, edged with seaweed and miniature limestone cliffs. The winter sea was milk turquoise, a great bowl in sluggish motion.

The sun glares low over the horizon, shows its power, the sea is a silver reflection, the road gleams, dances with struck flint, Rowena has to half shut her eyes. The wind presses against her, against her eyes and mouth so that she is smiling, blinded over the pram, and yes, she is happy, in some way about as happy as she can be.

The wine has spread through her.

Tom's head is slumped back like a drunk's, around it the dim bedroom, the house, the music, the lit heads on the terrace spin out in a circle.

5

It is as hot outside as in.

'*Good* evening!' Hutch calls out as Rowena stands blinking on the steps. 'I was just volunteering to go and wake you up.' He pulls out a chair for her with his foot.

'There's plenty left,' Harry says, waving his hand over the table. It doesn't look appetising. Amongst the spilled glasses, the plates scattered with grains of rice and chicken bones, moths are dragging in circles, grounded in pools of amber oil.

'Aren't you hot in those overalls?' Diane asks. Her legs are spread, she is fanning herself with a sandal.

'Take 'em off,' shouts Harry.

Their faces under the light look yellowish and greasy. Their eyes have almost disappeared.

'Wine,' Harry says, searching for a glass for her. 'Wonderful wine.' His mouth is faintly rimmed with black.

'Eases the pressure of family life,' says Hutch.

Rowena starts collecting plates.

'Just relax,' Hutch says.

'Moths,' Rowena says. She sees Tom's head lolling, a dark spot on their bed where she has left him.

Rowena is making fruit salad. Watermelon, rockmelon, grapes, peaches, passionfruit, mangoes, plums: she has taken them out of their stained brown paper bags and lined them up on the bench. Whether to make it minimal and chic, just the melon and grapes say, or to throw in everything . . . Rowena has an idea, she has seen a picture somewhere, the watermelon carved like a bowl, the fruits spilling out of it . . .

The big knife has made her bold, slicing through cheeks of pink flesh . . . it comes away from the rinds with a sucking sound . . . take it all off . . . and then chop, chop into children's blocks, pink, all shades of pink, orange, tawny . . . The music throbs, Rowena chops, she is hot, she has never felt so hot. The kitchen is so crowded, its bin is overflowing, the benches are covered with plates, scraps, fruit . . . she has to work on a chopping board balanced on a chair, crouching, so that the buckles of her overalls bite into her, she can hardly move or breathe . . .

It is so simple. It works with the speed of a good idea. To unbuckle. Unpeel. To step out of the overalls, kick at them, and feel that trusty roughness, thigh against thigh. She gathers up rinds, pips, peel, and dumps them in the sink. Why stop there? Already she is moving easily, the T-shirt slips easily up her spine, cooling it, releasing her head. It's as if a breeze is suddenly blowing all over her body. She's in a hurry now. A glass splinters outside and there's laughter. *Wait.* Her breasts come loping out of their milk-stiffened cups, she could almost fear for them as she bends over her knife . . . the final touches . . . pants, you need two hands and they're over your knees, binding them, but – you just step out of them . . . She's wading in her own clothes, hands plunged up to the wrists in fruit, mixing it, the passionfruit sprays out as she squeezes its upturned pouch . . . She washes her hands.

Here is Rowena, descending a staircase, her bowl held out before her, while somewhere over towards the city there is a rude outbreak of car horns. New Year. She is only aware of the whiteness beneath her, this company of globes and triangles, trusting them with her own grave progress.

And the faces looking up at her are frozen, their mouths are frozen open as if they cannot open wide enough for the laughter, they are stamping their feet, clutching their chairs with laughter, like uncles who have had one of their own tricks played on them. Tears run down Harry's face. Hutch claps.

Something white flies by and catches on the vines. Clothing? Actions bring results . . . but she is beginning to feel a drop, a fatal fading of interest. She has already been delivered of one miracle. She is tired. She places the watermelon bowl on the table in front of Harry.

'Here you are,' she says.

David Malouf

A MEDIUM
1985

When I was eleven I took violin lessons once a week from a Miss Katie McIntyre, always so called to distinguish her from Miss Pearl, her sister, who taught piano and accompanied us at exams.

Miss Katie had a big sunny studio in a building in the city, which was occupied below by dentists, paper suppliers and cheap photographers. It was on the fourth floor, and was approached by an old-fashioned cage lift that swayed precariously as it rose (beyond the smell of chemical fluid and an occasional whiff of gas) to the purer atmosphere Miss Katie shared with the only other occupant of the higher reaches, Miss E. Sampson, Spiritualist.

I knew about Miss Sampson from gossip I had heard among my mother's friends; and sometimes, if I was early, I would find myself riding up with her, the two of us standing firm on our feet while the dark cage wobbled.

The daughter of a well-known doctor, an anaesthetist, she had gone to Clayfield College, been clever, popular, a good sport. But then her gift appeared – that is how my mother's friends put it, just declared itself out of the blue, without in any way changing her cleverness or good humour.

She tried at first to deny it: she went to the university and studied Greek. But it had its own end in view and would not be trifled with. It laid its hand on her, made its claim, and set my mother's friends to wondering; not about Emily Sampson, but about themselves. They began to avoid her, and then later, years later, to seek her out.

Her contact, it seemed, was an Indian, whose male voice croaked from the delicate throat about the fichu of coffee-dipped lace; But she sometimes spoke as well with the voices of the dead: little girls who had succumbed to diphtheria or blood poisoning or had been strangled in suburban parks, soldiers killed in one of the wars, drowned sailors, lost sons and brothers, husbands felled beside their dahlias at the bottom of the yard. Hugging my violin case, I pushed hard against the bars to make room for the presences she might have brought in with her.

She was by then a woman of forty-nine or fifty – small, straight, business-like, in a tailored suit and with her hair cut in a silver helmet. She sucked Bonnington's Irish Moss for her voice (I could smell them) and advertised in the *Courier-Mail* under Services, along with Chiropractor and Colonic Irrigation. It was odd to see her name listed so boldly, E. Sampson, Spiritualist, in the foyer beside the lifts, among the dentists and their letters, the registered firms, Pty Ltd, and my own Miss McIntyre, LTCL, AMEB. Miss Sampson's profession, so nakedly asserted, appeared to speak for itself, with no qualification. She was herself the proof. It was this, I think, that put me in awe of her.

It seemed appropriate, in those days, that music should be separated from the more mundane business that was being carried on below – the whizzing of dentist's drills, the plugging of cavities with amalgam or gold, and the making of passport photos for people going overseas. But I thought of Miss Sampson, for all her sensible shoes, as a kind of quack, and was sorry that Miss Katie and the Arts should be associated with her, and with the troops of subdued, sad-eyed women (they were mostly women) who made the pilgrimage to her room and shared the last stages of the lift with us: women whose husbands might have been bank managers – wearing smart hats and gloves and tilting their chins a little in defiance of their having at last 'come to it'; other women in dumpy florals, with freckled arms and too much talc, who worked in hospital kitchens or cleaned offices or took in washing, all decently gloved and hatted now, but looking scared of the company they were in and the heights to which the lift wobbled as they clung to the bars. The various groups hung apart, using their elbows in a ladylike way, but using them, and producing genteel formulas such as 'Pardon' or 'I'm so sorry' when the crush brought them close. Though touched already by a hush of shared anticipation, they had not yet accepted their commonality. There were distinctions to be observed, even here.

On such occasions the lift, loaded to capacity, made heavy work of it. And it wasn't, I thought, simply the weight of bodies (eight persons only, a notice warned) that made the old mechanism grind in its shaft, but the weight of all that sorrow, all that hopelessness and last hope, all that dignity in the privacy of grief, and silence broken only by an occasional 'Now don't you upset yourself, pet,' or a whispered, 'George would want it, I know he would.' We ascended slowly.

I found it preferable on the whole to arrive early and ride up fast, and in silence, with Miss Sampson herself.

Sometimes, in the way of idle curiosity (if such a motive could be ascribed to her) she would let her eyes for a moment rest on *me*, and I wondered hotly what she might be seeing beyond a plump eleven-year-old with scarred knees clutching at Mozart. Like most boys of that age I had much to conceal.

But she appeared to be looking at me, not through me. She smiled, I responded, and clearing my throat to find a voice, would say in a well-brought-up, Little Lord Fauntleroy manner that I hoped might fool her and leave me alone with my secrets, 'Good afternoon, Miss Sampson.'

Her own voice was as unremarkable as an aunt's: 'Good afternoon, dear.'

All the more alarming then, as I sat waiting on one of the cane-bottomed chairs in the corridor, while Ben Steinberg, Miss McIntyre's star pupil, played the Max Bruch, to hear the same voice oddly transmuted. Resonating above the slight swishing and breathing of her congregation, all those women in gloves, hats, fur-pieces, packed in among ghostly pampas-grass, it had stepped down a tone – no, several – and came from another continent. I felt a shiver go up my spine. It was the Indian, speaking through her out of another existence.

Standing at an angle to the half-open door, I caught only a segment of the scene. In the glow of candlelight off bronze, at three-thirty in the afternoon, when the city outside lay sweltering in the glare of a blue-black thundercloud, a being I could no longer think of as the woman in the lift, with her sensible shoes and her well-cut navy suit, was seated cross-legged among cushions, eyes closed, head rolled back with all the throat exposed as for a knife stroke.

A low humming filled the room. The faint luminescence of the pampas-grass was angelic, and I was reminded of something I had seen once from the window of a railway carriage as my train sat steaming on the line: three old men – tramps they might have been – in a luminous huddle behind the glass of a waiting-shed, their grey heads aureoled with fog and the closed space aglow with their breathing like a jar full of fireflies. The vision haunted me. It was entirely real –

I mean the tramps were real enough, you might have smelled them if you'd got close – but the way I had seen them changed that reality, made me so impressionably aware that I could recall details I could not possibly have seen at that distance or with the naked eye: the greenish-grey of one old man's hair where it fell in locks over his shoulder, the grime of a hand bringing out all its wrinkles, the ring of dirt round a shirt collar. Looking through into Miss Sampson's room was like that. I saw too much. I felt light-headed and began to sweat.

A flutter of excitement passed over the scene. A new presence had entered the room. It took the form of a child's voice, treble and whining, and one of the women gave a cry that was immediately supported by a buzz of other voices. The treble one, stronger now, cut through them. Miss Sampson was swaying like a flower on its stalk.

Minutes later, behind the door of Miss Katie's sunny studio, having shown off my scales, my arpeggios, my three pieces, I stood with my back to the piano (facing the wall behind which so much emotion was contained) while Miss Katie played intervals and I named them, or struck chords and I named those. It wasn't difficult. It was simple mathematics and I had an ear, though the chords might also in other contexts, and in ways that were not explicable, move you to tears.

There is no story, no set of events that leads anywhere or proves anything – no middle, no end. Just a glimpse through a half-open door, voices seen not heard, vibrations sensed through a wall while the trained ear strains, not to hear what is passing in the next room, but to measure the chords – precise, fixed, nameable as diminished fifths or Neapolitan sixths, but also at moments approaching tears – that are being struck out on an iron-framed upright; and the voice that names them your own.

A l a n   M a r s h a l l

'TELL US ABOUT THE TURKEY, JO ...'

1941

He came walking through the rusty grasses and seaweedish plants that fringe Lake Corangamite. Behind him strode his brother.

He was very fair. His hair was a pale gold and when he scratched his head the parted hairs revealed the pink skin of his scalp. His eyes were very blue. He was freckled. His nose was tipped upward. I liked him tremendously. I judged him to be about four and a half years old and his brother twice that age.

They wore blue overalls and carried them jauntily. The clean wind came across the water and fluttered the material against their legs. Their air was one of independence and release from authority.

They scared the two plovers I had been watching. The birds lifted with startled cries and banked against the wind. They cut across large clouds patched with blue and sped away, flapping low over the water.

The two boys and I exchanged greetings while we looked each other over. I think they liked me. The little one asked me several personal questions. He wanted to know what I was doing there, why I was wearing a green shirt, where was my mother? I gave him the information with the respect due to another seeker after knowledge. I then asked him a question and thus learned of the dangers and disasters that had beset his path.

'How did you get that cut on your head?' I asked. In the centre of his forehead a pink scar divided his freckles.

The little boy looked quickly at his brother. The brother answered for him. The little boy expected and conceded this. He looked at the brother expectantly and, as the brother spoke, the little boy's eyes shone, his lips parted, as one who listens to a thrilling story.

'He fell off a babies' chair when he was little,' said the brother. 'He hit his head on a shovel and bled over it.'

'Ye-e-s,' faltered the little boy, awed by the picture, and in his eyes was excitement and the thrill of danger passed. He looked across the flat water, wrapt in the thought of the chair and the shovel and the blood.

'A cow kicked him once,' said the brother.

'A cow!' I exclaimed.

'Yes,' he said.

'Go on, Jo,' said the little boy eagerly, standing before him and looking up into his face.

'He tried to leg-rope it,' Jo explained, 'and the cow let out and got him in the stomach.'

'In the stomach,' emphasised the little boy, turning quickly to me and nodding his head.

'Gee!' I exclaimed.

'Gee!' echoed the little boy.

'It winded him,' said Jo.

'I was winded,' said the little boy slowly, as if in doubt. 'What's winded, Jo?'

'He couldn't breathe properly,' Jo addressed me.

'I couldn't breathe a bit,' said the little boy.

'That was bad,' I said.

'Yes, it was bad, wasn't it, Jo?' said the little boy.

'Yes,' said Jo.

Jo looked intently at the little boy as if searching for scars of other conflicts.

'A ladder fell on him once,' he said.

The little boy looked quickly at my face to see if I was impressed. The statement had impressed him very much.

'No?' said I unbelievingly.

'Will I show him, Jo?' asked the little boy eagerly.

'Yes,' said Jo.

The little boy, after giving me a quick glance of satisfaction, bent and placed his hands on his knees. Jo lifted the back of his brother's shirt collar and peered into the warm shadow between his back and the cotton material.

'You can see it,' he said uncertainly, searching the white skin for its whereabouts.

The little boy twisted his arm behind his back and strove to touch a spot on one of his shoulders.

'It's there, Jo. Can you see it, Jo?'

'Yes. That's it,' said Jo. 'You come here and see.' He looked at me. 'Don't move, Jimmy.'

'Jo's found it,' announced Jimmy, his head twisted to face me.

I rose from my seat on a pitted rock nestling in grass and stepped over to them. I bent and looked beneath the lifted collar. On the white skin of his shoulder was the smooth ridge of a small scar.

'Yes. It's there all right,' I said. 'I'll bet you cried when you got that.'

The little boy turned to Jo. 'Did I cry, Jo?'

'A bit,' said Jo.

'I never do cry much, do I, Jo?'

'No,' said Jo.

'How did it happen?' I asked.

'The ladder had hooks in it . . .' commenced Jo.

'Had hooks in it,' emphasised the little boy, nodding at me.

'And he pulled it down on top of him,' continued Jo.

'Oo!' said the little boy excitedly, clasping his hands and holding them between his knees while he stamped his feet. 'Oo-o-o!'

'It knocked him rotten,' said Jo.

'I was knocked rotten,' declared the little boy slowly, as if revealing the fact to himself for the first time.

There was a pause while the little boy enjoyed his thoughts.

'It's a nice day, isn't it?' Jo sought new contacts with me.

'Yes,' said I.

The little boy stood in front of his brother entreating him with his eyes.

'What else was I in, Jo?' he pleaded.

Jo pondered, looking at the ground and nibbling his thumb.

'You was in nothin' else,' he said, finally.

'Aw, Jo!' The little boy was distressed at the finality of the statement. He bent suddenly and pulled up the leg of his overalls. He searched his bare leg for marks of violence.

'What's that, Jo?' He pointed to a faint mark on his knee.

'That's nothin',' said Jo. Jo wanted to talk about ferrets. 'You know, ferrets . . .' he began.

'It looks like something,' I said, looking closely at the mark.

Jo leant forward and examined it. The little boy, clutching the crumpled leg of his trousers, looked from my face to his brother's and back again, anxiously waiting a decision.

Jo made a closer examination, rubbing the mark with his finger. The little boy followed Jo's investigation with an expectant attention.

'You mighta had a burn once. I don't know.'

'I wish I did have a burn, Jo,' said the little boy. It was a plea for a commitment from Jo, but Jo was a stickler for truth.

'I can't remember you being burnt,' he said. 'Mum'd know.'

'Perhaps you can think of another exciting thing,' I suggested.

'Yes,' said the little boy eagerly. He came over and took my hand so that we might await together the result of Jo's cogitation. He looked up at me and said, 'Isn't Jo good?'

'Very good,' I said.

'He knows about me and everything.'

'Yes,' I said.

There was a faint 'yoo-hoo!' from behind us. We all turned. A little girl came running through the rocks in the barrier that guarded the lake from the cultivated lands. She had thin legs and wore long, black stockings. One had come loose from its garter, and, as she ran, she bent and pulled and strove to push its top beneath the elastic band. Her gait was thus a series of hops and unequal strides.

She called her brothers' names as she ran, and in her voice was the note of the bearer-of-news.

'Dad must be home,' said Jo.

But the little boy was resentful of this intrusion. 'What does she want?' he said sourly.

The little girl had reached a flat stretch of grass and her speed increased. Her short hair fluttered in the wind of her running.

She waved a hand. 'We have a baby sister!' she yelled.

'Aw, pooh!' exclaimed the little boy.

He turned and tugged at Jo's arm. 'Have you thought of anything exciting yet, Jo?' His face lit to a sudden recollection. 'Tell him how I got chased by the turkey,' he cried.

Olga Masters

THE LANG WOMEN
1982

Lucy was a thin, wistful wispy child who lived with her mother and grandmother and had few moments in her life except a bedtime ritual which she started to think about straggling home from school at four o'clock.

Sometimes she would start to feel cheerful even with her hands still burning from contact with Miss Kelly's ruler, and puzzle over this sudden lifting of her spirits then remember there was only a short while left to bedtime.

She was like a human alarm-clock which had been set to go off when she reached the gate leading to the farm and purr away until she fell asleep lying against her grandmother's back with her thighs tucked under her grandmother's rump and her face not minding at all being squashed against the ridge of little knobs at the back of her grandmother's neck.

Her grandmother and her mother would talk for hours after they were all in bed. Sometimes it would seem they had all drowsed off and the mother or the grandmother would say 'Hey, listen!' and Lucy would shoot her head up too to hear. Her grandmother would dig her with an elbow and say: 'Get back down there and go to sleep!' Lucy was not really part of the talk just close to the edges of it.

It was as if the grandmother and the mother were frolicking in the sea, but Lucy unable to swim had to stand at the edge and be satisfied with the wash from their bodies.

Lucy made sure she was in bed before her mother and grandmother in order to watch.

It was as if she were seeing two separate plays on the one stage. Carrie the mother performed the longest. She was twenty-six and it was the only time in the day when she could enjoy her body. Not more than cleansing and admiring it since Lucy's father had died five years

455

earlier. Carrie was like a ripe cherry with thick black hair cut level with her ears and in a fringe across her forehead. She was squarish in shape not dumpy or overweight and with rounded limbs brown from exposure to the sun because she and the grandmother Jess also a widow and the mother of Carrie's dead husband worked almost constantly in the open on their small farm which returned them a meagre living.

Carrie was nicknamed Boxy since she was once described in the village as good looking but a bit on the boxy side in reference to her shape. When this got back to Carrie she worried about it although it was early in the days of her widowhood and her mind was not totally on her face and figure.

Some time later at night with all her clothes off and before the mirror in the bedroom she would frown on herself turning from side to side trying to decide if she fitted the description. She thought her forehead and ears were two of her good points and she would lift her fringe and study her face without it and lift her hair from her ears and look long at her naked jawline then take her hands away and swing her head to allow her hair to fall back into place. She would place a hand on her hip, dent a knee forward, throw her shoulders back and think what a shame people could not see her like this.

'Not boxy at all,' she would say inside her throat which was long for a shortish person and in which could be seen a little blue throbbing pulse.

She shook her head so that her thick hair swung wildly about then settled down as if it had never been disturbed.

'See that?' she would say to her mother-in-law.

Jess would be performing in her corner of the room and it was usually with a knee up under her nightdress and a pair of scissors gouging away at an ingrown toenail. She never bothered to fasten the neck of her nightdress and it was an old thing worn for many seasons and her feet were not all that clean as she did not wash religiously every night as Carrie did. She spent hardly any time tearing off her clothes and throwing them down, turned so that the singlet was on the outside and when she got into them in the morning she had only to turn the thickness of the singlet, petticoat and dress and pull the lot over her head.

Carrie did not seem to notice although she sometimes reprimanded Jess for failing to clean her teeth. When this happened Jess would run her tongue around her gums top and bottom while she ducked beneath the covers and Lucy would be glad there was no more delay.

It was only the operations like digging at a toenail or picking at a bunion that kept Jess up. Sometimes she pushed her nightdress made into a tent with her raised knee down to cover her crotch but mostly she left it up so that Lucy hooped up in bed saw her front passage glistening and winking like an eye.

The lamp on the dressing table stood between Carrie and Jess so that Lucy could see Carrie's naked body as well either still or full of movement and rhythm as she rubbed moistened oatmeal around her eyes and warmed olive oil on her neck and shoulders.

The rest of the little town knew about the bedtime ritual since Walter Grant the postmaster rode out one evening and saw them through the window. It had been two days of wild storms and heavy rain and the creek was in danger of breaking its banks. Any stock of Carrie's and Jess's low down would be safer moved. Walter on his mission to warn them saw Jess with her knee raised and her nightgown around her waist and Carrie's body blooming golden in the lamplight for they were enjoying the storm and had left the curtains open. Walter saw more when Carrie rushed to fling them together and rode home swiftly with his buttocks squeezed together on the saddle holding onto a vision of Carrie's rose-tipped breasts, the creamy channel between them, her navel small and perfect as a shell and her thighs moving angrily and her little belly shaking.

After that the town referred to the incident as that 'cock show'.

Many forecast a dark future for Lucy witnessing it night after night.

Some frowned upon Lucy when she joined groups containing their children at the show or sports' day.

The Lang women's house had only one bedroom, one of two front rooms on either side of a small hall. The hall ran into a kitchen and living room combined which was the entire back portion of the house.

It would have been reasonable to expect them to make a second bedroom by moving the things from what was called the 'front room'. But neither Jess nor Carrie ever attempted or suggested this. The room was kept as it was from the early days of Jess's marriage. It was crowded with a round oak table and chairs and a chiffonier crowded with ornaments, photographs and glassware and there were two or three deceptively frail tables loaded with more stuff. On the walls were heavily framed pictures mostly in pairs of swans on calm water, raging seas and English cottages sitting in snow or surrounded by unbelievable gardens.

Even when the only child Patrick was living at home and up until he left at fifteen he slept in the single bed in his parents' room where Carrie slept now. He was fifty miles up the coast working in a timber mill when he met Carrie a housemaid at the town's only hotel. They married when he was twenty and she was nineteen and pregnant with Lucy who was an infant of a few months when Patrick was loaned a new-fangled motorbike and rounding a bend in the road the bike smacked up against the rear of a loaded timber lorry like a ball thrown hard against a wall. Patrick died with a surprised look on his face and his fair hair only lightly streaked with dust and blood.

Jess was already widowed more than a year and managing the farm single handed so Carrie and Lucy without a choice came to live there.

Lucy could not remember sleeping anywhere but against her grandmother's back.

Sometimes when the grandmother turned in the night she fitted neatly onto the grandmother's lap her head on the two small pillows of her grandmother's breasts.

She was never actually held in her grandmother's arms that she knew about. When she woke the grandmother's place was empty because it was Jess who was up first to start milking the cows which was up to twenty in the spring and summer and half that in the winter. Carrie got up when the cows were stumbling into the yard seen in the half-light from the window and Lucy waited about until eight o'clock when they both came in to get breakfast. Lucy was expected to keep the fire in the stove going and have her school clothes on. She usually had one or another garment on inside-out and the laces trailing from her shoes and very often she lied when asked by Carrie or Jess if she had washed. Carrie did little or no housework and Jess had to squeeze the necessary jobs in between the farm work. Carrie was content to eat a meal with the remains of the one before still on the table, clearing a little space for her plate by lifting the tablecloth and shaking it clear of crumbs, sending them into the middle of the table with the pickles and sugar and butter if they could afford to have a pound delivered with their empty cream cans from the butter factory.

Carrie trailed off to bed after their late tea not caring if she took most of the hot water for her wash leaving too little for the washing-up.

Jess grumbled about this but not to Carrie's face.

Once after Jess had managed on the hot water left and the washing-up was done and the room tidied she said in Lucy's hearing that she hoped Carrie never took to bathing in milk. Lucy had a vision of Carrie's black hair swirling above a tubful of foamy milk. Her own skin prickled and stiffened as if milk were drying on it. She left the floor where she was playing and put her chin on the edge of the table Jess was wiping down waiting to hear more. But Jess flung the dishcloth on its nail and turned her face to busy herself with shedding her hessian apron as the first step towards getting to bed.

This was the life of the Lang women when Arthur Mann rode into it.

Jess and Carrie inside following their midday meal saw him through the kitchen window with the head of his horse over the fence midway between the lemon tree and a wild rose entangled with convolvulus. The blue bell-like flowers and the lemons made a frame for horse and rider that Jess remembered for a long time.

'It's a Mann!' Jess said to Carrie who did not realise at once that Jess was using the family name.

The Manns were property owners on the outer edge of the district and they were well enough off to keep aloof from the village people. Their children went to boarding schools and they did not shop locally nor show their cattle and produce at the local show but took it to the large city shows.

But Jess easily recognised a Mann when she saw one. When she was growing up the Manns were beginning to grow in wealth and had not yet divorced themselves from the village. They not only came to dances and tennis matches but helped organise them and there were Manns who sang and played the piano in end-of-year concerts and Manns won foot races and steer riding at the annual sports.

They nearly all had straight dark sandy hair and skin tightly drawn over jutting jawbones.

Jess going towards the fence got a good view of the hair and bones when Arthur swept his hat off and held it over his hands on the saddle.

'You're one of the Manns,' said Jess her fine grey eyes meeting his that were a little less grey, a bit larger and with something of a sleepy depth in them.

Arthur keeping his hat off told her why he had come. He had leased land adjoining the Langs' to the south where he was running some steers and he would need to repair the fence neglected by the owners and the Langs neither of whom could afford the luxury of well-fenced land.

He or one of his brothers or one of their share farmers would be working on the fence during the next few weeks.

'We don't use the bit of land past the creek,' said Jess before the subject of money came up. 'The creek's our boundary so a fence is no use to us.'

Arthur Mann's eyes smiled before his mouth. He pulled the reins of his horse to turn it around before he said there would be no costs to the Langs involved. He put his hat on and raised it again and Jess saw the split of his coat that showed his buttocks well shaped like the buttocks of his horse which charged off as if happy to have the errand done.

Jess came inside to the waiting Carrie.

Lucy home from school was playing with some acorns she found on the way. Jess saw her schoolcase open on the floor with some crusts in it and the serviette that wrapped her sandwiches stained with jam. Flies with wings winking in the sun crawled about the crusts and Lucy's legs.

'She's a disgrace!' Jess cried trying to put out of her mind the sight of Arthur Mann's polished boots and the well-ironed peaks of his blue shirt resting on the lapels of his coat.

With her foot Carrie swept the acorns into a heap and went to the mirror dangling from the corner of a shelf to put her hat on. Jess took hers too from the peg with her hessian apron. She turned it around in her hands before putting it on. It was an old felt of her husband's once a rich grey but the colour beaten out now with the weather. It bore stains and blotches where it rubbed constantly against the cows' sides as Jess milked. Jess plucked at a loose thread on the band and ripped it away taking it to the fire to throw it in. The flames snatched it greedily swallowing the grease with a little pop of joy.

Lucy lifted her face and opened her mouth to gape with disappointment. She would have added it to her playthings.

'Into the fire it went!' said Jess. 'Something else you'd leave lyin' around!'

She looked for a moment as if she would discard the hat too but put it on and went out.

It was Carrie who encountered Arthur Mann first working on the fence when she was in the corn paddock breaking and flattening the dead stalks for the reploughing. Almost without thinking she walked towards the creek bank and stood still observing Arthur who had his back to her. He is a man, she thought remembering Jess's words with a different inference. His buttocks under old, very clean well-cut breeches quivered with the weight of a fence post he was dropping into a hole. He had his hat off lying on a canvas bag that might have held some food. Jess might have wondered about the food and thought of a large clean flyproof Mann kitchen but Carrie chose to look at Arthur's hair moving in a little breeze like stiff bleached grass and his waistline where a leather belt shiny with age and quality anchored his shirt inside his pants.

He turned and saw her.

As he did not have a hat to lift he seemed to want to do something with his hands so he took some hair between two fingers and smoothed it towards an ear. Carrie saw all his fine teeth when he smiled.

'Hullo . . . Shorty,' he said.

'No . . . Boxy,' she said.

She was annoyed with herself for saying it.

He probably knew the nickname through his share farmers who were part of the village life and would have filled the waiting ears of the Manns with village gossip. Carrie did not know but he had heard too about the nightly cock show.

Arthur thought now of Carrie's naked body although it was well covered with an old print dress once her best, cut high at the neck and trimmed there and on the sleeves with narrow lace. Carrie was aware that it was unsuitable for farm work and took off her hat and held it hiding the neckline. She shook her hair the way she did getting ready for bed at night and it swung about then settled into two deep peaks against her cheeks gone quite pink.

'Come across,' said Arthur, 'I'm stopping for smoko.'

Carrie nearly moved then became aware of her feet in old elastic-side rubber boots and buried them deeper in the grass. She inclined her head towards the corn paddock as if this was where her duty lay. Still holding her hat at her neck and still smiling she turned and Arthur did not go back to the fence until she had disappeared into the corn.

Carrie spent the time before milking at the kitchen table in her petticoat pulling the lace from the dress. Lucy home from school with her case and her mouth open watched from the floor. When Carrie was done she stood and pulled the dress over her head brushing the neck and sleeves free of cotton ends. She swept the lace scraps into a heap and moved towards the stove.

'Don't burn it!' Jess cried sharply. 'Give it to her for her doll!'

Lucy seized the lace and proceeded to wind it around the naked body of a doll that had only the stump of a right arm, its nose squashed in and most of its hair worn off.

A few days later Arthur rode up to the fence with a bag of quinces.

Lucy saw him when she looked up from under the plum tree that grew against the wall of the house. She was on some grass browning in the early winter and her doll sat between her legs stuck stiffly out. Arthur raised the quinces as a signal to collect them but Lucy turned her face towards the house and Arthur saw her fair straight hair that was nothing like Carrie's luxuriant crop.

In a moment Carrie came from one side of the house and Jess from the other. They went up to the fence and Lucy got up and trailed behind.

Arthur handed the quinces between Carrie and Jess and Jess took them taking one out and turning it around.

She did not speak but her eyes shone no less than the sheen from the yellow skin of the fruit.

'The three Lang women,' Arthur said smiling. 'Or are there four?'

Lucy had her doll held by its one and a half arms to cover her face. Ashamed she flung it behind her back.

Arthur arched the neck of his horse and turned it around.

'I'll buy her a new one,' he said and cantered off.

Neither Jess nor Carrie looked at Lucy's face when they went inside. Jess tipped the quinces onto the table where they bowled among the cups and plates and she picked one up and rubbed her thumb thoughtfully on the skin and then set it down and gathered them all together with her arms.

Then she went into the front room and returned with a glass dish and with the hem of her skirt wiped it out and put the fruit in and carried it back to set it on one of the little tables. Carrie's eyes clung to her back until she disappeared then looked dully on Lucy sitting stiff and entranced on the edge of a chair. She opened her mouth to tell Lucy to pick up her doll from the floor but decided Jess would do it on her return. But Jess stepped over the doll and put on her hessian apron and reached for her hat. She turned it round in her hands then put it back on the peg. Carrie saw the back of her neck unlined and her brown hair without any grey and her shoulders without a hump and her arms coming from the torn-out sleeves of a man's old shirt pale brown like a smooth new sugar bag. Then when Jess reached for an enamel jug for the house milk Carrie saw her hooded eyelids dropping a curtain on what was in her eyes. Carrie put her hat on without looking in the mirror and followed Jess out. She looked down her back over her firm rump to her ankles for something that said she was old but there was nothing.

In bed that night Lucy dreamed of her doll.

It had long legs in white stockings with black patent leather shoes fastened with the smallest black buttons in the world.

The dress was pink silk with ruffles at the throat and a binding of black velvet ribbon which trailed to the hemline of the dress. The face was pink and white and unsmiling and the hair thick and black like Carrie's hair.

Lucy lay wedged under the cliff of her grandmother's back wondering what was different about tonight. She heard a little wind breathing around the edges of the curtain and a creak from a floorboard in the kitchen and a small snuffling whine from their old dog Sadie settling into sleep under the house.

Lucy marvelled at the silence.

No-one is talking she thought.

Every afternoon Lucy looked for the doll when she came in from school. On the way home she pictured it on the table propped against the milk jug, its long legs stretched among the sugar bowl and breadcrumbs.

But it was never there and when she looked into the face of Jess and Carrie there was no message there and no hope.

The following Saturday Lucy could wait no longer and sneaked past the cowyard where Jess and Carrie were milking and well clear of it ran like a small pale terrier through the abandoned orchard and bottom corn paddock to the edge of the creek. Across it, a few panels of fence beyond where Carrie had first encountered him, Arthur was at work.

Under her breath Lucy practised her words: 'Have you brought my doll?'

She was saying them for the tenth time when Arthur turned.

She closed her mouth before they slipped out.

Arthur pushed his hat back and beckoned.

'Come over,' he said.

Lucy hesitated and looked at her feet buried in the long wild grass. I won't go, she said to herself. But the doll could be inside Arthur's bag hung on a fence-post.

She plunged down the creek bank and came up the other side her spiky head breaking through the spiky tussocks dying with the birth of winter.

Arthur sat down on some fence timber strewn on the ground and reached for his bag. Lucy watched, her heart coming up into her neck for him to pull the doll from it. But he took out a paper bag smeared with grease which turned out to hold two slices of yellow cake oozing red jam. When he looked up and saw the hunger in Lucy's eyes he thought it was for the cake and held it towards her.

'We'll have a piece each,' he said.

But Lucy sank down into the grass and crossed her feet with her knees out. Then she thought if she didn't take the cake Arthur might not produce the doll so she reached out a hand.

'Good girl,' he said when she began nibbling it.

The cake was not all that good in spite of coming from the rich Mann's kitchen. It had been made with liberal quantities of slightly rancid butter.

Lucy thought of bringing him a cake made by Jess and imagined him snapping his big teeth on it then wiping his fingers and bringing out the doll.

'I should visit you, eh?' Arthur said.

Oh yes! He would be sure to bring the doll.

'When is the best time?' Arthur said folding the paper bag into a square and putting it back in his bag.

'At night after tea? Or do you all go to bed early?'

Lucy thought of Carrie naked and Jess with her legs apart and shook her head.

'Why not at night?' Arthur said. 'There's no milking at night is there?'

Lucy had to agree there wasn't with another small headshake.

'What do you all do after tea?' said Arthur.

Lucy looked away from him across the paddocks to the thin drift of smoke coming from the fire under the copper boiling for the clean-up after the milk was separated. She felt a sudden urge to protect Jess and Carrie from Arthur threatening to come upon them in their nakedness.

She got to her feet and ran down the bank, her speed carrying her up the other side and by this time Arthur had found his voice.

'Tell them I'll come!' he called to her running back.

Carrie was in bed that night with much less preparation than usual and even without the last-minute ritual of lifting her hair from her night-gown neck and smoothing down the little collar, then easing herself carefully down between the sheets reluctant to disturb her appearance even preparing for sleep.

To Lucy's surprise her nightgown hung slightly over one shoulder and she was further surprised to see that Jess had fastened hers at the brown stain where her neck met the top of her breasts. Carrie had not cavorted in her nakedness and Jess not plucked at her feet with her knees raised. Lucy looked at the chair where Jess usually sat and pictured Arthur there. She saw his hands on his knees while he talked to them and curved her arms imagining the doll in them. An elbow stuck into Jess's back and Jess shook it off.

'Arthur Mann never married,' said Carrie abruptly from her bed.

Jess lifted her head and pulled the pillow leaving only a corner for Lucy who didn't need it anyway for she had raised her head to hear.

'Old Sarah sees to that,' said Jess.

Before putting her head down again Lucy saw that Carrie was not settling down for sleep but had her eyes on the ceiling and her elbows up like the drawing of a ship's sail and her hands linked under her head.

Jess's one open eye saw too.

Lucy had to wait through Sunday but on Monday when she was home from school for the May holidays she slipped past the dairy again while Jess and Carrie were milking and from the bank of the creek saw not only Arthur but a woman on a horse very straight in the back with some grey hair showing neatly at the edge of a riding hat and the skin on her face stretched on the bones like Arthur's. The horse was a grey with a skin like washing water scattered over with little pebbles of suds and it moved about briskly under the rider who sat wonderfully still despite the fidgeting.

Lucy sank down into the tussocks on the bank and the woman saw.

'What is that?' she said to Arthur. Then she raised her chin like a handsome fox alerted to something in the distance and fixed her gaze on the smoke away behind Lucy rising thin and blue from the Lang women's fire.

Lucy had seen Arthur's face before the woman spoke but he now lowered his head and she saw only the top of his hat nearly touched the wire he was twisting and clipping with pliers.

The horse danced some more and Lucy was still with her spiky head nearly between her knees staring at the ground. The woman wanted her to go. But Lucy had seen people shooting rabbits not firing when the rabbits were humped still but pulling the trigger when they leapt forward stretching their bodies as they ran. Perhaps the woman had a gun somewhere in her riding coat and breeches or underneath her round little hat. Lucy sat on with the sun and wind prickling the back of her neck.

'Good heavens!' the woman cried suddenly and wheeling her horse around galloped off.

Lucy let a minute pass then got up and ran down and up the opposite bank to Arthur.

He went on working snip, snip with the pliers until Lucy spoke.

'You can come of a night and visit,' she said.

Arthur looked up and down the fence and only briefly at the Lang corn paddock and the rising smoke beyond it.

'I've finished the fence,' he said.

Lucy saw the neat heap of timber not needed and the spade and other tools ready for moving. She saw the canvas on top, flat as a dead and gutted rabbit.

'I know why you didn't bring the doll,' she said. 'Your mother won't let you.'

A KNIGHT OF TEETH
1981

He came to the sleep-out calling, 'At first light we'll do the gutters!'

Half asleep I mumbled, 'Do 'em? gutters?'

'Yes, the storm's gone. The gutters. Find a few things.'

Gutters – roof or street? I didn't like heights, but someone would have to hold the ladder. Walking kerbs at dawn with an eccentric didn't appeal to me though at that hour there'd be few people about to see us scavenging.

Street gutters, however, lead to drains and stormwater pipes. Nobody would ever, ever get me into a stormwater pipe. I knew that if you went into a stormwater pipe a cloud would miraculously appear and its deluge scour all drains. The blast of air, the terrible roar, the awful circle of rubbishy foam.

So I shuffled into the house, knocked on the bedroom door and asked, 'Which gutter, Bert?'

I heard my aunt say, 'It's a nightmare, go calm him. Witches. Witches and demons. What are witch-gutters?'

I certainly hadn't thought of witches and demons. I remembered the blood-gutter in the bayonet he'd shown me.

'The gutters!' he yelled. 'The beach gutters. I'll wake you.'

Comforted, I returned to the sleep-out.

He fed us porridge, sausages and fried bread. He wore faded, over-size army khakies. Long baggy shorts, shirt and jacket. Sandshoes. Thin, tallish. When we got to the beach we went to the rocks at the south end. The sky yellowish, shot with red. The sea gathering for another storm.

He gestured to a crack in the rock from cliff to sea. 'Not a gutter.' He squatted beside a pool. Like a stone. 'Clack – clack.' He looked over his shoulder at me. 'Clack – clack.' He laughed, and showed a set of hinged dentures. 'Ole!' he cried. 'My lucky castanets.'

The closest birds moved further away.

He strode to the beach as the first sunlight touched the sand. Looking for glints. The glints I went to were bits of glass and bottle tops. By the time I'd found three coins he'd gathered thirty, a ring and a brooch. Whenever he felt he had to celebrate he clacked. His footprints made easy curves, mine were all sharp angles. At the end of the beach he stopped. 'Now for the real clackers,' taking the teeth from his mouth, holding them at arm's length. His chin now a lot closer to nose. 'How'll we go today?' he asked the teeth.

I looked around to see if we still had the beach to ourselves.

Clack – clack – clack. Not as loud as the castanets.

'I'll translate,' he said. 'We'll do better than most times, but not up to the best time.' The next question: 'Which end of the beach?' Clack.

'This end,' he interpreted.

He rolled his shorts as high as they'd go and waded into what he called the gutter, the underwater trench in the sand alongside the rocks, not big enough to be a channel. He lifted his foot, took from toes what he'd found and tossed it ashore. He shook his head when I held up rusted iron chain. He found brass buckles, coins, sunglasses. Sometimes he found so much he seemed to be hopping. His shorts and jacket darkened with water. For every find he tossed to me he dropped one into his pocket. His big toothless grins. Once, he lurched and almost went under. He balanced his pockets. Glancing at the beach he directed me to a glint. 'Left . . . too far . . . back, back . . . five paces left.'

When he waded onto the beach he looked like a soldier who'd lost his gear. He took the granny glasses I'd found and jammed them across his forehead.

'Bert,' he announced, 'Herbert, means army-bright, maybe war-bright, germanic, German. Bosch, my Dad called them. When I fought they were Hun or Kraut.'

Back in the gutter he found an upper plate, with golden eye-tooth. 'Vanity,' he cried, 'all is vanity.'

More teeth, gold and silver chains, rusted tobacco tins. Wet to the hips. He raised his arms.

'In Borneo,' he said, 'I waded to my chin. I was a wild man then but I kept the rifle dry.'

The rising tide forced him onto the beach. He emptied his pockets. All coins were for me, even the sovereign. Holding high necklaces and a bracelet he cried, 'I have bejewelled my daughters from these waters – not that they like to be reminded. Other days, money found is money mine. My daughters – your cousins – get what isn't claimed. Jewellery and teeth I list on cards in the milk-bar window. I once found a mesh purse with three hundred dollars in it. The cops had to give it to me in the end. They hated me. I used to send unclaimed teeth to the dental hospital. Too good to waste. Teachers got the students to guess the jaws they'd come from. Had a good mate there, he went to Canada. Then I had a blue with the professor who said I was upsetting the patients with my gifts. I tripped with a shoe-box full of teeth, everywhere. He said I was making a mock of the profession. He had five thousand dollars in his mouth. Nowadays I make things with unclaimed teeth.'

'Things . . .'

'Just things. Found a full ivory set last year. Swept down the river in the flood. From a washed-out graveyard.'

'Did you make a – thing from the ivories?'

'I made what was demanded by the find. By which I don't mean the teeth spoke to me.'

I smiled with relief.

'Guess what I made?' he said. 'A miniature something.'

'Necklace?'

'Nooooo – something demanded by thirty-two teeth.'

I couldn't guess.

'I made a miniature chess set. Used a jeweller's eye-glass. We'll play a game later.'

'I can't play,' I stammered.

'Teach you,' he said. 'It's tactics, you need tactics if you're going to get on. Two years ago a knighted industrialist lost his teeth here. Big in concrete –' he winked, '– I bet his enemies look small in concrete boots. Anyway, he was here, demonstrating his humble beginnings to camera and notebook when a dumper battered him. A week later I found three beautiful gold caps and a solid gold with diamond. A small diamond, nothing flash. To be seen in anger, perhaps.'

'He must have been pleased when you found them.'

'He wasn't.'

'Was there a reward?'

'No reward.'

'Then he was just another rich mean man.'

'I didn't return them to him.'

I was astounded. 'Were they broken?'

'Intact. Tactics, my boy. Can you imagine a millionaire pleased to get his teeth back? To let it be known he'd lost his teeth?'

The question I daredn't ask was put for me. 'What happened to the teeth? I might tell you some time.'

'Did you give them to the hospital?'

'I did not. The diamond would have had them drunk for a week. Good teeth pulled and wrong injections.'

I wondered if he'd smashed them for gold and diamond. I shuddered.

'Easy there,' he said. 'Drunken dentists, horrible, eh?'

Though we walked slowly up the beach his pockets clinked with trove.

'I lost my uppers in Cairns, the lowers in Syria fighting the French, no gas, no injection, nothing but wrench, wrench. Off you go soldier, says the ripper, and remember to gargle with salt water. He wouldn't let me keep one, not one. I reckon he sold them to the Arabs. Just one tooth, I begged him. Soldier, he said, you're a grown man, you can't put your tooth in a glass and expect sixpence. So off I go, groan, groan. The French near-killed him with a mortar. I've a soft spot for the frog. Free or Vichy. I've had five sets of repat clackers, I've found thirty-three in the sea.'

'Did you,' I asked, 'throw the diamond and gold into the sea?'

'Don't pry, boy.'

When we got to where the grass began he took the castanet teeth from his pocket and clacked his way through the tussocks to the road. I didn't hurry after him. He waited on the kerb. His clacking right hand. He took the teeth from his mouth. His hands whirling, clacking.

'Punch and Judy!' he cried, shoving the castanets into his mouth and his teeth into the pocket. 'Excuse me – wrong way,' and winked.

I looked back at the sea.

'Teach you chess,' he said, 'but first I'll put a card in the milk-bar window.' Fumbling in his shirt pocket for a pencil. I saw the milk-bar man open the door and lift a crate of bottles from the footpath. When he saw us he replaced the crate, closed the door, pulled the blind. He would not open to us.

'He's got awful teeth,' said Bert. 'Maybe he's tired of the cards. I suppose he gets jokers.'

'Did you advertise the millionaire's teeth?'

'You're too clever by half,' he said.

His chessboard was made from matches thickly varnished. He respected my reluctance to touch the toothed pieces. He allowed me to promote a pawn to queen. After a while we played draughts with beach coins as men. When I won my first game he rewarded me with florins. I pushed them back.

'Not enough?'

'I'd rather know about the diamond.'

'Well . . . the gold went into my gold bag, the diamond's in concrete.'

'Concrete?'

'Because its owner is big in concrete. A colossus in concrete. Sir Concrete.'

'Yes –?'

'Concrete. A great man. Would've been disrespectful to sell his diamond so I set it in wet kerbing near the new bridge.'

'Whereabouts?'

'You just keep away from it – not that I'm telling you the place.'

'You mean you pushed it in with your finger?'

'Yup.'

'The way you write your name in wet concrete?'

'You are never to write your name in wet concrete. You understand? Vandalism.'

'You must have marked the concrete,' I said cheekily.

'I gave it a perfect finish.'

'You couldn't have with a finger.'

'I used a bit of wood.'

'You could've bought things.'

'Your aunt doesn't know.'

'The millionaire doesn't know.'

For several years thereafter whenever I came across wet concrete I made a diamond shape in it. Several times I was chased by workmen or watchmen. Sometimes I made the shape from *Bert* four times. I saw the millionaire once. His eyes were hard. I did not see his teeth. When I drew a diamond shape in the air his two companions made as though to defend him and offend me. I continued across the checkered floor, entered a lift, ascended, got out, attended to my business, descended with the ghost of my uncle and walked across the checkered floor, two squares forward, one to the side, one forward, two to the side until close to the door, when I moved in threes and twos. With minor doubts.

Brian Matthews

THE FUNERALS
1989

They started coming through late on a Friday towards the end of February.

Summer had been searing. All over the district the smell of smoke, charred wood and incinerated gum leaves tinged the air and thickened with every breeze. Those paddocks that were not blackened by fire had gradually bleached white as dry bone; surrounding hillsides were scarred with random black corridors where fire fronts had ripped up slopes, exploding from tree top to tree top, scything undergrowth, hissing like lit fuses up hanging ropes of bark. Dust was everywhere.

And that was how they first appeared: as ballooning dust a few miles out. As if a semitrailer or a big road train was on its way into the township.

The dozen or so drinkers on the veranda of the pub were in a good place to give an opinion because they were on the highest ground in the town and looking straight down the main street. But beyond repeating that it certainly couldn't be trucks kicking up all that dust because the whole thing was moving much too slowly, no-one had any idea at all what was straggling down the road towards them. Some of the men started betting.

– A big semi with a busted rear spring. A schooner on it.

– A dollar says it's bloody Charlie Percival's cattle out through that bloody fence again.

– Travellin' circus. Just what we need.

– Mob o' sheep. They been threatenin' to bring 'em down through 'ere if the drought up north kept on.

But no-one was right and no bets were successful. It wasn't trucks, broken down or whole; or cattle or sheep or a circus. Or anything remotely like that. It was funerals. Ten, twenty, thirty, hundreds of them. Men bearing the coffins, women and men mourning behind, a few yards separating each procession. And the dust from those hundreds and hundreds of shuffling feet clouding back up the main road as far as anyone could see. Funerals.

At first the sheer shock, the exoticism, the utterly unbelievable nature of what they were seeing, overcame every other reaction for the onlookers. They literally gaped. Drinkers emptied from the pub. Elderly ladies crowded indecorously in front of the Country Women's Association clubrooms where they had been playing cards; a few women and the proprietor came out of the general store leaving the flyscreen door to close with a spring-loaded crash behind them. The garage man serving at his bowser had petrol brimming from the tank and splashing round his boots before either he or the owner of the car noticed. Everyone stood stunned.

All this time the funerals dragged slowly past until they were strung the whole length of Yardley's main street. Almost all the ghostly mourners wore traditionally dark clothes, though dotted among them were some who were dressed in white or coloured flowing robes. And there were at least two mourning groups comprised entirely of black people wearing what appeared to be some form of national dress. These groups followed not a coffin but the body itself, held aloft by bearers, wrapped in white and clearly outlined in all its final lineaments. Graven into all the faces were lines of the most profound and inexpressible grief. No-one was stoic. Both men and women frequently buried their faces in their hands or robes, faltering almost to a stop, convulsed with sobs or inner pain. And so the funerals passed, and continued to pass.

Among the onlookers, stupefaction changed through horror to terror only very slowly. Indeed, it was not till one of the men who had come tumbling out of the pub said in a kind of wondering tone that degenerated into loud panic:

– Hey! y' can't – y' can't hear 'em! Listen! Everyone! *Y' can't hear 'em.*

It was true. Though many, on that first terrible day, felt persuaded they could hear the shuffle and scrape of the mourners' feet, and others, during the days that followed, reported hearing snatches of sobbing and wailing and even brief, broken waftings of some intensely medieval-sounding chorus, the fact was that no-one was sure of any of this and that, in general, the grim, endless procession dragged by in a tense and unendurable silence. The silence of the dead.

This realisation broke up the onlookers and the people of Yardley fled behind locked doors as dusk settled on their gruesome main street. Phones ran hot. The local police, supported by two squad cars from distant Port Lincoln, the main town in the area, stood by for much of the night but were helpless. The cold flashing blue lights on their cars, ghosting across face after funereal face, only intensified the surreal dread that invaded them all.

At first light, after a night of whispered conversations and fitful dozings in rooms shuttered and locked against prowlers but not against the thick, stultifying heat, the townspeople awoke to find that daylight had not dispersed their collective nightmare. The funerals wound past ceaselessly. Black and brown and white and yellow faces tormented with sorrow. Sober suits, widow's weeds, white gowns, colourful ceremonial robes, rags and filth. Sandals, boots, slippers, high heels, bandages, smart western shoes, bare callused feet. Coffins shining and embroidered, plain and woody looking, ornate and flashing in the hot sun; battered boxes – some with lids, some without; adult coffins, children-sized coffins, white, lacy, pathetic babies' coffins. Bodies – wound in sheets, draped in rich material, laid out, contorted, gaping at the sky. After two or three days it seemed there could be no further variations. In Yardley, Death had proved itself, far beyond anyone's desire to know, at least as variable and as unpredictable as Life.

Many of the townspeople left within the first fortnight of the funerals, but while tourists continued to arrive the shopkeepers stayed. It was the tourists who started the practice of nipping across the street through the gaps in the endless procession; and it was a drunken tourist who, staggering from the pub into the road, discovered that there was apparently no way through the actual ranks of the funerals: he reeled back as if struck, but seemed not to have touched any individual mourner but rather to have encountered some collective force or repulsion. Whatever the explanation, nobody tried it again.

In any case, the novelty was short-lived. Few who came to gape and point could long remain resistant to the black oppression, the sense of huge sorrows, which emanated from the ever-passing funerals. People arrived in Yardley looking interested, humorously sceptical, tensely expectant, exaggeratedly nonchalant. They left looking shattered and, above all, *bleak*. The word was first used in this connection by one of the visiting journalists: he was right. A bleakness of the spirit, an inner aridity, a wildernessed soul – these were the results inevitably of exposure to the funerals. And so the tourist stream dwindled to almost nothing, the town's shopkeepers left. Within six months of the first appearance of the funerals, only a handful of 'official observers' were in permanent residence. Journalists occasionally returned to check up on things but none stayed more than the few days necessary. And the funerals passed and passed and passed.

There were flurries of heightened interest. One occurred when concerted attempts were made by police and the military to trace either end of the procession. They could not penetrate the clouds of dust, either at the 'start' or the 'finish' of the melancholy line. There was a point where the funerals simply were, and there was a point at the other end of the town where they simply were not. Nothing further could be discovered or deduced. Speculation that more might be learned when the rains came to settle the dust led to an intense focus on the slowly changing season and this was how it became clear, perhaps earlier than otherwise might have been the case, that although the whole countryside was mellowing into luminous autumn and green- ing just perceptibly in the early frosts and first misty rains, Yardley and its immediate surrounds remained locked in that fire-blackened and bone-white dusty summer. The season never did change, then or later; the rains did not come; the dust never settled.

Another moment of interest occurred when a journalist, returning briefly to Yardley to see if anything had altered, reported that the ranks of the mourners seemed filled increasingly with men – and some women – in military garb. By the time the influx which his article prompted was well under way, the funerals were thick with khaki-clad figures. If it were possible, the pain, the suffering and the loss on these ravaged faces was deeper and more intolerable to look upon than anything yet seen among the tragic processions. And while some of the bodies mourned were in roughly made boxes, others were carried in the arms of comrades, gaping wounds flowering with corruption, stick-like limbs jolting and randomly pointing, stretched mouths grinning with bone at the empty and relentlessly unchanging sky. Grotesque, obscene, unburiable.

The crowds left as quickly as they had arrived.

After eleven months of the funerals, workmen were brought in (at the expense of much haggling and acrimony since most of those approached refused to come) to begin building a high, cyclone fence round the entire area of the town and the 'affected roadway', as the authorities now called it. Such tourists as ventured near – and there were few – were warned off and at the same time press reports about the Yardley phenomenon, still surfacing in this and that newspaper, became subject to censorship. The immediate reason for the censoring, aside from growing official nervousness, was that a French medical researcher had linked the worldwide upsurge of suicides with the funerals. The black depression, the sense of insupportable sorrow and loss which so many people reported after viewing the funerals, had spread, according to this doctor, even to those who merely read about them or watched them on television. He called it the 'Yardley Syndrome', noting without explanation two common factors linking the recent suicide victims: they all, without a single exception, left notes; and they all struck a tone in their notes not of resignation, farewell, bitterness or failure, but of defiance, protest. Suicide manifestos.

The funerals had been passing for fourteen months by the time the fence was finished. It was topped with four strands of barbed wire and had one set of double gates for entry. When these were ready for padlocking, four soldiers in a Land Rover thoroughly checked the area after which the gates clanged shut on the indefatigable dead.

Press censorship, quietly and more rigorously tightened, ensured that the Yardley Funerals drifted to the margins of the news even if they were never wholly out of it. In a world fed daily with disasters, sensations and unimaginable evils, most abominations – children blown up or starving to death, innocent men and women bludgeoned in the streets, airliners bombed – were soon distanced, accommodated.

Various scientists, politicians, journalists and others remained in close touch with the Yardley Funerals (which continued to pass and re-pass through the eerie, empty township), committed to discovering either an explanation or a way of removing them, but failing to make any headway on either score.

One of the journalists, however, by a combination of good luck, instinct and dogged tracking down, discovered an article in an obscure academic journal, beyond the reach and beneath the interest of the censors, entitled 'The Yardley Funerals'. He had become convinced that some kind of document existed after investigating the activities of a former Yardley resident – a retired schoolteacher, who, it appeared, had taken a profound interest in the funerals. All the journalist's attempts to find this man had failed. Indeed, he had some reason to believe, on the basis of fairly tenuous evidence, that the teacher had been one of the first in a wave of suicides by self-immolation. (As many last notes explained, this horrific method was chosen in the hope that the obliterating flames would cheat the Yardley funeral processions of new mourners: for while there were many who aspired to be seen among the funerals after death, there were others for whom that possibility stood as the vilest of the funerals' many depravities.)

The journalist read the article with growing excitement, photocopied it and slapped it in front of his editor with a flourish:

THE YARDLEY FUNERALS

The Yardley Funerals may be the 'end' that we have all debated, feared, conjured with and predicted so tirelessly since Hiroshima. The process may be drawn out and very different from the sudden cataclysm we have been educated and terrorised into expecting, but I think it will be ineluctable.

The press of the world, for as long as they remained or were allowed to remain interested, talked much of the supernatural. Probably that is the only way to describe these strange and horrible occurrences. But when we have said, 'This is supernatural', 'These are ghosts', what have we said? What do we know that becomes a basis for action? Clearly, the answer to *that* is: nothing. There has been no action. No-one has known what to do. All anybody has done – including the experts in the occult who were much in evidence early but whose numbers dwindled rapidly – has been to stand and gaze. And since this, as we now know, induces in the watcher the blackest of depressions, no-one stayed around very long. What was never asked, but what I asked myself almost immediately was, not 'What are these?' but 'What are they *doing*?' To that question, I think I can give the beginnings of an answer.

I watched these macabre processions from the time they began. I studied them at least as closely as did anyone else. What no-one else seemed to see – or at least to take account of in any way – was this:

First: these are the twentieth-century dead. Though every conceivable burial custom, every possible nation, all the creeds, fads, beliefs and superstitions are to be found somewhere or other among these silent, shuffling crowds, there is nothing – not a costume, not an expression, not a ritual – that suggests any time other than broadly our own.

Second: even if we set aside for the moment the utterly fantastic, incredible and ghastly nature of what is taking place and take the events, as it were, at their face value – even then, the Yardley Funerals are not typical funerals. The grief and the pain and the loss far outweigh the cause: there is no funeral at which every single mourner is stricken publicly and visibly. But in these funerals, *all* the mourners without exception are suffering and suffering so terribly that their look of pain becomes transformed into that expression of impotent anger that one sees in Renaissance paintings of the damned.

Third: (obvious enough, but again no-one seems to have bothered with the implications); what we are seeing in the Yardley Funerals is the dead reburying the dead. Why – when all are dead – do some mourn while others are shrouded, coffined, or openly borne with the grave's decay grisly upon them? I have a speculative answer to this, supported tenuously by my observations. I think it might be the case that, in the Yardley funerals, the 'corpses' are those who died by violence, the mourners those who died natural deaths. There have been, after all, more than one hundred million man-made deaths in our century alone. Perhaps it is only just that those whose lives were cruelly cut off should now be the centre of attention when the dead re-bury the dead.

However that may be, it was through contemplating these aspects of the Yardley Funerals that I arrived at my own resolution of the question: What are they doing?

I am convinced that the funerals are a protest, a demonstration by the dead against the obscenity of mortality, especially as it presents itself in our time. It is proper that the twentieth-century dead should lead such a protest (I say 'lead' because I do not discount the possibility that the dead from the more distant past will soon be visible) because this century is Death's kingdom in time. No other century can lay claim to such carnage, genocide, slaughter, random extinction. It is right that the mourners should be so wretched, so harrowed, bereaved to the point of anger, for they mourn not individuals but the fact of death itself. They re-enact the funereal ritual to dramatise the pointlessness, the idiocy, the sheer injustice of mortality; of a life that comes to an often abrupt, uncalled for, unheralded, useless, ridiculous end amid the muck and earth. The dead, who are the afflicted ones, the ones who know it most intimately and most hopelessly, have risen in revolt against Death itself. Against mortality.

Their protest has been, in a way, successful. Human beings could not continue, could not convince themselves that purpose, order, striving are worthwhile if all the time their sense and perception of the reality of Death was acute and persistent. We all know that we will die; but not tomorrow. It is the other person who gets the fatal disease, has the tragic accident, the sudden seizure that cancels all. It is a careful balance we all nurture: death is real but 'it won't happen to me yet'. The Yardley Funerals are destroying this fragile balance. Death, so constantly on parade, has ceased to be a vague, unpalatable idea and has become an acute and persistent presence. That is why suicides are increasing. Suicide is the one, momentary and pre-emptive control we can exercise over mortality. And it is why those suiciding are defiant: they recognise they are both making and possibly joining a protest. Suicides will continue and increase in number. And those who don't suicide will evacuate their lives of all purpose and striving towards goals and order. The Yardley Funerals' constant presence shows them how ludicrous are such pretensions since they are carried out from start to finish in the black nullifying shadow of mortality. Heavy censorship and the human being's capacity for selective amnesia have slightly blunted this impact for the moment, but it will be in the end irresistible.

Finally: why have the dead appeared in, of all places, remote and tiny Yardley? I have no answer to this question, but if I were directing any investigations designed to illuminate these mysteries, I would pay close attention to that question. Why

Yardley? My own view is that research would discover that Yardley has been in the past the site of some abominable crime against humanity. Its position and remoteness would suggest a massacre of Aboriginals. It is in fact in the centre of what used to be Parnkalla land. Some pressure (I can only call it that – inadequately) beyond the margins of our reality, has made Yardley the first site of the protest of the Dead. 'First' because, logically, there must be others to follow. There are, after all, many more famous sites of human perfidy and cruelty than Yardley – though for all we know, whatever happened at Yardley may be, on some scale of abominations, beyond our understanding – as bad as anything we have heard of. I am convinced, in short, that the Yardley Funerals are only the beginning of our reunion with the outraged Dead.

For myself, I hope I have devised a way of achieving death without joining them . . .

In defiance of government embargo, the journalist and his editor were preparing to publish a feature based on what they agreed was an extraordinary and serious document, to suggest to a waiting world why the dead had erupted into the consciousness and view of the living in insignificant Yardley, when: in the space of one northern hemisphere night, one southern hemisphere day, their revelation became redundant. Suddenly, the world knew (in principle at least – people would soon guess or learn the details) why humble Yardley had achieved its unwanted and sinister distinction. For in the space of those twelve hours of light and dark, the dead broke through all over the globe, funerals appeared in country after country, and the world's press, beyond censorship now, shouted the names of the new, dishonoured and unignorable sites by virtue of whose unholy election all was at last revealed:

HIROSHIMA. GUERNICA. DERRY. AUSCHWITZ. BUDAPEST. DRESDEN. DACHAU. SHARPEVILLE. MY LAI. THE SOMME. SAIGON. WARSAW. PRAGUE. TREBLINKA. NAGASAKI . . .

THE BROWN PAPER COFFIN

1988

My face has always brought me problems. It's not that there is anything terribly wrong with it, feature by feature. In fact, it's a fairly ordinary face, squarish and a little blunt, nose long rather than short, mouth wide rather than narrow, eyes a dull blue, straight mousy hair. It's just that the effect of the whole thing is worse than merely the sum of the parts. The fact is, it's an *untrustworthy* face – I know it, I *recognise* the fact, and I can't do anything about it. I even sympathise with people who take exception to it.

The difficulty has been with me for as long as I can remember. At school I was punished quite often, I am sure, simply because I looked as if I *deserved* punishment. Traffic policemen react badly to me, as do dogs and bank tellers and teenage girls. The first time I tried to kiss Jane, she slapped me so hard that I had a slight concussion. I am blamed – quite gratuitously – for disturbances in bars, unpleasant smells, familiarity in crowds, and I am regularly suspected of evading fares on public transport.

Enough. But it *does* have a bearing on my decision that day in Mt Isa. It explains also, I think, my choice of accountancy as a profession; in its exercise I have no need to intrude my face between my work and my clients. It is true that if my clients *do* meet me, they are not reassured. But I have a most personable partner.

Well, having cleared the decks, as it were, I must proceed to the crux of the matter and introduce my mother-in-law, and this opens the door to all sorts of opportunities for misunderstanding; mothers-in-law have for so long been the butt of coarse jokes that it is difficult to avoid the stereotype. But all the same my mother-in-law, Beth, is – was – a friend.

It took her some time, it is true, to overcome her initial mistrust of me. But she did overcome it, and we went on, the three of us, to build an enduring and affectionate relationship. This bond between us has been reinforced rather than hindered by our decision – Jane's and mine – not to have children. As a result, Beth – who is a widow of longstanding – has become a frequent companion, not only at home but on outings and holidays.

Which explains – I am afraid in a rather long-winded fashion – how the three of us came to be driving westward along the Barkly Highway, a day out of Mt Isa. We had travelled northward across the border, and all the way up to Townsville; then westward, aiming for Darwin. We were not pressed for time, and our itinerary was only loosely mapped out. We drove my dark-green Volvo sedan, and carried some simple camping gear, enough to make us independent of motels for several nights at a stretch. It was early spring, and the climate was not yet as uncomfortably hot as it would become later in the year.

Towards the end of that day we turned off the highway onto a secondary road which looped away into the scrub and seemed to lead towards a slight rise in the land where the trees were a little taller and greener, promising water somewhere. We were all a little tired and jaded by the long hours of nothing but dry scrub and red dust, and looked forward to camping for the night. The side road took us to a small creek which crossed the road and flowed northward into some thicker bush.

'Look,' said Jane, pointing, 'there are buildings of some kind in there . . .'

I pulled up, and we all got out. It was true, through the scrub I could see the vague outlines of buildings a hundred yards off the road.

'Let's have a look,' said Beth, and the two of them headed off along the overgrown track. I remember thinking that they looked more like sisters than mother and daughter, both slim, tall, both with bright auburn hair – although Beth's certainly owed something to artifice.

I followed along behind.

The sun was getting low now, and the shadows were lengthening. We pushed our way through the last of the scrub into a clearing, and in the clearing were the buildings we had seen from the road. My heart sank a little as I took in the utter desolation of the scene. I had hoped, I think, to find some human habitation. But the buildings, although quite new, were deserted. Apart from the air of desolation there was something else about the place that puzzled me. It was a moment or two before it dawned on me that the buildings had never been completed, had in fact been abandoned before they were finished.

And as we walked around, it became obvious that at some time in the last year or so someone had set out to build a motel here. The framework was all there, the raw concrete of the main wing with its empty roofless foyer, the grey pit of the swimming-pool, a little stagnant water in the bottom skinned with dead leaves, the smaller buildings to the side which might have been store-rooms, scrap timber, rusty re-inforcing, empty cement bags ... Someone's great plan curtailed, left to erode slowly in the tropical bush.

'It's creepy!' Jane shivered.

It was true. I think it was the silence that gave a certain threatening air to the place.

'Never mind,' said Beth. 'It's shelter, and we needn't put up the tent tonight. What do you think?'

'I suppose so,' said Jane a bit dubiously.

I went to get the car.

In fact we made ourselves fairly comfortable, not in the main building, but in one of the sheds. By the time we had the primus going, tea made, the inflatable mattresses in place, the smell of food in the air, it didn't seem such a bad place after all. As night fell, the silence seemed no longer quite so oppressive.

We turned in early, soon after the short tropical dusk. I slept soundly enough, although I remember that I had very odd dreams, filled with strange insect-like creatures of brilliant gold and bronze and crimson. I woke once about two o'clock, and lay listening to the small night sounds with a slightly uneasy feeling. It seemed odd to be sleeping inside that echoing concrete shell, still smelling a little of raw cement, in the middle of the vastness of the bush. Then sleep claimed me again, deep this time, and dreamless, and only released me when the first brilliant rays of the sun touched my face through the open doorway.

I lay for a little while in the warm silence. The place seemed to have lost its air of slight menace, and seemed very ordinary and down-to-earth in the hot sunlight. Feeling encouraged, I slipped quietly out of my sleeping-bag, lit the gas primus and made coffee. I took the first cup to the corner where Beth had slept, knelt and set the cup by her head.

That was when I found that, sometime during the night, she had died.

It was one of those rare moments when I wish I hadn't long ago given up smoking.

Still, there was coffee. But first I checked that Jane was still asleep; then, that Beth was really dead. No doubt about either. I haven't seen many dead people; my father, my mother, a dismal corpse dragged from a creek near home. But death is unmistakable.

I took my coffee, went softly out into the sunlight, sat with my back to the warm concrete wall to consider.

I can't say that I was enormously surprised; Beth had a history of heart disease. It all stemmed from a holiday in Tasmania when she had a mild heart attack and refused to go to a doctor in case she was put in hospital, prevented from returning home.

So, no great mystery.

I decided, there and then, that I would grieve later. There were certain practical matters to which I would need to attend. First of all, we would have to report the matter to the police. Could I leave Beth – the body – here with Jane, drive to Mt Isa? Clearly not, unimaginable. Have Jane drive back, leave me here with . . . the body? I felt a little queasy. No . . .

Leave the body, both of us drive back? Equally unthinkable.

Take the body with us.

Yes, clearly.

And I felt the first slight pang of unease, then. Remembering – how could I forget? – my unfortunate face and its effect on strangers. I appear from the wilds with a body . . . the police officer takes one look at my face . . . unpleasantness, in one form or another.

But there was no alternative. And besides, I could hear Jane stirring inside the shed.

I won't dwell on those first moments after Jane awoke. Suffice it to say that she went quickly into mild shock, and it took a while to bring her back to some sort of normality. I made her sit outside in the sun, drink sweet coffee, swallow some valium from the first-aid kit. She wept a little, sobbed a little. Calmed slowly. I explained what we must do. She accepted the necessity. I packed up.

Neither of us felt like eating, so within a very few minutes I had our gear collected, packed, in the car.

All except . . . the body.

And here I struck a certain difficulty. Post-mortem rigidity had set in, and modern passenger cars are not designed to carry cadavers; not stiff ones, at least.

While Jane watched, in tears, I juggled with the body for a while, attempting various entries to the passenger space. No go. I pondered. Perhaps if I opened one window, left the feet protruding . . . too grotesque. I set my burden on the ground and took thought.

When all the impossible alternatives have been excluded, what remains . . .

What remained was the luggage rack.

'No!' said Jane. 'Not up there, not Beth!'

'It's not Beth,' I said. 'Beth's gone . . . it's a body.'

'Not up there . . .'

'There's nowhere else.' It had begun to dawn on me that there was another factor. Even if we managed to accommodate our burden inside the car, it was going to be a hot day, as hot as yesterday, and in that confined space, no air-conditioning . . .

Jane gave in, but fell to sobbing again.

There remained yet *another* problem. I had left the body in its sleeping-bag, and zipped the hood closed. Even so, the bundle was clearly identifiable as . . . what it was. It seemed unwise, an invitation to speculation, to carry such an easily identifiable burden exposed. Especially when the face at the driver's window – mine – would be in full view.

I remembered the discarded cement bags, multi-layered dusty paper, lying in one of the sheds.

Well, I won't labour it. A disgusting business – a dozen bags, several lengths of cord, some wire, a pair of old boards, and I had a bundle stowed atop the car, a bundle which might have been anything. It was time to go, before I began to dwell too heavily on the ridiculous and macabre incongruity of the whole business. Few find dignity in death, but this was really too much . . .

Yet what else could I do?

I urged Jane into the car, climbed in myself and started the engine. We began to bump along the track, and in the wind of our passage I could hear a small rustling from the torn edges of the paper bundle above us.

I turned onto the road and headed back the way we had come the day before, towards the highway and Mt Isa. Neither of us spoke until we reached the main road. I am sure that we were both thinking of the paper-wrapped bundle above us. And I wasn't at all sure that I was going to be able to cope all the way to Mt Isa.

'I'm going to be sick,' said Jane.

I pulled in to the side of the road and parked, got out, went round and opened the passenger's door. Jane looked very white and frail. I helped her out, led her towards the shade of some trees fifty yards or so off the road. She disappeared behind a patch of scrub, and after a moment I could hear her vomiting. It seemed to go on for a long time.

I went back to the car, got a bottle of water and a face washer, took them back into the thicket. Jane was sitting on a log, looking very pallid and ill. I gave her the water and the cloth.

'I don't think I can go back to the car,' Jane said, after she had cleaned up a little. 'Not while she's . . . up there like that.'

I didn't really know what to do. There just didn't seem to be any alternative, as far as I could see.

'Just rest for a bit,' I said. 'Then we'll decide what to do.' I sat down with my back against a tree, out of the sun. The temperature was well into the thirties already, I guessed, and it was going to get hotter. And the car and its burden were still waiting for us.

Once again I regretted not having a cigarette.

After a quarter of an hour or so I got up, went over to Jane, knelt beside her, put my arm round her shoulders. 'We're going to have to move soon,' I said.

'I just can't do it,' she said. 'It's too horrible . . .'

I was beginning to wonder if we might not have to unload the bundle and leave it hidden somewhere after all, when the decision was made for us.

I heard, from the direction of the road, the sound of the car starting up. By the time I jumped to my feet and ran out into the open it was already driving off in a scatter of gravel and a cloud of red dust. I caught a glimpse of two figures in the front, a hint of long hair – male or female I couldn't tell – and then it was gone, obscured by the rising pall of dust. I just stood there, speechless, long after it had disappeared.

I wondered who they were – hitchhikers, perhaps, camped nearby overnight, an old car broken down – who knows?

After a little I realised that Jane was standing beside me. I took her hand. We looked at each other wordlessly, and it seemed to me that Jane's spirit had lightened a little. Well, one problem was certainly solved, even if another had appeared in its wake.

'What do we do now?' said Jane.

'I guess,' I said, 'that we wait . . .'

And wait we did. For about two hours, before an empty road train appeared, thundering down the road on its way back from Darwin. The driver and his mate made room for us in the cab, shared their sandwiches and beer with us, and sympathised with us over the loss of our car.

'Ah,' said the driver, 'you'll get her back all right. Just bloody yobbos . . . maybe put a dent or two in it, but they'll ditch it in the Isa, I reckon . . .'

We hadn't – by some unspoken agreement – mentioned the car's cargo.

They set us down at the outskirts of the town, at the first motel, and we waved them out of sight. Luckily, I had my wallet in my pocket, with cash and credit cards, so we had no trouble getting a room.

'Had a breakdown, did you, dear?' said the girl on the desk, and I didn't disabuse her.

Once in the room, we collapsed on the twin beds. It was deliciously cool after the heat outside.

'Aren't you going to ring the police?' asked Jane after a while.

'Not just yet,' I said.

'Why not?'

'No hurry,' I said. 'We'll just leave it for a while . . .' Because, to tell the truth, I was beginning to see that it might not be quite as simple as all that. We walk into the nearest police station. Report our car stolen. Make and model, registration number. Fine. Then we tell them there is a body wrapped up in brown paper on the luggage rack. A body? Yes, officer, you see, it was like this . . .

And the policeman is looking at me, and saying to himself, well now, this fellow's up to no good, just look at his face; a body is it, well, we'll just have to see about that . . .

And then the sergeant, and the look again; then the detective . . .
and you won't be leaving town till this is sorted out, will you? And all
the time looking at me, running through the photographs and circulars
in his head, and haven't I seen this fellow before?

So in the end, when I finally picked up the phone I didn't call the
police, but the airline instead.

'Why on earth didn't you report it in Mt Isa?' said Philip, my solicitor,
looking very serious and moral on the other side of his shiny desk.
'We're going to have all sorts of problems getting this sorted out, you
know. I'm not at all sure that they won't charge you with concealing
a death or something. Why didn't you *report* it?'

'Philip,' I said. 'Look at me.'

'What do you mean?'

'Go on,' I said. 'Look me in the face.'

'Yes,' he said, after a moment. 'You have a point, I suppose.' He
sighed. 'We'll just have to see what we can do . . .'

The car was found a week later, stripped and abandoned, just outside
Cloncurry. Quite bare, nothing in the boot, nothing on the luggage
rack. I had a number of uncomfortable interviews with the police; but
Philip was with me, and I was after all a known quantity on my home
ground. In the end no charges were laid, and the worst that has happened is a long delay in probating Beth's will.

The worst, that is, except for the uncertainty. Somewhere out there,
somewhere in all those thousands of square miles of bush, Beth has
come finally to rest in her brown paper coffin. And we will never know
exactly where.

And I will have to do my deferred grieving in private. We thought
of having a memorial service; but in the end I simply couldn't face the
prospect of all those people looking at me, looking at my *face* and
wondering . . .

THIS AND THE GIVER

1991

The last time I saw my husband, there was a wilderness in me. It was borderless and sexual. I'd imagine my wilderness full of naked men playing leapfrog over my body. I'm walking towards my husband's house when I see him drive past. He doesn't see me because at that moment I've moved into the thicker, older shade stretching across the path from the Catholic cathedral. The footpath is strewn with seed pods. They are from a Blackbutt tree. Years ago I would sail these with my sisters in the lakes that formed in the poplar forest behind the house after heavy summer rain. When I look up again, my husband has gone. He was travelling away from the direction of his house. I have slipped the fingers of my right hand through the hole in my pocket. The hair beneath my pants is soft and flat. I keep walking and before too long reach a purple circle made of fallen jacaranda flowers. The freshest blossoms pop under my shoes.

In my wilderness there were no clothes and no flowering trees. The shade where I played with naked men was dark green and thick. Trees had not been planted in neat avenues. Fleshy leaves bent under our feet and bodies. No lilac bells fell around us. My husband wouldn't have liked it there.

Ricco's Hot Food van goes by. The smell of hot grease reminds me that all day I've eaten only caramel tart. Ricco's van is followed by a caged truck full of festival singers. The singers are clad in a variety of purple hues in an attempt to match the trees. The colours of some of the singers clash. I look up through a jacaranda tree and find the sky behind is a shade of deep grey. As a child, the October storms were always more exciting than the colour of the jacaranda flowers. My fingers return into the pocket and curl this time around the small box that holds the letter I've written to my husband.

The box feels cold and smooth. It is the small enamel Halcyon Days box my husband gave me the day we were married. Halcyon is the name of an Australian kingfisher with iridescent feathers. It is also a bird said by the ancients to breed its young on floating sea nests. These birds were able to charm the wind and waves to be calm for their breeding season. My husband taught me this in Ancient History in 1979 many years before he gave me the English enamel box with the same brand name.

'This and the Giver are thine forever.' The inscription on the lid of the box twirls in pastel-coloured writing made to look like ribbons. I wrote my letter on small rounds of paper, each round connected to the other in the way of a home-made Christmas decoration. Some of the pages are decorated with crooked flowers and cats, drawn by me when I had paused in the writing of my letter.

Instead of stopping at the post office to post the box and letter to my husband as originally intended, I carry on along to Victoria Street. I glance through the alley formed by a sandstone wall and the post office and see a view of the river I have never seen before. It strikes me that I am looking at another town's river, divided by an island I don't recognise. I walk faster then, to reach Pullen's Produce. I take a deep breath of the smell of chaff being bagged and smile hello at the man with the moustache who used to be little Craigie Pullen when I was also a child.

It isn't far to my husband's house. The house is at the dead end of Victoria Street. I walk the river way, along the track that runs though the paddocks that were once part of a dairy.

At the weeping fig outside my husband's house, I stop. Something is rustling in the tree. I part the curtain of leaves and almost believe I have found another wilderness. The boy with red hair who lives next door is tying his sister to the trunk. Her nipples are delicate and periwinkled. I hope her laughter isn't the brink of tears.

'Hello,' she calls out my married name. Her name, I remember, is Amber-Jane. The boy is too intent on his knots to say anything. I let the leaves fall back around them. When one calls out something, I'm already moving down the side passage of the house where I lived for seven years as the young wife of my favourite high school teacher.

My sugarcane cat appears unexpectedly. She steps out through the nasturtiums that grow thinly under the house. I found her as a kitten two years ago at the edge of a burning cane field. 'Hello. Puss, puss.'

I bend down to feel her warmth. 'Hello, little sweetheart.' The border privet is boiling over with milky blossom. I pick up my cat and walk away from the sickly smell.

Around the corner, the footpath has disappeared beneath a mat of mint and weeds. Everything feels out of control. I glance up to the far end of the garden and see the old timber and tin shed. Mulberry and persimmon branches arch over it. The old tin shed gets two round pages in my letter. Something like:

> Don't think I don't mourn for the vision we once shared. The
> old garden shed as a ramshackle hidey house for our children.
> Silkworms in shoe-boxes. Mulberry stained smiles.

I put down my cat and take the Halcyon Days box from my pocket and then the letter out of the box. This is a mistake. It spills from my fingers like a sprong of orange peel. When I try to fold it back so that each page is in its correct place, I find myself reading certain sentences. It is a letter full of lies. For instance, the pages about the shed make no mention of how fantasy men would come into the coolest corner of the shed to fuck me during the hot summer days. On these days my husband would come home from the school smelling of chalk dust and warm classrooms. I would make him a cup of black tea into which I would float the finest sliver of lemon I could cut. I would kiss his forehead.

On the under side of the Halcyon Days lid is a mirror. I abandon my attempt to make the letter chronological. The mirror's slightly convex. I want to see my eyes. They look worried because although I have no way of knowing when he'll be back, the irresistible desire to go into my husband's house has come upon me.

In summer his forehead was oily under my lips.

In our last summer, I couldn't help noticing how blackheads marched in a straight line along the middle forehead wrinkle, as if someone had begun to plot a dot graph onto his face. I remember this as my fingers find the spare key where it has always hung behind the loose shingle. My hand reaching up for it dingles the old brass bell.

Memories take flight from all the pictures and postcards I once stuck onto the chipboard walls of the veranda. I carry my cat in my arms for comfort and examine each picture with care. Some I have to take down in order to know who once sent them. Others are instantly recognisable. I know, even as I pull the pin out of a black and white cartoon card, that this is no card I ever received. The writing on the back is the same as the writing on the opened envelope lying on the window bench. I don't read the card. I put the pin back into the pinhole. But I've noticed two things anyway: that she calls him My Darling: that she signs off with lots of Bic biro kisses, smudged by her hand putting on the stamp. The envelope has been ripped open. He always used to open his mail with a bone-handled steak knife. Where his thumb has slitted through the thick paper of the beige Croxley envelope, her fast blue writing is torn. I read the name and address of the new woman in his life. I knew a girl at school with this name who always had nits. Licey Lisa. The school nurse was always having to shave her head.

The new woman's writing rushes. Each letter turns back upon the last in blue biro waves. When I turned seventeen, my husband, who was still my schoolteacher, gave me a black fountain pen made in another country. He had an aversion to biros he said. It's probably only a matter of time before the new woman's presented with the same gift.

I stand for the longest time in front of a photograph my husband ripped from a 1971 *Time Life* magazine. It pictures an Australian child in the middle of a flock of chickens. She has turned round as she runs through them to answer the summons of a foreign magazine photographer. My husband tore it out because he saw my face in the child's face. He used to hope our daughter would be born with some of this face in her. But I've always thought the face of the child is sad. The long hem of her blue and white checked dress casts dark blue shadows behind her knees. The skin of her legs is the same colour as the bark of the gum trees ahead of her in the photograph. I put this picture into my other pocket. I don't want the woman with the fast blue writing looking at the vision we once had of a daughter.

I know the woman has been in this house three times so far, because on each occasion, my husband has invited my younger sister around. The woman bakes cakes for my sister and more recently, gave her a handsewn nightdress. I have tearful conversations with my little sister. I can't understand her continuing friendship, I tell her, with the man I could no longer live with. *Don't you think it's odd*, I accuse in reference to the new woman sewing the little sister of the bolted wife, night attire. But my little sister refuses to enter into any games of malice.

For a moment, before moving deeper into the house, I stand in this room that will remind me forever of sitting very still in autumn, hiding hangovers from my little sister, drinking black coffee, as the sun filtered through the dying grape vine. I remember the stillness of my sadness, when what I really waited for was a reason to run. In autumn, my cat would bring inside giant grasshoppers. The whirring of their wings gave my indecision a noise. *Are you trying to fall?* My little sister once asked. Her baby was asleep on her breast.

What?! Could she know that I ran naked and fleet with men who were not my husband, in a wilderness that was nowhere near northern New South Wales?

Fall pregnant, Silly.

Ah. I'd bent my face over the circle of black coffee. My face was so full of lies it looked half, not one quarter of a century old. I didn't ever reply.

When I left my husband, my little sister sent wood. It arrived in the post, wrapped in surgical cotton wool such as her shell collection used to rest on. I use the wood as a long paperweight for letters. My little sister must have whittled and sanded it for many hours to make the grain so smooth. It's a splinter of red cedar from one of the old fence-posts on my parent's farm. Its tip is sharp enough to puncture skin. My little sister would say my name in an exasperated way if she knew I had arrived in town early this morning and spent the best part of the day writing a letter on tiny rounds of paper. She would take my elbow sorrowfully if she knew I was snooping in my husband's house.

I wrote the letter on the south side of the river from where the Catholic school and cathedral grounds look English in their formality. For energy, I bought a Pocock Bakery caramel tart, piped with mock cream. I wonder will my husband notice that some of the letter's little pages are sticky?

I stand for a moment at the doorway into the kitchen, watching how the afternoon light casts snowflake shapes onto the floor through the window etchings. When my cat was a kitten she used to try to play with these shapes, patting at them with her paws. I take off my shoes and tread softly. I have just caught sight of the noticeboard above the table that used to hold so many real photographs of me. Now it is full of pictures of the woman who writes so fast. She is long-limbed and pale. We're quite alike. I touch her nose. From the side it would be thin and long. The photo feels cold and I flinch – as though someone has just reached out and touched my nose with an icy, unfriendly finger.

On the kitchen table is an iced finger bun. *Reduced from fifty-nine cents to ten for Quik Sale.* He has taken one bite out of it and left it lying. Ants are carting away long straws of coconut. If the bun wasn't there I might've mistaken the coconut for ants' eggs. I step with care over that site on the floor where my husband crouched over me, pouring whisky down my throat. I was stretched out in the shape of a cross and I was naked. It was Easter. The house was full of sugar eggs he'd been given by schoolchildren who liked him.

My letter, I remember, mentions that night over three pages, back and front. It apportions blame:

> That night was my fault. I shouldn't have danced the skinned
> chicken towards you.

A skinless chicken looks like a deformed and decapitated baby. On the same night, before we'd eaten, I'd quick-stepped a raw chicken towards him and away. *The spore of the drumsticks*, I named the blooded trail on the kitchen counter.

Later on, when I'd woken up from the whisky, he had pulled on some shorts. He was sitting on the floor, nibbling at the head of a chocolate chook. His balls fell like a red, loose heart to the inside of his left thigh. They looked drained. He winced when a piece of foil from the Easter Chicken touched a filling.

In my letter I remind him of all this and of how soon afterwards the vine with the heart-shaped leaf, that had always grown through the shingles into the corner of the kitchen roof, died:

> An omen as much as anything else. A sign.
> My reason to run.

Now I carry my letter into the bedroom. I make the bed I made so often. It is just as tricky as ever – the sheets too small; the plank beneath the mattress to help the sag still in the way. On the bedside table is the book I've long been missing. Mildew has grown along the spine. It is frail mildew on spiky legs. A fainter mould has grown along the saddest pages I used to cry over.

On the desk where he used to mark school essays, he has been chopping up photographs. They're not the photographs that used to be on the kitchen noticeboard. They are the photos of me swimming naked at the coast. It was some kind of reconciliation effort. But that day, he hadn't even taken off his clothes. Not even his shoes came off. I remember his black school slip-ons spilling over with sand and how he had on a pair of wool-blend trousers with checks the colour of baked beans and burnt toast. Do a handstand, he'd called out. There was a rainbow.

He has cut that photograph the most brutally. I wish I hadn't come here. I wish I was already at my little sister's house, drinking tea and playing Rose Monsters with her children. I didn't want to know this. My legs, that were still brown from summer, have been lopped off at the knee. He has severed the rainbow near where it meets the sole of my left foot. I'm wrist deep in the wash of a wave. My bottom looks fleshy and lopsided.

I tread on his glasses as I pull out from under the bed the box where I know all my old letters to my husband are kept. I feel a sliver of glass enter the flesh under one big toe. My back creaks. The bed creaks. There are seven or more years of letters in this sturdy Club Port box. They're heavy to haul out the front door but I persist. I do this so that my husband and his new woman can't sleep and fuck over the top of them any more. Silverfish and cockroaches scatter as I pause. My sugarcane cat, squashed between gauze and glass, is watching as I wade into the front garden azalea thicket. The letters can turn into compost. I kick open the box. It is dark under the leaves and I'm crying. A disease on the underside of some leaves reminds me of the discolourations on the underflap of a chicken wing. My cat looks stunned in the last of the light and doesn't answer when I call out.

I dart. I dart back into the house and leave my letter.

Instead of then walking back down Victoria Street to where my car is parked and driving to my little sister's (who would be growing worried now that I hadn't arrived), I cross over the road. I walk to the bank manager's residence that has been vacant for as many years as I can recall. The *For Sale* signs are all fallen over and covered in pale yellow kikuyu. I wait on the veranda at the top of the bank manager's steps until my husband's car turns into the driveway. I'm eating a windfall mandarin when I hear him open and shut the back door. He sees my shoes first, at the kitchen doorway.

In that house across the road, my husband's crying. I scratch dried salt off my cheeks. The glow behind the veil of weeping fig leaves could be the children still in there with a torch. Or it might be the light from the flower of the cactus grown over the trunk, that only shines once every two years.

I think I see my husband's shadow moving large and sad behind the louvres. He has found the Halcyon Days letter in the corner room where my desk and books used to be. The louvres sound snappable as he shuts them. He always used to admonish me if I treated them roughly. He shook me once because the dust was so thick along them.

Then the lights of the veranda rooms go out and the inner ones flicker on. I think I smell the smoke of a spring fire twisting from his chimney. He's reading the letter. My cat's dribbling on his knee. In front of him, ants die in their hundreds. Every now and then he looks up from the letter to watch the ants, their small black haste in and out of hot knots of wood. Underneath, the coals glow and whimper. Each time he tears off one small page to throw into the fire, a small circle of sweat like a silkworm egg slides down his neck and is gone. He wears his broken glasses. My cat purrs. He keeps reading.

Frank Moorhouse

THE COMMUNE DOES NOT WANT YOU
1974

At the door of the commune I hesitated. What ectoplasmic shapes and indistinguishable bearded denim and mumbling cabalism throbbed here, Oh Lord.

I knocked. Do you knock at a commune door? (Too unflowing? Does it pre-empt their attention?) Do you just go in, affectionately, pacifically? Or is it by initiation?

A young man as fresh as a constable, no beard, came to the door, opened it and went back in.

'Hey,' I called, 'is this Milton's commune?'

'It's not *Milton's* commune, but he lives here, yes,' he said, over his shoulder.

'Is he in?' I asked the receding back but the man disappeared into a dark hole at the end of the hall.

Don't they have caution? I could be the enemy of the commune.

Any manners, residue of their middle class?

Any guidelines for the handling of callers?

I groped my way into the commune.

There appeared in the dim light, amid the raga music, to be a person in every room or the shape of a person. Were they the residents or were they callers? Or were they too answering the advertisement for the room? In a commune there is always this group sitting around the kitchen table reading or picking at themselves, toes or noses, drinking tea, and you don't know if any of them live there or whether you can sit in that chair or is that Big Paddy's chair or is that where Papa Milton always sits.

I'm too dressed. I reprimand my bow tie with a twist, a yank.

No-one looks up when I come in. Nose picking leads to brain damage.

'Hullo there.'

Someone dragged snot a mile along their nasal passage.

They have their heads down, reading upside-down newspaper wrapping or the labels on packets, drinking tea from enamel army mugs.

'Is Milton in?'

'I think he's in his room.'

I could not see who said this. I could not, for the life of me, see their lips move.

'Which is his room?'

'Just bang on the wall and shout.'

I was not going to bang on the wall and shout.

'I think he's with some chick,' someone else said, although again I saw no lips move.

I moved into the other room. It was not so much that I moved, more that the unreceptivity poked me out through a huge circular hole in the wall into yet another even darker room. They had knocked this huge circular hole in the wall, leaving rubble. I sat down on a lopsided beanbag chair, keeping one of my legs outriggered so that I wouldn't fall over. The beans always move away from me. A pig squealed out from somewhere in the chair. A pig. From under me.

In the dimness I saw a girl with long suffocating hair about her face – personality concealment – who said, 'Come here, Pushkin, did the nasty man sit upon you.'

'It wasn't my intention,' I told her, 'I like . . . animals . . . pigs.'

'Do you have a pig?' she asked.

'I did have a cat but it decamped. It went away. Greener pastures.'

'Cats only do that to people who ill-treat them.'

'Oh no – it just went away.'

'You must have ill-treated it.'

'No, cats just go sometimes – for personal reasons.'

'That's the only reason they run away – ill-treatment.'

'No, I like animals. I used to talk to the cat. Shaw said cats like a good conversation but you must speak slowly.'

'You hurt Pushkin.'

'I didn't mean to hurt Pushkin. I want to see Milton. About the vacant room. Is he with a chick?'

'Don't use the word "chick" with me if you want a reply.'

But. I was going to say to her that I never use the word but that it had hopped onto my tongue from the other room, from the Kitchen Klatsch, but, oh well, I let it go.

'The herbs look good – the watercress is growing well.'

'Anyone can grow watercress.'

I was going to tell her that in the story 'The Girl Who Met Simone de Beauvoir in Paris' the male in the story is based on me. That I have, despite my use of the word chick, agonised on the questions of liberation. I am imperfectly liberated, that's true, I wanted to reconstruct but parts were missing. Maybe they could be imported.

I told her instead that I went to a commune once in Phoenix, Arizona, where everyone was smoking dope and I was drinking Lone Star beer and they had a pet Red Indian who noticed this and came over to me and said, Wow man, you drinking Lone Star beer, give me some man, I love beer, I can't smoke this shit, where you from. I told him from Australia and he said he'd heard great things about Australia, like everyone drinks. I said yes everyone drinks, almost everyone. He said that sounded like the place for him.

At first she made no comment.

Then she said, 'Do you always talk so much – you're not a very "still" person are you? And I suppose that was meant to be a put-down of dope.'

How long, I thought, how long should I give Milton if he's with a girl.

'How is the commune coming along?' I asked, ploughing on with courtesy.

'Look, man, this is a house we all share. If you want to call it a commune you call it a commune, but for us it is a simple experiment in shared living with a polyfunctional endospace.'

Ah!! So that explains the knocked-down walls, the huge circular holes.

I had been told that, as for sharing, it was Milton who paid.

'Why do you wear a bow tie?'

'Oh that,' I looked down, as if it had grown there unnoticed by me, 'Oh . . . a bit of a lark . . . a bit of a giggle . . . a bit of a scream . . . a sort of a joke.'

She seemed to be staring at me severely.

I stumbled on, 'Oh, about clothes – I don't give a damn. A lark. Dress never worries me. I've got some jeans at home, actually.'

'Pity,' she said, 'I thought for a moment we'd have one male here who presented himself. Men think that caring about clothing is female. And therefore beneath consideration. See, sloppiness is another put-down of women. Dress for me is a way of speaking.'

'I like the idea of a sharing experience,' I said, 'learning to share Milton's money.'

'I find that offensive,' she said.

'Oh come now,' I said, 'it was a joke. I lived with Milton before – in the Gatsby House and he paid then. He paid for the jazz bands on the lawn, everything. I mean it wasn't a moral statement. Far be it from me . . .'

'I didn't know Milton then,' she said. She was, I could tell, not interested in knowing about anything which happened before her existence. She was not interested.

I don't blame her.

I began to stare at my hands, which an interviewer once said were 'nervous'.

Then I thought of something chatty to say, knowing about brown rice and communes and such. 'In Chinese restaurants it was always sophisticated to order boiled rice instead of fried rice. I always liked fried rice best but ordered boiled to be correct. Now I read Ted Moloney and he says ordering fried rice is quite acceptable and doesn't offend Chinese chefs.'

Again she made no comment. I think she was being 'still'.

She spoke, 'I don't find that in any way interesting – getting hung-up about sophistication and all that.'

'But I thought it showed . . . never mind . . . have you read the latest *Rolling Stone*?' I asked.

'I don't read newspapers,' she said.

'Oh, I read every newspaper.'

'You must have a very messed-up head.'

'I read the manifest content and I read the non-manifest content. I read the archetypes, osmotypes and the leadertypes. I see the ideological meaning and the unintended information.'

'I don't read any newspapers,' she repeated.

'Oh, I guess I really just read the manifest content. I've pretty much given up classifying news into Merry Tales, Fairy Tales, Animals Tales, Migratory Legends, Cosmogonic Legends and such. I don't do that much now.'

'I'm a dancer.'

'Oh yes?'

'I'm learning Theatre of the Noh.'

'It's a rich world – I'm learning Theatre of the Maybe Not.'

'Is that some sort of put-down?'

'I wonder if he's finished yet,' I said, nodding upwards, leaning across and stroking the . . . pig.

'Do you know Lance Ferguson?' she asked.

'No.'

'Do you know Sheena Petrie?'

'No.'

'Are you Australian?'

'Of course, from Sydney.'

'Strange that you don't know anyone.'

'I know *some* people.'

'Where do you live?'

'Here, here in Balmain.'

'No . . . !!'

'Yep – for ten years or more.'

'Incredible, and you don't know Lance Ferguson or Sheena Petrie?'

'Never heard of them.'

'Wow,' she shook her head to herself and made a coughing laugh, 'oh wow – you must live in a hole in the ground or something.'

'I guess,' I said glumly, 'they're Milton's new scene – I'm from his first scene.'

'And you say you know Milton?'

'Yes, of course.'

'You mustn't know him very well if you don't know Lance Ferguson or Sheena Petrie.'

'Ten years – I've known him for ten years. He was my closet friend, I mean closest friend. I haven't seen him for a few months.'

'Are you part of the Balmain Bourgeoisie?'

'No. Not part of the Balmain Bourgeoisie.'

'Who do you know?'

'Adrian Heber.'

'He's a spy. Everyone knows Adrian Heber.'

'He's not a spy.'

'Sheena won't believe this when I tell her.'

'I wonder if Milton's finished yet.'

I heard a lavatory flush. 'Maybe that's him,' I said.

'No, that's Harvey.'

'How do you know?'

'He has a weak bladder.'

I stare at my nervous hands again.

'I have no problems like that,' I reassure her.

Then I said, 'Perhaps I should go up or something.'

She then left the room, without saying where she was going, but she took the pig with her – as if I couldn't be trusted with it.

I fancied that I could still hear the bed squeaking above me.

I looked through the huge circular hole in the wall at the people still sitting around the kitchen table, picking at themselves. Nose picking can lead to brain damage.

I gave up. I went to the wall and banged and shouted, 'Milton!'

No-one answered.

I went back into the dim endospace and fought my way onto the beanbag chair.

'You!!' an imperious voice came from the ceiling and, looking up, I saw a hitherto unnoticed manhole-sized hole. A girl, not the girl with the pig, but a girl dressed as far as I could see in only a man's shirt was crouched there.

It occurred to me that I may have been watched the whole time – by the Commune Committee.

'Here's a note from Milton and your book back,' she called, and dropped a note wrapped around a stone, and a book.

The note read: 'Go away. The commune does not want you.'

The book he returned was Olive Schreiner's *Stories, Dreams and Allegories*.

'Did he like it?' I asked, trying to point attention away from the wounding note.

'He said he didn't open it. If you gave it to him he said, it must have had a malign intent. A way of spooking his equilibrium.'

Scratching his duco.

'He said that applying for the room under the name Buck Fuller was not considered a good joke by the commune and the commune was not fooled.'

And the commune did not laugh.

'Are you Sheena Petrie?'

'No.'

'Do you know her?'

'Of course. Everyone knows Sheena. She's Milton's best friend.'

'Is there a commune for people who do not fit very well into communes? Could you advise me?'

'I was instructed not to talk with you any further. You must go now.'

John Morrison

THE NIGHTSHIFT
1944

Eight o'clock on a winter's evening.

Two men sit on the open section of a tramcar speeding northwards along St Kilda Road. Two stevedores going to Yarraville – nightshift – 'down on the sugar'. One – old, and muffled to the ears in a thick overcoat – sits bolt upright, his tired eyes fixed on the far end of the car with that expression of calm detachment characteristic of the pipe-smoker. His companion, a much younger man, leans forward with hands clasped between his knees, as if enjoying the passing pageant of the famous road.

'It'll be cold on deck, Joe,' remarks the young man.

'It will that, Dick,' replies Joe. And they both fall silent again.

At Toorak Road a few passengers alight. A far greater number crowd aboard. Mostly young people going to dances and theatres. Smoothly groomed heads and white bow ties. Collins Street coiffures and pencilled eyebrows and rouged lips. Creases and polished pumps. Silk frocks and bolero jackets. They fill the tram right out to the running boards. The air becomes heavily scented.

The young wharfie, mindful of past rebuffs, keeps his seat. He can still see the road, but within twelve inches of his face a remarkably small hand is holding a pink silk dress clear of the floor. He finds it a far more interesting study than the road. Reflects that he could enclose it completely and quite comfortably within his own big fist. Little white knuckles, the fingers of a schoolgirl, painted nails – like miniature rose-petals. He sniffs gently and appreciatively. Violets. His gaze moves a little higher to where the wrist – a wrist that he could easily put thumb and forefinger around – vanishes into the sleeve of the bolero. Higher still. Violets again. Real flowers this time, to go with the perfume. From where he's sitting, a cluster of purple on a pale cheek. She's talking to a young fellow standing with her; her smile is a flicker of dark eyelashes and a flash of white teeth.

Dick finds himself contrasting his own immediate future with that of the girl's escort. Yarraville and the Trocadero. Sugar-berth and dance-floor. His eyes fall again to the little white hand so near his lips, and he sits back with an exclamation of contempt as he catches himself wondering what she would do if he suddenly kissed it. Sissy!

Old Joe's thoughts also must have been reacting to the impact of silks and perfumes.

'The way they get themselves up now,' he hisses into Dick's ear, 'you can't tell which is backside and which is breakfast.'

Dick eyes him with mild resentment. 'What's wrong with them? They look good to me.'

Joe snorts his disagreement, and the subject drops. Dick is only amused. He understands Joe. The old man has shown no disapproval of similar passengers who joined the tram at Alma Road and in Elsternwick. It's the name: 'Toorak'. It symbolises something. Poor old Joe! Too much courage and not enough brain. Staunch as ever, but made bitter and pigheaded with the accumulation of years. Weary of 'The Struggle'. Left behind. A trifle contemptuous of the young bloods carrying the fight through its final stages. A grand mate, though. And a good hatchman. That means a lot on a sugar job. With the great bulk of the old stevedore at his elbow, and the little white hand before his face, Dick is sensitive of contact with two worlds. Shoddy and silk. Strong tobacco and a whiff of violets. Yesterday and Tomorrow.

Flinders Street–Swanston Street intersection. They get off and push through the pleasure-seeking crowd on the wide pavement under the clocks. Another tram. Contrast again. Few passengers this time. One feels the cold more. Swift transition from one environment to another. Swanston Street to Spencer Street. Play to work. Light to darkness. No more silks and perfumes. Shadowy streets almost deserted. Groups of men, heavily wrapped against the cold, tramping away under the frowning viaduct.

'It'll be a fair bitch on deck,' says Joe, quite unconscious of his lack of originality.

'Yes, you can have it all on your own.'

No offence intended; none taken. They walk in silence. Joe isn't the talking kind. Dick is, but the little white hand and the glimpse of violets on a pale cheek have set in motion a train of thought that makes him irritable. He keeps thinking: 'Cats never work, and even horses rest at night!'

Berth Six, River. Passing up the ramp between the sheds they come out on to the wharf. Other men are already there. Deep voices, and the stamping of heavy boots on wood. The mist is thick on the river, almost a fog. Against the bilious glow of the few lights over on south side dark figures converge on one point, then vanish one at a time over the edge of the wharf.

Dick and Joe join their mates on the floating landing-stage. Rough greetings are exchanged.

'How are you, Joe?'

'What the hell's that got to do with you?'

'You old nark! Got a needle on the hip?'

'I don't need no needle. How's the missus, Sammy?'

'Bit better, Joe. She was up a bit today.'

'Line up there! – here she comes.'

As the little red light appears on the river the men crowd the edge of the landing-stage, each anxious to get a seat in the cabin on such a night. The water is very black and still, and the launch moves in with hardly a ripple. The night is full of sounds. Little sounds, like the rattle of winches at the distant timber berths; big sounds, like the crash of the coalgrabs opposite the gasworks. All have the quality of a peculiar hollowness, so that one still senses the overwhelming silence on which they impinge. In some strange way sound never quite destroys the portentous hush which goes with fog. Dick feels it as he follows old Joe over the gunwale and gropes his way through the cabin to the bows.

'It's quiet tonight, Joe. Can't be many ships working.'

'Quiet be damned. There's four working on north side. Where the hell're you going, anyway?'

'I'm going to sit outside.'

'You can sit on your own, then. This ain't no Studley Park tour.'

Dick doesn't mind that; all the same he isn't left alone. Other men are forced out beside him as the cabin fills. He finds it hard to dodge conversation. Racing. Football. Now if it was politics . . . The Struggle! Just a humour, of course. He has no fixed antipathies to nightwork, the waterfront or his mates. Nightwork means good money, three pounds a shift. A real saver sometimes. Many a time he's stood idle for days, then picked up a single night – enough to keep landlord and tradesmen quiet, at least. Two hours less work than the dayshift too. Nevertheless it's all wrong. Surely to Christ the work of the world could be carried on in daylight. So much waste and idleness during the day, and toil at night. Only owls, rats and men work at night.

'What's wrong, Dick? You're not saying much.'

'Just a bit dopey, Bluey. Not enough shut-eye.'

Damn them! – why can't they mind their own business?

The launch travels smoothly and swiftly. Quite safe. The mist is thickening, but there's a bit of light on the river here from the ships working on north side. Small ships, as ships go, but monstrous seen from the passing launch. Beautiful in a way of their own, too, with the clusters of lights hanging from masts and derricks. Little cities of industry resting on towering black cliffs. One can't tell where the black hulls join the black water.

Nameless bows, but still familiar to the critical stevedores.

'That's the *Bundaleera*. Good job. She worked the weekend.'

'The *Era*. She'll finish tonight.'

'The *Montoro*. They say there's only one night in her.'

Strange twentieth-century code of values. A collier which works Sundays is a good ship; a deep-water liner which works only one night is a bad ship.

'They can stick their Sunday work for mine!' Joe's voice.

'I suppose you get more out of the collection-box, you bloody old criminal!'

'That's all right. I only been to church twice in my life. The first time they tried to drown me, and the second time they married me to a crazy woman.'

Dick smiles to himself. A smile of affection for the old warrior. Joe's a good Christian, whether he knows it or not. There's a word for him: 'Nature's gentleman'. A hard doer and a bit of a pagan, that's all. Three convictions: one for stealing firewood during the Depression, one for punching a policeman during the '28 strike, and one for travelling on an expired railway ticket – also during the Depression. Across one cheek the scar of a wound received on Gallipoli. A limp in his right leg from an old waterfront accident. 'Screwy' arms and shoulders from too much freezer work in the days when every possible job had to be stood up for. 'Sailor Joe.' Dick loves him as any healthy youth can love a seasoned guide and mentor. They work together, ship after ship. They travel together, live near each other.

With a mutter of deep voices the launch chugs its way across the Swinging Basin. The mist continues to thicken. South side is just visible. Haloes of brassy yellow around lonely lights. Dismal rigging of idle coal lighters – grimy relics of the white wings of other days. North side can be heard but not seen. Beyond the veil ageing winches clatter at the coal berths and railway trucks crash against each other in Dudley Street yards. A man's voice hailing another comes across the water with extraordinary distinctness.

A few minutes later everything vanishes and the speed of the launch drops to a walking pace. Real fog now. Dick's eyes have been fixed on the ridge of water standing out from the bows. Twice since leaving Berth Six it has fallen in height, now it is but a ripple. Voices in the cabin are still cursing the cold, speculating lightly on the chances of reaching shore in the event of a collision. Dick wishes they'd all shut up. He's cold himself, but some of his irritation has gone. Here again is beauty – of a kind, like ships working at night, and the little white hand. Just two feet away the sooty water flows slowly past. It's easy to imagine that only the water moves, that the launch is motionless, a boatload of men resting in the perpetual night of a black river. To port, south side has ceased to exist, to starboard, north side is only the distant clamour of a lost world.

Nine o'clock.

The green navigation light of Coode Island.

Only the light. A bleary green eye, neither suspended nor supported. Green eye and grey fog. They pass fairly close. Too close, they realise, as the launch swings sharply off to port. New sounds come out of the night. Sounds of a working ship. Dead ahead, and not far away. Yarraville. Conversation, which has languished, flickers into life again.

'What the hell's that?'

'Don't tell me it ain't nine o'clock yet!'

'Just turned. Maybe there's a rockboat in.'

'There is. They picked up for her this morning.'

'We won't be long now – thank Christ! I'm as cold as a frog.'

'Listen to the dayshift howl when we pull in. It'll be ten o'clock when they get up the river.'

In two places, one on each bow, the fog changes colour. Two glowing caves open up, as if a giant had puffed holes in a drop-curtain. And in each cave the imposing superstructure of a ship materialises with all the bewildering play of light and shadow characteristic of ships at night. Rockboat and sugarboat. The *Trienza* and the *Mildura*. The comparatively graceful lines of the bigger ship don't interest the approaching stevedores. Their eyes are all on the *Mildura*, their minds all grappling with one question: how many nights?

'By God, she's low!'

'She's got a gutsful all right.'

'Three or four nights – you beaut!'

Under a barrage of jeers and greetings from the dayshift the launch noses in to the high wharf.

'You were a long time coming!'

'What're you growling at? You're getting paid for waiting.'

'Ho there, Bluey, you old bastard!'

'How are you, Jim? Left a good floor for us?'

'Good enough for you, anyhow. She ain't a bad job.'

'How many brands?'

'Five in Number Two Hatch. Grab the port-for'ard corner if you're down there. You'll get a good run till supper. Two brands.'

'Good on you, son!'

The nightshift swarms up the face of the wharf, cursing a Harbour Trust which provides neither ladder nor landing stage. Dick is last up, for no other reason than that Joe is second last. The strain imposed on the old man to reach the top angers his young mate. Damn their hides! All ugliness again. A man can never get away from it for long. The strange charm of the fog-bound river has gone. The black beams of the wharf, with the shrouded men clinging to them like monstrous beetles, symbolise all the galling dreariness of the ten hours just beginning. Symbolism also in the tremendous loom of the coal-gantry. Toiling upwards, always toiling upwards, with just a little glimpse of beauty now and then, like the mist, and the little white hand, and the ridge of black water streaming away from the bows of the launch.

'Shake it up, old-timer!' someone cries from above.

Joe's big boots are just above Dick's head. One of them is lifted on to the next beam. He waits for the other to move but the old man is still feeling for a higher grip for his hands. Dick's own fingers are getting numb. The beams are covered with wet coal-dust and icy cold. At either side the dayshift men are swarming down. Noise, confusion, and black shapes everywhere.

A sudden anxiety seizes Dick as Joe's higher foot comes down again to the beam it has just left.

'On top there!' he yells. 'Help this man up!'

Too late. Even as he moves to one side and reaches upwards in an endeavour to get alongside his mate, the old man's tired fingers give in. A big clumsy bundle hurtles down, strikes the gunwale of the launch with a sickening thud, and rolls over the side before anyone can lay a hand on it.

An hour later another launch noses away into the fog. Only two men. Both are within the cabin, one standing behind the little steering wheel, the other crouched near the open doorway with eyes fixed on the grey pall beyond the bows. Coode Island is astern before the boatman speaks.

'He was your mate?'

'Yes, he was my mate.'

'You got him out pretty quick.'

'Not quick enough. He hit the launch before he went into the water, you know.'

After: minute's silence. 'Does the buck know you've left?'

'I'm not worried. I wouldn't work tonight, not for King George. And somebody's got to tell his old woman.'

'I'm going right up to Berth Two. Will that do you?'

'Yes, anywhere.'

Anywhere indeed. And the further and slower the better. Not so much different from an hour ago. Mist, black water, and the crash of trucks over in the railway yards. But no men. One of them embarked now on a longer journey than he ever dreamed of. And in a few minutes there will be lights, and more lights. And voices, and the faces of many people. And not one of them will know a thing of what has happened. Princes Bridge, and the bustle of the great intersection. Trams, and St Kilda Road. And the big cars rolling along beneath the naked elms. The other world – violets – and the little white hand.

The little white hand. Funny. She'll be dancing somewhere now, and the grand old man with whom she very nearly rubbed shoulders –

'What was that?' asks the boatman.

Dick is startled to find he has spoken aloud.

'We don't know much about each other, do we?' he says without hesitation.

'What d'you mean?'

'Oh, nothing . . .'

Barry   Oakley

FOSTERBALL
1 9 9 1

As an eighty-year-old, I am flattered by your invitation to set down my impressions of Australian Fosterball, now that hologram television is here. I'm a little impaired because of concussion (of which more later) but can still put pen to paper. (How antiquated that sounds.)

The new technology is quite beyond me mentally and financially, so in order to write this piece I arranged for my son to collect me from my Twilight Village and drive me to his home.

He was not keen. Last time I watched Fosterball with him on his old wall-screen TV I became overstimulated and apparently ruined the afternoon for everybody. This time, he explained, as we hummed electrically to his house, he'd set me up and go out for the rest of the day.

An entire room has to be given to the new system – preferably large and windowless (exterior light can ruin the image). He took me in, sat me down at his Take-It-Ezy, a specially designed mobile seat, and explained the controls to me.

They were in the right armrest, around a small joystick, which enables you to move your chair to any part of the room. With the new hologram three-dimensionality, you have the option of experiencing from the sidelines or immersing yourself in the action completely.

For optimum effect (my son, who's in computers, has a regrettable turn of phrase) I should sit in total darkness for five minutes and meditate, imagining I was actually walking to the football ground in person. The latest thinking is that you should make a mental effort to move towards this miracle rather than sit there passively and let it overwhelm you.

It was now 1.45 p.m. My son, who is separated, overweight, bald and gloomy, closed the front door and went off, leaving the house to myself. As I waited, sitting alone in the dark, I contemplated life's strange symmetries. As a schoolboy, way back in the 1940s, I'd go every week to barrack for Melbourne, in the primitive grandstands or grass-and-dirt outers of football grounds all over the city. And now it would be like that again. With hologram television, my son had explained, you don't watch the match – you penetrate it, and it penetrates you.

I prepared myself by thinking of those far-off times. I recalled being hit in the face by a St Kilda supporter after I had cheered yet another Melbourne goal. In those days, Hawthorn and St Kilda always crept obediently to the bottom of the ladder as if it was the will of God, and their supporters were a small and dour group who never really expected their side to win a match. They would cheer and barrack in the first quarter, then gradually lapse into stoicism as their team inevitably fell back further and further.

I thought of the time in 1950 when I got out a book of poetry – Rilke's *Duino Elegies* – at half-time in the North Melbourne outer. I was jeered at: 'typical Melbourne-supporter sissiness, he's probably a poof.' Melbourne was the snob's team in those days. It took the players from the private schools, and you always felt uneasy at North Melbourne or Richmond or Fitzroy. But the Collingwood supporters were the worst. The meanest, the most fanatical, the most unbearable in victory and truculent in defeat. If Melbourne won at Collingwood, you cheered, but not too loud, and left the ground as soon as you could.

Melbourne's big men were always taller and better than Collingwood's, who never seemed to be over six feet. I can still see Jack Mueller putting his knees on to Gordon Hocking's shoulders, rising high, pulling down the mark, and falling over. Jack Mueller always fell over after taking a mark. There was time to do that in those days. All the Collingwood crowd could do was insult him: 'Get back to Germany, you fucking Kraut.' (The war had only been over five years.)

As Alf Brown, the *Herald*'s football writer, would invariably say: 'Once Melbourne swung into their long-kicking high-marking game, Collingwood's handball didn't stand a chance. The shortest way to goal is always straight down the middle.'

Two o'clock. I press the ON button. Nothing happens. I press it again. Still nothing. I sit waiting in the darkness. A shimmer, a hum, a tuning-fork fibrillation – an image is forming, ethereal, graspable, elusive: a can of Foster's.

Blue, silver, beaded with drops, it hovered there, huge, weightless, irresistible. I felt my youth returning to me. I hobbled into the kitchen, not so much for the pleasure of drinking as for the sensation of actually putting my fingers around the can. The coldness of it! Its incontrovertible reality!

When I returned, I opened the door onto a Fosterball ground. What vastness! The Bass-Strait roar it gave off! I made my way nervously to my seat – if I lost my balance, it seemed as if I could plunge headlong into the great amphitheatre itself.

Carlton versus Collingwood – in my room! In their fosterblue jumpers and silver shorts, Carlton, as they ran onto the ground, looked like twenty cans in flowing, up-and-down motion. They seemed to come straight at me, turning away only at the last moment to finish their circuit, as, behind the goals, beautiful young girls began their dancing and fostersongs.

Just before the ball was bounced, just as I was about to drink, fostertime! A blue electric flash cuts across the grandstands, the maddening, repetitive refrain begins, and 100 000 hands raise their cans high to invoke the Elliotts, the spirits of the game, in the hope that they would grant success to their team.

But when the game actually begins, I'm forced to back away. The players seem to run at the ball from each side of the room – two enormous ruckmen lumbering and then leaping, poised for a couple of amazing seconds over my head! A trick of light! I say to myself. A hologram haze! No more palpable than sunshine filtering through trees!

To prove it, I move my chair boldly into the middle of the room, and the effect is amazing. I was on the field, I was in the game, plunged into a dazzle of blueness and black and white stripes. I hear their grunts, the bullthumps of their boots; they rush, they bump, they curse, they come straight at me – and out the other side. Here comes Cumberpatch, the evil-tempered Collingwood full-back; I lash out at him with my fist – but he's run through me, and with hips and shoulder sends Fothergill to the turf!

Overcome, I wheeled myself all over the room, from the backline to the wings, from the wings to the forwards. I travelled through sights and sounds, I was dazzled by crystal diffractions, I spanned spectrums, I was in front of goal!

Blackadder, of Carlton, drop-punts the ball from the centre. My West St Kilda days with the Catholic Young Men's Society come back to me. Wasn't I the high-flyer of Alma Park? I got out of my chair and started the long run for which I and John Coleman used to be famous. I run, I raise my arms high, and my legs go from under me as if boneless!

My son found me slumped against a wall with the game still going on around me and through me. He revived me and drove me home to my lonely flat, his great foster-stomach pressing up against the steering wheel, and told me he would never be able to invite me again.

V a n c e   P a l m e r

THE STUMP

1 9 2 8

'See that stump!' Old Svenson used to say to any stranger he could get
hold of. 'Somet'ing like a stump, ain't it? It belong to the biggest tal-
lowwood you ever set eyes on, an' I lopped it off when I first come
here. T'irty feet from the ground.'

And little Oscar, hanging on to his grandfather's hand, would repeat
with the same perky tilt of the chin:

'T'irty feet from the gwound.'

He didn't know what the height meant, but he was sure it reflected
some vague glory on them both. Besides, he had become so used to
echoing his grandfather that he did it when he was half-asleep or
thinking about something else.

It was, indeed, a mammoth stump. It caught the eye of everyone
who came up the steep slope to the cleared tableland, for it was about
the only relic of the tall timber left. There were orange-trees, of course,
arranged as neatly in their ordered rows as soldiers on a parade-
ground, with the earth showing red and bare between. They provided
a miracle of blossom that made the very bees drunk in the early months
of the year, but usually their atmosphere was merely that of a tame
prosperity. Small orchards abutting on one another, white-painted
fences, growers who might be retired land-agents, flitting from the
store to the post office in their saucy cars. And a few imported shrubs
along the front, protected by palings from the night-wandering cow.
The forest and the scrub had gone, picked over first by the timber-
getters for pine and cedar, and then hacked down wholesale by settlers
hungry to make use of every inch of the rich, volcanic soil, so that now
there was no evidence of the great giants that had once grown there.

Except Svenson's stump! It stood on a grassy space between the
church and the school, and could be seen from the flat country below,
raising itself up like some white pillar of stone.

'T'irty feet from the ground,' old Svenson said, as though he had taken the measurements to an inch.

There had been no point in cutting it off so high up. None at all, for the stump was nearly as thick at the top as at the butt. In those days, though, old Svenson had taken a pride in going one better than the next man. He had been a sailor and was not so expert as some of them with the axe, so he evened matters up by putting his footboards in higher than the most foolhardy would have dared to venture. There was a triumph in stepping from his precarious perch on to the bare stump as the great tree heeled over and crashed, risking annihilation if it caught in another tree or kicked. It gave a fillip of excitement and adventure to the day's work.

Besides, it provided something to boast about, and that had always been a necessity to the little man. For forty years he had been boasting of one quality or possession after another, and his flickering eyes that peered out from behind their glasses still had a challenge in them. Didn't his smallholding of ten acres produce better oranges than any on the range? Hadn't his white Leghorns a record for laying? Wasn't his wife, when she was alive, known all over the district for her cooking? His trim, upright figure, with its stiff back and pointed, grey moustaches, was in itself an aggressive note of interrogation as he moved about the front by the store, holding little Oscar by the hand.

'Old Svenson – he'd shrivel up and die if he couldn't find something to skite about,' people said.

But he had been forced to give up one source of pride after another, conducting a strategic retreat down the years. His firstborn, Emil, who had promised to be such a brilliant youngster, had contracted a disease of the hip that had cut short his schooling and had left him lame and a little heavy-witted. He earned his living as yardman and billiard-marker in a hotel down the line, and would lick the boots of any-one who would buy him a drink. The old man had long ceased to boast about Emil.

Then his wife, that marvel among housekeepers, had died in hospital after a lingering illness. Hardly a memory was left of the days when she whisked one triumph after another from the oven. The second boy, Chris, was working in the canefields and never came south; and as for Anna – well, no-one quite knew what had happened to Anna. After creating some scandal by the way she carried on at dances with the young fellows who came up for the fruit-picking, she had gone to town as a waitress, and old Svenson was evasive when inquiries were made about her. At one time he implied that she had married an officer on an overseas liner, and at another that she was playing in the orchestra of a big cinema. But people ceased asking about her when the old man went surreptitiously to town one weekend and brought back Oscar, a little, puny fellow of eighteen months, who looked as if he had been reared at a baby-farm on separated milk. That satisfied them finally about Anna.

Yet in spite of these subtle and treacherous blows of Fate, Svenson still kept his aggressive old head up in public. There remained the stump, durable and securely rooted, a testimony to all sorts of things – his daring, his skill, the fact that he had been one of the pioneers.

'Forty year ago,' he would say, thrusting out his chin, 'there was not'ing in the way of risks I wouldn't take them days.'

He despised the men who had bought their orchards for cash and knew nothing of the long struggle with the timber. They were hardly more than immigrants, in spite of the way they took the lead in every-thing, running the Progress Association and electing themselves to the local council. While the stump remained, he would be able to look over the heads of people like these.

And, in addition to the stump, there was little Oscar. He fussed over the boy like an old hen over a single chicken and hardly ever let him out of his sight. Something inexplicable had happened to his own children, but he was going to make sure nothing of the sort happened to little Oscar.

'Hey, Oscar, come away from that grass,' his voice echoed out as he chipped among his orange-trees. 'Do you want for to get bitten by a snake?'

Or, when he was sitting on the veranda reading his newspaper:

'Now then, Oscar, don't climb any more on that fence. How many times do I tell you not to play the monkey like that!'

Oscar was a mild, flaxen-haired youngster, a little cowed by his early life in an institution, and didn't rebel against this martinet discipline. He even seemed to thrive and grow robust under it. His admiration for his grandfather took the form of aping him even in the smallest things, and when he was swaggering in front of the butcher-boy, telling him how many eggs he had collected, or what a big watermelon was growing at the bottom of the garden, he might have been the old man himself. The same perky walk, the same tilt of the chin, the same inflexions of the voice. Svenson never had the slightest difficulty in shaping him in his own image.

But it was not so easy to guard the stump. As the township in front developed, and became known as a holiday resort, there were attacks on the stump from all sides. First it was the proprietress of the new boarding-house, a prim, suburban lady with a fringe and eyeglasses, who argued that it was an eyesore and blocked the view from her veranda.

'Such a beautiful view it would be, too, if that thing wasn't planked down in the middle distance. Catching the eye and holding it like some ghastly tombstone. My guests all complain that it's a blot on the landscape.'

The schoolmaster was with her, not merely on aesthetic grounds, but because the youngsters had a habit of trying to climb it at playtime and there was always a danger of accidents. Other people wanted the relic removed for various reasons. It seemed to have the stigma of an earlier life about it, a crude, hand-to-mouth life, like the first attempts at building homes that most of them had turned into kitchens or outhouses covered with greenery.

The most formidable enemy of the stump, though, was the local councillor, for he had power and authority, and he wanted the obstacle cleared away for the deviation of a new road. A progressive type of man who had come late on the scene and bought his property instead of pioneering it, Rainey had no sympathy with sentimental ideas or associations.

'Old Svenson's been skiting about that stump for Lord knows how long,' he said. 'He's just about got his money's worth out of it by now. Anyhow he has no property rights over it, and it's a public nuisance.'

And the reply of the storekeeper, the land-agent, and his other henchmen on the council, was always:

'That's so, Mr Rainey: you're right there.'

But Svenson was militant in defending the stump's right to remain, and he had his supporters. They were mainly drawn from the original settlers, and they didn't talk much, but their tenacity could be relied on:

'Why can't Rainey let it alone?' one of them growled. 'The place wouldn't be the same if that old stump went down. It's a landmark.'

And the others, with an obscure sense of loyalty to the past, repeated: 'That's right. It's a landmark.'

The subject was always being raised when Svenson came out to the front for his mail, or sat in the store waiting for Oscar to be let out of school. Even his friends had a good-humoured way of barracking him about it, and their jokes never failed to make the old man bristle aggressively. A ruffled fighting-cock, he looked, with his white moustaches waxed at the points and his pale eyes glinting behind their glasses. Since the rheumatics had come on him he was less inclined to boast about his orange-trees, which were running to wood, or his fowls, now being killed off because of the price of corn, but any attack on the stump always roused his fighting blood. They would see whether Rainey was game to remove it! If he tried, he would raise a storm that would sweep him out of his place on the shire council. Yes, there were enough of the old hands left to counter such an attack; they could make their minds easy about that.

And so the stump remained. Even Rainey didn't seem anxious to take the first step towards removing it, in spite of his talk. He knew there was a considerable amount of feeling liable to be aroused if he acted – more than if he did nothing. Having political ambitions, he was aware of the risks of offending even the least of his future constituents, for it was easier to make enemies than gain supporters. As well let sleeping dogs lie – for a while, anyway. Svenson was growing old. You could see it in his figure, no matter how he tried to keep his head up and his spine straight when people were looking at him. There would come a day . . .

It did come, sooner even than Rainey expected. Old Svenson was chipping among his orange-trees one afternoon when the schoolmaster and the boy from the store edged down the track, bearing little Oscar on an improvised stretcher. They laid their burden down by the gate, hesitating. They seemed to be waiting for the two women who were following behind.

It was some time before the old man could take in what had happened. Oscar had been climbing the stump in the lunch-hour, it appeared, and had slipped at the top niche, 't'irty feet from the ground', as his grandfather had so often said. The schoolmaster didn't attempt to drive home the moral, but he had foreseen some such accident if the stump remained, and his long, solemn face said plainly enough:

'There, what did I tell you? Your own grandson. You see how chickens come home to roost.'

While the others were present the old man made light of the accident. Things like this were always happening. How many bad tumbles hadn't he had himself when he was a youngster! Tumbles from trees, from cliffs, and, later on, from the spars of sailing-ships rolling in gales round the Horn! Oscar would be back at school in a day or two, he affirmed, and the boy repeated in a dim voice that he would be back at school in a day or two. Not even a bone broken, the old man said, and the echo repeated that there wasn't even a bone broken. But when, next morning, he complained of his back, his grandfather rang up the ambulance and had him taken down to the railway, making up his mind in the train that he would consult the best specialist. Oh yes, the very best! Money – that was of no account. Emil hadn't seen a doctor soon enough; that was the trouble with him; but there were going to be no risks with little Oscar.

It was nearly a month before he returned, and during that time a few more wrinkles had accumulated on his forehead and his moustaches had lost their spiky aggressiveness. Little Oscar had injured his spine, the specialist had told him, and would have to lie on his back for at least a year; indeed, it was doubtful whether he would ever walk again. Old Svenson had become hard of mental hearing, and it took some time for the news to sink into him. When it did, he decided to sell his orchard, then come back to town so that he would be near the boy. No use trying to let the place! He wouldn't be likely to find a man who would look after it with the same care as he had. And what pleasure would it be to come back in a year's time and find the trees a mass of wood, with weeds round them three feet high?

There was no car to meet the train, and as he walked up the five miles of steep road in the moonlight he had time to ponder on all that had happened since he first made the ascent. The people he had loved and taken a pride in – his wife, the two boys, Anna, and now little Oscar. Not much left to boast of now! ... But he didn't want to think or look back; it gave him a pain in the head and made the climb more slippery. With all their talk of progress they hadn't improved the grades much since he first struggled up with a sailor's kit on his back behind Doherty's bullock-team.

As he rested after the last abrupt rise, he was faced by the stump, looking white in the moonlight and durable as stone. For a long while he stood peering at it with his short-sighted eyes, his chin thrust out aggressively as of old, and his body rigid as hardwood. Then a little vein seemed to burst in his head, and he stumped off to where Rainey lived among his orange-trees in the big white house overlooking the lower slopes.

'You can root out that stump,' he said, when Rainey appeared at the door.

The local councillor was in his pyjamas and already half-asleep. He looked at Svenson, whose eyes seemed pale and blind in the glare of light from the hall.

'Eh?' he said thickly.

'That stump,' repeated the old man. 'You can root it out now. I give you leaf. Yes, I myself give you leaf. You can burn it or root it out. It's stood too dam' long already.'

It was his final surrender to life.

'Too dam' long already,' he could hear Oscar echo faintly as he drifted off through the orange-trees.

Ruth Park

THE HOUSE TO THEMSELVES
1988

The two girls watched the broad back of Mrs Pearson vanish between the bearded quince trees at the bottom of the hill. Instantly a new and enchanting air stole through the house; their elongated reflections leaped gnome-like in the brass platter over the mantel; the smell of new bread was like a charm.

'I like it best of all when Mum's gone out,' said Margaret. 'I like it when we're by ourselves.'

Her friend Dossie, who had come over to spend the afternoon, was a pale pudding of a child with thin hair and a solemn, elocutionary manner.

'Let's go and see how the baby is,' she suggested.

Margaret said: 'Wait a moment.' She stuck her head through the window and shouted grimly towards the back of the house. 'You lie down and be a good dog, Petey, or I'll wallop you,' though there was no sound except the somnolent chinking of a chain.

She slid along the floor, pausing by the stove to spit sizzlingly on its polished surface. Dossie considered an instant and then spat too, watched the droplets round themselves and dance on the glossy black.

The baby was asleep, his fuzzy head sticking out of a blue cocoon of blanket. They looked for a while at his pouchy cheeks and the shadows where his eyebrows were going to be. Then Margaret, with a calm, proprietary air, hit him a smart slap on the head.

'Oh, won't you get it!' said Dossie breathlessly. The baby wrinkled up a red face and showed a toothless half-moon.

'You shut up, gummy,' said Margaret, peering interestedly down the baby's throat as he yelled.

'Can I bash him, too?' asked Dossie.

'Sure,' said Margaret open-handedly. 'He's my brother isn't he?'

Dossie raised her hand with a thrilled, half-frightened feeling. Then, far away as a seagull on a sandbar, there sounded a voice, broken and attenuated by the wind.

'Bugger!' said Margaret. 'It's Cheap Billy.'

She raced out into the kitchen. Dossie started after her. Then she came back and gave the sobbing baby a kiss on his forehead, tucked him strangulatingly under the blue rug, and left with the firm, decisive tread of Mrs Pearson.

Margaret was already on the veranda. Up the track came a small bowed figure in a pudding-basin hat. He drove an old weary mare with a yellow cart behind her. Every now and then Cheap Billy lifted his head and uttered a long soprano howl in which words reared their heads for an instant and then sank again, indistinguishable from the coloratura notes.

'He's saying "Bone, rags, bottles and bags",' translated Margaret proudly. 'But he buys anything. Once he gave Mum thirty cents for two jars of her chutney. And another time he bought Petey's old rug that had fleas in it, so we couldn't keep it.'

'But he can't come here when your Mum's out,' cried Dossie. 'What would we say?'

'I know,' boasted Margaret scornfully. 'I'll say Mother's out and we have nothing to sell, thank you.'

Dossie said quickly: 'But then he'll know we're by ourselves and he might come in and do things.'

Margaret stared at her friend, half-dismayed comprehension in her eyes. Things! Might kidnap the baby perhaps, or steal the silver sugar basin in the sitting-room cabinet. Might take all the chooks in the henhouse. Or perhaps might choke Dossie and herself to death in the course of doing all those unimaginable and unnameable things that happened to little girls who spoke to strange men.

'Pooh! He's only old Cheap Billy,' she said uncertainly. But it was too late anyway. The mare plodded to a stop in front of the veranda, and Cheap Billy, with a big cobbled hessian bag on his back, came and stood at the foot of the steps. They stared down at him; at his skin like chamois leather; his hair growing in little spikes over his frayed collar; his eyes as red and hard as garnets; the curious humps and wrinkles in his boots; and his little smooth, dirty-nailed hands curled around the rail of the steps.

Margaret said hoarsely: 'Mum says we haven't got anything to sell today, Mr Cheap Billy.'

'Ach!' he said in disappointment. 'But your mumma promised me some picture frames when I was here last. Maybe she forgets? You go and ask her, liddle girl.'

The two girls stood there, their hands frozen in their pockets, their faces frozen with embarrassment. Dossie wanted to go to the door and call out: 'You said you didn't want those frames to be sold, didn't you, Mrs Pearson? All right, I'll tell him.' But her feet, nailed to the veranda, would not move.

The man had seen at once that the children were alone. He heard the chain jingle in the backyard and knew the dog was tied up. He rubbed a knuckle under his nose, pondering his chances.

'You got any old clocks, any old tools your daddy do not want, maybe?' he asked. His wrinkled boot rose to the next step, and his hand slid up the rail. Margaret swallowed, and Dossie squeaked:

'We haven't got anything, Mr Cheap Billy. Honestly we haven't.'

'Maybe if I go inside for a liddle, and have a look around, I see something, yes?' he suggested. He came up another step, and the girls smelled a dry musty odour rising from him, as though he often slept under houses and in woodsheds.

He looked thoughtfully at Margaret, her long coltish legs and pink rosette of a mouth. Margaret felt a strange prickling sensation run over her, as though her blood had turned in its course and was flowing back the way it had come. All at once the simple sounds of the countryside, the little creaking of a cricket, the chuckle of the water in the dam, the remote yelp of a magpie, took on a mysterious significance as though she were never to hear them again. She said in a sudden basso croak: 'I'll tell my father on you!'

He spread out his hands. 'Now, why? Your daddy and I are very good friends, very good. I just don't want to go away without buying something. You understand. You are smart liddle girl.'

Dossie stared at Margaret, standing there paralysed. Dossie knew that at any moment the small man with the dirty hands and his smooth coaxing voice would come up the remaining steps. There slid through her mind a picture of her friend and herself with their throats cut like the sheep she had once accidentally seen on a drought-stricken farm.

'Wait!' she croaked. 'I'll find something for you. You wait here.'

Ignoring Margaret's anguished snort at being left alone, she darted into the laundry that opened off the veranda. She looked frantically about. There was a big basket of dry washing there, the hem of a torn slip hanging over the side. Dossie gulped with relief. These old things wouldn't matter. Mrs Pearson wouldn't mind. She staggered out with the basket. Cheap Billy was on the top step. He seemed a little disappointed when he saw Dossie with the basket, but when she set it down he ran his fingers quickly through its contents.

'Not much good,' he grunted. 'One dollar only.'

He scrabbled in his pocket, hitching up his coat so that a medley of waistcoats and cardigans showed. He thrust a dollar coin into Dossie's trembling hand and hoisted the basket to his shoulder. With hurry in his heels he descended the steps, something of frustration or regret in his small garnet eyes. The old mare raised her grey muzzle and coughed as the whip flicked around her wealed shoulders. Cheap Billy did not look back as the cart moved away.

Margaret turned on Dossie and hit her hard on the ear.

'You've sold Mum's washing, shirts and tablecloths and everything for a measly dollar,' she shouted, her eyes blazing with fury and relief. 'You silly bugger!'

Dossie held her stinging ear. Amidst her shock and confusion a recognition of injustice stood firm.

Margaret's eyes, their fire rekindled, filled with hope.

'We'll set Petey on him! We'll send the dog after him!'

She rushed to the back of the house and hauled the drowsy black pup out of the kennel. He opened one eye and looked filmily at her, grinning at her shrieks and pleas. Then he rolled on his back and showed her and Dossie his bended paws. Margaret sat down in the scattered straw of his bed, weeping loudly.

Dossie looked at her friend with new eyes. She felt disdain and dislike. Margaret had let her down; she was only a silly bugger after all.

'And I'll tell Mrs Pearson she slapped the baby, too,' she thought.

Bruce   Pascoe

THYLACINE

1982

In the Australian bush at night you could find a lost sixpence or the feldspar in a piece of quartz, you could find the buckle off a dog's collar or a sooty owl in a tree. But you'd never find a pound note or an ant and you'd never find an old sepia photograph or why things are the way they are, although men will look for it there and some of them all of their lives.

And so Douglas was looking again, even though he'd told his brother he was going to check the chooks. That cold winter luminescence shone with such a fierce white light. Ah, it's a cold star. A cold star bearing the steely light of a cold moon, bearing that light without blinking, allowing it to find old sixpences and feldspar, dog's buckles and sooty owls, but very little else. More than enough light for some things but not enough for vision.

Old iron shines like new milled steel, a shovel blade glints sharp from the work in gravelly soil, trees shine like chandeliers, the dam like a disc of stamped plate. All these old things gleam anew. The barbed wire's rusty knots shine with frost, spider's webs are jewelled like the most precious things hung from the pale necks of the world's most desirable women.

Douglas checked the chooks and they stared at his eyes. Stupid chooks. He closed his fingers around the neck of a hen, and it blinked one eye but didn't move.

He checked the wire where he'd made the repair, and it was still intact. Six chooks they'd lost, and not a murmur. No feathers. No wild cackles. No fox dashing about in panic and blood lust. Just a chook off the roost and a neat hole in the wire. Douglas didn't know this animal. Clarrie said dingoes or native cats, but Douglas knew he didn't believe it himself. He knew the bush better than that, but Clarrie was the sort of bloke who always needed to propose a solution even if he knew it was wrong; anything to fill a gap.

When they'd found the human skulls, Clarrie had said it was just old-timers caught in a fire, even though Clarrie must have seen the strangeness of the sockets. Old Pearson had died out in the bush, killed by a tree that slipped back off its stump and drove his leg into the ground. Pinned him there. The bull ants stripped him clean. Clarrie had seen Pearson's skull and must have seen the difference in these others, but he just rolled them away with his boot and said it must have been two old timers. Clarrie was like that.

Douglas saw the stones but didn't bother to tell Clarrie; he'd only argue back. So he'd returned later and picked them up and seen how the long one matched the hollow in the flat one. Douglas placed them in the crook of a tree near where the skulls had been found. Where he could put his hands on them again.

The brothers got on all right. They could put in a row of fence-posts in a day and say no more than was needed to accomplish the task; and to put in a row of stringybark posts you don't need to say a lot. There's holes and posts and a straight line. If the posts ram tight, and the eye slips along the flat faces of each post, the job's done.

Douglas didn't need people. He sold the tickets at the local dance because it meant you could stand out on the veranda and listen to the blokes yarn and maybe add your piece about the last flood, but it was a way of meeting people without going through the bother of trying to balance a noisy china cup on a saucer and think of something to say at the same time.

And the women always made him nervous. And dancing. Dancing was plain impossible. He watched other blokes dance, blokes like him, bush workers, timber millers, cow cockies, and yet they could get around; some of them just glided about.

He'd watched the women's bodies like the other men, but he'd never really met one he wanted. During national service the boys had played up a bit, and that time he'd gone up to Candelo with the cricket team he didn't come back for three days. But not anyone you'd want to marry, stay with always; and anyway who'd have him? Short freckly bloke on a broken-down dry ridge farm. Women round here knew where the gravel pits were.

He'd never asked Clarrie. He'd never asked Clarrie anything much. Clarrie wasn't the sort of bloke you asked anything of. He guessed that Clarrie had knocked about a bit. Those trips to Bombala to sell cows sometimes took a while, but Clarrie never seemed – never seemed lonely or anything. Clarrie always had everything worked out. Douglas thought he'd know if anything worried his brother. When the old man had died, Douglas had watched, stunned, as tears dropped out of his brother's eyes. Clarrie had wiped his face with a rag and said, 'Dad taught me everything. All I know about the bush and that. That's all,' and again he had plunged his spade into the broken clay of the grave.

They got on all right, but there were times when Douglas liked to get away. The nights at the dances, the other blokes and the music, watching the women, and just something different. And nights like this, with the cold moonlight. He didn't tell Clarrie, you couldn't, but he knew some poems by heart. All the schoolbooks were still on the shelf.

Probably never occurred to Clarrie to throw them out. The sixth grade reader, *Modern Short Stories*, and that book of French poems that came with their lounge suite at the clearing sale.

He didn't feel like it tonight, but sometimes he'd said those poems looking over the dam and down to the river: 'Slowly, silently, now the moon/Walks the night in her silver shoon ...' Shoon, Shoon. He'd worked it out that it must be shoes. Their teacher had just expected them to know, but then she was the sort of jackass who'd never seen the paws of a sleeping dog in the frosty moonlight. How many people had?

He'd worked out how to say some of the French poems, too. He'd looked in amazement at the sheet music while cleaning up after a dance one night and a folded sheet fell from the back of a book, '*Non, je ne regrette rien*'. He wondered what it meant, but he found '*Alouette, gentille Alouette*', and suddenly the words and the song snapped to the front of his brain and he turned back to '*Non, je ne regrette rien*', and he worked out how most of the words must sound; but he'd never told Clarrie. Clarrie wasn't the sort of bloke you could.

What was that?

He didn't move. He didn't even let his heart beat any differently after its initial hesitation. He could feel the hair on his shoulders and across his neck edging upwards, but he didn't move. There it was again. A growl like he'd never heard before. He didn't allow his head to move, but his eyes swivelled and saw it almost straight away. After all, he was a bushman, and this was his yard, and his eyes found the strange object in it instantly. And look at it! What an animal!

The beast had been looking at the house but felt the man's eyes find his own, and they looked at each other, and the barbs of glance hooked in the eye flesh. Memories and visions are made thus.

The animal was gone in the next instant, and Douglas knew he'd be gone, but he followed him to the edge of the timber and stopped by the fence. Douglas spoke and his voice, clear and hard in the sharp white air, chased and found the beast.

'*Je vous regarde* – I saw you, dog, or – wolf. That's what you are. I saw you, tiger dog – Thylacine.' What a word to pitch into the moonlight.

Even as it ran, the animal heard the yelling and the strange word that was its name, and the sound would stay. Thylacine! It stood on the dry ridge among the shards of quartz and swung its heavy head to look down into the valley, knowing it was safe. Surely nothing could spirit itself through time so quickly. But a voice could, and did again.

'I know you're up there, tiger. I saw you.' The two knew each other. The wolf would remember the voice and the man would never forget the beast. In this universe of beings, these two were fused by the light of a silver moon. Both hearts beat; the tiger on the ridge, the man in the valley.

'I saw you, tiger.' There are some things, the man knew, which could never be denied. A man's spirit is built thus.

But animals are as logical as men, and Douglas had stood out in the bush where he knew the tiger must pass. The feldspar shone in the shafts of moonlight, the eucalypt leaves hung like small, bright scimitars of snipped tin, and the dog was there. Douglas could feel its presence by the way his hair crept beneath his collar.

'I know you're there, dog.' At the first word, before the muscles of the legs had flung the bones into flight, the animal's eyes had seen the other's eyes above where the voice had come out of the moonshine. 'I saw you, Thylacine. You can't deny that.'

Some night, man's logic and beast's logic diverged. The man knew he'd keep seeing it, although not so close to the house again. Chickens weren't that attractive. Not to a wild animal. Foxes and chickens were built for each other, but Tasmanian Tigers – well, they could take chickens or leave them, and when men were around, they left them.

But some nights, out of the bush came that quiet sound. No chase, no guns, just the sound. You looked out for things like that. You didn't get too close to snakes, you kept out of the way of eagles, and, especibally, you kept out of the way of men. But this one kept on being there. You never heard it; it was always where you couldn't smell it. And then, just that noise, not growling, just the same quiet sounds. No harm came, but you avoided things like that, if you could. It was better without the moon. The man wasn't there without the moon.

'Hey fellas, old Jack reckons he's seen a Tasmanian Tiger out by the river.' Bob Ridgeway had turned his big, red face over his shoulder to yell to the other blokes.

'Bull,' said Arnold Carter. 'Old Jack's been on the white lightning again.' Old Jack didn't like Carter, so he shut up.

'He just said so,' persisted Ridgeway. 'Didn't yer Jack; while you was settin' traps.' Jack didn't speak. His eyes were affirmative, but his shoulders looked as if his head was hoping its bloody mouth would stay shut.

'Keep the cork in the kero bottle, Jack,' said Carter, who knew how to use words like the whipping end of a roll of barbed wire. Jack flinched. 'Anyone else seen a Tasmanian Tiger?' Carter let the last words leer. No-one spoke. Douglas shuffled the last few dance tickets, and the group began chuckling and slapping broad shoulders. Jack slipped out into the moonlight back to his camp. No-one noticed. Silly old Jack, seein' bloody tigers now. Poor old coot. Trust bloody Arnold to stick in the boot, eh!

The last Palma Waltz bleated to a close, and the hall was packed up. Douglas cast an eye over the sheet music on the piano, but this new bloke didn't use the same stuff that the other pianist had used. Whatever happened to the other fella, Douglas wondered. Some blokes just disappear. Always a bit strange, that fella. Always quiet, never quite met your eyes. Except every now and then while he was playing, he'd look up and you'd catch him, and wonder what he was thinking. Not the Pride of Erin, that's for sure. Douglas wondered what *Non, je ne regrette rien* had meant. Could foreign words tell you anything more about a man?

With the new moon, the chooks began to disappear again. Sometimes Douglas would wait for the tiger in the bush. He would crouch beside the river and wait for the dog to highstep through the shallows to hide its track. 'Hullo, Thylacine. I saw you again.' But you couldn't tramp around the bush every moonlit night pretending to track a chicken thief. Clarrie'd get sick of it.

In bed, Douglas would think of the tiger, those swift glances they had shared. They got to know each other. Douglas could see the dog's frustration in the glances now. 'Here's that man *again*.' It was almost like tipping your hat. The man would greet the beast with its name, and the beast would recognise the man, recognise the voice long before the end of the split second it took to find the eyes above the voice. The man became an annoyance, like a new-fallen log across an old path, an owl that snatches the bandicoot you've tracked all the way from the creek. To the tiger, the man became just another night animal, and the man knew it and revelled in that pride.

Douglas lay in bed with the moon on his face, the pillow like a field of snow. Yes, it was as though the beast no longer thought of him as a man, but as an animal of the night, a clever one that would sometimes appear. Not an enemy, but an equal, and strangely, Douglas's heart strained with a feeling like – then his throat went tight. He was proud, but it was more than that, it was almost like –

The blast of the shotgun rattled the window pane by Douglas's face. He sat up in bed with that strange animal cry still with its hooks at his chest. He saw Clarrie with the shotgun. Clarrie turned and looked up at Douglas's moon-white face at the window.

'I just shot at a wild dog. It won't get far. There's enough blood over here to fill a bucket.' Clarrie came over to the window holding up a finger dipped in the blood.

'Thought I'd better do somethin' to stop you trampin' around the bush every night.' Douglas stared at the blood on Clarrie's finger and felt the hair prickling under his pyjama coat. The claw of the beast's cry slowly released, but now there was another sensation leaching from the wound the sound had made.

Moonlight nights were terrible after that. Douglas lay in bed, and the words of poems crept across his mind, trying to close up a wound with the soft stitches of the sounds and rhythms. If, in the eleven books the brothers owned, he'd found 'Tyger! Tyger! Burning bright', he would have read it to his heart and hoped that the wounds would heal.

But he didn't know those words and his mind sought for words that it didn't, couldn't know. If they'd had the seventh grade reader, he would have found it in there, but he didn't go to seventh grade. He was just a bushman.

Elliot   Perlman

THE REASONS I WON'T
BE COMING
1994

People seldom have a genuinely clear understanding of probate. They
are full of misconceptions about it. I've grown accustomed to this. It
doesn't surprise me any more. It shouldn't after twenty-four years with
the Office of Probate in what is now called the Department of Justice.
Maggie says people are afraid of it. She says that since they associate
it with death in some way and don't really understand it in the first
place, they're afraid of it. People are afraid of what they don't understand.
Maggie often says this. She's angry with these people. I've told her that
most people don't understand most things. She says that most people
are *afraid* of most things. Maggie is a social worker by training but she
works for the Department of Treasury now.

The topic arises when people ask me what I do. Maggie and I look
at each other and then I start at the beginning, with the basics of
probate. The Supreme Court grants a certificate to the effect that the
will of a certain deceased person has been proved and registered in the
court and that administration of the deceased's effects has been granted
to the executor proving the will. Maggie says I've lost them by this
stage. We never get to what I actually do.

We must have known the Gibsons for almost thirty years. Maggie
thinks it's more. I actually prefer Fran to Brian, but whenever we're
out with them there's always that preliminary stage where Maggie talks
to Fran and Brian talks to me. It's there right after the *hellos*. It can
take up to half an hour. Brian starts off with the state of his business
which he then links to the economy. He owns a newsagency. He
quotes figures and talks about trends, both in his business and in the
economy generally. He goes through phases. A while ago he seemed
very fond of the *trade-weighted index*. More recently it was the *current
account deficit* and *microeconomic reform* which he wants to introduce
in his newsagency. He puts his arm around my shoulders and talks

earnestly about the *fundamentals* which are or aren't in place (I can never remember) and about our *major trading partners.*

This preliminary stage usually ends with Brian attracting the attention of Maggie and Fran, and then with a mischievous grin, he asks what I do, again. He has a very loud laugh. Maggie thinks it's more than thirty years.

They have been our good friends for a long time. Maggie and Fran used to work together before Maggie went to the Treasury. They were really there for us when we lost Sarah. That's when you see what people are. Brian wouldn't go home. He said he didn't think it was good for us to be on our own and we never were. He said he would keep the media away and he did. If it wasn't Brian and Fran or Maggie's parents, it was the police. We seemed to be constantly putting the kettle on. The police were really terrific. We don't blame them. Maggie says blame is useless. Some things are unsolvable. They worked long and hard on the case. Some have become close personal friends of ours. I don't think the public really appreciate the work they do. When they started the Neighbourhood Watch in our area we were one of the first to join.

Not long ago, we received a printed invitation in the mail to the Gibsons' thirty-fifth wedding anniversary. The paper was tan and the lettering was gold. It said we had three weeks to RSVP. I've always wondered how they worked that out. Why three weeks and not four, or two? The Gibsons had booked the Regency Room at the San Remo Reception Centre. It was to be black tie. Maggie had left the invitation on the dresser in our room. She didn't mention it through dinner. She was talking to Griff, her father, about the ozone layer. He's not very concerned about it. She's been trying to make him more aware. Griff has lived with us in Sarah's old room since Maggie's mother passed away about two and a half years ago. He's not bad for seventy-eight. He's been trying to teach himself the guitar ever since we all heard a special on Radio National about a year back. Maggie's very good with him.

We listen to the radio together quite a lot, particularly Maggie and me. We listen in bed at night before we go to sleep.

One night in bed, as we lay on our backs having turned the radio off, Maggie asked, 'Do you ever wake up with an inexplicable . . . panic inside you?'

'Panic?'

'Yes, a sort of general non-specific . . . panic . . . in your stomach . . . that quickens your pulse?'

I thought about this for a moment. Although it was the middle of the night and her question was apropos of nothing in particular, I knew I had better give my answer some thought. Maggie can take people very seriously. She often does. Where was she leading with this question? She was waiting for my answer. She was probably describing something she has felt. Perhaps it is a feeling she is ashamed of. She doesn't always want to have to be strong. She has told me this.

'Yes. I have experienced something like that.'

'I thought you had,' she said and rolled over on her side.

Although it was my annual leave I had taken work home. You realise as you get older that you're really only hurting yourself if you put off your work, annual leave or not. We had formed a committee at work to undertake a client services program. It was me that pushed for the committee to be widely representative. Although it wouldn't be meeting until a few weeks after my return, I thought I would take the opportunity of this quiet time to draft a few proposals, nothing definitive, perhaps starting with a working definition of 'client'.

Maggie had a flexiday so she slept in while I worked on the draft proposals. At ten o'clock I brought her in a cup of tea. She had been listening to the radio but had turned it off when I came in with the tea.

'What were you listening to?'

'*Life Matters*.'

'What's that? I don't think I know that one.'

'It's the new name they gave to *Offspring*.'

'Oh,' I said and put the tea down on her bedside table.

'What was it about this morning?'

'Breastfeeding,' she said, bringing the teacup to her mouth. 'Is Dad up yet?' she asked.

'Yes, I've made him some toast and he's taken it outside. Are you still going to take him to the library today?'

'Yes. I'd better. He's got a couple of things that will be overdue soon.'

'What else?'

'What else *what*?'

'What else are you going to do today?' I asked.

'Well I've got shopping to do . . . and I'd wanted to write to Bruce.'

'Haven't you started that letter yet?'

'No. No, I haven't. He wants some more money you know.'

'Yes, I know.'

'How did *you* know?' she asked.

'He said it, didn't he? Doesn't he say something about money in his last letter?'

'*I* got the impression he wanted money from the phone call . . . when he called me at work.'

'Do you want to give him more money? How much does he *really* need in Nepal?'

'You've decided, haven't you. You have an agenda,' she said.

'No. I haven't decided. I haven't decided.'

Maggie sat up with a pillow at her back and said after a while, 'I haven't decided either.'

'It's terrific that he still writes . . .'

'And calls.'

'From Nepal of all places, after all this time.'

'He wasn't calling from Nepal.'

'Still. He's a good boy.'

'He certainly knows how to take care of himself. Nothing more we can teach him,' Maggie said, puffing the sheet up to her neck.

'Will you be working all day?' she asked.

'Not *all* day.'

'Would you do something for me today?'

'What?' I asked her.

'I'd like you to write to the Gibsons, to RSVP to their wedding anniversary invitation.'

'I could just call them, except I'll never get off the phone if Brian answers.'

'I'd like you to write to them telling them we won't be coming.'

There was an awful banging sound coming from another room, like a hollow wooden box being slapped. It startled me.

'What the hell's that?'

'It's Dad. He's been having terrible trouble with notes because he won't press the strings down hard enough. The reason he gets the muffled sound is 'cause he won't press the strings down hard enough.

It's important that he feels he's achieving something, making some progress, or he'll get discouraged.'

'Why do you say he *won't* press hard enough?'

'He could but he won't. He's too soft. Is there any more tea?'

I don't think Maggie has been enjoying her work recently. It's not so much the administrative component. She knew this would be a feature when she accepted the position. I think she even takes comfort in it now. I can understand that. I suspect that when Fran accepted a position with ACOSS Maggie was privately concerned that Fran's contribution to the community would be greater than hers. No matter what I said, I don't think anything has really dispelled that concern. Is it a valid concern? No, not really. There's a strong policy analysis component to Maggie's work. She's even privy to certain inside information. She knows in advance the proposed expenditure cuts, their size and where they'll fall. She sees the guidelines for the proposed Human Resources cutbacks. She even sees the lists of personnel, in all government departments, whose services will no longer be required. She has her finger on the pulse of public policy in a macro sense that I would have thought she'd find rather exciting. She used to find it exciting, but not lately it seems.

I must admit I've had my moments too, moments when I've felt I'd lost that sense of challenge. When you're caught up in a new program though, it's hard to remember ever having felt that way but I have felt it from time to time. You can even get blasé about things. I remember that within only a year of being granted a Higher Duties Allowance I took it for granted.

Sitting there in the study one day last week, with the sunlight coming through our trees and falling softly onto the pages of the draft proposals, I had to work hard to be at one with Maggie's dissatisfaction. Griff was in the garden with his guitar. He likes to hold it to him.

Maggie came in from the car and unloaded the shopping bags onto the bench beside the sink. When Griff heard her he brought his guitar inside and looked inside the plastic bags. I was listening to the rustling and talking. Maggie put the kettle on. Griff put the guitar on the kitchen table. Maggie ran the tap water, not hard but firmly over certain fruit and vegetables in our sink. I couldn't see it from the study but I knew this was what she was doing. I thought we might have a salad for lunch.

I was first in bed that night but not by much. Maggie was sitting at the dresser, taking off her face. It was a bit nippy so I brought out the flannel pyjamas, my stripey ones. Maggie saw me in the mirror and gave a little smile.

'Those pyjamas are so . . . you,' she said.

I smiled a little. 'What do you mean?'

'They are just . . . *you*,' she said and went back to her face, 'but they're too stripey. I can't look at them.'

I got into bed and she couldn't see much of them any more. Then she got into bed. We listened to Phillip Adams on the radio. I thought Maggie seemed sad.

'What are you thinking?' I asked.

'Lots of things . . . and nothing.'

'Should we talk about some of them?'

'Did you know that Sarah had once asked how we got married, about the decision to get married, the mechanics of it, the proposal and who was told first, etcetera?'

'I didn't know that. She was very romantic, wasn't she? I mean, right from the early days.'

'There were only early days.'

'Yes, of course, I know, Maggie.' I reached for her hand. 'You told her the way it all happened?'

'Yes,' she said removing her hand to apply her hand lotion.

'You always knew what you wanted, didn't you?' I said resting my hand on her shoulder.

'Why . . . why do you say that?'

'Because of the way it all happened. I was much too scared. I would never have said anything without your . . . encouragement.'

'But you did,' she said.

'I just said *yes*. Do you remember? It was about the time we were meant to be going camping, near Mount Disappointment.'

'What do you mean you said *yes*?' Maggie asked.

'Well I obviously didn't say *no* or we wouldn't be here, would we?'

'But I didn't *ask* you anything.'

'Yes you did,' I insisted. 'I remember it clearly. It was night time. We were in your parents' front room. They were in the kitchen. We were talking about what your parents would say about us going camping. We'd never been away alone. You said they wouldn't like it and that we might just as well tell them we were getting married because, as far as they were concerned, couples shouldn't go away alone together until after they're married.'

Maggie sat up. 'Yes, I remember. You said you didn't agree with that. You said it was old-fashioned but that you would respect it.'

'And *you* said we shouldn't respect it . . . then you asked me if I was ready . . . and *that's* when I said *yes*,' I reminded her.

I took Maggie's moisturised hand and put it between the covers and my stripey flannel pyjama top. She sat still. We were quiet for a moment, remembering.

'There's a logical inconsistency there,' Maggie said.

'Where?'

'Even the way you tell it now –'

'Which is the way it happened,' I jumped in.

'Even the way you tell it now, it sounds as though I was asking if you were ready to disrespect my parents' views for the sake of our camping trip, not if you wanted to get married.'

'Look, I don't remember the exact words after all these years but I remember the effect it had on me, and I said *yes*. Don't you think it's getting late?' I said, turning off the bedside light and snuggling up next to Maggie who stayed sitting upright.

'But I would know what I was asking!' she said.

'Yes, of course,' I said tucking my nose into her hip, 'but you might not remember *now* what you meant *then*.'

I was getting sleepy warming up next to her. The moisturiser smelt nice.

There are two forms of probate that may be granted, the common form and what may be called the solemn form. It's only when there is a dispute as to the validity of the will that probate in solemn form is employed.

I listen to the news. Maggie's away. There's a flood river alert for rivers north of somewhere I don't think I've been. Bad news on the debt front is faced squarely by the Prime Minister. He says we can't keep living above our means. I guess that's true. He says the government will set an example in 'belt-tightening'. It's the harsh medicine we have to have to make up for the excesses of the last decade. I feel a bit sheepish.

The all-ordinaries are down. Griff's in bed. He's not feeling the best. He doesn't understand why Maggie's not here. There's something about the recent Uruguay round of GATT talks. Where are my golf clubs?

She said she just needs some space. That's all she really needs at the moment. I can run things alone for a while. We're out of that multi-purpose spray stuff. We use it on the kitchen table but it says it's appropriate for bathroom use as well. I might take my work into Sarah's room, just to keep an eye on Griff. There's nothing I can get for him. It's probably best that he keep dozing. The more he sleeps the better. I'll get him some lemons when I go out. I don't mind the supermarket. It's got everything you need. Poor thing!

I gather some pens and my papers and take them in to Griff. He's sleeping soundly. I've got the mail too. Never anything exciting. Nothing but envelopes with windows. There's one from work too, from the department. I'm on leave, what do they want? They never write to me.

When there is a dispute it's usually determined pursuant to Part IV of the *Administration of Probate Act*. The Act provides a lot of room for the exercise of judicial discretion, which is probably a good thing.

I should respond to the Gibsons' invitation. I wouldn't go on my own. I wouldn't like to. I'd have to hire a dinner suit and everything. I'll drop a present around sometime. It feels silly writing to them. What do you say? I don't write many letters. Never did. Perhaps I'll give them a call? Maybe Brian can get away for a game of golf. He works very long hours. They have to in that game. I don't like leaving Griff though. He doesn't look good. We're out of lemons. How can a family be out of lemons? I'll give Brian a call. *Our major trading partners!* He's so funny. Who are our major trading partners?

Hal Porter

FRANCIS SILVER
1962

One grows relievedly older and less an amateur: the high noon of middle age is free of the eccentricities of the innocent, one's senses are correctly disposed, one does not permit oneself the pleasure of discreditable actions; altogether, reality has no frayed ends. One can, at worst, fortify oneself with memories. Nevertheless, there is one disconcerting, even disenchanting, thing: what one oneself remembers is not what others remember. In this, women as annalists are terrifying. One expects them to get their recollections as exact as the amount of salt in Scotch broth. Beyond the practical area, of course, one has no illusions: if a woman talks about democracy or eternal peace or disarmament one sees instantly and with the most telling clarity that these things are pure nonsense. One does not, however, expect a handful of salt or no salt at all in either Scotch broth or memories, but what one expects, and what one gets – oh, dear. Take my mother for example.

As eldest son of a family of seven I got the best of her memories, partly because mothers of that period had time to make their special offerings to firstborn sons, partly because her enthusiasm and salesmanship were fresh. Among her recollections the most recurrent were of Francis Silver.

Right here, I must indicate that mother was multi-loquous, gay and romantic. Whatever else a large family tore from her, it was not her vivacity. She sang all the time, particularly, I think I remember, on ironing day. The pattern of this day was that of a holy day; there was an inevitability, a feeling of religious ritual. It was always Tuesday, always shepherd's pie day. To mother's heightened singing the kitchen-range was stoked with red-gum until a mirage almost formed above its black-leaded surface on which the flat-irons had been clashed down. The piled-up clothes-baskets and the kauri clothes-horse were brought into the kitchen; the beeswax in its piece of scorched cloth was placed ready. These preparations over, and while the irons were heating, a tranquil overture began. Mother and the washerwoman took each bed-sheet separately and, one gripping the bottom edge, one the top, retreated backwards, straining the sheet taut in a domestic tug-o'-war, inclining their heads to scan it for signs of wear then, this done, advancing towards each other with uplifted arms to begin the folding. These retreatings, advancings, inclinations and deft gestures, repeated sheet after sheet, had the air of an endless figure of a pavane in which, sometimes, I attempted to represent the absent washerwoman. It was while thus engaged, and later, while mother was ironing, and between her ironing-songs which were more poignantly yearning than, say, her friskier carpet-sweeping or cake-mixing-songs, that I recall hearing much about Francis Silver.

As a young woman mother lived in a middle-class seaside suburb of Melbourne. Plane-trees lined the three-chain-wide streets from which cast-iron railings and gates, and paths of encaustic tiles of Pompeian design, separated two-storeyed brick houses overtopped by Norfolk Island Pines exuding sap like candle-grease. These houses had such names as *Grevillea, Emmaville, Dagmar* and *Buckingham*. Stucco faces of gravely Grecian cast stared in the direction of the beach on to which oranges thrown from P&O liners rolled in with sea-lettuce, bladderwrack and mussel-shells. A bathing enclosure advertised HOT SEA-BATHS and TOWELS AND BATHING-DRESS FOR HIRE. Mother strolled the Esplanade, tamarisk by tamarisk, or sipped lemon squash spiders in the Jubilee Café with the apparently numerous young men who were courting her. Of these beaux, two young men, one from the country, one from another suburb, were favoured most. In marrying the country wooer, my father, and darning his socks and bearing his children and darning their socks, mother left the suburb for a country town set smack-flat on the wind-combed plains of Gippsland. She also left behind Francis Silver, whom she never saw again, at least not physically. He lived on, remarkably visible, in a special display-case of her memories.

Since the time of mother's young womanhood was pre–Great War there had been a conventional and profuse to-and-fro of postcards. She had garnered several bulging albums of them. The most elaborate cards, in an album of their own, were from Francis Silver. These had a sacred quality. In my eyes they belonged to Sunday. My parents were pagan enough to regard the church merely as a setting for wedding, baptism and funeral services, but, largely for us children, I suspect, though also because of what had been dyed into the texture of their late-Victorian childhoods, they were firm about the sanctity of Sunday. On this day mother played on the piano, or sang, hymns only. We were forbidden to whistle or go barefoot. Reading was restricted to *The Child's Bible*, *Sunday at Home* or *Christie's Old Organ*. Apart from meals of great size and gorgeousness the only permissible secular pleasures were to look through the stereoscope at Boer War photographs or at Francis Silver's postcards.

Hypocritically careful, we resisted licking our fingers to turn the interleaves of tissue-paper because mother hovered wrestling with herself. Invariably, at last, she could resist herself no longer. Perhaps a postcard of stiffened lace, *moiré* rosettes and spangles would set her off. Her eyes and her voice would detach themselves in focus and tone from the present.

'Yes,' she would say in this unique, entranced voice, 'Francis Silver sent me that after we'd had a tiny tiff near the Williamstown Time-ball Tower. We had gone for a stroll to St Kilda to listen to the German Band. When we got there the ferry-boat to Williamstown was at the pier – the dear old *Rosny*. It was such a perfect day we decided to go across to Williamstown. There was a little man on board playing a concertina. I had on – oh, I remember it so well – a white *broderie anglaise* dress and a hat with enormous peach-coloured silk roses on it. And a parasol of the same peach with a picot-edged triple flounce. I'd made Francis Silver a buttonhole of Cécile Brunner roses. And when we were on our way back, he threw it from the *Rosny* into Port Phillip Bay because I wouldn't talk to him. It was all because I refused to give him my lace handkerchief as a keepsake. How silly it all was! I'd have given him the hanky if he hadn't said he was going to sleep with it under his pillow. And the next day he sent me this card. But I was quite firm, and didn't send the hanky. It was mean of me, I suppose, but I was terribly well brought-up.'

All mother's memories of Francis Silver were of this vague, passionless kind. The time seemed eternally three o'clock in the afternoon of a deliciously sunny day, band-music drifted cloudily in the background, no-one hurried or raised voices, there were no inflamed rages or cutting malices. It was a delicate game of teasing played in Sunday clothes and while wearing mignonette. It had its fragile rules no-one would be untamed enough to break. As people walking on the fresh boards of a new floor soil it in gingerly and gentle fashion, so did mother and Francis Silver serenely walk the floor of their affection.

From accounts as lame as this, of incidents as small, flat and pointless as this, it amazes me, now, that so vivid and important an image of Francis Silver became mine.

As I saw it, Francis Silver was extraordinarily handsome in a certain way. He had a shortish, straight nose, a little black moustache with curled-up ends, lips clearly cut as a statue's, white teeth, small ears with lobes, definite but not untidy eyebrows, tightly packed black wavy hair, and an olive skin. His hands were hairless and supple; the half-moons showed even at the roots of his little fingernails. He had a light tenor voice he exhibited in such songs as *Only a Leaf, After the Ball, 'Neath the Shade of the Old Apple Tree*, and *She Lives in a Mansion of Aching Hearts* – songs laced with misunderstanding, regret and tears. He was a picture-framer go-ahead enough to have his own business. In the sense of handling Christmas supplement oleographs and 'art photographs' of Grecian-robed women holding waterlilies or bunches of grapes he was artistic and sensitive. He smoked Turkish cigarettes, did not drink, was popular with other sensitive young men, wore a gold ring with a ruby in it, was very proud of his small feet and loved the theatre.

Throughout the years, mother had provided these and many more details, partly by anecdote, partly by a system of odious comparisons ('Mr Willoughby's eyebrows are much untidier than Francis Silver's'), partly by setting a standard we fell far short of ('You must press back the quicks of your fingernails each time you dry your hands: the half-moons on Francis Silver's nails, even on the little fingers, showed clearly'). It was incredible what we children knew of him: he disliked mushrooms, tomatoes and ripe apricots, he had cut his hand at a Fern Tree Gully picnic, lost his father's gold watch in Flinders Lane, had four sisters, used Wright's Coal Tar Soap, and was double-jointed.

During all the years of talk not once did mother call him anything else but Francis Silver, never Mr Silver, and certainly never Francis, despite the fact that, seemingly to us, she had given him every consideration as a possible husband. This possibility was never directly expressed. We presumed from constant obliquities. At one stage of my early adolescence, when I was sullenly inclined to regard father as the malice-riddled offspring of parents like Simon Legree and the Witch of Endor, I yearned to be the son of a merrier, more handsome and talented father. I knew exactly whom, and spent much time practising in various ornate handwritings names I greatly preferred to my own . . . Hereward Silver, Montmorency Silver, Shem Silver, Fluellen Silver.

My placid actual father (it was his placidity I regarded as a sinister malice) was as aware as he was of anything of mother's indestructible interest in Francis Silver. It was a sort of joke with him which, as children, we loved: Francis Silver was so often a bore.

'Woman, dear,' father would, for example, say, seeing mother and some of us off at the railway station when we were going for a few days to Melbourne, 'if you are not back by Friday, I'll assume you've put the children in a comfortable orphanage, and have run off with Francis Silver. I shall, therefore, set up house with Mrs Tinsley.' This, to us, was hilariously funny: Mrs Tinsley was a gushing woman who irritated father so much that he went and talked to the pigs when she appeared. If mother displayed herself in a new hat or dress, badgering father for an opinion, he would say, 'Now, woman, dear, you know you look very nice. You must have a photograph taken for Francis Silver.'

'Jealous beast,' mother would say.

This light-hearted chyacking about Francis Silver made him appear forever twenty-four, forever dashing, forever harmless. He was the legendary Gentleman first to his feet when Ladies entered; he daily cleaned his shoes, and the *backs* of his shoes.

Once only did this image of him take on sootier colours, and throw a disturbing shadow. This happened the one time I ever heard my parents really quarrel. What the quarrel was about I shall never know. To my alarm I was trapped in its orbit without the nous to consider flight let alone perform the act of flight. There mother and father were, upbraiding each other ferociously, in the glare of kitchen day-light, she songless and shrill and stripped of her vivacity, he loud-mouthed and stripped of his dry-tongued placidity. At the height of heat mother dashed a colander of French beans to the linoleum and, crying out, 'I wish I'd married Francis Silver!' rushed from the kitchen, slamming its door, then the vestibule door, next her bedroom door. Horrified as I was at the quarrel itself which seemed the disreputable sort of thing poor people, common people or drunk people did, I was more horrified at this vision of Francis Silver as a mother-stealer. I had the impression father was startled; the framework of his being somehow showed; he seemed much less a father, nuder of face, younger, like nothing so much as a bewildered man. I began to pick up the beans so as not to look at him directly, but I absorbed him foxily. He was, as it were, reassembling himself and dressing his face again, when the kitchen door opened quietly. The slam of the bedroom door had scarcely died but mother had done something neatening to her hair.

'I have,' she said, 'just caught a glimpse of myself in the glass.' It was a girl's voice. She tried a smile. It was too weighed out of balance with uncertainty and rising tears to succeed. 'I was quite hideous with temper. I'm sorry, Henry. Of course I didn't mean . . . honestly . . .'

'Woman, dear,' said father, 'Francis Silver would have been a lucky man if you had married him. Out to play, boy, out to play,' he said, crossing to mother who began to cry. I knew he was going to sit her on his knee. That night we had festive jelly with bananas and a dash of port wine in for pudding: a sure indication that, although he wasn't mentioned, Francis Silver was still in the house. Nevertheless, it was several months before I forgot him as a peril and could see him again as the eternal charmer.

When mother died at the age of forty-one I was eighteen.

Several hours before she died, her singing foregone forever, her gaiety tampered with by the demands of dying, I was alone with her for a while. After saying what, I suppose, all dying mothers say to eldest sons, most of it trite, she asked me to take Francis Silver the album of postcards he'd sent her twenty-odd years ago.

'I know what the girls are like,' she said of my sisters. 'They'll marry and have children, and let the children tear them up. I'm sure he'd like to have them. He's still alive, and still in the same place, I think. I've looked in the obituary notices every day for years.'

I began to cry.

'Stop that,' she said, as though I were breaking some deathbed rule, 'and listen. There's something else. In my little handkerchief-drawer there's a pink envelope with his name on it. It's got a lock of my hair in it. Before I married your father I was going to give it to Francis Silver. But I decided against it. Burn it, throw it away, anything. Don't tell your father. About the album doesn't matter. Not about the envelope. Be a good boy, and promise.'

In agony I promised.

It was not until several months after the funeral that I told father of mother's wish about the postcards.

'Yes,' he said, 'your mother told me she'd spoken to you. Women,' he said, giving me that two-coloured look which at one and the same time questioned my knowledge and informed my ignorance, 'are strange, strange mortals, and this is a strange gesture. He was very devoted to your mother, and may like to have them as a memento.'

'Would *you* like to take them? It might be better if you took them – more – more suitable.' I was trying a man-to-man briskness.

Father looked me over, and came to his decision about what I was up to.

'Why?' he said. 'Why on earth would it be more suitable? I've never met Francis Silver in my life. Anyway, you promised your mother, didn't you? Which issue are you trying to avoid?'

That my father did not know Francis Silver astonished me. Reading between the lines of mother's tales I had pictured Francis Silver and father, stiff-collared, in pointed button boots, carrying heart-shaped boxes of chocolates in their hands, and arriving (often) at the same moment on the basalt doorstep of mother's front door.

'I'm not avoiding anything,' I lied. 'Are you sure . . . are you absolutely sure you've never met him?'

'I am absolutely sure.' He looked me over again. 'I'll be looking forward to hearing about him. And, although I've never met him, I think, in the circumstances, it could not be considered too much if you conveyed my kind regards.'

Despite my deathbed promise, I had had hopes of finding father willing to return the postcards to Francis Silver. I'd justified these hopes by telling myself that Francis Silver would be more touched by receiving the album from his widower rival than from the son of the woman he had hoped to marry, from the son he might have had himself. My father's defection meant I should have to keep my promise. About this I was not really happy. At eighteen I conceived myself cynical; disillusionment was daily bread.

The next time I travelled to Melbourne the album went with me. As well, I took the pink envelope which I had not destroyed – there had been no moral pause, no sense of treachery in the betrayal. On her death-bed, I told myself, mother had tangled her values, her judgment had been marred. I ... I ... considered that the anguished man I would be meeting would be doubly consoled by this more personal memento.

I had no sooner arrived at the Coffee Palace in which I was staying in the city than it became imperative to set about handing over the album and the envelope: mother had been dead for four months; the cards with their velveteen forget-me-nots, their sequins, and intricately folded and embossed layers, the envelope scented from its long secret life in the handkerchief-drawer, were too precious and unfitting to lie about for even an hour on the public furniture of a room that had been occupied by unknown, impermanent, maybe sinful people. As though preparing to meet God or have an accident, I had a shower, and cleaned my teeth, for the second time that day, put on all my best clothes, my new shoes and tie, and took much trouble with my hair. With the envelope in a pocket, and carrying the album as though it were frangible time, and dreams of finest glass, I set out for Francis Silver's.

Since all this happened before World War II and postwar vandalism, the picture-framing shop had not been contemporised: it was still turn-of-the-century elegant in a slightly abraded way. Three etchings with the enormously wide creamy mounts and narrow black frames fashionable at the period were disposed behind the plate-glass on which, in Gothic gold-leaf, was the name I had heard all my life, the name in my mother's handwriting on the pink envelope containing the piece of her hair she'd called a lock. I went into the shop. There was no-one behind the counter. The sound of elfin-cobbler hammering came from behind plush curtains, black, on which were *appliquéd* pale gold lyres, and which obviously concealed a workroom. When I rang the small brass bell attached to the counter by a chain the tiny tap-tapping continued for a few moments, and then ceased. I heard no footsteps, but the curtains were parted. A short, fat man stood behind the counter.

'And what,' he said in a light and somehow wheedling voice, 'can I do for *you?*' His small eyes (Beady, I said to myself) stitched over me in an assessing way. He was the most strikingly clean-looking man I had ever seen, composed of the blackest black (his suit and tie and eyes and semicircular eyebrows) and the whitest white (his shirt, the handkerchief protruding from one sleeve, the white slices of hair curving back from his temples).

'I should like to speak to Fr . . . to Mr Francis Silver, please.'

He lowered his lids while pretending to pick something languidly from his sleeve, and to flick delicately with fingertips at the spot nothing had been picked from.

'You are,' he said, interested in the fact, 'thpeaking to that very perthon.'

I was not prepared for this, a disillusion not cut to my template. My face must have run empty.

'I athure you,' he said, 'I am Franthith Thilver. Have I been recommended? You *mutht* tell me by whom. You want thomething framed?'

'My . . . my mother . . .' I said, and placed the album on the counter. 'My mother sent this. Postcards.'

'To be framed?'

He opened the album.

He turned over several pages. 'My dear,' he said. 'My dear, how thcrumptiouth!'

I saw on his hand the ring with the ruby mother had told us about. I saw the fingernails with each half-moon even on the little fingers, unmistakably revealed.

'Jutht look! I've theen nothing like thethe for . . .' He pushed out his lips in a deprecating smile, '. . . for more yearth than I care to thtate publicly. I uthed to have a pothitive mania for them.'

'They are yours,' I said. 'They *were* yours. You sent them to my mother. Years ago,' I finished uncertainly.

'I did? Gay, reckleth boy I wath! May one have little lookieth?' He took one of the cards and examined its back. 'Tho I did! My handwriting hathn't changed a bit. How ekthtrordinary, how very ekthtrordinary! And now they are to be framed?'

'No,' I said. 'No, not framed. Mother thought you'd like to have them back.'

I knew I was expressing mother's wish very badly, but could do nothing else: the situation had become bewildering not only to me but also to Francis Silver who said, 'Oh!' There was, moreover, something beyond the bewilderment of a clumsy social situation; there was something wrong. Francis Silver had not asked me who had sent the postcards. Some film clogging natural curiosity, even polite inquiry, some flaw in his humanity, made him seem careless and carelessly cruel.

I did not want to say it but I said it: I told him my mother's maiden name.

He became fretful: the past was not for him. Nevertheless he acted good manners of a sort. 'Now, let me thee,' he said, and he put the tip of his forefinger on his forehead in an absurd thinking posture. He pouted.

'My dear,' he presently said, 'the mind ith blank. Abtholutely! Nothing thtirth in my little addled brain. I'm very, very naughty. But you muthtn't tell your mother. I thhould be *tho* humiliated. You mutht tell her I loved *theeing* them but I couldn't *deprive* her of them. It'th a wonderful collection and in *faultleth* condition. Oh, if only my friend Rekth were here ... he *adorth* pothcardiana, if I may coin a phrathe, abtholutely adorth.'

Scraps of the past were blowing about my brain like the litter at the end of a perfect picnic.

'And you don't remember my mother?'

He could have smacked me.

He tossed his eyes heavenwards but not too high.

'Be reathonable, *pleathe*! More than twenty yearth! One would adore to remember, of courthe. But too much water under the bridge. There've been too many people, too many, many people. I *thaid* I wath terribly humiliated. I couldn't akthept them now, could I? You take them back. And thank your mother very, very much.' He smiled a conspirator's smile, grasped my wrist and squeezed it boldly yet furtively. 'I know you'll keep my ghathtly thecret, just *know*. You've got a nithe kind fathe, haven't you? But there've really been too many people. I'm thure your mother ith ath charming ath you. But I don't remember her at all.'

I detached myself. Without a word I left the shop.

The album of cards remained with whom I'd promised to give it.

By the time I had returned to the Coffee Palace through the sort of exquisite day I used to imagine a pretty mother and a jaunty Francis Silver flirting through along the seafront, I had made up an outline of lies to satisfy and comfort my father for whom I felt the truth, as I saw it, to be of the wrong shape. By the time, days later, I was home with him, I hoped to have filled in that outline with unassailable detail: I dared not shock him. As my first adult chore, my initiation task, I would make a fitting Francis Silver for him, one that matched the Francis Silver of mother's recollections.

In the room at the Coffee Palace I looked at the pink envelope older than I. For one weak moment I felt like making a film-actor's gesture and kissing it. I remembered in time it was not mine to kiss. It was no-one's. In that room with its Gideon Bible on the glass-topped bedside cabinet, its ecru net curtains, its oatmeal wallpaper and petty frieze of autumn virginia creeper, I burned the envelope. In its first resistance to flame it gave up its ingrained scent. It twisted, fighting the flame and itself. It emitted a stench of burning hair. It writhed and writhed in an agony I could not bear to watch.

Katharine Susannah Prichard

THE GREY HORSE
1928

He was young, a draught stallion, grey, and Old Gourlay worked him on the roads.

Old Gourlay kept the road in order on the back of Black Swan and lived with his housekeeper in a bare-faced, wooden box of a house beside the road, where it loped over the mountain to Perth, by way of the river and half a dozen townships scattered across the plains. Gourlay was a dry stick of a man, and deaf; but Grey Ganger – the beauty of him took the breath like a blast of cold wind. There was nothing more beautiful in the ranges, not the wildflowers, yellow and blue, on the ledges of the road, nor the tall white gums gleaming through the dark of the bush from among thronging rough-barked red-gums and jarrah.

A superb creature, broad and short of back, deep-barrelled, with mighty quarters, the grey stallion carried Old Gourlay, on the floor of the tip-dray, uphill in the morning, curveting with kittenish grace, as though the tip-dray were a chariot; prancing and tossing his head so that silver threads glinted in the spume of his mane. He brought loads of gravel downhill, gaily, prancing still, with an air of curbing his pace to humour the queer, fussy insect of an old man who clung to the rope reins stretched out beside and behind him.

Wood-carters who worked on the Black Swan road envied the old man his horse. They wanted to buy him; but Gourlay would not sell the Ganger. Their great, rough-haired horses laboured along the bush tracks and came slowly down the steep winding road, sitting back in the breeching, the roughly split jarrah for firewood stacked on the carts jabbing their haunches.

O'Reilly had offered good money, cash down, for Grey Ganger; he had told Gourlay to name his own figure. But Old Gourlay shook his head. Nothing but cussedness, it was, O'Reilly declared. Gourlay had not enough work for the Ganger: a less powerful horse would suit him better, cost less, and be easier to manage. O'Reilly would have liked to mate the Ganger with his Lizzie when he found he could not buy the horse. Lizzie was a staunch enough working mare, shaggy and evil-smelling, with a roach back, and splay feet, but she had been 'a good 'un in her day', he said.

Gourlay would have none of that either.

'Aw – aw,' he stuttered; 'she's rough stuff. He's only a baby. There'd be no holding him if –'

Old Gourlay had pride in his horse, enjoyed crying his measurements, the size of his collar. The Ganger was always in good condition, close-knit and hard, his hide smooth and sheeny as the silk of a woman's dress. Not that Gourlay seemed to have any affection for him: rather was there hostility, a vague resentment in his bearing. He nagged at Grey Ganger as though he feared and had some secret grudge against him.

But no-one envied Old Gourlay his horse more than Bill Moriarty, who, against the advice of every fruit-grower in the district, had taken up the block of land adjoining Gourlay's, and had planted vines and fruit-trees to make an orchard there, a few years before Gourlay, Mrs Drouett and the grey stallion had come to live on the Black Swan road. As he cleared and grubbed, burnt off, and cultivated his land, Young Moriarty had watched Gourlay and Grey Ganger.

On the wildest, wettest nights he had seen the flickering, loose golden star of Gourlay's lantern as he went to feed the Ganger and shut him into his stable for the night. He had been up when the old man pulled the board from across the stable door in the morning, and the Ganger, released, dashed round the small, muddy square of the yard, flinging up his heels, snorting and gambolling joyously, with such a clumsy, kittenish grace that Moriarty himself would laugh, and sing out to old Gourlay: 'He's in great heart, this morning, all right.'

Gourlay would mutter resentfully, and swear at the Ganger, clacking the gate of the stable-yard to, as he went up to breakfast. Nothing annoyed him more than to see Grey Ganger disporting himself.

When first he and his housekeeper had come to live at Black Swan, Old Gourlay had made those trips to feed and shut the Ganger in his stable for the night with zest, swinging his lantern religiously and whistling. And he had gone afterwards into the shed beside the stable, where a bed was made up, put the light out there and slammed the door. But Young Moriarty had seen him stumble uphill in the starlight, or when he thought all Black Swan was sleeping, open the back door quietly, and go into his house.

Black Swan people did not appear to mind where Old Gourlay slept, really. They were too busy in their orchards or clearing and cultivating land for vines to bother much about what their neighbours were doing. Besides, Gourlay's and Mrs Drouett's story had gone before them. Nobody expected Old Gourlay to sleep in the shed beside the stable. Even the children going along the road to school, as they passed Gourlay's, said mysteriously to each other: 'He's got one mother up-country . . . and living here with another.'

The neighbours were kind and friendly enough when they met either Gourlay or Mrs Drouett. Their story had created a slightly romantic sympathy. It was said Old Gourlay had been a well-to-do farmer with a wife and family when Laura Drouett had come his way. He sold his farm and left his family to go away with her. They had wandered about for years and grown old together.

Mrs Drouett had been a comely woman and still kept her figure tight at the waist. Her hips were thrust out from it, plump and heavy; she had a bosom and a fringe of brown curly hair, which she wore above the withered apple of her face when she was dressed for the afternoon, or going driving with Mr Gourlay. She was older than he, perhaps, but better preserved; deaf also, and nervy, under the strain of living with Mr Gourlay, 'seeing how I am placed', as she explained to Young Moriarty when he hopped over the fence to talk to her, and cheer her up, sometimes.

Old Gourlay did not like Bill Moriarty hopping over the fence to talk to Mrs Drouett.

'He's as mad as a wet hen if he finds me having a yarn with the old girl,' Bill explained to O'Reilly. 'She's a decent sort . . . a bit lonely . . . and I've been trying to get round her to make the old man lend me his horse, now and then.'

O'Reilly laughed. He thought he guessed what was at the back of Old Gourlay's mind. Bill was a good-looker, thickset and swarthy, with crisp dark hair and blue eyes set in whites as hard as china, and so short-lashed that they stared at you unshaded from the bronze of his face. Though he was still more or less coltish, Young Moriarty, O'Reilly knew, was working too hard, and too much in love with a girl who lived down on the flats, to be bold with any woman or give Tom Gourlay cause for doubting the fidelity of his Laura. But O'Reilly could not resist rubbing it in when, a few days later, the old man stopped him on the road, not far from where Bill was pruning his vines.

'Good cut of a fellow, that,' he shouted, waving an arm towards Moriarty. 'Isn't a better made man in the ranges. Ever seen him stripped? By God, he's got good limbs on him.'

In the evening, mean-spirited and vindictive, Gourlay gave Mrs Drouett the benefit of that praise of Bill and the gall he had stewed in all day. The old woman cried; but she was coy and self-conscious with Young Moriarty next time she saw him. She put on her brown hair in the morning and pulled the strings of her corsets tighter. Old Gourlay guessed what he had done, and was madder than a wet hen, though Bill, for all Laura's youthful figure and hair, saw only her poor grandmother's face. He was soaked with the sight and shape of Rose Sharwood, her warm bloom; thirsty with desire for the sound and the smell of her. He was all a madness for Rose. So when he could not get a horse to do his spring ploughing, he went again to Old Gourlay. He had asked before for the loan of his horse, and the old man had refused him, churlishly enough, but with excuses. And Bill had not pressed him. But this was different. It meant a great deal to him, getting that ploughing done.

Black cockatoos had whirled about the clearing, shedding their wild cries high in the air that morning. A long spell of dry weather was breaking and Bill Moriarty needed a horse to cultivate between his vines after the rain.

'How's it for a loan of the Ganger to plough my orchard?' he asked Old Gourlay, leaning over the weatherworn saplings of the stallion's yard.

'Nothing doing,' Old Gourlay growled.

Moriarty explained the difficulty he was in. He was hard up. He could not buy a horse: he could pay for the hire of one by the day. But every man in the district with working horses was waiting for the rain and required his horses to plough, and make the most of the ground while it was soft. Young Moriarty could not get the promise of a horse from anyone. And it meant everything to him, to have the earth turned and sweetened about his vines, this year; all the difference between a good, or a poor, yield of grapes. Bill let Old Gourlay know, with all the sentiment he could muster, that he was praying for a good harvest because he wanted to get married. He soft-pedalled about Rose, and the skinflint of an aunt who threatened to take her away to the Eastern States at the end of the autumn if Bill had not built a house and married the girl before then.

Old Gourlay pretended not to hear half of what he was saying.

'T-too busy to do any ploughing,' he said. 'Rain'll w-wash away half the road up by The Beak . . . Couldn' spare the Ganger . . . plenty of work for him to do on the road . . . Too much for one man and one horse.'

He stuttered away from the subject, irritably. Moriarty let him go, watching the stallion as he frisked and plunged about the yard where the grey sapling posts and rails, silvered by the early light, shook as he bumped against them.

'Ever mate him, Mr Gourlay?' Young Moriarty yelled.

'No!' The old man's eyes leapt, sharp and startled in the weathered fallow of his face. 'There'd be no holding him if ever I did.'

So that was it, Bill thought. He and the Ganger were in the same boat. Old Gourlay would thwart them both if he could; defeat their instincts. Vaguely Bill understood that what Gourlay resented in the Ganger, and in himself, was their youth and virility, when the sap had dried in his old man's bones.

It was beginning to rain as Bill went back to his work.

'Mean old blighter,' he muttered. 'Had two women himself, and won't give a handsome animal like that his dues. Him breaking his neck . . . and me too.'

Young Moriarty went out to the road to meet O'Reilly as the wood-carts came downhill that evening, looking top-heavy, the wood piled high on them red and umber with rain, the shaggy, brown-furred horses stepping warily for fear they might come down on the slippery road beside which the feather-white torrents of rain-wash were flying.

Moriarty asked the wood-carter for the loan of his mare, Lizzie, some Sunday soon, when he was not using her. He told O'Reilly how Old Gourlay had refused to let him have the Ganger although the stallion spent most of his time on Sundays galloping up and down and cavorting about his yard beside the stable; and how he had explained to Gourlay what it meant to him to get his ploughing and harrowing done just then.

O'Reilly knew about Rose Sharwood and that Bill wanted to marry her.

The rain beat around them as they talked, Bill hatless, hugging himself in the coat of his working clothes buttoned up to the throat; O'Reilly, his tarred overalls shining, his ruddy, unshaven face with dropped lip and lit eyes laughing from under his sodden hat. The raindrops quivering on its brim ran and fell as he laughed, getting the gist of Young Moriarty's grievance, and the way he proposed to pay for the hire of old Lizzie.

Squalls swept up over the purple and green of the plains all the week, flung themselves against the ranges, scattering hailstones, and passed on inland. A film of fine, chill rain veiled the timbered hills about Black Swan for days. Then the sunshine of late spring leapt, shimmering on the water lying down on the flats, and drying the land in the hills quickly.

O'Reilly did not appear with Lizzie that Sunday. Moriarty was desperate. Rains had lashed the blossom from the almond-trees along the boundary of his fences. The tooth of green was everywhere; the flame of young leaves. Down near Grey Ganger's stable and yard, where Moriarty had put a row of nectarines below the vines, pink flowers were spraying widespread, varnished branches. It would soon be too late to conserve moisture for the vines. And the thought that Rose would go away with her aunt if he did not do well out of his grapes that year, overhung Young Moriarty like a doom.

But the next Sunday morning, while the Ganger was galloping about his yard, just from his stable, as fresh and beside himself as Bill had ever seen him, O'Reilly brought old Lizzie to cultivate the orchard.

O'Reilly and Bill stood watching the Ganger's gambollings for a moment, laughing and exclaiming their admiration. Then they got to work. O'Reilly drove the mare as they ploughed, across the crest of the hillside, while Bill, stooping along before Lizzie, cleared stones and pruned branches out of the way. O'Reilly ploughed well down the slope before he swung Lizzie from an upper to a lower furrow, uphill and along, downhill and along.

The Ganger came to the end of his yard as he sighted them. He watched Lizzie curiously, snorted as she passed, and galloped up and down, throwing himself about to attract her attention. When they had finished ploughing that side of the hill, Moriarty and O'Reilly spelled

Lizzie while they went up to the lean-to Bill lived in, for a meal.

They left her down near the fence where the young nectarines were in blossom. The grey stallion was trembling against his yard as they did so; taut, the breath blowing in gusty blasts from his nostrils. Lizzie swung her bland, white-splashed face towards him and blinked at him from behind her wide black winkers. Her tail moved gently. A hot, herby aroma reached the men. Young Moriarty went to lead her away, as if to avoid trouble and propitiate Old Gourlay. But it was too late. Grey Ganger rushed and broke his fences. He whirled round Lizzie, charging Moriarty. Bill got away from his plunging fury and flung heels. He picked up the dead branch of a fruit-tree as though to defend himself, or beat off the Ganger. O'Reilly ran away over the broken earth of the hillside.

The noise of the breaking fence and the stallion's whinnied blast brought Old Gourlay running from the house. Mrs Drouett jiggled marionette-wise on the back veranda for a moment; then when she saw what was happening at the bottom of the paddock, near Young Moriarty's flowering fruit-trees, she put her hands over her face and scuttered into the house again.

Old Gourlay writhed beside the fence, brandishing his whip and shrieking in a frenzy of rage. Moriarty tried to explain, but Gourlay would have no explanations. He was deaf to what Moriarty was saying, though he heard O'Reilly laughing up under the almond-trees. He knew well enough there was only one explanation, Old Gourlay, and Moriarty was not likely to give that.

'It's a put-up job,' he spluttered; 'a buddy put-up job. I'll have the law of ye for it. Taking the bread out of a man's mouth. There'll be no holding him now.'

And there was not. Gourlay was right about that. At the sidings there was no keeping the Ganger from passing mares; and he was as flighty as a brumby, on the roads. He dragged Gourlay, powerless at the end of his reins, behind the tip-dray as they came downhill, the old man looking more than ever like some dry, twiggy insect as he jogged there, shrilling fiercely. He was at his wits' end, and went in danger of his life, trying to manage the stallion. He could talk of nothing but the life the horse was leading him; and worry about each new incident in his career, as if an only son had kicked over the traces and was disgracing him in the district.

Mrs Drouett got nerves with it all. She went about with her head in a shawl and said she was ill. She and Old Gourlay quarrelled incessantly. Their voices could be heard cracking and rattling at each other in the evening. Nothing seemed left of their old passion except its animosities. But when Mrs Drouett took to her bed, Old Gourlay became alarmed. He thought she might die, and he threw up his contract for mending the road to stay at home and nurse her.

Without telling anyone in Black Swan what he was going to do, or where the horse was going, he sold Grey Ganger then. O'Reilly called him by every name he could think of. But Gourlay would not have forgone his vengeance for a fiver. As it was, he had taken less for the horse than O'Reilly, and many another man round Black Swan, would have given. He sold his house and land too; and he and Mrs Drouett went to live nearer town, where, if people were not as kind and friendly, at least they were less free with their neighbours' property.

Moriarty married Rose Sharwood soon after old Lizzie had foaled in O'Reilly's paddock beyond The Beak. At the end of the winter it was. His vines did well in that fifth year: he had expected so much from them. He dried currants, raisins, sultanas, and sold them at top prices on the London market. Even Rose's aunt was satisfied with the cheque he showed her from his agents.

It was not until the following season that 'the bottom fell out of the market for dried fruit', as fruit-growers about Black Swan said. And about the same time Rose gave birth to a son.

Bill was not sorry when the baby died, a few months afterwards during the summer. He believed it was better for a weakly child, as for a sick chicken or calf, to die. But the birth, brief screaming existence and death of the small puckered red creature were a shock to him. He had not reckoned on a child from him being a weakling; and Death, like a hand out of the dark, had gripped, shaken, and squeezed life out of the youngster. There was something brutal and unfair about the whole business. If the thing was to die, why had it ever been born? Young Moriarty was dazed, numb and angry under the shock.

As he worked out of doors, milked the cows he had bought to make up for the falling price of dried fruit, fed pigs and fowls, ploughed and harrowed the orchard, or cleared land for fodder crops, he still glanced often down to the Ganger's yard. Through his numbness and anger about the child, the cleaning of sties and cowyards, breaking of earth, slopping of milk into pig-troughs, thoughts of the stallion were fugitive.

Life with Rose was not what he imagined it would be. It was mostly a fitting-in of domestic jobs, talking about the cost of things, eating frugally, and sleeping without touching her. He had taken her as he wished, sometimes; and now she pushed him away, saying he was 'low . . . a lustful brute'.

Moriarty was depressed about it. He had not expected Rose to be like that; his joy in her to fade so soon. As he toiled, ploughing, harrowing and pruning, he was conscious of belonging to the fecund earth and life, and yet of being apart from them.

Rose did not want any more children; she dreaded having another baby. It seemed simple and natural enough for a man and woman to have children. But not for Rose, or for him . . . He snipped the shoots from a budding fruit-tree . . . Perhaps they were burnt cats who feared the fire, he and Rose.

He noticed that grass had grown in the Ganger's yard and under his stable door.

Rose herself had no strong feelings, he was sure, except for the things that did not matter: dust in out-of-the-way corners, pennies spent unnecessarily. But she was keen on the scent of any hankering Bill might have for another woman, and so shrewish about it that for the sake of peace, at least, he had come to heel. He no longer sought other women.

But Lord, what was there to live for? His days tasted all the same to him, from dawn till dark, flat and dull. He worked hard but without the old zest. Couch had made its appearance in his orchard, his tilth was not what it had been. He invariably struck a bad day if he had cows to sell; and he missed the best price for eggs.

He was a fool, Moriarty told himself, as Rose had often said. He had been wrong about Rose; he had made a mistake about the orchard. There was no money in fruit, fresh or dried. He worked as hard as any of O'Reilly's draught horses for food and a roof over his head: and that was all there was to it. He was sick to death of pottering about pigsties, cowyards, fowlhouses, fruit-trees; and he supposed he would go on pottering among them, and being sick to death of them. It was the rut of life he had made and must stay in.

As he sprawled before the fire that evening, morose and weary, this was swarming over him, the thoughts crawling in and out of his brain and breeding, as did fruit-fly on rotting nectarines in his orchard.

O'Reilly swung into the kitchen.

'That draught stallion of Old Gourlay's,' he said, 'he's been bought by Purdies. Standing the season at The Beak farm and will travel the district. Be up at my place this day next week . . . Thought you'd like to know.'

Moriarty went to see the horse when he was at O'Reilly's stables. As the groom led him out, the stallion came, arching his neck and tossing his head.

Grey Ganger was more beautiful than he had ever been; no longer skittish, but imperious, his quarters moulded to perfection, the grey satin of his skin sheening under its dapples as he moved. Bill walked across and stood beside him, rubbing a hand over his shoulders, the anguish of his dissatisfaction with life breaking.

'I wish it was me, old man,' he groaned. 'I wish it was me. It's all I'm fit for really.'

Tim   Richards

OUR SWIMMER

1992

Seeing films has corrupted the way that we remember things. Our minds will now perform sophisticated technical operations. We can isolate the subject in the frame, we can enhance or colourise, we can edit our memories into dazzling montage sequences. Now I find that when I remember Marianne Topp, I see her moving in a stylised, filmic way, as if some mental process has extracted every second frame of memory to create a more artistic, expressionistic version of my emotional attachment to her.

Marianne was an extraordinary-looking girl, her dark hair so often pulled up in a bun that emphasised the curve of her neck, her cheeks, and her red-charged lips. Yet the essence of my attraction to her wasn't the way that she looked or moved. It was Marianne's voice that stole my heart – a low carnal mutter, not so studied as the Mae West mutter, but with the same coarse-textured depth. Her voice had a natural insinuation that sent blood racing to vital outposts. And she fully understood the power of this weapon. Her speech was always so measured and deliberate. Everything about Marianne was perfectly composed.

I was browsing in Chapters Bookshop, scanning the blurb of a paperback. The book must have been *Oranges are Not the Only Fruit*, and she must have been looking over my shoulder.

If you like Jeanette Winterson, you should read *The Passion*.

I turned to face the voice, to tell the woman with the pulverising voice that I'd read *The Passion* and adored it. Then I saw that the speaker was Marianne Topp, whom I'd only ever worshipped from a distance, and her mouth had broken into a soft, slightly embarrassed smile, and I was in love then, instantly. I was seventeen, and, like just about everyone else, I was in love with Marianne Topp.

Marianne Topp kept so much to herself that people seldom associated her with her mother Beatrice, the most forceful presence in Hampton. When Mrs Topp's newspaper was left to soak in the rain, she made sure that the paperboy responsible was punished. Wayne Burgess was locked up in stocks for two days. This punishment would have gone on for a week, but the matriarch relented when the boy's doctor testified to his epilepsy.

I was playing cricket with Sam Morrissey the day that Sam was found out. Beatrice Topp discovered that Sam was the author of obscene letters sent to her daughter at the Topps' Favril Street home. Two senior teachers ripped Sam off the field and took him to be interrogated by Mrs Topp. You didn't need to be Einstein to predict the outcome. My mother went to console Sam's mum, who was a friend she knew from tuckshop duty.

Having confessed to the crime, Sam was condemned to death. On the day of the execution, the Principal pulled six boys out of the matriculation geography class. He took them to the school oval, where they were told to construct a pyre out of old desks and broken chairs. Mrs Topp decreed that Sam should be taken up in a cherry-picker, from which he would be lowered by rope onto the flaming pyre below.

All of Hampton gathered for the execution, which had been scheduled for just after sunset on March twenty-ninth. Mr Paterson, the sportsmaster, was assigned the task of restraining Sam in the basket of the cherry-picker. He was an unpleasant man well suited to the unpleasant task. Sam's bellows were so loud that Mr Paterson was forced to gag him while Mrs Topp read a list of his offences to the crowd. She was wearing her favourite purple jumpsuit.

Mrs Topp said that Sam had written anonymous letters in which her daughter – she didn't name which daughter, but everyone knew she meant the eldest, Marianne – was described as a cheap slag who'd jazzed so many old men that her mother had been forced to install a condom machine at the foot of her bed. Few of us had ever heard such a vile attack against an innocent girl. When Beatrice Topp called for a volunteer to light the pyre, dozens of outraged Hamptonians rushed forward.

Flames speared out into the night sky. Sparks and embers wafted off above the orange-faced gathering. Dramatic relief gave the yellow cherry-picker the appearance of a sad mechanical giraffe. When Mrs

Topp nodded, Mr Paterson eased Sam out the side of the bucket. For a few seconds, it seemed as though Sam was trying to swim across the sky. He flailed and shrieked as he dangled on the rope being lowered toward the rising flames.

Finally, Mrs Topp raised an arm to halt the execution. Sam was reprieved. His death sentence was commuted to permanent banishment from Hampton, and after that evening he was never seen in the suburb again. Not so long ago, someone told me that he's gone on to do valuable research work in immunology. But we'd all got the message.

If you took Beatrice Topp lightly, you'd live to regret it. It might be pointless for me to tell you all of this. You really can't conceive of such power unless you've experienced it first-hand.

Ruthless as she was, Mrs Topp was not a political leader. No-one elected her, and official authority resided with the mayor. But Mrs Topp held sway in Hampton. She represented our suburb at the summits that detailed the latest advances.

I remember how impatient we were for her return from the International Geometrical Forum in New York. We expected that Mrs Topp would come back with the New Knowledge. Everything we thought certain could be stood on its head by some astonishing development; the square triangle, or the refutation of Pythagoras.

That was the winter of unprecedented snows. The winds blasted up from the Antarctic and snap-froze birds in flight. Port Phillip Bay iced over for the first time in memory. Children skated across the rough surface, and fishermen dropped lines through holes in the thick ice. You'd see vandals strip palings off fences to fuel the bonfires they lit on the beach. Smelly Old Ryan, who lived in the telephone box outside the post office, was taken in by church people who feared that he would freeze to death, but they were so chilled by his incessant prophesying that they passed him on to the community welfare officer.

Old Ryan bellowed that we were going to be buried alive, that God was revisiting us with the fruits of our mediocrity. He didn't actually use the word Repent!, but you knew what he was getting at. Not that we would have repented. We were too curious, too used to these astonishments to be fazed by them. So we waited for Beatrice Topp and did what we could to keep warm.

I often played squash with my friend Yuri at the fitness centre by

Hampton railway station. After a match, we swam a few lengths, or sat by the pool and watched Marianne Topp cruise through her 10 000-metre training regime. We were entranced by the rhythmic thrust of her muscular arms breaking the surface. We fixed our gaze on the dark tufts of hair under her arms, and the glorious dark locks she dragged through the blue water, and the sheer magnificence of the so-womanly body packed into Marianne's black one-piece swimsuit.

Like most of the students and staff at Hampton High, I worshipped the enigmatic Marianne Topp. What's more, we were expected to worship her.

At school assembly, the Principal would detail Marianne's latest achievements in the pool. He told us that Marianne had swum nine seconds inside Janet Evans's official world record for 800 metres freestyle. Even her 400 metres was two seconds faster than Janet Evans's record for that distance.

Marianne Topp, the Principal told us, is a uniquely talented young woman who upholds the finest traditions of the school. If you look closely at her performances, you will see that Marianne is a negative-splitter. She's even stronger at the end of a race than she is at the beginning. In that, he emphasised, there is a lesson for us all.

After a spirited round of cheering, I heard a boy behind me say that he'd give anything to be Marianne Topp's bicycle seat, and when I turned around to see who it was, I saw that Mr Simonescu, the woodwork teacher, had heard the remark, and was smiling lasciviously.

All the teachers were hot for Marianne, the women as much as the men, but Marianne made a point of ignoring their attentions. She did them a favour. Being a teacher wouldn't have saved them from the cherry-picker.

We all knew that Marianne Topp would have been an Olympic gold medallist if her mother had allowed her to represent Australia, but Mrs Topp was a fierce anti-nationalist. She would have had Hampton secede from the Australian Commonwealth if it was possible for a suburb to secede.

Australia is lazy and complacent, Mrs Topp would say, too satisfied with living vicariously through its sporting heroes. Hampton has to make itself a model for what's possible.

For Marianne to have represented Australia would have been an unthinkable treachery.

Nevertheless, the school celebrated its negative-splitter in a very Australian fashion. The administration building was two storeys high, with a vast expanse of white wall facing to the west. The Principal instructed the senior art teacher to design a mural portrait of Marianne Topp. Each day, a group of fourth formers was sent out to bring the project to life. It took them a full term to complete an immensely beautiful, six-metre-square portrait of our swimmer. Each of her lips was the size of a tall sixth form boy lying on his side, and every lunchtime you would see a cluster of students gathered below Marianne's image. Swooning.

Marianne had one or two friends, but she wasn't part of a group. She didn't identify with heroes or pursuits the way that some kids identified with Nick Cave, or football, or weekend alcoholism. She gave the impression that she was entirely self-sufficient, that she had everything she needed emotionally, or thought that she had. I don't mean to suggest that Marianne was stuck-up or arrogant. She was guarded. Her smile, magnificent as it was, was a this-far-and-no-further smile.

What happened to Mr Topp? I asked my mother.

She dispensed with him.

Then how could she get to have so much power without any backing? What made her want to take over?

I don't think that she ever planned to take over. She just seemed capable at a time when people needed someone who seemed capable. She was co-opted by our neediness. We snaffled her.

But what could we need so much that we were prepared to be treated like shit?

I didn't say need. I said neediness. It's a different thing altogether.

The ice began to crack and melt. The skies turned a darker, cloudless blue. A rumour plague broke out. There were rumours that the Geometrical Summit had collapsed. The participants were said to have been devastated by the discovery of a previously unknown real number between sixteen and seventeen. The seventeen-year-olds among us feared that the new number might affect eligibility to take the driving test at eighteen.

Marianne was due to turn eighteen in October. When she broke her own unofficial world record for the 400 metres freestyle in September, the Principal called a half-holiday. Students wishing to commemorate Marianne's achievement were encouraged to visit Ron Dorfmann, the tattooist in Hampton Village.

I remember a very proud Jane Nelson unbuttoning her blouse to show us where Ron had etched the letters MT above the nipple on her perfectly shaped left breast. Poor Jane was mortified when we explained the double entendre.

But Marianne-madness was like that. Someone discovered that she loved expensive Belgian chocolate, and within days Hampton post office was jammed with parcels of chocolate addressed to Ms M. Topp. At times, Marianne seemed to be the only person in Hampton not affected by Marianne-madness. We were all hopelessly distracted, waiting for her mother to return, and waiting for Marianne to betray just a hint of vulnerability, a vacuum of neediness that we could be sucked into.

I told Yuri that he was crazy to spend his savings buying chocolate for Marianne. I told him that he was inviting her contempt. But I never confessed to Yuri that I slipped $200 to a waitress at Coriander's Deli for a white coffee cup that still had Marianne's lipstick print on its rim. A perfect smear of Black Tulip.

Looking back at my chance meeting with Marianne in Chapters Bookshop, I see things that self-consciousness prevented me from seeing at the time. In flickery, stylised motion I see the fraction of a second when Marianne forgot about the impression she was making, and became someone capable of speaking her adoration for literature. She put her emotions on the line.

˙ hold that moment in freeze-frame. We are connected, perhaps ridiculously, by the strength of our mutual feeling for the work of an author neither of us will meet. We are as powerless before this feeling as any character in a fiction by Jeanette Winterson. How is it that I can now isolate this feeling and find the audacity to call it love?

A few days later, I was standing in the shaded quadrangle between school buildings, hanging out with Yuri and some other friends, when Marianne Topp strode between clusters of gawping students to present me with a novel, *Love in the Time of Cholera* by Gabriel García Márquez. No particular sign of affection, or even eye contact, just, You might like to read this, before she disappeared through the crowd.

Thanks . . . Marianne, I called out after her, scarcely able to believe that I'd spoken her name out loud. My friends had lost the power of speech entirely.

Inside the front cover of the hardback novel was a note written on a slip of paper. Marianne's handwriting was as stylish as she was, and equally impenetrable. I spent the best part of that afternoon deciphering her short message. '*After Hours* is playing at the Colosseum on Saturday night. You can meet me in the foyer. M.'

The Colosseum was a very grand name for a fleapit cinema that used to stand opposite the post office, where Safeway supermarket is now. The pavement outside the cinema was a favourite hang-out for warring philosophers. If you were short of entertainment on a Saturday night, you could practically guarantee a violent stoush between the followers of Quine and the Wittgenstein loyalists.

One old woman always used to sit next to the doorway of the cinema holding a placard, DEFEND COPERNICUS! When someone asked her to do this, she let out a machine-gun blurt, The New Knowledge is a farce! The New Knowledge is a lie! Topp must be stopped! The New Knowledge is a farce!

My nerves were shocking. I was back and forth to the toilet. What on earth was I doing having a date with Marianne Topp? My stomach was buckling. I tried to calm myself by singing. I love singing, but the only songs that came to mind were songs about panic, and apprehension, and death. Who the fuck did I think I was to be meeting Marianne Topp at the cinema? I brushed my teeth at least a dozen times, and brushed my tongue as often.

Outside class, Marianne nearly always wore black, sometimes black and white, very occasionally a bright red jacket, but mostly shades of black to match her hair. Which is not to forget the deep, lascivious red of her lips.

Hi, Richard. Have you been waiting long?

I didn't want to admit that I'd been in the foyer since the manager unbolted the front doors. I might have grown a beard while I'd been waiting there.

I don't remember anything about *After Hours*. We hardly spoke before the film. Marianne saw a woman she knew and spoke to her for ten minutes, while I smiled an idiot smile, and shifted my weight from foot to foot. I've never been a student of body language, but I knew enough to realise that this engagement wasn't about tit-feeling in the dark, or even hand-holding, which was just as well because someone had installed a sprinkler system in my palms.

What I do remember is that Marianne wore a fantastic, subtle perfume that activated with the rise of her body temperature. Two-thirds of the way through the feature, my nose got hooked on an updraught of irresistible scent, and I was so far lost in Swoonsville that Marianne had to send out a search party when the film ended.

She must have known what she was doing to me, but what did she want? Not a kiss, though I would have sold my parents into slavery to kiss Marianne's full red lips. I thought then that my neediness, my undisguised adoration, might have been a quaint joke to her, that she was drawing strength or resolve from my own obvious weakness. But now I am inclined to believe that she wanted someone to trust, but didn't dare cross the line to a territory where her fears and desires would be exposed.

I walked her home. We said very little. A few comments about the books we'd read, and the films we'd seen.

I see you at the pool, she said.

Well, yes. Actually, I'm a drowner.

There was the slightest hint of a smile. I know, she said. You ought to get some coaching.

When I asked her if she knew when her mother would come home, she became uncomfortable and didn't answer. I certainly wasn't going to interrogate her, to ask her what it was like to be Beatrice Topp's daughter, or to be so often home alone with her two sisters. Instead, I asked her what she'd do when she left school.

I just have to get out of Hampton. I'm suffocating here.

C'mon, I joked, where in the world would you find somewhere more exciting than Hampton? I never cease to be amazed by this place.

It's possible to have too much imagination, she said.

We were at the front gate of her house then. Her German Shepherd was barking. Marianne moved her hand so that it briefly touched the back of mine.

Thanks, that was nice, she said.

I reconstruct this scene in my mind. I doubt that I could have played it any differently, not even if I'd known that it was the last time that I'd ever see Marianne.

Shortly before dawn, two days later, a light plane flew into Hampton, using a four-lane stretch of Ludstone Street as a landing strip. When it took off thirty minutes later, the plane struggled to squeeze through a gap between overhead power lines. Among its passengers were Marianne Topp and her two younger sisters, Beth and Cicely.

The Topp girls left in a big rush. Their house was a mess. Hampton people speculated that they may have been taken against their will, but it was impossible to compare the scene they left behind with how they lived ordinarily because the Topps had never invited anyone into their home.

Their moonlight departure became widely known when Federal Police disclosed that they had been keeping watch on the activities of Beatrice Topp. Federal agents alleged that she had been in Hong Kong conducting unauthorised land deals. At a time when she ought to have been gleaning the New Knowledge from the International Geometrical Summit, Beatrice Topp had been flogging sections of Hampton to a consortium of Asian and American business interests. No-one knew what had been sold, or the legal status of her transactions, but one thing was certain, Hamptonians could no longer imagine that they lived at the centre of their own small world.

A friend with access to police intelligence suggested that Mrs Topp had fled to Switzerland or Kenya, and that she had arranged for her daughters to be brought to her. That was as close as the police ever got to locating any of the family.

In her absence, Hampton's matriarch was tried by criminal courts, being prosecuted first for fraud, then for various misappropriations. As the hostility toward her grew, new charges were brought. Soon, Beatrice Topp was being tried for crimes that hadn't seemed so much like crimes at the time; abuse of public trust, conspiracy and false imprisonment. Each week, another case against Mrs Topp passed through the court, and she was sentenced to a further term of imprisonment. And so it went on, till whatever Hampton needed to purge itself of had been thoroughly evacuated.

If anything, the airbrushing of Marianne Topp was crueller than the vilification of her mother. It was permissible to speak your outrage at the treachery of Mrs Topp, but Marianne's name could not be spoken. It was as if she had been a heroine of the Third Reich, or a collaborationist entertainer in Vichy France. Marianne's name was removed from the school's honour boards, her photographs taken down from the corridor walls, and the same students who had produced the superb mural portrait of Marianne were sent up the scaffolds to slather it over with garish yellow paint.

It is a difficult period for me to speak about. Shock and confusion kept me at one step removed from feelings that might have been totally destructive. I seem to have lived in a permanent dream, a festival of imagined departures and passionate reunions.

My most frequent dream was one in which Marianne taps on my window late at night, and tells me she has to go. I am so overwhelmed by this that I can't question why, or express my feelings for her, or say any of the proper things. There is no kiss. But in the dream it seems enough that she's chosen to tell me.

She is rushing for the plane when I remember that I still have her book. What about your Márquez? I call. She halts, and turns, and there is the miraculous coalition of the two gestures that I least expect from Marianne Topp; a relaxed, totally unrestrained smile, and a single tear. A moment in which everything is exposed entirely. I want you to have it, she tells me, before rushing to her appointment at the makeshift airstrip.

I *did* have Marianne's book, and I've read it many times in the intervening years. *Love in the Time of Cholera* turned out to be a novel about the postponement of fated love. The two lovers finally unite, gloriously and miraculously, when it least seems possible. How many times have I read Marianne and I into that scenario? I want more than anything to believe that she chose to leave behind the Márquez novel because it articulated her most fervent hopes for our relationship. In spite of everything, we would one day be reunited.

But I'm not such a fool that I can't admit the possibility of coincidence. Who can say that Marianne gave even a moment's thought to how I might construe or misconstrue a subtext? Maybe it was just an accident that I had her book when she was forced to leave.

Six years have passed. I often wonder whether Marianne kept swimming. I keep a close eye on major swimming championships. Only in the last eighteen months have swimmers begun to approach the unofficial world records that Marianne swam when she was Hampton's darling.

After a long period of procrastination, the Federal Government decided to compensate the business people who had been stung by Beatrice Topp's illegal transactions. Though this spared Hampton from foreign ownership, the suburb couldn't insulate itself against changes brought by market forces. The cinema was forced to close, and the High School that was so much the heart of our community was sold to developers. The High School buildings were demolished, to be replaced by gauche but costly new residences.

During the demoliton of the two-storey administration building, I became friendly with Josef, a plump, black-bearded Romanian who operated a massive bulldozer. I managed to persuade Josef to gently tilt a portion of the west wall so that it could be recovered with its yellow-coated brickwork intact. The retrieved expanse of wall, one and a half metres high and three metres wide, stands on my back patio, leaning against the garage.

After receiving advice from conservators at the State Museum, I began to excavate a portion of the Marianne Topp mural. It's a laborious process, scouring away the thick coat of yellow plastic paint, while trying to keep the submerged level of portrait undamaged. Friends joke about my enterprise, and refer to the wall as The Hampton Shroud.

Gradually, the outline of Marianne's fabulous red lips has begun to emerge. When they are finally retrieved, I might use the lips in photo-composites or treatments, but just now it is enough that they will be retrieved. There is a romantic side of me that wants to believe that everything worth retrieving can be retrieved.

Still, I have a cynical side too. My cynicism reminds me that it's not a Michaelangelo that I toil on, but the rushed work of spotty fourth form art students. In many ways, my quest is as pathetic as it is heroic.

The air got terribly cold when I was working on Marianne's upper lip last Sunday. I could barely flex my fingers to operate the spatula. Feeling something brush against my ear, I looked up from my work to see a brief, majestic flurry of snowflakes. My heart almost seized with joy. This was the first snow that I'd seen in Hampton since that extraordinary winter when the Bay iced over and small birds snap-froze in flight.

Henry Handel Richardson

'AND WOMEN MUST WEEP'

1934

'For men must work'

She was ready at last, the last bow tied, the last strengthening pin in place, and they said to her – Auntie Cha and Miss Biddons – to sit down and rest while Auntie Cha 'climbed into her own togs': 'Or you'll be tired before the evening begins.' But she could not bring herself to sit, for fear of crushing her dress – it was so light, so airy. How glad she felt now that she had chosen muslin, and not silk as Auntie Cha had tried to persuade her. The gossamer-like stuff seemed to float around her as she moved, and the cut of the dress made her look so tall and so different from everyday that she hardly recognised herself in the glass; the girl reflected there – in palest blue, with a wreath of cornflowers in her hair – might have been a stranger. Never had she thought she was so pretty ... nor had Auntie and Miss Biddons either; though all they said was: 'Well, Dolly, you'll *do*,' and 'Yes, I think she will be a credit to you.' Something hot and stinging came up her throat at this: a kind of gratitude for her pinky-white skin, her big blue eyes and fair curly hair, and pity for those girls who hadn't got them. Or an Auntie Cha either, to dress them and see that everything was 'just so'.

Instead of sitting, she stood very stiff and straight at the window, pretending to watch for the cab, her long white gloves hanging loose over one arm so as not to soil them. But her heart was beating pit-a-pat. For this was her first real grown-up ball. It was to be held in a public hall, and Auntie Cha, where she was staying, had bought tickets and was taking her.

True, Miss Biddons rather spoilt things at the end by saying: 'Now mind you don't forget your steps in the waltz. One, two, together; four, five, six.' And in the wagonette, with her dress filling one seat, Auntie Cha's the other, Auntie said: 'Now, Dolly, remember not to look too *serious*. Or you'll frighten the gentlemen off.'

But she was only doing it now because of her dress; cabs were so cramped, the seats so narrow.

Alas! in getting out a little accident happened. She caught the bottom of one of her flounces – the skirt was made of nothing else – on the iron step, and ripped off the selvedge. Auntie Cha said: 'My *dear*, how clumsy!' She could have cried with vexation.

The woman who took their cloaks hunted everywhere, but could only find black cotton; so the torn selvedge – there was nearly half a yard of it – had just to be cut off. This left a raw edge, and when they went into the hall and walked across the enormous floor, with people sitting all around, staring, it seemed to Dolly as if every one had their eyes fixed on it. Auntie Cha sat down in the front row of chairs beside a lady-friend; but she slid into a chair behind.

The first dance was already over, and they were hardly seated before partners began to be taken for the second. Shyly she mustered the assembly. In the cloakroom, she had expected the woman to exclaim: 'What a sweet pretty frock!' when she handled it. (When all she did say was: 'This sort of stuff's bound to fray.') And now Dolly saw that the hall was full of *lovely* dresses, some much, much prettier than hers, which suddenly began to seem rather too plain, even a little dowdy; perhaps after all it would have been better to choose silk.

She wondered if Auntie Cha thought so, too. For Auntie suddenly turned and looked at her, quite hard, and then said snappily: 'Come, come, child, you mustn't tuck yourself away like that, or the gentlemen will think you don't want to dance.' So she had to come out and sit in the front; and show that she had a programme, by holding it open on her lap.

When other ladies were being requested for the third time, and still nobody had asked to be introduced, Auntie began making signs and beckoning with her head to the Master of Ceremonies – a funny little fat man with a bright red beard. He waddled across the floor, and Auntie whispered to him . . . behind her fan. (But she heard. And heard him answer: 'Wants a partner? Why, certainly.') And then he went away and they could see him offering her to several gentlemen. Some pointed to the ladies they were sitting with or standing in front of; some showed their programmes that these were full. One or two turned their heads and looked at her. But it was no good. So he came back and said: 'Will the little lady do *me* the favour?' and she had to look glad and say: 'With pleasure', and get up and dance with him. Perhaps she was a little slow about it . . . at any rate Auntie Cha made great round eyes at her. But she felt sure everyone would know why he was asking her. It was the lancers, too, and he swung her off her feet at the corners, and was comic when he set to partners – putting one hand on his hip and the other over his head, as if he were dancing the hornpipe – and the rest of the set laughed. She was glad when it was over and she could go back to her place.

Auntie Cha's lady-friend had a son, and he was beckoned to next and there was more whispering. But he was engaged to be married, and of course preferred to dance with his fiancée. When he came and bowed – to oblige his mother – he looked quite grumpy, and didn't trouble to say all of 'May I have the pleasure?' but just 'The pleasure?' While she had to say 'Certainly', and pretend to be very pleased, though she didn't feel it, and really didn't want much to dance with him, knowing he didn't, and that it was only out of charity. Besides, all the time they went round he was explaining things to the other girl with his eyes . . . making faces over her head. She saw him, quite plainly.

After he had brought her back – and Auntie had talked to him again – he went to a gentleman who hadn't danced at all yet, but just stood looking on. And this one needed a lot of persuasion. He was ugly, and lanky, and as soon as they stood up said quite rudely: 'I'm no earthly good at this kind of thing, you know.' And he wasn't. He trod on her foot and put her out of step, and they got into the most dreadful muddle, right out in the middle of the floor. It was a waltz and, remembering what Miss Biddons had said, she got more and more nervous, and then went wrong herself, and had to say: 'I beg your pardon', to which he said: 'Granted.' She saw them in a mirror as they passed, and her face was red as red.

It didn't get cool again either, for she had to go on sitting out, and she felt sure he was spreading it that *she* couldn't dance. She didn't know whether Auntie Cha had seen her mistakes, but now Auntie sort of went for her. 'It's no use, Dolly, if you don't do *your* share. For goodness' sake, try and look more agreeable!'

So after this, in the intervals between the dances, she sat with a stiff little smile gummed to her lips. And, did any likely-looking partner approach the corner where they were, this widened till she felt what it was really saying was: 'Here I am! Oh, *please*, take *me*!'

She had several false hopes. Men, looking so splendid in their white shirt fronts, would walk across the floor and *seem* to be coming ... and then it was always not her. Their eyes wouldn't stay on her. There she sat, with her false little smile, and her eyes fixed on them; but theirs always got away ... flitted past ... moved on. Once she felt quite sure. Ever such a handsome young man looked as if he were making straight for her. She stretched her lips, showing all her teeth (they were very good), and for an instant his eyes seemed to linger ... really to take her in, in her pretty blue dress and the cornflowers. And then at the last minute they ran away – and it wasn't her at all, but a girl sitting three seats further on; one who wasn't even pretty, or her dress either. But her own dress was beginning to get quite trashy, from the way she squeezed her hot hands down in her lap.

Quite the worst part of all was having to go on sitting in the front row, pretending you were enjoying yourself. It was so hard to know what to do with your eyes. There was nothing but the floor for them to look at – if you watched the other couples dancing they would think you were envying them. At first she made a show of studying her programme; but you couldn't go on staring at a programme forever; and presently her shame at its emptiness grew till she could bear it no longer, and, seizing a moment when people were dancing, she slipped it down the front of her dress. Now she could say she'd lost it, if anyone asked to see it. But they didn't; they went on dancing with other girls. Oh, these men, who walked around and chose just who they fancied and left who they didn't ... how she hated them! It wasn't fair ... it wasn't fair. And when there was a 'leap-year' dance where the ladies invited the gentlemen, and Auntie Cha tried to push her up and make her go and said 'Now then, Dolly, here's your chance!' she shook her head hard and dug herself deeper into her seat. She wasn't going to ask them when they never asked her. So she said her head ached and she'd rather not. And to this she clung, sitting the while wishing with her whole heart that her dress was black and her hair grey, like Auntie Cha's. Nobody expected Auntie to dance, or thought it shameful if she didn't: she could do and be just as she liked. Yes, tonight she wished she was old ... an old, old woman. Or that she was safe at home in bed ... this dreadful evening, to which she had once counted the days, behind her. Even, as the night wore on, that she was dead.

At supper she sat with Auntie and the other lady, and the son and the girl came, too. There were lovely cakes and things, but she could not eat them. Her throat was so dry that a sandwich stuck in it and nearly choked her. Perhaps the son felt a little sorry for her (or else his mother had whispered again), for afterwards he said something to the girl, and then asked *her* to dance. They stood up together; but it wasn't a success. Her legs seemed to have forgotten how to jump, heavy as lead they were . . . as heavy as she felt inside . . . and she couldn't think of a thing to say. So now he would put her down as stupid, as well.

Her only other partner was a boy younger than she was – almost a schoolboy – who she heard them say was 'making a nuisance of himself'. This was to a *very* pretty girl called the 'belle of the ball'. And he didn't seem to mind how badly he danced (with her), for he couldn't take his eyes off this other girl; but went on staring at her all the time, and very fiercely, because she was talking and laughing with somebody else. Besides, he hopped like a grasshopper, and didn't wear gloves, and his hands were hot and sticky. She hadn't come there to dance with little boys.

They left before anybody else; there was nothing to stay for. And the drive home in the wagonette, which had to be fetched, they were so early, was dreadful: Auntie Cha just sat and pressed her lips and didn't say a word. She herself kept her face turned the other way, because her mouth was jumping in and out as if it might have to cry.

At the sound of wheels Miss Biddons came running to the front door with questions and exclamations, dreadfully curious to know why they were back so soon. Dolly fled to her own little room and turned the key in the lock. She wanted only to be alone, quite alone, where nobody could see her . . . where nobody would ever see her again. But the walls were thin, and as she tore off the wreath and ripped open her dress, now crushed to nothing from so much sitting, and threw them from her anywhere, anyhow, she could hear the two voices going on, Auntie Cha's telling and telling, and winding up at last, quite out loud, with: 'Well, I don't know what it was, but the plain truth is, she didn't *take*!'

Oh, the shame of it! . . . the sting and the shame. Her first ball, and not to have 'taken', to have failed to 'attract the gentlemen' – this was a slur that would rest on her all her life. And yet . . . and yet . . . in spite of everything, a small voice that wouldn't be silenced kept on saying: 'It wasn't my fault . . . it wasn't my *fault!*' (Or at least not except for the one silly mistake in the steps of the waltz.) She had tried her hardest, done everything she was told to: had dressed up to please and look pretty, sat in the front row offering her programme, smiled when she didn't feel a bit like smiling . . . and almost more than anything she thought she hated the memory of that smile (it was like trying to make people buy something they didn't think worthwhile). For really, truly, right deep down in her, she hadn't wanted 'the gentlemen' any more than they'd wanted her: she had only had to pretend to. And they showed only too plainly they didn't, by choosing other girls, who were not even pretty, and dancing with them, and laughing and talking and enjoying them. And now, the many slights and humiliations of the evening crowding upon her, the long-repressed tears broke through; and with the blanket pulled up over her head, her face driven deep into the pillow, she cried till she could cry no more.

Deborah Robertson

THE CROSSING
1992

It is said that it was purple and that nothing like it had ever been seen before. The party stood on the riverbank and looked across the glittering water to the far side. They saw it amongst the dry grasses and papery barks. It is said that the young blind woman cried *Tell me more tell me more* and although it was only a smudge of colour shimmering in the heat haze, they said: *It is not like our flowers in England, it is wildly tall and waves in the breeze, it curls like an orchid but its colour is the passion of the African violet, nothing about it is ordered or well-behaved, each petal leads a separate dance.*

It is said he was a ticket-of-leave convict tending the grounds of the house on the river at Maylands. Edward Ackers turned the soil and plucked the weeds from the ground as he watched his employer and his employer's luncheon guests guide the young blind woman in their elegant stroll along the water's edge. Was it the lie he heard them tell? Or did the promise of such a flower inspire this rapist, this horse-thief?

Edward Ackers threw aside his spade, gathered the young blind woman in his arms and was in the water within a minute. The ladies on the land cried out, and the gentlemen hurried to free themselves of their coats and hats, but the powerful convict struck out against the river, clasping the young blind woman to his side. Her dress flowed like cream. There is no record of the words that Ackers spoke to calm her but her cry *Mother Mother I will see with my own eyes* soared like a gull through the blue air back to the party on shore.

The flower's fragrance, it is said, tears heart from mind. The strands of its musk draw melancholy and rapture from the body in such swiftly alternating currents that a person is struck helpless, sunk to her knees, for long and quivering moments.

On their return journey the young blind woman's cry rippled over the water towards her people. *I have seen the flower and it was just as you said.*

There was no more to be feared. She was as wet as an otter but safe. Edward Ackers was granted a full pardon and departed for the East Coast.

An annual performance now honours this event. The performance is called Two Who Have a Need for Each Other.

It is said that the tradition of these performances was continued by word of mouth until a time in the 1930s when the first organising committee was formed. It was then that the advertisement first appeared, a quiet enigma, in the columns of the *Maylands Gazette.* Year after year the initiated now seek it and the curious are enticed. The event is not what you would call a secret; it is shrouded for protection but not exclusion. Besides, it is not one to capture the public imagination. The drama it enacts does not have the appeal of, let's say, a football grand final.

This year there is a misunderstanding when the ad is placed. It has *always* appeared among the fetes and jumble sales of FORTHCOMING EVENTS. But things change, community newspapers change too, and this year the advertisement for Two Who Have a Need for Each Other is found in the new classified pages called POSSIBILITIES. The organising committee finds it alongside Men Seeking Women, Women Seeking Men, Seeking Same, Unmarried With Children, Travel Companion and 60s Plus Club.

This is a disaster, says Barry. *People will think we are a lonely hearts bureau.* Barry's memories of childhood are haunted by these yearly events. But he does not mention this. He simply says that it is important to keep tradition alive.

But Barry, our ad doesn't employ that discourse, says Max. *Our text does not inscribe that cartography of desire.* He reads from the newspaper:

TWO WHO HAVE A NEED FOR EACH OTHER

This summer's performance of courage and humility. An historic re-enactment. Interested participants must have their applications to the organising committee by the last mail Jan 30. Their decision will be final and no correspondence will be entered into.

I still think 'self-effacement' would have been better than 'humility', says Max.

But you haven't seen an enactment yet, dear, says Mary, *you are new to this. That hyphen word is not true to the poignancy of the situation.*

Mary doubts Max's motives in joining this committee. She thinks he is too dedicated a follower of fashion. And Max has his own problems with Mary. Her intense eye-contact and grey witch's hair unsettle him. But at this meeting, they must get down to business. *The Swan River Authority has agreed to restrict all traffic for one hour on the afternoon of Saturday, the fifteenth of February,* says Barry.

The applications do not exactly roll in but by the closing date the organisers have a dozen or so to assess. Despite the frame of tradition, each year the choice of the two participants seems like a task of fresh urgency. It is thought that, for many decades of the re-enactment, two people in symbolic costume played the parts of convict and blind girl. But over time the actors came to speak more of themselves. Other stories came to be told. Barry and Mary told Max about some of the past performers. Eight years ago they had chosen as Bearer the owner of a swimming-pool in which a neighbour's child had drowned. He carried across the river a woman who had suffered a paralysing fear of water since childhood swimming lessons at the Maylands jetty. In 1946, and again during the Vietnam War, women struggled to and from the purple flower carrying the uniform and kit of their dead soldier sons. Barry and Mary explained to Max their criteria for the selection of the Bearer and the Borne; a sense of composition and an eye for the contemporary. They were trying to create, they said, historic moments of expressive beauty. Repulsed by such language, Max relegated the applications to the categories of Beast and Burden but kept it to himself, kept the merest hint of these thoughts out of his eyes for fear that Mary might find them there, and know him.

On the fifteenth of February the purple flower is a smear of colour on the far bank. There are almost a hundred spectators gathered under umbrellas on the grass. They have eskies and blankets for the picnic that will follow the performance. In the crowd are those who have applied to enact their stories on the river. Only the organising committee knows its choice. The instant of surprise that bound the convict and the blind girl is cherished and preserved. Barry announces the name of the person who is to be carried across the water. With the help of his companion, Roger Thomas gets out of his wheelchair and shuffles slowly to Barry's side. As they look at him, there is but one thought in the mind of the crowd: *Auschwitz*. But when he speaks they hear *his* body, weak yet defiant, not a body belonging to history but before them now, of the moment. And he has something to declare:

I am forty years old. I am dying. I refuse all medical intervention. I will not be at the mercy of hope. I have AIDS. I am a scholar with no mark to leave. I wish to show my face.

Roger Thomas returns to his wheelchair. The crowd is anxious about him entering the water. Many times the river has been contested and defied, never has it been called upon to be kind.

I am not looking to be healed, he says suddenly, as if he knew their minds.

The name of the Bearer is announced. She disrobes and comes forward wearing a drab pair of old-fashioned green and gold Speedos. Irene Greenblatt holds a yellowed piece of paper above her head. She wants to explain:

This is my Certificate of Femininity. It is cancelled. I was ready to swim the race of my career; my life had been a preparation for this event. It was the eve of my competition. The International Olympic Committee has its rules. From the inside of my mouth they scraped some cells and put my womanhood under the microscope. I carry an extra Y chromosome, quietly sitting there, doing no-one any harm. I was judged too much a man. I was out. Today I will swim again and prove that I Am a Woman.

Roger Thomas stands and his companion helps him remove his tracksuit. The crowd sees his long, empty bones. He is wearing blue bathers, it is clear that they are brand new. In anticipation of this moment he has sought to look his best. Roger and Irene face each other: he is paper, she is clay.

The crossing begins, as it did for the convict and the blind girl, on the shore. Irene lifts Roger like a mother gathering the belongings of her dead son. The water laps her toes. He lifts his face to the burning sky like a sunbather. Irene turns on her side and takes Roger's body to her in the lifesaving position. They watch the spectators become smaller as they pull away from them and enter colder waters.

Roger is feverish; the water is astringent and soothing. He feels Irene's strong arm around his chest, her breast against his back, and he enjoys the quickness of his body, the effortless way it skims the water, like light. As she pulls through the water Irene feels rivets of tension locking her body. She hears Roger's threadbare breathing. Pelicans appear through cloud.

What school did you go to, Roger? she says.

And of course there is a face, a name, a place they both know.

It's a small world, they say, and Roger swallows water.

His cough sounds like it will break open his body. Irene turns him on his belly and supports his thin torso; he is figurehead to her boat. The vegetation on the far bank becomes clearer, the blond grasses blow about like hair. The purple flower flaps in the breeze. They both have their suspicions. But they must save their strength; they do not speak.

The triangle of purple silk is wired to the end of a star picket. Neither Irene nor Roger is capable of disappointment. Roger lies on the wet sand and realises that he is too ill for this performance. This is not the ceremony for the loss of himself that he was seeking. The river water smells bad on his skin. Irene stands beside him and stretches, hurting. There had been no younger body within her waiting to claim this day.

Roger is coughing again. *You don't want to die here,* she says, patting his hand.

We'll just take it nice and slow, she says, carrying him back into the water.

She adjusts herself to the load and the tedium; it occurs to her that this is just like the everyday. Roger gives himself over to his senseless pain, her stranger's arms, the wind, the sun, the water. And the shore finally comes closer. They see the spectators assemble on the sand.

A couple of heroes, she says. *We're going to make it.*

That'll do me, says Roger.

As they reach shallow water the children try to run forward to greet them but they are held back. Tradition has it that the carrier and the carried must touch grass before the journey is complete.

Irene moves through the crowd with Roger in her arms. She places him gently in his wheelchair. Max is there, taking notes. The children break free and run to them. The etiquette of the occasion does not permit applause, but the children cannot be restrained from this too, and they gather around them, cheering, clapping in their flat-handed way. Roger and Irene take a deep, professional, gracious bow. For the children. Mary studies the Bearer and the Borne. She watches their eyes. What she sees in their eyes she has seen before. She has seen it year after year after year.

Penelope Rowe

THE INNOCENTS

1992

Isobel Paraguay had come to live at the convent under Reverend
Mother's legal guardianship when both her parents had died in the fall
of Singapore. Isobel was then three years old and without another
living relative in the world. Reverend Mother was her grand-aunt. It
was a most unusual arrangement but these were unusual times and the
Bishop had given his consent. Now Isobel was nearly five and a quaintly
serious little girl moving happily around the convent in a quiet and
unobtrusive way. Reverend Mother used the child's modest inheritance
wisely and kindly to make Isobel as happy as possible. An unexpected
bonus was the delight (reserved delight) that the little girl brought to
this community of childless women.

Isobel was quite accustomed to living with a large group of people,
whether it be the students in term time or just the Community in
holiday time. She had her own room in the infirmary which was pink
with a rose-sprigged flounce around the kidney-shaped dressing table,
a little stool in front of it that also wore a flounce, a bed with a pink
bedspread and a small desk and chair beside the bookcase that held
her collection of picture books, three mountain devils that Mother
Porter had brought back from a retreat in Katoomba, a shell that she
could hear the sea in and a framed picture of her mother and father
that had come in her luggage from Singapore. Sitting on her pillow
was a little furry bunny that her mother had given her on her third
birthday, just before she had sent Isobel south. The bunny was her
most loved possession.

She was too young to start school but she took part in many of the
school activities in the playing fields and swimming-pool and, of course,
in the chapel. Already she had developed holy knees, toughened pads
of skin that she sometimes picked at so that scabs developed. When
the students went home at three-thirty, one of the novices would collect

Isobel and escort her through the convent bush to the little summer-house or to the beach, where Isobel could paddle happily about while the novices had their permitted hour of speech for the day. She would then be taken back to the convent and given a glass of raspberry cordial and two slices of shortbread. The nuns did not mind if she wandered through the deserted classrooms and drew on the blackboards with the coloured chalks that she loved, provided that she cleaned off the drawings when she was finished and banged the dusters out the window to get rid of the chalk dust. Sometimes she went to the sacristy to help Mother Sacristan clean the brass candlesticks and the incense brazier and the sanctuary lamps.

If Mother Sacristan was in a good mood and not rushed she let Isobel pull the bell rope but supervised carefully, telling her about the dangers of being carried up to the roof. She told Isobel that once she had been ringing the bells when some visitors had been shown into the belfry. To everyone's horror, a member of the party had jumped to his death out the belfry window. 'I didn't think my ringing was that bad,' Mother Sacristan said to Isobel.

Some days she sat in the ironing room and watched Mother Patrick starching and ironing the nuns' frilly caps. Once she had tried on one of them but Mother Patrick had told her to take it off at once. Sometimes she was allowed to fold the underpants and pair the stockings, though. Other days she helped Mother Percy press out the little communion wafers and understood that she must be very respectful of them even though they were not consecrated, whatever that meant. Once or twice she had eaten some of the left-over, uneven wafer, but it didn't have much taste and stuck to the roof of her mouth. Mother Agnes never minded if Isobel crept in and sat under the huge organ in the choir loft while she was practising. Isobel loved that. She loved being surrounded by sound. Not only could she hear it. She could feel it, she thought. It wrapped itself around her like a warm hug.

Every evening Isobel spent an hour with old Mother Leddingham, who was officially supposed to give her a music lesson. The fact was that the old nun, Reverend Mother realised, had grown senile. She fussed around with not enough to do and often interrupted Reverend Mother at her paperwork. It kept her occupied for a while. She and Isobel got on famously. They met in the piano cells and Isobel sat at the piano. Mother Leddingham, fluting, piping, trilling, tittupped hither and yon, moving with a dainty shuffle rather like a Chinese lady with bound feet, telling Isobel all the matters that concerned her. She was teaching Isobel to recite the psalms and gave her long recitations from Dickens about Mr and Mrs Veneering and all the little Veneerings, and Pip and Sam Weller. 'Would you object to an Aged P?' she asked Isobel quite often and Isobel opened her eyes wide and shrugged, crossed her ankles, neat in their white socks, and swayed back and forward on her chair. 'What larks, Pip!' Isobel giggled. Often she had no idea what Mother Leddingham was talking about.

All the nuns wore men's fob watches tucked under their capes, but Mother Leddingham carried hers in a box in her pocket. It was a bedside clock rather than a fob and in summer she kept it wrapped in hydrangea leaves inside the box. These, she told Isobel, kept the watch cool and in perfect working order. She needed to check the time constantly because there were a large number of special prayers that she had to say at given intervals and she became very distressed if her routine was thrown out. As a consequence there was not much time in the hour for actual music lessons but Isobel could play C major and 'Faith of our Fathers' with the right hand.

Thus was Isobel's little world and she was very happy in it, fitting in with the routine but able to amuse herself perfectly well when alone. But her very favourite time came in the evening after Mother Infirmarian had supervised her bath, brushed her hair, heard her prayers, tucked her into her cosy pink bed, whispered 'Goodnight, God bless' and gone, switching off the light as she did so. Now Isobel was alone with her bunny.

Isobel slips down deep into the bed, pulling the bedclothes high up around her ears. First she stretches her legs as far as she can, right out into the cold lost corners, then she snuggles them up tight, her knees up to her tummy as she rolls onto her side. Then she tucks her hands, flat palm to flat palm, neatly into the cosy gap between the tops of her legs. For a minute or so she lies quite still, enjoying the snug safe feeling it gives her. Then to feel even safer she stretches out an arm and pulls Bunny off her pillow and tucks him down there between her legs too. If she squeezes her legs together really tightly she can feel Bunny pressing up against her and it gives her a gentle tickly feeling in the part that, for want of any other word, she thinks of as her front bottom. For a little while she lies still, enjoying the sensation, her breath coming a little faster, her cheeks growing hot. Then she pulls Bunny out and pushes him down the front of her pyjama pants. Oh! Oh! The furry softness! The love and hug of it! She gives a little gasp. Then she starts to rub down her front bottom. The tickly feeling becomes stronger, sweeter, she is gasping loudly, the tickle becomes a pounding and she starts to thrash about under the bedclothes oh! oh! oh! faster, faster, until slowly slowly a big wave of heat falls over her and she falls onto her back, crying out with pleasure. For a minute or so she lies motionless, drowned in the feeling. Then, ever so gently, she pulls Bunny back up and cuddles him against her cheek, smelling the musky, friendly special smell, and she drops off to sleep almost instantly, breathing deeply, reassured, secure in her little convent world.

The first intimation that Reverend Mother had of these proceedings was when she was approached by Mother Infirmarian, who expressed an opinion that she had heard Isobel having some kind of fit several times now and she wondered if Reverend Mother felt a doctor should be called. Reverend Mother was astonished at this. Isobel was a thriving child. They'd never had a minute's trouble with her. Fits! Fiddlesticks! She would come tonight to investigate.

My goodness gracious me, thought Reverend Mother. The child *is* having a fit. She rushed into the room and hauled the blankets back. Isobel was lying there gasping, her back arched, a look of what seemed to be intense anguish on her face, dimly lit by moonlight.

'Isobel. Isobel,' said Reverend Mother in panic. 'Whatever is it, child? Isobel.' Isobel seemed to snap back into awareness. The sight of Reverend Mother towering over her in the darkness gave her a terrible fright. She pulled Bunny out of her pyjamas and clasped him tight to her chest, her heart pounding with exertion and fear.

'My dear, whatever are you doing?' asked Reverend Mother, in confusion.

'I'm playing with Bunny,' said Isobel in a whisper.

'Playing with Bunny? What sort of game are you playing?'

Isobel hesitated. It was a sort of private game but . . . 'I rub him on my front bottom . . .'

'You what?'

'I rub him on my front bottom.'

'On your what?'

Isobel could sense that something very unsettling was happening. 'My front bottom.' The whisper was all but inaudible now.

'Give me that at once,' snapped Reverend Mother, overwhelmed by the monstrousness of what she was hearing, and she snatched Isobel's beloved Bunny from her and left the room.

Isobel lay still. A horrible new feeling was coming over her. As if she was coming to know something that never again could she unknow and nothing would be the same from then on. And she knew she had been bad. Otherwise Reverend Mother would not have taken Bunny.

Reverend Mother was shaking with distress as she knelt in the chapel attempting to restore calm to her outraged nerves. She could scarcely credit such a thing. She knew that she could not deal with this herself so after a few heartfelt pleas for wisdom she decided that there was nothing for it but to consult Monsignor in the morning, terrible though it would be.

She did not feel able to say anything to him face to face so she requested a confession wherein she might whisper about Isobel and the terrible thing she was doing.

'I am troubled about my niece, Isobel, Monsignor. She . . .' There was a pause. Reverend Mother's breath was rapid. 'She is breaking the sixth commandment.'

'I beg your pardon?' said Monsignor and Reverend Mother could see that he was no longer slouching inside the confessional. 'The sixth commandment?'

Reverend Mother was flustered. 'Impure acts,' she stammered. 'Taking fits. By herself.'

'Ah,' said Monsignor, understanding and disgust dawning. He too was flustered. This wasn't the sort of thing you discussed with a nun. A heavy embarrassment hung between them. 'I shall leave you a book,' he said finally. 'Go along now.'

True to his word, the next morning after mass he handed Reverend Mother a heavy book, wrapped in brown paper.

'I have marked the relevant section for you,' he said. 'There will be no need for you to look at anything else.' (He was worried that the book, VITALOGY: *An Encyclopedia of Health and Home, 1929*, could become an occasion of sin for the nun. But it was a risk he had to take.)

Sitting at her desk, a cluster headache threatening, Reverend Mother examined the book's contents, 1 *Materia Medica*, 2 *Secret of Longevity*, 3 *Hygiene*, 4 *Mental Therapeutics*, 5 *Psychology*, and 6 *Moral and Sex Hygiene, Marriage and Child Culture*. It was this section 6 that Monsignor had marked. She turned to page 812 and read the incomprehensible heading, 'Self-Pollution'. Oh, God spare us and save us! What was it all about?

There were two grainy photographs of one D. S. Burton and the captions read:

> This illustration of D. S. Burton was taken before the habits of secret vice had begun to tell on him. The next photo was taken three years later, when he had become an inveterate victim of the vice. The doctor's opinion was, 'If this young man escapes the asylum he and his parents will be fortunate.'

Reverend Mother looked at the young man with the deeply lined face, the dark rings under the eyes, the wild gaze. She had seen before and after pictures in Isobel's *Cole's Funny Picture Book* but never of self-polluters – things like before and after taking to a life of crime, before and after taking to tobacco, before and after taking to drink. This was the first time she had ever heard of self-pollution in all her life. She turned the page and read the sections Monsignor had marked lightly with pencil.

> There are various names given to the unnatural and degrading vice of producing venereal excitement, either by hand or in other perverted and unnatural ways. It is a vice common to both sexes. The following are some of the symptoms of those addicted to the habit: inclination to shun company and society; frequently being missing from the company of other members of the family; the person cannot look anyone steadily in the face and will drop the eyes or turn away the gaze as if guilty. Health is notably impaired. There will be a slowness of growth, weakness in the lower limbs, unsteadiness of hands, loss of memory, weak eyes, loss of sight, and then will come stupidity, spinal affliction, emaciation, insanity and idiocy, the hopeless ruin of both mind and body. Few, perhaps, ever think or know

how many of the unfortunate inmates of our lunatic asylums
have been sent there by this dreadful vice. Were the whole truth
of this known it would alarm parents more even than dread of
cholera or smallpox. The too frequent use of meat, coffee, late
suppers, etc. strongly tend to excite animal propensities which
directly predispose to vice.

It was written by Professor Standish, Licentiate of the Royal College
of Physicians, clearly a force to be reckoned with.

Reverend Mother leaned back in shock and as she did she saw
Bunny lying on the corner of the windowsill. Disgustedly she seized
the filthy thing and walked with all possible speed to the convent
boiler room, where a strong fire was always burning. She pulled back
the furnace cover, the flames leaped and she hurled Isobel's occasion
of sin into the fire. Shaking with emotion, the cluster headache in full
thrumming agony over her left eye, she returned to the chapel, where
she appealed to God and His holy Mother to guide her in rescuing
Isobel.

She thought initially that it might be sufficient to show Isobel how
Our Lady always slept with her arms crossed over her chest outside
the sheets, but rejected this as insufficient. After all, if the grip of this
vice was as insidious as Professor Standish's book implied, drastic
measures were called for and she could not supervise all the time.
Without disclosing the reason she gave instructions to Mother
Infirmarian.

'There is no need to discuss this with Isobel. Please do as I say and
tell her it is my express wish.'

So, every night after her bath, which she must now take in her
underpants, Mother Infirmarian pushed Isobel's hands in large fleecy-
lined slippers which she then bound tightly on with long strips of
cotton cloth. Once Isobel had knelt and said her night prayers she was
firmly tied by both wrists to the top bedposts.

'There now,' said Mother Infirmarian the first evening. 'Reverend
Mother says you must sleep like that from now on. You have been a
very naughty girl.'

'Can I have Bunny back?' whimpered Isobel, trembling with fear.

'Absolutely not,' thundered Reverend Mother when Mother Infirmarian conveyed the request. 'Tell her I have burnt the disgusting thing

and tell her that if she ever misbehaves again I shall get the doctor to her. He will punish her even more severely!'

So, nearly five-year-old Isobel and Reverend Mother lost their innocence at the same time. While Reverend Mother now understood more readily the term 'the devil finds work for idle hands', and considered herself a sadder and wiser person, Isobel grew quieter, she dropped her head when addressed, dark lines appeared under her eyes, she developed an astigmatism, and she began to stutter so badly that some of the nuns thought she might be brain-damaged. Reverend Mother watched these degrading results of the secret vice with horror, determined on ruthless vigilance from now on, and thanked God she had been granted the opportunity to take action so that with His love and mercy further deterioration of her grand-niece would be prevented and the child would survive to make amends for her wickedness.

DAVE BRINGS HOME A WIFE

1903

All was joy and merriment at Ruddville. There was no grumbling, no dissension, no dissatisfaction of any kind. Even Dad took things cheerfully, and became frisky and light-hearted as a fat lamb. The longest days seemed short hours, and home was simply heaven. Dave was the cause of all the love and felicity. Dave got married, and brought his wife home to live with us. A fine wife she was, too – a slim, jolly girl with red hair. Lily White was her name, and we took a great liking to her. So did Dave. Lots of young fellows down at Prosperity had tried hard to win Lily, but she rejected them all with contumely. Dave thought all the more of her on that account.

The welcome we gave Lily when she arrived seemed to add twenty years to Dave's life. Our display of affection quite overpowered him, swelled his breast with gratitude, and filled his eyes with tears as large as hailstones. All of us except Bill and Tom and me met them at the gate, and kissed Lily freely. We hesitated when it came to hugging her, but Sarah shoved us forward, and said, 'Ain't y' goin' t' kiss Lily? She's your sister now.'

Then we took courage and waded in – though we wouldn't have hugged Sarah herself for a fortune, unless it was on her solemn assurance that she was going far from home and would never return.

After us, Dad stepped forward.

'Well,' he said, removing his hat to expedite the performance, 'if she be your sister, she be my daughter,' and he commenced vigorously where we left off. When Dad finished with Lily, Sarah took possession of her, and hugged her again, and put an arm round her waist, and conducted her up the veranda steps into Dave's little room, where she took her hat off for her, and kissed her some more, and showed her the newly papered walls – papered for her special comfort, and a new bed curtain and draping, and a coloured pincushion and a pair of flower-vases and a wardrobe and other knicknacks and pieces of furniture which Sarah had robbed her own room of to surprise Lily with and make her happy.

And Lily was happy. She sat on the bed, and said so. She spoke fondly of Dave, too.

'It was hard parting with Mother,' she murmured, 'but I don't mind when I know I have a good husband.'

And tears came into her eyes, and Sarah kissed them away, and said, 'No-one knows it better than I do, dear. He was always my favourite brother,' which was a fib, because Sarah always reckoned Dave a nuisance, and never tired of wishing him married. She seemed to think that a wife was the worst infliction she could wish Dave. Then Sarah broke into tears, and Lily kissed them away.

'There, my sister,' she said, and changed the subject.

She turned it onto Sarah's future, and they became very confidential. Sarah smiled happily at Lily, and said she couldn't say for certain when it was to be; it might be at Easter twelve months or the following Christmas. It all depended. But Lily wasn't to mention it to a soul – not even to Dave. And when Lily gave her solemn word not to divulge the secret, they kissed each other again and said, 'We're sisters now forever.' Then they returned to the veranda, where Mother and Dad and the rest of us were trying to entertain Dave. But Dave was a hard bridegroom to entertain. He didn't hear a word we had to say to him.

'Thought you was lost,' he said, eagerly grabbing Lily by the arm and leading her inside to sit on the sofa.

Four weeks passed, and the home was merrier than ever. And Lily and Dave were as happy-looking as a garden. Dave was proud of his Lily. He rarely left her side. Lily knew the run of the house, too, now and understood our ways, and addressed us all by our Christian names, and called Dad 'Father'. Lily was never untidy, either, and always came to her meals in a dress and sat beside Dave with a buttercup in her hair. And she would talk cheerfully all the time, and point out resemblances between Mother's eyes and Dave's, or Dad's nose and Bill's. Lily was an observant young woman.

In the afternoons Sarah would take Lily for a walk. Often they would go down to the paddock, and keep Dave company till nearly tea-time. On other occasions they would go visiting together, and sometimes they would ride to the store or to the railway station. And Sarah would give her side-saddle to Lily, and ride in a man's saddle herself. Sarah was fond of Lily. She couldn't do half enough for her. And Lily loved Sarah. Mother said she never knew two young people to be so devoted to each other. And Dad reckoned it was fortunate for Dave that Sarah wasn't Joe.

Four more weeks elapsed. Sarah and Lily were not so fond of each other now. They didn't go anywhere together at all. Somehow they avoided one another, and Lily would go down the paddock alone, and remain with Dave till he knocked off work. Mealtimes, too, lost all their cheerfulness. All the good-fellowship had gone from them. There was scarcely any conversation carried on at the table, and Sarah was nearly always absent from it. While we were eating she would be working and banging things about in the kitchen. Sometimes Dad would miss her and, looking up at Mother, he would ask, 'Where's Sarah?' and Mother would change colour, and mumble a clumsy apology, which would make Lily fidget, and look along her nose; and frequently Lily would refuse a second cup of tea, which she was badly in need of, and leave the table before she had finished and, with Dave at her heels, would retire to her room. But Dad was not a man to notice little things, and sometimes he would add with a yell, 'Well, why the devil doesn't she come and get her tea?'

Dave and Lily isolated themselves, spent a lot of time in their room, and we wondered what was the matter. We couldn't make it out, and Joe asked Sarah one night what it was all about. Sarah, who had her sleeves rolled up, making bread, dug her fists deep into the dough, and said, 'Pshaw! The little cat!' Then she turned the dough over, and slapped it down hard on the table, and punched it with her other f... Joe chuckled, and said he could never understand why women couldn't agree.

'Could you agree with anyone,' Sarah snapped, 'who expects you to do all the cooking and washing and slaving, and to run about and clean up after them, while they sit down and act the lady?'

'That's nothing,' Joe said flippantly. Joe enjoyed Sarah when she was angry.

'Oh, isn't it, nothing?' And Sarah leant on the dough with both hands, and glared at him after the manner of Dad. 'Then let her do it if it isn't. I'm not going to stay here and scrub and wash her dirt for her any more, that's one thing. Anyway, the least she might do is to clean her own room, and make her own bed of a morning, instead of titivating herself as soon as she gets up – scenting herself, too! And dolling her old red hair to come out and sit down to breakfast, as if she was Lady Muck or somebody!'

And Sarah waded into the bread again.

Joe grinned some more, and said, 'You're jealous, Sal.'

'Jealous! What of?' Sarah fired up. 'Of that cat? With her red hair? Pooh! If it was mine, I'd get some lamp-black and change its colour.'

Joe went away smiling, and Dave, with a warlike look on his face, entered the kitchen. Dave was looking for a fight.

Sarah didn't look at Dave.

'Any matches here?' Dave asked, manoeuvring for an opening.

'There's some there,' Sarah jerked out, walloping the dough as though it were a carpet.

Dave glanced round the room for a second or two, then rested his eyes on Sarah.

'What have you been doing to Lily?' he drawled at last.

'Who says I've been doing anything to Lily?' And Sarah flashed her big eyes on Dave.

'Well, I know you insulted her,' Dave replied.

'Well, if asking her to do her own dirty work is insulting her,' Sarah snorted, facing Dave with a big cake of dough in her hand, 'then I did – and I'll do it again – and what's more, you can tell her so.'

'You're very funny,' Dave sneered, and walked out. Dave was no match for Sarah in a row.

Dave went across to the barn, where the husking was being carried on by lamplight, and confided his troubles to Dad, and, in the interests of peace, suggested building a house for himself.

'Leave them alone,' Dad said. 'Don't take any notice of them; they're all the same; they'll drive you mad if you do.'

Dad didn't look upon the idea of building another house with favour. Dad never approved of ideas that cost money. And for the time being Dave took his advice.

But one evening, when loud screams issued from the house, and we all stampeded from the milking yard, and found Sarah mauling and clawing Lily, and trailing her about over the backs of chairs, matters were brought to a head.

'It's not a bit of good,' Dave moaned to Dad, after peace was restored.

'I must have a house of my own, or else I'll clear out and look for work somewhere else.'

'Well,' Dad answered slowly, 'I'll see if I can't get a bit of timber somewhere, and put you one up.' Then, realising to what length he had committed himself in the way of expenditure, he exclaimed, 'Dash the women, they're always fighting about something or other!'

After tea Dad sat on the veranda and cooled down, and ruminated for a long time. Then he called Dave and Joe together, and discussed the position with them.

'There were a house down on that old farm of Grogan's,' Dad said. 'Is that there yet?'

'Some of it's standin',' Dave drawled. And Joe remarked, with a chuckle, that he was once 'nearly putting it all in the dray and bringing it home for a calf-pen'.

'Tut! Tut! Not at all, not at all,' Dad said in disapproval. 'That were a snug little place when Grogan lived there first – forty-five year ago, believe me.'

'Forty-five year ago,' from Dave.

Joe chuckled again.

'Yes,' Dad said sententiously, 'I don't think it's any older than that. Let me see' – he made a mental calculation in the dark – 'Yes . . . no . . . yes . . . no – no, it's not more than forty-two.'

'Just about time for the sap to dry,' Joe sniggered.

'When it's pulled down and trimmed a bit with the adze, and put up again,' Dad went on enthusiastically, 'it'll look a different place. It'll look just as well as this, believe me.'

'But you'll want some new timber,' Dave put in anxiously.

'Well, yes, maybe,' Dad grunted, 'but not much, you'll find, not much. There's a lot of material in that house when you come to go over it all. I rermember it well.'

Then he said he would go with the dray in the morning, and bring the building home; and that night Dave and Lily went to bed in a happy mood, and lay awake for hours evolving and discussing plans and specifications for their new home.

E. O. Schlunke

THE ENTHUSIASTIC PRISONER
1945

Henry Holden decided to get an Italian prisoner of war after he had seen several at work on Esmond's farm. Esmond was building a shed, and it was beautiful to see how they ran to get the things he needed, how they rushed to carry anything he picked up, and how they seemed to take it for granted that they were there to do all the heavy work while the boss gave the orders.

When the captain in charge of the PWCC had a preliminary look over Henry's place he tactlessly asked him if he was an invalid; he saw so few signs of work being done and so many of neglect. He wasn't at all keen on letting Henry have a PW; he didn't think he was the type to handle them successfully, but, on the other hand, he was eager to get his 'hundred'.

When the PW arrived, Henry was decidedly disappointed with him at first sight. He did not look obliging and polite; he didn't even look like an Italian. He had a tremendous amount of fuzzy brown hair; his eyebrows were so large and dense they nearly surrounded his eyes, and thick hair grew all round his neck and jutted out of his ears. His small, bright eyes glinted sharply from among all the hair; not at all like the large, soft and servile eyes of the Italians at Esmond's. In fact he reminded Henry of a big brown bear, with his air of having great physical strength and tremendous determination. When the military truck drove away Henry had an uncomfortable feeling of having let himself in for something.

He directed Pietro to his room, and while he was settling in, tried hurriedly to work out a plan of what to do with him. There was, of course, plenty of work to do, but it wasn't so easy to start a man who didn't understand English, or know Australian farms. In a few minutes Pietro appeared.

'Worrk,' he said, briefly and determinedly.

Henry abandoned his half-formed plan to let him have the first half of the day off to get settled. Getting quite panicky, he thought of a number of jobs, only to realise he didn't have the necessary materials. In desperation he decided to repair a fence. He pointed to the fence, and to some tools and tried to explain to Pietro.

'Unnerstan, reparare,' said Pietro.

Pietro picked up the shovel and pick, and started hunting for a 'leva'. Henry soon realised that he meant a crowbar, but he couldn't remember where his was. Pietro looked at him in astonished reproval. When they started off, Pietro carrying all the heavy tools while Henry carried the wire strainer, Henry felt better, though he was sure that Esmond's men would have offered to carry the wire strainer too.

They did little good with the fence although Pietro was obviously eager to work. It really needed a lot of new posts and wires, and Henry had neither. They tightened what wires were there and braced and stayed some of the key posts in a makeshift manner. Pietro liked the wire strainer, apparently he had never seen one before and he was greatly intrigued with the way it worked.

'Very ni, very ni,' he said.

But when they were going home for dinner he glanced disapprovingly at the propped-up posts.

'No good, no good,' he said.

Henry usually had a nap after dinner, which lasted well into the afternoon if the day happened to be warm. But Pietro apparently didn't know about 'dinner hours'. He waited outside the door for a while, then knocked and said, quite politely but very firmly, 'Worrk.'

Henry went out and remembered the woodheap. It cheered him immensely. He had recently brought in a load and it would take Pietro several days to chop it up. It would be a great stand-by. Pietro could work there all the afternoon. He lay down while Pietro chopped with great vigour, but he could not sleep or even relax properly because of his problem. His wife and children, too, kept asking him questions about Pietro; they were rather awed by him.

He heard the rumble of the wheelbarrow on the veranda several times, and sounds of cut wood being tipped out. Then Pietro knocked on the door. He pointed to a great pile of wood and said, 'Sufficiente?'

'No, not sufficient,' said Henry, 'chop more.'

Pietro looked at him with a blank expression.

'No unnerstan,' he said, and before Henry could work out another way of expressing himself, he inquired, 'Sufficiente one day? Two day? Tre day?'

'Tre day,' Henry admitted reluctantly.

Pietro smiled broadly and looked surprisingly pleasant as he did so. 'Plenty sufficiente,' he said, closing the argument.

Henry went and got his hat. He could hear the wind banging a loose sheet of iron on the roof of the machinery shed. They would begin by nailing it down. But when they got on the roof Pietro discovered that half the sheets were loose. Henry gave him nails and directed him to fasten down the flapping sheets. But Pietro was hunting round for causes. He discovered that the rafters were rotting, and demonstrated it by giving one a hard hit with the hammer. It split from end to end, and a couple of sheets immediately blew off the roof.

They spent the afternoon cutting trees in the scrub and trimming them for rafters, though nothing was further from Henry's intention and inclination. He cut down a few little trees while Pietro cut a lot of big ones. Pietro always took the heavier end when they loaded the rails, but even so Henry became exhausted. Round about four o'clock he decided to go home.

'Sufficient,' he said.

Pietro consulted a diagram he had made.

'No sufficiente,' he said. 'Encora four.'

They went on working.

At tea that night Pietro met all the family. There was a flapper daughter, three younger boys, and a baby. He was particularly interested in the baby. He made some queer foreign noises at it, and to everyone's surprise it showed unmistakable signs of affection for him. He asked Mrs Holden if it was breastfed, and when she told him, in some confusion, that it was not, he wanted to know why. Then he gave her detailed and intimate directions, mainly by signs, about how to ensure an abundant flow for the next baby. The flapper daughter half smothered a lot of embarrassed giggles, and the boys nearly 'busted' trying not to laugh. Henry felt that he ought to reprimand Pietro for his indelicacy, but didn't know how he could make him understand.

The next day Henry felt stiff and sore. He decided to relax, but Pietro kept calling him on to the roof; sometimes for advice, but mostly to help him in fitting rafters which were too big to be 'poseeble solo'.

They finished re-roofing the shed by the weekend. Pietro wanted to know if they would cut some fence-posts next week to repair the fences. Henry thought of how he would suffer if he had to work on the other end of a crosscut-saw with a tireless bear like Pietro. He said, 'No, some other work.'

But he didn't like the way Pietro looked at him, so he decided to hide the crosscut-saw.

On Sunday Esmond's Italians came to visit Pietro. They must have told him all about what was going on at their place, because on Monday morning Pietro wanted to know why Henry was not preparing his soil for his crops, like Mr Esmond. Henry looked a bit guilty, then he tried to explain that he used different methods from Esmond's. Pietro was not satisfied.

'Mr Esmond good resultare? No good resultare?'

Henry had to admit that Esmond's results were good. He also had to confess that his own results were often bad.

'Provare similar Mr Esmond,' Pietro suggested enthusiastically. 'Poseeble very good oat, very good weet.'

'Tractor broken,' said Henry. He was always overwhelmed by a feeling of hopeless apathy in the autumn, and he couldn't face the strain of all the preparations necessary for his worn-out plant.

'Me look?' asked Pietro, and was off before Henry could say anything to the contrary.

Pietro had a thorough look over the tractor and scarifier. He made a list of all the new parts needed, which he laboriously translated into English with the help of his little dictionary. He explained that he was not a mechanic, but he had had a lot of experience with military vehicles. He suggested that Henry go to town and get the necessary parts, and Henry went, glad to get away from the responsibility of Pietro for an afternoon.

While Henry was away Pietro 'polished' the toolshed and the farm-yard. When Henry came home, rather late in the evening, and somewhat the worse for wine, he thought he had come to the wrong farm until Pietro came out of his room and carried his parcels for him. He was in an exalted mood and gave Pietro an orange for his services. But Pietro spoiled the effect by telling him of several things he had forgotten to bring.

At the table that night Pietro objected to Mrs Holden giving the baby honey to stop it crying.

'No good, 'oni, no good,' he said.

But she continued to exercise the lawful rights of a mother. Suddenly the baby vomited. Pietro made an angry noise, jumped up and put the honey away in the cupboard.

'No good, no good,' he said, so emphatically that she was startled and impressed.

Henry found that he couldn't tell Pietro much about overhauling farm machines. He stood by to tell him where tools, parts and materials were kept; frequently he found it easier to get them than to explain; sometimes when Pietro was held up and impatient Henry found himself running just like one of Esmond's Italians, until he remembered his dignity as a 'padrone'. They had an auspicious rain when everything was ready, and Henry's land was never worked into better condition.

The tractor ran very well. Pietro assumed a jealous control of it and appeared to be very happy on it no matter how long he worked. The arrangement suited Henry extremely well. He felt free for the first time since his prisoner arrived. He had plenty of time to turn over all the vague plans he had in his head.

When Pietro finished working the land he suggested again that they cut some fence-posts. But Henry was ready with his own plan. Pietro was to paint the house. Pietro agreed heartily; the house certainly needed painting. They went to have a good look at the walls. Not only had the paint peeled off, but much of the plaster was cracked and loose.

'No good paint,' said Pietro. 'Prima plaster.'

But the thought of all the work and expense involved in plastering horrified Henry. He said authoritatively, 'Paint sufficient.' And he got a trowel and demonstrated how the rough plaster could be smoothed off sufficiently. He handed the trowel to Pietro, who made what appeared to be a similar movement. But the result was vastly different, at least a wheelbarrow-load of plaster fell off the wall.

'Plenty similar,' he said, and knocked off another square yard with a flick of his wrist. Henry gave in.

Henry was kept very busy mixing the plaster and carrying it to Pietro. It had to be mixed in small lots and applied immediately, Pietro said, otherwise it would fall off just like the previous coat.

When it was finished Henry brought out the paint. Pietro was very interested in the 'colore'. But when he discovered that it was to be a drab, uniform stone-colour all his eagerness vanished.

'No good, no good,' he said, 'similar dirt.'

He wouldn't take the brush when Henry offered it to him.

'Brush no good,' he said. 'Troppo old.'

Henry tried the brush and had to admit it was worn out. He decided to go to town and get a new one. Pietro wanted to go too; to get his hair cut. Henry left him at the Control Centre and went to do his shopping. When he walked into the general store, where he did most of his business, he had an uneasy feeling that he was being followed. He turned and saw Pietro carrying the two big tins of stone-coloured paint. He had that brown-bear look about him which Henry hadn't liked the first time he saw him.

The manager of the hardware came up to them. He saw by the look in Henry's eye that he wasn't sure of himself, so he turned to Pietro, who appeared to know exactly what he wanted. Pietro held up the tins.

'Colore no good,' he said.

The manager remembered having advised Henry against a uniform drab colour, and immediately set out to help Pietro. He quite ignored Henry's somewhat indistinct, 'No, it's all right. I'll keep it.'

He showed Pietro a colour card and he selected a very light cream, a bright blue and a black.

'One big crema, one little blue, one little little nero,' he said.

The manager was, as he would have said, intrigued. He tried to discover what design Pietro had in mind, and Pietro demonstrated as best he could, attracting a lot of attention from other shoppers, who began to gather round. Henry became most uncomfortable.

'I won't have it at any price,' he protested, 'everyone who goes past will die laughing.'

'Ah, garn!' said a big voice from the back. 'Let him have a go. It couldn't look any worse than it's looked for the last twenty years.'

Then a couple of ladies joined in.

'How interesting!' said one. 'The Italians are so artistic, aren't they?'

The other one said, 'I remember seeing the adorable Italian cottages painted just like that; you must let us come and see it, Mr Holden.' She happened to be the wife of Henry's long-suffering mortgagee, and her word carried some weight with him. Quite a number of others voiced favourable opinions before Henry and Pietro carried out their cream, blue and black paint.

Pietro took endless pains over the painting, and all the time he was at it Henry felt resentful, despite the fact that many people came and admired it. He comforted himself by compiling a long list of heavy jobs Pietro would have to do when he was finished. He had the interpreter prepare a translation so that there would be no 'no unnerstan' business, and when at length the house was finished he gave Pietro a week's program, consisting mainly of firewood carting and post-hole digging.

But that day it rained; a splendid soaking rain, and during the night it cleared. Henry was wakened early in the morning by the roar of the tractor starting. He was puzzled and rather annoyed; Pietro was up to something. Then he realised that Pietro had taken it upon himself to make the all-important decision of the year – that the time was right to start sowing the wheat.

Henry thought with some indignation of the program he had given Pietro, but he also realised that it was much more important to get the wheat sown while the soil was moist. He lay thinking for a long time of ways in which he could reassert himself, and all the time he heard the noise of Pietro's preparations. He stayed there because he always hated the worry of working out the proportions of wheat and fertiliser, and adjusting the machines accordingly, and all the other important details necessary for a successful sowing season. When he finally went out, Pietro hurried up to him, his face aglow with enthusiasm.

'Oh, rain very nice,' he said. 'Terra very nice. Poseeble very good wheat this year, similar Mr Esmond.'

He pointed to the tractor hitched to the sowing combine and the farm cart loaded with supplies of seed, fertiliser and tractor fuel.

'After brekfus me take trattore and wheat machine. You bring carro; allora we commence before Giuseppe and Leonardo on farm Mr Esmond.'

'Okay, Pietro,' said Henry.

Rosie Scott

QUEEN OF LOVE

1989

It had never occurred to me that I would make old bones, but now that I'm here, at rest, with all the years mounted up behind me, it has turned out to be more refreshing than I ever imagined. Here I am, eighty years old, a survivor of the holocausts of this distraught century, being fed and kept warm like a baby, nodding off into my private day-dreams whenever the spirit moves me. It is more like a state of grace than anything.

There are few distractions in this friendly house of death, with its scent of daffodils and floor wax, the murmur of television in the draw-ing room where all the dears, full of mumblings from the past, are staring at the screen, stranded on their seats like old rumpled seals.

I sit in the room watching the days come and go, and find a shapely pleasure in cataloguing my past desires, going over them in my mind until I am word-perfect. I am an ancient librarian holding my dusty photographs up to the light.

I have never been the sort of woman who lived through a man, or my children for that matter; thinking my thoughts has taken up a lot of my time. The great slow tracking of my mind wheeling through the world is a happiness I share with no-one.

Even now I am still the same, but there has been one change which surprised me, although like all revelations it is quite likely I knew about it all along. The memories which keep my bones warm and make me smile are all of lovers long-dead, their beauty and the power of their loving.

People could say this was grotesque of course. In the ordinary course of events, a grandmother like myself, sitting in this expensive nursing home paid for by a loving family, would be thinking of religion, or family, or her health. With my straight back, aristocratic face, flyaway hair soft as duck down, perfumed as I am with talc and baby oil, I am no sex at all, I am simply an object of veneration to my visitors. I receive them with genuine if absent-minded love. My great-grand-children come so dutifully washed and dressed and brushed in my honour, their innocent faces overawed by the purity of age, the serenity of my surroundings. All the time, my mind circles lazily around old delights, day after day, hour after hour.

But I do not feel any shame, because to me this state of affairs is not grotesque. If the truth be known, and that is, after all, what I am most interested in at this time in my life, it would be simpler to say that I feel very privileged. Most women I know are only too happy to close their legs and hearts forever against a lifetime of men tearing into their soft flesh with or without the invitation. They spend their old age in thankful release, healing up their fearful wounds. All the love and pleasure has been burnt out of their most intimate centres. I, blessed lover that I am, still bathe in the afterglow, my papery skin is still warm from decades of well-placed caresses and consummated delights. And it seems only natural that I dwell on these past pleasures while I am slipping off into death.

Loving was not only a great delight to me always, I believe now it was the wheel that turned my life over and kept me alive all these long years. There are many other things of importance to me, but sex has always been the deep and delicious undercurrent flowing beneath my life and thoughts, an occupation as real as anything else I did.

It seems to me that few humans have done justice to the beauty of it, or even admitted its true spiritual worth, as a source of life, a miraculous rejuvenation. This is also so with love between the same sexes, blessed as it is. Hucksters, pornographers and all religions have trampled and sullied it – the word 'sex' itself, ugly, short and medical as it is, is proof of the common currency of their vinegar-thin views.

Even my favourite poet Yeats, who wrote some painfully honest poems about sex in his last years, was still ashamed and disgusted at his own late-developing raptures. Of course I am no match for the seedy greatness of those late poems, even in my thoughts, but at least there was never a time when I did not appreciate the beauty of a man, nor did I ever regret any longings or loves.

For me sex is a great richness, a transformation of every facet of existence. A trick of light, the way a man holds his head, a sudden rush of recognition, an ache for all the male beauty forever unattainable.

A dance, fleshed out by smouldering fantasies, a heartbeat of time so intense it is almost unbearable, wallowing in velvet so soft you can feel each hair brushing against your skin. Even a friendly miscalculation when all the grandeur of it suddenly goes out of kilter and the bumps and pimples of mortal flesh are laid bare to the light in one glorious comical anticlimax.

I was never a promiscuous woman, more the reverse, because there were only very few men who touched the nerve lying so close to my surfaces. But once they did there was a permanent change made somewhere in my cell-structure and that was that. It was as if each lover imprinted himself forever.

That was the miracle of it to me, the fact that a man, beautiful, moving against my skin like a wild animal, delighting me with his fine arts, could leave his trace, a permanent scent that I would carry through life.

Of course, I made false starts, watching men sigh and groan and plead under the spell of a perfumed girl who didn't know any better. But my own intelligence and meeting Mick saved me from all the fabrications of tragic romance and coy falsities in one clean blast, and the two of us looked set for eternity.

My body has always responded only to certain cues, very precise and divine indications of magic. Those qualities in men which stirred me most deeply are difficult to describe; it is like trying to dissect a butterfly. But I know them by heart.

There is nearly always brown hair, curls, an ebullience matched with grace, a face both scornful and tender, qualities of self-containment, intelligence, a dry wit, courage. A solid body with that bloom to the skin, competent hands, a touch of hardness, street wisdom. I knew that rare mixture whenever I saw it, and for all my breeding and background, it was rarely 'gentlemen' who set my heart beating. Hooligans, working men, were the ones that had that irresistible flash, that experience of life as they walked past me like warriors.

My beloved Mick had all these virtues and more, and so I was prepared to give up my class, my status, my family if need be to have him. It didn't have to come to that of course, my parents being too good as judges of character, and untainted by the curse of snobbery.

I can still see him now, the day we met. He had a strong body, hair curling down his neck, he spoke in a quiet voice. He was brown from the sun, his pants work-stained, his larrikin eyes alight when he caught sight of me. You could see he wasn't slow, his face alive with considering as he noticed my best white dress and my hair hanging down my back. The instant we met and looked at each other I wanted him in my bed. Eighteen and virgin as I was, I knew instinctively what sort of power lay in the big quiet body as he stood there in my father's yard.

In our wedding photograph we looked sly and merry and knowing, there was nothing of the shrinking violet about either of us. For all the world, as my eldest said once, as if we couldn't wait.

There was that powerful stance of his, his tender eyes brimming with vitality, and as for me, I showed none of the child-bride's usual shyness. I was smiling and every inch of me was willing. Young as we were, we were full of the pleasures of our new station.

There was nothing misleading about our innocent lust either, for we were equally matched as it turned out, although we both had our low times. The tensions and troubles that came between us were just more fuel for our night-time fires. And towards the end, when we were both more peaceful with one another, we knew, luxuriously, that even with all the joy and tumult of the world raging past us, we could always have each other.

He would come home from work with that soft bloom of dust and weariness on him, so tired he could hardly speak, but he seemed to draw sustenance from me. His eyes lit up so beautifully when he saw me that he glowed and looked startlingly alive.

I would kiss my beautiful husband, sit on his warm thigh, his delicious mouth on my neck, ride astride his knee, leaving a round of secret moisture there, glistening like a kiss. That was our private joy, the eroticism of married life, our licence for the unlimited pleasure of monogamy. While the children were sleeping like little dolls in their dark beds, mouths open, dreaming of horses galloping, we had our own supple fantasies, we were lost in our own trance.

In the dark when he was above me, his shoulders gleaming in the shadows, breath rasping on my neck as his hard warm body moved against me, his eyes closed with the sweetness of it, damp curls on his neck, smelling of clean sweat, I knew that was my mortality, my religion, the secret engine which pulled me through the world.

After he died, no-one could come near me for years. It wasn't as if I was living in purdah out of convention or necessity either, because there were plenty of suitors. It was simply a physical imperative – I could not let another man touch my skin.

When it finally happened and I met someone, he was so unsuitable that even my dear children were scandalised. I was a disgrace and an embarrassment because of course that was in the dead fifties when women sleepwalked through their days in those icy uplift bras and frilly aprons, while children lived their lives as bland as buttons with no-one to give them an underview.

Neither of us was interested in love at that time of our lives – but there was his white white skin, his decadent mouth, that sly look from under his eyelids which went straight to the hair at the back of my neck. Pat was a young adventurer, full of grace and ease in himself; he took his time over everything, shrewd, so that his lovely attentions lasted for hours.

Our fantasies meshed the day we met, he a builder's labourer in work pants and bare white chest, tattooed; me an older woman, barefoot, perfumed, scarlet nails, moving slowly with the heavy summer afternoon.

After the first time, I remember vividly how he lay back on the pillows like a lord. His eyes narrowed against the smoke of his cigarette and he gave me that lazy half-smile of total well-being. Lying there, his pale body glimmering in the shadow, looking at me with his hooded, blue Irish eyes, lovely as an angel – that was something, it was nourishment after all my days of loneliness. Our love-making was slow and creamy and relentless; they were times of intensity, drowning in the sheets in the long afternoons. He would always want more, pirate that he was, with that smile of his, his expert hands stroking me, unwilling at first, back into delirium.

When he left our town I was sad but not shattered, for unlike the breakup of many love affairs I'd seen, there were no sour memories or recriminations. There were images I kept in my mind's eye – his mouth, swollen after I'd kissed it, a certain spicy smell of male sweat, dust, apple-scented soap, the supple line of his white back as he bent over in the half-light to undress me.

And of course there was my next lover – blond, troubled, closed – infinitely attractive to women with his elegance and sombre blue eyes, an actor, very clever, always full of little calculations. He was a lost soul as well, a male siren, a cruel despot who taught all the women in his life lethal games. Our time together went smoothly as cream on the surface with the money, theatre parties, my job as tutor at the university, but all the time there was this deadly subterranean river flowing between us. I was always on the edge of drowning in it, in the aching sweetness of total submission to him, and its twin – rage at my self-annihilation.

I remember nights when I was so slippery wet he could not hold me, he called me his child, his pet, but I could not answer my mouth was so dry after our perverse games. He would whisper all his mockeries and commands softly in my ear as we made love, tell me about his other women in that deep cultured voice of his, and always, whatever he did, I was his whenever he wanted me, weeping, liquid, open in his arms.

I was his beautiful, assured woman during the day, and at nights a begging waif, his own creation, enmeshed in his ferocious needs. The voluptuousness of loving like that strung me out to an impossible pitch, and I became heartsick, a fool, my energies drained. I was a grandmother by then and could have been living in peace instead of chasing this man, undignified, my clothes too young, my face anxious at all the sugary parties we went to.

When he took up with a younger woman and began to teach her all his little scorching tricks I was sick with desire. I tried to lure him back, to compete with that lovely smiling girl, pleading with him to kiss me even when her scent was still fresh on his skin. Then one humiliating night I knew I had had enough. It was as if I closed off from this whole new frequency he'd tuned me into, and those sounds of distress, ecstasy and disgust ceased entirely.

No-one has ever talked to me about deep and private places like this in their lives; there is something too aching and ruttish about such behaviour for comfort. But I have a feeling that most people have experienced that hot shiver at some time, a sensation occasionally more delicious, certainly more terrible, than simple loving. He was a dark angel, this man, with his magnificent obsession with power and cruelty, his only means of showing love.

It would be boorish of me, not to say false, to deny his gifts, the exquisite pain and pleasure he provided and the dangerous territories he took me across, but I am glad I emerged safe, with only a few tender spots to keep me company when I have need of a little stimulant. Now that I am old I can say this about myself with just enough kindness and irony to keep it in perspective.

My second husband was pure sunshine after those dank delights. He was a giant of a fellow, huge, woolly, talented, kind – a comely man. We had no need of passion after our respective roller-coaster lifetimes. The sensual seep of our enjoyment together was more subtle, and slower, like luxuriating in a still, warm pond. I have such a loving memory of the two of us walking everywhere hand in hand. We were like those moth-eaten lions you see basking at the zoo. They are way past their prime, too experienced to make any unnecessary movement, but they are still observing the world closely from the sleepy slits of their wicked yellow eyes.

We gave each other comfort, and dignity and all the kindness we had. When he died, I believed my time was up as well, that I had had enough love to last me for the rest of my days.

Thus it is that the wheel keeps turning in our lives. It still seems strange to me that I am sitting here, an old woman, dreaming of these past loves, my limbs once so tender, now weighted down by age and infirmity.

But there is no real end to things, another discovery I have made recently. Even now sometimes I still catch myself thinking like a young girl, as I lie in my single monastic bed in the nursing home, my old heart beating strongly in my breast. I dream of pleasures that might still be, and then the power of love in me is like a fire, leaping out and lighting up the world.

Thomas   Shapcott

MARTIN FALVEY

1991

Martin Falvey was a man who had long been accustomed to order. In a disorderly century and a scattered, disorganised town that in itself was part of a new and therefore still inchoate country, he was not at all abashed. In primary school he had discovered mathematics, chess and music. Later, while his fellows were sweating for the afternoon glory and exertion of football or the sticky exertions of motorcycles and the engines of cars, Martin would be cool in the upper room of the Grammar School, at the desk that overlooked the inner quadrangle (constructed in Scottish Revival Gothic out of sandstock bricks and local stone). Martin had graduated to scientific theory and the formulations of Albert Einstein.

Martin was not without his quiddities, even as an adolescent. He kept a large glass bottle full of aniseed balls in his school satchel. He had an orderly but distinctly eccentric interest in collecting witchetty grubs. It might be thought that one witchetty grub is very like the–ext. Not so, Martin would have hastened to assure you. Not only the specimens themselves, but documentation and even tangible evidence of their habitat was an essential component of his researches, and of his collection. In his bedroom he had a wall of shoe-boxes, each tabulated. Inside them were his witchetty grubs, together with, variously, rotted tree trunks or limbs (site details provided in Martin's neat handwriting), composted dungheaps, earth shelters in rainforest edges, any place where the grub might be found. Although witchetty grubs have one celebrated virtue – they are known to be a delicious nutty food, much favoured by Aborigines and bush-tucker men – Martin was more concerned with matters of discipline and documentation. He watched their life cycle intimately, and kept a dossier and timetables.

At university, Martin was already wise in imposing order upon himself and his environment. He mildly chastised his tutors, he had laboratory assistants in fear and trembling. Martin's gentle gaze once reduced the professor of Organic Chemistry to a complete revision of his previous theories, a revision equally influenced by Martin's solemn documentation of genetic structures using an obscure rainforest parasite as specimen. Martin was expected to take up a scholarship to Aberdeen University, the acknowledged centre of Martin's chosen field, scientific research into rainforest ecology.

Instead, he joined the Public Service.

Although nothing had prepared Martin for the fantasy of a true bureaucracy, yet in a sense everything had.

To begin with, he arranged his desk systematically. His In-tray was replaced with a three-tier model, marked In, Inner, Innermost. He became feared as a generator of memos. He kept every scrap of paper, particularly notes scribbled by officers senior to him; these were filed punctiliously under name, not subject. He had himself elected as staff representative at management meetings. The list of agenda items began to run to two pages. He became a master at 'business arising'. Very soon he was in regular consultation with the chair, initially to advise him on the order of agenda items; later to instruct him. He developed a hard line in the cutting remark.

Martin was not liked, he recognised. He was fawned upon by under-lings. He was monarch of the morning tea break. Life, on the whole, seemed pretty good. The office replaced the laboratory as centre of operations.

Then Rosamund appeared.

Martin had evolved a particularly hard line with women. He knew his Sexual Harassment Code to a fine point, and always stopped a millimetre short of technical breach. He used the expression 'my dear' indiscriminately to both genders, and in a way designed to freeze the blood. After reducing a victim to blank despair or throttled rage, he would defuse the situation with something from his card-file of jokes and limericks, told with a 'me and thee' confidentiality, and if the scenario was right, with a firm, friendly grip of the arm or shoulder. Martin knew his position was inviolable.

Rosamund changed all that.

To begin with, her qualifications were higher. She used the phone, and never sent notes or memos. She worked through morning tea break and in the afternoon. Most threatening of all, she found Martin

Falvey a fascinating object of study. She could not get enough of him.

Rosamund was also very beautiful, in an offbeat fashion: she was tall (taller than Martin), she had Irish green eyes, unimaginably blue-white skin, and a carefully roughened-up tangle of carroty red hair. She had no eyebrows, and at first glance appeared to have been dragged from some forest pool, something green-shaded and mysterious. Rosamund had a voice soft as rainwater, and as persistent. She charmed men out of all caution. She expected Martin to be one of them.

Martin knew she was not frivolous. After the first shock (he realised he had been grinning foolishly all day), he understood he had to initiate different strategies.

One morning he brought a shoe-box with his witchetty grubs in it. The secretaries were curious, then recoiled. One of his underlings was instructed to demonstrate the techniques of witchetty grub ingestion. With uncharacteristic alacrity he escaped to the toilet. Rosamund was fascinated.

'I've read so much about these,' she murmured, then devoured the lot.

Martin was speechless. He watched her dusting down her fingers. He caught sight of the delicate tip of her tongue to her lips. The thought went through his mind: now I know what women feel like when they have been raped. He loved his witchetty grubs, he had only been joking.

'But they taste marvellous. Do you breed them commercially?' she pondered, as it were, half aloud.

Martin felt protective. 'I have twenty-four boxes,' he had to affirm, for the sake of precision and to show he was no amateur. 'You are the first person to have eaten one.' She raised her non-eyebrows. 'One of mine,' he corrected.

'Why?' she asked. 'I recommend them.'

He felt he should almost thank her, but instead he said, 'I study them. For ten years I have been undertaking a process of selective breeding. Smaller heads, bigger, fatter bums!'

The secretaries tittered. They had been preparing to flee. Martin's face was flushed.

'Fascinating,' Rosamund murmured. 'This I must see.' And he knew he was well and truly in for it.

No-one had ever been allowed into his tiny flat. Martin knew better than to allow the amateur semioticians in his community access to whatever tell-tale signs might reveal vulnerability, enthusiasm, individuality or address. His wearing apparel at work was conspicuously inconspicuous. His haircut, regular. He was as aware of the dangers of too-polished shoes, as of sneakers or (horrors) suede. So with his flat.

When Rosamund called around to see him the next Saturday afternoon (the exact address, even phone number, were ridiculously easy to track down), she was standing in his small living room before Martin fully realised her determination.

That murmuring voice cloaked a more than usually agile body, a body made for swimming through water, circling and flashing its tail and fins, here and not here almost before you looked. Except that Rosamund was here and remained here, in his front room, at two o'clock this Saturday afternoon while Martin still had his Electrolux vacuum cleaner out and an apron around his tidy waist.

Martin knew he had a further vulnerability. He had guarded it severely but even so it was something that constantly endangered his credibility and deflected his ambition in the eyes of others. Martin, in appearance, looked like the young Cary Grant.

He knew that his father, in his mid-thirties, had been constantly required to show proof of age whenever he entered a hotel – which was not often, Martin was always pleased to add when the anecdote was produced for the edification of Doubting Thomases.

Good looks are a burden for the serious minded, Martin knew, though they could be used in gaining minor advances. Martin had no wish to be taken up as a 'young protégé' by some high-ranking senior. He thought of himself as a 'young prodigy'.

He longed for the day when he would look hard, intense and serious. In his bedroom he kept a framed photograph of Gustav Mahler, the one revealing the enormous brow and the noble profile. Martin knew that Mahler, as a brilliant and ambitious young conductor in Budapest, was a boyish-looking hero. Why had Hollywood trivialised everything? Who thought the word 'hero' any more? His mother had said, 'Well, here's my little hero!' to him as a child. It meant everything. These days, it meant only a cynical rebuke, an ironic scythe in the tall poppy field.

Martin had no doubt he had heroic potential: dedication, application, intelligence. No matter what the Harkness or the Fulbright or the Rhodes Scholarship people thought, this much was beyond question. He suspected dishonest referees, or the enemies that congregate to foul one's best efforts – like the scorn finally bestowed on his witchetty grub thesis. He knew he lacked the ability to ingratiate himself. This was where the Cary Grant likeness was truly galling. That arch (*very* arch) ingratiator!

The problem, he knew, was expectation. Everyone expected a Cary Grant out of him. Even his mother eventually succumbed to the disease and he had ruthless delight in demonstrating himself a surly Marlon Brando in her kitchen.

At work, he had been initially furious because of the Cary Grant clubmanship and the fatuousness of people's expectations. Later, they had learned as perhaps Cary Grant's acquaintances had learned, the film image is only a projection of light and shade. Humans are something different, even their blood turns into a destructive acid once the heart stops. Humans are infinitely corrosive.

Rosamund, standing in his apartment with every expectation of being charmed by the Cary Grant boy in him, would be severely tested.

He had learned, of course, the strategies of expectation and discomfort his stereotyped good looks could be applied to.

'You've caught me out,' he said, meaning to disarm her before the rout. 'But here you find me. This is the plain fact of me. That's if you're looking for evidence, and not intuitions.' Martin was not without guile. He re-tied the knot in his apron as a clove-hitch. 'I can only offer lemongrass tea,' he added.

Rosamund sat down. The untenanted furniture (Martin had a brilliant eye for major garbage clean-up days in his suburb) became instantly a friendly centre for confidences. Martin had never realised the cosiness of this room. He spent his spare time either in bed cogitating, plotting, or plummeting into sleep, or in his study. There his computer referred him to delicious self-referential problems. His three current obsessions were all-consuming when he sat at his computer. The witchetty grub 'solution'. The grid of public service strategies (he regarded this problem as a simple card-game). And his endless solitary games of chess.

'Martin,' it was the first time Rosamund had used his given name, 'Martin, you're so delicious I could eat you up.' Her voice eddied around him like mossy streams but he was instantly reminded of her tongue as it had deftly groomed her lips after her witchetty grub feast. 'And of course you must have *known* my craving for lemongrass. With you nothing is fortuitous.' She smiled and he had to keep himself from grinning in return. His grin was the real disaster, Hollywood tinsel.

'Do you play chess?' He could see she had absorbed every inch of the room in her innocuous glance. Instantly he knew he had made a tactical error. She was already heading for the computer room. He had left the door ajar.

He thought of the computer virus, would her mere presence implant it and set it gobbling up his precious storage systems? Not the witchetty file; oh not that, please!

She stopped at the very door. 'Did you know I am into funnelwebs?' she murmured like the very silk of new-spun gossamer, like the distant buzz of drowsy summer wasps. 'I have just completed my PhD.'

Martin saw her working towards him; he nervously stroked his hair as if a spider had scuttled across his scalp. He had an old interest in arachnids, but could always be taken by surprise.

'As a child I used to keep huntsman spiders, the family *Sparassidae*. My favourite ruse was to place one of my pets inside a matchbox and gently allow the tail of the abdomen out. Then I would gently squeeze the box tighter. It would produce its silk. Fascinating. I was always charmed by that.'

Her fingers flittered in front of her, as if spinning.

'But huntsmen are really huntswomen. The male is generally quite insignificant. Not like the truly splendid *Atrax formidabilis*, the funnel-web. There we have a battle of equals. Equal size, equal strength, equal venom. When he approaches her web the male must make the right signals. And when he reaches her he must be quick; he must press the female's jaws apart with his front legs, in order to mate. Otherwise her love-bite would be more than the poetic *death* of the medieval court love-poets.' Her laugh was tiny, a whistle of breath through empty shells. 'I got to love my funnelwebs, too. I almost regret achieving that PhD.'

'And do you still have your . . . specimens?'

'I knew you would ask me that.' She reached out her hand and led him back to his group of ill-assorted chairs. He did not resist. 'I knew you would understand. One does grow attached to something that has offered so deep, so intense a study. When you brought in your witchetty grubs I had a moment of revelation. About you. So gentle, so industrious, so introverted. Mmmm, and so tasty.'

Was she mocking him? Martin knew he must give nothing away. 'You, my dear, were a cat. So greedy.'

'You did ask me.'

'So greedy and so thorough. I knew, then, it would be a fight to the death.'

'It's hardly a battle,' she whispered. 'Shall I help you with the lemongrass tea?'

Three hours later as she stroked her long sheathed paws along his limbs and murmured 'Relax, Martin, relax', Rosamund also began to muse upon her PhD research. 'Funnelweb toxin attacks the nervous system directly. The site of action of the toxin is probably not on the main cell body of the nerve but at the junction between the end of the nerve axon and the muscle or gland cells. The effect of the toxin is to release abnormal amounts of acetylcholine and noradrenaline.'

'I am supposed to be listening?' Martin also murmured, not a normal tone with him.

'What is really interesting is that it is a sort of flooding, an overplus. We die by excess. Death by funnelweb is so poetic.'

'Witchetty grubs are a force on the side of life. They convert waste, rubbish and compost to high nutrients.'

'Only man and monkeys are susceptible to the bite of funnelwebs. Only the primates.'

'The witchetty grub is a perfectly harmless creature.'

'But it is puzzling. There is no reason to suppose that there is any fundamental difference between the invertebrate and the vertebrate nervous systems. There is no toxic effect in rats, mice, guinea pigs, cats or even rabbits. I know; I've tried.'

'Witchetty grubs have a soft, affectionate nature.'

She reared back.

'Rot! You do not know passion!'

It was obvious Martin would have to prove his mastery of the subject. He went in like a man.

'The hunting wasp was what I used to terminate my spiders,' Rosamund remarked, as they washed up in the kitchen. 'It is quite determined, it will even follow the spider down into the web, to sting it and then lay its eggs. The spider becomes a supermarket for the larvae.'

Martin noted the new strength in her voice. Had he given her something she had been starved for? He wondered. Certainly, for himself, there was a glow. He had ventured into the web and had made the right signals. She had been fairly conquered.

He contemplated whether to show her his collection of witchetty grubs. Or not? He smiled up at her with a sort of disarming self-protection, yes very much like Cary Grant.

Christina Stead

GUEST OF THE REDSHIELDS
1934

On the second of January, when I was wondering how I should stave off my creditors on the fifteenth, Mr James Redshield visited me and acquainted himself with my home. It is a studio on the eighth floor, furnished with casement-cloth curtains, grass mats, a typewriter, a chair, a stove, and a lawyer's filing cabinet. Shortly after, I was invited to the castle of the Redshields for the weekend. In the afternoon we rode, with a small party, through the beech and chestnut forest, where deer abound, and over the pastures of the estate. The weather was showery, with gleams of sunshine; and so that we should not be encumbered with waterproofs, our host ordered out two small donkey-carts, which followed us at a strategic distance, with rugs, mackintoshes, galoshes and umbrellas. Outriders, discreetly passing behind distant clumps of trees, warned off picnickers, poachers and billposters; with them, a small band of waiters carried provisions hot and cold, which were prepared for us in a small clearing, when the sun shone, around four o'clock. A small cloud driving over the scene caused a band of footmen in livery to rise modestly from behind bushes and hold in readiness umbrellas and a waterproof canopy to cover the trestle tables. Our ride terminated and we encountered no untoward accident.

After a peaceful evening with my cultivated hosts, I retired to my room, one large and compendious. The curtains and wall covering were of the same silk and same design. When the door was closed I found myself in a floral bower, mossy and perfumed. In a cabinet at my bedside was an exhaustive collection of cigarettes of the strength and provenance I am used to. A bookcase contained the English poets bound in shagrin, the French poets in morocco, the Arabian Nights, with augmentations, in oasis goat, a private edition of the journals of the most famous prose-writers and poets in parchment, and the secret annals of the Papacy, the Quai d'Orsay, Scotland Yard and the lost archives of Gortchakov bound in sharkskin. A universal dictionary, a rhyming dictionary, a thesaurus, an illustrated bestiary, inks of various colours and consistencies, pencils of all hardnesses, penhandles of many shapes, and pens of steel, quill and gold, were all fitted into a combination lectern and writing desk, which held also a dictaphone, an improved pantograph for writing by hand, and a stenotype machine. The modern poet could desire no more.

A small handbook on the table explained that by pressing buttons in the entry I could change the wallpaper and curtains, or cause a series of spot, flood, and footlights to play, so that the aspect, perspective and size of the room would alter entirely. If I wished, the walls would slide back, leaving me enclosed in a pavilion of glass, transparent from within but not from without, so that I might ruminate in privacy on the rich and rolling demesne.

In a small glass-and-metal bar, fruits, soft and alcoholic drinks, coffee and mineral waters, cakes and comfits, bromides and sedatives, and bouillons in hot flasks stayed to comfort the wakeful guest. But I will not attempt to indicate the infinite advantages of this room: time can destroy but cannot compass them.

I sat in an easychair with adjustable back and foot and placed one dangling foot on a small brass knob planted in the dais on which the bed stood. The platform immediately rose and the bed, all in a moment, sank into the ceiling without a trace, while the floor, perfectly carpeted and unencumbered, permitted me to stretch my legs, when I felt kinaesthetic. On reading in the book of directions that the walls were soundproof, I took up a violin which lay on a table of calamander wood and silver, and began to play the Chaconne of Bach. A moment after finishing, I heard a light tap, which, I imagined, was on the shutters. I loosened these, but only the tempered wind was there. I looked forth. A rolled-up ladder was attached to the balcony, and at a careless tap of my cigarette, it unwound and invited me to descend directly into the park. The full but cloudy moon shone irregularly on the cockscombed glades, rounded knolls, ideal vistas, terraces and wildernesses sweetly artificed, which appeared momently along the serpentine paths; and here fountains, a well of dark sound, a jet of snow, and there watercourses, dulcet with pools, resonant with pebbles, with flute and lyre, descanted in the woods. In an hour I returned, wound up my ladder, closed the shutters and thought of sleeping.

I had begun to undress, meditating lazily, when again I heard a soft rapping, louder than before. 'Surely,' said I, 'that is something within the wall, a click-beetle, or death-watch, a rat running over the beams, the hot-water pipes vibrating.' But I said: 'Come in.'

A maître d'hôtel immediately entered the room through an invisible door in the wall, served by a secret passage. This mode of access was to avoid the embarrassment a guest feels at hearing a *passe-partout* turned in his lock: moreover, since the passage was overheated, aliments could be conveyed along it without turning cold. The man had a silver-backed tablet in his hand, and, addressing me with a mathematically modulated courtesy, he asked if I would take anything on waking in the morning, and whether it should be tea, coffee, cocoa, or some other thing I might suggest. I said I would take tea.

'Ceylon, China, Russian or Indian tea?' he asked delicately, with pencil poised.

'China tea,' said I.

'Black or green?' he asked.

'Black,' said I.

'And of what flavour: Pekoe, Orange Pekoe, Congou, Oolong, Soo-chong, Pekoe-Soochong, Poochong or Bohea?'

'My mother liked Soochong,' said I.

'With, or without, an admixture of dried tea-flowers, or jasmine flowers?' he continued.

Said I: 'With jasmine flowers.'

'Now may I trouble you,' he said politely, 'to know whether you like it hot or cold, and with or without lemon, or milk or cream, and sugar?'

'With milk and sugar.'

'As to the milk,' said he, 'will you have whole milk, skim milk, condensed milk, buttermilk, cream or whey?'

'Whole milk,' I said, much taken aback.

'Should it be, sir,' he said, 'from the Guernsey or the Jersey herd?'

'Guernsey,' I cried.

'Then as to the sugar,' he said, 'will you have cane sugar (white or brown), beet sugar, palm, maple or sorghum sugar?'

And when I replied: 'White cane', he inclined and inquired: 'From Cuba, the Philippines, Queensland or Natal?'

'Cuba, then,' I said, thinking that no more discrimination could be required, even of a guest of the Redshields.

Sensing my fatigue, he asked softly: 'May I suggest the Province of Camaguey?'

'Even so.'

'Good, and as to form, loaf, granulated, crystallised, or soft?' he asked; and I replied: 'Loaf!'

'Now sir,' he said, in a firmer tone, 'what will you eat?' In haste I replied, ere he could begin his inexorable enumeration: 'Bread and butter.' But the words had not left my mouth before his ingeniously insinuating vocables were upon me with, Wheaten bread, corn, oats, barley or rye bread, gluten or protein bread, and if wheaten, as he took the liberty to suppose, whether that made from spring patent (high protein), ordinary spring patents, clears (first spring), soft winter straights, hard winter straights, hard winter patents or hard winter clears, and whether new baked, or old, hot or cold, and whether crumb or crust, and in what form, whether Danish, Swedish, German, French or English (for example), and, my choice being made, whether aërated or salt-rising bread, and in what shape, plain or fancy, tin, cottage, twist, roll or crescent?

But now I arose quietly from my thrice-sprung seat and said in a soft voice: 'Nothing it is to me, if maître d'hôtel you be, or fiend or dream, or the three: but take my word, I am only a poet, and I cannot cope with the verbal resources of your universal larder. Let me only not starve! Thank you, good night!'

At these words, the butler, flitting, gave a soft submissive smile, like one, too courteous, that has not been well understood: he bowed himself to the wall and suddenly disappeared. I shut my eyes and drew a bottle at random from the automatic bar, and soon after falling asleep, dreamed I saw Gargantua pouring from an ever-running bottle the active ferments of a monstrous digestion.

You can well imagine that when I reached home again, and my mother asked me: 'Well, did you eat well at the Redshields'? At least, I suppose they have pure food, if their servants are not thieves', I was in a position to rejoice her heart.

Dal Stivens

THE MAN WHO BOWLED
VICTOR TRUMPER
1945

'Ever hear how I bowled Victor Trumper for a duck?' he asked.

'No,' I said.

'He was a beautiful bat,' he said. 'He had wrists like steel and he moved like a panther. The ball sped from his bat as though fired by a cannon.'

The three of us were sitting on the veranda of the pub at Yerranderie in the Burragorang Valley in the late afternoon. The sun fell full on the fourteen-hundred-foot sandstone cliff behind us but the rest of the valley was already dark. A road ran past the pub and the wheel-tracks were eighteen inches deep in the hard summer-baked road.

'There was a batsman for you,' he said.

He was a big fat man with a chin like a cucumber. He had worked in the silver mines at Yerranderie. The last had closed in 1928 and for a time he had worked in the coal mines further up the valley and then had retired on a pension and a half an inch of good lung left.

'Dust in my lungs,' he said. 'All my own fault. The money was good. Do you know, if I tried to run a hundred yards I'd drop dead.'

The second man was another retired miner but he had all his lungs. He had a broken nose and had lost the forefinger and thumb of his right hand.

Before they became miners, they said, they had tried their hand at many jobs in the bush.

'Ever hear how I fought Les Darcy?' the big fat man asked.

'No,' I said.

'He was the best fighter we have ever had in Australia. He was poetry in action. He had a left that moved like quicksilver.'

'He was a great fighter,' I said.

'He was like a Greek god,' said the fat man reverently.

We sat watching the sun go down. Just before it dipped down beside the mountain it got larger and we could look straight at it. In no time it had gone.

'Ever hear how I got Victor Trumper?'

'No,' I said. 'Where did it happen?'

'It was in a match up at Bourke. Tibby Cotter was in the same team. There was a man for you. His fastest ball was like a thunderbolt. He was a bowler and a half.'

'Yes,' I said.

'You could hardly see the ball after it left his hand. They put two lots of matting down when he came to Bourke so he wouldn't kill anyone.'

'I never saw him,' I said, 'but my father says he was very fast.'

'Fast!' says the fat man. 'He was so fast you never knew anything until you heard your wicket crash. In Bourke he split seven stumps and we had to borrow the school kids' set.'

It got cold and we went into the bar and ordered three rums which we drank with milk. The miner who had all his lungs said:

'I saw Tibby Cotter at the Sydney Cricket Ground and the English were scared of him.'

'He was like a tiger as he bounded up to bowl,' said the big fat man.

'He had even Ranji bluffed,' said the other miner. 'Indians have special eyesight but it wasn't enough to play Tibby.'

We all drank together and ordered again. It was my shout.

'Ever hear about the time I fought Les Darcy?' the big fat man asked me.

'No,' I said.

'There wasn't a man in his weight to touch him,' said the miner who had all his lungs. 'When he moved his arm you could see the muscles ripple across his back.'

'When he hit them you could hear the crack in the back row of the Stadium,' said the fat man.

'They poisoned him in America,' said the other miner.

'Never gave him a chance,' said the fat man.

'Poisoned him like a dog,' said the other.

'It was the only way they could beat him,' said the fat man. 'There wasn't a man at his weight that could live in the same ring as Les Darcy.'

The barmaid filled our glasses up again and we drank a silent toast. Two men came in. One was carrying a hurricane lantern. The fat man said the two men always came in at night for a drink and that the tall man in the raincoat was the caretaker at one of the derelict mines.

'Ever hear about the kelpie bitch I had once?' said the fat man. 'She was as intelligent and wide awake as you are. She almost talked. It was when I was droving.'

The fat miner paid this time.

'There isn't a dog in the bush to touch a kelpie for brains,' said the miner with the broken nose.

'Kelpies can do almost anything but talk,' said the fat man.

'Yes,' I said. 'I have never had one but I have heard my father talk of one that was wonderful for working sheep.'

'All kelpies are beautiful to watch working sheep but the best was a little bitch I had at Bourke,' said the fat man. 'Ever hear how I bowled Victor Trumper for a duck?'

'No,' I said. 'But what about this kelpie?'

'I could have got forty quid for her any time for the asking,' said the fat miner. 'I could talk about her all day. Ever hear about the time I forgot the milk for her pups? Sold each of the pups later for a tenner.'

'You can always get a tenner for a good kelpie pup,' said the miner who had all his lungs.

'What happened when you forgot the pups' milk?' I said.

'It was in the bucket,' the fat miner said, 'and the pups couldn't reach it. I went into the kitchen and the bitch was dipping her tail in the milk bucket and then lowering it to the pups. You can believe that or not, as you like.'

'I believe you,' I said.

'I don't,' said the other miner.

'What, you don't believe me!' cried the fat miner, turning to the other. 'Don't you believe I bowled Victor Trumper for a duck? Don't you believe I fought Les Darcy? Don't you believe a kelpie could do that?'

'I believe you bowled Victor Trumper for a duck,' said the other. 'I believe you fought Les Darcy. I believe a kelpie would do that.'

The fat miner said: 'You had me worried for a minute. I thought you didn't believe I had a kelpie like that.'

'That's it,' said the miner who had all his lungs. 'I don't believe you had a kelpie like that.'

'You tell me who had a kelpie like that if I didn't,' the fat miner said.

'I'll tell you,' said the miner with the broken nose. 'You never had a kelpie like that but I did. You've heard me talk about that little bitch many times.'

They started getting mad with each other then so I said:

'How did you get Victor Trumper for a duck?'

'There was a batsman for you,' said the fat man. 'He used a bat like a sword and he danced down the wicket like a panther.'

Kylie Tennant

LADY WEARE AND THE BODHISATTVA
1969

On any flight between Sydney and Melbourne there would be at least one Australian woman exactly like Lady Weare. She was half a stone overweight, and her knitted woollen suit, which she wore because she expected Melbourne to be cold, did nothing for her figure. Her hair was going grey and she couldn't waste time at the hairdresser's. Her husband and children loved her anyway. Her immovable face, which made her look like Queen Victoria, was more haughty than usual because her new shoes were giving her hell. She had bought them yesterday especially for this trip and they were too tight. She would continue to wear them because they were expensive and elegant. They exactly matched her off-white handbag. She also carried a shabby brief-case full of papers which she needed for her speech at the conference in Melbourne, and other papers for the committee meeting in Adelaide.

The briefcase didn't match anything except Lady Weare who was worn with a lifetime of work. It was as much part of her personality as the glasses she wore when she was reading, something indispensable which must not be mislaid.

The passengers tramped aboard the plane into an atmosphere something like plunging into a warm feather pillow. They looked about them as their ancestors must have done when transported, a look of bravado mixed with caution and the dreadful knowledge that they would be sitting next to strangers and might be expected to speak to them. Lady Weare took her seat and gave her companion an icy glance which crossed one even more icy. The man buried himself in his paper. Lady Weare took out a clip of statistics from her briefcase and bent her head over them. Shutting her eyes as the plane prepared to take off she ran through her accustomed prayers. She had been on so many flights she couldn't remember them all and this was only a bus run. But she prayed nevertheless that if anything happened someone would look after Jim and the children. She then went on to pray from force of habit for the long list of friends, connections and some undesirable characters who needed help. They would have been very surprised to know this praying was going on. Others she prayed for from old affection's sake. Lady Weare prayed the way other women knitted. She filled in odd moments and kept herself busy. She did not pray for herself because that might have been undignified.

She merely hoped that whatever hellish thing Melbourne had in store she might meet it without failing. She never refused to go to Melbourne, but it was her hoodoo city, a black jinx. Every time she went there something appalling happened, some bad luck, some disaster. She had gone to work in Melbourne when she was eighteen and suffered every humiliation and misery imaginable for someone young and poor. Now that she was old and rich Melbourne still lay in wait for her like a trap. On one visit, a year ago, she had stayed there for a week and congratulated herself that nothing had happened. But she reached the airport to come home to find that fog prevented her plane from leaving. The scene at the airport became more and more crazy – thickened with noise, crying children, crowds milling desperately as planes piled up. Lady Weare was there for six hours trying to get away and being met by rudeness; at last like a refugee refusing to struggle, sitting in despair, then listening to the unintelligible roar of the loudspeaker, realising finally that she was being called.

And what about the time she had been lost in a strange suburb after midnight and all the houses were dark; there was no-one to tell her the way? And the other time when the hotel made a mistake in her booking and she could not even find any of her friends and was given a couch in a stranger's living room? Other people might find Melbourne charming. To Lady Weare it was a disaster city. But she never refused to go there; that would be to admit a failure of nerve.

She eased her feet out of the tight shoes. The man next to her stirred and turned his flinty, suspicious face towards her. 'Excuse me,' he said. 'Aren't you Jill Weare? We met at the Amorys'. Did you ever find out what happened to Ernest?'

His face split into a smile so friendly that Lady Weare immediately stopped looking like Queen Victoria and became Jill Weare. They talked warmly and almost excitedly all the way to Melbourne because they were interested in the same committees. Lady Weare forgot she was going to her hoodoo city until she came down from the plane into the middle of a heatwave wearing a woollen suit.

'Lovely weather it's been for the Festival.' The driver of the government car thought he might as well be nice to the old bag, because she might be important if a car was sent to meet her. 'The whole fortnight it's been like this, sunshiny and glad to be alive.'

Lady Weare said, 'I am willing to place a small bet that tomorrow it will be raining heavily.'

'Ah, don't say that.' The driver was of a cheerfulness to match the weather. 'Why would that be, then?'

'I am here,' Lady Weare said sardonically. 'It never fails.'

'From Sydney then?' The driver nodded understandingly. He knew about Sydney people.

The house where Lady Weare was to stay for the two nights of her visit was old and had a friendly garden. The sunlight came through windows as though into a Dutch painting. Apples in baskets, pears in baskets, were lying on the marble table by the back door. The terrace had a grapevine just losing its leaves. Her host and hostess, when she had changed into summer clothing, introduced her to friends who came fluttering in; the wine cellar and the Western Australian native plants; and the children of the doctor who lived next door. There was a Persian cat and an old mastiff. When evening came and they all drove into the city in the bigger of the two cars, Lady Weare's host even found a place to park outside the restaurant where they dined before the conference.

The evening was a great success and on the way home, in the warm caressing night with the lights velvety and flowerlike, they laughed as though they were young and careless. As they sat in the kitchen having a last drink together Lady Weare's hostess exclaimed that it was raining.

In the morning, the Melbourne Lady Weare had known, the Melbourne of misery and wretchedness, was weeping with the grey skies that wept as though the rain was a loss to them. Lady Weare spent the morning transacting business for her husband. She felt gay – relieved – what could happen? She was to lunch with a professor at the University, who brought two friends to meet her. They asked what she was doing that afternoon. She told them she would be leaving early next morning for Adelaide, but that afternoon was for enjoyment. 'I thought I would seize the chance to go to the Art Centre. My daughter will be quite disgusted if I don't see it.' She assured them that she was quite capable of finding her way by tram across the city, and they drove her to a tramstop.

The rain was now being discharged as a vicious barrage, missing nothing. Lady Weare felt quite cheerful in her raincoat and knitted suit. Her feet were hurting her, the rain splattered into the tramcar. Well, if this was all there was to Melbourne this time, it was quite bearable. The Art Centre amused her with its neo-Aztec heaviness. There was nothing pleasanter than walking – even with aching feet – around an art gallery by yourself. You could stop to examine something you liked and were not hurried on to look at something you didn't want to see.

Lady Weare decided she would look at the Eastern art. You couldn't look at everything. She had never appreciated the Hindu convention – as simple really as comic-strip balloons – whereby gods with as many arms as a spider sat in the middle of this halo of limbs. It reminded her of the Italian picture of a man walking his dog and the dog had a whole blur of legs. What was the word? – 'gimmicky'.

She strolled from one magnificent scroll painting to the next. They were old, faded, brown, with intimate details of houses appearing when you looked closely. And strolling thus, dignified and not thinking about anything in particular except the pain in her feet, Lady Weare with her catalogue and her handbag, her cream-coloured raincoat, her glasses – for looking at the details closely – her sensible cloth turban – for rain, Melbourne rain – came upon the Bodhisattva.

She had noticed a number of these female Bodhisattva figures in the Asiatic paintings she had been studying. What these spirit-women were doing besides being decorative she had not the slightest idea. They posed around the edges of whatever heavenly or religious action was going on, representing some principle, perhaps. She would never know. But Lady Weare's Bodhisattva was quite different. A bronze statue about life-size, she came writhing up like a flame of goddess, dancing-girl, narrow-waisted, all dark energy.

Lady Weare peered at the Bodhisattva's face under its curved headdress. The eyelids were tilted, the narrow curved mouth was tilted in a smile at once menacing and unearthly. Perhaps she was representing some principle, but the hands that were holding a hammer and gong looked like just a beautiful woman's hands. Lady Weare felt drawn towards the Bodhisattva. Here was the embodiment, she felt, of all that she was not. This Bodhisattva had never sat on a committee or chaired one. She would not be worried or elated or try too hard.

Lady Weare admired the Bodhisattva a little wistfully and walked away. She walked back. She gazed intently at the figure of the spiritual being. Something was trying to get through to her. She looked again more closely. The clenched hand of the figure showed a worn place where people had touched it on the bronze knuckles. There were notices asking people not to touch anything. Nevertheless Lady Weare cautiously put out her ungloved hand and touched the hand of the Bodhisattva. She felt that the Bodhisattva would like that. It might make her feel, in this strange place, that she was receiving the deference to which she was accustomed.

Touching that worn bronze was like touching one of those electric machines in a penny arcade. A current of force prickled through Lady Weare so astonishingly that she touched the hand again to make sure. Then she hurried away – rather shaken. She found herself gazing at some Papuan deathmasks. Upstairs, the day darkened around her as she looked at a Raising of Lazarus and then a Vision of Hell. Even the portraits looked very dead. I must go, she thought desperately, beginning to be afraid. But she hesitated, stumbled on with those painful feet more excruciating now, until at last, exhausted, she found herself outside in the rain.

Opposite the Art Centre, beyond three streams of traffic, trams were arriving and departing almost empty at a strip of grass, while outside the Art Centre a group of people waited to run across to the trams, looking for a break in the line of cars.

If I were not so faint-hearted, Lady Weare thought, I would take a chance – dash across. The woman beside her took a break in the traffic and darted forward, and Lady Weare hesitated, almost went with her. The woman was about her age, had the same cream-coloured raincoat. Her grey hair was showing under just such a head covering as Lady Weare wore. If *she* could do it, Lady Weare thought, looking up the rushing traffic for the next break, can't I?

There was an exclamation from someone in the group and a thud. Lady Weare turned back to see the woman's handbag – so exactly like her own – lying in the wet roadway. The woman herself – where was she? Lady Weare looked in the wrong place because the woman had been flung forward by the car that had hit her such a long way beyond her handbag. Lady Weare felt a dreadful sinking. The traffic was still flashing past. No-one stopped. She could not get across the road. Finally she managed to struggle over and ran towards the woman who was lying in the rain and the dirt.

'Don't touch her!' a man ordered. He was standing sternly, saying nothing, with a group forming a kind of defensive ring. They had their lips tight shut, they had sent someone for an ambulance, they were waiting for the police, they were keeping off inquisitive people, doing 'the right things'.

The woman had her hand flung out, her fingers were clenched. Lady Weare wanted very much to take that hand in her own. Where the woman's face had scraped the road it was dirty and broken. As Lady Weare stooped down, the man said again, 'Don't touch her,' quite threateningly. The outflung hand shivered a little like the wing of a frightened bird. Then the fingers opened, stiffened, lay limp.

Lady Weare, under the hostility of the men from the car that had smashed into the woman, turned away. When she sat in the tram going home the hand of the woman kept quivering and then lying still. Around Lady Weare the kind of squalor that Melbourne provided especially for her darkened the dirty carriage. People with faces that are only seen in nightmares, mowed and leered at each other, read newspapers and smoked filthy stubs of tobacco. The floor was littered with repulsive garbage. An empty beer can clattered across the carriage. The colours ranged from deep soot to mid-mud. The landscape outside the windows could have been limbo.

The charming house, her warm friends, welcomed her. 'I saw an accident,' was all she told her hostess. 'It gave me rather a shock.' That night her host walked into the sharp corner of a wardrobe and was knocked unconscious. He was not badly hurt, but he lay on the floor with his hand flung out.

Next morning as she walked towards the plane for Adelaide, her rather chilly face set in its Queen Victoria repose, her feet hurt her worse than ever. The sun was shining in a cloudless sky and it was going to be a glorious day in Melbourne.

Arriving at the hotel in Adelaide she felt that even if it made her late for her meeting she would have a bath and change all her clothes. There was a Viennese maid of about her own age flicking about the bedroom. 'My shoes hurt me,' Lady Weare observed to the maid. 'If I had any sense I wouldn't wear them.'

'But, madame, they are so elegant!' The woman had a bright, sparkling look. 'Oh how I know the shoes that are elegant and hurt one's feet! When I come to this country I think: "One will not get good things there", and I buy *for forty dollars* a pair of crocodile-skin shoes. Think of it! And they hurt me so I can hardly walk onto the boat. They hurt me for years. They never wear out. At last I throw them away.'

Lady Weare sat down on the side of the bed. She regarded her elegant buckled shoes attentively while another maid came in and engaged in an animated exchange with the Viennese. I wonder if I am punishing myself, she thought. If so, I wonder what for?

Was it that if the shoes hurt her this might propitiate whatever provided the bad luck in Melbourne? That they would realise she didn't need more suffering? Ridiculous! Then she thought, I wonder if they mistook that woman for me? Ridiculous! She wondered what would happen next time she went to Melbourne, and shrugged. Then, with the icy expression which indicated her feet were hurting she took up her briefcase and set out, exactly on time for her committee meeting.

In three months' time, she knew, she would again be going to Melbourne.

Brenda Walker

LIKE AN EGYPTIAN
1990

When I went to high school I found a severed head in the library, as my mother had before me.

The library was not a mysterious place. It held fiction from the thirties, European classics and colonial poetry.

Above the books the long arched windows pressed blue against blue: jacarandas and summer sky. The air was pulpy with stale sweat. The ibis high-stepped on the asphalt outside. Little cats hid under the floor of the library in the crust of dried flood mud. Above the playground the arches of the phoenix palms hid the daytime folds of the flying foxes.

The head in the school library was protected from the climate and our fingers by a glass cube. It was raised to child level on a wooden stand inscribed with the date of embalming and the identity of an adventurer who turned his back on our corn-filled river flats and Moreton Bay figs. He sailed to London, then Cairo and became a famous Egyptologist. Somewhere he acquired the mummy of a young girl. I don't know if he unwrapped and removed the head himself but it was certainly he who had it shipped back to the school library. Here it remained, visibly glued inside its case, black and greasy and showing its yellow teeth. Patches of rusty fur covered the scalp.

The head is still there for the daughters of the town and will be there for their daughters. Ibis glimpse her from the windowsills. Cats stare up through cracks in the floorboards. They watch her as they litter and die in the heat. She disappears, their bodies dry and the next flood folds them under. They have no language to question her. Where is the cartonnage mask, the blue paint and gilt? Where are the patterned folds of linen with carnelian tucked inside? Where is the long hollow body with its bandaged hands? When Osiris was dismembered his wife knew no rest until she brought his limbs together. She gathered them

from the sky and the earth and the waters of the Nile. Our mummy
has no Isis. Just a little head with crumpled eyelids. She has no lovers
and no adornment, no body and no speech. She was an example to us
all. The last man who touched her snapped her thin dry neck and
parcelled her up for Australia.

Here are some questions for the librarian:

What did the Australian troops think of Egypt?

Sun, sand and syphilis.

What did they do there?

They burned the brothels in Cairo. The Egyptian women put too
high a price on themselves.

In free reading time the schoolgirls stand before the severed head.
Here is the home of the journeying spirit, exiled, exposed. But the
mummy is firm, brown fibre, while the faces peering in are insubstantial,
baffled by their own reflections. If they focus on the surface, trying out
model girl angles in the mirror of the glass, a little dry death lies always
behind their poses.

The Louvre contains its Egyptian artefacts in long galleries decorated
with wings and scarabs. The painting is unmistakably French.

Freud wandered in these galleries. He wrote a letter to the woman
who was to become his wife, describing the fiery sculptural reliefs, the
real sphinxes, he wrote, in a dream-like world.

In the Louvre there is a coffined mummy with the mask laid aside
to reveal the pattern of the bindings. Linen squares mitre into smaller
squares, so the face is framed and concealed, repeatedly. One wrapped
hand is uncurled for us to see and the other closes on itself, withholding
its darkness from the Parisian day.

In the British Museum a hieroglyphic frieze is painted on the wall
above the body of an Egyptian baby and a young child. They were
found in a single grave with a woman. Her body is now in Cairo. Who
divided the dry flesh of mother and child? What glory did it bring to
his Empire? Is it important for flesh to remain whole and together
throughout the millennia? Isis thought so. The frieze makes no comment on this situation. It is static, monumental.

According to the British Museum the Egyptians believed in imitative
magic. The representation of an object is the same as that object. How

else could the spirit ingest the images of roast quail on the walls of the tomb? To represent is to remember, and to predict. In the British Museum there is a papyrus from the Twenty-first Dynasty showing Nut, the goddess of the sky, arching over Geb, the earth-god. Her white body is stretched to an extremity. Geb is green, supine, with a thin erection. The distance between them is immense.

In *Ancient Nights* Norman Mailer imagines Egypt. His characters adopt postures of submission or exaltation. The spirit in the shadows of the Necropolis falls to his knees before the Ka of his great-grandfather. One is taken in a certain way, diminished, restored through an act with the sister and spouse of the aggressor. There is no obliquity in these exchanges. There are no dreams like Leonardo's childhood memory of the vulture perched on the side of his crib, inserting its tail into his mouth. There is nothing to puzzle Freud here. Just opportunists, zig-zagging through the social hierarchy. But what if Mailer is wrong, and the Egyptians were not simply Americans in fancy costumes? What if the Egyptian erotic had to do with

SILENCE

COMPOSURE

Some girls learn more than one lesson in the school library. They dance on the asphalt to the Bangles. They know that a woman wrote 'Heartbreak Hotel'. They know another way to walk

LIKE AN EGYPTIAN

Judah Waten

MOTHER
1950

When I was a small boy I was often morbidly conscious of Mother's intent, searching eyes fixed on me. She would gaze for minutes on end without speaking one word. I was always disconcerted and would guiltily look down at the ground, anxiously turning over in my mind my day's activities.

But very early I knew her thoughts were far away from my petty doings; she was concerned with them only in so far as they gave her further reason to justify her hostility to the life around us. She was preoccupied with my sister and me; she was forever concerned with our future in this new land in which she would always feel a stranger.

I gave her little comfort, for though we had been in the country for only a short while I had assumed many of the ways of those around me. I had become estranged from her. Or so it seemed to Mother, and it grieved her.

When I first knew her she had no intimate friends, nor do I think she felt the need of one with whom she could discuss her innermost thoughts and hopes. With me, though I knew she loved me very deeply, she was never on such near terms of friendship as sometimes exist between a mother and son. She emanated a kind of certainty in herself, in her view of life, that no opposition or human difficulty could shrivel or destroy. 'Be strong before people, only weep before God,' she would say and she lived up to that precept even with Father.

In our little community in the city, acquaintances spoke derisively of Mother's refusal to settle down as others had done, of what they called her propensity for highfalutin daydreams and of the severity and unreasonableness of her opinions.

Yet her manner with people was always gentle. She spoke softly, she was measured in gesture, and frequently it seemed she was functioning automatically, her mind far away from her body. There was a grave beauty in her still, sad face, her searching, dark-brown eyes and black hair. She was thin and stooped in carriage as though a weight always lay on her shoulders.

From my earliest memory of Mother it somehow seemed quite natural to think of her as apart and other-worldly and different, not of everyday things as Father was. In those days he was a young-looking man who did not hesitate to make friends with children as soon as they were able to talk to him and laugh at his stories. Mother was older than he was. She must have been a woman of nearly forty, but she seemed even older. She changed little for a long time, showing no traces of growing older at all until, towards the end of her life, she suddenly became an old lady.

I was always curious about Mother's age. She never had birthdays like other people, nor did anyone else in our family. No candles were ever lit or cakes baked or presents given in our house. To my friends in the street who boasted of their birthday parties I self-consciously repeated my Mother's words, that such celebrations were only a foolish and eccentric form of self-worship.

'Nothing but deception,' she would say. 'As though life can be chopped into neat twelve-month parcels! It's deeds, not years, that matter.'

Although I often repeated her words and even prided myself on not having birthdays I could not restrain myself from once asking Mother when she was born.

'I was born. I'm alive as you can see, so what more do you want to know?' she replied, so sharply that I never asked her about her age again.

In so many other ways Mother was different. Whereas all the rest of the women I knew in the neighbouring houses and in other parts of the city took pride in their housewifely abilities, their odds and ends of new furniture, the neat appearance of their homes, Mother regarded all those things as of little importance. Our house always looked as if we had just moved in or were about to move out. An impermanent and impatient spirit dwelt within our walls; Father called it living on one leg like a bird.

Wherever we lived there were some cases partly unpacked, rolls of linoleum stood in a corner, only some of the windows had curtains. There were never sufficient wardrobes, so that clothes hung on hooks behind doors. And all the time Mother's things accumulated. She never parted with anything, no matter how old it was. A shabby green plush coat bequeathed to her by her own mother hung on a nail in her bedroom. Untidy heaps of tattered books, newspapers, and journals from the old country mouldered in corners of the house, while under her bed in tin trunks she kept her dearest possessions. In those trunks there were bundles of old letters, two heavily underlined books on nursing, an old Hebrew Bible, three silver spoons given her by an aunt with whom she had once lived, a diploma on yellow parchment, and her collection of favourite books.

From one or other of her trunks she would frequently pick a book and read to my sister and me. She would read in a wistful voice poems and stories of Jewish liberators from Moses until the present day, of the heroes of the 1905 Revolution and pieces by Tolstoy and Gorky and Sholom Aleichem. Never did she stop to inquire whether we understood what she was reading; she said we should understand later if not now.

I liked to hear Mother read, but always she seemed to choose a time for reading that clashed with something or other I was doing in the street or in a nearby paddock. I would be playing with the boys in the street, kicking a football or spinning a top or flying a kite, when Mother would unexpectedly appear and without even casting a glance at my companions she would ask me to come into the house, saying she wanted to read to me and my sister. Sometimes I was overcome with humiliation and I would stand listlessly with burning cheeks until she repeated her words. She never reproached me for my disobedience nor did she ever utter a reproof to the boys who taunted me as, crestfallen, I followed her into the house.

Why Mother was as she was only came to me many years later. Then I was even able to guess when she was born.

She was the last child of a frail and overworked mother and a bleakly pious father who hawked reels of cotton and other odds and ends in the villages surrounding a town in Russia. My grandfather looked with great disapproval on his offspring, who were all girls, and he was hardly aware of my mother at all. She was left well alone by her older sisters, who with feverish impatience were waiting for their parents to make the required arrangements for their marriages.

During those early days Mother rarely looked out into the streets, for since the great pogroms few Jewish children were ever to be seen abroad. From the iron grille of the basement she saw the soles of the shoes of the passers-by and not very much more. She had never seen a tree, a flower, or a bird.

But when Mother was about fifteen her parents died and she went to live with a widowed aunt and her large family in a faraway village. Her aunt kept an inn and Mother was tucked away with her cousins in a remote part of the building, away from the prying eyes of the customers in the taprooms. Every evening her aunt would gaze at her with startled eyes as if surprised to find her among the family.

'What am I going to do with you?' she would say. 'I've got daughters of my own. If only your dear father of blessed name had left you just a tiny dowry it would have been such a help. Ah well! If you have no hand you can't make a fist.'

At that time Mother could neither read nor write. And as she had never had any childhood playmates or friends of any kind she hardly knew what to talk about with her cousins. She spent the days cheerlessly pottering about the kitchen or sitting for hours, her eyes fixed on the dark wall in front of her.

Some visitor to the house, observing the small, lonely girl, took pity on her and decided to give her an education. Mother was given lessons every few days and after a while she acquired a smattering of Yiddish and Russian, a little arithmetic and a great fund of Russian and Jewish stories.

New worlds gradually opened before Mother. She was seized with a passion of primers, grammars, arithmetic and story books, and soon the idea entered her head that the way out of her present dreary life lay through these books. There was another world, full of warmth and interesting things, and in it there was surely a place for her. She became obsessed with the thought that it wanted only some decisive step on her part to go beyond her aunt's house into the life she dreamed about.

Somewhere she read of a Jewish hospital which had just opened in a distant city and one winter's night she told her aunt she wanted to go to relatives who lived there. They would help her to find work in the hospital.

'You are mad!' exclaimed her aunt. 'Forsake a home for a wild fancy! Who could have put such a notion into your head? Besides, a girl of eighteen can't travel alone at this time of the year.'

It was from that moment that Mother's age became something to be manipulated as it suited her. She said to her aunt that she was not eighteen, but twenty-two. She was getting up in years and she could not continue to impose on her aunt's kindness.

'How can you be twenty-two?' her aunt replied greatly puzzled.

A long pause ensued while she tried to reckon up Mother's years. She was born in the month Tammuz according to the Jewish calendar, which corresponded to the old-style Russian calendar month of June, but in what year? She could remember being told of Mother's birth, but nothing outstanding had happened then to enable her to place the year. With all her nieces and nephews, some dead and many alive, scattered all over the vastness of the country only a genius could keep track of all their birthdays. Perhaps the girl was twenty-two, and if that were so her chance of getting a husband in the village was pretty remote; twenty-two was far too old. The thought entered her head that if she allowed Mother to go to their kinsmen in the city she would be relieved of the responsibility of finding a dowry for her, and so reluctantly she agreed.

But it was not until the spring that she finally consented to let her niece go. As the railway station was several miles from the village Mother was escorted there on foot by her aunt and cousins. With all her possessions, including photographs of her parents and a tattered Russian primer tied in a great bundle, Mother went forth into the vast world.

In the hospital she didn't find that for which she hungered; it seemed still as far away as in the village. She had dreamed of the new life where all would be noble, where men and women would dedicate their lives to bringing about a richer and happier life, just as she had read.

But she was put to scrubbing floors and washing linen every day from morning till night until she dropped exhausted into her bed in the attic. No-one looked at her, no-one spoke to her but to give her orders. Her one day off in the month she spent with her relatives who gave her some cast-off clothes and shoes and provided her with the books on nursing she so urgently needed. She was more than ever convinced that her deliverance would come through these books and she set about swallowing their contents with renewed zest.

As soon as she had passed all the examinations and acquired the treasured diploma she joined a medical mission that was about to proceed without a moment's delay to a distant region where a cholera epidemic raged. And then for several years she remained with the same group, moving from district to district, wherever disease flourished.

Whenever Mother looked back over her life it was those years that shone out. Then she was with people who were filled with an ardour for mankind and it seemed to her they lived happily and freely, giving and taking friendship in an atmosphere pulsating with warmth and hope.

All this had come to an end in 1905 when the medical mission was dissolved and several of Mother's colleagues were killed in the uprising. Then with a heavy heart and little choice she had returned to nursing in the city, but this time in private houses attending on well-to-do ladies.

It was at the home of one of her patients that she met Father. What an odd couple they must have been! She was taciturn, choosing her words carefully, talking mainly of her ideas and little about herself. Father bared his heart with guileless abandon. He rarely had secrets and there was no division in his mind between intimate and general matters. He could talk as freely of his feelings for Mother or of a quarrel with his father as he could of a vaudeville show or the superiority of one game of cards as against another.

Father said of himself he was like an open hand of solo and all men were his brothers. For a story, a joke, or an apt remark he would forsake his father and mother, as the saying goes. Old tales, new ones invented for the occasion, jokes rolled off his tongue in a never-ending procession. Every trifle, every incident was material for a story and he haunted music halls and circuses, for he liked nothing better than comedians and clowns, actors and buskers.

He brought something bubbly and frivolous into Mother's life and for a while she forgot her stern precepts. In those days Father's clothes were smart and gay; he wore bright straw hats and loud socks and fancy, buttoned-up boots. Although she had always regarded any interest in clothes as foolish and a sign of an empty and frivolous nature Mother then felt proud of his fashionable appearance. He took her to his favourite resorts, to music halls and to tea-houses where he and his cronies idled away hours, boastfully recounting stories of successes in business or merely swapping jokes. They danced nights away, though Mother was almost stupefied by the band and the bright lights and looked with distaste on the extravagant clothes of the dancers who bobbed and cavorted.

All this was in the early days of their marriage. But soon Mother was filled with misgivings. Father's world, the world of commerce and speculation, of the buying and selling of goods neither seen nor touched, was repugnant and frightening to her. It lacked stability, it was devoid of ideals, it was fraught with ruin. Father was a trader in air, as the saying went.

Mother's anxiety grew as she observed more closely his mode of life. He worked in fits and starts. If he made enough in one hour to last him a week or a month his business was at an end and he went off in search of friends and pleasure. He would return to business only when his money had just about run out. He was concerned only with one day at a time; about tomorrow he would say, clicking his fingers, his blue eyes focused mellowly on space, 'We'll see.'

But always he had plans for making great fortunes. They never came to anything but frequently they produced unexpected results. It so happened that on a number of occasions someone Father trusted acted on the plans he had talked about so freely before he even had time to leave the tea-house. Then there were fiery scenes with his faithless friends. But Father's rage passed away quickly and he would often laugh and make jokes over the table about it the very same day. He imagined everyone else forgot as quickly as he did and he was always astonished to discover that his words uttered hastily in anger had made him enemies.

'How should I know that people have such long memories for hate? I've only a cat's memory,' he would explain innocently.

'If you spit upwards, you're bound to get it back in the face,' Mother irritably upbraided him.

Gradually Mother reached the conclusion that only migration to another country would bring about any real change to their life, and with all her persistence she began to urge him to take the decisive step. She considered America, France, Palestine, and finally decided on Australia. One reason for the choice was the presence there of distant relatives who would undoubtedly help them to find their feet in that faraway continent. Besides, she was sure that Australia was so different from any other country that Father was bound to acquire a new and more solid way of earning a living there.

For a long time Father paid no heed to her agitation and refused to make any move.

'Why have you picked on Australia and not Tibet, for example?' he asked ironically. 'There isn't much difference between the two lands. Both are on the other side of the moon.'

The idea of leaving his native land seemed so fantastic to him that he refused to regard it seriously. He answered Mother with jokes and tales of travellers who disappeared in balloons. He had no curiosity to explore distant countries, he hardly ever ventured beyond the three or four familiar streets of his city. And why should his wife be so anxious for him to find a new way of earning a living? Didn't he provide her with food and a roof over her head? He had never given one moment's thought to his mode of life and he could not imagine any reason for doing so. It suited him like his gay straw hats and smart suits.

Yet in the end he did what Mother wanted him to do, though even on the journey he was tortured by doubts and he positively shouted words of indecision. But he was no sooner in Australia than he put away all thoughts of his homeland and he began to regard the new country as his permanent home. It was not so different from what he had known before. Within a few days he had met some fellow merchants and, retiring to a cafe, they talked about business in the new land. There were fortunes to be made here, Father very quickly concluded. There was, of course, the question of a new language but that was no great obstacle to business. You could buy and sell – it was a good land, Father said.

It was different with Mother. Before she was one day off the ship she wanted to go back.

The impressions she gained on that first day remained with her all her life. It seemed to her there was an irritatingly superior air about the people she met, the customs officials, the cab men, the agent of the new house. Their faces expressed something ironical and sympathetic, something friendly and at the same time condescending. She imagined everyone on the wharf, in the street, looked at her in the same way and she never forgave them for treating her as if she were in need of their good-natured tolerance.

Nor was she any better disposed to her relatives and the small delegation of Jews who met her at the ship. They had all been in Australia for many years and they were anxious to impress newcomers with their knowledge of the country and its customs. They spoke in a hectoring manner. This was a free country, they said, it was cultured, one used a knife and fork and not one's hands. Everyone could read and write and no-one shouted at you. There were no oppressors here as in the old country.

Mother thought she understood their talk; she was quick and observant where Father was sometimes extremely guileless. While they talked Father listened with a good-natured smile and it is to be supposed he was thinking of a good story he could tell his new acquaintances. But Mother fixed them with a firm, relentless gaze and, suddenly interrupting their injunctions, said in the softest of voices, 'If there are no oppressors here, as you say, why do you frisk about like house dogs? Whom do you have to please?'

Mother never lost this hostile and ironical attitude to the new land. She would have nothing of the country; she would not even attempt to learn the language. And she only began to look with a kind of interest at the world round her when my sister and I were old enough to go to school. Then all her old feeling for books and learning was reawakened. She handled our primers and readers as if they were sacred texts.

She set great aims for us. We were to shine in medicine, in literature, in music; our special sphere depending on her fancy at a particular time. In one of these ways we could serve humanity best, and whenever she read to us the stories of Tolstoy and Gorky she would tell us again and again of her days with the medical mission. No matter how much schooling we should get we needed ideals, and what better ideals were there than those that had guided her in the days of the medical mission? They would save us from the soulless influences of this barren land.

Father wondered why she spent so much time reading and telling us stories of her best years and occasionally he would take my side when I protested against Mother taking us away from our games.

'They're only children,' he said. 'Have pity on them. If you stuff their little heads, God alone knows how they will finish up.' Then, pointing to us, he added, 'I'll be satisfied if he is a good carpenter; and if she's a good dressmaker that will do, too.'

'At least,' Mother replied, 'you have the good sense not to suggest they go in for business. Life has taught you something at last.'

'Can I help it that I am in business?' he suddenly shouted angrily.

'I know it's a pity my father didn't teach me to be a professor.'

But he calmed down quickly, unable to stand for long Mother's steady gaze and compressed lips.

It exasperated us that Father should give in so easily so that we could never rely on him to take our side for long. Although he argued with Mother about us he secretly agreed with her. And outside the house he boasted about her, taking a peculiar pride in her culture and attainments, and repeating her words just as my sister and I did.

Mother was very concerned about how she could give us a musical education. It was out of the question that we both be taught an instrument, since Father's business was at a low ebb and he hardly knew where he would find enough money to pay the rent, so she took us to a friend's house to listen to gramophone records. They were of the old-fashioned, cylindrical kind made by Edison and they sounded far away and thin like the voice of a ventriloquist mimicking far-off musical instruments. But my sister and I marvelled at them. We should have been willing to sit over the long, narrow horn for days, but Mother decided that it would only do us harm to listen to military marches and the stupid songs of the music hall.

It was then that we began to pay visits to musical emporiums. We went after school and during the holidays in the mornings. There were times when Father waited long for his lunch or evening meal, but he made no protest . . . He supposed Mother knew what she was doing in those shops and he told his friends of the effort Mother was making to acquaint us with music.

Our first visits to the shops were in the nature of reconnoitring sorties. In each emporium Mother looked the attendants up and down while we thumbed the books on the counters, stared at the enlarged photographs of illustrious composers, and studied the various catalogues of gramophone records. We went from shop to shop until we just about knew all there was to know about the records and sheet music and books in stock.

Then we started all over again from the first shop and this time we came to hear the records.

I was Mother's interpreter and I would ask one of the salesmen to play us a record she had chosen from one of the catalogues. Then I would ask him to play another. It might have been a piece for violin by Tchaikovsky or Beethoven or an aria sung by Caruso or Chaliapin.

This would continue until Mother observed the gentleman in charge of the gramophone losing his patience and we would take our leave.

With each visit Mother became bolder and several times she asked to have whole symphonies and concertos played to us. We sat for nearly an hour cooped up in a tiny room with the salesman restlessly shuffling his feet, yawning and not knowing what to expect next. Mother pretended he hardly existed and, making herself comfortable in the cane chair, with a determined, intent expression she gazed straight ahead at the whirling disc.

We were soon known to everyone at the shops. Eyes lit up as we walked in, Mother looking neither this way nor that with two children walking in file through the passageway towards the record department. I was very conscious of the humorous glances and the discreet sniggers that followed us and I would sometimes catch hold of Mother's hand and plead with her to leave the shop. But she paid no heed and we continued to our destination. The more often we came the more uncomfortably self-conscious I became and I dreaded the laughing faces round me.

Soon we became something more than a joke. The smiles turned to scowls and the shop attendants refused to play us any more records. The first time this happened the salesman mumbled something and left us standing outside the door of the music-room.

Mother was not easily thwarted and without a trace of a smile she said we should talk to the manager. I was filled with a sense of shame and humiliation and with downcast eyes I sidled towards the entrance of the shop.

Mother caught up with me and, laying her hand upon my arm, she said, 'What are you afraid of? Your mother won't disgrace you, believe me.' Looking at me in her searching way she went on, 'Think carefully. Who is right – are they or are we? Why shouldn't they play for us? Does it cost them anything? By which other way can we ever hope to hear something good? Just because we are poor must we cease our striving?'

She continued to talk in this way until I went back with her. The three of us walked into the manager's office and I translated Mother's words.

The manager was stern, though I imagine he must have had some difficulty in keeping his serious demeanour.

'But do you ever intend to buy any records?' he said after I had spoken.

'If I were a rich woman would you ask me that question?' Mother replied and I repeated her words in a halting voice.

'Speak up to him,' she nudged me while I could feel my face fill with hot blood.

The manager repeated his first question and Mother, impatient at my hesitant tone, plunged into a long speech on our right to music and culture and in fact the rights of all men, speaking in her own tongue as though the manager understood every word. It was in vain; he merely shook his head.

We were barred from shop after shop, and in each case Mother made a stand, arguing at length until the man in charge flatly told us not to come back until we could afford to buy records.

We met with rebuffs in other places as well.

Once as we wandered through the university, my sister and I sauntering behind while Mother opened doors, listening to lectures for brief moments, we unexpectedly found ourselves in a large room where white-coated young men and women sat on high stools in front of arrays of tubes, beakers and jars.

Mother's eyes lit up brightly and she murmured something about knowledge and science. We stood close to her and gazed round in astonishment; neither her words nor what we saw conveyed anything to us. She wanted to go round the room but a gentleman wearing a black gown came up and asked us if we were looking for someone. He was a distinguished-looking person with a florid face and a fine grey mane.

Repeating Mother's words I said, 'We are not looking for anyone; we are simply admiring this room of knowledge.'

The gentleman's face wrinkled pleasantly. With a tiny smile playing over his lips he said regretfully that we could not stay, since only students were permitted in the room.

As I interpreted his words Mother's expression changed. Her sallow face was almost red. For ten full seconds she looked the gentleman in the eyes. Then she said rapidly to me, 'Ask him why he speaks with such a condescending smile on his face.'

I said, 'My mother asks why you talk with such a superior smile on your face?'

He coughed, shifted his feet restlessly and his face set severely. Then he glared at his watch and without another word walked away with dignified steps.

When we came out into the street a spring day was in its full beauty. Mother sighed to herself and after a moment's silence said, 'That fine professor thinks he is a liberal-minded man, but behind his smile he despises people such as us. You will have to struggle here just as hard as I had to back home. For all the fine talk it is like all other countries. But where are the people with ideals like those back home, who aspire to something better?'

She repeated those words frequently, even when I was a boy of thirteen and I knew so much more about the new country that was my home. Then I could argue with her.

I said to her that Benny who lived in our street was always reading books and papers and hurrying to meetings. Benny was not much older than I was and he had many friends whom he met in the park on Sunday. They all belonged to this country and they were interested in all the things Mother talked about.

'Benny is an exception,' she said with an impatient shrug of her shoulders, 'and his friends are only a tiny handful.' Then she added, 'And what about you? You and your companions only worship bats and balls as heathens do stone idols. Why, in the old country boys of your age took part in the fight to deliver mankind from oppression! They gave everything, their strength and health, even their lives, for that glorious idea.'

'That's what Benny wants to do,' I said, pleased to be able to answer Mother.

'But it's so different here. Even your Benny will be swallowed up in the smug, smooth atmosphere. You wait and see.'

She spoke obstinately. It seemed impossible to change her. Her vision was too much obscured by passionate dreams of the past for her to see any hope in the present, in the new land.

But as an afterthought she added, 'Perhaps it is different for those like you and Benny. But for me I can never find my way into this life here.'

She turned away, her narrow back stooped, her gleaming black hair curled into a bun on her short, thin neck, her shoes equally down at heel on each side.

Archie Weller

SANDCASTLES
1977

Hullo. My name is Tommy. I don't write too good, but I got all these things I want to say.

You know, when I walk down the street everybody stares at me. That's shame, like I was an escaped animal from the zoo, or a space-man or something. I'm just a coloured boy. Maybe that is why they all stare at me, because they imagine I might steal their car, or knock them down and take their money.

I think of money a lot, when I don't have any. When I got it, I don't think of anything except having my piece of fun. When I got money then I'm someone, but when I'm broke I'm just Tommy Caylun, the boong, shuffling down the street, with an eye out for the monaych – coppers. With money in my pocket I can pretend I'm a main actor, you know? I walk around like Marlon Brando, big tough Tommy.

But their scornful stares, that look right through me, show me what I really am.

I hate white people – or maybe I hate myself because I'm almost white. And that is all I'll ever be – an almost man. Whenever I start becoming good and try to settle down, something always happens and I'm back where I come from. Like last time, when I had a Wadgula girlfriend, and a Monaro, and a steady job. I told myself: Tommy, this is it. You right now.

But my cousin, Clemmy – who was on the run – come around home, one night, with a carload of stolen beer.

We all got blue-drunk and gang-raped this girl Clem brought along. Well, not really rape because she was drunk too, and asking for it. But, when police busted through the door, it looked like rape. You can't tell police nothing, when it's part-aboriginals involved.

So I got three years in Fremantle, I was only seventeen. It hurt me; that's the truth.

Down the Central Station, five CIB blokes punched me and Clemmy and the two Harrison boys up and down the room. But we give them our best because we only got our pride; when that's gone we may as well go out to some park to drink and die.

Any rate, I'm out now. I tell myself I will settle down now. But I am what I am. Or, rather, I am what the white people want me to be.

That white girlfriend of mine, she was pretty. She understood me, too. I met her at the Tech. school I was going to, where I was learning mechanics. One good thing about my Dad (and about the only good thing) was how he could fix up any old car. I learnt all I knew off him. I remember dusty days, in the hot sun, and rainy nights, with the electric light dancing with the wind. I would huddle into my hand-me-down clothes and watch every move his stubby, greasy fingers would make. I reckon he could of fixed an engine blindfold, he was that good. Every now and then he would glance down at me and explain, in his gravelly voice, what was where. Sometimes, he would raise a rare laugh and say I looked like a little joey 'roo. That was when he would forget the black skin my mother had given me and just remember I was his son and I could love him then.

He used to say him and me would go into partnership, when I got old enough and passed Tech. He was proud of me, you know.

Then Clemmy Jackson and Olman and Eli Harrison had to come along.

So, that was the finish of that; all Dad's dreams, I mean. It was the beginning for me. You might say I'd finally busted out of my white cocoon, hanging on a tree. But I wasn't a butterfly, you see. I was something bad, and black, and unsightly in my real world.

But I was telling you about my girl, I was going to marry.

One night, she and me took these pills. I learnt if you take pills with Coke, it makes you like you was drunk – well, happy really. Plastic joy, you might say. These Wadgulas have got funny tricks. Well, anyway, we was rolling around on the floor, laughing at nothing much, thinking about nothing much – at this party. Somehow, me and her got together. Kissing and cuddling, you know? Then we made love, and it was like nothing that had ever happened to me. She was so soft and gentle, and she gave everything. That's what got me, because most Wadgulas take everything off my kind. She quietened me down and showed me where I was going.

All that summer, me and her went everywhere together. I had this Monaro I bought off Uncle Butch for five hundred. Brother, she could move, all right! It made me feel like God or something, you know, to roar and rush up and down the streets. I hotted it up with floor shift, and foot-on-the-floor power, and mags, and bucket seats. I put a radio and cassette in it, and, with my knowledge, I kept the engine in good shape.

But you can't get away from nothing. One night, outside this pizza hut, these demons pulled us up. They tried to say I stole my Monaro, and shamed me in front of my girl. They had a good look at her, too, with a what-the-hell-are-you-doing-with-*him* sneer. They pulled me out, and trod on my toes, and scared the shits out of me. They made me look a fool, just to prove to themselves they was the men.

The people in the pizza hut stared, with hooded eyes, at another boong being picked up; the sluts in the one darkened car on the street (for it was past midnight) giggled at the two coppers – who promised, silently, to come back this way, later on, and pick them up for a quick free one someplace. The one Nyoongah there melted away into the shadows, not wanting to know about it. He knew that where there was monaych there was trouble: for him, or me, or any poor black bastard like us. You live and learn and live. The lights blinked down on me, bored-like. Even the jukebox couldn't give a damn, shouting out happily as I went through the third-degree, on the hot street.

I would like to punch the huge, fat policeman in the guts, and make him grunt. I would like to shout out, to all the world, that I am a man.

But I never did.

I put on my best aboriginal face, and closed my eyes and hung my head and called them sir – just as they wanted me to.

Afterwards, I could sense my girl, Jillianne, was just a little cold towards me. I think she was reminded that I was, after all, a quarter black. But I never cared. I was used to her kind of treatment. Any rate, it didn't last long. It did spoil our evening, though.

But when we went back to Tech., it was all right. It made me feel good making out I was a Wadgula. I met Jillianne's family, in their double-garage house at Subiaco. They thought I was number one, you know? Her old man got me a job in the Skipper Chrysler workshops.

But you can't keep being false forever. You can never escape from your people, either. They are always watching. Watching.

So my cousin come along and what happened, happened.

You can be what you like on the outside, but inside you are you.

In Fremantle, I met more of my cousins, and an uncle I never even knew I had. Nyoongahs, us south-west people, stick together in Freo, unless they are enemies. I never had no enemies, so I was right. I tell you, going into Freo is like having a bath. All the bullshit gets washed off you and you learn the truth. You come out clean, you might say.

That is why I do the given-up-don't-care shuffle around the streets and spend my dole money on getting drunk at Beaufort, or Guildford park, with my people. I live with my two cousins, and my woman, in a tent at Lockridge.

Not my Wadgula woman, Jillianne. A Nyoongah girl — Phyllis Kennedy — who I knew a little bit. She come to see me sweating it out in jail: Jillianne didn't. So what did you expect? She'd welcome me with open arms and a great big hullo-I'm-glad-you're-free-kiss? Buddy, she was off a month after I got put away, with a Wadgula lawyer. How she must of laughed at silly black Tommy, as she showed her aboriginal around to all the gawking squawking white crows.

Peck out your eyes. Peck out your life. Leave the bones to bleach, lost and forgotten, in the corner of some paddock.

That's when I started hating the white people.

Phyllis is pregnant for Paddy Needles, who took off when he found out. But I love her. Sometimes, when she's rasping away in her harsh voice, I feel disgusted with her and wish she would speak softer, and better English. I wonder why I can live with her, with her torn, dirty clothes and untidy hair and her smell. But it's not our fault. We got no water here, only a tap — and a creek that runs dry in summer. When Phyllis come out of Niandi she was given all these new clothes by that Girls' Home. But you can't keep nothing clean in this place. Besides, all her sisters come and take her clothes off her. Then — she got this pretty way of throwing her arms about that makes her look like a ballerina. And her hair *is* beautiful and soft. Her eyes, too, look at me with such warmth and happiness and trusting. We are very happy together.

Sometimes, however, she doesn't understand me, because I never belt her around; and I share everything with her, and worry about her, like an old chook. Even when she gets me wild, all I do is go for a walk, somewhere peaceful, and think.

No-one understands me.

They weren't me, brought up in my family.

Mum thought she was really good, marrying a white bloke, you know? She dressed in good clothes, and wore shoes when she went to town – and jewels. When we was given all our rights then she may as well have been a Wadgula. But before that, even, she could look a white person in the eye with pride.

Her first man, Freddy Jackson, was sitting back in Fremantle. (He was that uncle I never knew about.) What he done was get drunk on metho and paint cleaner (because coloured people wasn't allowed to drink legally, then) and run amuck in the Reserve, by the railway line. He got an axe and killed Mum's brother, who also had got drunk.

He got life for that, and had already done twenty years when I went there. He'd sort of grown onto the place, like a piece of fungus. He's not even a human any more. If they let him out tomorrow he wouldn't know where to go or what to do. They did let him out once, I remember, after he had done eight years, when I was about five years old. He come down to see Mum and his son Jojo, who was nine.

I won't never forget that night. Not that I knew what was going on. I didn't. It was just the violence, that was to be with me all my life, bursting in, that I remember.

It started off quiet. Dad, a couple of his mates, and Mum was getting drunk, playing poker around the kitchen table. Me and my true sister Geraldine, who was only two, and my half-brother, Jojo, was supposed to be asleep. But we always watched the Saturday Night Show.

We reckoned it was funny to watch Mum laugh, and stumble around the kitchen, and throw her body around in a dance for the white men. It was the only time Dad got happy.

They would listen to the radio, or Dad would drag out his guitar. Sometimes, one of Dad's mates would try to get a piece of Mum. We would giggle from our corner as the white fella fumbled Mum's heavy breasts, and threw floppy arms around her shoulders, and kissed her – and then dragged her, laughing, into the bedroom. Dad would laugh too: he didn't care. Only once, when Mum was pregnant, he got in one of his sudden violent rages, and tried to kill the unborn baby and Mum. But Jojo – who was fourteen then, but big and strong and sullen – stopped him.

But Mum only went with Dad's mates when she was blue-drunk and didn't know what she was doing. Next morning, when she was sober, she would straighten herself up and forget about it and pretend she was a white lady again. But Dad, over in his chair by the stove, looking like a cockroach, sort of, would cackle and grin, with his yellow teeth, and tease her about it. Then she would be ashamed and go away to cry.

Yeah, we used to laugh at the Saturday Night Show. But as we got older we became ashamed, then disgusted, then angry.

Nyoongahs lose their laughter young in life, you know.

But this night I am telling you about, we was laughing softly as huge Morry Gascoyne, who was a ringer in the shearing shed, tried it on with Mum.

Then there was a soft knock on the door.

Skinny-Jim (who we called Dad's brother) opens it and there stood . . . Uncle Freddy. I could see the front door from where I lay. It was raining and the rain run down Uncle Freddy's ragged clothes and formed in a pool around his feet; so it looked as if he had risen up out of that dirty puddle. It run down over his face, so it glistened in the light from the kitchen and looked like tears.

Uncle Freddy mumbled something to Skinny-Jimmy, who snarled back:

'No, you can't. Piss off!'

'Who's that?' Dad shouts.

'It's 'im. Come back to see his Missus.'

Us kids was wide-eyed watching this new twist to the show. We hardly ever had any visitors here; especially not Nyoongahs, who Mum discouraged. Any rate, as far as I could see this bloke was a stranger. But Dad and Skinny-Jim and big Morry seemed to know who ''im' was.

We could see something was up because Dad looked uneasy, and big Morry was going to get up. But then Dad grinned and motioned the giant to stay where he was.

'Bring him in, Jim. We ain't ignorant.'

Mum, she didn't know what was going on because she'd been drinking Vio Port, and whisky, and straight gin, all night, and she may as well have been dead.

Uncle Freddy come shuffling up the hall, with his prison gait; hands nervously shoved in his pockets. His hooded eyes flicked glances around the room without seeming to move.

He was only about thirty then but, in my mind, he looked ten years older.

He looked up and seen Mum and Mum seen him. Mum tried to struggle to her feet, but only fell off the chair. Her dress went right up her legs so her old petticoat showed.

No-one laughed. Not even us.

'So,' was all Uncle Freddy said. His eyes were bleared, like a fused light globe! Then he shrugged and turned to go.

That would have been an end of it, except for Morry Gascoyne (who thought of us all as boongs, and not worth a spit unless they was girls).

'So – what!' he bellows, and hauls poor dizzy Mum up by the arm. She leaned against the giant, and gagged, and hung her head.

'What you think of your woman now, the drunk little gin? Too good for a crazy boong like you. What did he do, sweetheart? Kill his best mate just to show how friendly he was? But we don't care, do we boys? This lovely piece of Black Velvet has kept us warm many nights.'

Uncle Freddy's hands sprung out of his pockets: big, knobbly, killing hands. He threw his head back and his eyes cleared. He gave a yell as he come in, swinging and kicking.

Morry let go of Mum, who fell back on the floor.

Then there was all buggeries let loose. Morry went down to one of Freddy's rights. Dad smashed a bottle over the black-haired head, before ending up, groaning, in the corner – his kidneys almost busted on him.

Skinny-Jim made a grab for a bottle then, but Freddy picked up a butcher's knife and put it right through him. Then the dark angry man worked over Morry Gascoyne so he wouldn't shear a sheep for a long time.

Mum had crawled over to us kids and hugged us to her.

Uncle Freddy busted every bottle in the house, and smashed the painting of the sorrowful white lady dressed in funny clothes, before he calmed down. Then he looked over at Mum, before dismissing her. He limped over to frightened Jojo, smiling with only his mouth. From out of his pocket he brought a medallion on a chain.

'I'm ya daddy, son. I bet ya forgotten me, unna? Well, any rate, I made this thing for ya to keep to remember me by. I won't never see ya again – Jojo.'

He was right. The monaych picked up Uncle Freddy, over at the camp, the next day, after Mum had rung them up. He came quietly, resigned and given up.

Skinny-Jim died.

They never let Uncle Freddy Jackson out again.

When I was in there all his teeth was falling out, and he talked to himself, and pissed himself sometimes. He was the joke of the jail, walking up to every new face – black or white – and promising to get them out on bail. Some people believed him, too.

When Dad recovered from his flogging, he laid into Mum and Jojo – just because Jojo was Freddy's son. Jojo ran away and lived by the Reserve, with his Auntie, for the next four years. He grew up rough and tough and dangerous, like his Dad. He always had a soft spot for me and Geraldine, though. When Jojo was thirteen, he went to work as a rousie on a shearing team. He come back home almost as tall as Dad and as strong as a bull. It was all right after that, because Dad was afraid of big Jojo, so he left Mum and us kids alone. Before, he used to flog us for any little thing. That is why I won't never flog my kids or woman, out at camp.

Yesterday, me and Phyllis went down to the beach. We kept out of the way of all the Wadgulas trying to turn black. We found a reef and waded around, looking for shells, Phyllis thought it would make the tent look pretty if we got some good shells. I went out deep and found some beauties; like trumpets, they were, and all orange and green and yellow, you know.

Some surfie blokes went by and whistled at Phyllis. Any Nyoongah girl is easy meat, they reckon. Even one who is six months pregnant. Other Wadgulas stare at us with their pale eyes, like they always do. But we don't care.

We sit in the shade of some rocks and talk quietly about what is happening outside in the world and inside Phyllis's stomach. That is our world.

Phyllis sleeps and I watch some little kids build a sandcastle.

The last time I built a sandcastle was when I become fourteen. I had just started Tech. and it was my birthday. Mum still believed I could be all right, you know. Turn out good.

She took us on a picnic down to the beach, to a place only she knew about. She used to come here, with her brother and sisters, when she was little and maybe she wanted to grab hold of her lost youth, or something.

That was fun. Jojo's Uncle Ronny, who was only a year older than Jojo himself (but that's how it works in Nyoongah families), drove us out there in his newly bought car.

There was just them two, Mum, me, Geraldine and the three young ones: all Nyoongahs together. We run around and played chasey and hidey. We swam and lay around, and ate a big feed, out of the picnic basket Mum had made. Ronny caught a huge fish and we seen some dolphins way offshore. No-one come to annoy us with their stares and muttered remarks. That was the best part.

Only one thing spoilt it when Mum brought out a flagon of wine. Jojo just stared at her and took himself off for a long walk.

But he came back to help us build the sandcastle. All us kids – even Ronny, who was twenty and a man, really. And Mum, too, sat at our side, running the white sand through her fingers, and giggling. It was a beauty of a sandcastle; with towers and walls and a moat; all covered in stones and shells and seaweed. Geraldine was Queen and I was King, whilst Ronny and Jojo was the enemies. The little ones ran everywhere, being nothing.

The King of sandcastles, that's me – all the way through.

When the sea come in and the sun went down, our castle was washed away, and we all went home.

I cried, and the others laughed. But, you see, for one whole day I had owned something beautiful, for the first time in my life.

Why do kids build sandcastles when they know the sea will come right in and wash them away?

Why do we dream, you might say?

All I ever do is dream.

I'm always going to do something, or be someone, or go somewhere – but I never move.

That's Tommy Caylun for you, all over.

Ida West

SNAKES

1984

When we were girls we used to watch snakes and the blue-tongue goannas having fights. The snakes would bite the blue-tongues, who would put up a good fight. The blue-tongue would crawl to a bunch of buzzies (bidgee-widgees or burrs), looking very sick, he would try to get under as far as he could. Each day we would go see the goanna. It would be there for a long time, but something they used to eat saved them. Perhaps it may have been the buzzies, I don't know, but they didn't die.

When I was going to school there were snakes everywhere. My brother, my sisters and I saw a log on the road on a culvert, there we saw all these baby snakes, there were more than a dozen. I don't know if there were two families, we didn't stay very long because we were not sure where the mother or father snakes were – they wouldn't be far away. Snakes have big families. The Marshall (the road from Emita to Robertdale) was a place for lots of snakes. Another time a female snake took to us. We found a big stone and hit her with it. It was just as well we did, but it was a cruel way to do it. We jabbed her stomach and all the baby snakes came out – some of the stuff got on my arm. We got home fast as we could and I washed my arm straight away. Dad told us we were never to be cruel. We, like all the children, had to carry a stick.

Dad used to go looking for water with a forked stick and when he found water he dug a well. We would go with him and the next morning often there would be a big water snake in the well, the red-bellied black snake. There were a lot of snakes on Flinders Island when I was a girl and where we lived at Killiecrankie there was a lot of scrub. There was a lagoon I had to go through, it was the only water at the place – our cows used to go through it in the thickest part and there were snakes all over the place. If we took the short cut through

Pinescrub across the hills, we had to watch out for the tiger snakes. The tiger snake has a head shaped like a diamond. They would get in the toilets up the backyard. A toilet was a large hole dug in the ground with a little house built over the top. It was hard to make it snake-proof. To keep the toilet clean we put ashes and Phenyle in it. If a snake got down the hole we put the sulphur down to get them out. We had the copperhead snakes which would come to the house or sheds looking for mice or rats. They were thin, long snakes and very cheeky. We had to put milk out, and be very quiet so they would come out to drink the milk and we would be ready with a stick to kill them. We had the whip snake and the grass snake. I was listening to Harry Butler talking about goannas, he said people think they are death adders. I was getting the cows in one afternoon, I was going with my stick when I saw what I thought was a goanna, I got a little closer to it but that was no goanna. I watched it crawl away, it was just like a death adder, the marks on it, thick body, and the thin rat-like tail. I went home and looked it up in a snake book. I told Dad I wasn't going along that track again. We got a dog to rouse the cows out. Dad reckoned there wasn't a death adder. He had never seen one, but I believe what I saw.

The women and the men all worked on Chappell Island amongst the tiger snakes and the 'Barking Brilla'. (The 'Barking Brilla' is the name for the snake-infested saltbush (barilla) on Chappell Island – the snakes make a warning noise when you get too close.) There were a lot of snakes there. The famous snake expert, Eric Worrell, told me they were the second most deadly snakes in Australia. The heads of this tiger snake on Chappell seemed to be bigger than those of the snakes on Flinders.

Herb   Wharton

WALTZING MATILDA

1996

Bunji and his old mate Knughy were droving horses in the outback. As the evening shadows lengthened they reached a billabong where the thirsty horses trotted down the sloping bank to drink heartily after their fifty-kilometre stage that day. Both Bunji and Knughy lived nomadic lives, wandering the stock routes droving sheep, cattle and horses, mainly for other people around the outback.

After the horses had watered, the two men looked around for a suitable camping place and unloaded their pack-horse under a big, spreading old coolabah tree which would shelter them from the wintry night dew. While Knughy hobbled the horses close by, Bunji gathered firewood. Looking through their meagre rations, he realised they were out of meat – and there was very little else in the packs except for a bit of flour, some tea and sugar and a few spuds and onions.

'We got no *yudie* (meat)!' he called out.

'Might be we get 'em *thum-ba* (sheep) later on,' Knughy said. 'Plenty meat then.' He walked back to the camp, where the fire was now alight and the billy filled with water. Both men sat around the camp fire waiting for a well-earned drink of tea.

At that moment, not two metres away, slowly lumbering down to the water like some prehistoric creature, they both saw this big old sand goanna. His long red tongue flickered as he walked along with the gait of a heavyweight sumo wrestler. Seemingly unafraid, he paid little attention to the two tired, hungry drovers. As it happened, the land this big old goanna strutted over was once their tribal kingdom.

Now this goanna might have been considered smart or brave, perhaps, walking in front of two hungry Murris like this. Or maybe he thought he was protected under some newfangled *withoo* (white) laws. In fact, his appearance was both foolish and fatal.

Both Bunji and Knughy jumped up, grabbed themselves sticks, and into the tuckerbag went goanna. As soon as the fire had produced enough coals and ashes, they scratched a long shallow hole in the ground, filled it with the coals and ashes, and cooked that big goanna.

'Proper bush yudi this one,' Bunji said later, savouring the tasty white flesh together with some johnny cake.

'A feast fit for a king,' Knughy agreed.

Bellies filled and pannikins brimful of tea, they sat around yarning, talking of the past, present and future. Bunji, who was about thirty, had been to school and was an inquiring sort of bloke. He'd worked in town and city and was an avid book reader, always in search of fresh knowledge.

Knughy, on the other hand, was old – how old, no-one seemed to know. Some other old men even declared that Knughy was old when *they* were boys long ago. How old he really was is anybody's guess. His education came from mustering and droving and Murri camps: his learning from the land. He could read the land like a book. For him it told stories just like printed words. Old Knughy had never learned to read printed words and he still signed his name with a cross – yet he could decipher cattle, sheep and horse brands and over the years he had gained much knowledge of his tribal land and its laws, both past and present.

As the sun sank lower and the trees cast longer shadows, the birds flew in to drink at the billabong, screeching and cackling. Some hovered at its edge, others perched on protruding logs. Then a mob of bleating sheep came cavorting down the bank to drink there too, spreading right along the edge of the billabong and taking over from the birds.

'Bloody stupid animals, thum-bas,' said Knughy.

'Yes,' replied Bunji. 'Only things sillier are people who try to work them without a dog.' Then an idea came to him. 'Hey, let's get one of them!' he said. 'Him fill up tuckerbag good and proper.'

'No, no,' said Knughy, 'too close to the road here. Might be station owner come along – might be *Ghunga-ble* (police) come along. Where you be then, hey?'

'Might be if Ghungie come I jump on horse and gallop away bush. Might be I jump into waterhole and swim away,' Bunji said.

'Might be you get caught . . . might be you drown . . . 'cause this is a funny waterhole, you know,' Knughy told him.

'Hey, what d' you know about this place?' Bunji asked. And now he recalled that it was called Combo waterhole, and it was supposed to be here the Jolly Swagman had stolen a thum-ba from Dagworth Station as he camped . . . maybe under this very coolabah tree. He had been surprised by the police, jumped into the waterhole and drowned. Bunji explained this piece of withoo history to Knughy in detail, and told him how it led Banjo Paterson to write the song 'Waltzing Matilda'.

'There's real, real history in this place, old man,' Bunji said.

'Might be this a good place, might be this a bad place,' the old man replied. His features were like dark, weathered leather. 'Might be this a real bad place . . . might be *whonboo* (ghost) here too.'

'What do *you* know about this place, old man? Tell me,' urged Bunji.

By this time the sheep had gone bleating away, the sun had set, a few frogs croaked in the billabong and from the tree branches came the subdued *carkle carkle carkle* of the roosting birds.

'You know,' Bunji said, 'I been reading and listening to a lot of different stories about that Jolly Swagman and don't know what to believe or think about him. What d'you reckon, old man?'

'Well, my boy,' said Knughy, knocking his bent-stemmed pipe against the coolabah tree before filling it with tobacco which he cut from a square, dark plug. 'Lotta history about here all right. Now you take that so-called Jolly Swagman – how d'you reckon a swaggie would feel jolly after tramping all day with his tuckerbag empty, belly pinching – might be his feet been aching too. Might be he had other problems, like he make 'em big *bhudie* (fire) in sacred place longa woolshed where they shear them thum-ba . . .

'I can tell you that long time before all that happen, people still came walking here. This waterhole was proper sit-down place then, with plenty yudie, plenty fish, sugar-bag (honey) too. These people, they all belonga this land and they say – if you want 'em tucker you take 'em yudie. There weren't no branded or earmarked animals in them days. The laws said you could take 'em yudie if you was hungry. And it might be, like that swagman, after they sitting down a while, they move on to hunt another place.

'By and by other tribes come with horses, cattle, sheep and all the proper yudie become scarce. People don't belong to land no more, the land belong to people, and the animals too. This mob, they start walkabout looking for proper sit-down place, and if they come to place where others sit down first, those people say, "You fella gotta move on. We here first, this our sit-down place."

'Now I don't know about that swagman. Might be he come along hopeful and happy, looking for sit-down place, might be he feeling real jolly with his tuckerbag empty, belly pinching and feet aching. Then them thum-bas come down to water while he's sitting under this coolabah tree with his billy on the boil. Well, he grabs one, butchers it up and has a big feed. He real Jolly Swagman then, belly bulging, tuckerbag full. He sits there singing, no worries – and that's when them Ghungies come riding silently along. They seen that thumba's fresh skin, no meat in it, in the creek bed. "Hey, that's strange," they think. Might be someone been steal thum-ba belonging to big fella boss owns country, owns animals – might be his own Ghungies, too.

'But he don't own Jolly Swagman. The Ghungies hear this happy singing and ride up, yelling: "We've got you red-handed! Where's your dilly bag with the yudi in it belonging to *mar-thar* (boss)?" – "I'm the singing swagman. Ya can have the squatter's meat. Take my bloody swag as well! Prison bars won't shut me in! I'll escape across the water!" – Then he jumps into the billabong, swims like a man possessed – until, with the opposite bank and freedom in his sight, suddenly he turns and begins to wave his arms like a band conductor, starts singing out of tune – and sinks.' Knughy paused. 'One of them Ghungies, I bin told, remembered that swagman's song, and that's how the music came about.' He refilled his pipe, then went on: 'Others say the swagman was swearing at the Ghungies as he sank, screaming: "I'll come back to haunt youse, you hacks of landed gents!" And then he sank beneath the muddy brown water – pulled down with cramps, some say. But others say that other, more knowing eyes were watching from their hiding-place, and the Jolly Swagman was pulled down by the great water spirit, the *Munta-gutta*.'

As Knughy paused again to tamp down the tobacco in his pipe, from across the water came a screeching sound like a banshee, followed by loud splashing sounds like a flock of ducks landing. It was so loud it startled the horses feeding close by. Hobble chains clinked and horse bells donged as the animals gave restless jumps.

'What you reckon that is?' said Bunji nervously.

'Oh, maybe it's ducks landing – but then they usually sing out. And maybe that screaming sound is curlews.' Knughy shrugged. 'But to get back to the history of that swagman. Here's another version. Might be he came from that big sit-down place over that way' – he pointed with arm extended in a south-easterly direction. 'Well, over there they have been having this big Bubblie and they bin fighting with the Ghungies. Afterwards this swagman goes walkabout, see, and might be he starts this bhudie (fire) in the mar-thar (boss cockie) sacred site, where them thum-bas are shorn. Then he comes along here, happy and singing, heading back to his proper sit-down place. But soon he begins to feel hungry and tired, so he camps here under this tree. He feels in his dilly bag – nothing there, no yudie, no *mhuntha* (bread); he got tea and sugar, billy can, swag, butcher knife. That's all. His belly's pinching. Soon some thum-bas come down thirsty – they want *gummu* (water). Well, that Jolly Swagman, he's real happy now. He grabs one of them thum-bas and soon he's singing again, no worries. The billy can's boiling, the dilly bag's full of yudie and his belly's bulging. He's singing so loudly he can't hear the horses coming . . . the Ghungies ride up and find him. They don't know for sure if he stole that thum-ba or set that bhudie in the mar-thar sacred place, but they say, "We got ya now, red-handed! Give yerself up, we're the law!"'

Once again old Knughy paused to refill his pipe. 'And that's when the Jolly singing Swagman made his fatal mistake,' he continued. 'He decided to go for a swim.'

'But didn't he make a mistake when he stole that sheep and burnt down the shearing shed?' Bunji interjected. 'He might have got away with both those things.'

'No, no,' Knughy replied. 'Young fellas like you should learn from this story.'

'What can I learn?' asked Bunji. 'Don't steal sheep, be careful where I light a fire, don't try to escape from lawful custody – is that all, old man?'

Knughy shook his head emphatically. 'The point is this: under no circumstances should you dive into deep water with a full belly. That's what killed that Jolly Swagman, my boy – going for a swim on a full belly.'

Bunji closed his eyes and sat silently for a moment, pondering this new-found information. Then, his eyes still closed, he asked: 'But what about them sounds, what about the Munta-gutta, what about the *whonboo* (ghost), what about –' He rambled on, but soon discovered he was talking to himself. For Knughy had silently slipped away, rolled out his swag, and was soon snoring his head off.

Bunji got up, looked around warily, then pulled his own swag closer to the old man. His mind was in turmoil. What could he believe? What was fact, what was fiction? What was reality, what was myth? Was history true or false? Suddenly he recollected an image of the past, and recalled the words of wisdom from his mother. She had always insisted: 'My boy, never but *never* swim on a full stomach.'

Could that really have been the cause of the death of the Jolly Swagman, he wondered.

Patrick White

BEING KIND TO TITINA

1964

First mother went away. Then it was our father, twitching from under
our feet the rugs, which formed, he said, a valuable collection. We
were alone for a little then. Not really alone, of course, for there was
Fräulein Hoffmann, and Mademoiselle Leblanc, and Kyria Smaragda
our housekeeper, and Eurydice the cook, and the two maids from
Lesbos. The house was full of the whispering of women, and all of us
felt melancholy.

Then it was explained to us by Mademoiselle Leblanc that she and
Fräulein Hoffmann had gone out and sent a telegram to Smyrna, and
soon the aunts would arrive in Egypt. Soon they did: there was our
Aunt Ourania, who was less stern than she seemed to be, and Aunt
Thalia – she was the artistic one – nobody, said Fräulein Hoffmann,
could sing the German *Lieder* with such *Gefühl*.

Soon the house began to live again. There were always people on
the stairs. There was a coming and going, and music, in the old house
at Schutz. That year my eldest sister Phrosso thought she was in love
with an Italian athlete, and my brother Aleko decided he would become
a film star. The girls from Lesbos hung out of the upper windows after
the dishes had been stacked, and tried to reach the dates which were
ripening on the palms. Sometimes there was the sound of dates plopping
in the damp garden below. The garden was never so cool and damp as
when they brought us back from the beach. The gate creaked, as the
governesses let us in through the sand-coloured wall, into the dark-
green thicket of leaves.

My eldest sister Phrosso said it was awful, awful – mouldy
Alexandria – if only they would let her wear high heels, or take us to
Europe, if only she could have a passionate love affair; otherwise, she
was going to burst. But it did not occur to me that our life was by any
means insufferable. Though I was different. I was the sensible one, said

the aunts; Dionysios is a steady boy. Sometimes I felt this bitterly, but I could not alter, and almost always I derived an immense pleasure from the continuous activity of the house: my second sister Agni writing essays at the oval table; the two little ones giving way to tempers; the maids explaining dreams in the attics; and at evening our Aunt Thalia playing the piano in the big *salon* with the gilded mirrors – her interpretation of Schumann was not equalled by that of Frau Klara herself, Fräulein Hoffmann said, not that she had been there. Our aunt was very satisfied. She crossed her wrists more than ever. She sang *une petite chanson spirituelle de votre Duparc* to please Mademoiselle Leblanc, who sat and smiled above her darning-egg. I believe we were at our happiest in the evenings of those days. Though somebody might open a door, threatening to dash the light from the candles on our aunt's piano, the flames soon recovered their shape. Silences were silenter. In those days, it was not uncommon to hear the sound of a camel, treading past, through the dust. There was the smell of camel on the evening air.

Oh yes, we were at our happiest. If my sister Phrosso said it was all awful, awful, it was because she had caught sight of the Italian athlete at the beach, and life had become painful for her.

That was the year Stavrides came to live in the house almost opposite.

'Do you know,' I informed Aunt Ourania, 'these Stavrides are from Smyrna? Eurydice heard it from their cook.'

'Yes, I know,' our aunt replied rather gravely. 'But I do not care for little boys, *Dionysi mou*, to spend so much time in the kitchen.'

It hurt me when our aunt spoke like this, because more than any of us I was hers. But I always pretended not to have heard.

'Did you know them?' I had to ask. 'These Stavrides, Aunt Ourania?'

'I cannot say I did not *know* them,' Aunt Ourania now replied. 'Oh, yes,' she said, 'I *knew* them.'

It seemed to me that Aunt Ourania was looking her sternest, but as always on such a transformation, she began to fiddle with my tunic, to stroke my hair.

'Then, shall we know them, too, Aunt Ourania? There is one child, Eurydice says. A little girl. Titina.'

But our Aunt Ourania grew sterner still.

'I have not decided,' she said at last, 'how far we shall commit ourselves. The Stavrides,' she said, clearing her throat, 'are not altogether desirable.'

'How?' I asked.

'Well,' she said, 'it is difficult to put.'

She went on stroking the short stubble of my cropped hair.

'Kyria Stavridi, you see, was the daughter of a chemist. They even lived above my father's shop. It is not that I have anything against Kyria Stavridi,' she thought to add. 'For all I know she may be an excellent person by different standards. But we must draw the line. Somewhere. Today.'

Then my Aunt Ourania looked away. She was herself such a very good person. She read Goethe every morning, for a quarter of an hour, before her coffee. She kept the Lenten fasts. Very soon after her arrival, she had ordered the hair to be shorn from the heads of all us boys. We were to wear the tunics of ordinary working-class children, because, she said, it was wrong to flaunt ourselves, to pretend we were any different. She herself wore her hair like a man, and gave away her money in secret.

'Still,' my Aunt Ourania said, 'there is no reason why you children should not be kind to Titina Stavridi, even if her parents are undesirable.'

Her eyes had moistened, because she was so tender.

'You, Dionysi,' she said, 'you are the kindest. You,' she said, 'must be particularly kind to poor Titina.'

For the present, however, nothing further happened.

Our life continued. After the departure of our parents, you could not say anything momentous took place. There were always the minor events, and visits. Our Aunt Calliope, the professor, came from Paris. She made us compose essays, and breathe deep. My brother Aleko wrote for a course on hypnotism; Phrosso forgot her athlete, and began to notice a Rumanian; my second sister Agni won her prize for algebra; and the little ones, Myrto and Paul, each started a money box. With so many unimportant, yet necessary things taking place all the time, it did not occur to me to refer again to the Stavrides. Or perhaps it did cross my mind, and I made no mention of them, because our Aunt Ourania would not have wished it. So the days continued more or less unbroken: the sun working at the street wall; the sea water salting our skins; the leaves of the ficus sweating in the damp evenings of the old house at Schutz.

When, suddenly, on a Tuesday afternoon, there was Kyria Stavridi herself sitting in Aunt Ourania's favourite chair beside the big window in the *salon*.

'Which one are you, then?' Kyria Stavridi called, showing an awful lot of gold.

'I am the middle one,' I replied. 'I am Dionysios.'

In ordinary circumstances I would have gone away, but now I was fascinated by all that gold.

'Ah,' Kyria Stavridi said, and smiled, 'often it is the middle ones on whom the responsibilities fall.'

It made her somewhat mysterious. She was dressed, besides, in black, and gave the impression, even at a distance of several feet, of being enclosed in a film of steam.

I did not answer Kyria Stavridi, because I did not know what to say, and because I had noticed she was not alone.

'This is my little girl, Titina,' Kyria Stavridi said. 'Will you be kind to her?'

'Oh,' I said. 'Yes.'

Looking at the unknown child.

Titina Stavridi was standing at her mother's elbow. All in frills. All in white. Wherever she was not stuck with pink satin bows. Now she smiled, out of her oblong face. Some of the teeth appeared to be missing from Titina's smile. She had that banana-coloured skin, those rather pale, large freckles, the paler skin round the edges of the hair, which suggested to me, I don't know why, that Titina Stavridi might be a child who had long continued to wet the bed.

Just then my Aunt Ourania came into the room, to which our maid Aphrodite had called her. She put on her man's voice, and said:

'Well, Kyria Stavridi, who would have expected to see you in Alexandria!'

Holding out her hand from a distance.

Kyria Stavridi, who had got to her feet, began to steam more than ever. She was exceptionally broad in her behind. Kyria Stavridi was bent almost double as she touched my aunt's fingers.

'Ah, Mademoiselle Ourania, such a pleasure!' Kyria Stavridi was bringing it out by the yard. 'To renew acquaintance! And Mademoiselle Thalia? So distinguished!' Kyria Stavridi said.

Aunt Ourania, I could see, did not know how to reply.

'My sister,' she said, finally, 'cannot come down. She is suffering from a headache.'

And Kyria Stavridi could not sympathise enough. Her breath came out in short, agonised rushes.

After that, they spoke about people, which was always boring. 'Dionysi,' my aunt said, during a pause, 'why don't you take Titina into the garden? Here there is really nothing for children.'

But I did not move. And my aunt did not bother again.

As for Titina Stavridi, she might have been a statue, but an ugly one. Her legs seemed so very thick and lifeless. All those bows. And frilly pants. By moving closer I could see she had a kind of little pockmark on the side of her lumpy, freckled nose, and her eyes were a shamefully stupid blue.

'My husband,' Kyria Stavridi was saying, 'my husband, too,' she murmured, 'does not enjoy the best of health.'

'Yes,' said my Aunt Ourania, 'I remember.'

Which somehow made her visitor sad.

Then all the others were pushing and rushing, even Phrosso and Aleko, the two eldest, all entering to see this Kyria Stavridi from Smyrna, and her ugly child. Everybody was introduced.

'Then I hope we shall be friends,' Kyria Stavridi suggested, more to us children, because it was obvious even to me that her hopes of our aunts were not very high. 'Dionysios,' said Kyria Stavridi, 'will be, I feel, Titina's little friend. He has promised me, in fact. They must be the same age, besides.'

This made my sister Agni laugh, and Aleko gave me a pinch from behind. But my little brother Paul, who was never in two minds about anything, went straight up to Titina, and undid one of her satin bows. For a moment I thought Titina Stavridi would begin to cry. But she did not. She smiled and smiled. And was still smiling when her mother, who had said all the necessary things, presently led her out.

Then we were all laughing and shouting.

'So that was Kyria Stavridi!' my sister Phrosso shouted. 'Did you notice the gap between her front teeth?'

'And the bows on her dreadful Titina!' Agni remarked. 'You could dress a bride in all that satin!'

'Do we have to know such very vulgar people?' asked my brother Aleko.

Then our Aunt Ourania replied:

'You are the one who is vulgar, Aleko.'

And slapped him in the face.

'Aleko, you will go to your room.'

This might have shocked us more, Aleko the eldest, already so strong, if Myrto – she was the quiet one who noticed things – had not begun to point and shriek.

'Look! Look!' Myrto shouted. 'Titina Stavridi has done it on the floor!'

There, in fact beside the best chair, was Titina's pool. As if she had been an untrained dog.

At once everyone was pushing to see.

'Such a big girl!' Aunt Ourania sighed.

She rang for Aphrodite, who called to the Arab, who brought a pail.

After that I began to suspect everybody in our house had forgotten the Stavrides. Certainly the two girls from Lesbos had seen the Kyrios Stavrides singing and stumbling at the end of the street. He had put his foot through his straw hat. But nothing was done about Titina, until one hot evening as I searched the garden with a candle, looking for insects for a collection I was about to make, Aunt Ourania called me and said:

'Tomorrow we must do something about Titina. You, Dionysi, shall fetch her.'

Several of the others groaned, and our Aunt Thalia, who was playing Schumann in her loveliest dress, of embroidered purple, hunched her shoulders.

'Oh!' I cried. 'I?'

But I knew, and my aunt confirmed, it could not have been otherwise. It was I who must be the steadiest, the kindest. Even Kyria Stavridi had said that responsibilities often fell to the middle ones.

On the following afternoon I fetched Titina. We did not speak. But Kyria Stavridi kissed me, and left a wet patch on my cheek.

We were going to the beach, on that, as on almost any other afternoon.

'Oh!' moaned my sister Phrosso. 'The old beach! It is so boring!'

And gave Titina a hard pinch.

'What, Titina,' asked Agni, 'is that?'

For Titina was wearing a blue bead.

'That is to keep away the Eye,' said Titina.

'The Eye!'

How they shouted.

'Like an Arab!' cried Myrto.

And we began to chant: '*Titina, Titina, Arapina* . . .' but softly, almost under our breath, in case Mademoiselle should hear.

So Titina came to the beach, on that and other afternoons. Once we took off her pants, and beat her bottom with an empty bottle we found floating in the sea. Then, as always, Titina only smiled, rather watery certainly. We ducked her, and she came up breathless, blinking the sea out of those very stupid, deep blue eyes. When it was wet, her freckly skin shone like a fish's.

'Disgusting!' Phrosso decided, and went away to read a magazine.

You could not torture Titina for long; it became too uninteresting.

But Titina stuck. She stuck to me. It was as if Titina had been told. And once in the garden of our house at Schutz, after showing her my collection of insects, I became desperate. I took Titina's blue bead, and stuck it up her left nostril.

'Titina,' I cried, 'the holes of your nose are so big I'd expect to see your brain – if you had any,' I shouted, 'inside.'

But Titina Stavridi only smiled, and sneezed the bead into her hand.

In my desperation I continued to shout pure nonsense.

Until my Aunt Thalia came out.

'Wretched, wretched children!' she called. 'And *you*! Dionysi!'

During the heat of the afternoon my aunt would recline in a quiet room, nibbling a raw carrot, and copying passages from R. Tagore.

'My headache!' she now protested. 'My rest destroyed! Oh, my God! My conjunctivitis!'

On account of the conjunctivitis Aunt Thalia was wearing her bottle-green eye-shade, which made her appear especially tragic. Altogether Aunt Thalia was like a masked figure in a tragedy.

So that I was shocked, and Titina Stavridi even more so.

On the next occasion when I fetched her, her mother took me aside and instructed me in detail.

'Your poor Aunt Thalia!' She sighed. 'Night and morning,' she made me repeat. 'Bathe the eyes. Undiluted.'

'What is this bottle you have brought me?' asked Aunt Thalia when I presented it.

She was standing in the big *salon*, and the sleeves fell back from her rather thin, but elegant arms.

'It is for the conjunctivitis.'

'Yes! Yes! But what is it?'

Aunt Thalia could grow so impatient.

'It is a baby's water,' I replied. 'Night and morning. Undiluted.'

'Oh! Oh!' moaned our Aunt Thalia as she flung the bottle. It bounced once on the polished floor.

'Disgusting, disgusting creature!'

'It's probably a very *clean* baby,' I said.

It sounded reasonable, but Aunt Thalia was not consoled. Nor did I fetch Titina again. I must say that, even without the episode of Kyria Stavridi's prescription, we should not have been allowed to see Titina. For the Stavrides were always becoming involved in what our aunts considered undignified, not to say repulsive, incidents. For instance, Kyria Stavridi was butted in her broad behind by a piebald goat in the middle of the Rue Goussio. Then there was the thing that happened in our own street as Despo and Aphrodite, the maids from Lesbos, were returning home at dusk. The two girls were panting and giggling when they arrived. We could hear them already as they slammed the gate. What was it, Despo, Aphrodite? we called, running. It was to do with the Kyrios Stavridis, we gathered, who had shown them something in the almost dark. Long afterwards it was a matter for conjecture what the Kyrios Stavridis had shown our maids, though our sister Phrosso insisted from the beginning that she knew.

In any case, Titina Stavridi withdrew from our lives, to a distance of windows, or balconies.

Once indeed, I met her outside the grocer's, when Titina said:

'It is sad, Dionysi. You were the one. You were the one I always loved.'

So that I experienced a sensation of extreme horror, not to say terror, and ran all the way home with the paperful of sugar for which Kyria Smaragda had sent me.

But I could not escape Titina's face. Its dreadful oblong loomed in memory and at open windows, at dusk especially, as the ripening dates fell from their palms, and a camel grunted past.

So much happened all at once I cannot remember when the Stavrides went away. For we, too, were going. Our Aunt Ourania had paused one evening in doing the accounts, and said it was time to give serious thought to education. So there we were. Packing. Fräulein Hoffman began to cry.

Once I did happen to remark:

'Do you suppose the Stavrides have left already? One sees only shutters.'

'That could be,' said Aunt Ourania.

And Aunt Thalia added: the Stavrides were famous for moving on.

Anyway, it was unimportant. So many events and faces crowded into the next few years. For we had become Athenians. In the dry, white, merciless light, it was very soon recognised that I was a conscientious, though backward boy. Time was passing, moustaches growing. Often we children were put to shame by the clothes our Aunt Ourania would make us wear, for economy, and to contain our pride.

Most of the other boys had begun to think of going to brothels. Some of them had already been. Their moustaches helped them to it. But I, I mooned about the streets. Once I wrote on a wall with an end of chalk:

I LOVE   I LOVE   I LOVE

And then went off home. And lay on my empty bed. Listening. The nights were never stained with answers.

It was soon the years of the Catastrophe. We moved to the apartment at Patissia then. So as to have the wherewithal to help some of those poor people, our Aunt Ourania explained. For soon the refugees were pouring in from Anatolia. There were cousins sleeping on the tiled floors, and our Aunt Helen and Uncle Constantine in the maids' bedroom; the girls from Lesbos had to be dismissed. Give, give, ordained Aunt Ourania, standing with her arms full of cast-off clothes. My youngest sister Myrto burst into tears. She broke open her money box with a hammer, and began to spend the money on ices.

Oh, everything was happening at this time. Our eldest brother, who had given up all thought of becoming a film star, was in Cairo being a businessman. Our sister Phrosso had stopped falling in love. She was again in Alexandria, trying for one of several possible husbands. There were the many letters, which filled me with an intolerable longing for damp gardens and ficus leaves. Once I even wrote a poem, but I showed it to no-one, and tore it up. It was sometimes sad at home, though

Agni might sit down at the piano, and bash out *Un baiser, un baiser, pas sur la bouche* . . . while the aunts were paying calls.

Then it was decided – it was our Aunt Ourania who decided things – that as Dionysios was an exceptional, but reliable boy, he should leave school, and go to our Uncle Stepho at the Bank. Then there would be so much more to give to those poor people, the refugees from the Turks in Anatolia. It was exciting enough, but only for a little. Soon I was addressing envelopes at the Bank. The dry ledgers made me sneeze. And my Uncle Stepho would send for me, and twist my ear, thinking it a huge joke to have me to torture at the Bank.

So it was.

Summer had come round again: the eternal, powdery, white Athenian summer. The dust shot out from under my shoes as I trudged along Stadium Street, for although I had intended to spend my holiday at Pelion, Aunt Ourania had at once suggested: Will your conscience allow you, with all those refugees sleeping on mattresses in the hall? So I had stayed, and it was intolerable. My clothes were damp rags by eleven o'clock in Stadium Street.

When I heard my name.

'Dionysi! Dionysi?'

It was a young woman. Or girl. Or girl. Who sprang from one of those little marble tables, where she had been eating a water-ice, on the pavement, at Yannaki's.

'Oh,' she continued, 'I thought. I thought it was *some*one. Dionysios Papapandelidis. Somebody I used to know.'

I must have looked so stupid, I had caused this cool, glittering girl to doubt and mumble. She stood sucking in her lips as though to test to what extent her lipstick had been damaged by the ice.

When suddenly I saw, buried deep inside the shell, the remains, something of the pale, oblong face of the child Titina we had known at Schutz.

My surprise must have come pouring out, for at once she was all cries and laughter. She was breathing on me, embracing even, kissing the wretched beginnings of my thin moustache, there in the glare of Stadium Street. I had never felt so idiotic.

'Come,' Titina said at last. 'We must eat an ice. I have already had several. But Yannaki's ices are so good.'

I sat with Titina, but was nervous, for fear I might have to pay for all those previous ices.

But Titina almost immediately said:

'I shall invite you, dear Dionysi.'

She was so glad. She was so kind. The curious part of it was: as Titina fished in her bag for a cigarette, and fiddled with the stunning little English lighter, and a ball of incalculable notes fell out on the marble table-top, *I* had become the awkward thing of flesh Titina Stavridi used to be.

'Tell me!' she begged; and: 'Tell me!'

Dragging on the cigarette, with her rather full, practised lips.

But I, I had nothing to tell.

'And you?' I asked. 'Do you live in Athens?'

'Oh, no!' She shook her head. 'Never in Athens!'

This goddess was helmeted only in her own hair, black, so black, the lights in it were blue.

'No,' she said. 'I am here on a short visit. Jean-Louis,' she explained, 'is an exceptionally kind and generous man.'

'Jean-Louis?'

'That is my friend,' Titina answered, shaping her mouth in such a way I knew my aunts would have thought it common.

'This person, is he old or young?'

'Well,' she said, 'he is mature.'

'Does your mother know?'

'Oh, Mother! Mother is very satisfied things have arranged themselves so well. She has her own apartment, too. If this is the world, then live in it. That is what Mother has decided.'

'And your father?'

'Papa is always there,' Titina said, and sighed.

As for myself, I began to fill with desperate longing. Here was Titina, so kind, so close, so skilled, so unimaginable. My clothes tightened on me as I sat.

And Titina talked. All the time her little bracelets thrilled and tinkled. She would turn her eyes this way and that, admiring, or rejecting. She would narrow her eyes in a peculiar way, though perhaps it was simply due to the glare.

'Tell me, Dionysi,' she asked, and I experienced the little hairs barely visible on her forearm, 'have you ever thought of me? I expect not. I was so horrible! Awful! And you were always so very kind.'

The fact was: Titina Stavridi did sincerely believe in her own words, for she had turned upon me her exquisitely contrived face, and I could see at the bottom of her candid eyes, blue as only the Saronic Gulf, I could see, well, I could see the truth.

'There is always so little time,' complained Titina, both practical and sad. 'Dionysi, are you free? Are you free, say, this afternoon? To take me to the sea? To swim?'

'But this is Greece,' I said, 'where men and girls have not yet learnt to swim together.'

'Pah!' she cried. 'They will learn! You and I,' she said, 'will swim together. If you are free. This afternoon.'

And at once time was our private toy. We were laughing and joking expertly as Titina Stavridi pared away the notes, to pay for all those ices we had eaten at Yannaki's.

'First I have an appointment,' she announced.

'With whom?' I asked.

I could not bear it.

'Ah!' She laughed. 'With a friend of my mother's. An elderly lady, who has a wart.'

So I was comforted. There were *youvarlakia* for lunch. Nobody could equal Eurydice at *youvarlakia*, but today, it seemed, sawdust had got into them.

'You will offend Eurydice,' Aunt Thalia had begun to moan. 'You have left her *youvarlakia*.'

I decided not to tell my two, dear, stuffy aunts of my meeting with Titina Stavridi.

It became the most unbearable secret, and to pass the time – to say nothing of the fact that I should probably have to pay Titina's fare on the rather long journey by bus.

'Oh, no,' she was saying at last, there on the steps of the Grande Bretagne. 'Call a taxi,' Titina insisted, which the man in livery did.

'Money is for spending,' she explained.

On the way, as she rootled after the lovely little lighter, I was relieved to see her bag was still stuffed with notes.

For the afternoon she was wearing a bracelet of transparent shells, which jostled together light as walnuts.

'That,' Titina said, 'is nothing.'

'My friend,' she added, 'advised me to leave my jewels in a safe deposit at the Crédit Lyonnais. One never knows, Jean-Louis says, what may happen in Greece.'

I agreed that the Crédit Lyonnais offered greater certainty.

It was like that all the way. As her body cannoned off me, as lightly as her bracelets of shells, Titina revealed a life of sumptuous, yet practical behaviour. She accepted splendour as she did her skin. All along the beach, that rather gritty Attic sand, Titina radiated splendour in godlike armour of nacreous scales, in her little helmet of rubber feathers.

'Do you like my costume?' she asked, after she had done her mouth. 'Jean-Louis does not. *Ça me donne un air de putain.* So he says.'

At once she ran down into the sea, shimmering in her gorgeous scales. I was glad to find myself inside the water.

Then we swam, in long sweeps of silvery-blue. Bubbles of joy seemed to cling to Titina's lips. Her eyes were the deeper, drowsier, for immersion.

I had asked the taxi to drop us at a certain bay along that still-deserted coast. The shore was strewn with earth-coloured rocks. The Attic pines straggled, and struggled, and leaned out over the sea. It was a poor landscape, splendid, too, in its own way, of perfectly fulfilled austerity. I had hoped we should remain unseen. And so we were. Until a party of lads descended half-naked on the rocks. Several of them I had sat beside in school. Now they seated themselves, lips drooping, eyes fixed. They shouted the things one expected. Some of them threw handfuls of water.

But Titina squinted at the sun.

Faced with these gangling louts, of deferred muscle and blubber-lips, anything oafish in myself seemed to have been spent. Was it Titina's presence? My head, set firmly on my neck, had surveyed oceans and continents. I had grown suave, compact, my glistening moustache had thickened, if not to the human eye.

Presently some of the boys I knew plunged in, and were swimming around, calling and laughing in their cracked voices. Their seal-like antics were intended to amuse.

But Titina did not see.

Then, as we were standing in the shallows, squat, yellow Sotiri Papadopoulos attempted to swim between Titina's legs.

'Go away, filthy little boy!'

How she pointed!

Titina's scorn succeeded. Sotiri went. Fortunately. He had often proved himself stronger than I.

Afterwards I sat with Titina, dripping water, under the pines. She told me distantly of the visits to Deauville, Le Touquet and Cannes. Reservations at the best hotels. I was only lazily impressed. But how immaculate she was. I remembered Agni, her goosey arms, and strings of wet, swinging hair.

Titina produced *fruits glacés*.

'We brought them, Jean-Louis and I, from the Côte d'Azur. Take them,' she ordered.

First I offered her the box.

'Ach!' she said. 'Eat! I am sick of them. The *fruits glacés!*'

So I sat and stuffed.

For a long time we remained together beneath the pines, she so cool and flawless, myself only hot and clammy. She began to sing – what, I really cannot remember.

'Ah,' she exclaimed, lying back, looking up through the branches. 'They are stunted, our poor pines.'

'That is their way,' I told her.

'Yes,' she sighed. 'They are not stunted.'

I walked a short distance, and brought her *vissinada* from a roadside booth. We stained our mouths with the purple *vissinada*. All along the Saronic Gulf the evening had begun to purple. The sand was gritty to the flesh. I believe it was at this point the man with the accordion passed by, playing his five or six notes, as gentle and persuasive as wood-pigeons. Unlike the boys earlier, the man with the accordion did not stare. He strolled. I think the man was blind.

'*Ach, Titina! Titina!*'

I was breathing my desperation on her.

The darkness was plunging towards us as Titina Stavridi turned her face towards me on the sand. A twig had marked her perfect cheek. She lay looking into me, as though for something she would not find.

'Poor Dionysaki,' she said, 'at least it is unnecessary to be afraid.'

So that I had never felt stronger. As I wrestled with Titina Stavridi on the sand, my arms were turned into sea-serpents. The scales of her nacreous *maillot*, which Jean-Louis had never cared for, were sloughed in a moment by my skilful touch. I was holding in my hands her small, but persistent buttocks, which had been threatening to escape all that afternoon.

'*Ach!*' she cried, in almost bitter rage, as we heard her teeth strike on mine.

Afterwards Titina remained infinitely kind. The whole darkness was moving with her kindness.

'When will you leave?' I dreaded to ask.

'The day after tomorrow,' she replied. 'No,' she corrected, quick. 'Tomorrow.'

'Then why did you say: *after* tomorrow?'

'Because,' she said simply, 'I forgot.'

So my sentence was sealed. All the sea sounds of Attica rose to attack me, as I thrust my lips all over again into Titina's wilted mouth.

'Goodbye, Titina,' I said, on the steps of her hotel.

'Goodbye, Dionysi. *Dionysaki!*'

She was so tender, so kind.

But I did not say anything else, as I had begun to understand already that such remarks are idiocy.

All the way to Patissia, the dust was thick and heavy on my shoes.

When I got in, my Aunt Calliope, the professor, had arrived from Paris.

'Our Dionysi! cried Aunt Calliope. 'Almost a man!'

She embraced me quickly, in order to return to politics.

We had never cared for Aunt Calliope, who had made us write essays and things, though her brothers loved her and would quarrel with her till the white hours over any boring political issue.

'The Catastrophe,' my Aunt Calliope had reached the shouting stage, 'was the result of public apathy in one of the most backward countries of the world.'

My Uncle Stepho was shouting back.

'Hand it over to you and your progressive intellectuals, and we might as well, *all*, decent people, anyway, cut our throats!' bellowed Uncle Stepho, Vice-President of our Whole Bank.

'But let us stick to the Catastrophe!'

'The Generals were to blame!' screamed my Uncle Constantine.

'All Royalists! Royalists!'

Aunt Calliope was beating with her fists.

'What can one expect of effete Republicans? Nothing further!'

'Do not blame the Republicans!' Aunt Ourania dared anyone.

'The Royalists have not yet proved themselves.'

Aunt Calliope started to cackle unmercifully.

'Better the Devil,' thought Constantine.

Aunt Ourania frowned.

'Still, Kosta,' she suggested, very gravely, in the voice she adopted for all soothing purposes, 'you must admit that when blood flows our poor Greece is regenerated.'

My Aunt Thalia, who had been crying, went to the piano. She began to play a piece I remembered. Sweet and sticky, the music flowed from under her always rather tentative hands.

The music gummed the voices up.

Then my Aunt Calliope remarked:

'Guess whom I saw?'

Nobody did.

'That little thing, that Titina Stavridi, to whom you were all so kind in the old days at Schutz.'

'Living in Athens?' asked Aunt Ourania, though the answer must remain unimportant.

'Not a bit of it,' Aunt Calliope said. 'I have run into her before. Oh, yes, several times. In Paris.' Here Aunt Calliope laughed. 'A proper little *thing*! A little whore!'

It was obvious from her expression that Aunt Ourania was taking it upon herself to expiate the sins of the world, while Aunt Thalia forced the music. How it flowed, past the uncles and out of the room, all along the passages of our shrunken apartment, which seldom nowadays lost its smell of *pasta*. The intolerable Schumann pursued me as far as my own room, and further.

Outside, the lilac-bushes were turned solid in the moonlight. The white music of that dusty night was frozen in the parks and gardens. As I leaned out of the window, and held up my throat to receive the knife, nothing happened. Only my Aunt Thalia continued playing Schumann, and I realised that my extended throat was itself as stiff as a sword.

Michael Wilding

THE MAN OF SLOW FEELING
1970

After the accident he lay for weeks in the still white ward. They fed him intravenously but scarcely expected him to live. Yet he did live, and when at last they removed the bandages from his eyes, it was found he could see. They controlled what he could see carefully, keeping the room dimmed, the blinds down, at first; but gradually increased his exposure to light, to the world around. Slowly his speech came back. He blocked for some time on words he could not remember, could no longer enunciate; but gradually his vocabulary returned. But he had lost sensation, it seemed. He could not smell the flowers Maria brought into the small private ward. And when she gave him the velvety globed petals to touch, he could not feel them. All foods were the same to him. The grapes she mechanically bought, he could only see. They had neither touch nor taste for him. If he shut his eyes and returned to darkness again, he did not know what he was eating. Yet he was not totally without sensation – it was not as if he were weightless or bodiless. He was conscious of lying in bed day after day, his body lying along the bed – perhaps because the constant pressure reached through to his numbed nerves. But the touch of Maria's fingers on his cheeks, the kiss of her lips against his, he could not feel, nor mouth the taste of her.

And yet as he lay alone in that small white room odd sensations came to him, brushed him with their dying wings. As if, lying there with only his thoughts and imaginings, he could conjure back the taste of grapes, the soft touch of Maria's hand, the searching pressure of her kiss. They surprised him, these sensations; often they would make him wake from a light sleep as if a delightful dream had achieved an actuality: but when he awoke he was always totally alone, and remembered nothing of any dream. It was often, as he lay there, as if someone had actually touched him, or forced grapes against his palate, and he would want to cry out at the unexpectedness of it. If imagination, it could only have been triggered by the workings of his subconscious. He mentioned it to the nurses, and they said that it could be that he was getting his sensations back. He did not argue with them, pointing out that there were no correlatives to the sensations, no objects provoking them. It was like a man feeling pain in a foot already amputated: a foot he would not be getting back. The sensations were the ghosts of feelings he had once had, nerve memories of a lost past.

Released from hospital, Maria took him back to the house in the country. They made love that first night, but he could not feel her full breasts, her smooth skin, and making love to her was totally without sensation for him. Its only pleasures were voyeuristic and nostalgic: his eyes and ears allowed him to remember past times – like seeing a sexual encounter at the cinema. The thought came to him that the best way to get anything from sex now was to cover the walls and ceilings with mirrors, so that at least he could have a full visual satisfaction to replace his missing senses. But he said nothing to Maria. He said nothing, but he knew she realised that for him it was now quite hopeless.

He was woken in the night by a dream of intercourse, the excitement of fondling a body, the huge relief of orgasm. He lay awake, the vividness of it reminding him bitterly of what was now lost to him.

The early days back in the house he found disorienting. Within the white walls confining the ward experience had been limited for him; he saw little, encountered little; the disturbing nerve memories were few. But released, now they swelled to a riot, as if exposure to the open world had revived dormant, dying memories for their final throes. Released, his body was a continual flux of various sensations, of smell, of taste, of touch; yet still with no sensations from his experiences. He could walk beside the dung heap at the field's corner, ready to manure the land, and though he inhaled deeply hoping its pungency would break through his numbness, he could experience nothing. When Maria was not looking, he reached his hand into the dung: he felt nothing. A visual repugnance, but no physical sensation, no recoil of nausea.

Yet at tea suddenly the full pungency of the foul dung swept across to him, his hand unfeelingly holding a meringue was swamped in the heavy foul stickiness of the dung. He left the table, walked across to the window that looked out onto the wide lawns. There was nothing outside to provoke his sensations; and if there had been, how could his touch have been affected from outside? His touch and smell had not, as he'd momentarily hoped, returned. Maria asked what was the matter, but he said nothing. He went to the bathroom, but oddly did not feel nausea. He expected to, biting that momentarily dung-drenched meringue. But his stomach recorded no sensations. His intellect's interpretation had misled him; his mind was interpreting a nausea he would have felt in his past life, an existence no longer his.

Yet in bed as he reached out to fondle, hopelessly, Maria who made love with him now more eagerly, more readily, more desperately, uselessly, pointlessly than ever before, his stomach was gripped by a sudden retching nausea, and he had to rush to the bathroom to vomit.

'My poor dear,' said Maria, 'oh my poor dear.'

He wondered whether he should rest again, to recover the placidity he had known in the hospital. But to rest in bed, although he could read or hear music, meant his life was so reduced. At least to walk round the fields or into the village gave him stimulation for those senses that remained.

But activity seemed disturbing. And provoked a riot of these sense memories, these million twitching amputated feet.

Then, one day, he realised his senses were not dead.

It was a compound realisation, not a sudden epiphany. In the morning he had driven the car and, going too fast over the humpbacked bridge that crossed the canal, had provoked a scream from Maria. He had asked in alarm what was the matter.

'Nothing,' she said, 'it's just that it took the bottom out of my stomach, going over the bridge like that.'

'I'm sorry,' he said, 'I didn't realise I was going that fast. I can't feel that sort of thing now.'

Indeed he had forgotten, till she reminded him, that the sensation existed.

They made love at noon, not because he could experience anything, but because in his dreams and in his waking nerve memories, he so often re-experienced the ecstasy in actuality denied him. He perhaps half hoped to recapture the experience. But never did.

Maria got up to cook lunch, absurdly spending great labour on foods he could not taste, perhaps hoping to lure his taste from its grave. She rushed from the kitchen to his bed when he gave a sudden cry. But he was laughing when she reached the room.

'Sorry,' he said. 'It's just that like you said, your stomach dropped out going over the bridge, and that must have reminded me of it. It just happened this minute, lying here.'

She touched his brow with her cool hand, whose coolness and presence he could not feel. He brushed her away, irritated by her solicitude. As he ate his lunch, he brooded over his cry of alarm. And later, buying cigarettes in the village shop, for the nervous habit he realised that had always caused him to smoke, not the taste, he came on the truth as his body was fused with the sudden aliveness of intercourse, the convulsive ecstasy of orgasm.

'Are you all right, Sir?' the shopkeeper asked.

'I'm fine, fine,' he said. 'It's, it's' (it's nothing he was about to say mechanically, but it was ecstasy); 'it's quite all right,' he said.

Walking back, he was elated at realising sensation was not denied him, but delayed. He looked at his watch and predicted he would taste his lunch at four o'clock. And sitting on the stile at the field corner, he did. In excitement he ran, his meal finished, to tell Maria, to tell her ecstatically that the accident had not robbed him of sensation, but dulled and slowed its passage along his nerves. When he tripped on a log and grazed his knee without any feeling, he knew, ambivalently, that in three hours the pain would be registered: he waited in excitement for confirmation of his prediction, in anxiety about the pain it would bring.

∽

But his knowledge was a doubtful advantage. The confusions of senses before had been disturbing, but not worrying. It was the prediction now that tore him with anxiety. Cutting his finger while sharpening a pencil, he waited tense for the delayed pain, and even though cutting his finger was the slightest of hurts, it filled three hours of anxiety. He worked out with Maria that the well-timed cooking of food could appetise his tasteless smell-less later meal; but few meals could produce rich smells three hours before serving. He could not do anything the slightest nauseating, like cleaning drains or gutting chickens, for fear of the context in which his senses would later register and produce in their further three hours the possibility of his vomiting. Defecation became nightmarish, could ruin any ill-timed meal, or intercourse.

And ill-timed intercourse would ruin any casual urination. He toyed with the idea of keeping a log book, so that by consulting what happened three hours back, he knew what he was about to feel. He experimented one morning, and in a sort of way it worked. For he spent so long noting down each detail in his book, he had little time to experience anything. He realised how full a life is of sensations, as hopelessly he tried to record them all.

He developed a device, instead, consisting primarily of a small tape recorder which he carried always with him. He spoke a constant commentary into it of his sensate actions and, through earphones, his commentary would be played back to him after a three hours' delay, to warn him of what he was about to feel. The initial three hours, as he paced the fields, were comparatively simple, though he worried at the limitations it would impose on his life and experience, having to comment on it in its entirety, each trivial stumble, each slight contact. But after three hours had passed, and his bruised slow nerves were transmitting his sensations, the playback came in. And he found he could not both record his current activities in a constant flow, and hear a constant commentary on his three-hours-back activities, momentarily prior to his sensations of those past ones. He braced himself for the predicted sensation that his recorded voice warned him of, and in doing so forgot to maintain his current commentary for his three-hours-hence instruction. And maintaining his commentary, he forgot to act on the playback and lost the value of its warnings. And returning again to it, intent on gaining from its predictions, he began to follow its record as instructions, and when he caught the word 'stumble' from his disembodied voice, he stumbled in obedience, forgetting to hold himself still for the sensation of stumbling. And what, anyway, warned of a stumble, was he to do? Sit passively for the experience to flow through him and pass? What he had recorded as advice seemed peremptory instruction, terse orders that his nerves responded to independent of his volition. The playback possessed an awful authority, as if the voice were no longer his, and the announced experiences (which he had never felt) foreign to him: and at each random whim of the voice, distorted parodically from his own, his sensations would have inevitably to respond. And he the mere frame, the theatre for the puppet strings to be hung and tugged in.

He could never coordinate commentary and playback: the one perpetually blocked the other, as he tried to hear one thing and say another. And he would confuse them and having spoken a sensation into the microphone before him would immediately prepare to experience it, forgetting the delay that had to come. His sensations became as random to him as before in that maze of playback and commentary and memory. And when he did accidentally, reflectively, re-enact the activity his playback warned him to prepare for, then he had to record another warning of that activity for his three-hours-later sensation: and it was as if he were to be trapped in a perpetual round to the same single repeated stumble.

He abandoned notebooks and tape recorders. He sat at the window awaiting his sensations. Sex became a nightmare for him, its insensate action and empty voyeurism bringing only the cerebral excitement of a girlie magazine, its consequence a wet dream, the tension of waiting for which (sometimes with an urgent hope, sometimes with the resistant wished-against tension) would agonise him – keep him sleepless or, in the mornings, unable to read or move. And the continual anxiety affected his whole sexual activity, made him ejaculate too soon, or not at all; and he had to wait his three hours for his failures to reach him, knowing his failure, reminded of it cruelly three hours after his cerebral realisation.

He could not sleep. Any activity three hours before sleep, would awaken him, bumping into a door, drinking wine, switching off a record player. The sensations would arouse his tense consciousness. He tried to control against this, spending the three hours before sleep in total stillness and peace, but the tension of this created its own anxiety, produced psychosomatic pains: of which he would be unaware until they woke him.

He thought back with a sort of longing to his hospital bed, when without stimulation he had experienced only the slightest of sensations. But in those bare walls of the bare room, he might almost have been in a tomb. If life were only bearable without sensation, what was the life worth that he could bear?

⌒

Maria came back from town one day to find him dead in the white, still bathroom. He had cut his arteries in a bath in the Roman way, the hot water, now rich-vermilioned, to reduce the pain of dying.

Though, she told herself, he would not have felt anything anyway, he had no sensation.

But three hours afterwards, what might he have felt?

Gerard Windsor

WEDDING PRESENTS
FOR BREAKFAST
1983

I acquired my mother-in-law by accident. But that's another story. The present point is that just recently I lost her.

The day after this epic turn of events I sat, unshaven, spooning breakfast into my jaded system. My wife sat opposite. We had disposed of certain issues with early-morning dispassion – hours of sleep tallied, milkman's bills, other items of that moment. The flow had dried up. The atmosphere was desultory. I had not thought of the deceased for quite some hours. My wife seemed relaxed and guileless; her chin was retracted. (My wife's chin could dispose of many a stronger man than I.) Then, cool as you please, half in the act of getting up and turning her back to me, she said, 'Mother never opened her wedding presents.'

The coffee being poured into my mouth ceased all vital motion. It simply sat there, a still pool, stagnant. My wife continued to affect the pose of one who has just emitted a supreme inconsequentiality. My mind took off at an alarming rate – for that hour of the morning. My mother-in-law had not married recently. My wife was in fact the fruit of her one and only union. Indeed, years had elapsed between conjunction and this recent, final disjunction.

Gravity proved overwhelming, and the coffee seeped slowly away, leaving my mouth free. 'I heard correctly?' I inquired.

'What?' said my wife.

She was playing with me, I saw. 'Your late mother's supreme act of retention.' I needed the slight tinge of combativeness to draw my wife into the open.

'I understand it,' she said.

'You!' I exclaimed. The remark sorted oddly with my wife. She is an acquisitive woman, much given to a role as a receiver of supplies of manchester, silverware, household items, etc. I looked at her suspiciously.

Never one to share my more personal pleasures, she was making herself a cup of tea. She still had her back to me. 'If you use your imagination it makes complete sense,' she reprimanded me.

'Hang on,' I said. 'Did you ever ask her why she hadn't opened them?'

'Of course. She said there was no need. She had the Hardy Brothers list.'

'And you really thought that explained it?'

'Of course not.' She actually turned round and faced me. 'As I said, you just have to use your imagination.'

'My imagination was never able to contain your mother. My scope was far too puny and limited.'

With even, exaggerated enunciation my wife said, 'It was a statement to Dad.' Then she turned away and actually walked out of the room.

'Saying what?' I called after her, but she ignored me.

Unaided, I applied myself to the puzzle. The statement, if statement it was, could only have been of ill-intent. Yet, to my perhaps naive eye, the old lady had displayed only average hostility towards her spouse. Given her normal outlook on the world, she was almost remarkable in her temperateness. Hence, I deduced, the statement, although undoubtedly malevolent, was subtly so. Once I had seen that much, the rest was easy. The statement had been a warning. My mother-in-law's commitment to the marital state had always been qualified and conditional. Legally, and perhaps by other imperatives, she had been forced to the ultimate validation of sexual union. But as long as the wedding presents remained unopened, the match remained unconsummated. Neither husband nor wife could touch those very singular gifts traditionally given exclusively to married couples for their mutual enjoyment. The presents remained strictly, *qua* presents, intact, virgin – boxed, wrapped, carded. They were as ripe for return to Hardy Brothers or sender as for defloration by my now late in-laws.

My admiration for the old woman was momentarily, but quite effusively, purged of all begrudging elements. She had produced a warning of quite splendid ominousness.

My wife returned to the kitchen. She looked brisk. Continued conversation with me was not on her mind. But I was proud of my insight; I wanted her to know I had cracked her code. I shook my head in tribute and said, 'The old lady certainly had style.'

'Don't be ridiculous,' said my wife, turning sharply. 'She never had the slightest sense of dress or decoration. Or taste at all for that matter.'

My marriage is like that. Overbearing obtuseness. I try to duck and let it pass. 'I mean I can't imagine a smarter way of letting the old man know there was an annulment round every next corner.'

'You can be so absurd,' spat my wife, and this time the jaw was planted firmly down the wicket. 'It was a very happy marriage.'

Facts are for flying in the face of. For some people. Reason, abuse, are both impotent. Just let the irrationality come, and use it as a source of wonder. Man's jaded experience constantly needs new stimuli. Viewed in this mature, sophisticated way, my wife's howlers can be a most fertile source of gaping and amazement. 'So what was the great statement saying?' I tried to be sweetly teachable.

'Some people!' grieved my wife. Then, with a largesse of maternal condescension, she explained to me. 'She was totally dependent on him. That's what she was saying. She wanted it known he was to be the sole supplier of her needs. Other people's presents would have been just a reminder that she'd taken favours from outsiders. He was her husband. He had to work through the Hardy Brothers list and supply her with everything himself.' My wife bent her head slightly and gave me that quizzical look meaning 'Do you understand now, dear?', and then her expression shot back into neutral before passing immediately into a simper. 'It was all rather sweet, really,' she said.

That was a rebuke of course. Need I say I was not the least bit convinced. My wife's charming romance was a complete fantasy – totally unlikely – deriving in no way from the actual characters whose lives it was embroidering. I made no attempt to make my wife see this stark logic. She is not open to reason. The adventure of my life consists of adapting myself to her unshakable fatuities. And indeed, from one point of view, it means there's never a dull moment. Some right contortions I have to perform to keep our two-planet galaxy from disintegrating.

I retrieved a slice of toast, spread margarine evenly and to the edges, and wondered whether the palate demanded honey or vegemite. No need was crying out. I divided the slice, and made one sweet, the other savoury. It was difficult to choose which I should eat first. Upstairs my wife made noises indicative of a return to the environs of my company. I seized the honeyed slice, and tended rather to bolt it, racing against the drips that oozed over the rim on every side.

'Chaos,' said my wife, bursting through the door. 'That's all this place ever is.'

Carefully I dusted a few crumbs from my fingers onto the plate. 'I'm finished,' I reassured her. Her flurried manner, in fact, was misleading. There was no crisis or urgency about. It was all merely a statement – in this case to me. 'Actually,' I said, 'I wouldn't mind a word with you.'

My wife opened the fridge. 'I'm listening,' she said. And I knew she was too. Our marital life demands that when I want her attention, I go through the paces of making an appointment. To keep the ploy effective, I use it sparingly. She feigns indifference, but I know she listens.

'I don't want to get philosophical,' I began, 'but, on the question of the presents, where are they now?'

My wife rarely lets up. 'Now, how on earth is that philosophical?' she asked.

I waved this red herring away. 'Just that my imagination seems to be in gear at the moment, and the phenomenon of the presents raises all sorts of questions.'

'I don't see . . .' she began, but thought better of pursuing that line. 'The presents are safe,' she said.

I took the bull by the horns. 'What are we going to do with them?'

'Do with them? Nothing! And what's *we* got to do with it? The presents are no business of yours.'

This was all so much bluster and smokescreen. My wife in fact sat down, and although her chin was forward there was an unmistakable foxiness about her. 'The presents,' she said, 'stay where they belong.'

'Which is with us, surely,' I said. 'You're the sole heir. They don't belong anywhere else.'

'Don't you have any feeling for the dead?' She was quite scathing. 'Can't you try and attune yourself to their spirit?'

This was a new tack for my wife, a plain woman at all times. Black was black and purple was purple, and pity help anyone who dealt in pastels. The dead only existed insofar as they were of use to the living. Sensitivity to their tunes was a new line for her altogether. I wondered what was going on. By this time I had finished breakfast, and I believe I was reasonably alert. 'Well,' I tried, 'what does her spirit communicate about her wedding presents?'

'My, oh my,' riposted my wife, 'what's happened to the little man with all his fanciful notions and flowery talk? The old lady's gesture should hit you in the eye.'

'I'm still too affected by her death,' I said. 'Please just tell me about the presents.'

'She's never opened them. She wouldn't want them opened now. She'll have to take them with her.'

'But she can't take them with her. That's usually the point.'

'Spare me your wit! The presents are to be buried with her.'

For a lingering moment my wife intended to repeat her trick of leaving the table on her big line. But the temptation to keep a ringside seat for my reaction was too great.

I saw all that happening even as her latest absurdity landed at my feet. 'For the love of Mike,' I cried, 'have you got religion or something? She's not Pharaoh or his wife or any other Egyptian for that matter. If she didn't need those things in this life, she's hardly likely to need them on her journey to the next.'

My wife remained unperturbed by this outburst. 'If you weren't at the mercy of your own wordspinning,' she said, 'you'd see it was the only possible thing to do with them.' She paused, and then added, 'Unless, of course, avarice is allowed into it.'

She thought she'd stymied me on that one. But I was too outraged to fall for cute attempts at cowing me. 'Avarice has nothing to do with it, and well you know it. Self-indulgent quirkiness, that's all this plan is. And there's no way I'm going to allow it to end up in such waste-fulness.' A cogent thought occurred to me. 'In any case, they won't all fit in the grave.'

'I've bought two plots,' she said. 'There'll be two coffins. I'll put some things in with her, some in the box next to her.'

I actually stood up. 'This is your own mother you're talking about.'

'Pooh, pooh,' she said. 'I've never noticed you display such concern for my family before. The old lady will be delighted to be lapped about by her presents.'

'Well, I'm going to take them off her. She had quite long enough to have a good go of them. It's someone else's turn now.' I felt I had put the moral point quite squarely.

My wife resorted to legalisms – a sure sign she was on the defensive. 'Interfering with graves is a criminal offence.'

'I'll plead overwhelming grief. One last look and embrace. Hamlet wasn't charged. And I'm a relative. They'll have to believe me.' I let the challenge sink in.

'You throw all those presents down there, and the moment the last mourner leaves the graveside I start digging.'

'No you don't,' said my wife, and this time she did stand up, and she pushed her chair back in. 'I've hired two guards. They'll be there till the earth settles and the slab goes on. Hang the expense. It's only your money.'

I find it unaccountable that marriages are so commonly regarded as dull, inevitably dull. My wife and I have no difficulty in giving one another constant stimulation. As the worthy woman turned her back on me, I felt every tingling hormone rushing to aid the genesis of my next move. Indeed there must have been a superfluity, for I was yanked roughly down a new alley of approach. 'Hey,' I called out. 'How do I know you really will put those presents in the coffins?' I'm sure I heard a step falter in the front room. 'For that matter, how do I know there still are presents in those boxes?' There was silence. Ha, ha, I smiled. Got her on the run.

Tim Winton

MY FATHER'S AXE
1983

1

Just now I discover the axe gone. I look everywhere inside and outside the house, front and back, but it is gone. It has been on my front
veranda since the new truckload of wood arrived and was dumped so
intelligently over my front lawn. Jamie says he doesn't know where the
axe is and I believe him; he won't chop wood any more. Elaine hasn't
seen it; it's men's business, she says. No, it's not anywhere. But who
would steal an axe in this neighbourhood, this street where I grew up
and have lived much of my life? No-one steals on this street. Not an
axe.

It is my father's axe.

I used to watch him chop with it when we drove the old Morris
and the trailer outside the town limits to gather wood. He would tie a
thick, short bar of wood to the end of forty feet of rope and swing it
about his head like a lasso and the sound it made was the whoop! of
the headmaster's cane you heard when you walked past his office. My
father sent the piece of wood high into the crown of a dead she-oak
and when it snarled in the stark, grey limbs he would wrap the rope
around his waist and then around his big freckled arms, and he would
pass me his grey hat with bound hands and tell me to stand right back
near the Morris with my mother who poured tea from a thermos flask.
And he pulled. I heard his body grunt and saw his red arms whiten,
and the tree's crown quivered and rocked and he added to the motion,
tugging, jerking, gasping until the whole bush cracked open and birds
burst from all the trees around and the dead, grey crown of the she-
oak teetered and toppled to the earth, chased by a shower of twigs and
bark. My mother and I cheered and my father ambled over, arms
glistening, to drink the tea that tasted faintly of coffee and the rubber
seal of the thermos. Rested, he would then dismember the brittle tree

with graceful swings of his axe and later I would saw with him on the bowman saw and have my knees showered with white, pulpy dust.

He could swing an axe, my father.

And that axe is gone.

He taught me how to split wood though I could never do it like him, those long, rhythmic, semicircular movements like a ballet dancer's warm-up; I'm a left-hander, a mollydooker he called me, and I chop in short, jabby strokes which do the job but are somehow less graceful.

When my father began to leave us for long periods for his work – he sold things – he left me with the responsibility of fuelling the home. It gave me pride to know that our hot water, my mother's cooking, the living-room fire depended upon me, and my mother called me the man of the house, which frightened me a little. Short, winter afternoons I spent up the back splitting pine for kindling, long, fragrant spines with neat grain, and I opened up the heads of mill-ends and sawn blocks of she-oak my father brought home. Sometimes in the trance of movement and exertion I imagined the blocks of wood as teachers' heads. It was pleasurable work when the wood was dry and the grain good and when I kept the old Kelly axe sharp. I learnt to swing single-handed, to fit wedges into stubborn grain, to negotiate knots with resolve, and the chopping warmed me as I stripped to my singlet and worked until I was ankle-deep in split, open wood and my breath steamed out in front of me with each righteous grunt.

Once, a mouse half caught itself in a trap in the laundry beneath the big stone trough and my mother asked me to kill it, to put it out of its misery, she said. Obediently, I carried the threshing mouse in the trap at arm's length right up to the back of the yard. How to kill a mouse? Wring its neck? Too small. Drown it? In what? I put it on the burred block and hit it with the flat of the axe. It made no noise but it left a speck of red on my knee.

Another time my father, leaving again for a long trip, began softly to weep on our front step. My mother did not see because she was inside finding him some fruit. I saw my father ball his handkerchief up and bite on it to muffle his sobs and I left him there and ran through the house and up to the woodpile where I shattered great blocks of she-oak until it was dark and my arms gave out. In the dark I stacked wood into the buckled shed and listened to my mother calling.

I broke the handle of that axe once, on a camping trip; it was good hickory and I was afraid to tell him. I always broke my father's tools, blunted his chisels, bent his nails. I have never been a handyman like my father. He made things and repaired things and I watched but did not see the need to learn because I knew my father would always be. If I needed something built, something done, there was my father and he protected me.

When I was eight or nine he took my mother and me to a beach shack at a rivermouth up north. The shack was infested with rats and I lay awake nights listening to them until dawn when my father came and roused me and we went down to haul the craypots. The onshore reefs at low tide were bare, clicking and bubbling in the early sun, and octopuses gangled across exposed rocks, lolloping from hole to hole. We caught them for bait; my father caught them and I carried them in the bucket with the tight lid and looked at my face in the still tidal pools that bristled with kelp. But it was not so peaceful at high tide when the swells burst on the upper lip of the reef and cascaded walls of foam that rushed in upon us and rocked us with their force. The water reached my waist though it was only knee-deep for my father. He taught me to brace myself side-on to the waves and find footholds in the reef and I hugged his leg and felt his immovable stance and moulded myself to him. At the edge of the reef I coiled the rope that he hauled up and held the hessian bag as he opened the heavy, timber-slatted pots; he dropped the crays in and I heard their tweaking cries and felt them grovelling against my legs.

During the day my mother read *They're a Weird Mob* and ate raisins and cold crayfish dipped in red vinegar. We played Scrabble and it did not bother me that my father lost.

Lost his axe. Who could have stolen such a worthless thing? The handle is split and taped and the head bears the scars of years; why even look at it?

One night on that holiday a rat set off a trap on the rafter above my bed. My father used to tie the traps to the rafters to prevent the rats from carrying them off. It went off in the middle of the night with a snap like a small fire cracker and in the dark I sensed something moving above me and something warm touched my forehead. I lay still and did not scream because I knew my father would come. Perhaps I did scream in the end, I don't know. But he came, and he lit the Tilley lamp and chuckled and, yes, that was when I screamed. The rat, suspended by six feet of cord, swung in an arc across my bed with the long, hairy whip of tail trailing a foot above my nose. The body still flexed and struggled. My father took it down and went outside with its silhouette in the lamplight in front of him. My mother screamed; there was a drop of blood on my forehead. It was just like *The Pit and the Pendulum*, I said. We had recently seen the film and she had found the book in the library and read it to me for a week at bedtime. Yes, she said with a grim smile, wiping my forehead, and I had nightmares about that long, hairy blade above my throat and saw it snatched away by my father's red arms. In the morning I saw outside that the axe head was dull with blood. After that I often had dreams in which my father rescued me. One was a dream about a burning house – our house, the one I still live in with Elaine and Jamie – and I was trapped inside, hair and bedclothes afire and my father splintered the door with an axe blow and fought his way in and carried me out in those red arms.

My father. He said little. He never won at Scrabble, so it seems he never even stored words up for himself. We never spoke much. It was my mother and I who carried on the long conversations; she knew odd facts, quiz shows on television were her texts. I told her my problems. But with my father I just stood, and we watched each other. Sometimes he looked at me with disappointment, and other times I looked at him the same way. He hammered big nails in straight and kissed me good-night and goodbye and hello until I was fourteen and learnt to be ashamed of it and evade it.

When his back stiffened with age he chopped wood less and I wielded the axe more. He sat by the woodpile and sometimes stacked, though mostly he just sat with a thoughtful look on his face. As I grew older my time contracted around me like a shrinking shirt and I chopped wood hurriedly, often finishing before the old man had a chance to come out and sit down.

Then I met Elaine and we married and I left home. For years I went back once a week to chop wood for the old man while Elaine and my mother sat at the laminex table in the kitchen listening to the tick of the stove. I tried to get my parents interested in electric heating and cooking like most people in the city, but my father did not care for it. He was stubborn and so I continued to split wood for him once a week while he became a frail, old man and his arms lost their ruddiness and went pasty and the flesh lost its grip upon the bones of his forearms. He looked at me in disappointment every week like an old man will, but I came over on Sundays, even when we had Jamie to look after, so he didn't have cause to be that way.

Jamie got old enough to use an axe and I taught him how. He was keen at first, though careless, and he blunted the edge quite often which angered me. I got him to chop wood for his grandfather and dropped him there on Sunday afternoons. I had a telephone installed in their house, though they complained about the colour, and I spoke to my mother sometimes on the phone, just to please her. My father never spoke on the phone. Still doesn't.

Then my mother had her stroke and Jamie began demanding to be paid for woodchopping and Elaine went twice a week to cook and clean for them and I decided on the Home. My mother and father moved out and we moved in and sold our own house. I thought about getting the place converted to electricity but the Home was expensive and Elaine came to enjoy cooking on the old combustion stove and it was worth paying Jamie a little to chop wood. Until recently. Now he won't even do it for money. He is lazier than me.

Still, it was only an old axe.

2

Elaine sleeps softly beside me, her big wide buttocks warm against my legs. The house is quiet; it was always quiet, even when my parents and I lived here. No-one ever raised their voice at me in this house, except now my wife and son.

It is hard to sleep, hard, so difficult. Black moves about me and in me and is on me, so black. Fresh, bittersweet, the smell of split wood: hard, splintery jarrah, clean, moist she-oak, hard, fibrous white gum, the shick! of sundering pine. All my muscles sing, a chorus of effort, as I chop quickly, throwing chunks aside, wiping flecks and chips from my chin. Sweat sheets across my eyes and I chop harder, opening big round sawn blocks of she-oak like pies in neat wedged sections. Harder. And my feet begin to lift as I swing *the* axe high over my shoulder. I strike it home and regain equilibrium. As I swing again my feet lift further and I feel as though I might float up, borne away by the axe above my head, as though it is a helium balloon. No, I don't want to lift up! I drag on the hickory handle, downwards, and I win and drag harder and it gains momentum and begins a slow-motion arc of descent towards the porous surface of the wood and then, halfway down, the axe-head shears off the end of the handle so slowly, so painfully slow that I could take a hold of it four or five times to stop it. In a slow, tumbling trajectory it sails across the woodheap and unseats my father's head from his shoulders and travels on out of sight as my father's head rolls onto the heap, eyes towards me, transfixed at the moment of scission in a squint of disappointment.

I feel a warm dob on my forehead; I do not scream, have never needed to.

The sheets are wet and the light is on and Elaine has me by the shoulder and her left breast points down at my glistening chest.

'What's the matter?' she says, wiping my brow with the back of her hand. 'You were yelling.'

'A dream,' I croak.

3

Morning sun slants across the pickets at me as I fossick about in the long grass beside the shed finding the skeleton of a wren but nothing else. I shuffle around the shed, picking through the chips and splinters and slivers of wood around the chopping block, see the deep welts in the block where the axe has been, but no axe. In the front yard, as neighbours pass, I scrabble in the pile of new wood, digging into its heart, tossing pieces aside until there is nothing but yellowing grass and a few impassive slaters. Out in the backyard again I amble about shaking my head and putting my hands in my pockets and taking them out again. Elaine is at work. Jamie at school. I have rung the office and told them I won't be in. All morning I mope in the yard, waiting for something to happen, absurdly, expecting the axe to show like a prodigal son. Nothing.

Going inside at noon I notice a deep trench in the veranda post by the back door, it is deep and wide as a heavy axe-blow and I feel the inside of it with my fingers – only for a moment – before I hurry inside trying to recall its being there before. Surely.

I sit by the cold stove in the kitchen in the afternoon, quaking. Is someone trying to kill me? My God.

4

Again Elaine has turned her sumptuous buttocks against me and gone to sleep dissatisfied and I lie awake with my shame and the dark around me.

Some nights as a child I crept into my parents' room and wormed my way into the bed between them and slept soundly, protected from the dark by their warm contact.

Now, I press myself against Elaine's sleeping form and cannot sleep with the knowledge that my back is exposed.

After an hour I get up and prowl about the house, investigating each room with quick flicks of light switches and satisfied grunts when everything seems to be in order. Here, the room where my mother read, here, Jamie's room where I slept as a boy, here, where my father drank his hot, milkless tea in the mornings.

I can think of nothing I've done to offend the neighbours – I'm not a dog baiter or anything – though some of them grumbled about my putting my parents into the Home, as though it was any of their business.

I keep thinking of axe murders, things I've read in the papers, horrible things.

In the living room I take out the old Scrabble box and sit with it on my knee for a while. Perhaps I'll play a game with myself . . .

5

This morning when I woke in the big chair in the living room I saw the floor littered with Scrabble tiles like broken, yellowing teeth. Straightening my stiff back I recalled the dream. I dreamt that I saw my body dissected, raggedly sectioned up and battered and crusted black with blood. The axe, the old axe with the taped hickory handle, was embedded in the trunk where once my legs had joined, right through the pelvis. My severed limbs lay about, pink, black, distorted, like stockings full of sand. My head, to one side, faced the black ceiling, teeth bared, eyes firmly shut. Horrible, but even so, peaceful enough, like a photograph. And then a boy came out of the black – it was Jamie – and picked up my head and held it like a bowling ball. Then there was light and my son opened the door and went outside into the searing suddenness of light. He walked out into the backyard and up to the chopping block in which an axe – *the* axe – was poised.

I felt nothing when he split my head in two. It was a poor stroke, but effective enough. Then with half in either hand – by the hair – he slowly walked around the front of the house and then out to the road verge and began skidding the half-orbs into the paths of oncoming cars. I used to do that as a boy; skidding half pig-melons under car wheels until nothing was left but a greenish, wet pulp. Pieces of my head ricocheted from chassis to bitumen, tyre to tyre, until there was only pulp and an angry sounding of car horns.

That does it; I'm going down to the local hardware store to buy another axe. It's high time. I have thought of going to the police but it's too ludicrous; I have nothing to tell: someone has stolen my axe that used to be my father's. A new axe is what I need.

It takes a long time in the Saturday morning rush at the hardware and the axes are so expensive and many are shoddy and the sales boy who pretends to be a professional axeman tires me with his patter. Eventually I buy a Kelly; it costs me forty dollars and it bears a resemblance to my father's. Carrying it home I have the feeling that I'm holding a stage property, not a tool; there are no signs of work on it and the head is so clean and smooth and shiny it doesn't seem intended for chopping.

As I open the front gate, axe over my shoulder, my wife is waiting on the veranda with tears on her face.

'The Home called,' she says. 'It's your father . . .'

6

The day after the funeral I am sitting out on the front veranda in the faint yellow sun. My mother will die soon; her life's work is over and she has no reason to continue in her sluggish, crippled frame. It will not be long before her funeral, I think to myself, not long. A tall sunflower sheds its hard, black seeds near me, shaken by the weight of a bird I can't see but sense. The gate squeals on its hinges and at the end of the path stand a man and a boy.

'Yes?' I ask.

The man prompts the boy forward and I see the lad has something in a hessian bag in his arms that he is offering me. Stepping off the veranda I take it, not heeding the man's apologies and the stutterings of his son. I open the bag and see the hickory handle with its gummy black tape and nicks and burrs and I groan aloud.

'He's sorry he took it,' the man says, 'aren't you, Alan? He –'

'Wait,' I say, turning, bounding back up the veranda, through the house, out onto the back veranda where Elaine and Jamie sit talking. They look startled but I have no time to explain. I grab the shiny, new axe which is yet to be used, and race back through the house with it. Elaine calls out to me, fright in her voice.

In the front yard, the father and son still wait uneasily and they look at me with apprehension as I run towards them with the axe.

'What –' The man tries to shield his son whose mouth begins to open as I come closer.

I hold the axe out before me, my body tingling, and I hold it horizontal with the handle against the boy's heaving chest.

'Here,' I say. 'This is yours.'

Amy Witting

THE ENEMIES OF TIME
1991

'Not the Domesday Book, Alice, please,' said Lex Warren to his wife, but without optimism.

Dinner was over at the Warrens'. Coffee, port and brandy were on the table and the diners sat chatting. They were Lex and Alice Warren, Lex's mother Marjorie, who was a member of the household, Marjorie's friend Ronald, the Anglican clergyman, who was also a poet, Evan the retired headmaster and his wife Jean, young Doctor Thomas Vence and his wife Dorothy, who were newcomers. Newcomers could not be long in the town without learning that Alice's ancestor Edmund Rees had settled the district in 1828. The Vences had learnt this and were being offered an introduction to the family scrapbook.

'But I'd love to see it,' said Dorothy, who came of a pioneer family and had her own handful of trumps to play. 'I'm fascinated by history.'

Lex got up with resignation and fetched the heavy manuscript book, his mother moved cups and glasses to clear a space for it in front of Alice, Dorothy changed places with her husband and Alice opened the book.

'Not much left of poor Edmund, I'm afraid. Just this cutting from the *Sydney Gazette* when the governor came to visit. Notice the trivial detail: when they fired the salute, the cannon backfired and took off the convict's leg. Mentioned in passing. And Edmund's death notice. Don't you like the stately prose? "Of a pulmonary complaint long since contracted."'

Dorothy was staring at the page. 'I know what that was,' she said. 'It was my great-great-great-grandfather's bullet in his lung.'

Alice was staring at the page, too, without speaking.

'Oh, you didn't know. You didn't know about the duel. I've shocked you. I'm so sorry.'

Laughing, Lex leaned across and passed his hand before Alice's eyes. He withdrew it, disconcerted, as she did not stir.

'I've always thought it so romantic, fighting a duel over a lady's honour. And so long ago. I'm sure my ancestor was the villain. He was a well-known besmircher of ladies' honour ... and a first-rate shot, of course. It makes a nonsense of duelling doesn't it, when the villain can shoot straight? Not at all like Westerns.'

'Dorothy,' said her husband, 'kindly remove foot from mouth.'

'Am I making things worse? Oh, dear, I am so sorry.'

Lex touched Alice's hand and put a glass of brandy beside it.

Marjorie said in haste, 'I do think it's romantic. There's that portrait in the living room. You see it every day and take it for granted, and all at once you're looking at quite a different person.'

Alice surfaced among them, shaking her head.

'Not offended. No, not at all. But shocked, yes. Such a strange experience, like falling through space.'

'Falling through time, perhaps,' said Ronald. 'The lighting changed, dead figures stirred and time was not.'

'Yes, that's right. And shock isn't the word, either. I don't know the word.'

'I take that plunge whenever I read T. S. Eliot:

> The nightingales are singing near
> The Convent of the Sacred Heart,
>
> And sang within the bloody wood
> When Agamemnon cried aloud,
> And let their liquid siftings fall
> To stain the stiff dishonoured shroud.

You heard that nightingale, I think, Alice. But I do it willingly for my own pleasure. It could be alarming if one didn't intend it, if the present gave way beneath one's feet. I haven't had that experience.'

'It's an extraordinary coincidence,' said Jean. 'It isn't an experience that would come one's way often.'

'I am thinking,' said Dorothy with compunction, 'that it was real. That he really suffered and died, your ancestor. It hadn't been real to me that way before. So I suppose I got a jolt, too. When I saw. The old villain didn't get off scot-free, you know. He had to get out of town and he must have hated that. That's when he took up his land, which is why we know the story so well.'

Ronald reflected that Alice might well forgive the past offence more easily than the present competition. Charity, he said to himself reprovingly. Have charity.

Lex said, 'I think we could all do with a drink. Who's for port?' To Dorothy, who was a very pretty woman, he said kindly, 'Cheer up. You haven't shot anyone.'

'I still feel guilty.' Dorothy accepted a glass of port. 'I needn't have come out with it quite like that.'

'You'll admit,' said her husband, 'that you tend to the dramatic.'

'I don't judge from your extremely privileged standpoint, of course,' said Ronald. The doctor looked discomfited and drank port. 'But I think it is that the subject matter called for drama, not that there was any leaning towards drama in Mrs Vence.'

Alice spoke.

'Please understand that I have not had a bad experience. You are right. Time seemed to vanish and I was there, feeling frightened for him, really loving him and – so ridiculous – I was telling him, "Live! Live! You have to live or I'll never be born." Dear me, it does sound so odd.'

'On such slender threads does human life depend,' intoned Ronald, and was so annoyed with himself that he was silent for some time. He had promised himself to get through the evening without quoting poetry, too.

'Sometimes,' said Evan, 'just one word or a phrase will bring the past back, sights, smells and all. Do you remember that farmer in the North of England, Jean? Where was it, dear?'

'Yes. Ainwick.'

'So it was. It was just after Australians had been declared aliens and had to show passports, and it hit the ordinary English people very hard. We were having a beer in the snug at the Black Swan when this farmer came up and apologised for it. He said, "What about 1940? We didn't want to see your passports then."'

'That was neatly put,' said the doctor.

'It certainly affected me. There I was, I was coming down the gang-plank and I even knew what thoughts I'd been thinking then. I could feel the weight of my pack and smell the water and I was worrying about my boots. There was a spot that was rubbing and I was wondering if it would get worse and if so what I ought to do about it. I had to laugh afterwards because all my life I'd wanted to see England and all I was thinking about then was my boots. And all that came back when the farmer said, "What about 1940?"'

Ronald thought of Proust's madeleine. Could a phrase bring back sensation as truly as the taste of a little cake?

Evan went on, 'I think Ronald has it, you know. It's the subject matter that's dramatic.'

Marjorie nodded. 'Best word forward, when you speak of time. You know, Lex, when poor old Estelle got her hair dyed you said she was having a tug-o'-war with time. That was very vivid expression from you. You don't normally use metaphor.'

Lex grinned. 'Got her heels dug right in, poor old girl.'

Marjorie sighed. 'Haven't we all?'

'More or less deeply, yes.' Ronald had suffered enough silence.

'Oh,' said Marjorie. 'The tea boy at the sanatorium!' She explained to the Vences, 'I did social work before I married. This wasn't long after the war – I said tea boy, but he was a charming young man, a Yugoslav. He'd gone up a grade – the patients were promoted by grade according to their progress, you see, and he'd been promoted and made tea orderly, so he was making out to be so proud of his white coat. I said to him, "Boris, how many uniforms is that so far?" and he told me, "Cub scout, boy scout, cadet, Yugoslav Air Force, Royal Air Force, company airline pilot, tea orderly . . . if you plot the graph of time and glory, she would go so . . ."'

Marjorie's finger traced the graph in the air.

'He was laughing while he drew his graph of time and glory. I thought it was so touching, I've never forgotten it.'

'But that's a poem,' said Dorothy. 'I'd have remembered it, too.'

'So it is a poem,' said Ronald. 'I believe we have hit on something. Marjorie is right: best word forward when we speak of time. That is, when we speak of time we speak with art, because art is the enemy of time. No, we are the enemies of time and art is our weapon.'

Lex grunted. 'Much good that does us in the long run.

'Oh, yes. We win our little battles, but we lose the war.'

Marjorie said, 'We'll have no more of that subject, thank you.'

The change of subject broke up the party. The guests stirred and prepared to leave.

At the door Dorothy, smiling nervously, offered her hand to Alice.

'We're not going to be Montagus and Capulets, are we?'

'Of course not, my dear.'

'Bygones,' said Lex. 'Bygones. There has to be one good thing to say for the old enemy, after all.'

Fay Zwicky

ONLY A LITTLE OF SO MUCH
1985

Help me up with the last button, says Aunt Eva, my mother's youngest sister. According to the scales even Krupp the Murderer puts his personal signature on, I weigh exactly thirteen and a half stones, she says. It never poisoned the spirit to see a bit of flesh. Too much, they're telling me but who listens? The same all my life – for this I should be bereaved? Why eat, says nurse, the Brünnhilde, with respect mind you. Why sleep is my answer to Miss Rheingold. Legs and arms were never wicked to us stage people. Or bosoms, bursting from the good life wherever it was. What's wickedness I'll tell you is something else. Don't let that button become your emotional problem – a safety pin does in this place! Here! Please God you wonderful younger generation won't drop the cheese when the fox says 'Sing!' Plums all day if you want!

Your mother was the skinny one. Pickled in dill and vinegar like her cucumbers, stuffed into glass jars like stiff hussars. Living decently while the earth trembled, may she rest in peace! A ruin at thirty following you and that messiah, your brother, round with a wettex. Your father couldn't come in the back door with his shoes on, and a colonel in the war! No wonder he looked other places, excuse me for saying so but you're old enough ... you needn't search your soul for answers either. 'What's a little dirt in a family?' I'd say, sorry as usual. 'You always were a fool,' she'd come back like a tiger. 'You ought to know about dirt. You bring enough of it into this house.' Harsh you're thinking? She didn't eat enough for kindness ...

Your father liked his food, poor thing. A hedonistic streak going nowhere. I'd run up a chocolate soufflé for support and other reasons. I made one the day after the ad came in the *Chronicle*. 'A celebration! Hello cello!' I said, my breath coming and going. 'They don't need this rubbish,' she shouted, swinging open the oven door with a bang. The soufflé sank in the sudden cold like a dead creature. 'He's putting on enough weight as it is. And your fanny needs now a duet stool!' 'It can't be your doing then,' I said under my breath, sharp fingers pinching my hammering heart. Don't look so worried, kid! *I'm* still here. Save worry for the final judgment. You're pretty enough for Miss Australia even if you are *her* daughter! A heap of cucumbers and four dead souls, ninety per cent water! Do you wonder I couldn't marry? Sisters! I could only take a little of so much ...

It wasn't my first endeavour in the Personals, by the way. *That* was an Armageddon! The perilous primrose path any time but, remember, I was no vision according to the authorities. Plump however. Some said womanly but no man around to make sense of it. Everyone acting as if they knew a thing or two. And I believed! I believed. 'Always stuffing your face!' 'How much on truffles this week?' 'Get your fat bottom off my seat!' And so forth. A Goldilocks with bears and no porridge. A full life of nothing and me crackling inside my thin skin like a Christmas duck!

The first – that hiker and waltzer! – turned out a tuner and I'm not talking fish. A race dying for you lot with your televisions and nuke boxes rocking and rolling. No Beethoven but who is so lucky? Deaf he wasn't but blind, yes. That such a man could call himself special, humorous, substance and character and ready to match an attractive female – I wrote Rubenesque with the returnable photo – for refreshing interludes of levity. Levity! I used to think it was a Jewish word. Him, me and the guide dog and your mother's wettex chasing us into every corner – a collaboration!

And who was he to say the family piano was finished? Finished! It sounded always good to me. You won't find filigree flowers and candleholders like that any more. Straight from the Steinway factory in Leipzig with your grandmother, I told him. Maybe the F sharp in the middle stuck a bit now and then. I could still get off lots of runs in the Minute Waltz – just under a minute in my prime – and plenty oompah and what-have-you on the left in the Tannhäuser arrangement. I practised like a fiend when your mother was out, pretending I never touched it. She always had to slave over her fiddle! Hours of scrape and scratch and for what? New hammers, he said, prodding away. That'll cost extra, he said. Who asked about cost? I started weeping like the fool that I was, thirteen and a half stones of autumn dream streaming like Niagara!

And what was Mr Substance and Character doing in the middle of the flood? Building an ark for my bones? Why, poking away at the F sharp stuck forever like it is today in spite of my runs. Who notices, kid? Your mother showed him the door. And to me, 'Don't bring any more of that trash into the house again!' with other profanities I won't soil your ears with. Screaming 'You need a psychologist!' and worse, waving her soapy rubber gloves over my plait like Mickey Mouse and him still on the path to the gate with his dog. Sorry as usual, I didn't ring anyone for a time, having trouble getting breath back . . .

All right, Miss Nosey. I promised no lies. The best last. Water drop by drop will also split stone. I was on the way to splitting when the colonel comes back from the war with his boots and medals and I start on the soufflés, making no demands on anyone. *Anyone*, mark you, patience my middle name almost. What was is what will be is by now my philosophy so no picture needed this time. Flesh may be flesh – how could I doubt? – but spirit no gherkin regiment either, even if I did believe everything for what it wasn't. I'm not religious, God forbid, but if I was, then God would be a musician. Or maybe an actor – Shakespeare only, with a little Schnitzler for luck! This time, please, a real *Musikant*! Beethoven he doesn't have to be. Never forget your musical talent comes from me, not your scratching mother! My prayer, kid, was heard and noted. Even a soufflé murdered couldn't wreck the day!

Every word comes back. Handsome professional cellist. And French! Twenty years under Toscanini. Warm and dynamic calibre to share hopefully dancing. Sense of laughter. Legally unencumbered. Photo appreciated but not essential – can you imagine? Another late bloomer exactly my age and ready to romp, the French culture a bonus. *Ça va sans dire*, Flaubert! That surprises you, doesn't it? I took to languages like a duck to troubling waters. Not educated like your generation but honoured, yes, honoured to match this person in intellect and frolicsome invigorations. I hid the *Chronicle* from your mother and communicated immediately. A woman of passions and ideas, I wrote, and ready always for gracious dining and something personal.

I am in levitation hours after first meeting – a Jewish word I told you it must be! – no questions in my mind. Size, shape, IQ high or low, my fate was written in his fancy! Kismet come true, my heart in throat and sleeve together! See for yourself the picture – a life-member of the Pleasure Principle Club, isn't it? Wonderful dancer and diner, a prince of eloquence – the entire holus-bolus! A pity all those genius Jews took precious time trying to make us better than we are – Misery Marx, Sad-Sack Sigmund and the atom-bomb person whose name I am forgetting forever. A woman has to measure things according to pleasant or unpleasant. How it feels is her final standards. Still, I am asking him to play me the sad Swan of Saint-Saëns and occasional Kol Nidrei to curb enthusiasm for more frivolity!

Even your mother, smelling excitement in my life, is impressed. Enough to forget to tell the colonel to take his boots off. The matter is not for laughing, kid! 'France my spiritual home,' she murmurs in her spotless kitchen, wandering round his chair. 'Ah, Paris,' she sighs, wettex stranded on the sink. 'My dream place! Where men chase real women with life's experience and leave minors alone.' 'Who is minor in this house?' I say. 'Humph!' snorts the colonel waiting for his dinner in the corner. No soufflés these days, alive or dead, poor man!

Before I can nip her bud, he is telling her what a lot of this and that she has, a woman with life's contacts written all over her face – her *face*, mind you! – fine children, loving husband and military to boot, the works. 'Why so personal?' I ask. 'She's only my sister, the eldest, and can't play the fiddle for peanuts.' Thinking, of course, of my under-the-minute waltz. 'My youngest sister here,' she says, 'is only a baby in arms. She can't help it.' A baby? Thirteen and a half stones and fifty years? I want to shout but do not for fear of releasing my cat from the sleeping-bag. My paramour is thinking thirty-eight but since the word marriage has recently arisen I let the sleeping dog lie ...

What next you are wanting to know? So much so quick, my mind rocky with remembering. But never so dumb I couldn't tell who warned him off my grasses.

The day before we were booked for Paris, I get a postcard with the Eiffel Tower in colour which says for all to see, 'I have missed for so long France. Now I must miss you for the remainder of my days. Thanks for all the good times, never so good with my legal encumbrance but duties call me home, *adieu.*' I go to my room and shut the door, very quiet. Outside, I hear your mother, *my* sister, saying to the colonel, 'All for the best. He did the right thing.' 'Always right if you say so,' says your father, no smile in his voice. 'In this case, yes. It was for the best. She doesn't know her own good and never will!' *My* sister again.

I come out, swinging the door with a bang behind me. Ten feet tall and stronger than any tiger. '*You* asked him to stay away?' I say in a quiet voice unlike my own, coming slowly down the stairs. 'Yes,' she says, backing away. 'And he agreed with that?' I say, still coming down, still quiet. 'Yes,' she says again. 'And he just *agreed?* He didn't even *want* to see me again?' 'He said he would write to you.' 'What am I, then? A dead-letter office? And what,' I scream, no tears, 'are *you?*' Then I leap at her skinny throat, a creature dying of pain. I know she was your mother, excuse me, but also my sister! And they say women stick together!

Turn on the light, kid. It's getting quickly dark these winter nights. Over the basin is the switch! There goes the colonel again in his silver lining! No, he didn't break, dear. Put him carefully back with the others and we'll celebrate. The tablets go down easier with a drop. They won't find out, don't look so worried! You remind me of your mother when you look that way. Miss Rheingold will be along soon with that tuft of dog-grass she calls dinner. No, I won't calm down! Calm isn't my nature. Why calm when I'm nearly dust? Tomorrow's almost behind me and yesterday's here already! So what's to celebrate? Something, maybe, missing the first time around.

NOTES ON THE AUTHORS

Glenda Adams (b. 1940) is the author of the novels *Games of the Strong, Dancing on Coral* which won the Miles Franklin Award and the NSW Premier's Award, *Longleg* which won the National Book Council Banjo Award and the *Age* Book of the Year Award, *The Tempest of Clemenza*, and the short-story collection, *The Hottest Night of the Century*.

Ethel Anderson (1883–1958) was the author of three collections of short stories, *Indian Tales, At Parramatta* and *The Little Ghosts*, as well as several volumes of poetry and essays.

Jessica Anderson (b. 1916) is the author of a short-story collection, *Stories from the Warm Zone & Sydney Stories*, and seven novels, *An Ordinary Lunacy, The Last Man's Head, Tirra Lirra by the River, The Impersonators, The Commandant, Taking Shelter* and *One of the Wattle Birds*.

Thea Astley (b. 1925) is the author of sixteen books of fiction including the short-story collection *Hunting the Wild Pineapple*, and has won an array of literary awards including the Miles Franklin Award three times, the Steele Rudd Award, the Patrick White Award and the Australian Literature Society Gold Medal. Her most recent novel is *Drylands*.

Murray Bail (b. 1941) is the author of a short-story collection, *The Drover's Wife and Other Stories*, and three novels, *Homesickness, Holden's Performance* and *Eucalyptus*, which won the Miles Franklin Award.

Candida Baker (b. 1955) is the author of a novel, *Women and Horses*, and a collection of stories, *The Powerful Owl*. She edited the series *Yacker: Australian Writers Talk About Their Work* and also *The Penguin Book of The Horse*.

Marjorie Barnard (1897–1987) was the author of *The Persimmon Tree and Other Stories*. She collaborated with Flora Eldershaw to produce five novels by M. Barnard Eldershaw. She also wrote historical works, notably *A History of Australia*, and literary criticism.

Barbara Baynton (1857–1929) had her first story published in the *Bulletin* in 1896. Her short stories were collected in *Bush Studies* and she published a novel, *Human Toll*.

Jean Bedford (b. 1946) is the author of the short-story collection *Country Girl Again*, and *A Lease of Summer*, *If With a Beating Heart*, *Now You See Me*, the bestseller *Sister Kate* and three detective novels.

Carmel Bird (b. 1940) is the author of the short-story collections *Automatic Teller*, *The Common Rat* and *The Woodpecker Toy Fact*, and several novels including *Red Shoes*, *The White Garden*, *The Bluebird Cafe* and *Crisis*. She has also written two books of inspiration for writers, *Dear Writer* and *Not Now Jack – I'm Writing a Novel*. Her most recent books are a children's picture book, *The Cassowary's Quiz*, and a crime novel, *Unholy Writ*.

James Bradley (b. 1967) is the author of two novels, *Wrack* which won the Commonwealth Writers' Prize, the Fellowship of Australian Writers' Literature Award and the Kathleen Mitchell Award, and *The Deep Field*. He has also edited an anthology, *Blur*, and published a collection of poetry, *Paper Nautilus*.

David Brooks (b. 1953) is the author of four works of fiction, *The Book of Sei*, *Sheep and the Diva*, *Black Sea* and *The House of Balthus*, and has published collections of poetry and a book of essays, *The Necessary Jungle*.

John Bryson (b. 1935) is the author of a short-story collection, *Whoring*

Around, and two novels, *Evil Angels* and *To the Death, Amic*. He is also the author of a collection of reportage, *Backstage at the Revolution*.

Janine Burke (b. 1952) is the author of eleven books of fiction and art history including *Australian Women Artists 1840–1940*. She won the Victorian Premier's Fiction Award for her novel *Second Sight*. She edited *Dear Sun: the letters of Joy Hester and Sunday Reed* and is writing a biography of Albert Tucker.

Keith Butler (b. 1948) is currently writing a novel, *The Secret Vindaloo*, and teaching English and history.

Ada Cambridge (1844–1926) published a number of novels including *Uncle Piper of Piper's Hill*, *The Three Kings* and *A Marked Man*, and a short-story collection, *At Midnight and Other Stories*.

Peter Carey (b. 1943) is the author of six novels, *Bliss*, *Illywhacker*, *Oscar and Lucinda*, *The Tax Inspector*, *The Unusual Life of Tristan Smith* and *Jack Maggs*. His short stories appeared in *The Fat Man in History* and *War Crimes*, now published in *Collected Stories*. His books have won every major literary award in Australia. *Oscar and Lucinda* won the Booker Prize; *Jack Maggs* won the *Age* Book of the Year Award, the Commonwealth Writers' Prize and the Miles Franklin Award.

Gavin Casey (1907–1964) was the author of several novels and many stories including the collections *It's Harder for Girls*, later republished as *Short Shift Saturday and Other Stories*, and *Birds of a Feather*.

Brian Castro (b. 1950) has written six novels and many short stories and essays. He has won several prizes including the *Australian* Vogel Award, the *Age* Book of the Year Award and the Vance Palmer Award. He is currently writing a fictional autobiography.

John Clark (b. 1953) works as a labourer and with Aboriginal organisations. He writes poetry and stories and was involved with an oral history program of the Wathaurong Aboriginal Community.

Bernard Cohen (b. 1963) is the author of three novels, *Tourism*,

Snowdome and *The Blindman's Hat*, winner of the *Australian* Vogel Award. His forthcoming novel is *Hardly Beach Weather*.

Tom Collins (Joseph Furphy) (1843–1912) wrote short stories, poems and articles and is best known for his novels, *Such is Life*, *Rigby's Romance* and *The Buln-Buln and the Brolga*.

Matthew Condon (b. 1962) has written several works of fiction and has won two Steele Rudd Awards for his collections of short fiction, *The Motorcycle Cafe* and *A Night at the Pink Poodle*. His most recent novel is *The Pillow Fight*.

Peter Corris (b. 1942) has published forty-five books of fiction and a dozen non-fiction titles including *Fred Hollows: An Autobiography* (with Fred Hollows).

Raimondo Cortese (b. 1968) is the author of the short-story collection, *The Indestructible Corpse*. His plays include *Lucrezia and Cesare*, *The Room*, *The Fertility of Objects* and *Features of Blown Youth*.

Peter Cowan (b. 1914) is the author of several novels including *The Hills of Apollo Bay*, and several collections of stories including *Drift*, *The Unploughed Land*, *The Empty Street* and *The Tins and Other Stories*. He has also published a history, a collection of colonial letters and two biographies, and he has won the Patrick White Award.

Eleanor Dark (1901–1985) published many short stories and ten novels including *Prelude to Christopher* and *The Timeless Land* trilogy which consists of *The Timeless Land*, *Storm of Time* and *No Barrier*.

Luke Davies (b. 1962) has published two collections of poetry including *Absolute Event Horizon*, and a novel, *Candy*.

Frank Dalby Davison (1893–1970) was the author of the short-story collections *The Woman at the Mill* and *The Road to Yesterday*, and novels including *Dusty*, *Man-Shy* and *The White Thorntree*.

Liam Davison (b. 1957) is the author of a short-story collection, *The*

Shipwreck Party, and three novels, the most recent being *The Betrayal*. His novel *Soundings* won the National Book Council Banjo Award for fiction.

Marele Day (b. 1947) is the author of the Claudia Valentine mysteries, the most recent being *The Disappearance of Madalena Grimaldi*. Her most recent novel is *Lambs of God*.

Robert Dessaix (b. 1944) is the author of the autobiographical *A Mother's Disgrace*, the novel *Night Letters*, as well as (*and so forth*), a collection of stories, essays, talks and reviews.

Barry Dickins (b. 1949) is the author of *The Gift of the Gab*, *What the Dickins!*, *I Love to Live*, and plays including *The Death of Ronald Ryan*.

Garry Disher (b. 1949) is the author of five short-story collections including *The Difference to Me* and *Straight, Bent and Barbara Vine*. He has also published award-winning novels, children's books, thrillers, anthologies and textbooks.

Sara Dowse (b. 1938) is the author of five novels including *Sapphires* and *Digging*.

H. (Henrietta) Drake-Brockman (1901–1968) was the author of a short-story collection, *Sydney or the Bush*, and several novels, the best known being *Blue North*.

Robert Drewe (b. 1943) is the author of the novels *The Savage Crows*, *A Cry in the Jungle Bar*, *Fortune*, *Our Sunshine* and *The Drowner*. He has written two collections of short stories, *The Bodysurfers* and *The Bay of Contented Men*, as well as plays, screenplays, journalism and film criticism. His work has won many national and international awards and has been adapted for film, television, radio and theatre. His most recent book is *The Shark Net*.

Nick Earls (b. 1963) is the author of six books including *Zigzag Street* which won the Betty Trask Award in the UK, *Bachelor Kisses*, *Headgames* and *Perfect Skin*.

Delia Falconer (b. 1966) is the author of a novel, *The Service of Clouds*.

Beverley Farmer (b. 1941) has written three novels and four collections of stories including *Milk* which won the NSW Premier's Award for fiction, *Hometime* and, most recently, *Collected Stories*. She also won the Alan Marshall Award.

Helen Garner (b. 1942) is the author of the short-story collections *Postcards from Surfers* and *Honour and Other People's Children*. Her novels are *Monkey Grip*, *The Childrens' Bach* and *Cosmo Cosmolino*. Her most recent book is *My Hard Heart*, a selection of her short fiction.

Kerryn Goldsworthy (b. 1953) is a former lecturer in English at the University of Melbourne. She is the author of a collection of stories, *North of the Moonlight Sonata*.

Peter Goldsworthy (b. 1951) has published four collections of poetry, four collections of stories including *Bleak Rooms* and *Little Deaths*, and four novels. His most recent book is a collection of essays, *Navel Gazing*. His awards include the Commonwealth Poetry Prize and the Australian Bicentennial Poetry Prize.

Kate Grenville (b. 1950) has written five novels including *Lilian's Story*, which won the *Australian* Vogel Award, and *Dreamhouse*, *Joan Makes History*, *Dark Places*, *Albion's Story* and *The Idea of Perfection*. She is the author of a collection of stories, *Bearded Ladies*.

Marion Halligan (b. 1940) has written five novels, the most recent being *The Golden Dress*, and four collections of stories including *The Living Hothouse* and *The Hanged Man in the Garden*. Her many awards include the *Age* Book of the Year Award, the Steele Rudd Award, the Nita B. Kibble Award and the Pascall Award for critical writing.

Barbara Hanrahan (1939–1991) was the author of several novels including *Sea Green*, *Where the Queens All Strayed*, *The Frangipani Gardens* and *Dove. Good Night, Mr Moon* and *Michael and Me and the Sun*, were published posthumously.

Frank Hardy (1917–1994) was the author of the short-story collections *It's Moments Like These* and *The Yarns of Billy Borker*. His novels include *Power Without Glory* and *But the Dead are Many*.

Elizabeth Harrower (b. 1928) has written short stories and four novels, *Down in the City*, *The Long Prospect*, *The Catherine Wheel* and *The Watch Tower*.

Gwen Harwood (1920–1996) was the author of collections of poetry including *Bone Scan* and *Collected Poems*. She also wrote stories, essays, reviews and libretti. She received many awards including the *Age* Book of the Year Award, the Victorian Premier's Award, the Patrick White Award and honorary doctorates from the universities of Tasmania, Queensland and Latrobe.

Shirley Hazzard (b. 1931) is the author of a short-story collection, *The Cliffs of Fall*, and four novels, *The Evening of the Holiday*, *People in Glass Houses*, *The Bay of Noon* and *The Transit of Venus*.

Xavier Herbert (1901–1984) was the author of many short stories including the collection *Larger than Life* and several novels, *Capricornia*, *Seven Emus*, *Soldier's Women* and *Poor Fellow My Country*.

Dorothy Hewett (b. 1923) has published three novels, *Bobbin Up*, *The Toucher* and *Neap Tide*, an autobiography, thirteen plays and nine collections of poetry. She has won numerous awards including the Mattara Poetry Award, the Victorian Premier's Award and two Awgies.

Barry Hill (b. 1943) has written novels, poems, non-fiction, short stories including the collections *A Rim of Blue* and *Headlocks and Other Stories*, and a poetic cycle, *Ghosting William Buckley*. His awards include the National Book Council Award, the Anne Elder Poetry Award and the NSW Premier's Award.

Janette Turner Hospital (b. 1942) is the author of several novels and short-story collections including *Dislocations* and *Isobars*. She has won a number of international awards including the Canadian Seal Award for *The Ivory Swing*.

Jan Hutchinson (b. 1952) is the author of a collection of stories, *Desire and Other Domestic Problems*.

Susan Johnson (b. 1956) is the author of four novels, the most recent being *A Big Life*, and a memoir, *A Better Woman*.

Elizabeth Jolley (b. 1923) has published four collections of stories including *Fellow Passengers: Collected Stories*, a collection of essays, fourteen novels and a novella, as well as poetry and radio plays. She has won many prizes including the *Age* Book of the Year Award, the Miles Franklin Award, the National Book Council Banjo Award and the NSW Premier's Award. Her most recent novel is *An Accommodating Spouse*.

Gail Jones (b. 1955) is the author of two collections of stories. *The House of Breathing* which won the Steele Rudd Award, and *Fetish Lives*.

John Kinsella (b. 1963) is a poet, critic and writer of fiction, and is the editor of two literary journals, *Salt* (Australia) and *Stand* (UK). His most recent book is a collection of stories, *Grappling Eros*. He has won many awards including the WA Premier's Poetry Award, the Harri Jones Memorial Prize for Poetry, the John Bray Award for Poetry and the *Age* Poetry Book of the Year Award.

Terry Lane (b. 1939) is the author of seven books including *God: the Interview*.

Henry Lawson (1867–1922) was the author of many short stories including the collections *While the Billy Boils*, *The Country I Come From*, *Joe Wilson and His Mates* and *Send Round the Hat*.

Joan London (b. 1948) has written two collections of stories, *Sister Ships* which won the *Age* Book of the Year Award, and *Letter to Constantine* which won the Steele Rudd Award.

David Malouf (b. 1934) is the author of several collections of poetry and ten works of fiction including *Remembering Babylon* which won the first Dublin International IMPAC Prize. His most recent novel is

The Conversations at Curlow Creek. He has won many awards including the Miles Franklin Award, the Pascall Prize, the Prix Femina Etranger, the Victorian Premier's Award and the NSW Premier's Award.

Alan Marshall (1902–1984) wrote travel and history books as well as novels and short stories including the collection *Tell Us About the Turkey, Jo*. He is best known for his autobiography, *I Can Jump Puddles*.

Olga Masters (1919–1986) was the author of five books of fiction including the short-story collections *The Home Girls* and *The Rose Fancier*. She won several awards including the National Book Council Award.

Peter Mathers (b. 1931) is the author of two novels including *Trap* which won the Miles Franklin Award, and a short-story collection, *A Change for the Better*.

Brian Matthews (b. 1936) is the author of a short-story collection, *Quickening and Other Stories*, and a biography, *Louisa*, which won four major awards. He has also published criticism, essays, radio scripts, columns and sports writing.

James McQueen (1934–1998) was the author of five novels, the most recent being *The Heavy Knife*, and six collections of short stories. He has also written for children and young adults. He has won national and international short fiction awards.

Gillian Mears (b. 1964) is the author of three collections of stories including *Ride a Cock Horse* and *Fineflour*, and two novels, *The Mint Lawn* which won the *Australian* Vogel Award, and *The Grass Sister* which won several awards.

Frank Moorhouse (b. 1938) is the author of several short-story collections including *Futility and Other Animals*, *The Americans, Baby* and *Tales of Mystery and Romance*, and the novel *Grand Days*. He has won a number of prizes including the Adelaide Festival Prize for Fiction and the Australian Literature Society's Gold Medal.

John Morrison (1904–1998) was the author of two novels, a collection of essays and eight short-story collections including *North Wind* and *Stories from the Waterfront*. He was awarded the Australian Literature Society's Gold Medal for *Twenty-three Stories* and the Patrick White Award.

Barry Oakley (b. 1931) is the author of several novels including *Let's Hear it for Prendergast* which won the Captain Cook Bicentenary Award for Fiction, numerous plays, and literary journalism, columns and diaries.

Vance Palmer (1885–1959) wrote many plays, five novels including the *Golconda* trilogy, collections of poems, essays and stories including *Separate Lives*, *Sea and Spinifex* and *Let the Birds Fly*.

Ruth Park (b. 1922) is the author of almost forty books. Her ten novels include *The Harp in the South*, *Poor Man's Orange*, *The Witch's Thorn* and *Swords and Crowns and Rings*, which won the Miles Franklin Award. She has written twenty-seven children's books and won the Australian Children's Book of the Year Award and The Boston Globe Award for *Playing Beatie Bow*.

Bruce Pascoe (b. 1947) has written four works of fiction including *Shark*. He is a member of the Wathourong Aboriginal Co-operative.

Elliot Perlman (b. 1964) is the author of a novel, *Three Dollars*, which won the *Age* Book of the Year Award, the Betty Trask Award (UK) and was the joint winner of the FAW Book of the Year Award. He is also the author of a collection of stories, *The Reasons I Won't Be Coming*.

Hal Porter (1911–1984) was the author of three novels, three collections of poetry, four plays and seven collections of stories including *A Bachelor's Children*, *Mr Butterfry and Other Tales of New Japan* and *Selected Stories*. He won many literary awards and is best known for his three autobiographies, in particular *The Watcher on the Cast-Iron Balcony*.

Katharine Susannah Prichard (b. 1883–1969) was the author of numerous novels including *Working Bullocks*, *Coonardoo*, *Haxby's Circus* and her *Roaring Nineties* trilogy, and short-story collections including *Happiness*.

Tim Richards (b. 1960) is the author of *Letters to Francesca*, *The Prince* and *Duckness*.

Henry Handel Richardson (Ethel H. Lindesay Richardson) (1870–1946) was the author of several novels including *The Getting of Wisdom*, *Maurice Guest* and *The Fortunes of Richard Mahony*, and two short-story collections, *Two Studies* and *The End of a Childhood*.

Deborah Robertson (b. 1959) is the author of a short-story collection, *Proudflesh*, which won the Steele Rudd Award.

Penelope Rowe (b. 1946) has published three novels and two collections of stories, the most recent being *Disreputable People*.

Steele Rudd (Arthur Hoey Davis) (1868–1935) was the author of ten volumes chronicling the fortunes of the Rudd family including *On Our Selection*, *Our New Selection* and *Dad in Politics*.

E. O. (Eric Otto) Schlunke (1906–1960) published three novels and three short-story collections, *The Man in the Silo*, *The Village Hampden* and *Stories of the Riverina*.

Rosie Scott (b. 1948) has written five novels including *Movie Dreams*, a collection of poetry and a collection of stories, *Queen of Love*. She has won the *National Sunday Times* Playwright Award for the play on which the film *Redheads* was based.

Thomas Shapcott (b. 1935) is the author of ten novels, two short-story collections and fourteen collections of poetry. He has received numerous awards including the Struga Golden Wreath International Poetry Award, a Churchill Fellowship and an Order of Australia.

Christina Stead (1902–1983) wrote short stories including the collections *The Salzburg Tales* and *The Puzzleheaded Girl*, and eleven novels including *Seven Poor Men of Sydney*, *House of All Nations*, *The*

Man Who Loved Children, For Love Alone, Letty Fox: Her Luck and *Cotter's England*.

Dal Stivens (1911–1997) was the author of eight collections of short fiction including *The Tramp and Other Stories*, *Ironbark Bill* and *Selected Stories*, four novels including *A Horse of Air*, a book for children, and a book of natural history.

Kylie Tennant (1912–1988) was the author of nine novels including *The Battlers* and *Ride On Stranger*, two collections of stories including *Ma Jones and the Little White Cannibals*, as well as much non-fiction including her autobiography, *The Missing Heir*.

Brenda Walker (b. 1957) is the author of three novels, the most recent being *Poe's Cat*. She has also edited *Risks*, an anthology of fiction.

Judah Waten (1911–1985) published seven novels including *The Unbending* and *Distant Land*, and two volumes of autobiographical impressions and stories, *Alien Son* and *Love and Rebellion*.

Archie Weller (b. 1957) has published a collection of stories and has also written poetry and plays. His first novel, *The Day of the Dog*, won the Western Australia Week Literary Award and formed the basis of the film *Blackfellas*.

Ida West (b. 1919) is the author of a collection of stories, *Pride Against Prejudice*.

Herb Wharton (b. 1936) is the author of a novel, *Unbranded*, a collection of stories, *Where Ya' Been Mate?*, and many essays and poems.

Patrick White (1912–1990) was the author of two collections of stories, *The Burnt Ones* and *The Cockatoos*, twelve novels including *The Tree of Man*, *Voss*, *The Solid Mandala* and *The Aunt's Story*, as well as essays, plays and a self-portrait, *Flaws in the Glass*. He received the Miles Franklin Award and the Nobel Prize for Literature.

Michael Wilding (b. 1942) is the author of several novels including

Living Together, ten collections of stories including *Aspects of the Dying Process* and *This Is For You*, and a number of critical studies.

Gerard Windsor (b. 1944) is the author of six books including the series of memoirs *I'll Just Tell You This*, *Heaven Where the Bachelors Sit* and *I Asked Kathleen to Dance*. His short-story collections include *Memoirs of the Assassination Attempt and Other Stories*.

Tim Winton (b. 1960) is the author of six novels including *An Open Swimmer*, *Cloudstreet*, *In the Winter Dark* and *The Riders*, two collections of stories, *Scission* and *Minimum of Two*, and books for children. He has won numerous awards including the *Australian* Vogel Award, the Miles Franklin Award, and the National Book Council Banjo Award.

Amy Witting (b. 1918) has written two collections of stories, *Marriages* and *In and Out the Window*, three books of verse and five novels, *I For Isobel* winning the FAW Barbara Ramsden Award. Her most recent novel is *Isobel on the Way to the Corner Shop*.

Fay Zwicky (b. 1933) has published six collections of poetry, the most recent being *The Gatekeeper's Wife*, and one short-story collection, *Hostages*. She has won the NSW Premier's Award and the WA Premier's Award.

ACKNOWLEDGEMENTS

The editor and publisher are grateful to the following writers, agents and publishers for permission to reproduce their stories in this anthology.

Glenda Adams, 'A Snake Down Under' from *The Hottest Night of the Century*, Angus & Robertson, 1979; Ethel Anderson, 'Miss Aminta Wirraway and the Sin of Lust', first published in *At Parramatta*, 1956, reprinted by permission of HarperCollins; Jessica Anderson, 'Under the House' from *Stories from the Warm Zone & Sydney Stories*, Penguin Books Australia Ltd, 1987; Thea Astley, 'Petals from Blown Roses' from *Hunting the Wild Pineapple*, Penguin Books Australia Ltd, 1981; Murray Bail, 'ABCDEFGHIJKLMNOPQRSTUVWXYZ' from *The Drover's Wife and Other Stories*, Text Publishing, 1998; Candida Baker, 'The Powerful Owl' from *The Powerful Owl*, Picador, 1994; Marjorie Barnard, 'The Persimmon Tree', courtesy of the copyright owner Alan Alford, c/- Curtis Brown (Aust) Pty Ltd, Sydney; Jean Bedford, 'Country Girl Again' from *Country Girl Again*, Sisters, 1979; Carmel Bird, 'The Golden Moment' from *Automatic Teller*, Random House, 1996; James Bradley, 'The Turtles' Graveyard' from *A Sea Change*, Sydney Organising Committee for the Olympic Games, 1998; David Brooks, 'John Gilbert's Dog' from *The Book of Sei*, Hale and Iremonger, 1985; John Bryson, 'Children Aren't Supposed to Be Here at All' from *Whoring Around*, Penguin Books Australia Ltd, 1981; Janine Burke, 'The Cruelty of Mermaids' from *Island Magazine*, Winter 1990; Keith Butler, 'Sodasi' from the *Age Saturday Extra*, 28 November 1998; Peter Carey, 'The Last Days of a Famous Mime' from *War Crimes*, University of Queensland Press, 1979; Gavin Casey, 'Dust' from *It's Harder for Girls*, Angus & Robertson, 1942, reprinted by permission of HarperCollins Publishers; Brian Castro, 'Sonatina' from the *Sydney Morning Herald*, 26 March 1994, courtesy of Curtis Brown (Aust) Pty Ltd, Sydney; John

Clark, 'Johnny Cake Days' from *Australian Short Stories*, no. 46, 1994; Bernard Cohen, 'Life in Pieces' from *Hot Type*, Penguin Books Australia Ltd, 1996; Matthew Condon, 'The Sandfly Man' reprinted by permission of Random House Australia and the author; Peter Corris, 'Tie-breaker' from *Expressway*, Penguin Books Australia Ltd, 1989; Raimondo Cortese, 'The Preacher in the Tower' from *The Indestructible Corpse*, Text Publishing, 1998; Peter Cowan, 'The Voice' from *Fairleigh Dickinson Review*, 1963–64; Eleanor Dark, 'Serpents' courtesy of the copyright owner Michael Dark, c/- Curtis Brown (Aust) Pty Ltd, Sydney; Luke Davies, 'The Mind of Howard Hughes' from *Certifiable Truths*, Allen & Unwin, 1998, c/- Curtis Brown (Aust) Pty Ltd, Sydney; Frank Dalby Davison, 'The Woman at the Mill' from *The Woman at the Mill*, Angus & Robertson, 1940, reprinted by permission of HarperCollins Publishers; Liam Davison, 'The Shipwreck Party' from *The Shipwreck Party*, University of Queensland Press, 1989; Marele Day, 'Embroidery' from *Below the Waterline*, HarperCollins, 1999; Robert Dessaix, 'Sacred Heart' from *Red Hot Notes*, University of Queensland Press, 1997; Barry Dickins, 'Real Good Slide Night' from *I Love to Live*, Penguin Books Australia Ltd, 1991; Garry Disher, 'Amateur Hour' from *The Difference to Me*, Angus & Robertson, 1988; Sara Dowse, 'The Choice for Carlos Menendez' from *National Library of Australia News*, March 1997; H. Drake-Brockman, 'Fear' from *Sydney or the Bush*, 1948, reprinted courtesy of the copyright holder P. M. Drake-Brockman; Robert Drewe, 'Radiant Heat' from *The Bay of Contented Men*, Pan Books, 1989; Nick Earls, 'The Goatflap Brothers and the House of Names' from *Headgames*, Penguin Books Australia Ltd, 1999; Delia Falconer, 'The Water Poets' from *HQ Magazine*, June/July 1994; Beverley Farmer, 'A Man in the Laundrette' from *Home Time*, Penguin Books Australia Ltd, 1985; Helen Garner, 'The Life of Art' from *Postcards From Surfers*, Penguin Books Australia Ltd, 1985; Kerryn Goldsworthy, '14th October 1843' from *Picador New Writing 2*, Picador Australia, 1994; Peter Goldsworthy, 'The List of all Answers' from *Little Deaths*, Angus & Robertson, 1993; Kate Grenville, 'Dropping Dance' from *Room to Move*, Penguin Books Australia Ltd, 1985; Marion Halligan, 'The Ego in Arcadia' from *The Collected Stories of Marion Halligan*, University of Queensland Press, 1997; Barbara Hanrahan, 'Sisters' from *Iris in Her Garden*, Officina Brindabella, 1991; Frank Hardy, 'My Father and the Jews' from *The Loser Now Will Be Later to Win*, Pascoe Publishing Pty Ltd, 1985; Elizabeth Harrower, 'The Cost of Things' from *Frictions*, Sybylla Cooperative Press and Publications, 1982; Gwen Harwood, 'The Glass Boy' from *The Present Tense*, 1995, reprinted courtesy of the Estate of Gwen Harwood and the publishers ETT Imprint; Shirley Hazzard, 'The Picnic' from *Cliffs of Fall*, Macmillan, 1963;

Xavier Herbert, 'Kaijek the Songman', courtesy of Curtis Brown (Aust) Pty Ltd, Sydney; Dorothy Hewett, 'Nullabor Honeymoon' from *Women Love Sex*, Vintage, 1996; Barry Hill, 'Headlocks' from *Headlocks and Other Stories*, Penguin Books Australia Ltd, 1983; Janette Turner Hospital, 'After Long Absence' from *Collected Stories of Janette Turner Hospital*, University of Queensland Press, 1995; Jan Hutchinson, 'Extra Virgin' from *Desire and Other Domestic Problems*, Penguin Books Australia Ltd, 1989; Susan Johnson, 'Seeing' from *Women Love Sex*, Vintage, 1996; Elizabeth Jolley, 'Mr Berrington' from *Central Mischief*, Penguin Books Australia Ltd, 1992; Gail Jones, '"Life Probably Saved by Imbecile Dwarf"' from *The House of Breathing*, Fremantle Arts Centre Press, 1992; John Kinsella, 'The White Feather' from *Grappling Eros*, Fremantle Arts Centre Press, 1998; Terry Lane, 'Hickenlooper's Syndrome' from *Australasian Post*, 7 May 1994; Joan London, 'New Year' from *Sister Ships and Other Stories*, Fremantle Arts Centre Press, 1986; David Malouf, 'A Medium' from *Antipodes*, Chatto & Windus, 1985; Alan Marshall, 'Tell Us About the Turkey, Jo . . .', courtesy of Curtis Brown (Aust) Pty Ltd, Sydney; Olga Masters, 'The Lang Women' from *The Collected Stories of Olga Masters*, University of Queensland Press, 1996; Peter Mathers, 'A Knight of Teeth' from *A Change for the Better*, World and Visions Publications, 1984; Brian Matthews, 'The Funerals' from *Quickening and Other Stories*, Penguin Books Australia Ltd, 1989; James McQueen, 'The Brown Paper Coffin' from *Death of a Ladies' Man*, Penguin Books Australia Ltd, 1989; Gillian Mears, 'This and the Giver' from *Collected Stories of Gillian Mears*, University of Queensland Press, 1997; Frank Moorhouse, 'The Commune Does Not Want You' from *Tales of Mystery and Romance*, Angus & Robertson, 1977; John Morrison, 'The Nightshift' from *Stories of the Waterfront*, Penguin Books Australia Ltd, 1984; Barry Oakley, 'Fosterball' from *Millennium*, Penguin Books Australia Ltd, 1991; Vance Palmer, 'The Stump', reprinted by permission of HarperCollins; Ruth Park, 'The House to Themselves' from *Art in Australia*, Sydney Ure Smith Pty Ltd, 1950, courtesy of Curtis Brown (Aust) Pty Ltd, Sydney; Bruce Pascoe, 'Thylacine' from *Night Animals*, Penguin Books Australia Ltd, 1986; Elliot Perlman, 'The Reasons I Won't Be Coming' from *The Reasons I Won't Be Coming*, Picador, 1999; Hal Porter, 'Francis Silver' from *Selected Stories*, Angus & Robertson, 1971; Katharine Susannah Prichard, 'The Grey Horse', courtesy of Curtis Brown (Aust) Pty Ltd, Sydney; Tim Richards, 'Our Swimmer' from *Letters to Francesca*, Allen & Unwin, 1996; Deborah Robertson, 'The Crossing' from *Proudflesh*, Fremantle Arts Centre Press, 1997; Penelope Rowe, 'The Innocents' from *Unacceptable Behaviour*, Allen & Unwin, 1992; Steele Rudd, 'Dave Brings Home a Wife' from

Sandy's Selection and Back at Our Selection, Angus & Robertson, 1973; E. O. Schlunke, 'The Enthusiastic Prisoner' from the *Bulletin*, 1945, reprinted by permission of HarperCollins Publishers; Rosie Scott, 'Queen of Love' from *Queen of Love*, Penguin Books Australia Ltd, 1989; Thomas Shapcott, 'Martin Falvey' from *What You Own*, Angus & Robertson, 1991; Christina Stead, 'Guest of the Redshields', reprinted with permission from the publishers ETT Imprint; Dal Stivens, 'The Man Who Bowled Victor Trumper', courtesy of the copyright owner, c/- Curtis Brown (Aust) Pty Ltd, Sydney; Kylie Tennant, 'Lady Weare and the Bodhisattva', courtesy of the copyright owner Benison Rodd, c/- Curtis Brown (Aust) Pty Ltd, Sydney; Brenda Walker, 'Like an Egyptian' from the *Age Monthly Review*, June 1990; Judah Waten, 'Mother' from *Alien Son*, Angus & Robertson, 1952; Archie Weller, 'Sandcastles' from *Personal Best*, Collins, 1989; Ida West, 'Snakes' from *Pride Against Prejudice*, Australian Institute of Aboriginal Studies, 1984; Herb Wharton, 'Waltzing Matilda' from *Where Ya' Been Mate?*, University of Queensland Press, 1996; Patrick White, 'Being Kind to Titina' from *The Burnt Ones*, Eyre & Spottiswoode, 1964; Michael Wilding, 'The Man of Slow Feeling' from *The West Midland Underground*, University of Queensland Press, 1975; Gerard Windsor, 'Wedding Presents for Breakfast' from *Memories of the Assassination Attempt and Other Stories*, Penguin Books Australia Ltd, 1985; Tim Winton, 'My Father's Axe' from *Scission*, Penguin Books Australia Ltd, 1985; Amy Witting, 'The Enemies of Time' from *In and Out the Window*, Penguin Books Australia Ltd, 1991; Fay Zwicky, 'Only a Little of So Much' from *Room to Move*, Allen & Unwin, 1985.